Anyone's Daughter

Shana Alexander

Anyone's Daughter

The Viking Press
New York

First published in 1979 by The Viking Press
625 Madison Avenue, New York, N.Y. 10022

Published simultaneously in Canada by
Penguin Books Canada Limited

LIBRARY OF CONGRESS CATALOGING IN PUBLICATION DATA
Alexander, Shana.
  Anyone's daughter.

  Includes index.
  1. United States–Social conditions–1970-
2. United States–Moral conditions.   3. Hearst,
Patricia, 1954–   4. National characteristics,
American.   I. Title.
HN65.A673   309.1'73'0924   78–27697
ISBN 0–670–12949–6

Printed in the United States of America
Set in Videocomp Times Roman

Acknowledgments:
Random House, Inc.: From "I think continually of those who
were truly great" from *Selected Poems* by Stephen Spender.
Copyright 1934 and renewed 1962 by Stephen Spender. Reprinted
by permission of Random House, Inc.

for all the daughters

Contents

Contents

We could be anyone's daughter,
son, wife, husband, lover, neighbor,
friend. . .

—the "Tania Interview"

Opening
Reflection

Long before Patty Hearst's trial, even before her disappearance, her flight into the wilderness, before the awful incineration in the burning house in Los Angeles, before she stuck up the bank, even before she joined her captors and denounced her parents as "the pig Hearsts" and said, "I have chosen to stay and fight"—possibly while she was still in the closet in the hideout on Golden Gate—I became a captive of Patty Hearst and her story, whatever that story might turn out to be. In some curious contortion of reality, Patty was experiencing personally the very things that I had been sitting on the sidelines and writing about for twenty-five years.

I understood her because in some way she was the girl I had been, and in some way I was also her mother. I understood that a mother-daughter struggle was close to the core of her story, something similar to what had happened to me and my mother, and to myself and my own daughter, whom I was losing now. One of these daughters was taken entirely by accident. But all three were in rebellion and revolt.

I understood the peculiar attraction and tension between the kidnappers—seven young white university dropouts, five of them women, and one black escaped convict—and the shadowy legion of imprisoned black men in "Fascist Amerikkka," for whom the Symbionese Liberation Army felt such unbounded, uncritical compassion.

I understood the central role of the media in the entire event, all the way from Grandfather Hearst, who invented tabloid journalism, down to the modern hysteria that was taking place in California and around the world over Patty Hearst.

I understood that California itself was a character in the story. In fifteen years as a California correspondent for *Life* magazine I had learned that California is once-and-future America, the part of the country where everything happens first, and in a heightened mode.

I understood that none of the characters in the story understood any of the others; everyone was talking at once, and each was speaking a different language: the anguished parents, the defiant militants, the debased Panther rhetoric of the convict Cinque, the California authorities, the Berkeley radicals, the hot-breathing press, the psychiatric establishment, the regents of the University of California, the taxi drivers, the trial lawyers, and the sociologists—the whole Tower of Babel—and I felt sure that long after the case was over, we would all be talking about it still. To me the story was a Rosetta stone for our own time. Because that stone's inscription is repeated in three languages—not only in Egyptian hieroglyphics but in classical Greek and demotic as well—a single tablet became the key that unlocked the language of the pharaohs and opened up an entire lost civilization. Like the Rosetta stone, the Patricia Hearst story was readable three ways: It was a melodrama for the media, it was a metaphor for America, and it had a private meaning for me that continued to surprise. For starters, the kidnapping of Patricia Hearst would become the liberation of myself from the anxious lifetime grind of newsmagazine journalism. Although I didn't know it at the time, Patty emerged from her closet at about the same moment that I emerged from my own.

Early in March 1974, I was in Los Angeles, driving to meet a friend for lunch. Patricia Hearst had been missing for five weeks. My car radio was tuned to the twenty-four-hour news to which I had become addicted. As a journalist, my private life had always been helplessly and sometimes painfully entwined with the public events and figures I covered. Clowns, ball games, catastrophes, celebrities, were all mixed up with *me*. The radio droned incessantly about the case, which already had captured the fancy of the nation and, in particular, the shallow, capricious fancy of California's freeway-trapped audience. A sharp physical sensation occurred as the revelation hit: Patty was *my* story. It felt as if a light bulb had switched on over my head, the way they used to in comic strips, and simultaneously a rubber-tipped arrow had struck me in the breast.

As time passed and my life went along as a journalist, as a mother and as a daughter, I lost confidence at various times in everything but one thing: I understood this story. "There is a kind of snail in the Maryland marshes—perhaps I invented him—that makes his shell as he goes along out of whatever he comes across, cementing it with his own juices, and at the same time makes his path instinctively toward the best available material for his shell; he carries his history on his back, living in it, adding new and larger spirals to it from the present as he grows . . ." writes John Barth in *Chimera*. That is how I crawled through the saga of Patty Hearst.

The problem for a long time was not substance but form. "How can you begin to write the story when you don't know how it ends?" people used to ask. "If you ask that," I'd say, "you don't understand which story I want to write." To some degree, this was a cover-up of my inability to dope out the form. One difficulty was that my central character was offstage, so to speak; no one even knew whether she was alive. A more serious problem, technically speaking, was that the Hearst case was an interesting story about a fundamentally uninteresting girl. What happened to Patty and what then happened to America are akin to what happens when a pebble is tossed into a pond: The pebble disappears, the pond ripples. I was attracted by the ripples, not the stone.

When she was kidnapped, this unremarkable young woman had become the object of world scrutiny, focused through the media's compound, unblinking eye. Not just one world but the separate worlds of law enforcement and psychiatry; the tremulous eyes of many parents beside her own; the hard eyes of revolution; the wary-stary eyes of fugitives, prisoners, psychopaths, terrorists, and self-proclaimed outsiders of every stripe; and the professional attentions of the best lawyers and doctors money could buy, and others that could not be bought— all these were trained on Patricia Hearst. Yet she was invisible all the while, a pebble in dark waters.

To me, the story was not just the tabloid bonanza of all time, evolved directly from the billion-dollar formula that old man Hearst had invented. It was a California event, reflecting the people, the dynasties, the patterns, the attitudes of that fevered, rootless state. It was a linguistic event in which all the main characters spoke different languages. It was a newfangled media event in which the characters captured the reporters, in which the SLA (the Symbionese Liberation Army) in effect took hostage the press, forcing it to print each of its mad communiqués in full. It was a criminal event in which the outlaws acted from new compulsions, unmellow motives. The money demanded for Patty's release was not to enrich the kidnappers but to help the poor: a Robin Hood ransom—America's first. But all of it, the $2 million spent by the victim's parents on the People in Need free-food-distribution program, and the $4 million they put into escrow to await their daughter's return, was set up beforehand as a charitable foundation. Tax-exempt ransom money! Surely another first in the annals of crime. It was a family event, occurring at a time when the family as an institution was in disunion and despair, when real families withered and shattered, and pseudofamilies thrived. The SLA was itself a pseudofamily, as well as a homegrown American terrorist band that prefigured the Palestine Liberation Organization, the Baader-Meinhof Gang, and Italy's Red Brigades. It was a fiercely female event, woman-created and woman-driven. It was a pathological event, sickening in its violence, frightening in its new formulations of old concepts of responsibility, free will, crime, and punishment. It was a mythological event, crowded with uniquely American figments—Bonnie and Clyde, Superman, Perry Mason, Nigger Jim, and the Lindbergh baby all come to mind; and it was a descendant of much older, archetypal myths about evil dragons and captive maidens, about Sleeping Beauty, Persephone, Helen of Troy. It was not just any one of these, it was all of them; it was, to me, a kind of all-American pie.

Then, just about the time I got all this figured out, something disconcerting happened. The pebble reappeared. The real Patricia Hearst, the actual flesh-and-blood girl, was captured by the FBI in San Francisco. But even after she was tried for bank robbery and convicted, she remained, or some part of her remained, an enigma to all the world, and quite possibly to herself. I was never allowed to meet her, and though I sat only a few feet away from her in court every day, even at times, I am ashamed to say, staring through special close-up artist's spectacles at the pale face with the charcoal-smudge eyes, I was unable to read what I saw there.

The windows of novelty shops in the 1930s and 1940s used to display a trick holy picture (perhaps they still do), a portrait of Jesus in which the eyes appear sometimes open, sometimes closed. But when you walked up close to the window, pressing your nose against the glass in an effort to see how the artist had achieved his optical illusion, the figure's eyes dissolved into smudges, and you saw the image less clearly than at a certain remove. It was the same with Patricia Hearst. To see her clearly, a certain remove was required.

By the time Patricia Hearst was brought to trial, two years to the day after she had been kidnapped, her disordered story had acquired a certain shape. A baroque sequence of what had once seemed random events had arranged themselves, I thought, into the classical three acts. The drama even had a name: HERNAP, FBI teletype code for the case.

Act I begins on the evening of February 4, 1974, when a college girl is dragged half-naked and screaming out of the anonymity of her private life and deposited, like a bone, onto the front pages of the world. Offstage, in a burst of machine-gun fire, she becomes "Tania," girl guerrilla. Then she disappears. Nineteen months pass, which become known in the hyperbole of lawyers as the Missing Year.

In Act II she is locked in jail, invisible and incommunicado for four and a half months, seeing no one but her millionaire parents, her big-time psychiatrists, and her celebrity lawyers.

Act III is Patty's trial for having taken part in the armed robbery of the Sunset branch of the Hibernia Bank of San Francisco more than twenty-one months before.

By the end of Act II I had the stone at least partially decoded, and although I could not read its inscription entire, I knew that much more than the defendant would soon be put on trial: Four of our most powerful gods also would be weighed in the balance—the blessed American family, the sanctified free press, the holy men of modern psychiatry, and the almighty jury system, which has been an indispensable element of our concept of justice for nearly a thousand years. By the time the curtain rose on Act III, I had determined to cover and write about that event in full. The *device* of the trial would enable me to deal with much more than the trial; ordered by a trial's classic unities of time and space, the courtroom doings could serve as a kind of prism through which to refract the whole. No problem is too big to deal with if you can find a large enough plastic bag, the playwright Tom Stoppard once pointed out. The coming trial would be my plastic bag.

It is important to note the larger time frame in which the drama takes place. Act I, the abduction of Patricia Hearst and her metamorphosis into Tania, occurs in an unusual news vacuum within a special period of drift and doubt and moral numbness while Americans are attempting to come to terms with the domestic disgrace of Watergate and the international shame of Vietnam. When Patricia Hearst is kidnapped early in 1974, the Watergate scandal happens to be in temporary eclipse. For six weeks or so, offstage, a Washington grand jury has been pondering the possible criminality of men whose names we have come to know well—Haldeman, Ehrlichman, Mitchell, Colson, Dean, Mardian, Kalmbach, and Stans, as well as the unnamed "unindicted co-conspirator." By the time the names and faces of the nation's top political leaders are back on the front page, indicted now for perjury, conspiracy, obstruction of justice, burglary, forgery, destruction of evidence, and various other crimes, HERNAP is in eclipse. By May 18 the SLA is finished. Its only survivors—Patricia Hearst and William and Emily Harris—have disappeared. The rest of the gang was incinerated the night before in a house in Los Angeles—and the entire holocaust televised live on the evening news.

When President Richard Nixon finally resigns, on August 9, 1974, Patty's Missing Year is well under way. On September 18, 1975, she is captured with a pistol in her purse, and at the jail she gives her occupation as "urban guerrilla." Patty is twice kicked off the front page within the month when, also in California, two other armed women open fire. In Sacramento, "Squeaky" Fromme, a leftover from the Manson gang, attempts to assassinate President Ford. Seventeen days later, in San Francisco, Sara Jane Moore tries the same thing. Ms. Moore had worked as executive secretary and bookkeeper for the People in Need program during the ransom negotiations. At the same time, unknown to the Hearsts, she was employed as a double agent by the FBI.

While the media's huge eye is focused on San Francisco and the trial of Patricia Hearst, a new and unknown American politician, campaigning as an antipolitician and promising the American people that, if elected, he will never lie to them, is piling up an astonishing string of victories in the presidential primaries. In the fall of 1976, Patricia Hearst is sentenced to serve seven years in prison, Jimmy Carter is elected President of the United States, and a new era has begun.

The period of HERNAP was an unprecedented time in America, a time of Bicentennial, a time of disillusion, a time of terrible disorder in the land of the free and the home of the brave. Actual civil war raged in the land, in the opinion of the German-born Secretary of State who with extraordinary flair and intelligence was managing to hold the show together. Alas, Henry Kissinger could never acknowledge his own role in bringing that civil war about. In any event, they were wretched years as the nation clumsily conducted its painful political self-curettage at home and struggled to "wind down" a disastrous decade of war abroad. The disruption was felt at every level of national life, including the most intimate. As families dissolved, children ran off in record numbers. In April 1975 this springtime of disunion and anxiety acquired its extraordinary symbolic punctuation mark—Operation Baby Lift. Leaving Vietnam at long last, we took with us as many children as we could. We filled the skies with "war orphans," tiny peace symbols borne aloft in a final paroxysm of war guilt, sentimentality, and bad judgment. They were ferried out by the same pilots on the same planes that had flown in the bombs that had made them orphans in the first place, and then they were adopted by American families. Except, of course, that they were not all orphans. Many—no one yet knows how many—were the commonplace casualties of war: lost children; wounded and ill children; fatherless children; temporarily displaced children; children whose parents could not just then care for them; children whose parents genuinely wanted to get rid of them; children of the rich or corrupt or powerful who feared Communist reprisals—children of all kinds. And all these children, the fruits of Vietnam's and our own debacle, were brought here and hastily fitted—often very badly fitted, like battered bits of a jigsaw puzzle—into several thousand American families. Their new American "parents" believed the children had been "rescued." But many of the Vietnamese parents believed the children had been kidnapped.

Courts in California, Connecticut, Michigan, and Iowa have already ordered some Baby Lift children returned to their Vietnamese parents. The anguish of these parents was expressed in a letter written by a Vietnamese woman, now married to an American and living in California, seeking to recover two of her children, who had been adopted in Connecticut through an agency in Colorado known as Friends for All Children. This mother felt her children were sold by Friends for All Children as if "they were water buffalo, or ducks."

"To understand my story," she wrote, "think you are caught upstairs in a burning house. To save your babies' lives you drop them to people on the ground to catch. It's good people would catch them, but then you find a way to get out of the fire too, and thank the people for catching your babies, and you try to take the babies with you. But the people say, 'Oh no, these are our babies now. You can't have them back.' I don't understand. Vietnamese don't do like that with children. We love them too much for that."*

The concept of adoption in the United States is entirely different from that in Indochina. To us, it is a formal, legal procedure designed to make the child's new parentage permanent and irreversible, and to

*The *New York Times.* September 26, 1976.

render the old parentage legally nonexistent. The intent is to ensure the child's legitimacy, chiefly for purposes of property and patrimony, so that when both sets of parents die, the child is legal heir to the estate of the adoptive parents and, collaterally, has no claim on the estate of the natural ones. But adoption has a different meaning among the rural, rice-growing peoples of Indochina. There "adoption" is widespread, an integral part of the ancient pattern of child rearing, occurring within a large, loose network of distant and close relatives and village neighbors. Thus, the Vietnamese saw this final American euphemism as a *literal* baby lift.

Randolph and Catherine Hearst would have understood the Vietnamese mother's position, I thought when I read about it. I understood it myself very well. When Patricia Hearst was kidnapped, I was the anxious, guilt-ridden mother of one unhappy twelve-year-old daughter, who, due to the divorce of her parents and attendant alarums and excursions over many years, was temporarily homeless and had just been reluctantly packed off to boarding school. I was also by then an experienced journalist, but a journalist by default. At Patty's age I had studied anthropology and had worshiped Ruth Benedict and Margaret Mead. My anthropological Shangri-La was somewhere in the islands of the western Pacific, however, and an opportunity to do the fieldwork necessary to become an anthropologist myself then seemed out of the question. The primitive region that interested me was overrun by warring U.S. troops and what we used to call "Japs." If I were to practice anthropology—the close, undisturbed observation of unfamiliar peoples in their native habitats—it would have to be closer to home. I think that is why I became a reporter.

Yet another extraordinary thing about HERNAP was that at the time it happened, nobody knew anything much about the crime and punishment of kidnapping, including the FBI. The most American of all capital crimes was also the one that had been least studied or understood. That appalling ignorance has since been remedied in part by Ernest Kahlar Alix, a professor of sociology at Southern Illinois University, in a pioneering study, *Ransom Kidnapping In America, 1874–1974/The Creation of a Capital Crime.* * The FBI's *Uniform Crime Reports*, the main source of national crime statistics, did not even contain the appropriate data, and when Dr. Alix wrote to the Justice Department and to

* Southern Illinois University Press, 1978.

the Law Enforcement Assistance Administration requesting unpublished kidnapping statistics, he was told they were "not available in any form from any federal agency." Alix was forced to turn to the *New York Times*, but the professor emerged from the stacks and the microfilm rooms with a remarkable profile of his chosen crime. He had identified fifteen distinct varieties of "unlawful takings of human beings," from abductions for purposes of white slavery to political highjacking, and had concluded that of the fifteen, the crime of ransom kidnapping has a "unique ability to generate intense and pervasive societal reaction," in short, to alarm, because in none of the other fourteen varieties, is the victimhood perceived as so entire. As a result, society's perception of and consequently its punishment for *classic ransom kidnapping*—a crime in which the primary intent is the collection of the ransom, rather than some other motive such as revenge, terror, or sexual or political exploitation—has changed dramatically.

America's first ransom note was delivered in 1874 to the father of young Charles Ross, of Germantown, Pennsylvania. A wave of child-stealing had swept the East and the Midwest, and now two such thieves were demanding twenty thousand dollars for a stolen child's safe return. With the receipt of their letter, a new form of extortion was born; a new variety of illegitimate capitalism was invented—in fact, a new crime. In the hundred years since the abduction of Charles Ross, kidnapping had "evolved from a shocking but modestly punished act into a capital crime in forty-five states," as well as in federal law. Today "only murder [is] a capital crime in more jurisdictions."

Although the SLA could have known nothing of the 1874 Ross case, it almost seems as if Cinque and his followers had timed the kidnapping of Patricia Hearst to celebrate the centennial of the crime itself. Public interest in kidnapping had peaked in the early 1930s, and so had the actual incidence of the crime—twenty-seven cases in 1933—and then both had subsided again. The stimulus in each instance was, of course, the Lindbergh case. HERNAP set off a similar imitative crime wave: twenty-six kidnapping cases in 1974, of which twenty-three followed the abduction of Patricia Hearst. In all but perhaps one of these, easy money was the motive.

HERNAP served to focus and harden many attitudes toward crime and punishment that had been slumbering in the nation's collective consciousness. Most interesting in Professor Alix's work is to watch how the beleaguered President Richard Nixon, already defensive and morally on the run, with his third Attorney General, William Saxbe, jogging uneasily alongside, *used* the Hearst kidnapping to call for more law and order, more morality, more punishment.

The fight to abolish the death penalty at home and the gradual increase in the use of highjacking and kidnapping as weapons of political terror increased simultaneously in the late 1960s, and their fates became intertwined. In the ongoing debates over the effectiveness of capital punishment, kidnapping was singled out frequently as one crime that the death penalty does perhaps deter. In the conjunction of these forces, first California and then the federal government in 1970 passed laws providing for the death penalty in cases where fatalities occurred as a result of political or terrorist bombings. But in 1971 the National Commission on Reform of the Federal Criminal Laws—the McClellan Commission—called for life imprisonment as the maximum federal penalty for *any* crime.* At that time, death-penalty statutes existed in thirty-eight states, and about one hundred twenty capital cases were pending before the Supreme Court.

Opposition to capital punishment is based on two separate propositions; some opponents of the death penalty believe in one proposition but not the other, and some, like myself, believe in both. The first proposition, still widely debated, states that capital punishment does not deter serious crime, and often in fact encourages it by gratifying the killer's conscious or unconscious wish to be punished. The second proposition is that the death penalty in itself constitutes cruel and unusual punishment, and is therefore unconstitutional. This issue appeared certain to be settled at last by the Supreme Court in the *Furman* decision of June 1972. But even *Furman* was not really definitive, because nine separate opinions were filed in the five-to-four vote, covering a broad range of social, ethical, and constitutional concerns, and it was apparent that if a way could be found to eliminate the factor of racial discrimination from the way in which the death penalty is applied, the Court's position might well be reversed.

In a press conference on the night of the *Furman* decision, President Nixon, siding with the minority, said he thought the death penalty was necessary to deter kidnapping and air piracy, and that he hoped the Court's decision "does not go so far as to rule out capital punishment for kidnapping and highjacking." In March he urged Congress to re-

---

*Two committee members, Senators Ervin and McClellan, disagreed with the majority and favored retention of the death penalty for intentional murder and for treason.

store the death penalty for the crimes of assassination, treason, air highjacking, the murder of FBI men, prison guards, and other law enforcement personnel, and kidnapping. Many people found kidnapping out of place in Nixon's list; the other acts primarily threatened government itself, not private individuals. Later that month, the President also asked Congress to abolish insanity as a defense against murder charges and related federal crimes.

Over the next twelve months the administration's cry for law and order escalated as its own troubles mounted. Less than a week before Patricia Hearst was kidnapped, and while the Washington grand jury was still debating the criminality of the Watergate conspirators, President Nixon in his State of the Union address again called for the restoration of the death penalty for "especially heinous" crimes, such as a murder resulting from a kidnapping, and a State Department pamphlet entitled *General Security Tips for U.S. Businessmen Abroad* warned the businessmen not to expect their government to ransom them if they were captured by terrorists.

Less than two weeks after Patricia Hearst was kidnapped, Attorney General William Saxbe was talking even tougher. In a press conference Saxbe characterized the FBI's long-standing policy of taking no action in a kidnap case that might endanger the victim as a "dereliction of duty." And when the SLA demanded ransom in the form of a multimillion-dollar handout of free food for the poor, and Randolph Hearst agreed to try to comply with the demand, Saxbe voiced his opposition again. To the attorney general, the attitude of the victim's distraught father appeared to be somewhat soft on crime. Once more he called for capital punishment in kidnap cases. It was about that time that the governor of California, Ronald Reagan, expressed his hope that the free-food program might touch off an epidemic of botulism among the poor. (Reagan later explained he had intended this remark as a joke.)

Members of the Nixon administration continued to use HERNAP as a rationale for the death penalty, and March 13, just two days before the Hibernia Bank heist, the Senate after twelve hours of debate voted 54 to 33 to restore the death penalty. The measure was sent on to the House, but its fate there was uncertain, because, although House support was strong, the *New York Times* reported that "the Judiciary Committee [was] involved with the impeachment investigation of President Nixon."

The kidnapping of Patty Hearst sent seismic tremors through every level of American society, and the direct consequences of HERNAP in law-enforcement circles reached even beyond the increase in kidnap cases and the renewed public alarm over that particular crime. A scant six months after Patty and her kidnappers knocked over the Hibernia Bank, says Professor Alix, "Twenty-nine states had restored the death penalty, 147 persons had been condemned to die under the new legislation, and nine capital cases were pending before the Supreme Court."

With a start, one could now recognize still another oddity about the ripple pattern in the Patty pond. Long before the Vietnamese babies arrived here, before this nation was even founded, in fact, the new republic already included a large and permanently kidnapped population: the cargo of the slave traders, the kidnapped sons and daughters of Africa.

The last odd thing about HERNAP was this. Although the story had every element of melodrama save the central ones—it had no heroine and maybe no villain—this was not due to any lack in Patricia Hearst. Nor was it a consequence of the fact that until Act III its central character never appeared onstage. The difficulty was that what counted most was not the girl but her symbolic power. Her importance was in her absence. Her absence made waves, and the waves were interesting; in a historical sense they still are. While the drama was playing in the *theater of now,* the actors fought for a piece of the spotlight. Now the light has flickered out. Sometimes I feel I am composing a guidebook to the moon, describing a lunar landscape illuminated only by reflected and remembered light. But while it lasted we were hypnotized, and before it ended, Patty's misadventure managed to defile every one of our sacred symbols: purity, property, family, and flag. It pushed every emotional button. It raked up all the deepest fears of parent and child, rich and poor, men and women, blacks and whites, haves and have-nots, Left and Right, young and old. Invisible, absent, and enigmatic, Patricia Hearst became for a while the thumb in America's eye. HERNAP was Bicentennial American pie. Cut into the Patty pie wherever you wish, and you cut yourself a slice of American anguish: massive mistrust, mindless violence, media overkill, family breakdown, urban despair, racial rage, sexual dread. Change the sequence of words; call it sexual rage, racial dread, urban breakdown, family despair. However you sliced it, America's crisis was circular, a pie, a loop, a ring. A curettage seemed in order, but HERNAP was a story written upon a Möbius strip.

Act III began for me on a brilliant Monday in January 1976. On that day, and for the next eight weeks to come, time died, or rather, past and future died, and my consciousness shifted tense into the journalistic everpresent, the seamless tense of *now.* I had arrived in San Francisco five days before, and the airport taxi driver, young and black, had suggested during the drive into town that I might like to call him up some night for dinner, and he had offered his telephone number. If he was out, a woman would answer; that would be his mother.

Only in San Francisco! America's puritan ethic dried up somewhere in the course of the great westward migration. It shriveled up and fell off in the trek over the Great Plains perhaps, or it froze to death in the high Sierras; anyway, it never reached the Bay Area. San Francisco is different even from the rest of California. "This is Golden California," its police chief says. "And this is the most open city in the most open society in California."

If the major characters in HERNAP's last act had understood the many ways that California is different from the rest of America, the story might have ended differently. But open-minded as the people of San Francisco might be in other respects, they had no use at that point for their retrieved heiress. In his own street-smart way, the taxi driver appeared to have a more realistic appreciation of the city's climate than did any of the principals. "What the hell does she mean, she's 'for the people'? Listen, lady, *I'm* a people, and I'm not for the people!" he had said before dropping me off at the swinging new Nob Hill apartment house where I would stay during the trial.

Upstairs, I had set out my writing paraphernalia on the dining table in the "picture window," which yielded a narrow slice of stunning San Francisco view, even a snippet of Golden Gate Bridge. The modest two-room apartment was a gift from a friend, and I had rented furniture sight unseen from a motel-supply outfit; lots of chrome and blue velour. The spareness and impersonality of the furnishings pleased me. I wanted to live starkly here, conserve my energies, focus my attention. An ordeal was approaching for us all. One could even feel it inside the bare little apartment. It was the warm wind before a hurricane.

Week One

January 26–February 2

Monday, January 26

CR. 74-364-JC—*United States of America* v. *Patricia Campbell Hearst* —is scheduled to begin today in the United States District Court for the Northern District of California, the Honorable Oliver J. Carter presiding. The defendant is charged with two violations of the U.S. Criminal Code: armed bank robbery (U.S.C. #2113 [a][d]) and use of firearm to commit a felony (18 U.S.C. #924 [c][1]). Each count carries a maximum sentence of twenty-five years and a $100,000 fine. In the corridor outside the nineteenth-floor courtroom, the chief defense counsel, F. Lee Bailey, is dragging deeply on a cigarette and scanning an advance copy of the latest *Newsweek* with Patty's picture on the cover. In all, the magazine will publish ten Patty Hearst cover stories, and each one will break all previous records for newsstand sales. The public may detest Patty, but they cannot get enough of her. She is this year's girl you love to hate, and last year's, too.

Bailey wears a new pearl-gray suit, fine pink linen, and a tie of gray silk damask—the colors of a French king. The hand holding the magazine trembles slightly. The stiff attire of Bailey's pudgy sidekick, co–defense counsel J. Albert Johnson, vaguely suggests a military uniform; a Marine Corps insignia adorns his lapel. Reporters jam the corridor. More than three hundred journalists are here to cover this trial. Judging by the weight of international media manpower assembled in San Francisco, we are about to witness the biggest news event since World War II. The sixty-three of us fortunate enough to have a guaranteed seat pass

(19)

one by one through an airport-style metal detector operated by stone-eyed federal marshals and take our assigned places. From *her* assigned seat at her lawyers' table, the defendant smiles wanly at her parents and sisters, who are sitting in the front row, and she signals them a quick, secret wave. Below the table, emerging from a tailored sleeve, five pink and perfectly enameled fingers flutter like the frilly fin of a Siamese fighting fish.

Patty is costumed today like a tiny Eleanor Powell, jaunty navy pants suit, white bow-neck blouse, and looks very different from the first time I had seen her. That had been in this very same courtroom, at the arraignment the day after her arrest. Her parents had entered first that day, walking stiffly like the Player King and Queen, followed by three of their five daughters. Then a tiny figure had appeared, slouched in front of the high bench, one hand hooked in the back pocket of the corduroy trousers. Nothing to see from the back but a defiant posture, a soiled lavender T-shirt, and chopped and dyed red hair. When she took a seat we could see that Patty wore heavy horn-rims, like her father; and that though stick-skinny, at odd moments she looked matronly, like her mother. Who was she, this skinny girl who looked plump? This kid who looked old? This debutante who looked like a stoned-out doper, this braless Temple Drake wearing rubber sandals and chewing gum? Today, five months later, she looks every inch the proper Hillsborough girl. One still doesn't know what she is.

Comes a sharp *rap-rap* of the gavel. "Everybodypleaserisethecourtof-thehonorableoliverjcarterisnowinsessionpleasebeseated." Then one loud *rap*. From the bench: "It is now time to swear in the jury."

They fill the entire spectator section of the courtroom. A deep rumbling sounds as they rise, humanity getting to its feet. Two hundred and fifty strong, they look like the recently unearthed buried armies of China, ranks of life-size clay figures put upright after centuries. They are the largest panel of prospective jurors ever called in a federal trial here. The narrow-faced judge has black-rimmed spectacles and thin hair. Courthouse scuttlebutt says that a few years ago the Honorable Oliver J. Carter consulted a psychiatrist; he was having difficulty making up his mind. But today, running through the familiar boiler-plate instructions to the prospective jurors, he seems firmly in command. He advises them they can expect a trial lasting four or five weeks, five days a week, from ten to noon and one-thirty to four, with a ten-minute recess in midmorning and midafternoon. "Because of the nature of this case and the amount of publicity, this is going to be the most fully covered case that I know of."* The pressure of public interest makes it practically impossible in a big case for a juror to keep an open mind, so to protect them from such pressure, this jury will be sequestered. "You will be in the custody of marshals at all times." No radio, no television, no phone calls out or in except for emergencies, and all calls to be monitored. The jury faces are impassive. "Hotel rooms have been reserved for you. . . . You can go home first and get articles of clothing and personal necessities." Friends and relatives may bring things on weekends, but no visits will be permitted alone in rooms. There will be a common room with *monitored* television and radio. "If some of you wish to go to church, the marshals will escort you, and you may read censored newspapers." The rows of faces begin to look dubious. "While jury service under these conditions is onerous, the right to a jury trial has a long history. You can go to other places where that privilege does not exist." The defendant is charged with two things only: armed bank robbery and use of a firearm to commit a felony. "That's all. She's not charged with any other offense in this court at this time. Now, I'm going to go through you alphabetically and ask: Are you able to perform the service of a juror under the conditions of sequestration which I have described?"

"Marian T. Abbe," the clerk intones. She is a pretty, young airline stewardess and appears to be part Hawaiian or Japanese.

"Is it Miss or Mrs.?" asks the judge gravely, with utmost courtesy, as if he were about to perform a wedding.

"It's Miss, sir."

"Are you able?"

"Yes, sir. I can get leave from work."

The clerk goes down his list. Aiken? I feel I am able. Anderson? Yes, Your Honor. Aragon? Yes, sir. As the questioning drones along it

---

*A note on punctuation. In a trial manuscript of this length, traditional punctuation would have required a *pointillist* profusion of quotation marks of no conceivable value. I have therefore eliminated quotation marks wherever, as is more often than not the case, I have condensed or paraphrased a speaker's actual words. But wherever this system might risk misperception or ambiguity, traditional quotation marks do appear. In the further interest of clarity, I have refrained from the use of paraphrase in presenting the all-important final arguments of the prosecution and defense attorneys, and of the judge's charge to the jury. However, to eliminate needless repetition, these passages have been substantially condensed, although for further typographical tranquillity, the conventional ellipses do not appear. My purpose overall has been to preserve sense and meaning while reducing a trial that ran to endless trial-transcript pages to manageable proportions.

becomes obvious that Judge Carter is deaf, and soon I begin to wish I were, too. My mind floats, drifts away.

I never understood what McLuhan meant by "The medium is the message." *Or* "the massage." To me, the medium is the miasma. This media miasma is the pond in which the pebble sank, and we're all in there together, reporters and subjects alike. The entire swampy place is booby-trapped with paradoxes and contradictions. You begin to stumble over them the moment you wade out into the damned stuff. Which ones are the journalists these days, and which are the subjects, themselves the "news"? What is a Woodstein? What is a Barbara Walters? A Mike Wallace? Why does the *Washington Post* appear to have almost as many informers as the government? Who is spying on whom? And who issued the spy license? What is going on here?

Well, many things. For one, thanks in part to the invention of instant replay, *then* and *now* and *tomorrow* have merged, or fused, and everybody lives together in the seamless, everpresent tense of *now*. For another, it is no longer so important for something to have happened; it is mainly important for something to have been reported. Haskell Wexler dealt with the phenomenon brilliantly in his film *Medium Cool.* "You put him on the six, the ten, *and* the twelve-o'clock news," insists a black militant talking to a television reporter. "*Then* he be real."

"Take our pictures! We are the revolutionaries!" Jonathan Jackson had shouted to photographers in 1971 as he stood up with a satchelful of machine guns in the Marin County Courthouse. What he meant was, "Take our pictures so that we can see ourselves, and so the whole world can see us, and we will become more real, and more tangible to ourselves."*

The Symbionese Liberation Army had hung on to deadly cartons of notes and diaries, and Nixon had kept his fatal White House tapes for the same reason, I surmised. The President and the terrorists each were haunted by a feeling of being *onstage*. Thanks to television, they had all become actors, and sometimes it made them uncomfortable. To have things down on tape and in notebooks, as well as to see one's image on television and read one's words in the press, is to reassure oneself of one's own reality. Patricia's parents and her fiancé, Steven Weed, had also spoken of being haunted by the feeling of being onstage. Surely the seven SLA members and their black leader, Donald DeFreeze—*nom de*

*Gregory Armstrong, *The Dragon Has Come* (New York: Harper & Row, 1974), pp.125–26.

guerre General Field Marshal Cinque M'Tume—were engaged in guerrilla theater as well as guerrilla politics. The invisible Patty may have felt more like an actor than anybody. I suspected this feeling guided her behavior throughout HERNAP more than any political motive. Perhaps Tania was an actress in a play within a play. Sometimes Patty/-Tania seemed to be Marion Davies' revenge, the retaliation of womankind on the Founding Father for his enforced and relentless infantilization of the woman he loved.

Want to wade into the pond from another place? Why not start with Walter Cronkite, who according to the polls is our most trustworthy American. (Within the miasma, polls are the only navigation aid we have.) By the time Patty was recaptured, the public's swollen trust of men like Walter Cronkite had begun to be mirrored by the medium's *mistrust* of itself. By then we had watched Gerald Ford on television duck behind his Sacramento limo as the frame froze, and next week the vacant face of Squeaky Fromme in her peaked red clown's hat stared back at us from a thousand newsstands. A few days after, in San Francisco FBI headquarters, special-agent-in-charge Charles W. Bates had been recounting the heroic details of Patty's arrest at a news conference when all of the fifteen reporters he was talking to leaped to their feet and raced out of his office. The second attempted assassination of Ford had occurred just a few blocks away. The proximity of these fierce and female events frightened us on several levels. So now the somber masculine editors of *Time* and *Newsweek* appeared on television, seated right alongside Cronkite and John Chancellor, as if, in this newest crisis of journalistic franchise and accountability, the weight of men from the older, more stable medium of print was wanted to anchor the anchormen. Dilemma: Had Squeaky inspired Sara Jane Moore? Was coverage of Squeaky in any way *the cause of* Sara? What was Patty's connection to either or both? What was the media's own responsibility in all this? The immutable duty of the press was to report the news in full, these older and wiser heads from print proclaimed, though clearly at times it was a heavy burden. The noble-browed anchormen nodded. The pencilmen looked wary and sallow alongside their electronic colleagues.

Another thing about the miasma: Within it, everything seemed to be negotiable . . . not least Patty's own guilt. By then we had a President and a Secretary of State who were admired most, wrongly or not, for their skill as master negotiators—with Russia, with China, in the Middle East, with George Wallace, with the Washington power brokers, with the electorate. When Nixon appointed his own successor—or perhaps one should speak of Ford's annunciation—even the Oval Office was shown to be negotiable. There were no standards left, *no* rules, *no* accountability. Might this be part of the explanation for the feeling so many of us had that our peak as a nation had passed, that we were looking back nostalgically to a golden past more than we were looking forward boldly to a golden future—a profound change in our perception of ourselves.

During the Vietnam War I used to wonder why more Americans didn't respond with greater revulsion to the nightly napalming of children on the evening news. One reason, perhaps, was that television by then had become so pervasive that our public had developed terminal image-fatigue. Another reason might be that among all the peoples of the planet, Americans most lack a sense of history. It would figure.

Looking at HERNAP, one saw an entire cast of characters living out of time, without a sense of history; people who lived only in the Eternal Present. Patty Hearst had never read *Citizen Hearst,* W. A. Swanberg's 1961 prizewinning biography of her grandfather, nor had she seen *Citizen Kane.* Randolph Hearst, president of the mammoth Hearst Corporation, had not heard of our greatest press critic, A. J. Liebling. Catherine Hearst, a regent of the enormous University of California, was seemingly unaware of the students' deep loathing of the board of regents for its support, through its investment portfolio, of the hated government of South Africa. She seemed insensible to the added peril in which she placed her daughter by accepting Ronald Reagan's appointment to a second term as regent at a critical point in the kidnap negotiations. Ludlow Kramer, the "experienced" relief administrator put in charge of the People in Need program, let much or most of the food be lost, spoiled, or ripped off by the Bay Area's well-known legions of hoodlums and con artists. William Coblentz, the lawyer selected by Hearst to handle the ransom negotiations, and a regent himself, had no experience with blacks and no prison law experience or prisoner clients. Yet he was the man whom Randolph Hearst sent to San Quentin at another very delicate point in the ransom negotiations to check on whether two "SLA soldiers," Joseph Remiro and Russell Little, were confined under "humane" conditions and according to "Geneva convention regulations," or were imprisoned in some government-operated black hole. (Just weeks before Patty was kidnapped, these two young white men had been arrested in connection with the SLA's first crime, the murder of Dr. Marcus Foster, Oakland's distinguished new black superintendent of schools, and the wounding of his deputy, Robert Blackburn, a white man.) The man most observers considered responsible for the killings at Kent State, William Saxbe, was now the country's leading legal officer, the previous Attorney General, John Mitchell, having been sent to jail. As for the SLA, they seemed to have come to politics entirely *de novo;* their writings showed no political sense whatever or knowledge of the political past.

When people live out of history, when the *only* events are current events, when the only current in life is the electronic instantaneous, all the rules change. What kept Patty Hearst alive in our consciousness during the nineteen months she was gone was her absence. Her absence accounted for her continuous presence in the headlines and in our minds. The one thing that could remove her would be the end of Patty Hearst as a news story. *How* that story ended didn't really matter. This curious half-life of figures in the headlines is what frightens me about "current events."

F. Lee Bailey is strolling back into the courtroom. His beautiful duds now suggest the figure on a Mother's Day candy box. The first round of jury eliminations is over. More than half the panel has been excused. It is time for lunch. Out in the corridor, the television newswoman Marilyn Baker is bitching. Last night Patty's parents had called the judge at home and demanded to be seated in the front row. To make room for them, Judge Carter has kicked out a couple of reporters, and Marilyn is on her way downstairs to another courtroom to seek legal redress. She would enjoin Carter from giving away the constitutionally guaranteed right of the free press to sit in the front row. Only in San Francisco.

Carter reads the indictment aloud. Potential jurors must fully understand the nature of the charges. "A presumption of innocence clothes and covers the defendant throughout this proceeding. It is up to the government to prove that her plea of not guilty should be overturned beyond a reasonable doubt and to a moral certainty. I will define for you reasonable doubt at the conclusion of this trial." He asks Patty to stand and show herself to the prospective jurors. On her feet, she looks pitifully frail. Attorney Al Johnson steadies her bony elbow and holds her rolling chair. The judge has some general questions for the panel as a whole. "One, are any of you, as far as you know, acquainted with the defendant or members of her immediate family?" He asks the Hearsts to rise. Randolph, Catherine, Ginna (Mrs. Jay Bosworth),

Vicki, and Anne stand up and turn toward the prospective jurors, all five executing a right about-face with parade-ground precision, five profiles as expressionless as carvings on an Egyptian tomb. One hundred pairs of eyes gaze back. No, they are not "acquainted" with these people, whose faces, after two years of constant television and newsstand exposure, must be nearly as familiar as their own.

More questions. "Are *all* of you willing to give the defendant the presumption of innocence?" No one moves. These one hundred people seem to want more than anything in the world to be on this jury. Only a few speak out. A man from Oakland says his wife's brother was nearly beaten to death. "I'd hate to say so, but I think subconsciously I'd be tilted against . . . Well, it was kind of a shock seeing the old gent lying there with blood running down his face." An angry-looking black woman says her son was involved in a crime. "I did not attend his trial," she adds, scowling at Catherine Hearst. They are excused, and when the clerk again calls the roll, we are down to seventy-four potential jurors and Carter is still asking questions. Does anybody discredit witnesses with beards, long hair, or both? Finally, Carter announces that tomorrow he will draw thirty-six names by lot; the rest will be standbys.

Looking at the would-be jurors, I think them all alike, each one desperate to be *in on* it. Only four have answered yes, yes, indeed, they have an opinion of this case. Four straight answers in a pool of one hundred. Five months later, at the start of his own trial, SLA survivor William Harris, serving as his own lawyer, would give voice to my thoughts. "I think what we have here are people dying to get on this jury. Maybe because it's a big case. But that is not fair. It is not right for them not to tell the truth, not to talk about their deepest feelings."

It is not just the jurors who long to be in on it. So do the judge and prosecutor, and neither man has been reluctant to make his feelings known. Californians tend to be outspoken. When the great migration began, the more timid people must have stayed home, and the bolder ones headed west. In Eldorado almost everybody yearns for the spotlight, likes to preen in the sunshine and be recognized. This tropism is what California is all about. Oliver Carter, sixty-five, has recently been in poor health with serious coronary problems, and the weekend before the trial, he was forced to submit to emergency surgery to repair a broken blood vessel in his neck. Chief United States Attorney for the Northern District of California James R. Browning, Jr., forty-three, is a Nixon appointee who has not tried a case in seven years. Both men see this case as the capstone of a long career in government service. Sad to say, their visions are accurate. Three months after the trial ends, and before passing final sentence, Judge Carter will suffer a fatal heart attack, and the task of determining the extent of Patricia Hearst's punishment will fall to a man who has never even seen her, Judge William H. Orrick. After reviewing the 4,582-page trial transcript and a voluminous posttrial psychiatric study made by the federal Probation Department under Carter's orders, Orrick will sentence her to serve seven years in prison. At about the same time, Browning's government career will quietly end when President Carter, despite preelection promises to keep politics out of the Justice Department, replaces him with a Democratic appointee.

The canons of judicial ethics require a judge to "abstain from public comment about a pending or impending proceeding in any court." But a few days after Judge Carter was assigned to the Hearst case, an extraordinary interview appeared in the *New York Times*. Speaking with unusual, if not unprecedented, frankness for a sitting judge on a pending case, Carter told the reporter, Lacey Fosburgh, that the Hearsts didn't intimidate him one bit. He'd been on the bench twenty-five years and had known Patty since she was a little girl. He had been a dinner guest at the Hearsts' home. The Carter family has been in California as long as the Hearsts, the judge added, even though the Hearsts may have owned the mines and the Carters worked in them. "Heavens, you can't be around California and not know Randy. You can't be in public life and not know Randy. But he doesn't scare me at all. I've got people, forebears, buried all around, at just as many places as he has. All their money and power falls off me like water off a duck's back." The issue to be decided is: How credible is the defendant? "Legally, it boils down to a question of whether you believe her, and how much you believe her. The tales she tells are very horrible. It's kind of like—not to be facetious—you don't know whether to cry or to vomit."

Tuesday, January 27

Dawn. I look out at my toy view. Framed by two white high rises is a narrow slice of blue water; above it, brown hills, sky. The blue is slashed at the waist by the brick-red line of the Golden Gate Bridge, and freighters and navy ships pass underneath. Sundays there will be many small white triangles of racing sailboats. San Francisco is a toy city. Hills and high rises offer toy views of water framed by masonry. Toy ferries, toy cable cars, toy people. Old and new juxtaposed. Quaint, clean, new-painted, fresh. Class structure, too, is well defined here; lots of wealth and lots of poverty are arrayed on these pointy hills. The place is in human scale, 750,000 population; you can walk everywhere. People are friendly. San Francisco has a special sense of its own gaiety, which degenerates too easily into whimsy. The toy city delights the little kid inside every adult; it appeals to the adolescent dreamer, the wanton, the wanderer, the free soul, the drunk. No accident that Irish coffee, a kid's way to get drunk, was invented here. North Beach is a Disneyland for childish sex fantasies. This is a city of writers, yet its newspapers are scarcely more consequential than comic books. The editorial matter reads as if produced by Dear Abby, the ad copy by Xaviera Hollander.

The Federal Building's large Ceremonial Courtroom, reserved for show trials, is veneered in executive teak. Bench, counsel tables, jury boxes, entrances, and exits—all are as formally arranged as an Elizabethan stage. Only the drama is shapeless, at least to those of us who have never seen a trial before. We see only random movements, sequences, comings and goings, no form or agenda apparent. To us the action is less like watching a play than watching an aquarium.

The bailiff raps his gavel twice. We rise as if he were tapping on the glass. Feeding time. Otherwise, we sit passively attentive, watching. The big fish is Bailey, a grouper or sheepshead bass, all massive head and strong shoulders. Perhaps later he will become a shark, swim upside down, and attack. But for now he is benign. Browning is a

(28)

pipefish, reed-slim, long-legged, brushed, and bespectacled. If this place were an aviary (which it is not; no sudden movements, cries, or flights here; even the tempo is underwater, beneath the bluish light from the high fluorescent ceiling), Browning would be a secretary bird. The twelve jurors and four alternates who will occupy the jury box are a school of fish, two rows moving as one, sixteen pairs of eyes, sixteen heads, turning back and forth from lawyer to witness stand, shifting gaze at the tap of a pointer from the giant movie screen to the artist's easel on which various pieces of evidence are displayed. The press box for top-rank reporters, exactly across the courtroom from the jury box, holds a similar school of fish—sixteen reporters who mirror the jurors' every twist and turn. For forty-six court days the witnesses—individual marine exotica, no two alike—will enter, testify, and exit. Shoals of spectators—marshals, stenographers, the regular courthouse herring— drift in and out, changing shifts at regular intervals.

Patty's team of lawyers sits at the big oak defense table, stage left, led by Bailey and cocaptained by dear, sentimental Fat Albert, packed like a blowfish into his belt-in-the-back bus-driver suit. The others are Thomas May, the handsome, brilliant ex-prosecutor from Boston with steel-colored eyes; the appeals expert, Henry Gonzales, the big, swarthy blackfin from Tampa; John McNally, Bailey's chief investigator, a blue-eyed and baby-faced former New York City detective who once captured Murph the Surf; and gray Theodore Kleines from Garrett, McInerney, the San Francisco law firm that looks after the affairs of the gigantic Hearst Corporation. A very catholic kettle of fish.

The prosecutors at their matching table, stage right, wear suits of no-wrinkle fiber, thin-rimmed spectacles, thin mouths. Second in command here, some say really first, is F. Steele Langford, chief of the Justice Department's Criminal Division, a bureaucrat from Washington with the protective coloration and speech habits of a clam. Langford has just won a conviction against Sara Jane Moore. All specialized psychiatric testimony will be handled by a jut-jawed, Ivy League barracuda, David P. Bancroft. Least among the prosecutors is the eellike Dennis Michael Nearney. *Do not underestimate these men,* I scrawl in my notebook. Dead center and motionless, sitting so still he might be barnacled to the back wall of the tank, hangs the black-robed judge.

Al Johnson has arranged a special seat for me this morning, only a few feet from the Hearsts. I watch Catherine, a mother strikingly more beautiful than any of her five daughters, swivel clear around in her seat and fix a gimlet eye on each potential juror as he or she stands up to answer the standard questions. All morning I have avoided meeting Catherine's gaze. The situation between us is awkward. Although I interviewed Patty's father many times during the Missing Year, her mother and I have not met. We did have one brief telephone conversation, right after the holocaust, but it ended abruptly and mysteriously with Mrs. Hearst's saying, "I don't think I care to talk to you," and hanging up the phone. The next day I read in the papers that she had broken her wrist. I have been watching her this morning out of the corner of my eye. She looks brightly Lana Turnerish, yet also strangely Chinese because of the tilt of her eyes and the full skin of her eyelids. But now, suddenly, just before the bailiff raps, Randy smiles, beckons to me, then formally introduces his wife. She smiles at me and we shake hands. "Come home, all is forgiven," she says, mysterious as ever.

"These benches sure are hard on the tail," says Randy.

Wednesday, January 28

The jury lottery is well under way. As each name is called, that person is asked to rise and go sit in or alongside the jury box. The box fills in and overflows with faces—black, white, brown; old, young; male, female. Like a sheet of photographic paper developing in a darkroom, slowly a composite panel of humanity forms.

"Has anybody *not* heard about this case? I don't think it's physically possible to live in this world and not have heard about it, so I'm going to speak to each one of you privately." Carter sounds like an emcee on a quiz show explaining the rules of the game that is about to begin. Swiveling abruptly from the jury box to face the press box, he announces, "We are going into another, adjoining courtroom, to interrogate these jurors individually. The marshals are not going to allow *you* to charge *that* courtroom, or you will be thrown out bodily!" With that he skedaddles through a side door. This judge may appear bumbling and in poor health, but he has just managed, very deftly, to box out the press. In the granite Siberia of the corridor, the outraged reporters mutter darkly about the First Amendment. But NBC's Carl Stern, himself a lawyer, explains that the press is frequently excluded during *voir dire* questioning, for the excellent reason that it is the only way to prevent a prospective juror from reading in the paper about the questions asked of previous candidates. The questions are intended to trick jurors into revealing their prejudices. If jurors know the tricks ahead of time, they can evade them.

The judge has further infuriated the reporters, and stunned certain lawyers, by permitting Patty's parents to remain inside the locked courtroom during the *voir dire* proceedings. Outside, the atmosphere of dull anger, of professional frustration unleavened by the least bit of journalistic enterprise, recalls the caged, useless, stupid feeling one has when trapped in the press bus of a presidential candidate. I dismiss myself from this silly stakeout and go home.

If they won't let me write about the trial, very well, I'll sit here in my goddamn picture window and write about California. I have known from the very beginning, from that moment nearly two years ago on the freeway when I realized I was going to tackle Patty's story, that it could have happened nowhere else. I know the Golden State. My mother was born here, in Grass Valley, then a small gold-mining town, not a hundred miles from where I am sitting right now. Later, like Lana Turner, she went to Hollywood High School and after that to the University of California at Berkeley, where, like Patty, she probably exercised in the Hearst Gymnasium. Then she went to New York and married my father, a composer of popular songs. He wrote "Ain't She Sweet?" when I was born and "Happy Days Are Here Again" when my sister arrived. I grew up in New York City, but I spent a good part of my childhood in California and most of my married and working years there.

California is shaped like a dogleg. As America was to Europe, California is to the United States—a country built on an imagination of gold. El Dorado. In 1849 they found the gold. The miners married the whores; the place began to grow, to explode; one year later it had become a state. Today it is the richest, most populous, looniest state, and a host of other superlatives, but above all, it is *first.* Soothsayers once foretold the future by dropping molten gold into water. If we could drop the dogleg of California into water, we could forecast America. The sun moves from east to west, but as every long-suffering California reporter knows, everything else in the United States moves in the opposite direction. What happens today in California turns up tomorrow in the Midwest and only then arrives in the decaying and moribund cities of the East—those same cities where the press lords and pundits live, smugly convinced that they know what is going on in America. Even in urban renewal, California is first: Los Angeles has just built sixteen new downtown skyscrapers, an "instant skyline" with twelve million square feet of new office space. Right in the middle of it all is a taco stand, operated by a Chinese family, that advertises "Kosher-style Burritos."

Two gigantic forces of nature are always at work in California, usually at cross-purposes. Geologists call them the San Andreas Fault and the continental tilt. The week before my daughter and I left California for good, or so I thought, seven years ago, I had tried to write a farewell *Life* column about them.

Yesterday at 5:22 P.M. the seismograph at Cal Tech registered an earthquake centered about twenty miles east of San Francisco and measuring 3.3 on the Richter scale, the paper says. Out here, news bulletins like this one are routine. Daily the earth trembles, the land slides, freeways crash, smog boils. With the Santa Barbara oil spill, even our ocean is a sea of trouble on oiled waters. Turbulence is our way of life, convulsion the norm.

The earthquake scare started as something of a joke, but it is being taken seriously not only by doomsday fanatics but by all the mental-health experts out here, doubtless attracted to California by the rich plankton of distressed souls abounding in our turbulent societal waters. The assorted shrinks more or less agree that the cause of our earthquake obsession is what they call "free-floating anxiety." They think that because practically everybody out here has come here from someplace else, California probably has more of this dangerous stuff floating around in it than any other state. Personally, I often feel we are drowning in it. I have also from time to time felt we were drowning in smog, leisure, alcohol, wealth, poverty, bureaucracy, and barbecue fumes. My own anxiety about California is equal to anybody's, though I am not worried about its falling off. . . .

At this point I abandoned the pretense of writing the column, which would have been my last for *Life,* and it was my first rejection. They said they weren't going to print another one because I had by then been offered, and accepted, the editorship of *McCall's,* and in some quarters at the old stand this was regarded as an act of treachery after eighteen years' faithful service. I felt not traitorous but betrayed. Where was the farewell banquet and the gold watch? What was really worrying me was not California's earthquake but my own.

If California did let go, true enough, my own house would be one of the very first to be submerged. I had been divorced for four years by then, and my daughter, Kathy, was in the second grade. We lived above the beach on the leading edge of the doomed chunk, in an old house set high on a north-south axis. I had a huge new bed, bought after the divorce. From it, at twilight, I could watch the red sun sink into the sea and, later, without moving, could look leftward through windows in the opposite wall and watch the moon rise. On some nights there were foghorns and bell buoys, even an occasional train whistle, and just lately, when the jet traffic abated a bit, we had been listening to the ducks winging north on the spring flights.

The lovely room also contained a TV set, on which the faces of those of my neighbors who were celebrities appeared with regularity. I had been thinking a lot lately about the rise of the gossip industry and about the way that as mass society becomes increasingly anonymous we seem to need celebrities more and more. As that hunger grows, distinctions blur, masks become interchangeable, and what comes to matter least is the head, and most the hat it wears.

It was not surprising to me that California, the movie capital, headquarters of our national fantasyland, should continue its historic role as the country's leading manufactory of celebrities, and I was by profession a celebrity-watcher. Then, one day, after years of writing about movies and movie stars, it came to me in one awful flash that Judy Garland was Mickey Rooney was Elizabeth Taylor was Marlon Brando. After that I couldn't really write about movie stars anymore. If anyone can do anything, if all hats are interchangeable, if there is no business anymore that is *not* like show business, that's when *I* begin to feel the earth rumble, to sense the subterranean fissures widening, and to hear an ominous tinkling in the chandelier.

So much for the Fault. As for the tilt, every millennium, another foot or so of California disappears. Geologists spend a lot of time measuring its slow but inexorable westward slide. I wish somebody would study the slippage in the *other* direction. Nearly all of our national fads and foibles, political trends, and social seizures seem to begin in California. They appear along the Pacific shoreline like salamanders crawling up onto the beaches out of the sunset's fire to begin the trek. Eastward, ho! As a cradle of contemporary civilization, the sands of Santa Monica rival those of the Nile Valley. Consider hula hoops, bikini suits, skateboards, smog alerts, encounter groups, jogging, open sex, swinging singles, BankAmericards, Frisbees, McDonald's, *I Ching,* Zen tennis, topless cocktails, and black power. Consider the taxpayers' revolt— Proposition 13. Consider picture windows. Think of it! The very flesh and profile of today, all blooming first in the warm California sunshine! The place is prototypical America. The entire state is a series of stage sets, from the forced-perspective streets of San Francisco to the faded, painted backcloth of Los Angeles. The apparent unreality of California may be what is most real about it. The place is continually in the process of becoming, perpetually emergent, like a darkroom image developing in its chemical bath, and what is liveliest about America, most ener- getic, most dissatisfied with things-as-they-are, most ardent for things- as-they-might-be, most rootless, most forward-looking, most superfi- cial, most contemporary, most independent, most existential, most flimsy, all piles up along our teeming western edge. When Patricia Hearst was tied up and blindfolded and dragged off into the night, she wound up in a closet in Daly City, a postwar Bay Area real-estate development of pink-and-green ticky-tacky houses built directly on top of the San Andreas Fault. By the time the SLA arrived there the place was something of a municipal scandal. Its cheap stucco houses already had begun to crack along the foundations, slide down the cliffs, and crumble into the sea.

Week Two

February 2–8

Monday, February 2

In all, jury selection at the Hearst trial will grind along for four and one half court days. During these *voir dire* proceedings, fifty-six prospective jurors are interrogated in detail by judge and counsel behind closed doors. Both to gain perspective on Patty and to keep my court-reporting hand limber despite the press lockout in Judge Carter's courtroom, I decide briefly to leave town. Today I cross to the other side of the Golden Gate and drive north to the bizarre Frank Lloyd Wright–designed Marin County Courthouse. This curious, sprawling structure is painted a hideous octopus-pink, and it lies clamped like a giant stucco squid along the top and sides of its green ridge of hill. Inside, for several months, the trial of the so-called San Quentin Six has been taking place behind a bulletproof plastic shield. The Six, all black convicts, are charged with multiple counts of murder and conspiracy growing out of the 1971 prison uprising in which the legendary George Jackson and five others were killed. The legal maneuverings leading up to this trial have been going on ever since. Long after Patty's case has been decided, these six defendants will still be sitting here, chained and shackled into their chairs.

Tuesday, February 3

I spend today wondering about what I saw yesterday and waiting for tomorrow.

Wednesday, February 4

At last, today, at ten o'clock, Patty's trial begins. People have been lined up in the street since seven. Many in the 150-person queue are young lawyers eager to study the defense tactics of the master; others are psychologists, kids, housewives, students, and the usual courthouse eccentrics—the pigeon lady, the bearded derelict who carries a law book. Number one in line, a hospital nurse and the mother of five children, has arranged to work the night shift for the duration of the trial. "I want to make my own decision what Patty is like," she says. "Besides, this is history." Inside, reporters outnumber spectators by eight to one. We sit in absolute silence in our assigned and numbered press seats for a full quarter hour until suddenly Catherine Hearst jumps to her tiny feet. Only then do I hear the two sharp raps of the gavel and see Judge Carter enter upstage right, his narrow head poking out of his robes like a turkey caught in a black sack. How did Catherine know he was coming? Can she see around corners? No matter, it has begun. Two years to the day from the day she was kidnapped, Patty Hearst's trial is finally under way.

First comes the yo-yoing of the peremptory jury challenges. In silence, as if a tennis match were in progress, the clerk carries a list of jurors' names back and forth between the two teams of lawyers. Huddled over the list of prospects, Patty, Bailey, and Johnson look like three horseplayers handicapping the big race. The twelve jurors and four alternates who have survived the legal choose-up are the least memorable citizens on the original panel. Blacks and oddballs have disappeared. One female juror is part Oriental. One man has a beard. The others are entirely unremarkable, average even in height and weight, almost aggressively neutral. Seven are women; five are men. They wear wash-and-wear drip-dries and carefully composed expressions. Nobody smiles; nobody frowns. Nobody takes notes. Just now they look a bit stunned as the clerk swears them in and the judge instructs them: "The ability to be fair and impartial is an attitude, as well as an act. Remember your duty to withhold your final judgment until you have heard all the evidence and until you have heard the instructions given you by the court. Do these things in logical order. One of the hard things to do in deciding cases is to wait until you have heard it all." One must strain to hear Carter's light voice. The Ceremonial Courtroom has a defective sound system, which will plague us throughout the trial.

"Remember, you are not to discuss . . ." the judge says, wagging a schoolmasterish finger before sending the jurors out of the courtroom so the lawyers may argue some last-minute motion. Nervous, Patty begins to pour water into Styrofoam cups and pass them around the table to her lawyers, as if she were a hostess at a sorority tea. Carter administers to the press a stern and patronizing rebuke. In future, reporters are not to rush up to the counsel when recess is declared. There will be no press conferences in his courtroom, and no whispering. "I have not allowed you a preferred position here in order to talk to *one another!*" I feel humiliated, and grateful the jury is not present. In a big case everybody in the courtroom feels on trial—lawyers, spectators, press, judge, and jury.

Bailey argues that the second count of the indictment—use of firearm to commit a felony—is "duplicitous," which turns out to mean not "deceptive" but "doubled." He wishes to exclude certain other matters and to prohibit the prosecutor from bringing up events in his opening statement before the evidence itself can be presented and dealt with by the defense.

"I understand what you are saying, Mr. Bailey. As we say upcountry, you can't unring a bell."

"You can't get a skunk out of a courtroom once you bring it in," Bailey replies.

In the defense view there are four skunks. Skunk One is Patty's boast on the sixth SLA tape that she robbed the bank. Bailey claims that Patty was forced to make the tape and that one of the kidnappers, Angela Atwood, wrote out the actual words.

Skunk Two would be testimony that more than a month after the robbery, Patty sprayed Mel's Sporting Goods store in Los Angeles with machine-gun fire in order to rescue her SLA companions Bill Harris and his wife, Emily. Such testimony would indicate that Patty was familiar with the use of automatic weapons, as well as loyal to the SLA.

Skunk Three would be testimony from Tom Matthews, the Los Angeles youth whom Patty and the Harrises have been charged with kidnapping. During the night Matthews spent with Patty and the Harrises in their van driving aimlessly around Los Angeles, Patty told him she had taken part willingly in the Hibernia Bank robbery. Bailey contends she was forced to say this by the Harrises under threat of being "blown away." Further, the very presence in this trial of Tom Matthews would bring up evidence of other crimes (his own kidnapping) not related to the bank robbery.

Skunk Four is the notorious "Tania Interview," a purported autobiography written many months after the bank robbery and discovered by the FBI in a locked closet in the Harrises' apartment. In it Patty again says, partly in her own handwriting, that she was a willing participant. Once more, Bailey contends that Patty was coerced, and he has a battery of psychiatrists standing by to prove it.

The government, for its part, sees all of the proposed psychiatric testimony as one great big skunk and asks the judge to exclude mention of it from Bailey's opening statement on the grounds that Patty's defense is not *insanity*. It is *duress:* She did what she did because there was a gun at her head. "A psychological or psychiatric *explanation* ought not to be a psychiatric *justification,* " says Bancroft, and he speaks of the "circus atmosphere" already created by the defense, especially in the media. He hopes these jurors will not be among "the suckers who are born every minute."

I lunch by myself in the courthouse cafeteria. How slow I am to get the hang of all this! I turn out to be a trial illiterate, a courtroom primitive without the slightest concept of ordinary criminal procedures, let alone the particularities and subtleties of this special case. What to do? I do not take shorthand, nor can I afford to buy the daily trial transcript that the court reporters sell at a dollar a page to the lawyers and to the big news outfits like the *New York Times.* Besides, the official transcript provides both more and less information than I require. But I do have a guaranteed press seat, center section, third row, on the aisle. So long as I occupy this seat every day, come rain, snow, gloom, or walking pneumonia (all of which, in time, do come), nobody can throw me out. So I will manufacture my own transcript, homemade, to suit my own needs.

I walk around the corner to a stationer and buy a couple of large pads with blue covers. Eventually my homemade transcript will fill seven and a half of these reassuringly legal-looking, fifty-page pads. To hell with court stenographers; they are fallible beings, human ear trumpets who funnel every word through trained fingers into the little, terrier-sized tripod that sits between their legs. At twenty-minute intervals they scurry out and speak their coded stenotype notes into a tape recorder while the actual words of testimony are still fresh in their minds. Later, typists plug earphones into these same tape recorders and type up what they hear. This typewriting becomes the official transcript; not what is said, but what the court reporter hears, taps out, then speaks, followed by what the secretary hears and types. My home-baked, one-person transcript will be, for my purposes, an improvement on the original. It could even be more truthful, as a painting is more truthful than a photograph. I will stay loose, work freehand. During the dull stretches of testimony I will force myself actually to *write paragraphs*. I will be impressionistic and put down what interests *me*. I prefer this plan on journalistic grounds (no reporter tells the whole truth; he tells the parts he thinks important) as well as on artistic ones.

After lunch, when court resumes, I notice the defense table is sprinkled over with cough drops. Bailey's team is obsessed by bad breath; they consume mountains of lozenges, Clorets, deodorizers. May eats mints; McNally and Gonzales chew deodorant gum. Johnson carries a tiny vial of spray breath freshener. As he prowls about the courtroom he employs it discreetly, but with relish, like a man with a solid-gold toothpick.

The judge denies each lawyer's motion to limit the other's opening statement. Evidence will be admitted at the proper time, he says, provided the proper foundation is laid. Warning both sides they "proceed at their peril," he sends for the jury and smiles thinly, visibly eager to begin. "An opening statement is a narrative preview . . . a bird's-eye view of what the case is all about," he tells the jury.

The pattern of a criminal trial seems to be very like the formula for organizing a long magazine article. As my first editor explained it years ago, "First you provide a menu. You tell 'em what you're gonna tell 'em. Then you tell 'em. Then you tell 'em what you told 'em." This corresponds to the legal sequence we shall follow: opening statements, prosecution's case, defense case, prosecution's rebuttal case, defense surrebuttal, prosecution's closing argument, closing defense argument, prosecution's final final. The prosecution gets the last word because it has the burden of proof. All the defense must do to win its case is raise a reasonable doubt of the defendant's guilt in the jurors' minds.

U.S. Attorney James Browning is well suited to offer a bird's-eye view. Balanced on storklike legs, he inclines his head toward the jury, clears his throat, unrolls his menu. "Ladies and gentlemen, my purpose in speaking to you at this time is to acquaint you with the evidence. The evidence will show that on April 15, 1974, at nine-forty A.M., the Hibernia Bank was held up by five persons, one male and four females, one of them the defendant, who had been kidnapped ten weeks prior by one or more of these same people . . . the group called itself the Symbionese Liberation Army. . . . The government will call various witnesses to this bank robbery—customers, bank employees, and pass-ersby." Clumsily, he hoists some large pasteboard maps onto an easel and picks up a pointer. He indicates the location of the bank, the position of its two surveillance cameras, check desks, and tellers' counters, the positions of various bank personnel and customers, the two getaway cars parked outside.

The bank opened at nine A.M. At nine-forty customer James Norton came in, leaving his mother in the car outside. He was followed through the door by customer Zigurd Berzins and then, almost immediately, by five bank robbers, who have been identified by the FBI as Nancy Ling Perry, who entered first, followed in order by Patricia Hearst, Camilla Hall, Patricia Soltysik, and Donald DeFreeze. Four carried sawed-off carbines; Soltysik had a handgun. Patty's gun was the only one with a straight clip. The other automatic rifles had curved "banana" clips, which hold more bullets. For the benefit of those jurors who, like myself, know nothing about guns, Browning explains that the clip is the thing that contains the bullets, which are forced out of it and into the firing chamber by a spring mechanism. I am grateful and make a note.

At the defense table, Patty Hearst is expressionless; she rarely even looks at Browning's charts.

Browning indicates the bank guard's position with his pointer and says, "You will hear the bank guard, Mr. Shea, testify that he saw the defendant approach him with her weapon and say, 'The first person who moves gets his M-F head blown off!' You will hear a second witness testify that he heard the defendant say something like 'Get on the F floor. We are not fooling around!' You will hear a third witness testify he saw DeFreeze near the safe-deposit counter and saw Patricia Hearst pointing her weapon directly at Mr. Ryan. He asked her, 'Do I lie down here?' He got no reply, but he lay down anyhow. Camilla Hall confronted Mr. Bower. Nancy Ling Perry confronted Zigurd Berzins virtually eyeball to eyeball. DeFreeze removed Mr. Shea's revolver. The whole robbery lasted two, maybe two and a half minutes total, and most of it was recorded by surveillance cameras. Perry was between the entryway and the manager's desk. Soltysik you will see clearly in the film leap over the teller's counter and go toward the vault. DeFreeze stands at the corner of the wall and the left, or west, end of the counter. Camilla Hall is to the east. Patty Hearst is between them in the middle area of the counter.

"Each camera took four hundred frames of film. A regular movie camera goes at a rate of twenty-four frames per second. If you reprint each bank frame six times, therefore, you can make a kind of jerky movie which is true in time to actual events. We will show you such a movie and tell you how it was taken. We will show it both in full speed and in slow motion. You will see DeFreeze, Perry, and Patty Hearst turn their weapons toward two new customers coming into the bank. Nancy Ling Perry fires at and wounds the two customers. You will see the ejected shell casings fall from Perry's weapon. You will see the defendant, Patricia Hearst, looking at her watch. You will see her checking her weapon. You will see that her fingers are in the area of the trigger. You will see her hand move freely on the weapon. Various employees and customers in the bank will tell you they heard things like 'SLA! SLA!' 'This is a robbery!' 'This is Tania!' or 'This is Patty Hearst!' One person heard 'I am Patty Hearst!' One person heard 'Everyone down! Hit the floor!' One person heard a male voice counting, 'Nine oh one, nine oh three, nine oh five.' "

During this recital I glance at Patty. She appears to be reading a book in her lap.

"People in the bank will say they heard two short bursts of gunfire: d-d-d-d-t! d-d-d-d-t!" Imitating the machine gun's stutter, the U.S. attorney sounds like what he once used to be—a small boy playing cops and robbers.

"After the robbers left the bank, a man named Eddie Washington was sitting in his parked car when he noticed a red Hornet drive up and park behind him. He will say he saw Patty in the back seat, that she was the last one out of the car, and that Bill Harris was the driver. Four cars were used in the getaway, two original cars and two switch cars, the change being accomplished in the parking garage of the Japanese Cultural Center.

"Witnesses outside the bank will testify that the robbers exited in the following order: Hall, Soltysik (carrying the money), Perry, Hearst, DeFreeze. One shot was fired outside the bank. One witness thinks Patty fired the shot; another witness thinks it was DeFreeze. In any event, the shell casings have been recovered, and the ballistics markings on them are similar to the marks on a live round found inside the bank, near the area where DeFreeze was standing. Finally, the jurors will hear that one witness was alert enough to get a partial license number of one of the getaway cars."

Now comes the first mention to the jury of the disputed SLA tapes. Browning says that on April 24, nine days after the robbery, a cassette was found taped to the steps of Woodrow Wilson High School in San Francisco. The jury will hear Patricia Hearst's voice on this tape. They will hear her say, "Greetings to the People. This is Tania. On April 15 my comrades and I expropriated $10,660.02 from the Sunset branch of the Hibernia Bank. . . . My gun was loaded and at no time did any of my comrades intentionally point their guns at me."

Browning shifts his story to events that occurred one month later, in Los Angeles, during a shoplifting incident at Mel's Sporting Goods store. At about four-fifteen on the afternoon of May 16 a security clerk heard "the sound of cellophane being stuffed into a coat" and looked up to see Bill Harris stealing a pair of socks. He managed to get one handcuff on Harris as they scuffled. Emily Harris tried unsuccessfully to intervene. The government will produce a .38 revolver taken from Harris during the struggle. The clerk will identify a 1970 Volkswagen van parked across the street. He will describe how he saw Patricia Hearst lean out of the van's front window, on the driver's side, and fire a volley of shots at him.

Patty, eyes downcast, sits absolutely motionless as Browning describes how she sprayed the area with lead, how the Harrises ran to the van and they all drove off, how the clerk gave chase in his car, and how, as the van was stopped in traffic, he saw Patty leap out and commandeer another car, the Pontiac in which the three of them then disappeared.

Patty leans toward Bailey's ear. It is easy to read her lips from my seat across the courtroom thirty feet away. "I did not," she says.

Browning says that markings on the shell casings recovered from Mel's match one of the weapons later found in the closet of the San Francisco apartment where Patty was arrested.

At seven P.M. on May 16 the fugitives passed a Ford van with a "For

Sale" sign in its window and persuaded its owner, eighteen-year-old Thomas Matthews, to get into the van with them. He was held captive for twelve hours. They tried at several places to buy a hacksaw and, when they found one, removed the handcuff from Harris' wrist. Then they all went to a drive-in movie and watched *The New Centurions.*

"You will hear Matthews testify that Patricia Hearst told him that she had been a voluntary participant in the Hibernia Bank robbery and that it had been carefully planned and rehearsed . . . that each person in the robbery was instructed to move his weapon only a few degrees, so as not to shoot one another accidentally. She also told him how she had fired her weapon at Mel's that afternoon. She said she felt lucky to have glanced up from her newspaper when she did and have seen the Harrises in jeopardy."

The next morning at seven Matthews was abandoned along with his van. He went home and at first didn't mention to the authorities that he had seen Patty Hearst. The Harrises had warned him not to, and besides, he had received good treatment from his abductors. But the following day, after watching the SLA's televised death by fire in a burning house, and after hearing the newscasters say that the Hearsts still did not know whether or not their daughter had been burned alive, Matthews went to the FBI.

Seventeen months later, Browning continues, on September 18, 1975, the defendant and the Harrises were arrested separately in San Francisco. The Harrises occupied an apartment at 288 Precita Avenue. The defendant was living at 625 Morse Street, more than a mile away. A number of documents were found at the Harris apartment, both type-written and handwritten, including a series of questions and answers, some in the defendant's handwriting. *Why did you rob the bank?* "Because we needed the money." And "because we wanted to illustrate that Tania Hearst was alive." *Why did you choose this bank?* "Because it had a good getaway route." And "because of the bank cameras." A type-written diary, also found at Precita Avenue, with interlineations in Patty's handwriting, states that the perpetrators of the bank robbery intended it to be "well-planned but flamboyant."

So much for the government's opening argument. It is two-fifty-five P.M. as we file out. In the corridor I note Catherine's black dress, black pumps, black stockings, black crocodile handbag. It appears to be the same outfit Patty had begged her on the second SLA tape not to wear because it made her feel her mother considered her already dead. Filing back into the courtroom, Catherine is first in her seat.

It is now time to hear the defense's opening statement, and the jury is brought in.

Tension hangs across the courtroom like a trapeze net. Brick-faced, with Brillo sideburns, dressed in a formal dark-blue suit, Mr. F. Lee Bailey approaches the jury and begins to speak quietly and without notes. "Ladies and gentlemen, ninety percent of what Jim Browning has told you is not in dispute."

In a low, intimate tone of voice and the simplest possible language, the lawyer tells a story. In 1973 a man was assassinated in Oakland. He was Dr. Marcus Foster, superintendent of schools, "and the following day, the world heard for the first time, at least to my knowledge, of an organization of terrorists that called themselves the Symbionese Liberation Army. . . . On January 10, 1974, Joseph Remiro and Russell Little were arrested after a shoot-out with the police [near] their apartment in Concord, whereafter the building was burned. On the following day, an arson warrant was issued for Nancy Ling Perry, who was identified as an SLA member, and who was the person that in August of 1973 rented that very same apartment.

"Patricia Hearst was then nineteen years of age. She had led, as it pertains to this case, a most ordinary life. She was a college student; she was living with a graduate student whom she had been associated with for some years. She was a completely apolitical creature: She had no interest in radical politics, causes, or anything of the like, did not attend meetings, or get involved in projects of this sort. She was living in Berkeley with Steven Weed and somewhat concerned about the security of her apartment, to which end a burglar-alarm system had been installed.

"On the evening of February 4, two years ago tonight, a form showed up at the door. And although Miss Hearst's first inclination was to advise Mr. Weed not to take the chain off, before she could make a decision or articulate her concern, the door was opened, and the young lady was talking about an auto accident and a need to get to a phone. Very shortly thereafter, there burst in by force Donald DeFreeze and William Harris, who threw Miss Hearst to the floor and held her down, at the same time disabling Mr. Weed, who was subsequently beaten rather badly. . . .

"This was the SLA terrorist group. As they yanked Patty Hearst forcibly from her home she began to resist, and they clouted her hard in the cheek with the butt of a rifle, causing her a serious injury."

Neighbors came out, and anyone who showed curiosity was fired upon. The prisoner was placed in the trunk of an automobile "and taken to an apartment, she knew not where. She was blindfolded at all times and thrown into a closet in which there was no light. . . ."

Miss Hearst spent the next six to nine weeks in a closet. We don't know precisely how long. The SLA had several purposes in kidnapping her: One, it gave them bargaining power to negotiate for the release of Little and Remiro. Two, these crazy people actually thought that if they could put food on the street for poor people and thus earn the support of the have-nots, they could overthrow the United States of America. Three, they wanted to show the Establishment that they could convert one of its own members to their terrorist beliefs.

Until World War II, torture was the traditional way one got prisoners to change their minds. Now there is a new technique, variously called brainwashing, coercive persuasion, mind control. "Donald De-Freeze, you will learn, who gave himself the grandiose name General Field Marshal Cinque, had read some books in prison about mind control." In Miss Hearst he thought he had a vulnerable prospect, a nineteen-year-old girl who could rather easily be persuaded that she had been abandoned by society, abandoned by her parents and by the representatives of law enforcement. He could convince her these people were now her enemy and would kill her if she tried to escape. Furthermore, if she were compelled to become an outlaw, he need be even less concerned with the possibility of her attempting to flee. And so, "for perhaps the first time in the history of bank robbery, a robber was told to identify herself during the commission of the act," and she was also told that if she messed up in any way, she would be blown to bits.

The first warrant issued for Patty's arrest named her only as a material witness. But the SLA wanted her *charged* as a bank robber, so they told her this was merely a government trick to get her to give herself up to the FBI. If she did, the FBI would shoot her and blame it on the SLA, Bailey says. The SLA also wanted Patty to confess publicly to her voluntary participation in the robbery, and she did. But the jury will be shown that Angela Atwood wrote the words Miss Hearst spoke on the tape and that she made a bad slipup.

In fact, says Bailey, every single one of Patty's taped messages was read from a draft written by others. But after William Saxbe, the Attorney General, told the press, "She is nothing but a common criminal," the SLA shrewdly told Patty, "You have been *defined as a criminal*" by the government of the United States. Now you can never

convince an American jury that you did *not* want to get into that bank."
A month later, on May 17, when Patty watched on live TV as the police burned and shot to death all the other members of the SLA, it confirmed to her in the most vivid possible way that everything the SLA had told her was true.

Bailey's story so far has been simply and powerfully told. Unquestionably the jury is impressed. When he arrives at the moment of his client's arrest, in the apartment on Morse Street, his rich voice deepens, slows. Miss Hearst had been so conditioned to the idea that *FBI* was synonymous with *"Kill! Kill Patty Hearst!"* that upon hearing the shout at her doorstep *FBI!* "the degree of her terror mounted to the point which is probably the highest that a human being can stand without passing out, and"—here his voice drops dramatically—"she became incontinent."

For twenty months, Bailey continues, Miss Hearst had been kept literally a prisoner of war. She had every opportunity to escape "but also every opportunity to believe she had nowhere to go." We will hear testimony from three distinguished medical specialists in the field of brainwashing, experts either originally appointed by the court or persons who have since agreed or even asked to testify for her defense. All these experts agree that Miss Hearst's is a classic case, a textbook example of the type of coercive persuasion undergone by American prisoners of war in Korea and in Vietnam. Against these intolerable pressures, Patty held out longer than one could expect of a combat-trained male, but inevitably her will was broken. It broke while she was still held captive in the closet. The SLA "was a foreign army just as much as the ones that we battled overseas, intending as much, if not more, harm to the United States. . . . Her terror was real. But for the kidnapping of Patricia Hearst, there would have *been* no bank robbery," Bailey concludes, "and she would not be here today."

Spectators and journalists alike have been deeply moved by this spare, eloquent, even elegant summary of the case. Two of Patty's sisters and several reporters leave the courtroom in tears.

The kitchenette beside my front door is equipped with an infrared plate-warming light over the stove, perfect for slowly melting squares of cheese while I sit at the writing table at the other end of the room. Warm cheese, cold yellow apples, wine, Fresca, soup, and bushels of fresh broccoli steamed in my Chinese pot—this will be my peculiar, solitary fare for the next eight weeks. When a court day ends, I am usually too tired to do more than watch the television re-cap of the trial, eat, and fall onto the hard, rented bed. The trial drains strength from all alike—reporters, lawyers, jurors, witnesses, spectators. Nobody is good for much afterward. But this evening, when Al Johnson telephones, I invite him to stop by for a drink.

Over the months Patty has been in jail, her defense lawyers and I have developed a wary friendship. Occasionally we dine together, accompanied by Linda Bailey, Lee's adorable third wife. Linda, a practical-minded young woman, looks and dresses like a movie starlet; she is partial to wigs, falls, spike heels, and lamé. A former New Zealand airline stewardess, she reminds me of rare antipodal delights, of koala bears and kiwi fruits—soft and fuzzy outside, juicy and sweet within. Frequently the four of us are joined by another reporter or two, everybody eating and drinking splendidly on the Hearst tab.

The man F. Lee Bailey would most like to have been, had he not had the extreme good fortune to be F. Lee Bailey, is Hildy Johnson, the savvy, wisecracking reporter in *The Front Page*. The famous trial lawyer vastly enjoys the hard-drinking, swaggering company of newspapermen; he understands their fears, and he gives them what they need: colorful quotes, gaudy facts, quantity and quality bullshit, and, very often, truth. Bailey takes risks with reporters. He dares to be indiscreet; he takes chances on their honor. If he can ever find time and bread enough to quit practicing law for a while, Bailey knows just what he would do: become a full-time writer himself. He has written a bestseller, *The Defense Never Rests,* about his big cases, but he longs to attempt a novel. He has known its plot for twenty years: A great criminal lawyer conceives and commits the perfect crime and intends to be punished for it. But his greatest rival, an equally brilliant criminal lawyer, elects to defend the killer and get him off to face a worse fate: life with the knowledge of his crime. Each man knows all the courtroom tricks there are. Each man is attempting simultaneously to bamboozle the other and dope out the truth. In one man's case his life is at stake; in the other, his reputation, which among such men amounts to the same thing.

Bailey's sidekick, Al Johnson, is damp-eyed, overworked, smart, shy, complicated, and, like his childhood friend, Boston Irish. Al is as tough as Lee, but he lacks the flamboyance. Whereas Bailey's personality can be grating, Johnson's tends to have a soothing effect on almost everybody. By the time the trial got under way Johnson had logged several hundred hours visiting Patty in jail, sitting knee to knee with her and chain-smoking, in a small, airless room—"the iron phone booth"—where attorneys and clients meet privately and face to face, without the bulletproof glass, television monitors, and bugged telephones that separate prisoners from their other visitors.

Johnson was the pivotal figure in HERNAP's Act II. During this crucial four-and-a-half-month period, the defense managed an arpeggio of medico-legal-propaganda delays, arguing on each occasion that the client simply was not yet ready to stand trial because she was still, in Johnson's oft-repeated refrain, "incapable of cooperating in her own defense." Johnson's assignment was to restore that capacity, which is to say, to preside over the demise of Tania and make sure the defiant girl guerrilla of the Missing Year was dead and buried before the trial began. Whoever Patty Hearst may be right now, Al Johnson knows better than anyone else in the world. What, I often wonder, does the kidnapped-heiress-turned-revolutionary make of this cynical, shrewd, sweet, overripe, Archie Bunker–style ex-Marine and her only confidant? For myself, I liked him the moment we met.

Call him anytime, Al always said, and on that first day he had groped in his wallet for a business card. But he had been handing out cards all over San Francisco, and the only one he could find was not the lawyer card but the other, the one advertising his services as a magician. Al is known professionally as The Great Zombo, and the card proclaiming his availability for weddings and private parties pictures a cartoon of a chubby aviator in goggles and leather flying helmet riding on a magic carpet above the legend

> THE GREAT ZOMBO
> "MAGIC FOR ALL SITUATIONS"
> *By Appointment*

The last time I had seen either of Patty's lawyers outside of court was last Friday, at a final pretrial lunch of soft-shell crabs and hard-sell Bailey in the dining room of the Mark Hopkins Hotel. Johnson, as usual, was with Patty down at the jail, thirty miles away. Bailey had told me then that the government's two psychiatrists were feuding, and that the defendant was in such poor emotional shape that even the prosecutors were losing their stomach for the coming trial.

"Jim Browning told me last week, 'Plead her guilty to *anything*, and I'll dismiss the case,'" Bailey had said. "I told him, 'Dismiss *all* the charges, then I'll talk to you.' Jim said, 'You know I can't do that. The

American people won't put up with it.' And I said, 'You're damned right they won't.' "

Bailey also emphasized, as Johnson always did, that Patty's life was in considerable danger. Terrorists, counterterrorists, and assorted crackpots, paranoiacs, and misguided patriots all wished her ill. "You wouldn't *believe* the threats that are coming into the jail," he said. "If the judge had let her out on bail, there was no way her life could be protected. *No way!*"

As with his previous big cases, Bailey was planning to write about his new client; in fact, her story would be the subject of his next book. The novel would have to wait a little longer. Income from other, extralegal activities had become especially important in recent years. He also presided over a TV talk show and published a magazine. He gave frequent public lectures, at good fees, as well as legal seminars for trial lawyers. He was franchising the helicopters manufactured by the Engstrom Helicopter Company, which he owned. Its manager was a one-time client, former Marine captain Ernest Medina, of My Lai–massacre fame. Himself a former Marine fighter pilot, Bailey today flies himself around his busy world in one or another of his own aircraft.

His rise to the top had been, as the press frequently pointed out, "meteoric." In 1952, during the Korean War, Francis Lee Bailey had been a bored Harvard sophomore. He quit college, joined the Navy, transferred to the Marines, learned to fly, and, by a fluke, wound up as his squadron's chief legal officer. For his last seventeen months of duty, he prosecuted, defended, investigated, and judged military cases. On the side, he moonlighted with a civilian lawyer and accumulated so much practical experience that once he got out of the service he was able to talk his way into Boston University Law School, even though he lacked a college degree. After being graduated first in his class, he embarked on his dazzling courtroom career.

Barely three months after being admitted to the bar, he won his first case when the jury acquitted an auto mechanic accused of chopping up his wife. A year later Bailey, then thirty-two, found glory in the Sam Sheppard case: He argued before the Supreme Court that Dr. Sheppard had not had a fair trial because of the judge's failure to insulate the jurors from the vicious anti-Sheppard campaign in the *Cleveland Plain Dealer.* The opposing attorney, representing the State of Ohio, was William Saxbe. Bailey won a landmark eight-to-one decision and later an easy acquittal for Sheppard. He went on to defend a spectacular series of cases, and won most of them. Dr. Carl Coppolino, an anesthesiologist, was acquitted of murdering his mistress's husband (though later convicted of killing his wife). Albert DeSalvo, the alleged Boston Strangler, was convicted of robbery and other offenses but not of the string of sex murders of which he was accused. Bailey got four alleged plotters off scot-free in the Massachusetts $1.5-million Great Plymouth Mail Robbery. In Medina's court-martial the captain was acquitted so briskly that the panel of officers voted to smoke an extra cigarette before announcing their verdict, to make it look better.

But despite this series of Alpine peaks, Bailey had been in a valley for the past couple of years. He had become too enthusiastic about one of his clients, Glenn Turner, the cosmetics franchiser and "Dare to be great!" man, and when the government indicted Turner for mail fraud, Bailey was indicted, too. After an eight-month trial, which ended in a hung jury, the government dropped the charges against Bailey, but during this harrowing period the lawyer had had to borrow $400,000 just to stay afloat. "It was the worst thing that ever happened to me," Bailey told me. "I couldn't try any cases. I couldn't get any income. People stayed away in droves." His practice plummeted, and he had to disband a legal stable of twelve attorneys. Fortunately, his boyhood chum J. Albert Johnson was around to keep Bailey's Boston office open. When Bailey was in law school, his first job had been working nights for Johnson's law firm. Now Johnson was helping him out again.

A month after the charges against Bailey were dropped, an emergency call from Randolph Hearst reached Bailey at the state penitentiary in Jackson, Mississippi, where he was visiting a woman on death row. Hearst thought his daughter, who had been represented since her capture, a week earlier, by young Terence Hallinan, under the guidance of his eighty-one-year-old father, Vincent, needed new or additional counsel right away. Bailey said his plane was parked nearby, and he told Hearst he would fly to San Francisco at once. He paused just long enough to call his buddy Johnson, who was on a first-degree murder case in Niagara Falls. Then, each at the controls of his own plane, both lawyers headed west. By week's end Bailey had met Patty at the jail, won her approval, and concluded his arrangements with her original counsel and with her parents, who would be paying the bills. His agreement with the Hearsts called for him to defend Patty in at least two trials: the charge of bank robbery in federal court in San Francisco, and the California case in Los Angeles, where Patty was a codefendant with the Harrises for the shoot-up at Mel's Sporting Goods and related offenses. For the Hibernia Bank case he would charge the Hearsts only $125,000 plus expenses, which of necessity would be vast, but he instructed all "subcontractors"—persons and firms aiding in the preparation of the defense—not to bill the Hearsts any higher than they had the average of their last twenty clients. Their new lawyer had a strong feeling that "the Hearsts have been ripped off enough already." From the start, Bailey enthusiastically accepted his role as defender of the rich against the venal chiseling of the multitude.

"Did *Patty* accept you and Al as her lawyers right off?" I had asked over lunch at the Mark Hopkins.

"She said she did. Handling a criminal case is a problem of management. Money alone will not win a lawsuit; it only gets a lawsuit prepared to be won. What you need most is the confidence and trust of the client. A lawyer has two obligations: One, I've got to be good, but two, she's got to believe I'm good."

Our interview had migrated upstairs from the hotel dining room to the Bailey-Johnson apartments. On the eve of the trial the defense team was moving to another, newer hotel, the Stanford Court. Moving day at this all-male ménage reminded me of a road trip I once made with another migratory all-male tribe, Ricky Nelson and his band. The rock band existed in a midden of used condoms and gnawed chicken bones. These middle-aged migrants traveled with tape recorders and legal briefs instead of guitar strings and comic books, but the sense in their apartments of happy masculine dishevelment was the same. Now all the legal memoranda, the liquor, the half-empty fruit bowls, the Maalox and Gelusil, the tape-recording gear, the silk neckties and Gucci shoes, were being dumped in big cartons by three of the young Boston Irish cop-type investigators who work for Bailey. Ignored, the red message light on the telephone winked without letup. The bathrooms were damp with old towels, and the toilets were like unflushed latrines. The place looked as if a general staff billeted in a very expensive hotel had just won a major victory and were hastily evacuating to even grander headquarters.

While his lieutenants packed, Bailey was busy manufacturing a master tape of the seven SLA messages all on one cassette. The amplified, braggadocio voices of the dead terrorists counterpointed the moving-day banter of the living men. When Al reappeared, Bailey switched off the mad tirade of the General Field Marshal and asked, "What do you want, asshole?"

"Lee, please. General Field Marshal Asshole, if you don't mind."

The noted Harvard legal scholar Alan Dershowitz had written the briefs for Patty's case. "In a heavy case, I'm apt to send it over to Alan," Bailey had said, "because law students know more damn law than anybody. In this case the key issue will be how the jury is instructed. Because Patty is a kidnap victim, the ordinary rules don't apply. Ordinarily the robbers' presence in the bank proves their intent to rob the bank. But if the accused is a kidnap victim, and there is an unbroken chain of custody by the kidnappers, there can be no inference that she was there intentionally. It is just as likely she was there unintentionally."

One of Bailey's expert witnesses would be a quadruple-threat man, Dr. Martin Orne, a psychologist and a psychiatrist who is also a hypnotist and polygraph expert. Bailey himself knows a great deal about hypnosis and has taught courses in its legal aspects. Patty had already weathered a three-day test on Bailey's favorite item of detective hardware, the polygraph, and "she did real well."

The afternoon was late, the cartons long gone. At the door of the suite, Bailey smiled. "By the way, I think I can get Catherine to see you now." This was startling news.

"How is she holding up?" I asked.

"Mrs. Hearst is a terrible pessimist. Deep down she thinks that, despite the apparent genius of counsel, her daughter will go to jail."

Al Johnson is pale and splotchy when he arrives for a drink after court, bearing a present from Lee. It is a copy of the master cassette, so that I can listen to the entire sequence of the seven SLA messages. Al has not slept for two nights. Personal troubles compound his professional problems, and he has other bad news. "Catherine has changed her mind again. Now she won't talk to you. She says you wrote that Patty smoked pot at school."

"Al, you know I didn't write that! She just doesn't trust me."

I mention a rumor that before the kidnapping Patty and Steve Weed had not been getting along. "That's putting it mildly. She hated him! For six months she'd been thinking about suicide, she wanted so desperately to get out of that marriage."

"Why not just call it off?"

"She was weak. Her mother was out buying china. The wedding juggernaut was rolling, and she didn't know how to stop it."

I understand, having once been in the same position myself. Al says he was, too.

Al is upset because an extract of Weed's book, *My Life with Patty Hearst,* had just appeared in a magazine, despite all of Bailey and Johnson's warnings. "It may influence the jury. Besides, it's a lie. He says she seduced *him,* that she initiated the pot and sex experiments. Sure, she was infatuated with him, she moved into his place, but the experiments were his idea, not hers."

Randoph Hearst's hangout, the posh Pacific Union Club, on Nob Hill, is too stuffy and rarefied for a man like Al Johnson. But clearly he could use a place to relax, steam, swim, cool out, so I offer him my spare key to the sauna and pool downstairs, and we have another drink. Before he leaves, Al offers to get me an official front-row seat at the trial, on the Hearsts' own bench, and urges me please to "use our office anytime, the secretaries, the Xerox, whatever you need. Tomorrow I'll bring you the transcript of today's hearings." Then, with a whiff of Vitalis and a shy smile, The Great Zombo is gone.

It is difficult not to believe Al has been sent over to leak some of this. But which was the important part? How much was leak, how much truth? Is he sure himself? For me, the stunner is his admission that Patty had been desperate enough to get out of her coming marriage to consider suicide, for if this is true, disturbing questions arise. Was she desperate enough to get herself kidnapped? Even if she did not actually engineer her own abduction, would not the SLA's abrupt intervention in her life seem like a blessing in disguise, a providential deus ex machina in army fatigues and combat boots? If Patty was always, by nature, the weak person with no will of her own whom Al has just described, what becomes of the notion that Cinque regressed and brutalized her until he *destroyed* her strong will? What becomes of the famous brainwashing premise, on which her entire defense rests and which is now about to unfold?

Thursday, February 5

Last night the heavens opened. Surging thunder and lightning swept the city, a truly operatic storm. This morning every peak and pinnacle in this spectacular city of hills is white; San Francisco's first snowstorm in eighty-seven years.

In court Patty looks terrible. She is dressed in a dowdy brownish wrapper over an orange turtleneck, which emphasizes her pallor, and she looks like an inmate in a 1930s prison movie. The government's first witness is the bank manager who pushed the burglar alarm which automatically activated the cameras. Judge Carter bends toward the jury and, in the kindly, all-the-time-in-the-world voice he always employs when addressing these special people, says, "What Mr. Browning proposes to do now is read a stipulation. A stipulation is something to which both parties agree. You may accept that evidence without further proof."

Browning stipulates that, one, the Hibernia Bank *is* a bank and, two, that Ron Ceraghino *is* an auditor, who, following a robbery at the bank, determined there was a loss of approximately $10,690 in lawful moneys of the United States.

The second witness, Vernon L. Kipping, is an FBI photography expert. He explains how the bank's automatic cameras work, slipping easily into worn, photography-lecture cadences. "A motion-picture projector has a lot in common with a sewing machine. A needle makes a stitch; a projector projects a frame. . . ." While the jury listens politely Bailey amuses himself, and us, by strolling with exaggerated slowness across the courtroom, head cocked alertly toward the old-maidish witness. He ends up leaning on the back of the jury box in a posture of sober regard. Only the spectators have been able to see his face, the mocking air, the thin, Johnny Carson smile.

I hate technical explanations of how things work, and my attention wanders toward the figure on the bench, the quizzical face and birdlike head above the robes. Carter parts his thin hair in the old style, straight down the middle, like his decisions. He enjoys an even contest in his courtroom. Lawyers have told me that if one side appears to him stronger than the other, Carter will tend in his rulings to favor the weaker side. Well-matched opponents make a better ball game, but I'm not sure I like to find the sports mentality on the high bench. I am puzzled, too, by Carter's statement that the Carter and Hearst families are well acquainted. It is true that the San Francisco Establishment is small and tight enough so that, more than in any other American cosmopolis, "everybody knows everybody." But when I had asked Randy about the family friendship, he had said, "I think his father was involved in some dispute with the paper at one time. But I scarcely know the fellow." Either Hearst felt he had to say this, or Carter is more of a name dropper and social climber than he appears. He appears now both benevolent and irritable, first a pixie, then a fussbudget. He is meticulous and frail. He scratches his head. He peers over his glasses. He closes his eyes to rest them; sometimes he does fall asleep.

San Francisco's legal fraternity had hoped Carter would let this case pass to the next man on the circuit, the capable Judge Alphonso Zirpoli. What concerned the lawyers was less Carter's health than his lack of "firmness." They didn't really consider him "tough enough" for the Hearst case. Carter *could* have passed up the case but he didn't. Judges have as big egos as lawyers do. Indeed, it must be a fearsome sight, the well-developed ego of a mature federal-court judge. I imagine a large organ, something white-and-purple-veined, engorged, a living eggplant pulsating under the black robes. This is only the first day of the trial, and already I know I would not ever like to be a judge. However, if I must one day *be* judged, I would settle for Oliver J. Carter.

Comes now our first glimpse of Bailey's famed skills at cross-examination. "Is it not correct that when you convert from thirty-five millimeter to sixteen millimeter, the shape of the frame changes?"

"Yes, it's like running a CinemaScope movie on TV."

"I think the jury has the essence of motion-picture technology at this point. . . . Mr. Kipping, the second version of the film you showed us hones in on the center section. *Why did you crop out the rest?*"

"To show the expression and demeanor of the subject."

"You were aware, as you made the edited version, that there were serious questions about whether the defendant was covered at all times by people carrying weapons?"

The witness appears not to understand, and Bailey repeats, as if speaking to a slightly retarded person, "At the time you made the film, you were aware there was a serious question whether she was covered at all times by the others' weapons?"

KIPPING (deliberately misunderstanding): I had no knowledge she was in fact covered.

BAILEY (hard): Are you learning for the first time today, Mr. Kipping, that there is a question about whether she was covered in the bank?

KIPPING: I saw no evidence that she was under the gun.

BAILEY (airy): Was it your purpose, when you made the edited version, to blank out evidence that she *was* under the gun?

"Absolutely not!" says the witness. But the lawyer has successfully raised doubt in the jury's mind about whether and, if so, to what purpose the government has meddled with this crucial film.

The Hearsts' new lawyer is tough and smart. Certainly he is earning his $125,000 fee. Indeed right now Bailey seems a great bargain. I recalled the spooky, intimidating day we first met, very soon after he had rather hastily been hired. I knew him then only by reputation: the scrappiest, most audacious, best-known, and possibly best criminal lawyer in the land. Suddenly this man's professional concerns and my own had a great deal in common, and it seemed important to me that we meet soon. Although Bailey worked out of Boston, it appeared he retained a Washington press agent, and through him an appointment had been arranged. I was invited to visit Bailey's Massachusetts home one September weekend, after spending the night at my daughter's boarding school in Concord, nearby.

It was a beautiful New England autumn weekend, but the visit with my daughter had been grim. She seemed miserable and would scarcely talk, and I could find no way to penetrate her armored, icy reserve. I could only hope that, in time, the school would take hold. We had no alternatives. I resolved to be better prepared for my next encounter.

Driving along the Cape Cod highway through a dazzle of red and gold leaves, I constructed imaginary Perry Mason dialogue:

BAILEY: *What can I do for you?*

S.A.: *Trust me. This one is the case of your life, and mine, too. I've been on your client's side ever since I started looking into her story, only five weeks after she was kidnapped.*

But, of course, he never asked me that question, or any other. Bailey doesn't ask, he *tells,* and when I finally got to see him he told me exactly how he intended to defend his latest client.

Earldor Circle, several miles off the highway, looked like an incipient housing subdivision deep in the woods. Winding streets and sewers and power lines were in, but no lots yet sold. It appeared to be yet another Bailey business venture, this one a speculation in suburban real estate. Bailey's own spread covered several acres atop the highest hill, and its relaxed architecture was more Las Vegas than New England. A helipad adjoined the parking lot and, when not in use, the helicopter was parked inside a hangarlike extension of what realtors used to call the rumpus room.

Although F. Lee Bailey's fights have always been on the side of the law, visiting him at home felt a little like calling on a retired gangster, or perhaps a Prohibition czar. The large, queer, rambling house was sparely but expensively furnished, and spotless. It suggested the VIP passenger lounge of a just-built airport in a remote province. The helipad, the elaborate, multitelephoned, in-house office, and the small fleet of airplanes parked nearby all implied a Perry Mason professional setup, just the image Bailey always says he is trying to avoid.

Linda Bailey met me at the door. Her attitudes were conventional and middle-class, her only obviously liberated aspects being her beautiful, unbra'd breasts. It would have been easy to read her as a cookie of little brain, but probably a mistake. Linda and I made small talk in the huge glass living room while we waited for Mr. Big. The onetime New Zealand airline stewardess is Bailey's third wife, and the extraordinary Maori hand-carved totem-pole lamp had been a wedding present two years ago. She has been considering covering the six-foot carved brass coffee table with a sheet of glass to reduce housework, as she is so often away. Yes, she travels everywhere with Lee. He gave her a new Mercedes three years ago, but she has yet to learn how to drive. They are rarely at home longer than a day or two at a time.

Mr. Big turned out to be medium height, sleepy-eyed, affable, sexy-voiced, and vain, a chain-smoker who continually combed his hair. Despite his cordiality, he did not engender much warmth. But I felt great intelligence, a vibrating ego, controlled power, and controlled impatience. I had a strong feeling he could scarcely wait for me to leave. The tension was tremendous; perhaps he was putting me on. Bailey seemed to train on put-downs the way other men train on push-ups. The man frightened me a little. Did I frighten him, too, or bore him, or was he merely eager for me to get out of there so he could have a beer and relax and unloosen the too-tight trousers of his creamy gabardine suit?

The hospitality was curious, stiff. Linda had said proudly, "Lee never needs makeup on TV. He's got that good J&B complexion." But no drink was offered. Linda heated frozen hors d'oeuvres and served black instant coffee from an open galley off the living room, but she did not herself join us. It was like being back on Qantas, and I had a feeling a drink would cost me a dollar, and for two dollars I'd get earphones.

As soon as Lee began to speak about his case, the personalities, the legal strategies, the difficulties, the probabilities, Linda discreetly withdrew. He struck chords and stated themes I was to hear, with variations, many times. If the FBI had done its job properly, there wouldn't be any Tania, for example, because the FBI would have rescued Patty before she became Tania. If Bailey won in San Francisco, as he expected, the scene would then shift to Los Angeles, where the prosecutor was not so concerned—as Bailey thought Browning was—that he might appear to be knuckling under to pressure from the Hearsts. "Browning's glad I'm in the case because it means a fight, not a fix." With a less aggressive lawyer than Browning, it might have appeared that the government was going easy on Hearst's daughter, in return for the Hearst press's support of Ford over Reagan as the Republican candidate in an election year.

"How did you work things out with the Hallinans?" I asked.

"The first thing I wanted to avoid was the appearance of lawyers getting into a pissing contest. So I've made my peace with Vince, and he will remain as a consultant on the case."

"What is Patty's present mental state?"

"She's in a transitory stage right now." The word "transitory" suggested that Bailey's client has already undergone some kind of psychological shift in the four weeks since she had been arrested and photographed giving the raised-fist guerrilla salute. First she was Patty, then she became Tania: The critical point in it all, I thought, was when the second personality switched off. When, and how, did Tania die?

That's crucial, Bailey agreed. "But in any case, she'll never be the girl she was. She's a third person now, and not all that spaced out. If you do get to see her, you'll find a little girl who never had any place of her own before, who was always closely watched, even before she joined the SLA. I think she likes that jail cell. This is the first time in her life that nobody's watching her. She cries easily, but people in jail do that."

I mentioned a confidential *Newsweek* file I had seen describing one of the SLA writings, leaked by the prosecution. (In fact, though I didn't know it at the time, it was a part of the "Tania Interview.") Patty had called Catherine a bigot, a pill-head, and a drunk.

"Aren't you going to have trouble handling Patty's terrific hatred of her mother?" I said.

"Not at all," he replied. "All daughters say stuff like that about their mother. If it wasn't Patty Hearst, no one would think anything of it."

Driving away, I realized he was right. I had had similar thoughts about my mother lots of times, and my father, too. I just never dared write them down.

Bailey had said I could talk to Patty, provided she was willing, as soon as she had recovered sufficient emotional equilibrium. He did not think this would take long. For several weeks after that, night and day, without success, I had left telephone messages for Al Johnson in San Francisco, trying to confirm the promised appointment. Finally I called Bailey back at his hilltop. It was another lovely fall Saturday afternoon. Genial and expansive, Mr. Big said Johnson had been scrambling so fast in the pretrial maneuvering that even Bailey couldn't get hold of him. A woman psychiatrist, Dr. Elisabeth Richards, had been found to treat Patty in prison. "We won't try to bail her. It's too dangerous. She's getting a couple of death threats a day. Al has applied for a weapons permit. The Red Guerrilla Family is after him." And then, casually, and so fast I barely saw it whiz past me, came the curve ball: Bailey himself controlled "all book rights" to Patty's story. As he has on his other big cases, he intended to write a book about HERNAP, centered on the coming trial and "incorporating previous material." The work, he implied, was already under way.

After lunch, spectators find an enormous movie screen, the size of an outdoor billboard, has been set up in the left rear corner of the courtroom, between the press box and the bench. The jury will now see the bank film for the first time, as narrated by Tom Padden, the senior FBI agent on the case. Blue tie, gray suit, tall gray man.

CARTER *(bending his turkey neck toward the jury):* All right, ladies and gentlemen, we're going to turn the lights out now. [He grins like a merry skull.] No hocus-pocus, please!

The lights dim, and enormous, ten-foot-high figures rush onto the screen—huge, lurching shadows carrying automatic weapons. First Nancy Ling Perry dashes in, then DeFreeze in his floppy Abzug hat, then Camilla Hall, and now Soltysik vaults over the counter in a single bound and soon flies wildly back toward the camera with a sack of money in her fist. The gigantic phantoms skitter across the bank floor, shouting to one another in total silence except for the click-click-click of the movie projector. Twice the specter of Patty in black coat and wig looks back over her shoulder at DeFreeze. Her movement is ambiguous. The jury must decide whether she is seeking instruction from a cohort or cowering under his gun.

The courtroom twilight lasts for a long ninety seconds. During this time the real Patty watches the screen Patty intently. Her mouth is open, and she is swallowing hard, licking her lips, holding the table edge with whitening knuckles. When the lights go up, her eyes are wet.

Bailey rises. "No questions, Your Honor."

The government next calls the clerk, who testifies that on the morning in question she "heard metallic noises." Browning reaches behind the court clerk's desk and fishes up a semiautomatic carbine with a big manila FBI identification tag dangling from the webbing strap. In two quick strides, he is across the courtroom and beside the jury, pulling back the bolt and ramming it home. *Tock!* "Was it similar to this sound?"

"It could have been."

The next witness, the bank guard, is an elderly man with a shaky voice, thick glasses. He "saw four men . . . four persons . . . in a doorway . . . four abreast. . . . They stepped forward and divided, two and two. . . ." His testimony is impossible to follow.

Carter says, "I want to know which was male and which was female."

"It appeared to be a female wearing pants."

"What did she say?" The judge is becoming crotchety.

"She said, 'First person puts up his head, I'll blow his motherfucking head off!' " So the dread words have been uttered. In the old man's quavery, dry hole of a mouth, they really do sound obscene.

"Is the person who spoke those words now here in court?" Browning asks.

"She's over there. . . . You want her name?"

Mr. Bailey rises to cross-examine, cream dripping from his whiskers. "What is your age, Mr. Shea? . . . Ah, sixty-eight. And how long have you been a bank guard? . . . Um-hum, seven months." Lightly: "I take it this was your first robbery?" Leaning on the witness box, friendly, wearing a tiger's sleepy smile, Bailey asks Shea to repeat his description of the female bandit. What comes out is hodgepodge.

"Miss Hearst, would you rise, please?" She stands up, pink-polished fingertips braced against the table top to steady herself, perhaps ninety-five pounds, the size-six dress hanging on her frame like a shroud.

"Now, Mr. Shea. What would you say is the height and weight of this lady?"

"'Bout five foot six, a hundred and twenty pounds."

"Mm-hmm. Thank you. Now, would you go to the chart and point out to the jury the *position* of the female bandit you were describing when you told the agent she was five feet six inches tall and ten feet from the door. . . ."

A witness led into a contradiction in his testimony senses the trap an instant before it closes. He becomes intractable, like a small child. Doggedly, the decrepit Mr. Shea marches out of the witness box and points to an orange sticker marked F.

"Have you been informed, Mr. Shea, that position F was occupied by Nancy Ling Perry and not by the defendant?"

It is time for recess. Outside, in the corridor, the defense is feeling pretty good. Round One is clearly theirs. Randolph Hearst lights a cigarette and giggles. "I wouldn't put any money in that bank, if I were you."

After recess Bailey concludes his demolition of Mr. Shea, drawing from him the admission that he could neither see nor hear clearly on the day of the robbery and that he subsequently had an ear operation, obviously unsuccessful.

The next important witness is James Norton, a hospital therapist, who was making a deposit when he saw the bank guard suddenly shoved against the wall by the black man in the floppy hat, and next found himself looking straight down the barrel of a gun held by a woman who ordered him to lie on the floor or she would blow his fucking head off. He identifies Patty as the woman. Norton had hesitated before complying with the command because "they had been filming *The Streets of San Francisco* at the hospital, and frankly, I thought this was more of the same." Laughter from the spectators, smiles from a few jurors.

CARTER: Stop this outburst! This is not a place to come and laugh! This is not a movie house!

Earlier, jesting about "hocus-pocus," Carter had suggested his courtroom *was* a movie house. But, like most judges, Carter has a selective sense of humor, and none about the majesty of his own position.

Inside this courtroom the press is sequestered as much as the jury. During lunch we discover that the day's big Patty Hearst story is not even in San Francisco. The *Chicago Tribune* has just published huge chunks of the notorious "Tania Interview," and in response, the Harrises have released a statement accusing Patty of selling them out in order to free herself. The two stories underscore the double nature of the trial. Patty is being judged simultaneously in this courtroom, where she remains cloaked in her "presumption of innocence," and in the media, where her cloak was torn to shreds long ago. Bailey and Johnson are shrewd media managers who manipulate the trial press like a bunch of Muppets. Edward Bennett Williams, once Bailey's mentor and still his hero—perhaps his only one —calls Bailey an "ink junkie," hooked on his own press. But Patty's ordeal-by-press began long before Bailey came into this case. Patty was never *not* on trial in the media; she was suspected from the beginning of plotting her own abduction. Despite denials by everybody, including the U.S. government, public skepticism persists. That Patricia Hearst was a genuine kidnapping victim is as difficult for many Americans to believe as the notion that President Kennedy was the victim of Lee Harvey Oswald acting alone. It may be that no matter whom Patty and her parents had chosen to represent her, her lawyers would have had no choice but to run two defenses concurrently: one before the judge, for the jury and the record; the other an "instant replay" before the television cameras, for the press and public. Lest it be imagined that the U.S. government is any less anxious than the defense to try its case in the media, it is well to remember that the "Tania Interview" was leaked the same week Patty was captured, but it was so damning the papers refrained from printing it. The instant the jury was locked up, however, the papers rushed into print with Patricia Hearst's "innermost thoughts" during her time with the terrorists:

> After a couple of weeks, I started to feel sympathy with the SLA. I was beginning to see what they wanted to accomplish was necessary, although at the time it was hard for me to relate to the tactic of urban guerrilla warfare.
>
> My comrades were willing to help me learn the political and military skills that I was lacking as long as I was willing to struggle to become a guerrilla soldier. . . . Before I made my decision to stay with the cell, Cin talked to me about the changes I'd gone through. . . . What some people refer to as a sudden conversion was actually a process of development, much the same as a photograph is developed. . . . When the members of the unit decided I could stay with the cell, the decision was

unanimous. . . . Like someone said . . . I'd been brainwashed for twenty years, and it only took the SLA six weeks to straighten me out.

Tania's comments about her parents are extraordinarily bitter:

> I told Cin right away that I didn't think my parents would cooperate —that they had no love for me, and I had none for them. I'm glad it turned out the way it did because, if I'd been closer to my family, I would have been a different kind of person. . . . My decision to join the SLA would have been a lot harder. . . . I would have been much more prone toward developing into a Fascist rather than a freedom fighter.

Patty's description of herself as a "freedom fighter" is no more persuasive, at least on the face of this document, than is Donald De-Freeze's grandiose designation of himself as a "Field Marshal." SLA rhetoric is loonily overblown. Yet amid the lush verbiage, one paragraph of the "Tania Interview" rings with the faint, clear bell of truth: "What you have to understand is that if I'd been a different person, a typical 'rich bitch,' I would have been treated a lot differently. Nobody would have wanted to talk to me after about a week." Right there, perhaps, might be the kernel of it all.

Once more it is time for the ritual twice-daily plunge for the elevators and the scramble down to the television press room on the seventh floor, a huge, fluorescent-lit cube arbitrarily lifted out of the vast empty acreage of gray bureaucratic floor space within the Federal Building and designated Hearst Press Room for the duration of the legal carnival upstairs. Within it, each press organization has staked out its own area, an untidy clutter of desks, phones, lights, cameras, telexes, trash, and typewriters. The various media organizations are encamped in this arid space like separate groups of nomadic desert tribesmen, rival and wary though essentially friendly, bound together on the same long, straggly pilgrimage to the same Mecca: a verdict in the case. Along one side of the room is a permanent setup of lights, a large, battered table bristling with microphones, and a few chairs. Here each day, and sometimes twice a day, the lawyers reenact the trial upstairs, staging a condensed instant replay for the benefit of the cameras. It is an opportunity for the opposing counsel to angle, color, expand, or sharpen testimony, to make charges and offer explanations they could never get away with in court. Bailey relishes these sessions; they give him a second chance to score points and wisecrack with the press. He tosses out quotes like a coloratura throwing roses.

"Mr. Bailey, are you satisfied you demolished Mr. Shea?"

"He did not go writhing to the floor in Perry Mason fashion . . . but I'm satisfied the jury has some questions about his accuracy."

"Did your client comment to you on Mr. Browning's opening statement?"

"Yes." Pause. Silken grin. "She was not favorably impressed."

Friday, February 6

When Bailey rises to cross-examine James Norton, canary feathers are hanging out of his mouth. His purpose is to get Norton to waver on his earlier identification of Patty as the female bandit who ordered him onto the floor. The film is to be run again, this time in slow motion. Twenty-seven seconds into the film, Norton identifies the lady, "but not *where* I first saw her." Bailey's trap is about to spring. "Mr. Norton, I would like you to examine this document." In his original FBI interview, the day after the robbery, Norton had identified a different lady at a different location. Bailey stands patiently, one hand resting lightly on the edge of the witness box, his eyes turned heavenward. It is a long, long wait. Then: "There is *no mention in that document* of Patty Hearst threatening you or using obscenities. . . . Mr. Norton, do you recognize John McNally?" Bailey's ace investigator, the burly ex-NYC cop, beams like a seraph over at the defense table. "Did you not tell Mr. McNally that you believed Patty is guilty and that nothing could convince you otherwise?"

"No, I did not. I know how my mother feels, but I have an open mind."

"Did you not hear your mother say to Mr. McNally, 'I hope they stick it to her!'?" At the defense table Patty gasps. Norton denies it. McNally interviewed his mother at home and talked to him at the hospital.

"Mr. Norton, don't you think the fact that for the past eleven years you have lived with your mother might have [delicate cough] *tainted* your recollection?"

During recess, reporters caucus in the corridor. "Bailey's working the faggot angle pretty hard."

"But does a San Francisco jury care?"

After the recess court resumes with a third running of the film—this time cropped to show the defendant only, in extreme close-up, so that she appears as a monstrous, gun-toting automaton, the Patty balloon in Macy's Thanksgiving Day Parade. Twice, the huge head half turns toward Cinque, behind her, and appears to speak. The government contends we are seeing Patty tell Mr. Norton to get on the fucking floor. The defense claims Patty said only what the SLA told her to say: "I am Tania" or "This is Tania Hearst!" The second set of mouth movements is not speech at all, but Patty's gasps as she hears the sound of gunfire. Save for the tick-tick-tick of the projector, the darkened courtroom is deadly quiet, but this appearance of speech on the silent screen gives the trial its most dramatic moment.

Bailey later tells reporters he has sent a print of the film back to the famous Itek Labs in Cambridge, Massachusetts, the same outfit that analyzed the Kennedy-assassination film, in order to demonstrate scientifically that his interpretation of Patty's mouth movements is correct. But how can even Itek prove what someone is saying on a silent film? Muttering portentously of "lasers, scanners, and computers," Bailey and Johnson disappear into the elevator for lunch.

The afternoon's evidence includes aerial photographs of the bank. Frisky as an otter, Bailey wins an affectionate laugh from the press when he says, "I certainly do not object to any helicopter pictures, Your Honor." Thanks to tireless self-promotion, it is well known around town that Bailey's major nonlegal enterprise is his helicopter company.

One has nearly forgotten that two elderly men were shot during the robbery. We meet them this afternoon. Eugene Brennan, a deliveryman, just "felt a little sting in the stomach" and found out when he woke up in the hospital that a bullet had struck his liver, cracked a rib, and come out his side. His buddy, Pete Markoff, "felt a thump, like being kicked in the behind. After that, I don't know what happened."

"No questions," says Bailey.

The remainder of Friday is given over to various witnesses to the robbers' getaway. Bailey has no difficulty pointing out discrepancies between their testimony today and what they told the grand jury nearly two years before, his implication being that the prosecutors had assisted the witnesses in making their identifications.

When we adjourn, Catherine Hearst precedes her husband and daughters down the aisle, still impeccably groomed and coiffed after a full day in court. "Flawless!" a press photographer exclaims. "Catherine Hearst is the most perfect woman I've ever seen . . . and I once spent a weekend with Grace Kelly."

Steven Weed had told me the same. "Never saw her with a hair out of place. But Randy, he didn't even mind coming to the dining table still in his silk pajamas."

But the week's real stunner comes on the drive home, when Richard Threlkeld remarks offhandedly, "Of course, everybody knows it was Emily Harris who shot the pregnant woman."

Threlkeld has been CBS-TV's man on the case from the beginning, and his zinger concerned a quite different SLA bank robbery. One Monday morning in April 1975, at which time Patty had been "missing" for eleven months, several robbers burst into the Bank of America branch in Carmichael, California, a suburb of Sacramento. Myrna Lee Opsahl, pregnant mother of four, was standing in line shortly after nine-thirty A.M., waiting to deposit Sunday's church receipts, when she was hit in the stomach by a shotgun blast at almost point-blank range. The woman was rushed to the hospital, where the surgeon on duty was her husband. Dr. Opsahl had been unable to save either his wife or their unborn child. According to Threlkeld, "everybody" also "knows" that Patty Hearst drove the getaway car. Under the law, therefore, he says, she is considered a coconspirator, guilty of felony murder, and can be charged with murder, even though she was never inside the bank. Furthermore, Patty was so overwrought right after her capture last September that she confessed the whole story to her mother on Catherine's second visit to the jail. The mother's reaction had been to go straight to the FBI.

Threlkeld's story is a shocker on several levels. Murder in California is once again a capital crime. Under the fighting leadership of Governor Ronald Reagan, Californians have recently voted to restore the death penalty (abolished by the state legislature during ex-governor Edmund G. "Pat" Brown's regime). One of Reagan's staunchest supporters in the fight has been his fellow regent Catherine Hearst. In June 1974, when I first arrived in California to study the Hearst kidnapping, Governor Reagan, toying with the idea of tempering justice with mercy, had instructed his aides to come up with some form of execution "more humane" than the gas chamber, yet something still sufficiently unpleasant to act as a "deterrent" to potential murderers. What the governor was really hunting for, said the *Los Angeles Times,* was something midway between an instantaneous and tasteless poison—not nasty enough—and crucifixion.

Threlkeld's tale sounded so incredible that, after brooding about how best to check it out, I decided to ask Johnson point-blank. "Absolutely not true," he said, jowls shaking with indignation. "It didn't happen that way at all. The truth is that Patty told *us* the story, and *we* told the FBI."

Patricia Hearst and her misadventures had been the focus of my professional life for nearly two years, and had made me almost a commuter from Long Island, New York, where I live, to the Bay Area. Now, at the end of her first week of trial, I had much to ponder, beginning with my own complex relationship with the defendant, her parents, and her attorneys. I had been working on my own book for eighteen months before Bailey entered the case. Indeed, by that time mine was one of more than a dozen Hearst-books-in-embryo, and three Patty books already had been published. But my project had the tacit approval at least of Randolph Hearst, as well as of the family lawyer, William Coblentz, an old acquaintance of mine. It was Coblentz who had originally introduced me to the Hearsts, saying that since Patty books were inevitable, it might be wise for the family to cooperate with one more-or-less respectable journalist. Patty's mother emphatically did not agree, but Randolph Hearst had remained ever affable, ever available. Each time I saw him, however, he made the point that "the real story is Patty, not me." Although I thought then that the "real story" was everything but Patty—as I expressed it at the time, "I want to write the doughnut, not the hole"—nonetheless, her reentry on the scene, complete with a lawyer who was also a would-be biographer and who controlled all access to the client, had set up a certain literary conflict of interest.

Bailey faced the conflict, if that is what it was, with characteristic bravura. Throughout the pretrial months he had given me repeated assurances that I would see Patty "when she was ready." This moment never occurred, but on the very last weekend before trial, Bailey had made me an offer I couldn't refuse. Certain critical documents existed by that time that shed light on the emotional state of Patricia Hearst before her capture and after. One of these was the "Tania Interview." But an even more interesting one was a confidential psychiatric report,

162 pages long, prepared by two of the four doctors who had originally examined the prisoner, within days of her capture, at the request of Judge Carter. The purpose of these examinations was to determine whether the defendant was legally capable of standing trial. Carter was obliged to call for such examinations, he said, because Patty's first attorneys, the Hallinans, had themselves raised the whole issue of Patty's mental health in spectacular fashion. Five days after her arrest, the Hallinans had filed the damnedest bail affidavit anybody around San Francisco had ever seen. It said that after she was kidnapped, Patricia Hearst was held for weeks in a tiny closet, bound, blindfolded, and in the dark. During her first ten days "she was unable to dispose of her body wastes." Nobody spoke to her except Cinque, and he told her "she would be executed unless the ransom demands were complied with." During this period she was given liquids to drink. Then,

> when the blindfold was removed, she felt as if she were on some LSD trip; everything was out of proportion, big and distorted. She heard constant threats against her life . . . was told by her captors that her parents had abandoned her . . . that [if the FBI found the SLA hideout they] . . . would bust into the house with drawn guns . . . and she would undoubtedly be killed in the general massacre. After a month of this sort of treatment, she was in such a condition that she could stand for only 60 seconds or so, and would then fall to the ground. . . .
>
> . . . she was taken to the bank . . . given a gun . . . told that . . . if she made one false move . . . she would be killed instantly. . . .
>
> Finally, under the pressure of these threats, deprivations of liberty, isolation and terror, she felt her mind clouding, and everything appeared so distorted and terrible that she believed and feared that she was losing her sanity, and unless soon freed, would become insane. . . . A short while before her arrest, she began to experience lucid intervals in which her sanity briefly reappeared, and during one of these she began to doubt that her parents were involved in any plan for her destruction . . . but when the FBI agents appeared, she thought that she would instantly be killed. When this did not happen, her mind began to clear up again, but the first full realization that she had been living in a fantasy world whose terrors could be resolved by merely returning to her family or even consulting the law officers, occurred when her mother, her father and her sisters hugged and kissed her.

The troubles to flow from this lurid affidavit were terrible and manifold. Set aside for a moment the fact that the document conflicted with previously disclosed information on Patty's actions after her kidnapping, and that it made no reference to numerous documents in the government's possession in which Patty in her own handwriting described how she had willingly, enthusiastically joined the SLA, forsworn her parents and even denied her own identity as Patricia Hearst; how she had stuck up one bank and, at the very least, made detailed plans to rob others; and how she had joyfully joined the revolution. Although the public was not yet aware of the nature and extent of these documents, Patty and her attorneys surely knew that the FBI had carted off boxloads of this incriminating stuff and had also recovered an arsenal of weapons from her apartment, including some of the guns used in the Hibernia Bank robbery. There was even a stolen "bait bill" from the Carmichael bank cached in Patty's refrigerator.

On the good side, one might have argued that the psychiatric examination could stop the clock from running on the new Speedy Trial Act. Conceivably it could have produced a consensus that the defendant was wacko and therefore not responsible for her acts in the Hibernia Bank or for anything else that may have happened between that time and her arrest. It could perhaps have gotten her transferred from jail to the relative comfort of a "secure" psychiatric institution. It could perhaps have preserved her from the necessity of testifying against others; if she was nuts, how could she be expected to remember anything? How could such "memories" be taken seriously? On the other hand, if Patty was found capable of performing the functions of a defendant, she could be cross-examined on every detail of her story, and if the least bit of it proved false, she could be convicted of perjury. Even that was not the worst. The Hallinans' affidavit violated basic rules of legal strategy: It disclosed Patty's defense in detail and bound her to it; it left her lawyers almost no room to maneuver.

One possible explanation for the affidavit seemed to be that somebody really wanted Patty to remain in jail just then, no matter what. Equally plausible was the notion that Randolph and Catherine Hearst could not bear to see their daughter in jail, no matter what. Perhaps the Hearsts' chief concern was for their own public image: "We'll do *anything* for our daughter!" had been their posture from the very beginning. On the other hand, the family may just have been getting bad legal advice. Maybe dynastic concerns, rather than legal ones, were dictating strategy. Perhaps other, still-hidden considerations in the HERNAP constellation had compelled the bizarre step. Even today, no one knew. In any event, the affidavit and the reaction it engendered were a signal to the Hearsts that new or at least additional legal counsel was urgent. Less than a week after her capture, Patricia Hearst's legal position appeared to be as messy as her mental state and her public image.

Upon receiving the astonishing affidavit, Judge Carter had appointed a panel of three doctors to examine Patty. Service on such a panel is not compulsory, and the following day, without comment, one of the doctors declined to serve. A replacement had to be found fast. Until Carter received the medical report, he said, he would continue to refuse bail and would also refuse a defense request that Patty's parents need not observe the regular jail visiting hours. "What you are telling me is that I should make special rules for Miss Hearst, and I am not going to do that."

So what it had come down to in the pretrial wrangling was the perennial question: Was Patty Hearst "an ordinary person"? The over-riding aim of the prosecution, and a concern seemingly shared by the judge, was that nothing be done for, or allowed to, this defendant that would not be permitted or offered "an ordinary person." Outpatient psychiatric care, for example, would not be available to "an ordinary person," so Patty couldn't have it, either. It struck me that several extraordinary measures were taking place in other current Bay Area trials. In Marin, for example, six defendants had been appearing daily in court since March, each man wearing twenty pounds of iron chains. In Sacramento a young woman in a long red robe was daily carried in and out of a courtroom with her eyes squeezed shut. One would have a hard time proving that Patty Hearst was less ordinary than Squeaky Fromme or the San Quentin Six.

The press said that Catherine Hearst did not trust the Hallinans, who are well known in the Bay Area as defenders of sensational cases and radical causes. Terence "Kayo" Hallinan frequently handles drug as well as political cases; perhaps his father's most famous client had been Harry Bridges. Catherine, said the *New York Post,* had been heard to refer to the old man as "the anti-Christ."

A preliminary psychiatric report was filed on October 4 by the panel of four doctors whom Carter eventually appointed. It said Patty was legally sane but somewhat diminished in her capacity to cooperate in her defense because of her emotional state, a consequence of the severe stress of the past twenty months. Not surprisingly, the doctors recom-mended that Patty would benefit from some pretrial psychiatric treatment, assuming there was to be a trial, and it gave the court a list of possible treatment facilities. Finally, the doctors promised Judge Carter that "detailed reports to the Court will be provided by us individually within the next ten days." All this was a professional way of saying that while the doctors could not agree on what, or how much, was the matter with the girl, some immediate treatment certainly couldn't hurt.

Two of the subsequent individual reports were one page long. The third one was a collaborative effort by Louis Jolyon West, MD, chief of psychiatry at UCLA, and Margaret Thaler Singer, PhD, the clinical psychologist from the University of California at Berkeley, who was brought in at Dr. West's request to administer a full battery of psychological tests. It went on for 136 pages, plus bibliography, footnotes, and *curricula vitae* of its authors.

Carter accepted all the reports and then ordered the trial to proceed within ninety days under the terms of the Speedy Trial Act. He declared the reports confidential and inadmissible as evidence. Only three copies existed, and all three were placed under court seal. Anyone who revealed the contents to anybody save the judge or one of the attorneys risked prosecution for contempt of court. Eventually the hefty West/Singer psychiatric report would turmoil the trial of Patty Hearst just as much as the Hallinans' bail affidavit. Indeed, it was these two remarkable documents—each intended with the purest of motives to help a girl in deep trouble—that set the law and psychiatry on their collision course and guaranteed the sustained shambles that was to take place over eight grueling weeks in Judge Carter's courtroom.

Two days after the Hallinans' affidavit was filed, Susan B. Jordan, the young attorney whom Emily Harris had asked to represent her, had turned up at the jail and shown reporters a note on a torn scrap of yellow paper. "I want to see you. P. Hearst," it said. (Ms. Jordan later said she was prevented from seeing Patty by Vincent Hallinan.)

So far as the public knew, this five-word note was the sole expression from Patty since her arrest of what *she* wanted. Not a single other direct word would be heard from her until she took the witness stand. Everything was filtered through her family, attorneys, or jailers. From the prisoner's point of view, Act II was entirely a dumb show.

But lawyers were atwitter all over town, and most said the case was being mishandled. "Poor Randy's at his wit's end," Coblentz told me. I asked him why the Hallinans couldn't just be fired. "Patty doesn't want 'em fired. She likes them. Besides, Randy can't do it. They're representing *her.*"

Maybe so. But the power of the Hearst dynasty was represented by Randolph's older brother, William Randolph Hearst, Jr., and that week Patricia's uncle flew in from the East to warn that the corporate image of the entire Hearst empire was at stake, and an Establishment attorney had better be hired fast.

That same week Randolph Hearst made several crucial phone calls, one to Edward Bennett Williams in Washington, D.C., possibly the most highly regarded criminal lawyer in this country. Williams is famous as the triumphant defender of everybody from the mobster Frank Costello to the *Washington Post.* His most recent legal triumph had been to rescue ex-governor John Connally from professional death-by-drowning in Mr. Nixon's spilled milk.

"What do you want?" Williams asked Hearst.

"I want her out on bail."

"Can you guarantee she won't run?"

"I can't promise anything."

"Then why the hell are you talking to me? You better get straight with your daughter first."

Williams also was unwilling to share the case with any cocounsel. "When I take a case, I want total candor and total control." Hearst couldn't promise either.

Williams strongly recommended that Hearst turn to his old friend the respected San Francisco attorney James Martin MacInnis, but this gambit had already been tried, and Patty had called MacInnis an asshole. Hearst's next call was the one to the law offices of F. Lee Bailey.

Just a week ago, on the Friday evening before trial, a few hours after I had left Bailey and Johnson in their disordered suite at the Mark Hopkins, my apartment doorbell rang. Standing in the hall was one of Bailey's young men, and he was holding an enormous liver-colored legal envelope. This was the offer I couldn't refuse. The envelope contained the entire confidential West/Singer report, as well as the twenty-seven-page "Tania Interview." In showing me both documents, Bailey had acted with characteristic audacity, and had faced me with the same dilemma he intended to lay out for the jury: Which version of Patty Hearst do *you* believe, the doctors' or the SLA's? Is she the Lady or the Tiger?

It took the entire weekend to read it all. At the competency hearing Carter had called the West/Singer report "verbose." This turned out to have been an understatement. The report was an extraordinary document that swiftly became irritating in its reiteration of the obvious and amplification of the minimal. Its table of contents listed ten chapters and seven "attachments," one of them a ten-page single-spaced listing of the authors' vast professional credentials. As an example of the report's prose style, here is an excerpt from Chapter III, "Family Background."

> Hearst is one of the world's most familiar family names. The San Francisco branch is now a daily international topic of conversation because of the events involving Patricia. However, the name of Hearst has been famous in America and especially in California since the Twentieth Century began. William Randolph Hearst was the topic of several biographies. One is still widely circulated, *CITIZEN HEARST* by W. A. Swanberg (New York, Scribner & Sons, 1961). Swanberg's choice of title probably stems from the title of a classic film by Orson Welles, *CITIZEN KANE,* said to have been suggested by the life of William Randolph Hearst. At least part of the message of *CITIZEN KANE* is that a person of great wealth and fame does not always find happiness, in fact these distinctions may militate against it, and that the normal, basic qualities and needs of such a person are likely to be so obscured by the public image that a simple human cry goes unrecognized.

This interpretation of *Citizen Kane* may tell one more about the writer than it does about the film or the subject of the biography.

The doctors said Patty had undergone several personality changes. They had seemingly descried a seeming case of multiple personality in which there were four separate defendants:

A. Patty   February 20, 1954—February 4, 1974
B. Tania   February 4, 1974—May 17, 1974
C. Pearl   May 17, 1974—September 18, 1975
D. Pat   September 18, 1975—to present time

"Patty" had seemingly metamorphosed into "Tania" the instant she was kidnapped. After the fire in Los Angeles, the Harrises began to call Tania "Pearl" because it was too risky to address Tania in public. But when the jail interviewing began, none of the prisoner's three previous names seemed quite right to the doctors, so they settled on "Pat."

The surprisingly scanty substance of these jail interviews is chewed over a half-dozen times. Chapter IX, for example, runs from page 88 to page 135, rediscussing what has already been said *ad nauseum.*

Switching from film critic to psychiatrist, Dr. West describes his patient's fourth personality, "Pat," in this manner:

> Pat was a painfully constricted, tearful, bewildered and deeply regressed young woman. . . . She could hardly talk about her nineteen months in the hands of the SLA. This reticence is not seen in a normal person who returns from a prolonged, unusual, even terrifying experience and who can hardly wait to pour out the story. Pat resembles, more than anything else, a returned prisoner of war, one who has endured an experience that cannot be revealed for fear that the unbearable emotions of that ordeal will return and tear the fragile survivor apart.

Dr. West then goes over and over the same material like a pants presser. The verbosity becomes amazing as he rehashes it first in Chapter V, "Present Illness," and then a third time in three more chapters, entitled "Psychiatric Diagnostic Formulation," "Medico-Legal Formulation," and "Discussion."

I turned next to the "Extended Report," by Dr. Singer, a separate document from her psychological-test findings. Despite her professional objectivity, Dr. Singer's maternal instincts seemed to have been stirred by the plight of this unfortunate, multiply-abandoned, multiply-misunderstood girl. Among Singer's test findings, Patricia's answers to a sentence-completion test were particularly affecting.

"The underlined words below are the sentence starters," Singer writes. "The responses suggesting the 'immediacy' of her associations are as follows."

I want to know	"how to crochet"
Our family	"comes to visit me"
I feel	"O.K."
Much of the time	"I smoke"
If I	"was out of here I'd like it"
Friends	"come to see me"
My mother	"she's been good"
My clothes	"don't fit me"

My greatest trouble	"is the present and the past, and I guess the future, too"
My stomach	"it's there"
My father	"he's been good"
My worst habit	"is smoking"
I envy	"people who are free"
At night	"I go to sleep"
My looks	"they're average"
The dark	"it's there, I mean"
My chief worry	"is this case"
When I get out	"I'm going to see my friends"
My health	"is all right"
Death	"you have to accept it"

Dr. Singer now comments, "A second group of responses suggesting some concerns or longer term factors are"

My school work	"was a drag"
The future	"doesn't look like much"
I suffer	"in silence"
There are times	"when I feel like dying"
My mind	"it's hard to concentrate"
My imagination	"runs wild"
Most men	"are assholes"
I feel	"death"
Many of my dreams	"I try not to remember"
I cannot understand what makes me	"cry"
Secretly	"I am depressed"
My childhood	"I don't remember it that good"
Suicide	"is out of the question"
Fighting	"makes me sick"
I feel most proud	"of nothing"

"The third group of interest are some miscellaneous responses," Singer says.

The training	"happened"
Money often	"destroys people"
Working	"is good"
My greatest longing	"is to be with people"
God	"is the supreme being who made all things"
Religion	"I can't relate to it"
The laws we have	"I don't understand them"
Earning my living	"I can do it"
Most people	"are content"
I am very	"strong"
Children	"I really like them"
Girls usually	"grow up and get married"
My greatest ambition	"is to help people"

Dr. Singer's "Extended Report" moves beyond the ordinary presentation of test findings to include small essays on such subjects as "Ms. Hearst's attitude toward being examined" (docile, cooperative, troubled), "Ms. Hearst's conversational style during the examining period" (long pauses, dislocations, and discontinuities of space and time), and "Ms. Hearst's susceptibility to coercive persuasion." The last was particularly informative, despite its windy style, because it was the basis of the defense.

MS. HEARST'S SUSCEPTIBILITY TO COERCIVE PERSUASION

Included among the factors that contributed to making Patricia Hearst particularly susceptible to being coerced into "cooperating" with her captors were . . .

1. *Uncertainty About Self*

a. During Patricia's childhood, she had a prolonged period of significant close contact with a caretaker [a harsh governess who looked after Patty until the age of nine] upon whom she was very dependent and who frequently told her that she was a child unwanted by her parents. Cinque, upon whom she also found herself dependent, also told her that her parents rejected her, punctuating his message with threats of pain and with actual brutality. She was particularly vulnerable to Cinque's method because his technique rekindled her old childhood doubts about her self-worth.

b. As a schoolgirl, Patricia had a poor opinion of herself and was more vulnerable to feeling put down by her classmates and associates than would be someone who felt secure about her own worth and proud of her accomplishments. Part of her defense against her uncertainty about herself was to behave in a "haughty" manner to her classmates. [This haughtiness has been described by several schoolgirls who knew Patty in her pre–Steven Weed period.]

c. At the time of her capture, Patricia was mildly depressed. She was unsure of her plans for the future and was in the process of redefining her educational goals. . . .

d. During the first two days of her testing Patricia behaved at times as though she considered herself guilty of some sort of serious transgression. For example, on one occasion she inadvertently touched with her cigarette a small, worthless plastic disk that came from the examiner's tape recorder and that had been put on the edge of the ashtray. Patricia apologized profusely and dusted the disc carefully to remove all traces of her cigarette ash. Her manner was that of a pathetic little girl who had done something terribly wrong.

e. During the administration of the Rorschach test, Patricia admitted in a confessional manner that she had failed to mention images of a sexual nature that she had perceived when viewing the inkblots. Again her manner was one of confessing to a transgression, a style of communicating that is characteristic of prisoners of war or others who have been browbeaten by their captors.

2. *Ambivalence Towards Her Parents*

a. Again, perhaps related to her prolonged period of childhood contact with a noxious caretaker, Patricia developed a feeling of some alienation from her parents. As she grew older, she particularly felt unable to make contact with her mother other than on a shallow, surface level. Therefore, Cinque's rhetoric about social dissidents, including Patricia herself, being rejected by people like her mother, fell on fertile soil. She was able to believe, for example, that her mother, who was (not unusually) photographed wearing black clothes, did so because she regarded Patricia as already dead.

b. During her formative years, particularly in adolescence, Patricia had often felt herself to be a "prisoner" of the Hearst family tradition. This is not an unusual experience for children born into prominent, affluent families. . . . The ambivalence that children naturally feel towards their parents can be heightened in someone like Patricia, who feels resentment at being constrained by a prominent family, yet reaps the rewards of special privilege.

c. As a young adult, Patricia was [making] . . . a natural move toward independence. Her new life with Steven Weed was a statement of her willingness to deviate from the life-style exemplified by her family. . . .

3. *Characterological Lack of Inner-Directedness*

a. Patricia's school history is noteworthy for its pattern of discontinuity. Although some of her moves from school to school were made for understandable reasons, others appear to have been based on caprice and determined by her response to superficial considerations: friends who were there, transitional relationships that she accepted or rejected, whimsical notions about what would be best for her. At no time was her choice of a school predicated upon some carefully thought-out long-range plan for acquiring an education.

b. . . . In comparison with some of her more studious, thoughtful classmates or with the more mature friends whom she met through Steven Weed, Patricia was not an intellectual, a deep thinker, or a conceptualizer. She was not inclined to explore issues with depth or logic, nor was she given to introspection or to dwelling on inner psychological processes. Furthermore, Patricia was politically naive and unconcerned with the political issues that absorbed many of her contemporaries. She was not informed about the positions or opinions of various political revolutionaries, nor was she aware of the arguments they utilized or the styles with which they declaimed their positions. Therefore, when faced with a barrage of intense political propaganda from Cinque and his followers, Patricia had no inner frame of reference that would enable her to understand their behavior or put her experience into some perspective. . . .

c. Patricia's trait of responding to the immediacy of situations is demonstrated in her adjustment to life in jail. . . . As an example, she showed the examiner her cell with the demeanor of a little child proud to show off her very own special place, expressing pleasure at the meager appointments and the little tiny objects she had collected during her short term behind bars. She appeared to be very content with her situation.

4. *Psychological Suggestibility*

a. Patricia was always prone to take on the ways of those around her. As a child, she adapted more "responsibly" to the demands of her parents than did her four sisters. As a young woman, taking her first tentative steps toward independence by living with Steven Weed, she adapted swiftly to both the style of life and the friends he provided. She wore Weed's Boy Scout shirt, used his old billfold, and was willing to sit and listen to his friends, who were older than she, talk about topics about which she knew nothing and in which she had no interest.

b. Patricia's natural style of talking can best be described as informal, and is typical of the casual form of communication currently in vogue among the young. Her way of phrasing ideas is elusive and her reference points are non-specific. In sharp contrast to this is the language style she used on the tapes she was required by Cinque to make for propaganda purposes. Under circumstances of stress and duress, she employed the verbal style of her captors. Of course, the passages marked by crisp wording, clear phrasing and a rehearsed manner were written out for her beforehand, disclaimers to the contrary notwithstanding.

c. During psychological testing Patricia reported that her subjective experience resembled what she had felt when she was interacting with Cinque, namely that he knew everything she was thinking. In fact, her style of communicating with me during my administration of the psychological tests did indicate that she thought I "knew" what was going on in her mind. She used references that were meaningless to me, and did not recognize the need to fill me in with respect to whom or what she was referring.

The weekend's reading left me stunned, sad, and embarrassed. Going over the doctors' reports, I felt like a Peeping Tom staring into the emotional boudoir of the young woman who for so long had intrigued me from afar. But I also felt a new rush of maternal concern and of empathy for her ordeal. The psychobabble of these doctors was far more affecting than the florid rhetoric of the Hallinans. The creature the doctors described appeared to be a classic shell-shock victim; that much was clear from—or perhaps clear despite—all the grandiose verbiage. But then how was one to deal with the other document, Tania's purported "autobiography"? The two documents read like a photographic double exposure. Superimposed on the doctors' picture of the pathetic shell-shock victim was Tania's first-person self-image of a young girl strongly impressed by a very idealistic and brave set of values. As Tania saw it, the objectives of the SLA were admirable. And they were. She could not see that the methods proposed to achieve them were psychopathic. The SLA, it appeared, had invented a new formula for compounding insanity.

Week Three

February 9–15

Monday, February 9

This morning Patty will take the stand for the first time. But the jury will not be present. Only the larger jury of the media will be on hand when Judge Carter considers a defense motion that Patty's various statements about being a willing participant in the bank robbery should not be admitted into evidence because they were not made voluntarily. Bailey would also like to keep the jury from hearing about the shoot-up at Mel's Sporting Goods in Los Angeles. He is still fighting hard to keep the skunks out of the courtroom.

Alone and palely loitering at the bare oak table, the defendant looks beautiful for the first time. Her long white throat rises out of a Byronic collar of salmon-pink silk, spread out over a velvet jacket the color of port wine; pale and perfect skin, aquiline features, charcoal smudges for eyes, the whole softly framed by fine, coppery hair. The face is *quattrocento,* but the palette is Rembrandt's. When she moves and settles into the raised, pulpitlike witness box, one of the sketch artists lends me his close-up glasses, and the powerful lenses make a corona of golden light around the edge of the cream and auburn and copper girl. The image at the center shimmers slightly. The aquarium has found its mermaid.

Bailey is brisk. Who was with Patty when the tape in which she describes taking part in the bank robbery was made?

In a faint monotone: "Donald DeFreeze, Nancy Ling Perry, Patricia Soltysik, Camilla Hall, William and Emily Harris, William Wolfe . . ."

(85)

A long pause here. The voice trails off, she appears to go blank, and Bailey has to prompt her. How about Angela Atwood? Oh, yes . . . and then Cinque said they were going to make a tape to show I participated in it . . . so everybody sat down on the floor, and Angela Atwood wrote out some words. Cinque took Patty into the closet, and she read by flashlight while he operated the tape recorder.

Bailey reads from a transcript of that tape: " 'I am obviously alive and well. As for being brainwashed, the idea is ridiculous to the point of being beyond belief. . . .' Was that your language or the language of Angela Atwood?"

"Angela Atwood."

And if she had refused to say these words, what would have happened?

Patty's cheeks redden. Her eyes fill with tears. "I was told that—um —that I'd be killed."

Were the words true or false? Patty doesn't appear to understand, and Bailey has to rephrase the question to get the answer he seeks. "False."

Judge Carter sits with lips pursed, listening hard. Bailey looks physically different today, as if he had sharpened himself to attack. He is no longer a sheepshead bass, more like a pike or a barracuda circling the coppery mermaid.

So much for Skunk One, the taped confession. Now the oral one, the Matthews boy. What kind of van were they riding in? Well, it had benches in the back. Emily was driving, and William Harris said to Matthews, "You recognize her, don't you? That's Tania."

From the moment she was kidnapped until this moment, how many times had Patty been threatened with death? Her answer is inaudible, and the judge asks her to speak up. Soft but clear now: "Hundreds of times."

Now Skunk Three, the written confession. Patty describes being driven by the man who rescued her, Jack Scott, the former Oberlin coach and "sports activist," to a farmhouse hideaway in Pennsylvania, where she heard talk of a book he would write about the SLA. What sort of book? She makes helpless, fishlike gestures with her tiny hands, finally saying weakly, "About how great they were."

Patty was given a long list of questions and instructed to write out the answers as a basis for her "autobiography." Was she generally truthful in supplying these answers? Silent shrug. Hesitation. "Yes."

Who else came to the farmhouse?

Here marks the start of a long Lorelei siren song, a naming of names of coconspirators, aides, friends, SLA hangers-on. Eventually thirty-eight persons will be drawn into the fatal net. Not the least name, the tiniest minnow, will be permitted to escape through the meshes she begins now to weave.

Who came to the farmhouse?

Paul Houck, a professor from Canada. Wendy Yoshimura.* Phil Shinnick.†

Anyone else?

Long pause. Then: "No."

"Any attorney?"

"No."

"How about Jay Weiner?"

Like a frightened pupil finally producing the answer teacher wants: "Oh, yes, Jay Weiner. He was a friend of the Scotts."

We are told that the "Tania Interview" is entirely untrue, that she was forced to help write the book because the fugitives were running short of funds.

Browning rises to cross-examine and thumps down onto the witness stand a monumental pile of photographs. The girl's eyes widen; she shrinks in fear. Lillian Gish could not do it better, but in Patty's circumstances, the exaggerated reactions of a silent-movie heroine are believable.

"Is this the closet where you were held?"

Patty looks, closes her eyes for a moment. Then: "Yes." She was in this closet until sometime early in March and was then tied inside a garbage can and transported to another closet in another apartment.

The bail affidavit describes Patty's imprisonment "in the closet." "But you say now there were *two* closets," Browning prods. Patty admits she signed an incorrect affidavit, knowing it was incorrect.

How about the "I have chosen to stay and fight" tape of April 3? She closes her eyes; a long blink, a slight frown. Again she looks scared. She doesn't recall making that tape and doesn't know who composed it.

---

*Ms. Yoshimura, a three-year fugitive from justice, was living with Patty when they were arrested together at 625 Morse Street. Steven Soliah, Patty's lover and also a resident of the apartment, was arrested the same day at another location. He was later tried for and acquitted of the Carmichael bank robbery.

†Shinnick, a member of the sports faculty at Rutgers University, had been a 1964 Olympics contender as a long-jumper. Eventually he would serve fifty days in jail for contempt for refusing to cooperate with the FBI.

"They would bring in a sheet of paper, and I would read it."

Browning's questions get tougher. Is it not correct that just before making this tape, the SLA told Patty she was free to leave? Well, the War Council said . . . that is, DeFreeze told her, first, that they had decided that she could either join the SLA or be killed. Later, when they told her she had a different choice—join or go home—"I didn't believe them."

Browning reads from the SLA's final tape: " 'Neither Cujo [William Wolfe] nor I had ever loved an individual the way we loved each other, probably because our relationship wasn't based on bourgeois, fucked-up values. . . .' Do you recall those words?"

"Could I see them?"

"You have a right to see them if you don't recall," Carter says. One cannot tell whether the judge is being solicitous or sardonic. It is apparent that Miss Hearst has been well prepared by her lawyers. She knows not to answer a question until she understands fully what she is being asked; she always asks to see the documents on which the government is basing its questions; she looks the prosecutor in the eye. This "voluntariness" hearing is giving Patty an excellent chance to accustom herself to the stress of the witness box and to develop stamina under cross-examination before she must face the jury.

It is a long, uncomfortable, wearying day. Something about merely being *in* a courtroom makes one feel obscurely at fault. Guilt falls on all impartially, like soot. The lawyers evoke guilt. The marshals reinforce it. The black-robed judge implies it. Minor witnesses tremble to be caught in an inconsistency or an omission in their testimony. A juror's private guilts are deliberately aroused and strummed upon by the lawyers for each side. This whole chamber steams with guilt, but to the natural-born criminal lawyer this place is not a sweatbox but an arena, a personal testing ground. The joy of combat is unmistakable in Bailey's definition of "not guilty" in his book. "A plea of not guilty means, 'Prove it.' By no stretch of the system does it mean 'I'm innocent.' "

"*Do* you, in fact, recall those words?" Browning repeats.

"No."

"Miss Hearst, did you participate in other activities with Mr. and Mrs. Harris with respect to banks?"

"*Objection!*" Bailey is on his feet, quivering. "That question goes far beyond the scope—"

"Sustained."

Browning, unperturbed, asks the witness if she recognizes a two-page typewritten document headed "Bakery." She shakes her head. "How about this one? A diagram headed 'Bank of America, Marysville'?"

"Objection!"

"Overruled. Answer the question please, Miss Hearst."

"Yes. Well, I mean, I wrote it."

Browning reads a marginal notation from the document: " 'Saw 7 employees, 1 young, manager is fat and black.' " Is this Miss Hearst's handwriting?

Bailey is on his feet, shouting, "Object! This is a fishing expedition, not a hearing! It is a violation of my client's constitutional rights! She demands a recess. It is not *right* to force her to incriminate herself."

Judge Carter is calm. "Let's quit this business of trying to outdo one another on documents, Mr. Bailey. I do not see this [question of voluntariness] as a segmented proposition. I see it as a whole proposition. . . . I want you to tell me what your point is. If you have one, state it."

"My point is that you're forcing her to answer questions which could expose her to further charges, and I will not permit her to do it."

Carter is becoming testy. "Tell me the nature of the charges, so that I can rule. Are these state charges or federal charges?"

Browning interrupts to say that Bailey waived his client's right against self-incrimination when he allowed her to take the witness stand.

Carter is exasperated. "You *can't* waive a constitutional right!"

The questioning resumes. Browning asks about fingerprints on the "Bakery" document. Narrow-eyed, flushed, pike snout thrust forward, Bailey insists that his client is instructed *not* to answer the question on fingerprints.

"Objection sustained."

In courtroom skills Mr. Browning appears outclassed, but he has other resources. He has twenty-seven typewritten pages of the "Tania Interview," with revisions in Patricia Hearst's handwriting, describing the kidnapping, the revolutionary politics behind it, the SLA's views on military action, and the terrorists' reaction to subsequent events. There is also a grimly detailed autobiographical description of the childhood, education, and family background of Patricia Hearst, as seen from Tania's new, revolutionary perspective.

In the history of terror, in the history of crime, surely no group suffered such excesses of literary manufacture as the Symbionese Liberation Army. Their logorrhea was chronic and possibly fatal. They wrote down *everything.* No idea, plot, scheme, scrap of political theory, no rag of secondhand revolutionary rhetoric was too trivial to throw away or too dangerous to commit to paper. Has Bill Harris been mulling over the wisdom of promoting the revolution by equipping "every disenfranchised, exploited person" with a pipe bomb sufficient to destroy a patrol car? Yes, and he makes a note of it. Where are the headquarters in San Francisco of the hated governments of Bolivia, Argentina, Chile, South Africa, Israel, Spain, Great Britain, the Philippines, and Japan? Patty Hearst in her round schoolgirl's hand neatly sets up an address list and heads it *"Consul General of."*

The members of the SLA were terrorists with the habits of graduate students. After the arrests, the FBI hauled more than seven hundred cartons of documents out of the Hearst and Harris apartments. The previously discovered SLA hideouts were similarly littered. These people were jackdaws of the radical Left. In addition to their own writings, they accumulated heaps of other revolutionary tracts, pamphlets, handbooks, posters. They left a paper trail behind them so wide that one might imagine that they were seeking rather desperately to be found out and stopped. The sea of evidence might also be interpreted as a sign of the SLA's overweening contempt for the pigs and for their inability to read and write or to comprehend the paper middens they were wading through. One item found in the half-burned SLA safehouse in Concord, amid the rubble that Nancy Ling Perry set afire the day after Remiro and Little were arrested and the terrorist cadre went into still deeper cover, was a green spiral notebook. It contained a list of twenty possible future victims to follow Marcus Foster. Some persons on the SLA hit list were alerted by the authorities; inexplicably, Patricia Hearst was not, and neither were her parents. The Hearsts never forgave the FBI for neglecting to tip them off, and the failure looks now like inexcusably sloppy police work. But it is conceivable that the authorities simply thought they had stumbled into the untidy lair of revolutionary crackpots, not serious killers. The fact is that the SLA was something new in the annals of American crime: It was both.

The SLA wrote, sorted, classified, and revised, manufacturing its revolution as it went along, working with the diligence of aardvarks. Night and day, without letup, it was busy formulating what it believed were original political coalitions—the great new symbiosis of all radical thought, the grand amalgam of every scheme ever invented to alleviate the suffering of the oppressed people on earth. The architects burned to put the theory to the test. The necessary time for theory to cure and mellow, to translate and modulate into action, simply did not exist. The SLA members lived on instant terror, instant politics, brewed like instant coffee, fast-frozen, and shot from guns. Their "politics" offered instant gratification of any rebellious impulse, no matter how half-cocked or half-baked. They were very American. The paper detritus they left behind, the laundry lists of potential assassination victims indiscriminately mixed in with *real* laundry lists, the scratch-pad notations of "cat food" and "sink stopper" scrawled on the back of the same envelope as the maps of banks and diagrams of homemade pipe bombs, did not indicate a shortage of scratch paper but a hopeless confusion of trivia and terror, of theory and action, a lost ability to discriminate between violent, rage-based revolutionary fantasy and reality. The seven hundred cartons of captured SLA documents were the ideological equivalent of the nondisposable, nonrecyclable, half-eaten, nondigested debris that litters the American landscape, the paper analogue of all the unfashionable junk forgotten, discarded, or bypassed in the search for newer, better, shinier, more nutritious junk, the objective correlative of all the leftover, left-behind waste of a consumer society gone mad.

Of all the captured documents, none is potentially more damaging to the defense than this "Tania Interview." Bailey will fight like hell to keep the jurors in innocence of it. Prosecutor Browning reads aloud from the incriminating manuscript:

> Q. The media has at times put across the theory that you were being brainwashed. . . . How do you feel about that?
> A. I think that that kind of cheap sensationalism is all you can expect from the media. From the moment I was kidnapped they consistently attempted to discredit the revolutionaries. After the first communique was received, the pigs reacted by hauling out "stress machines" [which] indicated that I was being tortured and kept awake 24 hours a day, and Randy announced that I was obviously drugged.
> I couldn't believe that anyone would come up with such bullshit! I guess that all the pigs expected me to keep my mouth shut, but I was furious. I refuted their lies in the next communique and they put away their "tricknowlogy" for a while . . . at least, until I announced that I was going to stay with the SLA. Then, once again, I was "under duress." If you believe the media you'd think that I was totally weird—according to them, I never mean anything I say, and I'll do anything I'm told.

"You say this material was dictated by the Harrises. Was anybody else forcing you to write those words? Was Wendy Yoshimura helping you?"

Patty's eyes open wide. "Oh, no!" The two words convey the only passion she has shown so far.

Browning wonders why Patty didn't try to escape. The flat voice returns. "I thought they might kill me." William Harris in particular was abusive. On four occasions during the Missing Year he gave her a black eye.

But after the group returned to San Francisco, were they not living in separate apartments, more than a mile apart? Yes, but "they knew where I was."

Couldn't she have gone to the police?

Almost whimpering: "I thought they would kill me. Or the FBI would . . ."

How about the incident in Los Angeles seventeen months before? Patty had been alone reading the paper when she looked up and saw the Harrises scuffling with the store clerk. Why grab a machine gun and open fire? Why not simply drive off?

"Where would I have gone?"

BROWNING: Did you prefer staying with the Harrises, who had threatened to kill you, to simply walking away from them when you had the opportunity? You could have walked away, could you not? [*Scornful.*] You *rescued* the Harrises!

PATTY (*resigned to not being believed, and somewhat scornful herself*): If I had walked away, the other members of the SLA would have come looking for me . . . and the FBI would, too.

During the midmorning recess the marshals escort Patty out the rear door. In the public corridor Al Johnson has an important message to get across to the press: Patricia Hearst is terrified of drugs and refused even to take birth-control pills for fear of getting cancer. Johnson is still fighting a pervasive rumor that his client is being fed sedatives to keep her sufficiently under his control. (A recent Associated Press report has it that Dr. West has been feeding Patty "antipsychotic drugs" in such heavy dosage "that they would themselves cause lethargy and disorientation.") Patty's sisters stalk the periphery of Al's briefing. "I'd like to tear that Jim Browning limb from limb!" button-nosed Vicki whispers. "*I'd* like to hit him in the eye!" Anne, the younger sister, replies: "I've just never felt this way before about *anyone!*" Shivering with delicious fury, the girls hurry back to their front-row seats alongside the sedate, side-by-side but never-touching totem figures of Mom and Dad.

Browning shows Patty a transcript of the tape in which she says she has "decided to stay and fight." Did DeFreeze force her to make such statements? "He said that I'd be killed." She is biting her lips now and seems on the verge of tears. Browning places another tape transcription in front of Patty. Fighting for composure, she carefully aligns the papers, microphone, and cup of water along the edge of the witness stand.

Bailey protests angrily, "We were never given these documents!"

BROWNING *(mildly):* They were given the tapes.

CARTER *(like an exasperated kindergarten teacher):* If documents are going to be used, would you give them the documents, please?

Browning leads Patty through an account of her escape from California at the height of the most extensive manhunt in FBI annals, of her hegira to Pennsylvania and then back to Las Vegas. She was driven cross-country from Oakland by Jack Scott and sheltered by Scott's parents. Although *Rolling Stone*'s long and detailed account of the Missing Year, published within weeks of Patty's arrest, had already informed the world of Jack Scott's role in the story, the senior Scotts have never before been publicly identified. Jack's father is elderly and mild; his mother has high blood pressure and is in frail health. They look like quiet Las Vegas motel keepers. I had met them last summer, along with Jack Scott and his wife, Micki, and their friend Bill Walton, the basketball star, at a press conference called by William Kunstler. The charming surprise of that otherwise standard denounce-the-government-for-harassment session was Walton, looking like a perfectly enormous version of Little Orphan Annie's dog and sitting at Mother Scott's feet throughout the session, he cross-legged in tattered shorts, she with gentle fingers curled in his tousled red hair.

It seems likely that the senior Scotts got mixed up in the Hearst case solely to help their beloved son Jack. But by naming the senior Scotts, Patty is laying them open to prosecution for aiding and abetting a kidnapping and harboring a fugitive. She is putting into effect the defense strategy imposed by Bailey and Johnson from the moment they took over the case.

Six months ago, sitting in the sweaty, smoke-filled "iron phone booth" at the jail, Johnson had told Patty, "You're gonna have to dump it all out, honey." Every daily visit since, Johnson reinforced those instructions: "Dump it out. Dump it all out." So now Patty is naming names, and Mr. and Mrs. John Scott are merely names, numbers five and six out of all the strangers, lovers, political sympathizers, and casual friends who tried to help her when she was underground and on the run.

On the way back from Pennsylvania to Las Vegas, Patty and Jack Scott traveled alone, staying in motels. Could Patty have left *then?* "Where would I have gone?"

The prosecutor reads another passage from the "Tania Interview," describing a family visit to Catherine's hometown of Atlanta. "Catherine is an incredible racist. . . . She went crazy. It was 'nigger,' and 'we're in jig town now.' There were no street signs in the black areas of Atlanta, and her comment about this situation was, 'Niggers don't need street signs.' "

"Did you tell the SLA that?" Browning asks.

Tiny voice. "I must have. It was part of the writing of the book."

"In other words, you would volunteer accurate information for the writing of the book?"

"Yes."

"Why did you do that?"

"I don't know."

A clerk whispers something to the judge, who abruptly announces the noon recess, although it is only eleven-thirty. In the corridor we learn the reason: the New World Liberation Front has just called the courthouse and said that somewhere in the twenty-story building a bomb is ticking.

After lunch the daughter flashes the mother a tiny, private smile just before climbing back up into the witness box; contrition, perhaps, for the Atlanta testimony. Mom's astonishing response is to fire back the wide-open grin of an Atlantic City Miss America contestant. The dazzling smile is bizarrely out of place; it is the impossibly white-toothed smile of a Wrigley's gum ad and belongs on an aquaplane behind a speedboat. Mom's smile haunts me. Much later I come across a fascinating bit of historical trivia: In the late 1930s Patty's mother, then Catherine Campbell, the belle of Atlanta, was a finalist in the nationwide Scarlett O'Hara contest to find an unknown actress to star opposite Clark Gable in *Gone with the Wind.* Close to forty years later, Catherine had whirled on Steve Weed and said, "Whatever happened to the real men in this world? Men like Clark Gable? No one would have carried off my daughter if there had been a *real* man there!"*

*Steven Weed, *My Search for Patty Hearst* (New York: Crown Publishers, 1976), p. 127.

Catherine Campbell Hearst is, before everything, a Southern girl. She would no more reveal her true feelings in public than she would sit with her legs uncrossed. Catherine *is* Scarlett: gallant, petite, opportunist, and forged of hardest steel. Nothing can vanquish the Southern girl's indomitable spirit, lower her tip-tilted chin, or redden for long her retroussé nose. "I'll think about it tomorrow!" Temples crumble, heart's dreams shatter, the South perishes, Atlanta blazes. The next morning Scarlett rips down the velvet draperies from Tara's walls and runs up a new and even more beguiling gown. "I'll worry about that tomorrow!" Brave little smile. Fade-out. Scarlett grown older might have looked very much like the beautiful but careful-not-to-crack, smiling, hard-edged woman that is Patty Hearst's mom.

Browning is still leading Patty through the "Tania Interview." "Did you write, on page four, 'In the fall of 1972 we'—meaning you and Steven Weed—'moved to Berkeley, and I got a job at Capwell's department store as a salesgirl and office clerk'?"

"Yes."

"And, on page eight: 'I ended up in a closet for about six weeks'?"

"Yes."

"How about this part? 'At the end of two or three weeks, Cin asked me if I wanted to have a class on how to defend myself with the shotgun. . . . The comrades felt that if the pigs came, I had a right to defend myself.' "

False, Patty says. Cinque never asked her anything.

"After a few weeks I started to feel sympathetic with the SLA." Did Patty write *those* words? No. How about this? "Gelina's [Angela Atwood's] poetry moved me to start thinking about ideas that were new to me, about revolutionary violence." No. On page 23 the manuscript states, "My mother appeared at press conferences dressed in black to urge me through her racist tears to 'Keep praying honey. . . . God will bring you home.' " Are those Patty's words? No. When did Patty become aware her mother wore a black dress? "I didn't know she did it."

"You don't recall speaking about a 'black dress'?"

"No."

I glance over at Mom. Again today she wears a black dress, with black shoes and bag and black stockings, and a folded black coat lies across her lap.

Now a passage about Catherine Hearst's behavior as a regent. "People like the Berkeley student body president would come over to the house to talk to her during the '60s, and her way of dealing with the situation was to direct them to the swimming pool and send out sandwiches. She always prided herself on how much the students like her. . . ." The rest of the typewritten paragraph has been crossed out and in Patty's hand is written, "when in fact they thought she was a corrupt right wing little bitch."

Randy Hearst leans forward, elbows on his knees, staring at the floor. Browning now switches to the bail affidavit: Did you know it contained errors? Yes. Then why did you sign it? Because the lawyers told me to sign. Then another switch. In the robbery rehearsals were you positioned so that the bank surveillance cameras would see you? Yes. Now a critical question: During the robbery was your weapon loaded? "I was told it was loaded."

Browning asks the clerk for people's exhibit number 19 and crosses jauntily to the witness box. Its FBI identification tag flutters like a pennant from the green webbing strap of the M-1 semiautomatic rifle. He hands the weapon to Patty, asks her to examine it, break the bolt, inspect the clip. Her tiny hands know precisely what to do. They look like the hands of an educated bank robber. Patient Dad watches his favorite daughter handle the weapon as a plumber would a wrench. Browning is stumbling, making slips of the tongue, referring to Tom Matthews as "Tom Harris," mixing up dates. Judge Carter chuckles; he seems to find this degree of clumsiness quite delicious.

On redirect, Bailey inquires whether Matthews was the *first* person Patty had told about the bank robbery. No, right after the robbery Cinque brought four black strangers to the Golden Gate hideout. He told Patty to identify herself to them and tell them about the robbery.

Bailey now questions Patty about another part of her testimony.

Okay, now you were asked by Mr. Browning whether or not a statement made by you . . . in June 1974 is true, particularly as to your alleged affection for William Wolfe. Did you, in fact, have any such affection . . . ? No. Did William Wolfe ever do anything offensive to you? Yes, he assaulted me sexually. How long after you were kidnapped? About a month. Was he the only one? No. Was it in the closet? Yes.

There is a sudden stir in the back rows, and we turn to see four very black-skinned persons, two men and two women in Afro hairdos and vivid clothing, like four magnificent birds newly arrived from a tropic jungle. Cinque's friends! Sternly, Carter says that potential witnesses are not permitted in his courtroom, so the four exotics and their attorneys—young white women in snappily cut pants suits—are escorted outside.

BAILEY: Who was present when you signed the bail affidavit?

PATTY: John Knutsen [a Hearst family attorney], Vincent Hallinan, Terence Hallinan.

And Terence told you that the source of this information was Wendy Yoshimura and others? Yes. And you pointed out the mistakes in the affidavit to him? Yes. Did you also point out that there were two closets, not one? No. And although John Knutsen told her not to sign a false affidavit, "Kayo Hallinan said I should sign." There was a fight, Vince Hallinan left the room, and Patty signed at his son's insistence.

Is it not a fact that the SLA told you that if your hideout were discovered, the FBI would kill all the people in the house? Yes. And did the SLA also tell you that the Attorney General of the United States, William Saxbe, had denounced you as a "common criminal"? Yes.

Where were you, Miss Hearst, on the evening of May 17, 1974? The defendant was in a motel in Anaheim, across the street from Disneyland, watching on television the fire in which six of her comrades were burned alive. Although the police and everybody else at the time believed that Patricia Hearst, too, was trapped inside the house, they had continued shooting, had held back the firemen, and let the house burn to the ground.

On re-cross-examination, Patty tells Browning that only Cinque was permitted to speak to the four exotic visitors; it would be "disrespectful" for other SLA members to address the blacks directly. Now some extraordinary new information: By that time the SLA had cut off all her hair. This is why it was necessary to wear a wig in the bank and to identify herself later to the four visitors as Patty Hearst. Cinque also ordered Patty to tell them about the robbery and to smile so she would look more like her photographs.

For what purpose was her hair cut? That was just the first thing they did. Did they ever discuss with you why they did it? No. How much did they cut? She looks downcast. All but one inch. Wasn't it a fact that they cut off your hair so that you *could* wear a wig? No, they said they wanted me to wear a wig so that I would look more like myself.

This puzzling reply is not pursued. Instead, after a whisper from coprosecutor Langford, Browning switches subjects once more and asks: As a matter of fact, William and Emily Harris were part of the bank robbery, weren't they? They were waiting outside, in the red car, were they not? When she says yes, Patty's lawyers break into smiles, for now she has put the Harrises directly into the Hibernia Bank robbery.

Browning inquires if the Hallinan affidavit is not again incorrect when it says "that you were made to lie in your own body wastes." Patty in her tiny voice and Bailey in his ringing Papa Bear tones exclaim simultaneously, "It doesn't say that." *"It doesn't say that!"*

The prosecutor picks up a sheet of paper and reads, " ' . . . was given food but was unable to eat any for a period of about ten days, and for all that period was unable to dispose of her body wastes.' What does that mean, Miss Hearst?"

Small voice, eyes lowered: "It means when they took me to the bathroom I was unable to use it."

So much for what an imaginative lawyer can do with an ordinary case of constipation. It is time for midafternoon recess.

The mermaid's song has been long and moving. By the time she leaves the stand a half-dozen of the toughest sob sisters in the American press are cluck-clucking, dabbing their eyes. No doubt our maternal hearts have been touched. From now until the end of the trial, we will be caucusing in courtroom corridors, meeting late at night for drinks and dinner after the exhausting days are over, reviewing the poor girl's predicament, and searching for ways to substitute journalistic chicken soup for the more traditional vitriol.

When court resumes, we meet two important new characters: David Bancroft, thirty-four, the soft-spoken Justice Department lawyer who will handle all the psychiatric testimony; and Professor Margaret Thaler Singer. After Dr. Singer completed her psychological tests for Dr. West, she undertook an elaborate linguistic analysis of the seven SLA tapes and has now concluded that although Patty was the speaker, she was not the author of the words. Dr. Singer is a woman of uncommon wit, probity, and scruples, HERNAP's Mary Poppins. There is no question in her mind but that she cannot discuss the case with any reporter until after it has gone to the jury. For a long time I cannot bear to tell her that before the trial even began, Bailey had shown me her lengthy report, along with all of Dr. West's materials.

Tall, pink-cheeked, staunch, and fiftyish, Dr. Singer takes the stand and testifies that her analysis of Patty's language style is based on more than twenty-four hours of personal interviews with the defendant, as well as on a careful study of the SLA tapes, Patty's old school papers, and some old letters on tape that Patty mailed to Steve Weed during a trip to Europe. Singer can identify the stylistic language pattern of each SLA member. Even before Patty and Bailey told her that the language on the portion of the tape in which Patty confessed to the robbery was written by Angela Atwood, Dr. Singer had concluded that the passage was written, not spontaneous, speech. Singer listens for pauses and for the sound of pages turning. When one reads aloud, the pauses tend to follow written punctuation; in spontaneous speech the pauses emphasize the meanings of individual words. One also uses a simpler style in speech, a more complex style when writing. But the tape on which Patricia admits to having participated in the bank robbery resembles neither her written *nor* her oral style. Consider this example: "In the case of expropriation, the difference between a criminal act and a revolutionary act is shown by what the money is used for. As with the money involved in my parents' bad-faith gesture to aid the People, these funds are being used to aid the People and insure the survival of the People's forces in their struggle with and for the People." This, says Dr. Singer, is simply not her style.

Cross-examining, David Bancroft wonders how Dr. Singer explains Patty's having given her occupation to the jail matron as urban guerrilla. Because Emily Harris, whom she feared, was present in the room. And why did Patty tell her friend Trish Tobin during a jail visit that, were she to issue a public statement, it would be made from a "revolutionary feminist perspective"? Because Patty had been coached by her captors to talk in those terms.

Citing Dr. Singer's written report to the court, Bancroft asks, "Is there any possibility that *your questions* suggested the answers given by Miss Hearst?"

"No. Miss Hearst was in such a state of tension and difficulty that I had to ask questions again and again, to make very sure I had correctly understood her very brief remarks . . . and to let her know I was offering her an opportunity to correct herself."

Well, doesn't that itself suggest that possibly the kindly Dr. Singer was leading or coaching the girl into giving "correct" responses? Singer stands firm. The language of the confessional tape is "heavy and convoluted . . . not in the style you yourself heard her talk in today, before I came on the stand. She speaks in very short, simple sentences." The prosecutor persists until the witness dismisses him with schoolmarmish finality. "The trouble is, Mr. Bancroft, that I'm talking about her style, and you're talking about her content."

It is 4:05 P.M. *I* think Dr. Singer has scored heavily, but the judge may not be so impressed. "I intend to keep an appointment now with my own doctor—who is an MD, not a PhD," he harrumphs, rising from his high-backed chair.

Tuesday, February 10

Last night there was another bomb scare. Today the voluntariness hearing resumes, but it is hard for me to concentrate on it. Very early this morning, in the office of her attorney, I met Wendy Yoshimura, and Wendy was an astonishment. She is the positive to Patty's negative, intensely alive, bright-eyed and bouncy, strong and slim, with thick, glossy black silk hair framing a wide-cheeked olive face. Such incandescence is unexpected in a shy, soft-spoken commercial artist who for several years had been a fugitive from justice and is now awaiting trial for illegal possession of weapons and explosives. Since her arrest, Patty's former roommate has been living quietly in Berkeley with a Japanese-American professor of criminology and his family, preparing for her trial.

Wendy, thirty-three, and her young attorney, James Larson, had been cordial but circumspect. I learned nothing that had not already been in the papers. In 1971 Wendy rented a Berkeley garage for her lover, William Brandt, a militant antiwar activist. When Brandt and two companions were arrested outside the garage a few months later, Wendy disappeared and remained a fugitive until she was arrested with Miss Hearst. The garage was filled with a huge cache of weapons and explosives, and Brandt was convicted of plotting to blow up military buildings and sent to prison for twenty years.

After dropping from sight in March 1972, Wendy joined the thousands of other radical young Americans living underground, Mao's invisible "urban guerrillas." Eventually she was fished up by Micki Scott to be a companion for Patty Hearst. Jack and Micki Scott were among the many people who ran a kind of informal underground railroad for radicals in hiding. It is assumed they first helped Wendy and later recruited her to help another fugitive, an offer her own code of honor would not allow her then to refuse. In any event, Wendy seems to have begun to steer Patty away from concepts of revolutionary violence and toward revolutionary feminism, and in the months before their capture, it was she who persuaded Patty to move away from the domicile and domination of the Harrises.

After their capture by the FBI, Wendy's case became a rallying point for thousands of Bay Area Japanese-Americans and other part-Asian peoples—Chinese, Koreans, Filipinos—traditionally the least vocal of California's many ethnic minority groups. These people came up with $150,000 in cash for Wendy's bail, which was later reduced to $25,000 when the judge recognized the extraordinary depth of Wendy's support. One man took the $2,500 he had been saving for his son's law-school education and pledged it to the Yoshimura bail fund because, as he wrote to the judge, "I know that Wendy would never turn around and hurt anyone who helped her. Betrayal brings disgrace to your family."

If the saga of Patty Hearst can be thought of as grand opera, nothing is more appropriate to the California *mise-en-scène* than this chorus of hitherto-invisible and unheard-of small-time gardeners and truck farmers marching out of the Oakland hills and up from Fresno and Salinas and the San Joaquin Valley waving Wendy's bail money in their work-worn hands. As a result of her chance involvement with Patty Hearst, Wendy became a kind of Joan of Arc and Emma Goldman to these almost-forgotten people; in turn, they became her jealous, vigilant, mistrustful guardians. Few groups in America have so much to be mistrustful about.

Tomorrow at noon I am to meet with Wendy's volunteer defense committee and try to negotiate terms for an interview. They are eager to raise money for her legal expenses, which will cost hundreds of thousands of dollars, but are determined to protect her from exploitation by the media. They are looking for the "right" journalist, and I am eager to help. Not only do I like Wendy very much. So far as I can see, she is the single heroic figure in this entire cast of characters, the one person since Patty was kidnapped to have offered her help and companionship without demanding money, love, fealty, attention, respect, or anything else in return. Wendy strikes me as a far more interesting individual than Patty. She is a mysterious figure, but her persona has weight. She may be the rarest fish in the tank, the creature who knows who she is, even if others do not.

Americans used to be Irish, Italians, Jews, Slavs, Negroes, Scandinavians—an arrangement of discrete ethnic blocs. As the melting pot is stirred, homogeneity increases; ethnic type matters less and personality type matters more. I preferred the pot unstirred. The stirring detached people from their ethnic roots and offered no replacement. One result is that the person with a strong sense of individual identity has become the model, the ideal sought and worshiped in the office and shrine of every shrink and faith healer and marriage counselor and psychotherapist in the land. No longer grace or virtue or hard work but self-knowledge, self-acceptance, and self-realization are the new American ideals. In these terms, too, Wendy Yoshimura and Patricia Hearst are positive and negative materializations of the same principle. Wendy defies classification; nobody quite understands who Wendy is except Wendy. *Everybody* knows, or thinks he knows, who Patty Hearst is. Some think of her as saint, some as sinner, some as rich bitch, some as spoiled brat, some as adventuress, some as pathetic victim. All except Patty seem to have a definite picture. Patty takes the old saying that one cannot be all things to all men and stands it on its head. Only to herself is she nothing, nobody, no one at all.

The voluntariness hearing continues. It is our second day without a jury. Anthony Shepard, the young caramel-colored man on the witness stand, wears a coppery Afro, a Fu Manchu mustache, a short-sleeved shirt that displays his muscles, and a tough-guy swagger. He was the clerk at Mel's, and he is studying to be a cop. A sense of barely controlled anger stretches between this man and Bailey like the rope each would like to wrap around the other's neck. But first Browning must lead him through his story. Shepard caught William Harris shoplifting a pair of socks and "attempted to put handcuffs on the gentleman. Emily Harris was on my back, attempting to protect Mr. Harris." Still struggling out on the sidewalk, Shepard had managed to snap on only one handcuff when "we were fired upon from across the street by an unknown vehicle." When he "saw an unknown suspect hanging out of the van window with a weapon, I proceeded to shimmy out of the street, behind a light stand. . . ."

The Harrises dashed across the street into the van and took off. The clerk gave chase in his own car. When both vehicles got stuck in traffic, someone jumped out of the van and approached Shepard with an automatic rifle held at port-arms position. It was "an individual with shoulder-length hair."

"Do you know who that person was?"

He knows it was not William or Emily Harris.

I glance at Patty and think of Wendy. In contrast to this zombie at the defense table, Wendy was so ... what? "Clear-eyed, smiling, strong, clean-haired, young, confident, cheerful, open," I write on my yellow pad.

"No questions," Bailey snaps.

"Whew!" Shepard shakes his head, very glad to avoid cross-examination.

Tom Matthews steps into the box, and we get our first look at the young man whom Patty and the Harrises are accused of kidnapping. He wears an open shirt, a half smile, and a shock of hair over his forehead. In contrast to this open-faced young man and to strong, cheery Wendy, Patty looks so—I still search for a word—"so dead," I write, though that is not quite the word I want, either.

Matthews testifies that after he got into the van, he was told that one of his companions was Patricia Hearst.

"Do you see that person here today?"

"She's sitting right next to Mr. Bailey," says Matthews, his smile waxing like a three-quarter moon.

This questioning is tedious. I take the opportunity to sketch the geometry of our rigid environment. Every day we occupy the same seats for the same number of hours. My assigned position is in the center section of the visitors' benches, right-hand aisle seat, second row. To my right, across the aisle, is a narrow section of seats reserved for the prosecution: government witnesses, FBI men, wives, and friends. In the front-row aisle seat is Tom Padden, the FBI man in charge. Behind him, directly across the aisle from me, sits one of the government psychiatrists, Dr. Harry Kozol, and his wife, Ruth. Already they have spent more than a month in San Francisco, waiting to testify. They wear the timid, anxious expressions of turn-of-the-century immigrants at Ellis Island. We exchange daily pleasantries. Mrs. Kozol enjoys watching my "Point/Counterpoint" debates on television; I admire the writing of their rebellious son, Jonathan, author of *Death at an Early Age.* But like the jurors in their slightly elevated box directly in front of and at right angles to us, along the right-hand wall, the Kozols and I are careful to keep our thoughts about this trial scrupulously to ourselves. We behave as if we were meeting at a bus stop, not in a courtroom.

The matching narrow section of seats left of the left-hand aisle is reserved for the defense team. The wives of Patty's lawyers sit here, as do the extra Hearst sisters and cousins for whom there is no room on the front bench. The front rows of this section are also the bullpen for the defense psychiatrists. Some come in and out of town as needed, but Dr. Louis Jolyon West, in the corner seat, has moved to San Francisco for the duration. He is ruddy, blond, large, cheerful, blue-eyed, and football-shouldered. Off duty, "Jolly," as he is called, occupies a Stanford Court hotel suite, alongside the Baileys and Johnson, across the street from the Hearsts' own Nob Hill apartment. (Sometime during the Missing Year, the Hearsts had sold the six-bedroom suburban Hillsborough mansion where the press besieged them during the early days after their daughter's kidnapping, and had moved into town.) Daily the doctor dispenses smiles, good-fellowship, reassurance, medical and psychiatric expertise, a flu pill here, a pat on the arm there; he is always ready with a friendly ear, a judicious, professional opinion, and a brief-case full of reprints of his own work. He is willing to listen, if not to talk, to the friendly reporters who cluster around him during recess, in the lobby, in the restaurant across the street, or in the hotel corridors. West occupies a position in the HERNAP entourage similar to that of a family priest in a medieval royal household. He hears confessions, soothes the weary, comforts the oppressed, and jollies everybody along. Every set of Canterbury pilgrims should have a Jolly in its entourage.

Like Tom Padden, across the way, West is a physically imposing man with a broad chest and large, fleshy features. Seated always at opposite sides of the courtroom, heading their opposing factions, West and Padden, the psychiatrist and the FBI man, are like twin tritons flanking the show. Both men are also key witnesses throughout the trial. Their daily attendance makes a mockery of Judge Carter's assertion that potential witnesses, such as yesterday's four blacks, are to be excluded from the proceedings.

Along the left-hand wall of the courtroom, at right angles to the defense section, is another raised jury box. This one is filled with two rows of specially privileged press, representatives of the wire services and major newspapers and television networks. Between the two facing jury boxes are the defense table, at left, and the prosecution table, right. The center spectator-press section, behind the stout tables, reserves the front bench for the Hearsts and for the sketch artists for television and newspapers. A second bench holds more artists; then come several rows of middle-rank correspondents like myself (I am officially covering the trial for *Newsday,* my hometown Long Island newspaper), who occupy the sixty-three reserved seats. Behind us are three or four rows reserved for accredited free-lancers who daily must scramble for places. The public is allotted only one or two rows of benches along the back wall.

I sit just behind the second row of sketch artists. A large spiral-bound drawing pad is balanced at an angle on each artist's thighs. One hand braces the pad and holds a fistful of spare pencils and inks for softening, shading, filling in finishing touches and details during slack periods; the other hand moves ceaselessly over white paper. As I watch over the artists' shoulders the figures in the drama reappear on the pads, interpreted in russet felt-tip pens, fine-line blue and black inks, or soft, smudgy lead pencil. The cameralike eye of the trained sketch artist snaps an instant detail—say, the muzzle, stock, and flapping tag of exhibit 19—and the hands reproduce it on the white sheet. The artists draw continually, even when nothing is happening, sketching jurors, press, the public at random, as if to keep the apparatus warmed for the next moment's necessity to record a cheek, a hairline, a gesture.

The Matthews boy, arms folded across his chest, is cheerfully describing how the SLA told him they needed money because it was expensive to be engaged in guerrilla warfare. Matthews likes everybody, including Patty. During the night in the van, "she kept patting me on the head, under the blanket, and asking me if I was all right."

Did she ever ask you to get a message to her parents? No. Ever talk about the shoot-up at Mel's? She said it was "a good feeling" to see her two comrades come running back across the street.

Bailey's cross-examination is brisk. Yes, a light blanket was over him the whole time he was in the van. No, he doesn't recall any lights inside the vehicle. He could tell by the sound whether the van's doors were open or closed. How often did Patty pat him on the head? At least twice, maybe four or five times. Did she express concern as to whether he was comfortable? Yes. Thank you, that's all.

As we rise for the lunch break Vicki Hearst suddenly opens her hand and flashes her sister a Day-Glo–orange rabbit's foot. The defendant's vacant, *dolorosa* face breaks into a startled grin, and for an instant Patty is beautiful again. But the grin vanishes, and I find then the word I have been searching for all morning: embalmed. Patty looks not dead, but rather as if she is being made up for her courtroom appearance by cosmeticians from Forest Lawn.

After lunch the jury returns briefly to hear testimony by an FBI ballistics expert, as well as a description by Tom Padden of the various cars and false identification papers used by the robbers. Wherever the jury goes, it is nudged and chivied along by the marshals, who surround it like tugboats around a big tanker. Each marshal wears a vast sunburst of hardware attached to his Western-style uniform: a gun and holster, a heavy set of keys, brass whistle on a chain, screwdriver and other tools clipped to the keys, and a radio on his belt with the speaker clipped to his shoulder. He also carries nightstick, flashlight, handcuffs, notebook in the back pants pocket, large shield on the breast, a smaller name badge and rank or unit badge, and a picket fence of pens and pencils clipped across his shirt pockets. To see one of these fellows suit up for duty must be like witnessing the vesting of a bishop.

The people who guard this jury, who keep it sequestered and safe from taint, take their responsibility with great seriousness. Last weekend the jurors voted to go to the movies. *Dog Day Afternoon* and *One Flew over the Cuckoo's Nest* were both playing. Because *Dog Day Afternoon* is about a bank robbery, the marshals vetoed that one and dutifully shepherded their charges to the most savage indictment of modern psychiatry ever committed to film. On subsequent weekends they took the jurors to see *Taxi Driver,* an almost unbearably graphic study of a psychotic, violent killer, and *Swept Away,* in which an empty-headed upper-class woman finds herself sexually switched on by a working-class man.

Now the matter of the four unwilling witnesses must be disposed of, so once more the jury is invited to leave, and as a massive, angry-looking, jet-black lady in orchid silk, lowers herself into the witness chair, Janey Jimenez, the young Chicana marshal who guards and escorts Patty, sniffs, "It's like a zoo in here!"

The black lady's lawyer is a slender young blonde in a white pants suit. On tiptoe, she whispers into her client's ear, and aloud she protests that Browning has sent out the same inadequate boiler-plate form letter to each of the four reluctant blacks. "Yesterday's witnesses were in this courtroom *by order* of Mr. Browning!" Patty's lawyers smile and comment audibly on the shape of the blond lawyer's buttocks.

The next black witness, Ronald Tate, illustrates the gulf of misunderstanding between these ghetto black people and the virtually all-white courtroom. Asked to give his address, Tate says, "I take the Fifth, because I'm motherfucking not going to any more . . ." or, rather, that's what white reporters hear and write down. But a black correspondent hears, correctly: "I take the Fifth because my mother 'n' father don't live there no more."

The third unwilling witness gives her name as Retimah X and also takes the Fifth. Susan B. Jordan, who represents these last two persons, is also Emily Harris' lawyer, and she is the person whom Patty asked to see right after her arrest. But if the defendant recognizes Ms. Jordan now, she gives no sign.

We are out taking the midafternoon recess when we hear the familiar shout, "Clear path! Clear path! Jury coming through!" and the court-wise throng in the smoky, T-shaped corridor parts like the Red Sea, pressing back against the marble walls to avoid contaminating the Chosen Ones, who file past us like ritual holy priests or idiots savants of Anglo-Saxon justice, under the watchful eyes of their marshals. Shrinking back, I find myself pressed right next to Susan Jordan, who whispers, "I have represented these people since 1974, and I still don't know how the government got on to them!"

After recess Judge Carter orders the reluctant witnesses to testify. Ms. Jordan protests that his ruling "harks back to the time of the Inquisition—"

"You might as well say Torquemada, too, and enlarge your complaint," the judge interrupts with a thin smile.

"Ms. Muntaz, did there come a time in 1974 when you met Cinque?" Browning asks.

Ms. Jordan whispers to her client, who responds, "I refuse to answer on the basis of my constitutional rights."

"And the Fourth, Fifth, Sixth, Eighth, and Ninth amendments," Ms. Jordan adds. This sets all the defense attorneys laughing aloud, and with these hoots of scorn the day's testimony draws to a close.

Downstairs the young women attorneys hold a press conference. "These people have good reason to resist testifying. They are caught between the two most powerful forces in San Francisco—the government and the Hearsts." Retimah X wears earrings made of iridescent blue feathers with polka dots, like trout flies tied to her ears. The feathers flap wildly as she reports, "My house was bugged! My phone was bugged! I have an eight-month-old son to take care of! I was first called by the grand jury a year and a half ago!" Since that time the bugging sounds and the anonymous phone calls have not let up, though she has several times changed her phone number and even moved to a new apartment.

"One doesn't *have to* testify if there are good legal grounds not to," Ms. Jordan explains to the reporters. Her point is well made in a case such as this.

Home from the trial, I find Al Johnson waiting in the lobby. He has stopped by for a swim. When we go upstairs to get him a towel, he asks diffidently if he may leave "Walther" behind. Walther is like a fretful wet baby to Al; where to park him is a constant preoccupation. Though he knows I have already seen the little German pistol in its woven leather pouch that he wears on his belt under his coat, revealing Walther still makes Al shy. He takes off his jacket like a man exposing himself. Then, the weapon safely stashed on top of my refrigerator, he grabs a towel and flees.

The trial is into its second week. How is it going? How do I know? The situation reminds me of the night long ago when I first saw *Death of a Salesman* and wept uncontrollably. The next day I ran into a friend, a florist, who had also been in the audience, and we fell upon each other like castaways who had once shared the same lifeboat. "Wasn't it marvelous!" I exclaimed.

"Perfect! Except for one thing," my friend replied. "Willy Loman's funeral wreath at the end was just a touch *too chic.*" Come to think of it, he was right, and that same ultrafine-tuned sense of nuance might have led my friend to say of this trial that, so far, Patty's defense has been just a touch too good. Her demeanor on the stand has been a shade too perfect, too controlled. She never says one word more than necessary. Her clothes are possibly a touch too dowdy. She is perhaps a touch too well prepared. Something about these proceedings is a touch too smooth. "Do not expect anyone to go writhing to the floor, Perry Mason fashion," Bailey has warned me a dozen times. But I do, I do. . . .

A knock at the door, and Al is back, pink and shining. Walther lies forgotten on top of the refrigerator. We have a drink and watch the news. Jack Scott is reportedly close to being indicted in Pennsylvania. "Good," says Al. "Joe Cottone, the U.S. attorney down there, is a hands-off guy. I had four murder cases with him." Suddenly weary again, Al looks at his watch. "Time to call the jail. Don't make any noise. She doesn't like it if she thinks anybody else is with me."

He dials, and after some banter with the warders, Patty comes on the line. "So what's going on in the can? . . . Oh, *you* just called *me?* No, I wasn't in my room. I just came in here now, and I'm going right out again. Did you have supper?" She tells him what was served at the jail. He lights a cigarette, loosens his collar, and asks how many mouthfuls of it she was able to eat. If Patty *is* a Manchurian Candidate, and Al is her control, she is lucky to have him. He is a genial fairy godfather; Walther never shows under his coat. A bizarre "friend" for a girl like

Patty, but these days her only one. With Patty, as with everyone, Al is unfailingly patient, cheerful, and entirely himself. They slip into a conversation they've had many times: planning Patty's "coming-out party."

"Have you been working on the menu, like I told you? . . . Good. By the way, whaddya gonna wear? . . . Naw, get something new. Better be a gown, a long gown. You'll have a lot to celebrate. . . . I've been thinking where to have it. It'll have to be someplace like Chasen's, because you're gonna be in L.A."

Patty asks Al his opinion of the two female lawyers. She had appeared impassive during the sniggering horseplay at the defense table. "I thought one of 'em stunk. The blonde. But the other one, if she wasn't a Commie, would be great. . . ." I wondered if Al knew that "the other one" was the attorney Patty had originally asked for, before himself *or* the Hallinans. "People who defend radicals have split allegiance," Al continues. "In the first place, that's unethical. In the second, you can't do justice to the client. Causes are dangerous, because often the cause will be at odds with the interests of the defendant. . . . That's what happened to Kayo. . . . Yes, you *should* go to law school"—fatherly, encouraging voice—"though *I* wouldn't ever hire you! You're too bossy!"

Poor girl. If she can exist at this simpleminded level, she must be well and truly lost. She might as well join her semiinvalid sister, who works at a convent, and live out her life as an impaired creature, a medieval recluse, embroidering, manicuring her nails, and doing good works.

Having spooned into Patty her evening's ration of applesauce, we go downstairs for dinner. This evening Al feels mainly like drinking and unloading a few troubles, and somewhere during a long and rambling chat, he permits the only criticism of Bailey I will ever hear cross his lips. It was Al who kept their law firm going for two years while Bailey fought the Florida indictment, but the costs were very high. When they finally got the big case, Al was outraged by Bailey's low fee. His partner has forgotten the two immutable factors that should determine legal fees, Johnson believes, "time spent and indispensability to client."

"How do you get Patty to eat?" I ask.

"Choo-choo."

"Huh?"

"You know, like you feed a kid. You say, here comes the choo-choo train. Open up now, food's going in."

Conversation circles back to Al's domestic life. He tells me about his fifteen-year-old son. "When I'm not there, he sits and waits by the door. When I'm in the living room, he sits by me on the couch. He doesn't say anything. When I make a phone call, he comes and sits by the phone. How can I let him down? I don't know what to do."

"For Patty you know what to do. The most impossible predicament in the world doesn't faze you," I say, trying to cheer him up.

But Al doesn't hear me. "Oh, well . . . I'm a very good con man. I worked since I was fourteen . . . in a drugstore . . . then the Highway Patrol. Then Boston Law School. I'm very good." Irish melancholy descends.

Wednesday, February 11

My phone rings at eight o'clock the next morning. "I musta been really out of it last night. I left Walther over there." When he comes to pick up his gun, dressed in still another of his odd bus-driver suits with the Marine pin in the lapel, Al looks scrape-shaven, damp-eyed, and dogged.

This is a critical day. If Judge Carter rules to admit the enormous amount of evidence in Patty's own words that she was a willing participant in the bank robbery, Bailey must then show that all of it—taped, spoken, and written in her own hand—was forced out of her while she was under immediate fear of death or great bodily harm; further, he must show that this immediate danger lasted from the moment she was kidnapped until the moment of her capture, more than nineteen months later. The defense is *duress,* but the duress was physical only up to a point. Once she joined the SLA it became mental, and was imposed jointly by her captors and by Patty Hearst herself because she had come to believe whatever they told her. Browning's task may not be easier than Bailey's, but it is certainly simpler. To win his case, he must convince twelve jurors beyond a reasonable doubt that Patricia Hearst is a liar.

Bailey finds it unseemly at best "and in my view a flat violation of the rights of the defendant [for the SLA] to create evidence against [her in order] to isolate her from the society from which she came and to which she might otherwise return—and then to have that [manufactured] evidence admitted in a court of law." A ruling to admit the "manufactured" evidence would encourage and even inspire other radical groups to attempt similar kinds of terrorist actions, he says. Now it is Bailey, rather than the SLA, who is attempting to politicize what would otherwise be a simple matter of law. Then he makes a purely legal point: An involuntary statement, to whomever made, cannot be admitted in evidence, and as Bailey has repeatedly pointed out, the tape, the manuscript, and the confession to Matthews all were involuntary, all made under duress. He recalls the threats to the victim that "we'll croak you if you ever try to go back into society" and implies that if the judge rules against Patty, the court will be lending its own imprimatur to such threats. Furthermore, "this defendant ought not to be convicted on statements forced from her [nor on] the notion that because her father didn't *do* enough, she was convinced by her captors that he put a short dollar on her head. To allow an American jury to carry out [the SLA's] predictions that, if she were to return, she would be cast in jail, because of evidence *they* had forcibly created, is an outrage. And I ask Your Honor to exclude that evidence."

Finally, the government's own evidence is in conflict with itself. They have offered a "writing" (the "Tania Interview") wherein Patty indicates that within two weeks of her kidnapping, she had voluntarily joined the SLA, "when the evidence is overwhelming that two weeks after this kidnapping she was praying and begging in very fervent tones that her parents comply with their demands. "We here today are disseminating a formula for terror. And terrorists abound in this city." Patricia's various revolutionary statements "don't comport in any way with the nineteen or twenty years of upbringing this young lady has had. . . . The court would be permitting the government to dirty up the defendant." Bailey's speech is full of menace. He speaks in a bullying tone, threatening the judge and waving the flag at the same time. He ends with a plea that, at the very least, Carter should exclude "all of Los Angeles, with the possible exception of Matthews."

The prosecutor's argument runs just as Bailey had told me it would. Normally, the burden of proof would be on the government to prove that Patricia had acted voluntarily, not under duress. However, "no government agency was involved in the alleged involuntariness because private individuals made these threats," not cops or overeager district attorneys. The evidence that force and intimidation were used is in the possession of the defense. Therefore, it should properly bear the burden of proof. . . . This fugue in double negatives is making my head spin.

Now Browning shifts to simpler logic. "The real question is whether the defendant may be believed. . . . The evidence submitted here does not suggest she was in fear of great bodily injury or death." She claims she was under duress when she wrote the Tania manuscript in late 1974. But she had told the same things to Tom Matthews many months before, and he says she was not then under duress. If she was under duress in the bank, why was she wearing a wig? If they wanted her to be recognized, why was her hair cut off? Does Patty look in fear of injury or death in the film? She does not. Patty had enough time alone with Matthews to ask him for help; why didn't she? She could have escaped when she was alone in the van, across from Mel's; why didn't she? During the trip east there were many more chances to escape; unless the Harrises trusted Patricia, why did they permit her to be alone? Especially, why was she permitted to remain alone in the van with a weapon? Why on earth, if the defendant were in fear of her life, would she rescue the very comrades she claims to have been so afraid of? Lastly, in evaluating her truthfulness, her admitted untruthfulness in the bail affidavit must be kept in mind. If the court forecloses the opportunity to present all this to the jury, it deprives them of "highly probative evidence. All evidence is *somewhat* prejudicial to the defendant," Browning concludes plaintively. "That's the whole idea!"

If the jury were present to listen to the government's damning list of questions, the case would be all over. But they are not present, and to them Patricia is still clothed in the presumption of innocence that Judge Carter spoke of. It will be Bailey's job throughout the remainder of this trial to answer Browning's penultimate question: He must make the jury understand that *rescuing the very comrades she lived in fear of* is precisely what "brainwashing" is all about.

Bailey appears to expand slightly inside his tight suit, and his color darkens a shade. "The burden of proof does *not* shift. We have submitted a memorandum on this which has been run back and forth through four centuries of law at the Harvard Law Library." How much, one wonders, is a California judge whose father was a California judge impressed by the Harvard Law Library?

The problem must be decided carefully, Carter says, "because it brings the Fifth Amendment into play" [the right of the defendant against self-incrimination by involuntary statements] and he declares a recess so he can consider the matter.

I am on a corridor telephone arranging the meeting with the Yoshimura Defense Committee when a herd of reporters comes thundering down the marble hallway, *Front Page* style, racing for the bank of phones. Carter has just denied Bailey's motion to suppress the evidence. He will let all four of Bailey's skunks into his courtroom, because he finds "by a preponderance of the evidence that . . . the statements made by the defendant after the happening of the bank robbery, whether by tape recording or by oral communication or in writing, *were* made voluntarily."

It is a severe blow for the defense. Despite Patty's aversion to medication, she is observed to swallow a pill. The jury files back, and the morning drones along with tedious FBI testimony documenting the chain of custody of the bullets, the begats of criminal testimony. The judge yawns openly. At his noon press conference Bailey is appealingly candid: Carter's ruling did not catch him unawares. Since the damaging materials had already been permitted in the government's opening statement, the only alternative to this morning's ruling would have been to throw the case out of court. While that would have been nice, "nobody has been hanging by his thumbs."

Will Bailey now put Patty on the stand? "The likelihood of her testifying has increased sharply this morning." His voice turns hard. "I imagine Cinque is sparkling in his grave. . . . A formula for the future treatment of kidnap victims is being laid out by this case. Follow it, and you can kidnap, extort money, involve an individual in crime, and then tell your victim: *'You have no place to go.'* "

I go now to Glide Memorial Church to meet the members of Wendy's committee. It is another tribunal. Hostility and mistrust thicken the air. To these watchful representatives of the counterculture and the Third World, reporters are all alike. My protestations of interest in Wendy are not believed. I am perceived as an incarnation of *Newsweek* and *CBS,* not as a human being. We are not introduced; they know my name but I don't know any of theirs, which increases my unease. We decide on a third meeting, this one to be in Oakland, at the offices of Wendy's attorneys. It is only as I am stumbling out that I realize one of the young inscrutables around the table has been Wendy herself, grim, unsmiling, unrecognized. I return to court chagrined and depressed.

(113)

Eighty-two-year-old Adela Rogers St. John is in town to cover the trial for a few days for the Hearst syndicate. Adela, the original Hearst sob sister, was one of my girlhood heroines. We meet now from time to time on television talk shows, where talking women are always in short supply, and Adela is one of the most dependable—sharp-tongued, sharp-eyed, with the face of a merry prune. Adela, Sybille Bedford, Dorothy Kilgallen, Mary McCarthy, Jessica Mitford, Rebecca West— why are so many of the best trial reporters women? Perhaps it is because a courtroom offers action rigorously contained, framed both in space and in time. To report it well requires not action but reaction. Trial writers are not private eyes; they do not go out and *do*. They sit still and figure, match pieces, dovetail fragments like archaeologists at a dig. They proceed by guesswork and intuition: Where is this lawyer trying to lead us? How much truth is this witness telling? Who is frightened? What is the jury thinking? The woman assembles the puzzle from its pieces. She fills in the frame, as if doing embroidery. She reacts selectively. Ultimately she judges.

One of the greatest of Hearst's reporters, Adela had not flinched when asked to describe her longtime boss and patron in an obituary for his own paper. Her description of the Old Man, as William Randolph Hearst was always known, was masterful: "No other press lord ever wielded his power with less sense of responsibility; no other press ever matched the Hearst press for flamboyance, perversity and incitement of mass hysteria. Hearst never believed in anything much, not even Hearst, and his appeal was not to men's minds but to their infantile emotions which he never conquered in himself: arrogance, hatred, frustration, fear."

When I had invited Adela out to dine, she suggested I come by her hotel instead. Now I find her sprawled on the couch in a gaudy, rumpled negligee, an uninhibited old lady taking floods of phone calls and horsing around in one of her favorite towns. We order room-service dinners, and I ask permission to test my tape recorder, which I do not completely trust.

ADELA: In the corridor, please. I don't care how often *you* hear it, but I've never heard my own voice.

S.A.: Which was your first trial?

ADELA: I started going to them with my father, when I was eight. The first trial I actually covered was when Delfin M. Delmas, the great New

York criminal lawyer, came out to the Coast. Delmas had defended Harry K. Thaw when he shot Stanford White. Since my father, Earl Rogers, was the greatest criminal lawyer in the West, I was sent to cover the trial. I'd just gone to work on the Hearst paper. Now, let's get one thing clear. I am aware that we fought a war in 1776, but that's the *end* of my dates. I haven't the vaguest idea when anything happened. Mr. Hearst used to say, "Adela sees it all as a tapestry, with everything happening at exactly the same time. She never sees one reel. She just looks and sees everything at once."

S.A.: You've seen them all. The Lindbergh trial, Leopold and Loeb, the Hall-Mills case. Where would you rank this one?

ADELA: One of the difficulties is that great trials are dependent on great lawyers, and there's not a good lawyer in that courtroom. *Darrow* defended Leopold and Loeb!

S.A.: What is Mr. Bailey?

ADELA: He's a clown, if you ask me.

S.A.: Would you have taken Ed Williams instead, if you'd been hiring her counsel?

ADELA: I would have taken a San Francisco lawyer. That's always been my policy. They know the local mores; they know the feelings; they know their jurors. If it says on their little pad, "He graduated from Santa Clara," that tells them something about him. Also, I think an out-of-town lawyer offends a jury. Randy should have hired your best San Francisco lawyers. I told him this at the time. If *they* wanted to bring in Mr. Bailey, fine. . . . You know, the Hearst family is almost like my own. Mr. Hearst was as dear to me as my own father. I loved him with *great* devotion, and I worked for him for thirty-five years.

S.A.: Did you ever know this granddaughter?

ADELA: No. Randy has always been one of my favorites, but I don't know his children at all.

S.A.: You have a flock of grandchildren. Do you think that family traits skip a generation?

ADELA: I'm not a great believer in heredity. I believe in environment. For example, I'm an alcoholic, and my father was an alcoholic. But I don't think that's hereditary. I think it's the fact that I was going to prove to everybody in the world that *anything* my father did was right. If he wanted to stay drunk, then it was right, so I stayed drunk to prove that I could do it, too. I may be wrong—I guess a psychiatrist would say I am—but anyway that's what I think.

S.A.: Have you had many dealings with psychiatrists?

ADELA: As little as possible.

S.A.: I rather suspected that. Have you covered many trials when there has been a lot of psychiatric testimony?

ADELA: Off and on. We used to call those people alienists back aways, and they popped in and out. But they were not taken with this great hero worship that we now award to so many of them. . . . This whole trial is kind of ass-backward, it seems to me, starting with trying the wrong crime. She is on trial for *having been kidnapped.* I think that's idiotic in the extreme. . . .

S.A.: How else is it idiotic?

ADELA: This judge to me is very ineffectual. One great thing about the Lindbergh trial, which was the best trial I've ever seen, was that Trencherd was a great, great justice. And being in New Jersey, he wore the robes, which helps.

S.A.: Different robes from Carter's?

ADELA: Has *he* got a robe on? I hadn't even noticed.

S.A.: Can you see the girl very well from your seat?

ADELA: No, but I've looked at her . . . nothing happens in her face. . . . I am not at all sure that this girl is . . . is in her right mind. . . . Oh, dear, I hope she lives through this. I mean that very sincerely. I'm not at all sure she's going to. Yesterday at one point she went so white.

S.A.: She's been menstruating continually for over a year. They can't stop it. That accounts in part for the terrible pallor.

ADELA: I have a feeling she's not going to live through the case. That's one of the reasons I'm here. Her health is very bad, and she's very down. Sometimes I think she may take the suicide way out. Has that occurred to you?

S.A.: Yes. Why do you think this particular kind of defense is being conducted? Remember during the Vietnam War when some general said, "We have to destroy this town in order to save it"? It seems to me they may have to destroy this girl in order to save her.

ADELA: A very interesting remark, my dear. Very. As I say, we're trying the wrong case, and it seems to me all very mixed up. I called up Randy as soon as I heard about Bailey. He suggested that there had been tremendous pressure from around the Hearst service, that Bailey was the greatest criminal lawyer, the biggest, and the one he ought to have. I said, "Well, I think you've made a tragic mistake, and I say it only because I think there's still time for you to rectify it."

S.A.: There's an excellent older man, Jim MacInnis, whom Randy wanted to use, but Patty said he was an asshole, which ended that idea.

ADELA: Well, she hasn't been the greatest judge of men that I've ever met.

S.A.: If this trial were really not so important in itself, but was looking ahead to other possible prosecutions—would it make more sense to put her through this?

ADELA: I think they may be fighting for something like not guilty for reasons of diminished responsibility. Put her in Camarillo [a state mental hospital] or one of those places for four or five years.

S.A.: Would she have to be there that long?

ADELA: I think in so public a case as this, they'd have trouble with less. She's not a popular figure, even with the young people.

S.A.: I know. She has *no* friends.

ADELA: Well, she's managed to do everything wrong that you could possibly do. The ironical thing is, you know, that Mr. Hearst wanted a daughter more than he wanted anything in the world. He had five sons, and he used to say, "Adela is my daughter, the daughter I didn't have." He said it often enough so that it was imprinted on my brain. When this first happened, I used to think, isn't it a shame, his own granddaughter! I mean, he would have *so* loved the story!

S.A.: If you reject the view of Patty as the zombie we see now and look for the girl she *was,* you can see a rather spunky, vivacious, sexy creature who said, "I like this teacher in my school, and I will seduce him, I will have him," and she did. *That* girl—the one who wrote that "Tania Interview"—is temperamentally like her grandfather, is she not?

ADELA: That's right. He was the smartest man *I* ever knew by about a hundred miles.

S.A.: If he'd known that his granddaughter had been kidnapped by a radical group and had joined or appeared to join them, how do you think Hearst would have reacted?

ADELA: I think he would have prevented it going as far as it did.

S.A.: You know, this girl was ashamed of being a Hearst. Maybe "ashamed" is the wrong word, but the burden of the name was too heavy. Steven Weed says that Patty felt her parents were "in the business of being Hearsts."

ADELA: I know it, but even so, it's an awful lot of shit. And you know that, and so do I. It's a word I don't like, but there are times when you can't say anything else. . . .

S.A.: How would W.R. have handled the kidnapping of his granddaughter?

ADELA: Mr. Hearst would have found her in a week and a half, I would think.

S.A.: You mean, with his own sources?

ADELA: I heard Mr. J. Edgar Hoover say to his Attorney General one afternoon, "Let me tell you something, *use the press.* They have solved more crimes than the FBI and the CIA and the Attorney General all put together. They have better men, more time, more people, more money, and more sense. They do a better job than *any* of us." I don't know how good reporters are anymore—I don't follow it enough —but in those days W.R. would have put Runyon on it. Runyon knew more people in the underworld than anyone else alive, and knew 'em *well.*

S.A.: Yes, but he didn't know radicals.

ADELA: There *were* no radicals then.

S.A.: Who covered Harry Bridges?

ADELA: W.R. had a man *living with* Bridges most of the time.

S.A.: Have you reflected on the miserable performance of J. Edgar Hoover's men in this case?

ADELA: All of their cases recently . . . they don't seem to exist at all. I don't know what happened, but at some point what had been the greatest body of criminal investigators in the world disappeared.

S.A.: Charlie Bates [special agent in charge of the FBI's San Francisco office and of the Hearst case] tells me nobody will talk to him, and nobody will talk to his men. They get the door slammed in their face.

ADELA: That's because they've run down in some way that I don't understand. Never have. The people who most wanted to see Mr. Hoover disappear off the face of the earth are the Communists. So I think that's what happened. They're very shrewd, they have enormous power in this country, and I just think they got Hoover.

S.A.: Almost the last thing Hoover did, one reads, was go to have lunch with President Kennedy. After that Miss Judith Campbell Exner was never heard of again.

ADELA: Honestly, Jack Kennedy slept with anything that didn't have four legs! And maybe a couple of *those,* I'm not too sure. I got mad at him one day and I said, "You know, dammit, I don't like this. You don't sleep with your wife's secretary in the White House! I won't have it! The White House doesn't belong to you. It belongs to *me!*"

S.A.: About Randy and Catherine—have *they* changed?

ADELA: I think she has. There's something about her that I don't quite understand. She has a wrong emotion of some kind. I don't know what it is.

S.A.: Does she seem a different woman now?

ADELA: I didn't know her well, but I would say that she is exactly the same woman. I went up to her the first day in court, and I said quite honestly, "I hope that if there's anything I can do, in my prayers, in whatever capacity, I hope you will remember me. I'm Adela St. John." And she said, "Why, Adela, what do you mean, you're Adela St. John? Of course! My goodness!" and she put her arms around me. It didn't seem to me phony, except I never thought I knew her that well.

S.A.: But in her *need,* she knew you.

ADELA: That's probably what it was. W.R. was very, *very* fond of Randy. . . . My goodness, I wish he was here. He'd think up something. He always did.

S.A.: I ask myself, what is the connecting thread in the Bailey cases? I think it's that his clients have been people perceived by the public as "ungettable off," and yet somehow Bailey does it.

ADELA: Well, that's what a good criminal lawyer does. See, Darrow was a great man, but he never won a case. Never. He used to say, "I am the great defender of lost causes," and my father used to say you can drop the *u* out of that, and it still holds. Oh, dear, how he disliked Darrow! When my father was defending him on the jury-bribery thing, he went over to him one day and said, "God damn you, if you don't stop looking guilty, I'm going to walk out of this courtroom and never come back. I'm up here sweating blood, trying to get you off as an innocent man, and you sit there looking guiltier than any client I ever had in my entire life!"

S.A.: In a way, you've just put your finger on what's wrong with *this* trial. There's no blood in it, and there's no *guilt* in it, and there isn't any *passion* in it. It's eerie. . . . I keep thinking I'm at Marineland.

ADELA: Exactly. You're going to stay here for the full length of the trial, I take it. Well, when you come to Los Angeles, let me know.

S.A.: I'd like to very much. Are you in the telephone book?

ADELA: Yes, ma'am! How did you guess that? *Nobody* has a listed phone anymore.

S.A.: Because you're a very straight dame. . . . By the way, I'm in the phone book, too.

Thursday, February 12

In the lobby of the Federal Building this morning a spectator was knocked down in the rush for seats and had to be hospitalized. Now the marshals have decided to admit the public in groups of sixty, one batch for the morning session, another for afternoon. The queue outside the building looks like the lines outside *The Exorcist.*

Patty appears unusually energetic today, talking rapidly, gesturing as if she were speaking in sign language, pointing animatedly at photographs of the closets, as if in some perverse way she is happy to see these awful old homes once more. Possibly late this afternoon, certainly by tomorrow, the defense case will begin. So this morning two of the biggest guns in academic psychiatry are drawn up on the defense side of the courtroom. The ruddy man is Dr. West. The handsome, saturnine fellow in the tweed jacket is Yale's Robert Jay Lifton, MD, accompanied by his wife, Betty Jean. Later a large, rumpled, European-looking couple will arrive from the University of Pennsylvania—Dr. Martin Orne and spouse. Bailey can hardly wait to rip the canvas off his three cannons and blow the government out of the water.

Now a parade of jargon-talking FBI agents identifies incriminating evidence found in the two SLA apartments. "This particular weapon was first observed by myself on the upper portion, more specifically, on the *shelving,* of the closet. . . ."

A U.S. Army technical manual on firearms, seized in the Harris apartment, bears Patricia's right thumb print. Bailey says there is no evidence that Patricia herself was ever in this apartment. Furthermore, the fingerprints of William Harris, James Kilgore, Kathleen Soliah, Emily Harris, Wendy Yoshimura, Steven Soliah, and Josephine Soliah are on the same manual. Steven Soliah, Patty's lover at the time of her arrest, was later tried for and acquitted of having taken part in the Carmichael bank robbery. Kathleen and Josephine Soliah are his sisters. James Kilgore, a former lover of Wendy Yoshimura, was Soliah's partner in a house-painting business.

During the noon recess reporters learn with a shock that there has been still another terrorist bombing. This time the target was San Simeon, a direct attack on the Old Man's castle-fortress. SLA sympathizers are suspected; later the New World Liberation Front will take credit for the explosion in which two small outbuildings were destroyed. Randolph Hearst says he is "shocked and outraged," but to hear his weary voice is to feel that there is no shock or outrage left in the man.

I had seen San Simeon first more than twenty years before—twenty-two, to be exact—in 1954, the year I arrived in California, sent out from New York by *Life* magazine to be a correspondent in its Los Angeles bureau. (That same year, also in Los Angeles, also in February, Patricia Hearst was born.) When my husband arrived a month or two after me, the very first thing we did together was to drive up the beautiful California coastline in the new car.

Two hundred miles north of our little house, above bluffs and tawny fields and great escarpments overlooking the Pacific, in the middle of a 77,000-acre spread, stood the marble pile of Spanish buildings and looted castles, gardens and pools and gargoyles and bell towers that is San Simeon. Eventually this grandiose mausoleum of power would become a state park; ever since Hearst's death, in 1951, his heirs had been trying to give it away, but the state government, sniffing a gargantuan white elephant, had been behaving with diplomatic skittishness.

Once, the place had been the bizarre dream castle a fearful old man had built for his true love, a lavish but hideous wedding-cake-in-stones hoarded up over centuries. Today, this monument to excess, this *imitation* of splendor, is also where the story of HERNAP most properly begins—for despite all her protestations, Patricia Hearst is not "anyone's daughter." She is the granddaughter of the Old Man, of William Randolph Hearst, and that is why she was kidnapped.

One day in January of the Missing Year, I made a second pilgrimage to San Simeon, by then the top tourist attraction in the California State Parks system and the only public monument in the Golden State that pays its own way. A drive to Hearst's remote pleasure dome from any direction is a tedious proposition, involving many hours on winding mountain roads. But a mutual friend of mine and the Hearsts had the use of a private plane. We intended to fly down from San Francisco, and hoped to save further time by landing on San Simeon's private airstrip.

"What are you doing with that adventuress?" Patty's mother asked my friend when he called to ask permission to land. Although I found Catherine's term for me quaint and rather appealing, it also struck me that if there *were* an adventuress abroad in the land at the moment, surely she was not I.

Flying south and low over the California coastal ranges, we saw mountains like undersea peaks of folded algae, a soft gray-green color with tree-spiked flanks, darker crests along the ridges, and a light airbrushing of fog across the topmost peaks. It was a landscape lunar in its emptiness, alongside the flat blue plate of the sea with its rim of turquoise-edged-in-white running right up to the Old Man's doorstep. Seen from the air, his white dream castle is a Moorish Disneyland atop a crumpled green doily of gardens, with the cars of tourists parked neatly as slippers tucked in at the foot of the hill.

In the tourist bus, as we wound our way up the six-mile driveway toward the castle, the smartly uniformed girl guide told us that the main house has a hundred rooms and ninety old ceilings. Each room was built to measure to contain the antiquities and ceilings, Gothic archways and stone fireplaces purchased abroad. Endless gloomy carvings and tapestries; Spanish Madonnas; an awful decor of cretonne and chipped cherubs. In the dining hall a dozen carved wooden saints, each one larger-than-life size, are deeply coffered into the ceiling. Walls lined with choir stalls are hung with silken banners above a fifty-four-foot-long table set with Vatican-scale silver candelabra and ketchup bottles —the latter intended as a reminder that San Simeon was, at heart, a "ranch." The loot of the world is piled up here. The place is a giant extrapolation.

"These columns are over two thousand years old. None of the capitals match—but they all blend," says the guide's disembodied voice. One feels enchanted, half-drunk from the overpowering smell of mimosa. "At one time," chirps the inane voice, "Mr. Hearst bought one-fourth of all the art in the world." Which way does she mean that? one wonders, stumbling on from room to room of hideous Spanish gloom, past the huge, blue-and-gold mosaic pool, like the Roxy Theater lobby underwater, where only servants swam. There is a movie theater here, too, of course, all garish red and gold. There is not just one of everything in this place but multiples of everything, none quite comfortable with the next. It is acquisitiveness run riot, a giant malignancy of decor. Anita Loos said Hearst wanted to be a great man more than anyone else she'd ever known. This place both expresses that longing and shows why he never made it. It is an enormous shambles.

Which San Simeon was he, the patron saint of this place? The Persian martyr who was sawed in half? Or Simeon Salus, the "fool for Christ," who went about naked and took special care of harlots? Or Simeon Stylites, the Syrian ascetic so wise he had to live upon a pillar to remove himself from the importunings of the multitude? The higher he built his pillar, the greater grew his fame. Letters arrived from the corners of the world; the throngs pressed closer; even emperors came. To escape, the saint was forced to spend the last thirty-six years of his life on a pillar sixty feet above the heads of the crowd—not a fitting altitude for the patron saint of newspapering. This Simon must have been Christ's own, the least known of the Twelve Apostles, remembered only for his zealotry.

Once, this was a quarter-million-acre spread, with ten thousand head of prize cattle. Much of the land was bought by W.R.'s father for fifty cents an acre, after the Civil War. George Hearst was a rough silver-and-gold king who drank, chewed tobacco, and swore; he was forty years older than his gentle, philanthropic estranged wife, Phoebe Apperson Hearst.* The next Mrs. Hearst, Millicent Willson, was estranged from W.R. for more than thirty years before his death, in 1951, and lived on another quarter-century, to the age of ninety-three, alert to the end. Though she always read the papers and adored television, vigilant nurses were under orders from her devoted youngest son, Randolph, to shield her from all knowledge of HERNAP. Millicent Hearst died during the Missing Year, perhaps the one and only newspaper-reader and television-watcher on the planet who did not know of the misadventures of Patricia Hearst.

In the gardens now, our tour group was examining a malevolent nine-foot Egyptian deity carved in black stone. "The lion-headed goddess of death and destruction," the canned voice intoned. Today the lion-headed goddess was queen of the hill, empress of the outdoor pool, the indoor pool, the lotus pool. Going down the hill at dusk, we passed a solitary zebra, all that remains of the world's largest private zoo, and all around, the lone and level sands stretched far away.

---

*Phoebe spent much of her time at her beautiful, isolated summer home in Pleasanton. Much later, the remote site was selected for a modern women's prison. By 1978 Pleasanton's best-known residents were Phoebe's great-granddaughter and "Squeaky" Fromme. Sara Jane Moore was still trying to gain admission.

The FBI's droning identification of various weapons continues after lunch. The carbines and M-1s seem unreal as they are handed about, like stage props in a war play. It is important to know whether or not Patricia had a weapon *capable* of being fired. On show today are the carbine Patty carried in the robbery, later found in her apartment, and an M-1 carbine taken from the Harrises' flat. The entire captured SLA arsenal includes another carbine, two shotguns, a revolver from the Harris apartment, and the revolver in Patty's purse—the one taken from the guard at the Hibernia Bank. Bailey has tried to bar any evidence from the Harris apartment on grounds that its prejudicial nature outweighs its probative value, but Carter has deferred ruling on that objection. In this curious trial, in which everybody is right, in which any jury decision would be a wrong decision, it seems appropriate that we have a Hamlet for a judge.

Patty's carbine was a .30-caliber, M-1 type of semiautomatic with a straight clip, or magazine, which holds fifteen rounds. The other robbers carried banana clips, each of which holds thirty rounds. All the SLA weapons had their barrels shortened, making them easier to conceal but also less accurate. The stocks were modified so the guns could be held at waist level and fired, rather than braced against the shoulder. Triggers and operating slides were also modified. A cache of homemade "Sear-trip" mechanisms in various stages of modification was found in one of the SLA hideouts. These are long, specially machined pins used to convert semiautomatic rifles into fully automatic weapons capable of firing 850 rounds per minute. And, yes, the FBI's expert has fired all these weapons personally to test their capabilities.

"Object!" shouts Bailey. "He did not! He keeps saying he fired these weapons automatically. He fired the *Harris* weapon automatically."

In cross-examination, Bailey demonstrates that Patty's weapon has a tendency to "hang up," to jam, and when this happens, "you could pull the trigger all day long and it wouldn't fire!" With a snort, he turns on his heel and walks off in disgust. The point has been to suggest to the jury that Patty's gun was possibly not even in working order, that she had deliberately been issued a faulty weapon because the SLA didn't trust her with an operative one.

FBI agent Tom Padden has been dozing. Now Bailey calls him to the stand to identify the all-important SLA tape no. 6, Patty's confession. Although only her portion of the tape has been transcribed, Bailey insists the jurors hear all the voices, including Cinque's long, ravening, paramilitary introduction. He wants the SLA wildness loud in the jurors' ears before they hear Tania herself speak. Browning is willing, and we hear Cinque's extraordinary monologue begin:

> Greetings to the People. And all sisters and brothers, behind the walls and in the streets. Greetings to the Black Liberation Army, the Weather Underground, and the Black Guerrilla Family, and all combat forces of the community. This is General Field Marshal Cin speaking.

Booming out over the silent courtroom, the gently cadenced, powerful voice makes my skin prickle.

> Combat Operation: April 15, 1974, the Year of the Children. Action: appropriation. Supplies liberated: one .38 Smith & Wesson revolver, condition good. Five rounds of 158-grain, .38-caliber ammo. Cash: $10,-660.02. Number of rounds fired by Combat Forces: seven rounds. Number of rounds lost: five. Casualties: People's Forces—none. Enemy Forces—none. Civilians—two. Reasons: Subject One (male)—subject was ordered to lay on the floor, facedown. Subject refused order and jumped out the front door of the bank. Therefore, subject was shot. . . .

Cinque's language sounds like a parody of a prisoner's "jacket"—the official record of his crimes and his infractions while in custody, written by the prison guards.

The field marshal's maniacal announcements continue:

> We again warn the public: Any civilian attempting to aid, to inform, or assist the enemy of the People in any manner will be shot without hesitation. There is no middle ground in war. . . . As a Black man, and a father, and as a representative of Black people, I would like to say that I, as well as many other Black people, have been watching the actions taken against Black people over in the City of San Francisco, and also in Berkeley and Oakland, by the racist agents of the ruling class. Like most of my people, I never trust anything the enemy says or does. I at first had thought that Operation Zebra* was really nothing more than a normal counterinsurgency operation to attempt to entrap SLA forces,

---

*A police dragnet of black males instituted by Mayor Alioto in response to twelve random killings of whites by blacks in the San Francisco streets. Alioto and the police chief have announced that the murders are initiation rites to a secret Black Muslim death cult to which admission can be gained only by shedding white blood. Save for the accident of timing, the SLA and Operation Zebra (the police-radio code name for the dragnet) are unrelated, so far as is known.

or more precisely to assassinate myself. I say "assassinate" because the enemy knows by now who I am. . . . I am the bringer of the children of the oppressed and the children of the oppressor together. . . . I am bringing the truth to the children and opening their eyes to the real enemy of humanity. . . . At this point, I am more inclined to feel, however, that Operation Zebra is a lot more than just entrapping the SLA . . . that Operation Zebra is a planned enemy offensive against the People, to create a race war, which could possibly be the only way the enemy can stop the SLA from bringing all the oppressed People together against the common enemy. Operation Zebra is even more than that. . . . We can expect in the next few months, under the guise of searching for the so-called Zebra Killer, block-by-block and house-by-house searches. And, of course, all weapons found in people's homes will be confiscated under the guise of stolen property, or that they have to be verified as not being the murder weapon. In short, the People will be disarmed. Operation Zebra serves yet even another purpose to the enemy. It is a means to remove as many Black males from the community as possible, at the same time forcing all the Black males to submit to FBI classification identification which is being applied in the form of so-called police passes. . . . My People, I warn you again, the only way, I repeat, the only way you will regain your life and freedom is to fight; the only way you will keep your guns is to use them. . . .

The next speaker, William Harris, escalates the level of rage still higher:

Pigs like Alioto wish to maneuver these white people into allowing the fascist army to sweep the ghettos and machine-gun or imprison the People. But anyone who by their racism and government-manipulated fear supports a genocide makes the grave error of forging his or her own slave chains. And if white people in fascist America don't think they are enslaved, they only prove their own foolishness. . . . Black people, more revolutionary than ever before, are armed and angry, and now the SLA is proving the Black people ain't alone, that the things the pigs have feared the most is happening, is growing. A People's army of irate niggers of all races, including whites—not talkers but fighters. The enemy recognizes that the People are on the brink of revolution and the enemy will do anything at any cost to prevent this. We ask the People, especially whites, to carefully analyze Operation Zebra, the Black-and-white horse of the times, and to understand who in reality sits in the saddle and holds the reins. Death to the fascist insect that preys upon the life of the People!'

At last Patty's voice comes on the tape:

Greetings to the People. This is Tania. On April 15, my comrades and I expropriated $10,660.02 from the Sunset Branch of the Hibernia Bank. . . . My gun was loaded, and at no time did any of my comrades intentionally point their guns at me. . . . To the clowns who want a personal interview with me—Vincent Hallinan, Steven Weed, and the pig Hearsts—I prefer giving it to the people in the bank. It's absurd to think I could surface to say what I am saying now and be allowed to freely return to my comrades. The enemy still wants me dead. I am obviously alive and well. As far as being brainwashed, the idea is ridiculous to the point of being beyond belief. . . . As for my ex-fiancé, I'm amazed that he thinks that the first thing I would want to do, once freed, would be to rush and see him. The fact is, I don't care if I ever see him again. During the last few months, Steven has shown himself to be a sexist, ageist pig—not that this was a sudden change from the way he always was. . . . Frankly, Steven is the one who sounds brainwashed. . . . I have no proof that Mr. Debray's letter is authentic [a reference to the taped message to the SLA from the French radical writer Régis Debray. Weed had gone to Mexico City to obtain it in a desperate move to establish some bona fides with the SLA]. . . . How could it have been written in Paris and published in your newspapers on the same day, Adolf? In any case, I hope that the last action has put his mind at ease. If it didn't, further actions will. For those people who still believe I am brainwashed or dead, I see no reason to further defend my position. I'm a soldier in the People's army. *Patria o muerte . . . Venceremos.*

As Tania's amplified voice fills the courtroom we can watch Patty's eyes moisten, then rapidly scan the jury, searching each face as they listen to her words. Tears begin to run down her cheeks. She sips water, strokes her hair from her brow; the ivory pallor of her face blotches red.

The day ends with agent Padden describing the arrest. Looking in a kitchen window, he saw two females, one white and one Oriental. He yanked open the door and shouted, "FBI—freeze! Freeze or I'll blow your head off!"

"Would you have blown her head off?" Browning asks.

"No, sir."

"Did she freeze at that time?"

"Yes, sir, she did."

In the corridor the women reporters huddle to compare notes on how many tears Patty shed. The clucking caucus of sob sisters serves as a cross-checking mechanism, so that the *New York Times* doesn't report one tear while three tears blot the *Daily News.* Carolyn Anspacher of the *Chronicle,* Helen Dudar of the *New York Post,* Theo Wilson of the New York *Daily News,* Linda Deutsch of AP, Linda Schacht of KQED, Jeanine Yeomans of NBC-TV—all these Jewish-mother hearts ache for Patty now. How differently one had felt about it just a few months ago, when the actual arrest occurred! Then, paradoxically, the torrential television coverage tended to trivialize the reality, to reduce the drama to the level of soap opera. Then Patty's suffering had seemed tragicomic. Now it is affectingly real.

When her family came to see Patty at the jail the very first time, at midnight, her mother had carried a bouquet of yellow roses and a white-orchid corsage.

"God has answered our prayers," Mom told reporters afterward.

"There is nothing she should be afraid of. . . . After all, she was kidnapped!" Dad said.

"I hope they throw the book at her!" a bystander volunteered. "Look at all the trouble that brat has caused!"

"It was such a calm ordeal," marveled a witness at the arrest scene.

"We knew we were going to find her. It was only a matter of time," said Charlie Bates.

"They have badges but no hearts," said Mom.

Wendy Yoshimura's father, a mild little gardener from Fresno, appeared next on television to say, "My daughter has always been for the underdog."

These people seemed to belong onstage at La Scala, not in a television news studio. Most of the things they said sounded like translations from Verdi. "After all, what did she really do?" *Mamma mia, cosa fa?* "The child was kidnapped!" *Ella mi fu rapita!* "It was such a calm ordeal!" *Era una prova tanta calma!* "Just look at the trouble she has caused everybody!" *Guarda! Guarda! I quali quella ragazza ha provato . . . !* Catherine's rich contralto could be imagined soaring over the other voices: *Loro hanno l'emblema, ma non hanno cuore!* And the policemen's chorus responding, "We knew, we knew. It was only a matter of time!" Then the sweet tenor voice of Mr. Yoshimura: *Mia figlia sempre è stata cogli sfortunati!* And Randy's baritone: *Oh quanto amore! Mia vita sei.* "Oh, what love! You are my life." Again the policemen's chorus, louder now: "Only a matter of time . . ." *Tantantara!* The honor of the Justice Department is restored. The populace rejoices. Everybody joins in a final chorus of self-congratulation. Even the FBI is redeemed! Up in heaven, *giocoso* at last, J. Edgar smiles down out of his FBI-limousine-transformed-into-fiery-chariot and shyly reaches over to squeeze Clyde Tolson's hand amid the candy wrappers under the lap robe. *Oh quanto amore! Exeunt* all, smiling happily.

Only the voice of Patty herself had not been heard.

I have been thinking further about where this long, tangled story really began. It wasn't only the house that Hearst built, not only his hideous castle-mausoleum overlooking the Pacific. The story started in two places, and neither was more important than the other: It was the confluence that counted. The other place was a cement rectangle, five feet by eight feet—the floor of the California prison cell in which a young black prisoner named George Jackson lived in solitary confinement. Every day for eight and a half years Jackson got down on his belly and did one thousand fingertip push-ups on his scrap of cold stone.

"You should have seen George's hands!" a young matron exclaimed to me one night in San Francisco, long after Jackson was dead. "After a while George didn't have fingertips anymore, just these black knobs. They looked like freshly-dug truffles."

In 1959 in Los Angeles, at the age of eighteen, Jackson was accused of having stolen seventy dollars from a gas station at gunpoint. He was routinely convicted and routinely handed over to the California Youth Authority, which gave him a routine sentence: one year to life. Before entering prison, he filled out a routine questionnaire:

Q. What do you want to be?
A. A writer.
Q. What do you like to do most?
A. Make love in the rain.

Imagine a great net dropped into the brine of American life, a net that sooner or later catches up everything, everybody, every issue in its dripping reticulations. The net grows; it bulges and heaves. It is a place of tangled weeds, dark waters. In both its form and content it suggests a plague of demons issuing from the mouth of a medieval saint. This net is the playing out over the next fifteen years of George Jackson's story. By now the net has become so full—so heavy with turtles, schools of herring and sardines, fiery water snakes, seaweed and sea creatures of every description—that it can never be hauled in. All one can hope to do is pull up a portion at a time and examine its glistening catch before its own weight pulls it back into the sea. Long ago this immense watery bag began to develop its own mythology. Today it even has its own mermaid. She is like no other mermaid—if any mermaid is like another—but she is the only possible mermaid for this particular net and seascape. One cannot reckon her story or understand her song without knowing something of the net George Jackson cast. Here, then, a crude topography of the net.

What do you want to be? A writer. What do you like to do most? Make love in the rain. Instead Jackson spent the next decade in prison, devoting himself to the fanatic perfection of his body and mind. In between the push-ups, he read politics, philosophy, literature. He became convinced that convicts, especially black convicts, are in fact illegal political prisoners, concentration-camp inmates of the California prison system. He became a professed revolutionary.

There are many Gulag archipelagoes. California's prison system contains the third-largest incarcerated population in the world—23,000 in 1974. Only the prisons of China and the USSR hold more caged men. The situation in California has changed somewhat, but at the time of HERNAP the California Department of Corrections had 7,500 full-time employees, an annual budget of $140 million, twelve maximum-security prisons, eighteen minimum-security prison camps, and fifty parole offices up and down the state, all of them under the command of Director of Corrections Raymond Procunier.

During his decade of incarceration George Jackson's defiance, sweetness, crazy courage, and indomitable strength made him the single prisoner most hated and feared by the guards and most beloved by his fellow inmates. Through his writings, Jackson became a legendary hero outside the prisons, as well. *Soledad Brother,* his collected prison letters, became a best-seller and was translated into fifteen languages. His second book, his political autobiography, was *Blood in My Eye.* Literary critics praised him; political theorists saluted him; young blacks idolized him, and so did many whites; brilliant and beautiful women fell in love with him. By 1970 Jackson had become an international symbol of the man the system cannot break.

Jackson was twenty-eight years old when, on January 13, 1970, after three years of increasingly violent racial confrontations within the California prison system, three black convicts were machine-gunned to death in the exercise yard at Soledad by white guards who claimed they were attempting to break up a fight. But the victims all were black; all were self-styled prison revolutionaries; all were followers of Jackson. Three nights later, in a different section of the maximum-security prison, a white guard was choked to death bare-handed and his body hurled over the railing of the fourth-floor tier of cells. Prison officials accused Jackson and two other black convicts, and the three became known as the Soledad Brothers. Their case attracted worldwide attention. Outside the prisons, feuding black and student left-wing groups, including both factions of the Black Panther Party, Eldridge Cleaver's Black Liberation Army, and the Communist Party, formed a united front in support of the Soledad Brothers. Inside the prisons, Jackson was regarded as a kind of black Lazarus, a fiery leader of slave uprisings in the tradition of John Brown and Nat Turner.

The turbulent movement for prison reform in California had many sources. To try to disentangle the history here would invite serious error and risk. Suffice to say that those sources included the civil-rights movement in the South and the black-power movement in the North, though of course these movements overlapped. In the prolonged series of peaceful sit-ins and bloody confrontations throughout the 1960s, which produced the new legal rulings that finally broke the grip of racism in the Southern states, the civil-rights movement was the occasion for many new contacts between whites and blacks, both Northern and Southern. The black-power movement was active chiefly, though not exclusively, in the Northern population centers—the big-city ghettos—and, to a degree, in the prisons. It was led by several militant black groups that were often at war with one another; and, like the civil-rights movement, it was quietly coached by political sophisticates of both colors.

All of this new activism, North and South, black and white, in prison and out, was in turn stimulated by Watts and the other highly visible racial confrontations of the decade. The various forces were *interreactive,* and the burgeoning prison-reform movement in California was one result.

The political catalyst in the Bay Area was Venceremos, the largest and most active radical group in the region until, in 1973, it splintered irredeemably, mainly over the old Maoist-Marxist question of terrorism versus mass organizing. The name came from Castro's rallying cry during the Cuban Revolution: *Patria o muerte, venceremos!*—"Fatherland or death, we shall triumph!"

In the 1960s blacks in prison began to see themselves as "political prisoners," as well as, and sometimes instead of, criminals. A new sense of black pride and spiritual rebirth suffused the fetid tiers of cells. Many of the men who later organized the black-power movement on the "outside" had acquired their new awareness and organizing skills on the "inside." The effects on the outside, in the black communities, were mostly to the good. But on the "inside," as the prisons became politicized, racial gang warfare increased alarmingly, and not just between blacks and whites; Mexicans and Chicano convicts constituted a third force in the West, as Puerto Ricans and a few Native Americans did in the East.

Jackson always denied he had choked the guard. But as he wrote to a friend from prison, "This charge carries an automatic death penalty for me. I can't get life. I already have it."

Soledad—"solitude." The tenderest, most passionate letters in *Soledad Brother* were written to two people: George's younger brother, Jonathan Jackson, and Angela Y. Davis, a young black philosophy instructor at the University of California at Los Angeles. Angela was a Marxist and the protégée of the refugee German theoretician of revolution Herbert Marcuse. She had been reared in a quiet, moderately well-to-do black family in Birmingham, Alabama. Her mother was a teacher; her father owned a filling station. Back in the hot summer of 1963 the city was at war. Dr. Martin Luther King, Jr., was leading protest marches in support of public-school desegregation. Eugene "Bull" Connor, the red-neck police commissioner of Birmingham, attacked the marchers with fire hoses and police dogs. One Sunday morning a bomb went off in a black church, and four girls in Sunday school were killed. One of those children had been a friend of Angela Davis.

Jonathan Jackson, the beloved "man-child," was reared in a poor black Los Angeles neighborhood. He worshiped his brother George with fierce but remote adoration. George Jackson had been sent away to prison when Jonathan was only seven years old. At sixteen, Jonathan met the young philosophy instructor. He and Angela were often seen strolling hand in hand around the UCLA campus. At seventeen, the man-child died in a hail of bullets outside the Marin County Courthouse in the climax of a suicidal attempt to free his brother.

San Quentin is a notorious and hideous old penitentiary that sticks out from green and pleasant Marin County into San Francisco Bay like a chronically infected appendix. On the morning of August 7, 1970, three black convicts were inside the Marin County Courthouse, on trial for their part in a San Quentin melee, when suddenly, in the back of the courtroom, Jonathan Jackson stood up. He held a satchel full of guns. "All right, gentlemen, I'm taking over now," he said, and tossed the weapons to the three convicts. His plan was to take hostages to exchange for his brother, but in the wild shoot-out that followed, four persons were killed, including Jackson, the judge, Harold Haley, and two of the convicts. A juror was wounded, and the prosecutor was paralyzed for life.

Angela Davis was accused of masterminding the scheme and of buying the guns. She was indicted for murder and conspiracy, and acquitted only after a cross-country FBI manhunt, nearly two years in prison, and a trial in the same futuristic pink-stucco Marin County Courthouse where young Jonathan had declared war on the state of California, and where the San Quentin Six were still on trial.

Angela's codefendant (until their two cases were severed) was another black man, Ruchell Magee, the only convict survivor of the massacre. Magee had held a shotgun taped to Judge Haley's neck while Jackson, the convicts, and their hostages made their way downstairs from the courtroom to a van waiting in the parking lot. Police and sheriff's officers inside the courthouse had held their fire for fear of injuring the hostages. But San Quentin prison guards, a different, harder breed of gunmen, were stationed outside, and when the van began to move, the guards opened fire with automatic weapons. Magee's shotgun discharged and blew most of Judge Haley's head off. But the autopsy showed that the judge was already dead from a machine-gun bullet in his chest, and Magee was charged with kidnapping.

Ruchell Magee was the original convict "Cinque." While researching the law and studying black history Magee had come across the story of Cinque M'Tume, an African slave who in 1839 led the first slave mutiny in the New World. It began off the coast of Cuba, aboard the poetically named Spanish slaver *La Amistad* ("The Friendship"), when fifty-three slaves climbed out of the hold one night and slaughtered the entire ship's crew except for two seamen, whom they directed to steer the ship back to Africa. But each night the sailors changed course and headed north, hoping to hit the southern coast of the United States. Instead their zigzag pattern led them to eastern Long Island, and a United States cutter took Cinque and his men prisoner about twenty miles from where I now live.

The rebel slaves were jailed in New Haven and charged with murder and piracy. A group of abolitionists undertook to defend them, and by 1841 their case was before the Supreme Court—the first civil-rights case ever to reach it. The most eloquent lawyer of the period, former President John Quincy Adams, argued the slaves' case and won an acquittal. The thirty-nine surviving mutineers, including Cinque, were freed and repatriated to Sierra Leone.* The abolitionist group, Friends of the Amistad, later merged with the American Missionary Association, and after the Civil War they turned their attention to the education of freedmen and founded more than five hundred black schools and colleges throughout the South, including Hampton, Howard, Atlanta, Berea, Dillard, Fisk, Huston-Tillotson, LeMoyne-Owen, Talladega, and Tougaloo. Tangled weeds, dark waters.

It must have been about 1968 that Ruchell Magee began calling himself Cinque M'Tume. But Magee's proud new nom de guerre was soon ripped off, just like everything else he had ever had. The thief was one of his own cell mates, a small-time crook named Donald David DeFreeze.

In 1968 a black-studies group called the Black Cultural Association was formed by prison authorities at Vacaville Medical Facility, and Magee and DeFreeze were among the original members. Vacaville, built in 1955 northeast of San Francisco on the road to Sacramento, is considered one of the premier "correctional facilities" in the United States. One part of Vacaville is the place where new convicts receive the psychiatric evaluations to help determine how "dangerous" they are, how stable, and what institution, with what level of security, will house them for their time behind bars. But Vacaville is also a prison mental hospital that attempts to treat acute and chronic forms of mental illness. Additionally, it is a research center—some would call it an experimental madhouse—where the treatment and management of violent offenders is studied. Its warden is a psychiatrist. His domain is a cuckoo's nest inside an iron cage.

By August 21, 1971, George Jackson was housed in solitary confinement in the maximum-security section of San Quentin that is officially called the Adjustment Center but commonly known as the Hole. Two days hence he was scheduled to stand trial for killing the Soledad guard.

*Back in Africa, in an all-American development that seems to have escaped the notice of his admirers in San Quentin, Cinque M'Tume became a successful small-business man—a slave dealer, in fact, and one of the more prosperous in his region and time.

But that Saturday, Jackson was gunned down on a flowery patio inside the prison compound, shot in the back during an alleged escape attempt. Three white guards and two white prisoners also were killed in the uprising. Three more guards had their throats slashed but lived to testify. Scarcely a month later, in the East, came Attica.

The last morning of Jackson's life began with a visit from one of his attorneys, Stephen Bingham, in the prison visiting room. Later, on the way back to the Adjustment Center, Jackson produced a gun and overpowered the guard who was escorting him. He tripped the mechanism that automatically either locks or unlocks all the cells at once, and when the solid steel doors slid open, six convicts, all black, stepped out into the corridor. (Twenty-one others remained in their cells during the frenzy of shooting and slashing that followed.) These six were indicted for the murder of the five whites and became known as the San Quentin Six. Nobody was ever indicted for Jackson's death; that was ruled a justifiable homicide.

After an incredible series of delays, the San Quentin Six case finally went to trial in March 1975. Officially designated *People of the State of California* v. *Stephen Bingham et al.,* the San Quentin Six trial would eventually become the longest, most expensive criminal trial in California history, lasting for more than sixteen months and costing the people of California more than $2 million. One of the many witnesses who appeared each day in shackles was the hapless Ruchell Magee. (With six convict defendants, five defense lawyers,* and multiple charges of murder, conspiracy, and assault, the case defies ready summation. A total of forty-six counts of conspiracy and thirty counts of murder was involved. The prosecution contended it could never prove which of the defendants committed which of the murders; therefore, it would concentrate on theories of "conspiracy" and "aiding and abetting." In sum, the government charged that the six convicts had been part of a conspiracy with Jackson to escape from prison by force. The defendants, on the other hand, claimed that the state of California had conspired to kill George Jackson because he was the leader of the prison militants, and that the six men on trial had been deliberately selected out of the prison population by the authorities to be punished for political activities.)

---

*When the Supreme Court ruled that an accused person has a right to choose his own lawyer, one of the Six, Hugo "Yogi" Pinell—like Magee, a man officially diagnosed by prison psychiatrists as a dangerous paranoid schizophrenic—decided to fire his court-appointed attorney and defend himself.

On August 12, 1976, long after the Patty Hearst trial was over, the sequestered jury brought in a mixed verdict in the San Quentin case: Three of the men were acquitted of all charges, two were convicted of assault, and one was convicted of conspiracy and the murder of two guards, after an eyewitness—another guard—testified that he had seen this prisoner with a gun in his hand and also saw him speak to Jackson briefly after the uprising began.

Once police and FBI undercover agents managed to infiltrate and split the various black militant groups and turn one faction against the other, they were in position effectively to weaken the burgeoning revolutionary black reform movement both inside and outside of the California prisons. To achieve this much had taken nothing less than a ten-year guerrilla war, with prison reformers, ghetto blacks, convicts, and radicals all lined up on one side, and the state of California on the other. The formation of the Vacaville Black Cultural Association may have been part of that war. Its Friday-night meetings, featuring black-power salutes, militant marching, and revolutionary slogans, probably served a double purpose. They were an attempt by prison authorities to diffuse some of the black political pressures building up inside the walls. But the close contact between prisoners and sympathetic visitors also provided a way to infiltrate police informers into prison-allied underground groups throughout California.

The SLA had connections with the prison movement. Willie Wolfe was the first SLA member to attend the BCA meetings. Later Bill and Emily Harris, Nancy Ling Perry, Russell Little, and Joe Remiro came, too, and formed close bonds with a number of prisoners. Donald De-Freeze was a moving spirit in the BCA and for a time its president. It is possible that DeFreeze at this time was a police informer, a paid snitch. Certainly he had been one in the past. His criminal record over the years prior to his escape listed more than twenty convictions, mostly on gun charges, with very little time served. And the circumstances of his "escape" from Soledad in March 1973—from a minimum-security boiler-room area where he had been assigned to work, alone, only the day before—strongly suggest that he was working for the authorities at the time he went over the wall.

DeFreeze made his way to Berkeley, and there he found bed and board with Patricia Soltysik. Since Soltysik had not attended any BCA meetings, her house was a safer place to hide out in than the homes of the other members of the still-germinating Symbionese Liberation Army. When Soltysik's former lover, Camilla Hall, the preacher's gentle daughter, returned from a trip to Europe, she, too, joined the Army. That summer, while Soltysik and the others went out to recruit and to train at a nearby rifle range, DeFreeze stayed indoors and kept house. His specialties were chitlins and ribs. The SLA loved his home cooking and they were plumb crazy about anything black. They spoke in ghetto argot, and soul food was their haute cuisine.

The real objective of the SLA was never to bring down the government of "Fascist Amerikkka." Freaked out and suicidal as these young people were, they were not *that* crazy. What drove them into ever greater paroxysms of violence was the imperative to prove to blacks that white revolutionaries are every bit as brave and trustworthy as black ones. The SLA suffered from extreme racial guilt of a virulent and terminal variety.

"Three passions, simple but overwhelmingly strong, have governed my life," wrote Bertrand Russell at the age of ninety-four. "The longing for love, the search for knowledge, and unbearable pity for the suffering of mankind. These passions, like great winds, have blown me hither and thither, in a wayward course, over a deep ocean of anguish, reaching to the very verge of despair." Similar emotions, run amok, drove the SLA into violence and death.

The shadow of clinical madness was heavy upon them, too. Donald DeFreeze had a long history of mental instability, in and out of prison. A gun freak, he had a record including twelve arrests in ten years, half of them for possession of firearms and homemade bombs. He had bought his first gun at the age of fourteen, intending to murder his father, he once told a probation officer, because the father used to beat the son with a hammer and had broken his arm three times. A letter he wrote in 1970 to Superior Court Judge William Ritzi is the best insight we have into DeFreeze's pre-SLA personality. It was composed in hopes the judge would grant probation, but after reading it, Ritzi concluded the author was safer behind bars:

I am going to talk to you truthfully and like I am talking to God. I will tell you things that no one has ever before know. . . .

I had Just gotten out of a boys school in New York after doing 2½ years for braking into a Parking Meter and for stealing a car, I remember the Judge said that he was sending me to Jail for boys because he said it was the best place for me. I was sixteen at the time and didn't have a home, life in the little prison as we called it, was nothing but fear and hate, day in and day out, the hate was madening, the only safe place was your cell. . . . I had only two frights, if you can call them frights. I never did win. It was funny but the frights were over the fact that I would not be part of any of the gangs, black or white. I wanted to be friends with everyone, this the other inmates would not allow, they would try to make me fright, but I always got around them somehow, they even tried to make a homosexual out of me, I got around this to. After 2½ years I found myself hated by many of the boys there.

When I got out of jail, people just could not believe I had ever been to Jail. I worked hard, I didn't drink or any pills nor did I curse. . . . But I was still lonely. I didn't love anyone or did any one love. I had a few girld friends but as soon as there mother found out I had been to Jail, that was the end.

Then one day I met my wife Glory, she was nice and lovely, I fell in love with her I think. . . . We had just met one month before we were married. My wife had three kids already when I met her.

We were married and things were lovely. . . . Then seven months later I came home sooner than I do most of the time from work and she and a old boy friend had just had relations. I was very mad and very hurt. . . . Then one day I found out that none of my kids had the same father and that she had never been married.

I thought that if we had kids or a baby we would be closer, but as soon as the baby was born it was the same thing I had begun to drink very deeply, but I was trying to put up with her and hope she would change.

But as the years went by she never did and she told me that she had been to see her boy friend and that she wanted a divorce because I was not taking care of her and the kids good enough, I was never so mad in my life. . . . I could have killed her, but I didn't. I through her out of the house and I got a saw and a hammer and completely destroyed everything I ever bought her and I mean everything!

For months later she begged me to take her back and she said she had made a mistake and that she really loved me. I was weak again. . . . I took her back. . . . But I couldn't face anyone any more. I started drinking more and more and staying at my job late. . . . I started playing with guns and firer works and dogs and cars. Just anything to get away from life. . . . I finely got into trouble with the Police for shooting off a rifle in my basement and for a bomb I had made out of about 30 firer works from forth of July.

I told my wife I would forget all that she had did to me. . . . But I was wrong again. I started playing with guns, drinking, pills but this time more than I had ever before did. I was arrested again and again for guns or bombs. I don't really understand what I was doing. She wanted nice things and I was working and buying and selling guns and the next thing I knew I had become a thief. . . .

You sent me to Chino [a California prison] and I lied to them and didn't tell them all the truth. They think I am nuts. . . . But you should not have never sent me back to her. The day after I got home she told me she had had Six relations with some man she meant on the street when I was in Chino. . . .

Sir Don't send me to prison again, I am not a crook or a thief nor am I crazy. I hope you will believe me. . . . Sir, even if you don't ever call me back or want to see me again Thank you for all you have done and all I can say is God Bless you,

Yours Truly,
DONALD DEFREEZE

Each of the SLA members was fresh from some severe emotional crisis in the summer of 1973, when the terrorist band was formed. Emily Harris had decided for ideological reasons to lead a more "open" sexual life and had begun an affair with Cinque, a painful arrangement for Bill Harris but one he felt politically obliged to accept. Nancy Ling Perry had split from her black musician husband, Gilbert Perry, and then began a tumultuous series of sexual connections with Russ Little and many others. Like Joe Remiro, Ms. Perry had been using drugs heavily for several years. After her marriage broke up, Nancy told a friend, "She'd drop acid and everything would go black inside her head. Sometimes she said she felt her mind being completely obliterated by her venom toward herself."* Radical politics and violence became her salvation from drugs.

Angela Atwood had broken up with her husband, Gary, and he had returned to Indiana. The lesbian lovers, Camilla Hall and Patricia Soltysik ("Mizmoon"), had split up twice, the second time when Cinque moved in with Mizmoon after his prison escape. Russell Little's girlfriend, Robyn Steiner, had left him and returned to Florida. The only SLA member without a clear psychosexual crisis in his recent past was Willie Wolfe, but Wolfe, an ardent Maoist, was most deeply involved in the prison-reform movement. In the two months before Patty was kidnapped, Wolfe had visited Vacaville forty-five times.

When Russ Little and Joe Remiro were taken into custody in early

---

*Weed, op. cit., p. 207.

1974 after their arrest for the Foster murder, they were confined in the Hole at San Quentin, allegedly in order to protect them from attack by black prisoners enraged by their crime. But prison officials found the two captured SLA soldiers excessively paranoid. Convinced that their food was being poisoned, the pair went on a prolonged hunger strike, and were weaned only when a jailer thought of sending out for Big Macs. The Apocalypse at hand, In McDonald's We Trust.

By the time the SLA kidnapped Patricia Hearst all its members were on their way to becoming suicidal psychopaths. They saw the abduction of Patricia not primarily as a kidnapping but rather as an act of war, the opening move in what was conceived as a sustained, to-the-death guerrilla uprising against the government of the United States. *This* was the "fascist insect" whose death these self-styled urban guerrillas pledged at the close of each communiqué. In these deranged minds, the millions of dollars' worth of free food for the poor that was demanded of Randy Hearst and distributed by the People in Need program was thought of not as ransom but as wartime reparations.

Donald David DeFreeze was probably only one of many paid professional informers in HERNAP's cast of characters. Colston Westbrook, a colorful black-studies instructor at Berkeley and a leader at the Black Cultural Association meetings back at Vacaville, had worked in Southeast Asia during the 1960s for Mullen & Company, an alleged CIA front. Walter Scott, the alcoholic, unstable brother of Jack Scott, was the informer who tipped off the FBI about Jack and Micki Scott's involvement with the fugitive Patty. Sara Jane Moore was the FBI's snitch inside the People in Need program.

Ms. Moore's court appearances at hearings concerning *her* crime were in dramatic contrast to Patty's. Sara Jane insisted on conducting her own defense, and in the middle of her trial she surprised and dismayed her attorney by filing a statement with the court saying she was not now insane and never had been. Ms. Moore's handwritten statement, entirely unexpected and unheard except by the fifteen spectators and eight reporters who happened to be in the courtroom, contained moments of considerable eloquence:

> No one has been charged with, nor is on trial for the assassination plots against Castro, Allende, Lumumba or other foreign leaders, nor for the actual assassinations in this country of Fred Hampton, George Jackson and the Attica inmates, to name only a few of the comrades deliberately murdered by the police.

When any government uses assassination, whether of political leaders in other countries or of its own citizens to put down dissent or to hide its own repressive actions, it must expect that tool to be turned back against it.

To those of you who share my dream of a new revolution in this land of ours, I say fight on. To those dedicated to keeping from the people what is rightfully theirs, I warn you never to turn your backs on those —on us.

For those and for other reasons, I am disinclined to participate in what promises to be a circus, though called a trial, nor did I want to put on someone else's shoulders the responsibility for deciding what is an already obvious, and to the government, necessary verdict.

So saying, Ms. Moore changed her plea to guilty and threw herself away, despite the efforts of the judge to prevent her by urging her to reconsider and by ordering more psychiatric testing. Under a 1972 law, pleading guilty to an assassination attempt on a President carries an automatic sentence of zip to life. Ms. Moore's sudden switch and her acceptance of responsibility for what she had done were in turn accepted by the court, and she was sentenced to life imprisonment, despite her own long history of mental illness, including at least five hospitalizations. Federal District Judge Samuel Conti used the occasion to assert his own belief in the salubrious effects of the death penalty. Ms. Moore would not have tried to kill President Ford "if we had in this country any effective capital-punishment law," he said.

What sort of person becomes an informer? People like Moore and Scott and DeFreeze all seem to lack strong convictions or identities to begin with. After a time in the Ping-Pong life of paid informers, they tend to become confused as to which identity is the true one—the revolutionary anarchist or the secret agent? It becomes tempting to be both, which is to say, to become schizophrenic. Crippled, such persons lose their anchor in reality and also lose their usefulness to their employer; they become an embarrassment, even a liability.

Sara Jane Moore's assassination attempt moved Harrison E. Salisbury to analyze the historic relationship between radical terrorists and police informers. It was a matter of each group's scheming to infiltrate the other, he wrote in the *New York Times*, each *requiring* the other to exist in order to ensure its own survival—a symbiotic interdependence, in fact, which he traced back to the last days of the Romanovs. "Violence inevitably stems from a police system that recruits (and educates) secret informers and provocateurs within a radical movement. The recruited agent almost by definition is an unstable, psychotic or psychopathic individual. His temptation to improve his status by engaging in or encouraging violence is almost irresistible. This is what touches off the fatal chain reaction. Violence feeds on violence and the question of who is informer, who is terrorist, becomes confused beyond comprehension even by the individuals involved."

The confusion was apparent in both Scott and Moore, and in De-Freeze. Even before he left prison, his usefulness as a snitch was probably over; it is possible his escape was a matter of mutual convenience. When DeFreeze ran into the mostly female and all-white, middle-class founders of the SLA, a strange catalytic action occurred. DeFreeze gave focus and substance to the others' free-floating guilt and rage; he gave them a black totem pole to dance around. To them he was charismatic, and so he *became* charismatic. Out of that catalytic action of personalities, many new identities were formed. The small-time punk Donald DeFreeze became General Field Marshal Cinque, a revolutionary terrorist. The middle-class white girls became "bad," so bad that two of them were able to walk up to Marcus Foster and shoot him in the back at point-blank range.

By mid-1973 Donald David DeFreeze, like the Manchurian Candidate, appears to have escaped his control and gone into the revolutionary-messiah business for himself. The SLA's first organizing meeting was held in June. In July an Alameda County grand jury reported on the extraordinary amount of violence, truancy, and vandalism in the Oakland public schools. The situation was unmanageable because the schools were infiltrated by outsiders. Drug pushers no longer hung around street corners, waiting for the kids to emerge; they came right into corridors and classrooms. A student photo-identification-card system was proposed, to distinguish genuine students from the troublemakers. In August the world heard of the Symbionese Liberation Army for the first time when the unknown group sent the press a "communique" declaring "revolutionary war" on the United States. Its first target was the new photo-ident system. The date was carefully chosen: August 31, 1973, was the second anniversary of George Jackson's death.

The identification-card program may have upset some Oakland blacks, particularly former prisoners, men who knew what it meant to wear a number and who were determined to spare their children that stigma. But mainly the plan upset the fledgling SLA. To them it appeared to be a Gestapo-like system of keeping track of potential enemies of the state; it looked like the beginning of apartheid in the United States. Alarmists and opportunists were quick to fan the natural paranoia of the ghetto, and matters turned sufficiently ugly so that at a school-board meeting on October 9, Oakland's newly hired and distinguished superintendent of schools, Dr. Foster, scrapped the ID-card proposal. But by then the self-proclaimed Army may have been too busy drilling, stockpiling weapons, and drawing up codes of war to read the papers.

On November 6 Dr. Marcus Foster was shot in the back in an alleyway by three hooded assassins, and his deputy, Robert Blackburn, was gravely wounded by a shotgun blast. The message to the media taking credit for the crime was marked with the SLA's emblem: a seven-headed cobra. The SLA had moved from revolutionary theory into revolutionary action by killing the wrong man for a nonexistent reason. Foster had been a beloved and respected civil-rights leader in Philadelphia before Oakland handpicked him to take over its delicate, difficult assignment. He was the first black school superintendent in California. The day after his death, Oakland police received another communiqué from the mysterious SLA. It said the murder was an "execution" to carry out a "Warrant issued by the Court of the People," and to prove that they had done it, they boasted that Foster had been shot with homemade cyanide-filled bullets—a fact hitherto undisclosed by the police.

The SLA intended the assassination to trigger the beginning of the revolution—to provoke counterviolence by the cops and to mobilize ghetto blacks to rise up and join the SLA in guerrilla warfare against the United States. Instead the Left was horrified. Assassinating Foster was not revolution; it was mindless political vandalism, similar to defacing a building or sabotaging a computer.

The police got nowhere in their investigation of the Foster murder until, on January 10, 1974, in Concord, California, near Berkeley, two men were stopped by police for driving a van in a suspicious manner through a residential neighborhood at one o'clock in the morning. One man pulled a gun and fled, but by dawn both men were in custody. Their names were Joe Remiro and Russ Little, and they said they were SLA soldiers Bo and Osceola. Eventually they received life sentences for the Foster murder. Remiro and Little were housed in the San Quentin Adjustment Center, and they spoke in their prison letters and communiqués of their joy at being incarcerated in the same dungeon that once held their beloved saint, George Jackson.

The Concord van turned out to be full of newly printed SLA leaflets as well as bombs and guns. By noon of the next day the eight other members of the SLA had gone underground; overnight, William and Emily Harris, Patricia Soltysik, Angela Atwood, Willie Wolfe, Camilla Hall, Nancy Ling Perry, and Donald David DeFreeze simply disappeared. But a hastily set fire in their Concord house only partially destroyed the trail. Part of the unburned evidence was the green notebook containing names of future SLA kidnap targets, including Patricia Hearst.

A few weeks later, Patty was kidnapped. On her first day of captivity, Field Marshal Cinque M'Tume entered the closet. He carried no mace and orb, no sword or baton. He was a contemporary field marshal: He carried a tape recorder and a flashlight. Crouching together on the floor, they made the first of the seven SLA communiqués.

On her second day in the closet, according to the "Tania Interview," a reading light was rigged inside her carpeted cell, and a deliberate, systematic program of political reeducation was begun. The first book issued to the SLA's first prisoner was *Blood in My Eye,* the posthumously published autobiography of George Jackson.

Friday, February 13

Sometime today the defense case is to begin, with Steven Weed expected as the first witness. The prospect has drawn additional mobs to the Federal Building. Schools are closed for the Lincoln's Birthday holiday, which further swells the crowd. The lobby churns with life like the surf at home off our Long Island beach when the blues are running and the anchovies fleeing ahead of them boil the waters white. It is impossible to keep one's feet; one just moves with the human current toward the banks of elevators. The crowd compacts itself—the Hearsts must have arrived—and photographers react as sharks to a chunk of meat. A camera clips my head. I stagger, recover, and am caught in the white-spotlight glare with the Hearst family as we all are shoved together into an empty elevator. Doors slide shut. Everybody within grins with the exhilaration of escape. Once, in New Zealand, I was penned inside a sheep-shearing shed along with President Lyndon Johnson, the entire Washington press corps, and several hundred excited ruminants made mad by the lights, the sounds, and the imminence of being shorn. This had felt like that.

"Can't you get some security?" I exclaim.

"Since the bomb scare, no one will come near us," says Catherine. In a corner of our elevator I notice a tiny person, well under five feet tall. "Our daughter Catherine," Mrs. Hearst says. The family's firstborn child is frail and almost transparent, about thirty-five years old, an eerie echo of her mother's beauty. Catherine had polio as a child and now, a reclusive semi-invalid, is employed by an order of southern California nuns. After her birth, the Hearsts had no children for ten years. Then came Ginna, now twenty-five and the wife of Jay Bosworth; Patty, twenty-one; Anne, twenty; and Vicki, eighteen, all delivered by cesarean section.

"That mob down there is waiting for Weed," I say.

"I hope they get him!" Vicki exclaims.

Squeezed beside Randy is Ted Kleines, the Hearst Corporation lawyer on the defense team. "We got another PIN [People in Need] lawsuit today," he reports. "Fellow claims somebody threw a rock at his car."

Randy giggles. "And he only waited two years to tell us? Did he include his address, so I can just mail the check?"

Today Patty is wearing a smart apricot silk shirt and gray flannels. But the girl herself looks terrible. The circles under her eyes are darker, her skin is grayer, her body thinner, her lips almost blue. The jury also looks different. They once marched in each morning like musical-comedy Mounties, stalwart, cadenced avatars of the middle class. But they have relaxed; only one male juror still bothers to wear a necktie.

Every person whom this case has touched has in some way been blasted by it. The morning *New York Times* carries a profile on Jim Browning that notes that the prosecutor has been divorced within the past year. He is forty-three and has a daughter, fourteen, and a son, thirteen. We also learn that he is a tennis player, a former president of the Young Republicans, and a hard worker who never leaves his office before seven-thirty and usually lunches in the building cafeteria. He was formerly chief trial deputy in the district attorney's office in San Mateo. His salary is $36,000 a year, and until now he has spent all his time prosecuting Vietnam draft resisters, welfare frauds, and suspected terrorists.

(145)

Bailey is easygoing in his cross-examination of agent Padden. "In any kidnap case it is rather important for the investigator in charge to attempt to psych out what the captors are doing and what might trigger them to kill the victim, right? This is an, ahem, a matter of continuing concern to the Bureau?"

"The safety of a hostage, the victim, is paramount," says Padden.

Bailey reviews the SLA's bloody history, rooted in the assassination of Marcus Foster. "So you were aware they would not stop short of murder." And, of course, the witness also recalls that Miss Hearst was considered a prisoner of war, to be exchanged for Remiro and Little? He does. Now the big point. The grizzled Padden has been involved in thousands of bank robberies. "Did you *ever* hear of a bank robber identifying himself by name?"

"No, but I *have* had them stay and ask people to call the police."

Padden acknowledges that Miss Hearst made little effort to conceal her identity, though she did wear a wig, and DeFreeze wore a funny hat. Is there some question in Padden's mind that she might have been under the gun of several of the others at the time? Yes, there is. Has Padden ever heard of prisoners of war turning against their own country? Yes. Is he aware of the existence of a fairly extensive U.S. government library on the subject? Yes. Did anybody in the FBI attempt to gain access to those materials? No. What was Patty's reaction to being arrested? She wet her pants. Have you ever had any others—among *all* the ones you have arrested at gunpoint—who reacted in that fashion? No, sir.

Bailey has sketched a face-off between a veteran FBI man, gun in hand, and two young women suspects, one of them so terrified she pees in her pants. It looks like a strong finish to his cross-examination until Browning, on redirect, asks the veteran agent if he has "ever heard of a prisoner of war who had been converted, and then committed a violent act" and gets exactly the same soft reply, "No, sir."

"And was there any reference to Patty Hearst as a prisoner of war in the tapes delivered *subsequent* to the time of her conversion?"

"No, sir."

Just before the noon recess the government rests its case, having presented thirty-two witnesses in seven court days. Over lunch we learn there has been still another extortion demand: The New World Liberation Front now wants a quarter of a million dollars from the Hearsts to finance the defense of William and Emily Harris—or else. Recalling the frightening scene in the lobby, I ask Ted

Kleines why someone does not insist on protection for the Hearst family.

"Randy won't accept private guards. He doesn't wish to seem privileged."

Court resumes ten minutes late. The room is tense, anticipating Weed's appearance. The lovers will see each other for the first time in two years. A bailiff waits at the door of the witness room, one hand on the knob. Patty is tight-lipped. "Mr. Bailey, you may call your first witness," Carter says.

"We call Steve Suenaga," says Bailey, and to the astonishment of all, a chubby, cheerful Japanese in glasses and a sweater comes hurtling through the door, shoved into the courtroom by investigator McNally. Weed's absence is not explained.

On the night of February 4, 1974, Suenaga, a student neighbor in Berkeley, returned from dinner in Chinatown and "saw a black gentleman in front of Patty's window." That was unusual, as not very many blacks attended Patty's parties. Suenaga ventured closer. The black man had a rifle, and he ordered Suenaga inside the apartment and told him to lie on the floor, next to Weed. What happened next? "The gentleman who was there proceeded to tell a young lady to tie me up. He told Patty Hearst to shut up or they would have to knock her out. The female said, 'No, they've seen us. We've gotta kill 'em.' " Suenaga heard a shotgun blast and heard Patty crying. "She was frantic. Weed looked bloody and beat up. He said, 'Call Randolph Hearst.' " Browning has no questions.

The next witness was studying in Mrs. Reagan's apartment, across the way from Patty's, when he heard screams, looked out the window, and saw two men stuffing a girl in a car trunk. He yelled, "Call the heat," the men closed the trunk, shooting began, and the witness ducked back inside.

The third student eyewitness heard Patty beg "please" and noted she was blindfolded. He ran after the kidnappers and was shot at by people following in a backup car. A fourth student saw Cinque standing with a machine gun at the head of the stairs and then a flash of blue, which she recognized as Patty's robe.

These witnesses move with crisp dispatch. Next comes Mrs. Reagan herself, an old woman, walking painfully to the stand on crutches. "I used to see her painting her furniture, washing her little rug," Mrs. Reagan says. "One of the nicest girls I ever met. I wish we had more like her." With a shock one realizes that this is the first representative of the American public to utter a kind word for Patty since the bank robbery.

When Mrs. Reagan heard the shooting, she thought people were celebrating the Chinese New Year. Then she looked out her window and saw two black boys carry Patty down the walk and shove her into a car trunk. After that, Mrs. Reagan endured "two or three hundred people"—cops, newsmen, and neighbors—in her apartment asking questions until five o'clock the next morning.

Why did Mrs. Reagan never tell the FBI about what she saw? "It was too hard on me. I had seen them carrying away someone's daughter, and I was too upset to talk about it." The prosecutor having no more questions, Mrs. Reagan hobbles from the stand. Halfway across the courtroom, the old lady pauses on her crutches, smiles merrily at the defendant, and waves a green handkerchief. Barry Fitzgerald never made a finer exit. Patty begins to weep. Bailey suggests a recess.

In the corridor the lawyer snorts and snarls. He is furious at Weed for holding a press conference that very morning to plug his new book, in which he says he believes Patty was "coerced," not brainwashed. Johnson says that at the press conference Weed "seemed insincere. We were afraid he'd impress a jury the same way."

Browning, too, has begun holding impromptu corridor press conferences. No, he was never worried about facing the famous F. Lee Bailey, he tells a reporter. "A juror *could* say to himself, 'Since he never loses, he must be right.' But I don't think we've got any that dumb."

Tom May glides quietly up beside me. "What did you think of Mrs. Reagan?"

"Terrific!"

The ex-prosecutor looks baleful. "I think we've got a dry jury. Not much humor there."

The moment has arrived for the defendant to take the stand in front of the jury for the first time. Bailey helps her walk across the courtroom, leaning gently on his arm, and the jurors watch the small, composed, but terrified-looking young woman give details of her family and school history. She was born in Los Angeles on February 20, 1954, the third of five sisters. She attended Marymount School in Los Angeles, a school in San Mateo, then St. Matthew's, Sacred Heart, Crystal Springs, and Santa Catalina in Monterey. After a year at Menlo College, she went on to the University of California at Berkeley, where she took classes five hours a day.

"Do you know a gentleman named Steven Weed?" Bailey asks, his voice gentle, quiet, matter-of-fact.

Yes, she says, he taught seventh- and eighth-grade math at Crystal Springs.

Patty was aware of the Foster murder and the SLA prior to her being kidnapped. "Black friends of Steven Weed" had told her about them. Coming to the evening of February 4, "while you were watching TV did something unusual happen?" Yes. Someone knocked at the door; three people forced their way in. One was Angela Atwood, one was Donald DeFreeze, and one was William Harris. This is the first time Patty has publicly named a living person as one of the kidnappers.

"What did they do?"

"Um [sigh] . . . um . . . Angela Atwood put a pistol in my face and told me to be quiet." Harris tied her hands. She was blindfolded and gagged but bit down on the gag "so they couldn't put it in as far as they wanted. Steve Weed was screaming—" Patty has begun to cry. Regaining her composure, she testifies that she heard firing and more screaming, was pulled to her feet and struck by a gun butt, "right here"—she points to her cheek—and briefly lost consciousness. She begins to cry again as she describes how she was dragged downstairs and stuffed into the car trunk, then transferred to a station wagon and shoved onto the floor, between the seats. Emily Harris drove; Nancy Ling Perry rode shotgun.

How would Patty describe her own situation? Swallowing hard to maintain her precarious control, she says, "I was bound, blindfolded, and gagged. They drove around for an hour or two."

"Did Cinque say anything?"

"He just said, 'Bitch, you better be quiet or I'll blow your head off. If you make any noise, we'll kill you.' "

"Do you know who Barbara Jean Mackle was?"

"They put her in a box and buried her." Patty sobs, then cries harder.

How did Patty feel when she was put in the closet? "I just was real scared."

Catherine Hearst looks over at the jury to see how they are taking her daughter's description of the dirty closet, its walls covered with old carpet. They look concerned but deadpan.

Patty's cheek was sore; she had no wristwatch and only the blue bathrobe to wear. An hour or two passed, she thinks, before they opened the door.

Who opened it? Cinque. Was he the only black person in this group?

Yes. What did he say to you? He said that they were the SLA and that I was going to be held as a prisoner of war. I'd be safe as long as their comrades Remiro and Little were. He told me I'd be hearing a lot about prisons. He said if I made a noise they would hang me from the ceiling. He said they had cyanide bullets. Nancy Ling Perry and Angela Atwood were standing outside the closet. They said I was a bourgeois, and it didn't matter if I got killed or not.

But of course the real bourgeois was not Patricia Hearst; it was the SLA itself. Of the group's eleven known members (including Remiro and Little), all were white and all were in their mid-twenties except for Donald DeFreeze, who was thirty-one. Only Joe Remiro (SLA name *Bo*), Mexican-Italian from San Francisco, could conceivably be termed working class, and that on his father's side only; his mother was a cousin of Mayor Alioto. DeFreeze was really underclass. Again with the exception of DeFreeze, all were highly educated, although Remiro's education after high school had taken the form of on-the-job training in Vietnam, where he had acquired invaluable practical experience as a combat grunt in a long-range reconnaissance platoon, engaging in one-to-one killing and taking part in numerous search-and-destroy missions during two combat tours. But all of the others, save Willie Wolfe, were at least college graduates—several held advanced degrees—and Wolfe was a prep-school–educated National Merit Scholarship finalist who had abandoned his studies in astronomy and archaeology to work full time for the cause of prison reform.

DeFreeze was a product of the black ghettos of Detroit and Los Angeles, but all the others came from suburbs and small towns. Their parents were professional people from traditional, stable families in which the mother was homemaker; the father, provider. Angela Atwood, née De Angelis (SLA name *Gelina*), was the daughter of a New Jersey Teamster official. She had originally come to California from the University of Indiana, along with Emily and William Harris. Harris *(Teko)* was another Vietnam vet and the son of a career army officer. The former Emily Schwartz *(Yolanda)* was the daughter of an Illinois insurance executive. Russell Little *(Osceola),* from Pensacola, Florida, was the son of a middle-level aerospace executive. Nancy Ling Perry *(Fahizah)* was the daughter of a furniture dealer in Santa Rosa, California, and a former high-school cheerleader and Goldwater girl. Patricia Soltysik *(Mizmoon)* was the daughter of two pharmacists from Goleta, California, and bisexual. One of her lovers was DeFreeze. Another was

Camilla Hall *(Gabi)*, the soft-spoken daughter of a Midwestern Lutheran minister. One of Camilla's love poems to Soltysik gave the druggists' daughter her SLA name, *Mizmoon.* Willie Wolfe *(Cujo)* was a doctor's son from Pennsylvania and, at twenty-three, the youngest of the group.

The young of the human species take longer to mature than any other animal, and a nest is needed in which to rear them. The best nest is the family, nuclear or extended, and marriage stabilizes the nest. "The family is the basic vessel of the human voyage," as Luigi Barzini says. But in the 1950s the vessel began leaking badly. In the 1960s the leaks got worse. Parents lost status. Their traditional authority was usurped by teachers, doctors, social workers, even television. By the mid-1970s unprecedented numbers of Americans were on the loose. The Bureau of the Census reported that the number of men living alone had risen 61 percent, and women alone, 30 percent, in only five years. Makeshift nests were needed, and almost anything would do. The proliferation of communes, counterculture families, religious and spiritual groupies, intense brotherhoods such as the Moonies, the Children of God, assorted Jesus freaks, and Hare Krishnas, the women's collectives, singles clubs, even such secret outlaw prison groups as the Black Guerrilla Family and depraved grotesqueries like the Manson Family—all were expressions of the need to create substitutes for the crumbling nest. One substitute was a style of intense communal living long practiced in Berkeley, California, which produced the SLA.

Assuredly the SLA was an extended family. Its members cared for one another in a multitude of changing patterns. Their shared and shifting love was something far more important and integral than merely having to "take care of one another's sexual needs within the cell," as one of their interminable writings had it. It was love on the run, love on the lam, love in a pressure cooker, love on the barricades, love all mixed up with political passion and suicidal despair, love born of broken hearts and cracking minds—for all of them the most intense emotional experience of their short lives.

Certain parallels with the Manson Family suggest themselves. In each case a group of women is clustered around a sexually hyperactive male. In each there is a tinge of diabolism, or at any rate cobra worship. Both groups were preparing for the Apocalypse. Both anticipated race war and attempted in different ways to precipitate it—the Manson Family by initiating what they called "helter-skelter," killing whites and trying to make it appear as if it had been done by blacks in order to bring down reprisals, and the SLA by killing a respected black civil-rights leader, a deed that by some pathological political miscalculation they thought would cause the ghetto people to rise up.

Although there is no doubt that Manson led his family, there has been considerable speculation about the role of Cinque. He was the leader of the whites but also their captive. He was their pet nigger as well as their essential nigger. Yet he made the tactical decisions, which were invariably disastrous as well as weird. (His original choice for assassination target Number One had been not Marcus Foster but Charles O. Finley.) After the robbery, when it became necessary to "break out of the massive pig encirclement" in the Bay Area, the Field Marshal moved his group to his home turf—Los Angeles. No other SLA member would have led them to that dead end.

A striking difference between the Manson girls and the SLA women was that whereas the Manson girls were strays and family rejects, the bewildered SLA mothers and fathers all were remarkably supportive, loyal, and loving parents.

The aura of boys' adventure book, the aroma of pirates, always characterized the SLA, as well as a kind of sugary, Victorian–greeting-card attitude toward children, a sentimentality uncontaminated by reality, as nobody in the SLA ever had any children. According to De-Freeze's letter to Judge Ritzi, none of the beloved babies to whom Cinque tenderly bids farewell in his tapes was his own child. All were his wife's offspring by other men, a provocation for his emotional troubles, the living evidence of his unmanliness.

Patty had been in her closet about twenty-four hours, she is saying, when Cinque returned and told her she was in People's prison. Patty begins to weep again. "He told me that I'd be treated in accordance with the Geneva Convention." He said that five other kidnappings were going on simultaneously across the country, and "I wouldn't be released unless all the demands of all the people who were kidnapped were met." She cries harder.

"In other words, each victim's parents, or whoever, would have to satisfy the SLA before *any* would be let go?"

Patty whispers, "Yes." She is breathing with difficulty, panting for air, as she says, "They accused my parents of crimes against the People. They said I could be tried for the crimes of my parents."

The Court of the People was going to try you for the crimes of your folks, is that it? Yes.

Did Cinque interrogate you? Yes. The conversation lasted several hours. What kinds of things did he want to know? About my family. She begins to cry much harder. ". . . the names of my sisters, where they lived, where my parents owned property, how old they were, about the Hearst Corporation . . ."

Patty, did you know very much about the structure of the Hearst Corporation or your parents' holdings at the time you were kidnapped? No. Did you have any idea how much money they had or could raise if the need arose? No. All right, did he ask you other questions about your family? Yes. Please tell us all that you can recall.

"I mean the way he was asking them, I thought he already knew the answers."

Were threats made? Yes, by many people, many times. She never knew if it was day or night. Then came a point where Cinque got really mad because "I wasn't answering the questions right," and he left her alone after warning her that she had better "get straight. He said I knew what he was talking about. And he just closed the door." She begins to cry again.

The next day's interrogation by Cinque lasted several more hours. The prisoner was given mint tea to drink. With her blindfold still in place, Cinque told her, " 'We are going to make a tape,' so that my parents would know I was still alive." Patty handled only the microphone, not the tape recorder itself. All the time she was in the closet, either she was blindfolded or else the person with her was masked, and Patty had a flashlight. The closet had no windows. A radio played all the time. They brought food, but she couldn't eat. They took her to the bathroom blindfolded.

It is time to play the first SLA tape for the jury, but it isn't here. Browning has to send downstairs to his office to get it. During the wait I borrow the binoculars; Patty's lips have turned blue. The attorneys are at the bench, holding a private conference with the judge on the newest extortion demands. The jurors are unaware of any of the bomb threats to the Hearsts. Nobody looks at Patty at all. Any injury now to Patty's family, coming on top of the death of the SLA members, would be a double load of guilt for this girl, too much, perhaps, to bear. I fear this latest threat to her family could drive her to attempt suicide.

We have waited nearly ten minutes. Bailey wisecracks, "As soon as the FBI finds its evidence we will continue this case." Everyone smiles except the witness. By the time the tapes are produced and marked into evidence the tape recorder won't play; something is jammed. Patty looks flippy. Her glance darts about the room. She coughs and sips water. Browning proposes an early recess, but Bailey says a long break is coming up in this trial over the three-day Lincoln's Birthday weekend, and he damn well wants these tapes played first.

"We're not going to have the jury sit around here cooling its heels any longer," Judge Carter warns. Johnson is grimly winding the tape spool with a pencil. Perhaps evil spirits have possessed the machine; certainly we are seeing a witch trial. Then Johnson discovers that the tape merely needs rewinding. While this is being done the judge makes petulant, childlike threats. "We are *not* going to sit here!" Bailey, dogged and furious, *wills* the tapes to play.

At last Cinque's voice booms out over the courtroom. "To those who would bear the hopes and future of our people, let the voice of their guns express the words of their freedom." The voice is big and deep. As Patty listens tears roll down her cheeks. Al Johnson stands in shadow behind her in the grim posture of the cop he used to be. Listening to the tape, I feel that we are all enchanted here in this room, all of us turning back into the person we were long ago. Cinque says that though he is the father of two children himself, he is willing to lose his own children for the cause. When he tells the Hearsts, "I am quite willing to carry out the execution of your daughter," Patty flinches as if she has been struck.

Then we hear her own breathy voice: "Mom, Dad, I'm okay. I'm with a combat unit; they also have a medical team." How preposterous it all sounds! Her amplified voice continues, as if she were drugged and numb. "I'm not being forced to say any of this. I'm starting and stopping the tape myself."

In her too-big, man-tailored dove-gray pants suit, the girl looks like a forlorn dress extra left over from a Busby Berkeley musical. The pathos of the last hour has been difficult to watch. Trembling, gasping, wiping tears, Patty has made us feel the terror of her capture, of being beaten and blindfolded and shoved into the closet, of her fear she was about to be buried alive. She approaches the edge of breakdown as Bailey leads her through a description of how that first tape was made, she crouching in the closet, terrorized, blindfolded, repeating each sentence as the brutal Cinque dictated it. Now, eyes downcast, she whispers how Cinque criticized her taped performance and then pinched her, hard. Where? Trembling more, she places a superbly manicured hand on her pitiful, scrawny chest. "My breasts . . . and down . . ." She points with a tiny finger but is unable to continue, choking back sobs.

BAILEY: Your private parts?

PATTY [*barely audible*]: Yes.

BAILEY: Was the blindfold replaced?

PATTY: I had it on all the time.

The jury is left to think *that* one over during the long holiday weekend, and we adjourn to the corridor, where Al Johnson, making sure this assault is not interpreted as a mere tweak, gives the moment its final *fortissimo*. "He didn't just pinch her. He lifted her up off the floor by her nipples."

Analyzing Watergate, Theodore H. White concluded that "the true crime of Richard Nixon was simple: he destroyed the myth that binds America together, and for this he was driven from power." I disagree. Nixon's crime was much simpler: He *was* a crook, after all. One who did more in that period to destroy "the myth that binds America together" was a nineteen-year-old college sophomore who had the bad luck to get kidnapped in spectacular fashion at just the time when the Watergate news had dried up temporarily. Some of the binding myths that Patty challenged are the belief that the free press is invulnerable to takeover; that crime doesn't pay; that parents love their children and vice versa; that if the G-men are really out to get you, there's no place to hide; and that once we withdrew from Vietnam the war would remain in Indochina, where it belonged, and not come home to roost in places like California. Most shattering of all, HERNAP cast doubt on the notion that some immutable, basic American distinction still exists between good guys and bad guys, white hats and black hats, and that you can tell what it is by looking at it. The SLA knocked that one into a cocked hat, put a feather in it, and called it not macaroni but revolution.

But although Patty shattered many myths, many golden bowls of complacency and all-American self-assurance, she also incarnated powerful new ones. For the young, Patty-as-Tania became the country's first existential heroine. Her poster bloomed red on thousands of college walls. Everybody else in our pop pantheon, from Billy the Kid to Lucky Lindbergh to John Glenn, was a variation on Jack Armstrong, your basic all-American boy. Patty was the first big-time all-American girl, and that, I am certain by now, was part of her original powerful attraction for me. One reason the story of Patty Hearst felt like *the* news event of my journalistic lifetime was that the protagonist was female. My fellow reporters had always been men, and although we all wrote about the same celebrities, we didn't have the same feelings about them. I had never longed to *be* a tycoon or an astronaut or a modern King Arthur, for that matter, reigning over a contemporary Camelot; to me, Carl Furillo and Gil Hodges were just ball players, never the boys of summer. We wrote about women headliners, too, of course, but I felt no kinship with starlets, ice skaters, or politicians' wives. These women seemed remote from whoever I was now or had ever as a girl dreamed of becoming. But I had been a bright girl, a protected, precocious, rebellious girl, and when Patty Hearst came along, I must have recognized her a little.

For many Americans of middle age, Patty performed another mythic function, nothing less than the acting out of their most secret fantasies. This girl was doing precisely those forbidden things that men and women of her parents' generation and background dream of with dread. She gets tied up and carried off against her will. She is a fairy princess abducted by demonic creatures—black men, lesbian women. She is initiated by them into unspeakable practices, unimaginable rites. Not just her body, even her mind is taken over—bound, chained, tortured, brainwashed. She loses all her free will; she becomes entirely submissive, a total victim, the ultimate "O."

Though some saw her as a victim, most Americans saw Patty then as an ungrateful child, a sexual and political adventuress who probably had set up her own kidnapping. She swiftly became a female hate object, a modern witch.

A people's myths are embodied in huge figures of collective fantasy, and these figments change with the times and circumstances. The European imagination in the Middle Ages and even later, for example, was haunted by flying female figures who consorted with black devils and feasted on human infants. Norman Cohn has shown that the great witch-hunts "derive from a specific fantasy which can be traced back to Antiquity. The essence of the fantasy was that there existed, somewhere in the midst of the great society, another society, small and clandestine, which not only threatened the existence of the great society but was also addicted to practices which were felt to be wholly abominable, in the literal sense of anti-human."*

---

*This and all following quotations from Norman Cohn, *Europe's Inner Demons* (New York: Basic Books, 1975).

Cohn traces the fantasy back to the second century A.D., when pagan Greeks and Romans imagined that the early Christians ritually held orgies and ate babies. Cohn is astonished to discover that as the fantasy evolves in the Middle Ages the witch-cult fantasy was strongest where Christianity was most devout. Cohn identifies the fundamental source of these fantasies as "the urge to purify the world through the annihilation of some category of human beings imagined as agents of corruption and incarnations of evil." The same dark human urge felt by these seventeenth-century kings, popes, inquisitors, and magistrates obsessed the minds of Nazis who sought to purify the world by ridding the planet of Jews and Gypsies. The gong of mindless hatred sounds again today in the pea brain of Anita Bryant, and she figures out that homosexuals "prey upon other people's children because they can't have children of their own." What the Europeans saw in, and got out of, their witch-hunts—an internalized scapegoat and handy whipping boy for the society's own errors and failures—our society got from the saga of Patricia Hearst.

"The urge to purify the world through the annihilation of some category of human beings imagined as agents of corruption and incarnations of evil." These are words to ponder. They are the basis for all the holy wars ever fought by mankind. They describe the urge that motivated the SLA to kill Marcus Foster and the urge that drove the Los Angeles police to cremate the SLA. They offer a frightening glimpse into the unconscious mind of the race.

In Patty, America found her first mythological daughter-image after many sons. We do not have a mother-image or a father-image of comparable power, perhaps because we are a comparatively young country. But we do have a Godfather figure, the *macho*-paternal-criminal-king. I suspect the Godfather is a male myth, essentially the product of a boy's imagination. The high priests of our Godfather cult are the overgrown boys of "investigative journalism" and the *macho* writers who dominate so much of our image-making industry: Mailer, Maas, Puzo, Coppola, Gage, Peckinpah, Spillane, Breslin, Hamill, and Talese come to mind. Many others have helped to promote the image. J. Edgar Hoover, Frank Sinatra, and Robert Kennedy did more than their share. So did various Capones, Costellos, Gambinos, Lucianos, and other real-life Corleones too perfidious to mention.

Before they ate the babies and so on, the seventeenth-century witches were believed to get into the spirit of things by kissing the anus and genitals of Satan, conceived as a gigantic black goat-god illuminating the demonic scene with light streaming from his horns and flames blazing from his eyes. Unlike the goat-god and his witches, the Godfather is not entirely a fantasy. Organized crime does exist, and it does run in families, and many of these families are what I suppose would be called Sicilian-American, although many others are Russian-American, black-American, Irish-American, and so on. Nonetheless, as a mythic bank of evildoers among us, the shadowy *mafiosi* of contemporary books and films do for our times what the witches did for theirs; they hint at an imaginary, hidden counterculture, an alien conspiracy in our midst that can be blamed for our own failures and excesses. In this country the American Communist Party and the Brotherhood of Masons have performed similar services over the years.

The development of the "Mafia-image" coincided roughly with several other developments: the rise of the self-made kings of capitalism —the bankers, railroad tycoons, industrialists, robber barons; the spread of literacy and newspapers to record and sanctify their rapacious achievements; and the arrival of waves of immigrants from Southern and Eastern Europe, wretched people with fevered imaginations (for the immigrants were the more vivid dreamers; the others didn't dare leave), who dreamed of a land of self-made entrepreneurs where the streets were paved with gold.

Other gangster and racketeer figures (which is to say, other images of criminal-businessmen) competed for our imaginations during the 1920s and 1930s, but the Mafia came back strongly after World War II, with the energetic assistance of its new journalist-biographers, young writers themselves just out of uniform. During the war, too, the real Godfathers and the U.S. government had first become business partners when the Mafia undertook to protect U.S. ports from Axis sabotage and to control the waterfront in return. These original government-underworld contacts were later expanded to include Cuban connections, CIA connections, Hughes and Las Vegas connections, and ultimately into the sexual democracy embodied in the delectable person of Judith Campbell Exner, who shared her favors simultaneously with mob boss Sam "Momo" Giancano, with the mythic Frank Sinatra, and with the President of the United States.

The Cosa Nostra and the Black Hand were a real force in the villages of Sicily and the slums of Naples. They still are. But before the Mafia fantasy flowered in America, as, in England and Europe, before the witch-fantasy took wing, resulting in the torture death of perhaps four million women, the fantasy-image of the secret, criminal-capitalist conspiracy among us already lay dormant in our imaginations. To understand how the Mafia has been able to stake its enormous claim on American public attention, one must demythologize organized crime and see it as one offshoot of the free-enterprise system. It is scary to imagine unseen enemies among us, but not so scary as to acknowlege that crime-business-syndicates or merchants of violence-for-hire are the *consequence* of certain fundamental values in American society rather than the cause. These values include the *macho* ideal, the supremacy of individual ambition over all other values, the hierarchical model of society, the uncritical acceptance of violence in ordinary life, and a certain willingness to bend the law and adjust moral standards in pursuit of our "higher values"—power, rampant free enterprise, wealth, and pleasure.

I find these values to be largely male values. I doubt if our society will change much so long as we continue to accept and operate by them. If it does not change, I wonder how much longer we can endure. I wonder whether and how women will be able to reject these male values without at the same time rejecting men. I wonder how the traditional female values of conserving, nurturing, protecting, sustaining, fine-tuning, balancing, bending, yielding, and gathering-in can be stirred into the value mix. Two figures lurk in the magic wood, male and female. I have about decided that the people who control this country, the men, in whom power resides, really like—do not just tolerate but *prefer*—an atmosphere of at least potential violence; they quicken to the sniff of unshed blood. They enjoy the dozing possibility of coiled hidden danger. The anticipation of imminent danger is a "high" more common among men than women. Woman's expectation is other—not a lion in the bush, a beast in the jungle, a dragon in the cave. She is more likely to dream of a frog-prince or a knight on a white horse. Alas, women's phantoms too seldom jump out and become flesh; alas, men's too often do.

In the period between the death of President Kennedy and the fall of President Nixon, just to set out some rough markers, new heroes and new villains appeared on the scene in record numbers, the white hats and black hats flipping back and forth like Arabian tumblers. Malcolm X flipped from pimp to prophet, Robert Kennedy from Joe McCarthy stooge to golden boy, Daniel Ellsberg from traitor to Paul Revere, Eldridge Cleaver from rapist to literary lion to political exile—and now to born-again Christian; Anita Bryant flipped from Mary Sunshine to Mrs. Grundy, Eugene McCarthy from hero of the cause to betrayer of the cause, George Wallace from narrow racist to broad-appeal populist, Betty Friedan from national joke to Founding Mother. These acrobatics produced unparalleled street theater. We saw confrontations from Watts to Kent State to People's Park to Wall Street, where the hard hats egged Mayor Lindsay—*there* was a white hat that disappeared fast from view!—while Teddy Kennedy sprang upward like a backward movie from the waters of Chappaquiddick to the heights of elder-statesmanhood. But no guerrilla theater was more powerful, more panoramic than the suffering Hearsts, the victimized Patty, the ruffian SLA. It had the classic elements of the fairy tale: the maiden abducted by a seven-headed cobra, enchanted by an evil genius, enslaved by a prince of darkness, put in a trance and compelled to do the fiend's bidding, captive of a magic spell from which she cannot voluntarily awaken.

Not only is Patty's story loaded with symbols; its characters think in mythological terms. "You don't name your group the 'Symbionese' Liberation Army, you don't invent a seven-headed cobra symbol,* you don't decide to capture Citizen Kane's granddaughter, you don't hold her for ransom for food rather than money, unless you are painfully aware that politics in the mid-seventies is a matter of imagery and iconography," wrote James Monaco.† You don't subject your own daughter to a public ordeal medieval in its cruelty, he might have added, unless the image of a loving family is more important to you than love or family itself, or unless you are extremely naive or very badly advised. Nor does a government put a pathetic kidnap victim on public trial unless its need is urgent and acute to demonstrate that *its* mythology is intact, that its dream of democracy still flies, that its rule of law still prevails.

A a mythic daughter, wanton, stolen, or strayed, Patricia Hearst wears a long train of embroidery in song and story trailing backward from the gritty good times of Temple Drake to the wagonloads of girls throughout history who are gone with the raggle-taggle Gypsies-o. But HERNAP's mythic roots go back even further in time, back to the two great classical myths of lost women. One of these describes a mother-figure and one a daughter; HERNAP encompasses both. First Patty is lured underground as Eurydice, the captive maiden, and later, as Tania, she becomes the underground queen. Whether that unlikely Orpheus,

*Technically, the SLA didn't "invent" their cobra; they borrowed an ancient Hindu symbol.
†James Monaco, "The Mythologizing of Citizen Patty," *MORE*, 1975.

J. Albert Johnson, really rescued Patty or killed Tania is a matter best left to scholarly speculation.

In the still earlier legend, Persephone is carried off and ravaged by Pluto, the dark king of the underworld, then put on the throne of hell to reign beside him as queen. The anguished mother, Ceres, goddess of agriculture, searches for her daughter everywhere, roaming the whole world to no avail. Finally Alpheus, a river god, brings news of the lost daughter. "While passing through the lower parts of the earth I saw your Proserpine,"* he reports. "She was sad, but no longer showing alarm in her countenance. Her look was such as became a Queen."† The heartbroken Ceres appeals to Jupiter, and a compromise is reached: Proserpine will spend half of each year in the underworld, and be restored to her mother every spring. The allegorical reference to the flowering of springtime is obvious, and here one could say that the legend does not quite fit. Patty was recaptured in the fall. On the other hand, it was really Tania who was recaptured then. Catherine Hearst did not get her daughter back until another spring—and then not without the intervention of judge, jury, and bail bondsman.

It is worth noting, and may perhaps be of some comfort to the psychiatrists who testified in Patty's behalf, that, in later legend, Proserpine becomes the goddess of sleep. Certainly Patty's doctors saw Patty most clearly as a Sleeping Beauty figure. The conception was most unfortunate for Patty, as I have come to think it is for any woman. The trouble with being a Sleeping Beauty is that you cannot get out of the trance by yourself; you have to wait for the prince. If the prince doesn't show up, or if he turns out to be the wrong prince, a frog perhaps, with a magic kiss you would just as soon forget about, well, hey-ho and that's life, and not only in fairy tales. Patty deserved better than she got—but which of us indeed does not?

It could, of course, be argued that Patty was "asleep" during her time with the SLA; that it was Cinque and his evil coven that stole her and shut her up in a tower and put her under a magic spell; and that, as three indentured Princes of the Good, it was the job of the defense psychiatrists gently to awaken her from the trance and lead her back to reality. Certainly this is the way her lawyers and her parents read the story, and myths are susceptible to many meanings.

In retrospect one can see that the SLA took possession of a part of

*Persephone was the Greeks' name for the goddess. The Romans knew her as Proserpine.

†*Bullfinch's Mythology* (New York: Modern Library, 1934), p. 50.

our collective imagination, and this occupation of our imagination had consequences in the real world. Such is the power of myth that scarcely a week after the Los Angeles holocaust, or *barbecue,* as it was already known in radical circles, an emergency meeting—a "war council"— united the Weather Underground, the Black Liberation Army, the Black Guerrilla Family, the New World Liberation Front, the August 7 Movement (named for the Marin County Courthouse shoot-out, August 7, 1970), and other left-wing groups in support of the SLA aims. The old SLA dream of a Symbionese federation had come true in its own ashes. The phoenix was rising. The war council decided to confer the Shao Lin Dragon Award, a mystically sacred posthumous decoration invented by George Jackson to honor the martyrdom of his brother Jonathan, on the six martyrs of the burning house. Carried away by its revolutionary passions, the war council even decided to give the Dragon to Patty Hearst—the first time a living person had ever received the award. That a living *white* person received it is still more extraordinary. Should Tania thereafter betray her new supporters, or in any other way sully the golden Dragon, there could be little doubt she would be marked for certain death. The Dragon helped make Patty, in Bailey's words, "a walking dead girl," a literal zombie.

By July 1974, less than eight months after the assassination of Foster, the phoenix fledged in the flame and ash of Los Angeles was fully grown, and the martyred SLA had been enfolded in its forgiving wings. The SLA's memory and even its politics were embraced and enshrined across the country in a special commemorative edition of the Weather Underground's clandestine journal, *Prairie Fire.* Myth had shown itself stronger than politics, stronger than reason. Perhaps it always is.

Week Four

February 16–22

Monday, February 16

During *voir dire*, Judge Carter had repeatedly warned prospective jurors against the press.* "They will get upon you like locusts," he said. Today we see the truth of the judge's prophecy when the whole trial apparatus—judge, jury, marshals, and press—turn out to view Patty's two closets. On a soaking-wet Monday morning, a legal holiday after the Lincoln's Birthday weekend, the city is quiet and empty, a cold rain falling. My taxi moves through deserted streets until we hit the 1800 block on Golden Gate. Then, pandemonium: The entire street in this black neighborhood of shabby apartments and run-down Victorian mansions converted into rooming houses has been blocked off, and is aswarm with trucks, cameras, lights, cable. It looks as if a big movie company were on location here, waiting for the principals to arrive. All the curlicued, paint-peeling balconies, gables, porches, bay windows, arches, and even some rooftops are crowded with curious onlookers, many in colored head cloths and white nightclothes. The scene is festive, like a Haitian primitive painting. The street is filled with prowling newscasters, a Who's Who of broadcasting all of them trailing yards of cable and searching for someone to interview who will say he once saw, or thought he saw, Patty here. Most residents won't talk, so the big, trench-coated reporters are reduced to interviewing round-eyed, giggling six-year-olds.

A car screeches to a stop in front of a four-story brick apartment

*John Bryan, *This Soldier Still at War* (New York: Harcourt Brace Jovanovich, 1975) p. 298.

(165)

building, and a bunch of burly marshals in raincoats shoulder their way through the mob of press people. In the middle of their huddle is a bright flash of color—Patty's raincoat. She is supported by the matron and Al, who look as if they were pushing a bundle of painted sticks. All disappear inside while other marshals hold back the crowds. A dinky and dented old Coast Guard bus pulls up, and the jury files out. Two more sedans full of men arrive, and with a start one recognizes the skinny chap in the fedora and checkered topcoat. Out of his judicial robes, Oliver J. Carter looks like an elderly shoe clerk. Save for Bailey and Browning, our entire cast of characters is on hand. The aquarium has broken, and the whole bizarre kettle of fish has spilled out into the city.

Only Patty, Al, the marshals, the jurors, and Carter get upstairs— no press. One juror is dimly visible through the window of the still-empty third-floor apartment that has a "For Rent" sign tacked to the fire escape. At the end of the street, through rain and fog, one can see the dull gleam of the Federal Building, fourteen blocks away. The SLA planned and executed its bank robbery in the shadow of FBI headquarters.

Now, in reverse order, everybody comes pouring back out of the building, and in a mad scramble, cars and television trucks pull away, tires squealing. I wind up bouncing around on top of some film cans in the back of the CBS truck, Threlkeld doing seventy as the press caravan chases the rickety jury bus through misty Golden Gate Park. In a dripping eucalyptus grove a class is practicing graceful Chinese shadowboxing. Others are doing headstands and meditating in the rain.

Daly City is a hillside of small bungalows, green, pink, and peach, inspiration for the song about "little boxes, made of ticky-tacky, filled with people just the same." Patty's car is driven directly into the garage of one house, and its pistachio-colored door is then closed, so there is absolutely nothing for the press here, either. The silent, raincoated jury plods between muddy flower beds to the front door. When it is time to leave, Patty is driven south to the jail, and we rush north along Highway 101, beside the stormy Pacific, cypresses and surf lashed by the strong winds, and for one exhilarating moment we pull alongside the jury bus, but bars and thick iron mesh on the bus windows make it impossible to see in.

Back in our press room, Al is ready with a blow-by-blow report. At Golden Gate, which was actually the SLA's second hideout, although we went there first, the jurors saw a closet five feet long, one foot seven inches deep, and seven feet high. Each juror went inside it and examined the rest of the apartment as well. Unfortunately the place had been renovated after the SLA left it in a rubble of dirt, slime, graffiti, and cockroaches, and the landlord had replaced the closet door, removed the doorknobs, and repainted. Johnson invited Carter to step into the closet, but the judge declined his offer to see the nail holes where filthy carpeting had once hung. In Daly City they saw the closet off the rear bedroom, two feet deep and five and a half feet long, where Patty lived for the first month. Each juror again went inside, had his attention called to some nail holes in the walls, and then viewed the bathroom. This was all the jury saw, presumably because it was all that Patty saw during her confinement. Patty had been reluctant to go on the tour at all and started crying as soon as she saw the first closet. "I hadda hold her up. I thought she was gonna faint for sure," Al says. This spell of weakness occurred before the jurors showed up. Al would have liked each juror also to sit down on the floor of the closet and close the door, but Carter refused that request.

The press conference appears to be over. But the sob sisters have a final question. Anticipating that the press would be barred while the jury or Patty was present, several of them had arrived at Golden Gate at about seven A.M. and, posing as prospective tenants, had inspected the vacant apartment. Is it not true that it has *two* closets, one of them large enough to contain a Murphy bed? Correct, says Johnson, and during the SLA's tenancy that closet did contain a Murphy bed, as well as a stockpile of tear gas, guns, and ammunition. Patty was confined in the small closet, not in the big one. No question about that.

In the afternoon I chat with several lawyers. First, Leonard Weinglass, an old friend, who now represents Emily and Bill Harris, rings me from Los Angeles to ask how the defense is going. I tell him I believe Patty's story and I think most of the other reporters do, too.

Weinglass thinks Patty's trial is being very poorly reported. No question she is in some kind of mental distress, he says, but it's very common. It happens to many people of privileged background who are exposed for the first time to revolutionary ideas and people, and then perceive the truth of what the revolutionaries are saying. They feel intense inadequacy and great guilt about themselves, and about their families and backgrounds. One way to defend Patty would be to say that what happened to her was "the result of a reality gap in her past."

The reason Steve Weed was not put on the stand, Weinglass believes, is that on cross-examination he would have testified that Patty was suggestible to any group of eight or nine people who held strong ideas about *anything.* "How is it that none of Patty's friends are willing to testify in her behalf if they know that by doing so they could save her up to thirty years in the can? Because the story isn't true. These kinds of people have terrific loyalty. Wendy would back it up if it were true, but Wendy isn't there, Weed isn't there, Steven Soliah isn't there."

"Shana, this thing is like grappling with Jell-O," William Coblentz had said to me back in March 1974, when he was trying to negotiate with the kidnappers and I was trying to begin writing the story. In a case built on Jell-O—political, moral, philosophical, and every other flavor of Jell-O—I soon discovered I badly needed some fixed point of reckoning, a lodestar by which to navigate this vast swamp of assertion wherein everybody seemed to have something to sell and something to hide, an ax to grind, a body to bury and another to exhume, a message to trumpet to the credulous, waiting world. From the very beginning, HERNAP had glowed like rotten wood.

The lodestar I chose was Charles Garry. If Vincent Hallinan is the elder statesman of San Francisco's considerable left-wing legal establishment, Garry is its dean. He is also the one man touched by HERNAP who knew all the others, knew the scene, knew the ropes, and knew the law. Garry had been a close friend of Marcus Foster, and he was one of the first people Randolph Hearst consulted after Patty was kidnapped. He is a Marxist, a man whose ideas about politics, race, and human nature, as well as economics, have been consistent over many years. He has wisdom, scars, a titanium ego, and a sense of personal honor that is basalt-hard. Not only is Garry a champion of blacks and of prisoners' rights, he has fought the death penalty, fought McCarthyism, fought for students' rights, has represented the Black Panther Party, the San Quentin Six, the Oakland Seven, Inez Garcia—he has defended the weak against the strong for more than thirty years.* Garry dresses with abandon in florid shirts and wild plaids, and his white hair is brushed over the fine bald skull from nape to brow. But the youthful, mod-silly getup fails to disguise the passionate, stern man within, the immigrant Armenian moralist who toils every day, Saturdays and most Sundays included, amid a rubble of books and briefs, under framed specimens of Day-Glo prison art and an illuminated manuscript of Stephen Spender's poem:

---

*His newest high-visibility client is the tragic People's Temple cult of San Francisco and Guyana.

I think continually of those who were truly great. . . .

Near the snow, near the sun, in the highest fields
See how these names are feted by the waving grass,
And by the streamers of white cloud,
And whispers of wind in the listening sky.
The names of those who in their lives fought for life,
Who wore at their hearts the fire's centre.
Born of the sun, they travelled a short while toward the sun,
And left the vivid air signed with their honour.

Unless he is in court, Charlie is almost always sitting there, under the poem, in his office, across the leafy plaza from the Federal Building, poring over legal papers or chatting with a client, and he is there on the afternoon of the Lincoln's Birthday holiday. Charlie is disgusted. This brainwashing defense will destroy Patty as a human being, he says. The only way to save her is to let her take her medicine. What's important is where her head is. If she was serious at the time about exchanging herself for Remiro and Little, she should have surrendered then. "Instead they pull some chickenshit bank robbery. How does that feed the hungry? How does that educate the masses? Lenin criticized those kinds of people. The Spanish Civil War was lost because of those same kinds of people. Terrorism *has* no politics, only the politics of terror. It brings on counterrevolution; it invites fascism. Agggghhhh! The Movement is moribund. Nobody who's a Marxist would relate to this shit."

Garry disagrees with Weinglass. He thinks that the first part of Patty's story is substantially correct. He believes she was a prisoner of the SLA, totally under their control and in their power at the time of the bank robbery; that she did not become a free agent until sometime after the crime for which she is now on trial. However, Garry is appalled by the legal tactics that are now being employed. "If she were my child," he says, "not my client, but my own daughter, I would prefer she plead guilty and spend five years in the pen, rather than put her through this kind of ordeal. I can't understand it, because her parents don't seem to be the sort of vindictive people who would allow a daughter to go through this if they could prevent it. Another thing: If she's convicted, she'll do bad time, as it's called, because she'll be in prison as a snitch."

Tuesday, February 17

By our third week we have shaken down into in-people and out-people. The carnival continues outside the courtroom, but inside, we think of ourselves as old pros. Opposing counsel exchange legal papers, slapping them down on each other's table like cardplayers throwing down tricks. Today will be Patty's worst ordeal yet. She will have to tell all the rest of her story again, this time to the jury. Over the three-day weekend, Bailey has flown his jet to Seattle and Los Angeles, addressed a meatpackers' convention, and conducted a legal seminar. He cannot relax, cannot slow down. He is smoking maybe forty Benson & Hedges a day and drinking maybe ten highballs—usually scotch and sodas at night, Bloody Marys or margaritas at noon. His weight worries him, and he puts saccharine in his morning black coffee. His belly bulges more than he would like over the waistband of the eight brand-new three-piece suits he has brought with him to San Francisco. But in court his tension does not show at all.

"What makes me run? I *burn,* dammit, that's why. I like to run," Bailey has written. His motor races *naturally.* When I met him for the first time, at his home in rural Massachusetts only a couple of weeks after he took over the case, he had been nearly as keyed up as he seems this morning.

On the witness stand, Patty is explaining why in her very first taped message she warned authorities not to rush in and try to rescue her. By then the SLA had told her that the FBI had stormed a house in Oakland, looking for her, and that if the SLA *had* been inside, Patty would already be dead. They would never surrender, Cinque said. They would shoot it out to the death first.

It is time now to play the second tape, received four days later. Johnson throws the switch, and we hear, "Mom, Dad, you don't have to feed the whole state." Her voice sounds brighter. "I would like to emphasize that I *am* alive. I'm well. I'm fine." It is the voice of Dorothy in *The Wizard of Oz* reassuring the little dog, Toto, that everything will be all right. "It's not a racial issue, it's a political issue. . . . I am being held as a prisoner of war. . . . I am not being left alone, I am fine! I am not being starved, beaten, or tortured. . . ."

The real Patty looks as if she were now suffering all three of these abuses. She dabs at her eyes with Kleenex. "Mom should get out of that black dress. As long as the FBI doesn't come busting in on me . . . that is my biggest worry . . . I think I can get out of here alive."

Bailey reminds us that the tape's "not unreasonable" demands—$70 worth of free food for every poor person in California—add up to $400 million. He asks Patty about the circumstances under which the tape was made. "Cinque came into the closet. . . . He had notes. . . ." She has again begun to weep. What is triggering the tears? Is it the reference to her mother in black or the recollection of Cinque? Or does she weep because she is betraying truth?

Can Patty remember anything of significance that occurred between the making of the second and the third tapes? She looks briefly bewildered and upset; then she understands the question. "Okay. They got real mad because my father was going to give two million dollars. They said he was just playing with my life. They said he could just write it all off."

On February 20, on a third tape, Cinque said that Hearst's $2 million was "an act of throwing a few crumbs to the people and forcing them to fight over it." The jury hears Cinque list the Hearsts' holdings: a silver mine and thousands of acres of land in Mexico, land in Hawaii, 70,000 acres of timberland in northern California, a cattle ranch near San Luis Obispo, orange groves in Florida, rice paddies near Sacramento, and homes in Hillsborough, New York, and San Diego, each valued at well over half a million dollars. Then comes the personal stock portfolio—large interests in IBM, Exxon, Safeway Stores, United Airlines, Hughes Airways, drug companies, paper companies, lumber companies, cattle ranches. There is a huge collection of antique paintings, Cinque says, in addition to Chinese screens and Greek pottery, including a group of twenty-four vases valued at $10,000 each; a collection of valuable Oriental rugs given Hearst by his friend the shah of Iran; other gifts from friends like Howard Hughes. . . . The Hearst Foundation is a tax loophole for the Hearst fortune. The $1.5 million that by now has been promised to the SLA from the foundation is but 50 percent of what the foundation is legally required to give away anyhow in order to maintain its tax-exempt status.

Can any of this be believed? I don't know. Now Cinque begins to list the assets of the Hearst Corporation: "annual profits of $78 million a year from *Cosmopolitan* magazine," for example. *That's* absurd, I know. But how about the next part? "Mr. and Mrs. Hearst have a personal fortune of hundreds and hundreds of millions of dollars." Is this whole tape an absurd Ali Baba fantasy, or is it at least partly true? When the world first heard the tape, it was impossible to judge. W. A. Swanberg had valued Hearst's publishing empire at $160 million, San Simeon at $30 million, the assets of the Hearst Foundation at his death at $44 million, and the yield from the immensely profitable logging operations at Wyntoon, the only one of Hearst's seven castles still in family hands, at $2 million a year. (When Hearst was living, not a tree could be touched.)

Sixteen years after Hearst's death, *Forbes* magazine estimated the total assets of his estate as "well over the $500 million mark, and approaching $1 billion in the estimable future." It was to protect all this from the depredations of the tax men and the possible folly of his heirs that the Pharaoh of San Simeon invented the Hearst Family Trust, a sort of charitable foundation run by thirteen trustees, of whom no more than five—according to the terms of the will—may be members of the Hearst family. Randolph Hearst is chairman of the Hearst Family Trust; his brother William is president. The trust holds all the voting stock of the Hearst Corporation; the trustees elect the corporation's board of directors, largely from their own ranks. Until the trust is dissolved, upon the death of the last surviving son or grandchild who was alive in 1951 (when the Pharaoh died), the will states, the trustees are independently in control of the fortune and family members are employees of the trust. The corporation, run by professional managers, owns and controls the great wealth, not the individual Hearsts. In sum, the whole thing is a tax shelter more gorgeous than San Simeon itself, and as its assets continue to multiply in near-perfect fiduciary hygiene, they could guarantee the Hearst heirs the largest family fortune in history. The arrangement led the SLA to claim that Patty's parents were figures of Midas-like wealth, and it led the Hearsts, equally afflicted with tunnel vision, though looking down a different tunnel, to claim they didn't really have very much money at all and were not a great deal better off than their Hillsborough neighbors. It helped explain the assertively unrich style in which they chose to live.

In the courtroom the tape continues to spin. Cinque is now demanding a total of $6 million in ransom, all of it to be used for the purchase of top-quality food at wholesale prices. No supermarket must make a profit off the poor. Cinque's harangue segues into a plea to "save the children" of the world:

> Cry out! Cry out for all the millions of children of all races who are starving and dying now, and not just cry out for the safety of one human being who just happens to be the daughter of an enemy of the People. Fight and cry out in the defense of millions and save the children, and by this action you will save also the life of one who has never seen the robbed or knew that the riches of her life were the spoils of the robber and murderer.

Cinque sounds passionate but stoned. The jury seems numb. Judge Carter appears to be fast asleep.

> You do indeed know me, you've always known me. I am that nigger you have hunted and feared night and day. I am that nigger you have killed hundreds of my people in a vain hope of finding. I am that nigger that is no longer just hunted, robbed, and murdered. I am a nigger that hunts you now. Yes, you know me, you know us all. I am the wetback. You know me. I am the gook, the broad, the servant, the spik. Yes, indeed. You know us all, and we know you, the oppressor, the murderer and robber, and you have hunted and robbed and exploited us all. Now we are the hunters that will give you no rest, and we'll not compromise the freedom of our children. Death to the fascist insect that preys upon the life of the People!

Then, to date this diatribe, the tiny, breathy voice of Patty Hearst: "Today is the nineteenth, and yesterday the shah of Iran had two people executed at dawn." A chill goes up my spine at hearing the powerful outburst again.

This tape was made after Patty had been in the closet about fifteen days, she says, with little hope of getting out. "I mean, I mostly thought I would be killed."

The SLA told her it intended to demand a prisoner exchange with Remiro and Little. "Did you have any hope the authorities would release these men?" asks Bailey.

"I hoped they would, but I knew they wouldn't."

You've told us you were blindfolded at all times except when you were allowed to bathe. How often was that? "I think once a week." When her blindfold was removed, the light hurt her eyes. Her hands looked huge and distorted. The bath mat seemed to be moving. As she describes this Patty's small hands flutter rapidly, as if she were doing a newscast for the deaf.

Though she knew "from their voices" that the only black in the group was Cinque, the white SLA members talked continually about their readiness to die for blacks. One day Cinque told Patty that the War Council was thinking about offering *her* a chance to fight for the People, too. Her alternative? To die. Here Patty's voice breaks, and she is unable to continue.

The third tape was made on the day before Patty's twentieth birthday. After it was received and broadcast, the prisoner was told repeatedly that "my parents weren't doing anything except trying to humiliate people and trying to provoke the SLA to kill me. . . . They were throwing the food at the people, distributing garbage. . . ."

It is now time to play the fourth tape, retrieved on March 9 from a San Francisco ladies' room. "General Gelina" (Angela Atwood) speaks first:

> To die a race and be born a nation is to become free [George Jackson's words]. It is the dream of the reactionary leadership that the enemy corporate state will *willingly* give the stolen riches of the earth back to the people . . . the goods that the people themselves have produced at the price of blood. To this our bullets scream loudly. . . . We will never say anything we do not fully and totally mean! . . . Poor people have been offered hog feed and been forced to stand in line in the cold like dogs for only a bag of cabbages. . . . But words don't make no bag of cabbages into meat. . . .

Mr. and Mrs. Hearst, listening for the tenth or maybe the hundredth time to this harangue, sit stiff-backed, untouching, unmoving. On the bench, Judge Carter nibbles at his nails. The SLA has been thinking of putting Patty into a "strip cell" like the ones in which Remiro and Little are confined on death row in "San Quentin Concentration Camp," Gelina says. Saxbe's statement that the FBI should burst in and get Patty, even if it meant killing her, "was no slip of the tongue, but was in reality a prematurely exposed government policy decision." The FBI is trying to set up Patricia Hearst to be killed and then use her death to rally support for Nixon's corporate dictatorship. Gelina demands that Remiro and Little be allowed to appear on live television and that this tape itself be published in full.

When it is Patty's turn, one hears a new firmness and bitterness in her voice. On this fourth tape one seems to hear the personalities of Patty and Tania speaking almost in fugue:

The SLA are not the ones who are harming me. . . . It's the FBI, along with *your* indifference to the poor. . . . I can't believe you are doing everything you can. . . . I don't believe that you are doing anything at all. . . . The news media has been assisting the FBI . . . promoting a public image of my father as a confused parent who has done all he can. . . . Immediate and complete cooperation with my parents have created a public image of me as a helpless, innocent girl who was supposed to have been abducted by two terrible blacks, escaped convicts. I am a strong woman, and I resent being used this way. If you had just done what the SLA wanted . . . I would be ready to get out of here. . . . Dad, I know that you get most of the food donated . . . and you have put very little money at all into the program. Mom, I . . . just wish that you could be stronger and pull yourself together from all these emotional outbursts. . . . You have got to stand up and speak for yourself. You seem to be relying on other people to make your decisions. . . . If it had been you, Mom, or you, Dad, I know that I and the rest of the family would do *anything* to get you back. . . . I'm sorry to think no one is concerned about me anymore. . . . I no longer seem to have any importance as a human being.

This part of her statement, at least, is manifestly true even now. The real Patty stares down at the tabletop, and Judge Carter snoozes as the amplified, disembodied voice booms out of the loudspeakers across the quiet courtroom.

I hope you will not think that I have been brainwashed or tortured into saying this. Please listen to me because I am speaking honestly and from my heart. . . . I have been reading a book by George Jackson called *Blood in My Eye.* I am starting to understand what he means when he talks about fascism in America.

By now nearly all the reporters watching her believe Patty's story. The tears, that gaunt face, make disbelief impossible. But for some reason—perhaps the reporters are being overly "objective," struggling too hard to keep their copy clean of emotional contamination—the public still believes she's lying.

"Please listen to me," Patty had begged her parents over and over. But they were unable to hear her, and she them. Parents and teenagers often feel they are speaking different languages, but in this bizarre and extreme situation it really seemed to be true. In my own conversations with Patty's father, the sense of stymied love, love frustrated by an impossible language barrier, was always there.

I'd met Randolph Hearst first at his office at the *San Francisco Examiner,* a few days after Patty and the Harrises disappeared. Had we but known it then, even as we talked the three fugitives were holed up across the Bay in a Berkeley fleabag, waiting for Jack Scott to complete arrangements to transport them to safety in the East.

Quiet, even hushed, Randolph Hearst's outer office was like the anteroom of a funeral chapel. A portrait of William Randolph Hearst stared down from on high like a manta ray. Randy's inner sanctum had two or three secretaries sitting outside his closed door, but the typewriters were still; even the telephones didn't ring; they just lit up. The inside looked rather like a library. Some film cans were stacked in a corner. A small desk and bookcase appeared unused. The books included works on coney-catching, revolution in Angola, and *Editor and Publisher's Yearbook.* There was a lamp, a plant, a few pencils, some silk flowers in a jar, but no photos or personal mementos of any kind. Old newspapers and correspondence were piled up on the cocktail table in front of the couch where Randy sat, a gray man in gray tweed, continually taking off his glasses and putting them back on. He had a naked, smooth-shaven face, Irish chin, fine eyes.

William Randolph Hearst's fifth and youngest son* has a gentlemanly giggle in his voice that is never altogether absent, not even when the voice breaks with pain, mystification, loss. Almost every conversation, no matter where it began, circled back to his daughter, and it almost always included a comment on his financial standing's being somewhat less than most people believe.

Although we often spoke of politics, the press, and other matters, he liked talking about Patty best, and he returned back and back to the subject like a tongue reaching for a sore tooth. *I* liked *him* from the start; in every way a nice man, a good man, and a very good man to

---

*By a fraction of a moment. In December 1915 Millicent Hearst gave birth to twin sons, Elbert Willson and Randolph Apperson Hearst. Elbert changed his name to David. The first three boys were George, William, Jr., and John.

be the father of a little girl. Perhaps not quite so perfect a daddy for big girls, girls who want bigger answers than he may be capable of giving. He reminded me sometimes of Robert Young in *Father Knows Best:* a movie daddy—uncritical, loving, nonjudgmental, relaxed, indulgent, laughter-loving, a sweet, rather soft guy.

Until he was fifty-eight years old, the life of Randolph Hearst recalled that of Henry James's hero in "The Beast in the Jungle"; he was the one man in the world to whom nothing really ever happened. A convivial sort, president of the Hearst Corporation and publisher of the *San Francisco Examiner* but not an especially strong executive (his older brother William had the real power), not much interested in politics, he dwelled genially and inconspicuously in the shadow of his father and his older brothers. Then Patricia was kidnapped, and his world for a time expanded. Who were these people who took her and what did they want? Searching for the answer, he became "open" for the first time to the demands of blacks, the poor, of convicts and rebellious youth. His moss-backed newspaper showed the change. He hired editor Reg Murphy away from the *Atlanta Constitution* to bring the *San Francisco Examiner,* flagship of the much-diminished Hearst chain, into the second half of the twentieth century. The paper improved noticeably. But then, as HERNAP dragged on and on, as the FBI lagged and the hunt slowed and the trail cooled, Hearst, too, began to change, to close again like a sea anemone that has been brushed by a swimmer's foot. But at our first meeting, indeed at all of them, he was a remarkably available, open, agreeable man.

Four long cigarette butts were already in the ashtray when we began to talk. He could appreciate his daughter's sympathy for prisoners and for the poor, he said. "I understand poverty of opportunity. But when it comes to things like shooting up banks, wearing bandannas, and pulling stickups, I don't understand. Though I do appreciate that she had to turn off her parents' old ways, and the old Establishment, in order to survive."

"Do you think she really believes the SLA line?"

"She believes it now. But until we get her back, you just don't know."

Hearst worried about his wife. "Catherine has high blood pressure. She has a nurse there all the time. She just doesn't want to talk to anyone now. When Steve Weed speaks about Patty's relations with her family, he doesn't really know what he's talking about. We never talked family. He's a bright fellow, but he's not sensitive to other people. After he began giving out interviews, I felt he was not being very fair. I mean, after we let him live in our house, he goes out and bubbles like a yeast cake. That's a breach of hospitality, to say the least."

It was always a small shock in talking to Hearst to recollect that newspapering is his business, that he was something more than a bereaved father. "The real story is Patty. Until she gets back, nobody knows what the hell to write. . . . No 'authorized version' of this thing is worth a damn. You don't want it, and I don't want it. It's a cheap way to go. It smacks of trying to make money on my daughter. What happened inside our house just isn't it. The story is what happened to Patty. You'll have to talk to her."

Hearst said he was smoking four packs a day and getting fat. He scratched his hands compulsively as he talked.

"Have you spoken to any of the other parents?"

"Yes. Dr. Wolfe called me after the last tape.* He was crying. He wanted to tell me what a fine young man Willie was. I said, 'Doctor, I watched that television and I thought my daughter was being cremated. I'm terribly sympathetic, but I think your son could have met a girl a little better way than kidnapping her.' I wasn't too excited about the son-in-law idea. I told him I did and I do have sympathy, but I couldn't exactly feel that the person who kidnapped my daughter was an upstanding young man!"

After lunch Patty describes the shotgun the SLA gave her to defend herself with. It had a cut-down barrel, a sawed-off stock, and no ammunition, and Cinque gave her lessons on how to break it down and clean it. Her only previous experience with shotguns was on a shooting trip with her father when she was thirteen. Looked at close up, through opera glasses, Patty appears much younger and more vulnerable than the hard-edged figure in the witness box.

"Did there come a time when one of the women came to you and talked to you about getting it on with someone?" Bailey asks. Yes, Angela Atwood. Where? In the closet. "She said that in the cell everybody had to take care of the needs of other people. She said I was gonna sleep with Willie Wolfe." The corners of Patty's thin mouth turn down, and she begins breathing heavily. "So I did." Wolfe came into the closet that same night.

---

*This was the final SLA tape, received several weeks after the holocaust in Los Angeles, on which "Tania" had eulogized her slain comrades and described her love for "Cujo" (Willie Wolfe): "the gentlest, sweetest man I have ever known."

What did he say and do? I don't remember. Did he take you out of the closet? No. He came into the closet, and he closed the door and . . . Patty's chest heaves; her breath comes in convulsive gasps, so that for a moment she cannot speak.

"Did he make you lie down on the floor?"

"Yes."

"And then what did he do?"

"Had sexual intercourse."

And one week later, did someone else come to the closet for the same purpose? Yes. Who was it? It was Cinque. Did he do the same thing? Yes.

During this testimony Catherine Hearst has first covered her eyes with her hand and then, in a gesture almost Japanese in its suggestion of abject submission to grief, bent forward and buried her face in her lap. Randolph just stares woodenly ahead.

A short while later, the SLA decided to move to a new hideout, and the blindfolded prisoner was tied inside a garbage can and loaded into the trunk of a car. "Then they took it out of the car and dropped it a couple of times." "It" is Patty; she has become an object, not a human being. When they opened the garbage can, she couldn't stand up. "Then they put me in another closet." Once more she begins to weep. She remained in the second closet a few weeks, until about April 1. "The SLA sent a communiqué to my parents that said I was going to be released, and it was like their idea of an April Fools' joke." Patty is crying uncontrollably.

Shifting focus, Bailey takes her back to the making of the fourth tape. Did she really believe then that the FBI would murder her and blame the SLA? No, she then believed only that she might be killed accidentally in a shoot-out.

When at last Patty was brought out of the closet and her blindfold was removed, "they were all sitting around in a circle"—here Patty draws a circle on the desk top with one dainty fingertip—"talking about beauty parlors and restaurants. Camilla Hall said we needed money. Cinque said we were going to rob a bank. . . . I couldn't believe they were really going to do it."

Cinque sent people out to case banks, and when they decided on the Hibernia Bank, Patty was afraid to mention that its president was the father of her best friend, Trish, because she feared "they might kill someone just because it was the Tobins' bank." What was the SLA's attitude toward killing people? That either you were with the People or you were a pig. And that killing a pig was—was what you were supposed to do.

BAILEY: All the time you were with them, did you ever hear anyone speak out *against* killing or violence?

PATTY *(shocked voice):* Oh, no!

Patty's normal weight is 105 pounds. She lost about fifteen pounds in the closet, and when she was let out, her legs were too weak for her to stand. What had you been eating? Patty furrows her brow like a little girl; she can't quite remember . . . beans and rice . . . water, coffee, tea. She seems remote, disinterested.

Does Patty know why that particular bank was chosen? It was on a corner. It had cameras and a guard. Cinque said the guard meant the bank was less likely to have good security; his mere presence would be depended on to frighten off thieves. The cameras were important "so that everyone would know that I'd been robbing the bank." She was also "supposed to say my name and give a speech: *This is an expropriation. The money is going to be used for the Revolution.*"

Bailey now asks the court's permission to play the fifth tape, received April 3. It contains as full out a revolutionary statement from Patty as we ever get: ". . . I wrote what I am about to say. It's what I feel. I've never been forced to say anything on tape, nor have I been brainwashed, drugged, tortured, hypnotized, nor in any way confused." Because we know that Patty's entire defense is based on the opposite contention—that she *was* brainwashed—these phrases sound like code, as if Patty were deliberately attempting to suggest the opposite of what her words in fact say. "Mom, Dad, I would like to comment on your efforts to supposedly secure my safety. The People in Need giveaway was a sham. You attempted to deceive the People, the SLA, and me." As the voice on tape accuses the Hearsts of deception one can see the face in the witness box literally turn gray. Gray with shame, I wonder, or in dread of what is to come?

My mother's acceptance of the appointment to a second term as a UC regent, as you well know, would have caused my immediate execution had the SLA been less than together about their political goals. Your actions have taught me a great lesson, and in a strange kind of way I'm grateful to you. . . . Steve . . . I've changed. Love doesn't mean the same thing to me anymore. My love has expanded . . . to embrace all people.

It's grown into an unselfish love for my comrades here, in prison, and on the streets. A love that comes from the knowledge that no one is free until we are all free.

Tears are rolling down Patty's face. She wipes them away with one hand.

I have been given a choice of being released in a safe area or joining the forces of the Symbionese Liberation Army and fighting for my freedom and the freedom of all oppressed people. I have chosen to stay and fight. . . . It should be obvious that people who don't even care about their own children couldn't possibly care about anyone else's children. . . .

The voice rolls on. Before us sits a classical image of suffering, dolorous beyond belief. Our lady of sorrows, gray lids downcast.

Dad . . . tell the poor and oppressed people of this nation what the corporate state is about to do . . . tell the people that the energy crisis is nothing more than a means to get public approval for a massive program to build nuclear power plants all over the nation. Tell the people that the entire corporate state is, with the aid of this massive power supply, about to totally automate the entire industrial state. . . . Tell the people, Dad, that all lower class and at least half the middle class will be unemployed in the next three years and that the removal of the . . . unneeded people has already started. I want you to tell the people the truth. Tell them how the law-and-order programs are just a means to remove so-called violent—meaning *aware*—individuals in the community . . . in the same way that Hitler controlled the removal of the Jews from Germany.

The connection of these words to the weeping, suffering child in the witness box is absurd. Al Johnson stands in a shadowed corner close behind her, grave. If Dorian Gray had started out with the face of a painted Italian cherub, halfway through his life he would look like Al Johnson now. The rhetoric is all Tania now, and she is rallying the black prisoners.

If I'm feeling down, I think of you. . . . We are learning together, I in an environment of love, and you in one of hate in the belly of the fascist beast. . . . Greetings to Death Row Jeff, Al Taylor, Raymond Scott [three black convict SLA sympathizers]. . . . We share a common goal as revolutionaries, knowing that Comrade George lives! It is in the spirit of Tania that I say: *Patria o muerte. Venceremos!*

Next a few near-hysterical words from William Harris:

To Black people, who lead our struggle for freedom, we have proved to be the racist punks of the world. . . . We have a long way to go to purify our minds of the many bourgeois poisons, but we also know that this isn't done through bullshitting and ego-tripping. It is done by fighting and, as the comrade has taught us, by stalking the pig, seizing him by his tusks, and riding his pig-ass into the grave.

Swiping at her streaming eyes with the full, open palm of her hand, Patty appears in total despair. A new female voice comes on the tape and says:

Up until now, the fascist media has printed our documents in full because of their vested interest in Patricia Hearst. From now on, however, since this pressure point no longer exists, the fascist corporate military state via the media will lie about and distort any information concerning the SLA.

Patty grows even more pallid and tearful. Now we hear the strong voice of Nancy Ling Perry. To her, Cinque is art and spirituality incarnate:

Cinque M'tume is a Black brother who spent many years of his life in fascist America's concentration camps. Cinque met literally thousands of Black, Brown, Red, Yellow, and White freedom fighters while locked down. Courageous comrade George Jackson was one among them. The spirit of all the brothers Cinque knows lives in him now. . . . Cinque M'tume is the name that was bestowed upon him by his imprisoned sisters and brothers. It is the name of an ancient African chief who led the fight of his people for freedom. The name means "fifth prophet," and Cin was many years ago given this name because of his deep instinct and senses, his spiritual consciousness, and his deep love for all the people and children of this earth. Cin's example has taught us . . . that he or she who is scared and seeks to run from death will find it. But she or

he who is not afraid and who actively seeks death out will find it not at
their door.

In this paranoid ranting, one can hear the parallel themes that run
through SLA politics and Charles Manson's notion of the black apocalypse he called "helter-skelter." Take these same fantasies and turn
them inside out, change black to white, run the film backward, and you
hear the very dreads that stirred the nightmares of Richard Nixon when
he ordered up his supersecret Huston Plan to detect foreign enemies in
our midst.

Paranoia rises from mistrust like steam from a dung heap. In the
years since World War II, we have earned our paranoia. Hiroshima
destroyed our sense of moral superiority. Joe McCarthy taught us to
mistrust legislators, diplomats, civil servants. The Cold War taught us
to mistrust foreign policy. Johnson, then Nixon taught us to mistrust
the presidency. Vietnam taught us to mistrust our sense of national
honor. Watergate taught us to distrust the appearances of moral character. Jimmy Carter may succeed in teaching those who still believe in
Him to distrust God. Assassins taught mistrust of crowds. Suicides
taught mistrust of solitude. We learned from the CIA to mistrust trust.
Experience taught us to mistrust the old sex manuals; further experience bred distrust of the new sex mechanics. Crime teaches distrust of
the system. The media have taught distrust of the word and the image.
Small wonder so many distrust themselves.
    Paranoia feeds on itself. People who hunt for spooks in every closet
and ghosts in every attic are rarely disappointed for long. Imagination
boils and grows like a thunderhead on an August afternoon. Acts of
violence that are in themselves random, and all the more frightening
because they are inexplicable, acquire meaning and design through
paranoid fantasy . . . and the urge to extend the design compels.
    What paranoid America dreads most are the lies it suspects it may
be built on. A nation born in revolution and nearly destroyed in civil
war now fears revolutionaries and blacks above all others, and fears
most an alliance between the two. Consider "Zebra." According to
Mayor Alioto and the San Francisco police, the Zebra killers were
blacks seeking membership in a secret, black, nationwide murder cult.
Shedding the blood of whites was the price of admission. Consider the
widespread belief that Donald DeFreeze was a police informer who

underwent mind-bending, Manchurian Candidate treatments while a prisoner at Vacaville and was programmed, probably by the CIA, to set up a terrorist organization in the Bay Area in order to discredit blacks and left-wingers and to bring down swift government reprisal. Result: the SLA.

How far is far out? Who's crazy now? Consider that at the very period in our history that the government at home was concocting the Huston Plan and abroad was waging an entirely illegal war in Vietnam and Laos and a *secret* illegal war in Cambodia, the CIA was secretly conducting Operation Chaos, its huge, clandestine, illegal espionage operation against blacks, student radicals, and antiwar dissidents that included "a computer system containing an index of over 300,000 names and organizations," most of them American, and apparently unconnected in any way with international espionage.* For that matter, consider the murder kit that the CIA kept hidden in its dark closet of dirty spook tricks: Indian arrow poison, shellfish toxin, poison diving suits, fluorescent tattoos,† death-bearing cigars. Alongside these comic-book devices, the CIA experiments with LSD and nuclear-radiation tolerance on unsuspecting servicemen seem refreshingly "normal."

In his book *The Choice,* Samuel F. Yette, a black journalist, argues that the government must choose one of three courses to deal with black people: "liberation, pacification or liquidation." The only honorable course is "liberation," but the American economy cannot absorb that many blacks into the mainstream; there are not even enough jobs for poor whites. The schools are falling further and further behind in their task of educating black youth. The prisons are full to bursting. The crime rate continues to rise. As for "pacification," it is simply "not possible." Some time ago, therefore, says Yette, the government concluded that its only hope lay in liquidation—destruction of the blacks. Concentration camps are secretly being built. Black-sterilization programs are being planned, and U.S. Naval Intelligence has already completed a study that indicates that few white Americans will object when these plans go into operation. But to create and sustain a suitable climate of race hatred, an ongoing program of violent, Zebra-like racial "incidents" is required.**

*Rockefeller Commission Report, 1976, p. 148.

†In Vietnam we had been having difficulty telling "our" Vietnamese from "theirs." Somebody in the CIA thought it would be good to mark "ours" indelibly.

**Though a Zebra trial ultimately was held, no convictions were obtained, and there is not a shred

Anyone who thinks Yette's book is far out has yet to encounter the works of Ms. Mae Brussell, who publishes *Conspiracy Newsletter,* in, of course, California. After the Hearst kidnapping, she put out a special issue in which she argued for forty closely reasoned pages that the SLA was a direct outgrowth of the CIA's Phoenix program in Vietnam and its purpose was to destroy the Left in America. In her view, Angela Atwood and others in the SLA were paid CIA agents. The PIN food program was a calculated disaster, a deliberate "provocateur action to hasten Patty's conversion to the SLA." According to Ms. Brussell, the CIA created the SLA with seven objectives in mind. In her words, the intention was to

1. Create widespread fear of kidnapping and suspicion of terrorist organizations.
2. Link U.S. terrorists to international guerrilla groups.
3. Discredit communes.
4. Escalate domestic fear of Mao Tse-tung, brainwashing, and Communist-style indoctrination.
5. Drum up support for the U.C.L.A. Center for the Study and Reduction of Violence (a massive, federally funded project to continue and expand secret programs already in progress at Vacaville Prison. In these studies American psychiatrists, working with Nazi doctors, experiment in controlling human behavior and turning prisoners into zombies, assassins, and informers through electric implants in their brains, and powerful drugs. "Surgical terror" to control prisoners is already a fact of life in California's Gulag Archipelago).
6. Discredit the poor; rehearse for massive food handouts; hand out condemned food (which will later cause botulism or cancer).
7. Halt prison reform movements dead in their tracks.

Ms. Brussell believes that the true aim of the U.S. government is to set up a police state and impose martial law. To that end, the CIA invents, staffs, and funds organizations like the SLA, sets up events like the murder of Foster and the kidnapping of Patty, and then arranges the cremation of its own no-longer-useful agents in the burning house in Los Angeles. Reading her pages is like sitting through a horror-movie triple feature: The fangs may be rubber and the blood

---

of objective evidence that a Zebra conspiracy did in fact exist. The killings probably *were* random; the only "link" was invented by the authorities and disseminated by the sensation-hungry media.

ketchup, but the back of the neck prickles nonetheless.

By the time Patricia Hearst's ordeal was at an end America had become a different world. Nixon and Kissinger had been toppled, and Vietnam was behind us. But the Warren Commission Report had been exposed as a cover-up; the assassination of Martin Luther King, Jr., was shadowed by real, not paranoid, doubts; U.S.-government murder plots against Castro and other heads of state had been revealed; and it was now clear that the entire intelligence-police-government-military network had been in corrupt cahoots for many years. Last year's conspiracy freak looked like this year's far-seeing visionary and, possibly, next year's Pulitzer Prize–winning investigative reporter.

Watching the defendant listening to the paranoid and pivotal fifth tape has been extremely painful because Patty's suffering is so apparent, her victimhood so total. When Fahizah signs off, Cinque's voice returns to issue SLA death warrants to "enemies of the People." Henceforth "all corporate enemies of the People will be shot on sight, and no more prisoners will be taken . . . since the prisoner is now a comrade and has been accepted into the ranks of the People's Army. . . . Subject may leave whenever she feels that she wishes to do so. She is armed and well capable to defend herself. This operation is hereby terminated."

Now the mad finale, a crazy rock anthem churns in the background —Cannonball Adderly's "Save the Children"—as Cinque bids goodbye to his own "six lovely black babies"—

Victor, Damon, Sherry, Sherlynne, Dawn, and Dee Dee . . . Just to say your names again fills my heart with joy. . . . Even when you may not see me, I am there. . . . Daddy wants you to understand that I can't come home because you and the People are not free. . . . I want you to understand that I have to fight for you and for all fathers and mothers who must stay home or who have not the courage to fight or the clear understanding yet that the greatest gift they can give their children is freedom. For you, my children, even when I may never see you again, know that I love you and will not for any price forsake your freedom and the freedom of all oppressed people. For you, I give all that a father could wish. I give you life without fear and exploitation. I give you love with a future, understanding that the price of freedom is daring to struggle, daring to win.

The all-American words of Bailey's old client and nemesis, Glenn Turner, echo from Cinque's dead mouth.

The music swells, then silence. The tape is a suicide letter, addressed to his own children and to the world, that foreshadows the *Götterdämmerung* in Los Angeles. During the final minutes of music, Carter smirks from on high, Lee Bailey makes a thumbs-down gesture of derision, and over in his shadowy corner, Al Johnson shakes with silent laughter.

BAILEY *(grinning):* Does Your Honor wish to take the afternoon recess?

The defense ends its second day of presenting testimony by attempting to sort out who wrote what. It is surprising to hear from Patty that the sections of tape no. 5 on the energy crisis and Jews in Germany were the work of Cinque.

Bailey dwells on the SLA's longing to be black. Patty says William Harris "wished he wasn't white, because then he'd be much more together." Emily Harris and Angela Atwood "wished they weren't white. Nancy Ling Perry just—I mean, she practically would have said she *wasn't* white, even though she was." Cinque's attitude was that although he could be with blacks, the best thing he could do would be to work with whites to try to make them better revolutionaries.

Cinque planned the robbery. Emily Harris and Camilla Hall rented the cars. The robbers had a number to use when communicating with one another. "Cinque was number one, Patricia Soltysik was number two, number three was Nancy Ling Perry, four was William Harris, five was William Wolfe, six was Emily Harris, seven was Angela Atwood, eight was Camilla Hall, and I was number nine." Curious that Patty can remember all this two years later, in such minute detail, yet West and Singer report she suffered from severe amnesia during all her jail interviews. But, of course, Bailey and Johnson must have carefully rehearsed this part of her testimony. It is important that in the jurors' minds every bit of responsibility for planning and carrying out the crimes with which she is charged be placed firmly on shoulders other than her own.

"Okay. Did Cinque tell you why he wanted you inside the bank?"

Her answer sounds like a country-and-western song title. "He Wanted Me to Be Wanted by the FBI."

The business of wigs and haircuts is still puzzling. At the close of the first meeting at which the robbery was discussed, Cinque instructed

Nancy Ling Perry to cut off all of Patty's hair. Two weeks later, in the bank, Camilla Hall, Angela Atwood, Emily Harris, and William Wolfe also wore wigs. It is still not explained why four people wore wigs to disguise themselves, whereas Patty's wig had the opposite function.

Patty has a cold and speaks in a soft, hoarse monotone. When she got out of the closet, Patty saw that the other SLA members were always armed and that the apartment had a large closet chock-full of weapons, gas masks, ammunition, and wigs and disguises of all kinds. Patty was shown the guns and taught how to "field strip," clean, and fire the carbine she would carry. Cinque and Nancy Ling Perry would have fully automatic machine guns, Patricia Soltysik would carry a handgun, and Camilla Hall would have "a twelve-gauge sawed-off shotgun, which is to say, a single-barrel, pump-action shotgun." It is as startling to hear this delicate young woman talk knowingly about weaponry as it had been earlier to hear her speak with authority about radical politics in Mozambique.

On the morning of April 15 Patty saw the rented red Hornet and the chosen disguises of her cohorts for the first time. "I think Angela Atwood had on like a medium-length, sort of medium brown-blond shag kind of wig, and Emily Harris, I think, wore like a short blond wig, pageboy type. And William Wolfe wore a gray wig, and William Harris' hair was dyed blond, I think."

Patty's descriptive style reminded me of her mother's friend, the dithyrambic Adalene Ross, who composes fashion-show copy for Matson Line cruises to Hawaii. Catherine Hearst has some rather odd ideas about the press, which may be understandable, and when Mrs. Hearst was at length prevailed on to tell "her side" of this whole story, she chose Ms. Ross as her sole authorized biographer. In due course, a piece by Ms. Ross entitled "The Private Ordeal of Catherine Hearst" was published in July 1974 in *The Ladies' Home Journal.* The article is heavy on Catherine's hobbies—stargazing, supermarketing, and the study of the genealogy of the ancient royal family of Hawaii stand out in my mind—and aglow with the warmth of the Hearsts' family life. "In all the time Patty has been gone, I have often thought how grateful I am for our wonderful family relationship," Catherine tells Adalene, and in case the reader has doubts, Ms. Ross adds a parenthetic aside: "(To the delight of her daughters, Catherine sometimes wears her wedding veil to their quiet, family wedding anniversary dinners at home.)" Visions of gravy stains danced in my head! But it was as easy to mock as to mourn; what I wanted was to understand.

The Hearst family appears to be an entire dynasty of estranged men and women living generation after generation in ill-concealed domestic torment. Not only did Patty's grandfather and great-grandfather live away from, but bound to, their wives; so did the ancestor before that. According to Swanberg, George Hearst, born in 1820 in Missouri, had a difficult boyhood in that "his father was interested in another woman, and his mother would only speak to him when necessary."* Patricia Hearst, in her generation, seems to have been the one to continue the family tradition. She, too, had two mates—a respectable one, her fiancé, Steven Weed, and the outlaw figure, Cujo.

When F. Lee Bailey got around to writing *his* exegesis of the trial, also for *The Ladies' Home Journal* (Al Johnson would choose *Good Housekeeping,* a Hearst-owned magazine, for his forum), he cast further light on Patty's urgent desire to be known as Mrs. Weed. "I think Dr. Kozol's testimony caused her more distress than anyone else's," Bailey wrote. "At one point he told the jury that she was 'embarrassed by the name Hearst.' I noticed that Patty had taken a sheet of yellow legal paper and was writing quickly. She passed the sheet to me. She had written: 'Was not *politically* embarrassed by name H.—was embar. because people would always ask me about H. castle instead of talking to me like a *person.* ' "

To all these Hearsts—to Patty no less than to her parents, albeit in a different way—their self-image as a family seemed to be as important as the family itself. It governed the parents' demeanor while Patty was gone; it dictated strategy at her trial. This image was defined by the standards not of San Francisco or of San Simeon or even of Atlanta, where Catherine Hearst was raised as the sheltered daughter of a telephone-company executive, but of Hillsborough and, still more narrowly, of Hillsborough's small but sturdy community of Roman Catholics, the church to which Randolph Apperson Hearst, an Episcopalian, converted in 1939 when he married Catherine Campbell, the belle of Atlanta.

Long before I ever heard of Patty Hearst, I knew Hillsborough. It is the district that in 1967 sent Shirley Temple to Congress, and when I first interviewed the potential congresswoman *in situ,* I had found the place a hotbed of social rest. Hillsborough's houses protect themselves behind high walls and hedges. At night the citizens sometimes stalk

*W. A. Swanberg, op. cit., p. 3.

their own estates, armed and drunk, hunting trespassers. The talk at the Burlingame Country Club, Hillsborough's Versailles, is of stock options and tax shelters, golf and street crime. Its members are rich in material wealth but paupers in imagination. Hillsborough does not produce people with flexible minds; its citizens suffer from premature hardening of belief. All in all, the place was without doubt the most boring enclave of privilege I had ever visited, lacking weather or even scenery to fall back on when in conversational distress.

Seven years later I was back again. Saturday, June 29, 1974, was to have been Patty's wedding day, and the maid of honor at her marriage to Steven Weed would have been Trish Tobin. That very day, at a Hillsborough party, Trish's mother, Sally, pulled me into a corner. "I was prepared not to like you," she told me tearfully. "But you seem like a nice dame, so I want to ask you: Why do they write all that terrible stuff about Patty? I've known her all my life. Such a bright, brave, *good* girl! How can they *say* those bad things?" Mrs. Tobin's round china-blue doll eyes blinked. "One time we went on a camping trip and Patty got a big splinter through her jeans. Micky is the splinter man in our family, but this time he was away and I had to take it out. Do you know what it's like to pull a three-inch sliver of wood out of a kid's backside? Patty must have been about eleven then, and she didn't make a sound. She was so incredibly brave! How can they write these terrible things about her? Tell me. . . ." She began to sob.

Ordinary words seem to have special meanings in Hillsborough. Another woman at the party undertook to explain the community to me. Hillsborough is a "nice" place, she said, "no different from parts of Long Island or Beverly Hills." Sure, people live well here. Sometimes they send their kids to the public schools; the public schools are "good." But the people are not "rich," they are "well-off." "I've known Randy since I was ten. How can they write all that stuff? How can they call their house a 'mansion'? It's just a nice home, with only six bedrooms. Is that so much for five children?" It is as if they cannot bear to be merely rich.

Hillsborough money is "old" by California standards, but these people, mostly Irish and Roman Catholic, still lust to be labeled "nice." They have been trying to live down their wealth for four or five generations. Their lace-curtain Irish attitudes are a hundred years old. But although "rich" is a pejorative word hereabouts, "power" is not. Mergers turn them on more than feelings do. They have appetite without sensibility. There are two kinds of people in the world, they instruct their children. One kind is born cautious, the other is not. This seems to me a screwy way to divvy up humanity, but it comes to them as naturally as eating and drinking, which they also do with vigor. Hillsborough is inhabited by a clannish people passionately defensive, without quite knowing why, of an extremely narrow way of life. Hibernia Bank president Micky Tobin, Trish's father, hates Pat Brown, the former California governor, even more than he despises the present one, Brown's son, Jerry. "Pat said the rich should *give away* some of what they have!" Micky told me, his eyes as narrow as his wife's were round. *"Why* should we? Why don't people *own* what they own?"

These are brutish and dim people. They live on a level of coarse resentment. The really, really rich, the Eastern aristocrats, the titled Europeans, may think Hillsborough does not know the contempt in which it is held. But Hillsborough knows, all right. It knows the world is a place where people will always try to take advantage of you—rob you, rape you, take you for a fool. The answer is to be overcautious. If you weren't born that way, better learn before they steal you blind. Theirs is a vestigial peasant attitude, and they are a vanished social "missing link" between the bog and the bourse, surviving behind the high hibiscus hedges in darkest country-club country.

In the report on Patty's injured mental state at the time of her capture, the court-appointed psychiatrists described a person of "flat affect" and shallow mind. They spoke of her intense preoccupation with her own body and of her hyper-*politesse* and an unusual concern with proper, hostesslike behavior, even when "home" was a jail cell. They mentioned her vagueness and diminished ability to focus her thoughts, her literal-mindedness, and the sense that she was a person living only in the moment, without past or future. They emphasized her limited awareness and the extreme narrowness of her concerns. In short, they described a typical denizen of the Burlingame Country Club. Perhaps Patricia's abduction did not make her regress to a childlike state but, in fact, accelerated her normally expectable development into a typical forty-year-old Hillsborough matron.

Bailey has asked Patty and the jury to watch the bank film again. So once more we see the defendant and her comrades skitter silently across the polished marble floors. Bailey directs the witness's attention to film frames 19 and 20, where Patty is squarely positioned in front of Camera A. What were Patty's instructions? To get into a crouch, move around, keep my balance, shift from leg to leg, and "if anybody in their area moved, to shoot to kill."

Bailey now proposes to show the film in close-up and slow motion, and he will ask Miss Hearst to describe four of her actions in more detail: One, she looks at her wrist; two, she looks down at something; three, her mouth "comes open"; and four, can she identify the frame in the film where she says the word "Tania"? So we watch it all for the fifth time. Patty cannot explain the wrist motion; she doesn't remember if she was wearing a watch. Opening her mouth was a reaction to the sound of gunfire. "I remember seeing the man get shot, his coat rip open —" She is very near tears again. Bailey asks the clerk for exhibit 19, then walks over to the box to show Patty her own carbine, its bolt only half closed, the way it was in the film. Wet-eyed, the defendant stares down at the weapon. Bailey establishes that when the bolt is not fully closed, Patty's gun could not possibly have been fired. In a Perry Mason finish to the longest day yet, he carries the gun over to the jury and draws its attention to "this silver portion right here"—the telltale partially open bolt. But my own lingering impression of the day is of two wet, round, disbelieving eyes.

Wednesday, February 18

A private bodyguard has at last appeared. He sits beside the Hearsts on a folding chair. Patty is dressed in deep Renaissance velvets the color of plums, and Bailey wears a strange new pale-green pinstripe the color of a $10,000 bill. Patty describes the gang's escape from the bank and the dividing of the spoils. The cash was split into nine equal piles so that any member of the group who got cut off from the rest would have his own funds. After each SLA shopping expedition, the money was pooled again and redivided. A more equitable redistribution of wealth could scarcely be imagined; in fact, symbiotic banking.

To prove that the whites, as outlaws, were now safe within the black community, Cinque proposed to haul in some strangers off the streets who would be happy to assist them in obtaining food, clothing, cars, and other necessities of life on the lam. He went out and soon returned with four adults and three small children—the reluctant and sullen Retimah X, Jamella Muntaz, Rasham, and Ronald Tate, whom we, but not the jury, have already seen. Patty's recollection of the names of these unusual people, their children's names, and their relationships is precise and detailed.

Did they make any comments about the SLA? A deep sigh. Yes, the woman Retimah said she had taped every SLA communiqué that had been broadcast. They had assigned Cinque the code name Jesus. All the children, ages nine, eight, and two or three, could recite the seven aims of the SLA in Swahili. One man, Rasham, said he was prepared to join the SLA right then. The SLA wanted to move out of their cramped quarters, and the blacks were pressed into service as rental agents. Finding a safe new apartment required several visits, and each time they came Cinque told Patty to identify herself as Tania and to say she had helped rob the bank. "And he said I should smile, so it would be easier to recognize me." Racial color blindness works two ways. We look alike to them, too.

Last week, just before the government rested its case, the jury listened to tape no. 6 in which Patty described the bank robbery. Does she recall the part where she says Steve Weed would be foolish to think that "once freed" she would want to go see him? Yes. Were those her own words, "once freed"? No, Angela Atwood wrote every word. Bailey grins as if he has just earned the price of his suit. To him, "once freed" is a critical SLA slip; it acknowledges that Patty was *not free* when she spoke the words. Bailey returns to the "once freed" point several times both during the trial and in the after-hours briefings he holds for the press, but I doubt whether the jury grasps its significance. In truth, I find it hard to keep the "once freed" business in mind. The point is so small that it seems to skid out of its fulcrum position in Bailey's construct of the case.

He moves along to another crucial piece of that construct. Was there any talk among the SLA members that the bank robbery had made Patty a criminal and any discussion of what that might mean to the official FBI view of the case? "Cinque said that I was wanted by the FBI . . . and that I'd be shot on sight if they found me."

"Did anyone talk to you about what would happen if you surrendered or were picked up?"

"That I'd be charged with bank robbery. And be tried for it." Bailey pauses to let that one sink in. For once Cinque, fifth prophet, had been right on target.

After the robbery the SLA moved from the racially mixed neighborhood of Golden Gate to an all-black area. The eight white SLA members, wearing black greasepaint and Afro wigs, moved by daylight, carrying all their guns and bullets with them. The racial fantasies were getting out of control; the entire SLA was playing nigger now. They were becoming reckless and infantile. Before abandoning Golden Gate, they filled the bathtub with "evidence"—a mixture of documents, acid, and excrement—and spray-painted a message: "Here it is, pigs. Have fun getting it."

Patty was no longer kept in a closet, but neither was she ever allowed to go out alone. All nine members of the band slept together in the front bedroom. Several weeks passed before Cinque suddenly decided the Bay Area was no longer safe. One evening he declared that they might actually, *right then,* be surrounded by FBI agents, and they left San Francisco that very night, driving south in a caravan of vans purchased by the four blacks with money provided by Cinque. One, a red-and-white Volkswagen, was the vehicle later used at Mel's. In Los Angeles everybody rendezvoused "in a park or something." Nancy Ling Perry and Patricia Soltysik rented a small, shabby house in an all-black neighborhood because "Cinque wanted to get busy doing what he called *search and destroys.*"

BAILEY *(languorous):* Search and destroys? Who was to be searched, and who was to be destroyed?

"Police."

"Police! Ah. And how was he going to go about that?"

"He was going to have everybody just go out and steal a car, and do the search and destroy, and then take over a house afterwards, and stay there. And every night do that . . ." Her voice trails off.

Only in America! A chain-letter system to spread Vietnam-style commando raids through the vast urban ghettos. The formula even had a gentle, flower-child aspect. "I mean, he said that sometimes it wouldn't be necessary to take over the home. Because the people would just welcome us . . ."

The house was rented from one Prophet Jones, a man who refused to believe they really were the SLA until Cinque pointed to the thin, nearly bald young woman and said, "That's Tania." To judge by her tone of voice and demeanor, Patty has no fear of people like Prophet Jones, Jamella Muntaz, Retimah X, or, for that matter, Cinque. She sounds far more comfortable than Bailey with these angry, loose-limbed, funky blacks

Was she, by this time, beginning to have hope that maybe she would survive, after all? "After I got through the bank robbery, I thought I might live." But escape "didn't seem realistic anymore." It seemed more realistic at the time that the FBI would kill her and blame the SLA.

The house was "really little," with broken glass all over the floor and no gas or electricity. Daily gun classes and drills in how to crouch, roll, and dive continued. All this was done in anticipation of open street warfare. "Everybody was talking about the search and destroys all the time. Willie Wolfe said he couldn't wait until we could become real urban guerrillas."

Patty speaks about "trigger housings" and other terms of weaponry with great familiarity. She appears today to be a far stronger witness than the frightened girl of yesterday. The purpose of the expedition to Mel's, she now explains, was to purchase boots and heavy clothing to wear on the search and destroys. On this day she put on a brown wig and glasses, as well as old green-and-white plaid pants, hiking boots, and a black sweater. They had plenty of money, and there had been no advance plan to shoplift anything from Mel's. But Patty had been trained "that if anybody ever got in trouble, that you were supposed to fire on the people that were attacking them and help them get away. It was in the SLA Codes of War, too . . . that . . . that anyone who didn't do that would be killed."

What were her instructions if an SLA member was struggling with a captor, so that it was risky to fire at one for fear of hitting the other? Patty looks confused again. "To fire over their heads, I guess . . . I mean . . ."

BAILEY *(hard):* Was that something *you* concluded or something you were specifically told?

Her confusion seems to deepen. Then, taking a deep breath, she says with conviction, "I wouldn't have fired at anyone!" Her tone is both helpless and scornful.

The Harrises each carried a handgun; two carbines, a shotgun, and another handgun were in the van. Precisely where were the weapons? "They were all on the floor of the bank [sic]." Patty had a clear shot through the open window, on the driver's side. Her response "was just like a reflex, it happened so fast." She aimed for the top of the building, to avoid hitting anybody. "I pulled the trigger. . . . The gun jumped out of my hand . . . bullets hit the bushes, the divider. . . ." She recovered the weapon and emptied the clip, then picked up the semiautomatic and continued to fire.

Later, at her own trial, Emily Harris would testify that it was only chance that took Patty to Mel's at all. She had impulsively decided to "go along for the ride." As it turned out, her last-minute decision saved Patty's life. Otherwise she would have perished with the others in the burning house.

The instant Patty opened fire, the Harrises came flying across the street, and they all took off. William Harris was "yelling at me because I didn't shoot sooner," and Patty was rolling and bouncing around in the back of the van.

At the time she saw the Harrises struggling with the clerk, did the thought of escape cross her mind? No.

"Were the other members of the SLA, other than the Harrises, still at large?"

"Yes."

"What was the penalty for failure to rescue a comrade in trouble?"

"Death."

"After the Harrises did, in fact, escape, and you were driving away in the van, did you consider at all the opportunity that might have been before you and was now gone?"

"Yes . . . I mean, I just couldn't believe I'd done what I did."

During recess we hear about still another death threat. Someone has called a Los Angeles radio station with the message "Randy Dies Today."

When we return, the courtroom has been set up for a multimedia extravaganza: A large rear-projection screen and two color television sets will show the jury the videotape of the burning house; extra microphones have burst into bloom. But first Bailey must clear up a few points. Patty explains that she smiled at Tom Matthews because the SLA had instructed her to smile at everyone, to make her look more like her well-publicized smiling pictures. But why did she tell Matthews that she had been in the bank voluntarily, that her hands were not tied under her pea jacket, that she had not been brainwashed, and that the bank robbers had practiced how to avoid shooting one another should it be necessary to open fire? To all these questions her answer is the same: She's sure she said it, if Matthews says so, but she doesn't know why.

At the drive-in movie they set up a prearranged distress signal—a paper cup upturned on top of the movie-speaker stand. But nobody showed up to rescue them. The next morning Bill ordered Patty and

Emily to steal a car. "I said I didn't want to do it. They said: 'Too bad.'" Pretending to be hitchhikers, Patty and Emily commandeered a car and kept the driver captive while they drove around most of the day, listening to the radio. In the afternoon Emily was able to buy a car, and they turned their hostage loose in Griffith Park. The three fugitives then drove to a motel across the street from Disneyland. It was early evening. Emily rented a room, and as the trio entered, Bill flipped on the television set. The shoot-out between the SLA and the cops was appearing live on the evening news.

Backstage yesterday during recess, we learn, Patty had been shown the television tape of the shoot-out, to confirm that it is the same fiery footage she had watched in the motel room. Now it will be the jury's turn. The courtroom is darkened, the film begins, and the familiar staccato voice of Los Angeles television newscaster Jerry Dunphy provides a running ad-lib commentary on the violent events we see—people running; cops crouching, ducking and pushing back black spectators; barefoot, openmouthed children flattening themselves back against walls; smoke and flames upstaging the palm-treed sunset; the ever-present sound of gunfire; occasional glimpses of snipers on rooftops. Dunphy describes the action as if it were an impromptu sporting event, which in a sense it was. Police radios crackle with assault-team code: Manhunt, Cobra. The action shifts. The SLA are really hiding in a different bungalow. Cops and newsmen run to the new location. Dunphy's hyped-up sportscaster voice praises the Los Angeles police "professionalism," and this brings a chorus of boos from a few spectators and younger reporters in the back rows of the courtroom.

On the bench, Judge Carter is biting his fingernails. Expressionless in the dim light, Patty in rusty velvet and pink silk is a diminutive Borgia queen. Her coppery hair, now grown long, is spread over her shoulders. Her face is a grim cameo in three-quarter profile, lit only by reflected light from the huge video screen. Vengeance is mine, it seems to say. Flames rise from the house. A camera crew staggers backward, tear-gassed. A "wounded person," body tied like a sack, is pulled across the screen. "Cops are moving 'em back hard," barks Dunphy, "preparing for their final assault." The SWAT (Special Weapons and Tactics) team moves in. CS gas is everywhere. A barefoot man in undershorts dashes past. Teams of newsmen, carrying cameras and mikes instead of weapons, run, crouching, through the lavender twilight. The SLA is being burned alive, barbecued in the shabby house, by an army of police who behave like Vietnam commandos. The cops run one way through

(197)

the smoke, the newsmen run the other way, each heavily laden with the gear of their trade, like teams of movie extras. It reminds me of a day, years ago, when fire suddenly broke out on the set of a cheap TV Western I was visiting. "Quick! Run through the smoke!" the assistant director shouted. "Indians, cowboys, everybody! Run! Again! Again!"

"I don't know *how* we'll use it," the man told me afterward. "But what great footage! And *free!* We can write a plot later."

The morning after the fire, five bodies charred beyond recognition, gas masks melted onto their faces, were removed from the ruins, put into plastic body bags, and delivered to the coroner's office. One female corpse was found eight feet outside the house; the woman seemingly had been trying to crawl to safety. The body of Camilla Hall was found jammed in the crawl space under the floorboards, fused to the remains of her burned kitten. By noon the coroner had made positive identifications from dental records. Only then did Catherine and Randolph Hearst learn that their daughter was not among the victims. Five of the six SLA members died from bullet wounds and smoke inhalation. DeFreeze's body, like the others, contained multiple bullet wounds, but the coroner said the fatal shot was a self-inflicted revolver bullet in the head.

Later, in its official report on the battle, the Los Angeles Police Department said the SLA arsenal had included four automatic weapons, six shotguns, six handguns, and the makings of pipe bombs, all found inside the house. The LAPD had opposed this force with 5,371 bullets from the SWAT team alone. It also used tear-gas rockets and tossed tear-gas canisters into the house. "Prolonged gunfire" completely wore out the barrel riflings and magazine springs of two M-16s and ten AR-15s. In all, more than 125 tear-gas canisters and 9,000 bullets were fired. On the scene were 321 police vehicles, two helicopters, 410 siege officers, and 196 crowd-control and security officers. The total police bill for eradicating the SLA came to $67,576.55; FBI charges were extra. The battle even had medals, of a sort. Police Chief Ed Davis ordered that some of the SLA's big double-aught shotgun shells be encased in Plexiglas cubes, and he awarded them as mementos to reporters who had covered the battle.

Throughout the showing of the twenty-minute film, Bailey and Johnson have been lounging in the shadows at either end of the jury box, flanking it like a pair of stone library lions. The last time Patty's parents saw this film, they believed their daughter was inside the house. But when the lights go up, the Hearsts appear entirely composed. Their daughter resumes her testimony.

During the evening of May 17 the trio in the Disneyland Motel continued to watch reruns and updates of the mass cremation, and Patty heard frequent speculation that she was inside the house, being burned alive by the cops and FBI—in short, that the SLA's prophecy had come true. Patty and the Harrises remained in the motel three days, then moved north to Costa Mesa, then to a Bay Area hotel for two days, and finally to an Oakland apartment. Meanwhile, on television, the nation watched the grieving, bewildered parents of the slain arrive in Los Angeles to claim their children's bodies. I had found the glimpses of these ordinary-looking people very moving. The weeping father of Willie Wolfe told a reporter he would try to get in touch with the parents of the others "slaughtered by these police officers. I'm going to do everything I can to put an end to this American John Wayne tradition," he added bitterly, gesturing with an imaginary gun.

"They loved America," said the Reverend George Hall, father of Camilla. "They were trying to say: America, wake up! What is happening to our great country?"

Los Angeles Mayor Thomas Bradley, a black ex-cop, praised the police, pointing out that not one bystander had been injured, even accidentally, despite the extraordinary amount of firepower. The six desperadoes had been told repeatedly by bullhorn to come out with their hands up. When they responded with a burst of gunfire, the only thing to do was fire back. The police dared not wait until nightfall. If they had lit the area with klieg lights and established a no-man's-land around the house, for example, one of the terrorists might have made a break for it, and the risk of injuring bystanders in the ensuing gunplay in the dark was too great. The gunmen had to be contained within the house. All this was standard police procedure, designed to ensure maximum safety to the largest number of people. Bradley had not attempted to direct or interfere with the police action in any way.

Later, Dr. Frederick Hacker, a Los Angeles psychiatrist and authority on terrorism who had been retained by the Hearsts as an adviser shortly after Patty's kidnapping, characterized the holocaust as "a deliberate public-relations attempt to terrify the populace and glorify the Los Angeles Police Department with another cheap Götterdämmerung." That the SLA had a self-destructive urge was "no justification for helping them to gratify it," he said.

Although the SLA's first act of terror, the assassination of Marcus Foster, had branded it as "adventurist," the ultimate pejorative of the Left, and other radicals would have nothing to do with it after that, the morning following the horrifying televised incineration, a spray-painted *graffito* appeared on the wall of a Berkeley supermarket: CAMILLA HALL LIVES! VIVA CINQUE! In death the SLA was not only still alive; it was at last legit.

In Los Angeles more than a hundred cops and FBI men were searching for Patty and the Harrises; it was the start of the biggest manhunt since the one for Dillinger. Numerous "sightings" eventually were reported, from Denver to Hong Kong, as if Patty were some sort of UFO, but there were no facts. The FBI was universally mistrusted. Nobody would talk. A 1970 Gallup poll had said that 84 percent of the public had a "highly favorable" opinion of the FBI. By the time Patty Hearst disappeared public confidence in the G-men was badly eroded; by the time she was arrested the figure was down to 37 percent. HER-NAP's occurring when it did put the government's credibility squarely on the line, and for nineteen months FBI Director Clarence Kelley was asked about Patty at every single news conference. By the time the case came to trial *Newsweek* estimated the FBI had spent $5 million trying to find the missing girl. Although the Bureau printed WANTED! posters in Spanish and distributed 60,000 flyers throughout Mexico and Central America—BUSCADOS POR EL FBI!—Patty never made the famous list of Ten Most Wanted Criminals. That would merely have drawn further attention to an already embarrassing situation; only four of the ten people then on the list were old-style criminals—dangerous bank robbers and killers. The other six were political fugitives who by then had managed to elude the government manhunt(s) for some time. Like Bernardine Dohrn, Cathy Wilkerson, Kathy Boudin, Mark Rudd, Susan Saxe, and Susan Powers, Patty and the Harrises simply dropped out of sight among the general populace. Following Chairman Mao's formula, they became invisible fish in the stream of the general populace.

Had it not been for the massive, televised overkill by the Los Angeles police, it is doubtful that they could have found such ready refuge "underground." To imagine the radical underground as a distinct stratum in American society is to fall for a media myth. But there is "a loose network of old friends and comrades from the decade of resistance [to the Vietnam War]. And here, with entrée, political fugitives ranging from draft resisters and military deserters to 'retired' protest bombers of the sixties find refuge, but it is a principled subculture of sanctuary.

It is rarely open to the violent fringe of the Left; until after the debacle in Los Angeles, it was not open to the SLA."*

Despite the disappearance of the survivors, the HERNAP story was too good to drop. It had acquired its own momentum, and the words "Patty Hearst" still brought reporters swarming to a press conference like flies. Colston Westbrook, Cinque's onetime instructor in black studies at Vacaville prison, was always available for a sexy interview. Coquettish and sulky in his weird goggles and crocheted, rainbow-colored cap, he speculated that five, perhaps ten members of the SLA were still at large and could indeed be backed by agents of a foreign government. Westbrook's rumored past as a CIA spook in Southeast Asia lent his statements a vague credibility. Joe Remiro, speaking from the Alameda jail, saluted Patty and the Harrises: "You are the true revolutionaries! You have made good the pledge of George Jackson to haunt the pig from the grave." Mrs. Christine Johnson, a neighborhood black woman who was seen staggering out of the besieged house after the shooting began, said Willie Wolfe had told her that the reason Patty was not inside was because "we sent her away out of love."

In point of fact, Patty told the jury, she was in Berkeley, meeting several of the people who would help her survive the FBI dragnet: Kathy Soliah, James Kilgore, and Jack Scott, "a writer and some kind of athletic director," who "offered to help get the three of us across the country to a safe place," where he planned to write "a propaganda book" about the SLA.

As for me, I remembered, I had gone home to Long Island to try to figure out what was going on, and what to do next. I had found bugs in my apple trees, weeds in the asparagus bed. My daughter had decided to live permanently with her father and stepmother; I was alone in the house. Patty's FBI "wanted" poster hung on the wall of our village post office. In a neighboring village some teenagers had sent a tape to the local radio station threatening to assassinate the police chief. In California schoolchildren on a bus bound for Disneyland had changed their minds and voted to visit the charred ruins on East Fifty-fourth Street instead. The SLA had passed into the folklore.

At the Sacramento County Courthouse, Remiro and Little were convicted of killing Marcus Foster and related crimes. The evidence was only circumstantial and scarcely added up to Thoreau's trout in the milk. At best, the jury saw a collection of minnows: guns, cyanide

*Vin McLellan and Paul Avery, *The Voices of Guns* (New York: G. P. Putnam's, 1977), p. 414.

(201)

bullets, SLA literature, and a map found in the Concord house that Nancy Ling Perry and Russ Little had rented as SLA headquarters. The most damaging testimony had come from Rudy Henderson, proprietor of Fruity Rudy's orange-juice stand, where Nancy once worked. He testified that shortly after Dr. Foster was murdered, Nancy confided to him that she, Wolfe, and DeFreeze had done the deed. SLA Communiqué No. 1 had arrived at Berkeley radio station KPFA the next day. That document, decorated with the seven-headed–cobra symbol, served "notice on the Board of Education and its fascist supporters that The Court Of The People have issued a Death Warrant on All Members and Supporters of the Internal Warfare Identification Computer System. This SHOOT ON SIGHT order will stay in effect until such time as ALL POLITICAL POLICE ARE REMOVED FROM OUR SCHOOLS AND ALL PHOTO AND OTHER FORMS OF IDENTIFICATION ARE STOPPED."

As I read this at my kitchen table in the empty house, the whole trout swam into view for the first time, not an evidentiary trout but a psychological one, which could explain the SLA's seemingly senseless first crime. Murder is not easy. In every tribe the new hunter must be blooded. Young marines at Quantico learn to yell "Banzai!" The Manson girls tested themselves on pigs and chickens before the knife was plunged into Sharon Tate's belly. Mayor Alioto had made tidy political capital out of the secret black society of Zebra killers who he said stalked San Francisco's hillsides, randomly murdering whites—any white—a boy on a bicycle, a honeymoon couple, an old lady. The new-made, self-made street guerrillas of the SLA had to prove to themselves that they, too, could kill. They had to move from theory to action. Foster and his deputy, Blackburn, shot down in an Oakland alley, became the instruments of proof. Almost anyone else would have served as well. SLA Communiqué No. 1 was the jubilant cockcrow that blood had successfully been shed.

The surging high of blood and revolution pounding hard now through their veins would carry them, raft riders on the white-water turbulence of shooting and looting, happy and high, strung out on violence, revolution, and righteousness, first kidnapping the evil millionaire's daughter and then redeeming her, converting her into an avenging female goddess—shooting the blood rapids faster and faster until their own inevitable, fiery deaths in Los Angeles.

Charles Garry believed that Remiro and Little would not have been convicted if they had refused to take the stand. Later, Patty would testify that the two "soldiers" were merely in the backup car; still others would whisper that Remiro and Little had not been present, were not even members of the SLA. They were just a couple of prospective recruits who got picked up by the cops, loyally refused to betray the SLA, were spurned by the principled Left, and ostracized to the degree that they could not even get a top left-wing lawyer to defend them. They are now serving life terms for conspiracy in the Foster murder and for a subsequent attempted jailbreak in which they tried to kill a guard by stabbing him in the throat with the perfect SLA murder weapon, a lead pencil.

In the courtroom, Patty is describing the start of the Missing Year. Because of her continually downcast, charcoal-smudge eyes, it looks from where I sit, thirty feet away, as if a blind girl occupies the witness box. After Cinque's death William Harris assumed the leadership of the three-man "army." "I was supposed to 'struggle' with them to rebuild the SLA and be sure the people who had died had not died in vain."

The time has come to play the final tape, the long eulogy to the slain, which was delivered to a Los Angeles radio station three weeks after the immolations. First Bailey draws from this seeming blind girl repeated assurances that she had nothing whatever to do with writing the words we shall hear. As the tape is threaded into the machine Patty really does close her eyes. The reason soon becomes apparent. This message is the most emotional of them all.

After the SLA's new leader, General Teko (William Harris), extends "profound feelings of revolutionary love and solidarity from the Malcolm X Combat Unit of the Symbionese Liberation Army to . . . the Weather Underground, the United Symbionese Federation, the New World Liberation Front . . . all elements of the Anti-Aircraft Forces of the SLA," and numerous other combat groups, real and imagined, the eulogy begins:

> The result of the encirclement by the CIA-directed force of FBI agents, Los Angeles City, County and California State pigs, with air support and reserve assistance from the United States Marine Corps and the National Guard, was that the People witnessed on live television the burning to death of six of their most beautiful and courageous freedom fighters by cowardly, fascist insects. . . . Our six comrades were not on a suicide mission, as the pigs would have us believe. They were attempting to break a battalion-sized encirclement.

As Harris recites the names of the dead, F. Lee Bailey tilts his wheeled seat back like a dental chair and stares ceilingward with the pained expression of a man having his teeth drilled. This seems a gratuitous insult to six newly dead young people, however misguided, and especially to their families—an insult to the very people in this whole bizarre and violent affair who are never mentioned at all at this trial, not by either side. It is as if these legal proceedings are occurring not only in a moral vacuum but in a human one as well. The ordinary American is simply Not Here. Except, of course, in the jury box.

Noting the position of the burned bodies, Harris concludes that the SLA had split into two teams, which

> were preparing to move out of the house by force. The heavy automatic-weapons fire from the front of the house was a diversionary tactic to force the pigs to concentrate some of their forces in the front. The two dynamite-loaded pipe bombs were to be used as fragmentation grenades to clear a path through the cringing pigs, who had started the blaze by firing incendiary grenades into the house. [The dead] died of smoke inhalation and burns before they could get outside. The pigs want us to believe that the fire was started by the SLA. This is pig shit.

Bailey's insolent posture says the same thing back to Harris. "The SLA uses automatic weapons and homemade bombs because the pigs have automatic weapons, artillery, and hydrogen bombs," Harris continues.

Raving now, Harris calls the Foster murder "the assassination of a jive-ass pig-agent school superintendent" and denies that the SLA women are "mindless cunts enslaved by giant black penises."*Cinque M'Tume was a great prophet, a beautiful genius, the embodiment of every black hero and martyr from Frederick Douglass to Martin Luther King, Jr. "Cin was the baddest member of the SLA and therefore our leader." In many ways, over and over, Harris insists that the fallen soldiers did not commit suicide. His evocation of valor, however demented, seems to demand of Bailey that he sit up in his chair.

When it is Emily Harris' turn to speak, she conjures up an image of spontaneous nationwide revolution:

> All comrades, dead and alive, in prison and out, underground and on the streets, are calling on all the people to conquer the fear and join the

*This was the first time the SLA had mentioned the Foster murder since the kidnapping.

battle, realizing what can happen when five hundred pigs surround a house and then are surrounded by fifty or one hundred or five hundred irate niggers firing from their houses, alleyways, treetops, and walls, with a straight and fearless shot, to bring down the helicopter, the SWAT squad, the LAPD, the FBI.

Judge Carter's eyelids close.
Comes the familiar, breathy, Jackie Kennedy voice:

Greetings to the People. This is Tania. Cujo was the gentlest, most beautiful man I've ever known. . . . We loved each other so much. . . . Neither Cujo nor I had ever loved an individual the way we loved each other, probably because our relationship wasn't based on bourgeois, fucked-up values. . . . Gelina was beautiful. Fire and joy. She exploded with the desire to kill the pigs. . . . She loved the People.

On the witness stand, Patty looks acutely uncomfortable. The eulogies sound real. Of all the tapes she made, this one must be the most excruciating to listen to, and the one she is most ashamed to repudiate. Now she is selling out the dead. She weeps again as we hear

Gabi crouched low with her ass to the ground. . . . Zoya, female guerrilla, perfect love and perfect hate reflected in stone-cold eyes . . . Fahizah taught me the perils of hesitation, to shoot first and make sure the pig is dead before splitting. She was wise and bad, and I'll always love her. . . . Cinque loved the people with tenderness and respect. . . . He helped me to see that it's not how long we live that's important, it's how we live, what we decide to do with our lives. . . .

The taped voice states, "On February 4th, Cinque M'Tume saved my life. . . ." It is hard to believe that Patty did not mean these words at the time she spoke them. The girl in the witness box is breathing heavily, gasping for air. The jury is staring at her openly as the voice says,

It's hard to explain what it was like watching our comrades die . . . a battalion of pigs facing a fire team of guerrillas, and the only way they could defeat them was to burn them alive. It made me mad to see the pigs looking at our comrades' weapons, to see them holding Cujo's .45, and his watch, which was still ticking. . . . What a difference between the parents of Cujo and my parents! One day, just before the last tape was made, Cujo and I were talking about the way my parents were fucking me over. He said that his parents were still his parents because they had never betrayed him, but my parents were really Malcolm X and Assata Shakur. I'll never betray my parents. The pigs probably have the little old mack monkey that Cujo wore around his neck. He gave me the little stone face one night. . . .

Patty looks so soft and vulnerable she is more like a blurry watercolor portrait of herself than a flesh-and-blood being. Her mother is weeping uncontrollably. The judge opens his eyes to glance over at Catherine, but I look away. To stare now seems indecent. The mermaid's long song resumes: Nancy Ling Perry and Patricia Soltysik killed Foster. Cinque shot Foster's deputy, Blackburn. Remiro and Little were in the backup car. The Harrises were not personally involved, but "they said it was good that he was killed."

We hear again, this time from the defense point of view, how the terrified girl, disguised in glasses and a wig, was driven cross-country by the Scotts. It must have looked like a scene from a Thornton Wilder play: four average Americans, all wearing spectacles, riding in a four-door sedan, kindly-looking John Scott driving, his wife beside him, and, sitting up straight in the back seat, the bewigged Patty and Jack. The Scotts talked about another son, Walter. "They said that—well, they loved him, because he was their son and Jack's brother, but that he was crazy and sometimes got drunk and beat his mother up." They warned that if Walter found out about Patty, he would go directly to the FBI.

Emily was driven east by Phil Shinnick, a friend of Scott's. Then Jack Scott returned to the West Coast to pick up William Harris while Micki Scott hunted for the farmhouse in which they would write the book. The place was to be "like a writers' retreat," Scott had said.

Before leaving California, Patty was given the new name Pearl. During these car trips or at any time at the various hideouts back East, did Pearl ever believe she had a chance to escape or to surrender to the FBI? Never. She thought that if she tried she would be killed. She feared not only the government but the Harrises, who had often said that mysterious "friends" would kill her if she disobeyed them. Pearl and the Scotts remained a couple of months in the Scotts' New York City apartment. Then, with the Harrises, Pearl spent several weeks at the farmhouse near Scranton, two more months at a farm near Jeffersonville, New York, and finally returned to Scranton for a few weeks before heading west again. At the Scotts' apartment another fugitive joined the group —Wendy Yoshimura, who called herself Joan Shimata.

BAILEY: Did you say "General"?

PATTY *(suddenly irritable):* No, *Joan.*

Did Pearl meet any other people during this period? Yes, Jay Weiner, "a friend of the Scotts," Paul Houck, "a professor from Canada," and another friend, Phil Shinnick. These people all knew "Pearl" 's true identity, but no one was concerned about security because everyone despised the FBI and "wouldn't tell them anything." Work on Scott's proposed book got under way. It was to be partly Patty/Tania/Pearl's autobiography and partly a political discussion of the aims of the SLA, which Scott found admirable. Lists of questions and answers were prepared by the Harrises, reviewed by Patty and Paul Houck, then tape-recorded. Once transcriptions were made, the Harrises had the tapes destroyed because Patty's voice sounded "forced," and her answers to the questions were "not radical enough." Patty helped type the manuscript, penciled in some corrections, and contributed some material "in her own language" to the final draft. But the part that describes her relationship with her parents is in the Harrises' language only. This section includes such phrases as "My parents hired nurses and governesses to take care of us because they didn't want to do it themselves. My parents were the last people that I would go to to talk about anything . . . my parents never listened . . . I hated my parents . . . I fell in love with Steve and I felt very secure . . . because Steve would change my name and rescue me from being 'a Hearst.' " But Patty assures the jurors she "didn't have anything to say about" these particular sentences.

"Pearl" was a "travel name," to protect Patty's true identity while the fugitives were on the road. The Harrises' travel names were Frank and Eva. Frank sometimes became angry with Pearl, Patty says, commencing to tremble again. If she "wasn't being respectful," Harris would hit her. During the Missing Year he gave her four black eyes. At least ten people knew Pearl's true identity during the Missing Year: the Harrises, the four Scotts, Phil Shinnick, Jay Weiner, as well as Paul Houck, and, of course, Wendy Yoshimura. But Patty makes it very clear that Wendy was never an SLA member, "just a fugitive."

In a sense, Wendy Yoshimura had been a fugitive all her life, first from her native land, which rejected her at birth. This event occurred behind barbed wire in a Japanese "relocation camp" near Death Valley,

California, during World War II. After the war her embittered parents, both American-born, returned to the island near Hiroshima that their forefathers had left a generation before, and Wendy experienced a kind of double exile, feeling no more at home in Japan than she had in the United States. Back in California, ten years later, after the American occupation of Japan had ended and there were no more jobs left at military bases for English-speaking Nisei like Wendy's father, the girl still felt alone, and now she was made to feel freakish as well. Because her English had deteriorated during her years in Japan, California school officials put the tall, shy twelve-year-old into the second grade. Not until college—when she moved away from Fresno's all-Japanese community and came to Oakland, became involved in antiwar politics, fell in love and went to Cuba with her lover, William Brandt, as part of a volunteer Venceremos Brigade to help harvest the sugar crop—did Wendy begin to develop a sense of "belonging." Soon after that, Brandt was picked up by police, and Wendy disappeared. In 1974 and 1975, recruited now by the Harrises as a companion for Patricia Hearst, the most wanted criminal in the country, Wendy was a fugitive still. Yet if anybody had reached out to Patricia Hearst during her ordeal and tried to help her for her own sake, with no ulterior motives, political, financial or personal, it seemed to be this Japanese-American young woman about whom so little was known.*

At the farmhouse, Patty testifies, she and Wendy and the Harrises spent their time jogging, practicing search and destroys, running obstacle courses, rehearsing rolls and dives, and training for armed combat, using weapons owned by the Scotts. In late September or October 1974 the group headed back west, first to Las Vegas, where Scott's parents operated a motel. A year later Patty was living in San Francisco with Steve Soliah and Wendy Yoshimura.

On the morning of September 18, 1975, when Tom Padden came up the back stairs, Patty was in the kitchen doorway. "FBI. Freeze!" he yelled. "Come out or I'll blow your head off!"

"When you first heard the words 'FBI,' what did you think?"

"I thought I was dead."

Patty was arrested and put in a cell next to that of Emily Harris, who

---

*When Wendy was first arrested, her attorney suggested she compose a brief autobiography, both as a means of killing time and as the first step in preparing her defense. So, in neat script on a blue-lined prison tablet, Wendy wrote out her life history. I found it a most affecting document.

told her she'd better not talk to her lawyers or the Harrises would be charged with kidnapping, "and that better not happen, or somebody would kill me." A woman deputy filling out forms asked Patty her occupation. "I just shook my head and said I didn't have a job." But the woman said, "We have to have an occupation," so Patty replied, "Urban guerrilla." She was brought into court almost immediately, wearing the same clothing in which she'd been arrested, and was photographed in the police car, grinning and giving a raised-fist salute. Why did she do this? "Because I . . . because I knew that's what I was supposed to do."

Patty's attorneys, the Hallinans, came to her with a bail affidavit based on information obtained "from Wendy and others," and although it was incorrect, Patty signed it at the Hallinans' direction.

"Do you recall on the twenty-sixth of September meeting me in San Mateo County Jail?"

"Yes."

"Up to that time had you understood that an application for bail would be pursued?"

"Yes."

"As a result of a conference we had, was that application *not* pressed, so to speak? And have you remained in the San Mateo County Jail from the time of your arrest in September until today?"

"Yes."

"And do you know why no effort has been made to get you out on bail?"

"Yes."

"Why?"

The prosecutor says the question is irrelevant. Bailey says his client's present state of mind is highly relevant, and Carter agrees.

BAILEY *(repeating his question):* Why?

PATTY: Because I'd be safer in jail.

And there we have it. Her "friends" were now enemies, her "enemies" friends. Her lawyers' patient program of "reverse brainwashing" seemed to be well under way.

Not that F. Lee Bailey had ever had much doubt it would work. Nor much reticence in talking about it, for that matter. I vividly recalled the day that Judge Carter ruled Patty legally fit to stand trial. For six weeks after her arrest reporters had nothing to report. Patty had languished in the relative isolation of the San Mateo County Jail, talking only to lawyers and doctors. She also had had long and cordial or short and painful visits with her family, depending on whose newspapers one read. Details of her existence were sparse. She chain-smoked; she was crocheting a ski mask for Al Johnson. She had talked to no members of the press except, of course, those to whom she was related by birth, and their reactions were unknown. Her normally gregarious father had ceased giving interviews. Her mother had labeled all reporters "ghouls," an attitude at that point not difficult to understand.

Now the ghouls, about a hundred-strong, had fought their way into Carter's courtroom and scrambled for seats. But it was impossible to see through the phalanx of burly marshals. Threats were coming to the jail and to the family every single day, Patty's attorneys told us, and security was tight. Then a crack had appeared in the row of beefy shoulders, and a small, pale girl was suddenly *there*, as if materialized by The Great Zombo. She was tiny and jailhouse sallow, with a copper coin's profile, Roman nose, red-gold hair gone dark at the roots, no makeup, dressed in a matronly brown pants suit. She had looked like a mental patient dressed in civvies for a court appearance. She also looked composed, but she did not look around. Directly behind her, in a straight line, sat her team, their faces rigid, formal, and familiar as figures painted on a billboard. Dad wore the patient, horn-rimmed glasses; Mom, the cotton-candy hair. F. Lee Bailey wore powder-blue stripes that nicely brought out the color of his eyes, which were narrow.

Browning had said his understanding of the law was that if a defendant is competent, proceedings must move forward, and he asked for the earliest possible trial date in accordance with the principles of due process. Bailey had said this was a unique case, "in civilian courts, at least," and that Dr. West and Dr. Singer's joint report was "one of the most detailed examinations of a criminal defendant I've ever seen." And he had added, "The preparation of a defense requires a person who is nondisabled. Your Honor, I have got to have more than a piece of meat to defend."

Browning had pointed out that two of the four court-appointed doctors explicitly said Patty was competent, adding, "The law says the defendant needs a 'reasonable' degree of rational understanding. It doesn't say she needs a 'maximum' degree of competence. Nowhere in Dr. West's report can we find conclusions she's *incompetent*. The Speedy Trial Act is not a defendants'-rights bill. It's a government's-rights bill."

"A public-rights bill," Carter had corrected him, adding that he would study the complex and lengthy reports further and rule in writing in a few days.

That night the Baileys and Al had invited me to a kind of semivictory dinner at the town's most expensive restaurant. Margaritas bloomed across the tabletop, and Linda was all in silver, with a curly red wig. Lee was happy with the day's work, glad to have it in the trial record, and on the front pages, that Patty had been treated like a prisoner of war for twenty months. In fact, he confided, Patty had been kept in the closet until three days before the bank robbery, and she was able to keep track of time only by her menstrual periods. Dr. West's report described all this in detail, he assured me.

A waiter distributed menus and without consultation Bailey had ordered for everybody: watercress soup and *fruits de mer*—creamed seafood in pastry cups. Another drink, more wine; he was growing expansive. "Watch out for Al," he had told me. "He's a con man, a *great* con man!"

During dinner Bailey kept talking. "Right now we are brainwashing her in reverse, using the good-cop–bad-cop approach. Frankly, it's not hard. She has a lot of confidence in Al, and she has no deep political convictions. She's easy meat."

"But how will you get her to betray the Harrises?"

"*They* betrayed *her!*" he had shouted. "They tried to make money by selling her story in a book! Look, a trial is a play. It's not a matter of who is right and who is wrong. It's giving the jurors a play they can relate to."

Then, sopping up the last bit of lobster sauce, he had pointed to his empty plate. "Ooooh, look!" he said. "I just ate a patty shell!"

Now Bailey is asking Patty to name the doctors who examined her at the jail. "*All* of them?" she says, and Carter permits himself a prim grin. But Bailey is after the name of the first person to whom she related the events about which she has been testifying. Doctors West and Singer, she says. Did Bailey or Johnson ever interrogate her about these events *before* the West/Singer psychiatric reports were filed with the court? No. Does Patty still fear the Harrises? "Yes. I think there is a good chance I could be killed, because—"

"May we approach the bench, Your Honor," Browning interrupts. Carter dismisses the jury in order to hear a motion on a matter of evidence. The government believes the defense is about to bring up the bombing two days ago at San Simeon, as well as the more recent threats made against the life of Randolph Hearst. These are events of which the jury is, and should remain, unaware, as they have no bearing on the case.

The jury certainly *should* know of the newest threats, Bailey says. On the final SLA tape William Harris endorses the very same organization that made the threats, the New World Liberation Front. San Simeon *was,* in fact, bombed, and "the usual radical garbage" aside, the NWLF communiqué attempted to extort still another quarter-million dollars from Randolph Hearst, to pay for the Harrises' defense. It also warned Patty to "stop the lying that is designed to free Miss Hearst and bury the Harrises." What does this new threat have to do with testimony on matters that occurred two years ago? Carter asks, becoming testy.

It is a typical example of the sort of thing that has terrorized his client from the day she was kidnapped by "these same people."

What "same people"? snaps the judge.

The Harrises, of course!

Browning explodes. "Can you prove any connection between the Harrises and the bombing of San Simeon?"

The judge is not pleased to be interrupted by the United States attorney. "I'll hear from you at the appropriate time, but I don't want these outbursts."

Whether the threat is real or not is obviously not relevant, Bailey admits. But whether Patty believes it to be real and to have been issued at the request of the Harrises in order to continue their two-year terrorization of her and her family is most certainly relevant. Further, it tends to rebut the notion Browning is trying to sell to the jury: that Patty has no fear of the Harrises.

I find the argument persuasive, but Judge Carter does not. "Mr. Bailey, I'm not going to have this blown up out of all proportion," he harrumphs, and he decides the jury should remain ignorant of the threats. Bailey demands it be in the record nonetheless that dangerous radicals remain on the loose and that his client and her parents remain their prime targets. "If that isn't relevant to this case, *she* isn't relevant to this case!" he cries.

Since the jury is still out, Browning brings up another matter: His opportunity to cross-examine Patty is fast approaching, and Mr. Bailey's direct examination "leaves out a considerable amount of time," approximately a year, during which period Browning has documents that indicate Patty was living in Sacramento and was "out casing banks with the Harrises. I want to cross-examine her on that."

"You may *not!*" Bailey fairly shouts.

But Browning says once more that he has a two-page "laundry list" of how to rob a bank, which list bears Patty's fingerprints, and he also has a record in Patty's handwriting of the actual surveillance of a specific Sacramento bank. Surely such documents are relevant to a bank-robbery case. Bailey reminds Carter that he has already ruled to exclude these documents. Carter says he'll rule again, if necessary, when the time comes, but he will not prejudge.

The jury returns, and Bailey makes a few final points. Although Patty had no intention of using the many guns found in her apartment, she kept them cleaned and loaded in case William Harris should drop by. Otherwise, "he would have started yelling and screaming." In fact, however, Harris had not dropped in. Nor had Patty ever visited the Harrises' apartment.

"Thank you," Bailey says. "That concludes direct examination."

It is late Wednesday afternoon, two days before the defendant's twenty-second birthday, and James Browning rises to cross-examine. His manner is quiet, his mode humdrum. Reminding us that Patty had said she was an apolitical person who was made aware for the first time by the SLA of the injustices of American society, Browning inquires about the books found in the defendant's apartment: works by Lenin, Marx and Engels, George Jackson, and Che Guevara, and titles such as *Who Rules America?, The Wobblies: The Story of Syndicalism in the United States, Guerrilla Movements in Latin America,* and *Explosives and Homemade Bombs.* With the possible exception of the last-named volume, all this sounds to me like the standard bookshelf of any college student of contemporary political movements. As Patty herself says, "I was interested in social change."

"Violent social change?"

"No."

As cross-examination proceeds the four defense lawyers watch Patty like new owners of a thoroughbred on a strange track. It is a fast track, and the filly looks good. Browning is inquiring about a sheaf of typed papers headed "Anarchism, Trotskyism, Marxism, Leninism, and Maoism," found in Patty's bedroom. She isn't positive who typed them, but believes it was Jim Kilgore. Before she can say more, Bailey rushes to the bench for another off-the-record conference, seemingly to deter any reference in the jury's presence to the Missing Year. While the lawyers whisper Patty flashes her sisters a near-invisible smile. And when Browning again inquires about Kilgore, there is a tiny bit of spunk to Patty's reply: "I told you. I met him in Berkeley. Before I met Jack Scott."

By day's end Patty has implicated twelve persons, and laid the groundwork for authorities in Alameda County to charge the Harrises with kidnapping. Important legal consequences will flow from today's events, but I am more interested in the psychological implications. All day I have been aware of the defense psychiatrists massed on the left side of the courtroom, watching intently, preparing themselves for their own days in court, their opportunity to offer professional, scientific explanations of this young woman's strange mental state, to spread out their years of study of human behavior like Arab merchants unrolling fine-woven carpets, bolts of Venetian damask, pennants of Chinese silks, before the jury's bedazzled eyes. Yet these psychiatrists look uncomfortable. During recess they huddle apprehensively with one another and their womenfolk. One is stringy, one is rotund, each is magisterial, and one is even piercing-eyed. None appears to like what he sees happening here. It is a poor mix, psychiatry and law. The courtroom is an adversary world. These men come from another world. They are dealers in nuance, brokers of doubt, ambiguity-graders by trade. A world of infinite shades of gray is their natural environment. A lawyer's world is black-and-white. Because Bailey is a criminal lawyer, his canvas is often slashed with red. If a pastel is needed, a subtle shade of gray or pink, the master painter will stir it up himself, mixing not a drop more than he needs. Bailey is a supreme courtroom artist. At times he paints by the numbers, filling in prescribed areas as all trial lawyers must, then adds a surprise impasto slash to show the maestro's touch. In cross-examination, he can paint a white area black or wash a red area almost white. Sometimes, for emphasis, he hurls a paint pot full in the jury's face.

Thursday, February 19

Describing to Browning her abduction and the geography of the double duplex-apartment complex in Berkeley, its walkway, stairs, ramp, and basement garages, Patty is so precise that a builder could reproduce the structure from reading the trial transcript. As the kidnap car sped through the darkness, she says, a policeman flagged it down, and Cinque warned her to be quiet "or we'll blow your head off." But the cop simply reminded the driver, Patricia Soltysik, to turn on her lights, and waved them on.

Browning questions the item-by-item details of the kidnapping as they are described in the "Tania Interview." Patty acknowledges that many statements of fact in the manuscript are correct, but "the whole tone is incorrect," she says, "because it was written to show that they were nice to me and that's why I joined them."

BROWNING: They lied to you about Weed, did they not?

PATTY *(tears starting):* They lied to me about a lot of things.

Reading from last Friday's testimony, Browning inquires about the watch she said the SLA took from her. Bailey interrupts: Patty said *wallet,* not *watch.* The error is the court reporter's, and it strikes me as a fairly substantial mistake, which encourages me to continue keeping my own home-baked transcript on the yellow legal pads.

Browning suddenly inquires about a ring Patty wears in the famous Tania-as-guerrilla photograph, the one that was sent to her parents on April Fools' Day and later became a best-selling poster. In it, she cradles a carbine and poses before the red cobra banner. Where did the ring come from? "Cinque." What type of ring was it? "Just a band." But she hasn't had the ring for at least a year. The jury looks at Patty intently.

Browning casually passes along to a few questions about her clothing and then asks about Cinque's interrogations in the closet. Cinque had inquired about her family in some detail, and "I told him about everybody I could think of—because I was sure he already knew it." The mention of *family* triggers fresh tears.

Then suddenly Browning is talking about rings again. What about the ring she was wearing when she was arrested? That was a different ring. Yes, but that ring has since been withdrawn, has it not, from the property custodian at the jail? Yes. (The next day the *New York Times* reports that the person who withdrew the ring was one of Patty's defense attorneys.)

Next Browning reminds us of the unwisdom of asking a question to which one does not know the answer. Browning presumes Patty was allowed elementary hygiene. "You *were* given a toothbrush, I take it?"

"I think it was just the toothbrush that everyone used." A compassionate shudder sweeps the courtroom. How revoltingly un-American!

A recurring dilemma for the legal illiterate like myself is to decide who is lying and who is just not telling the truth. It helps to be a journalist, a profession in which one seems to develop a sixth sense for truth, a not-quite-audible *ping* sound in the inner ear when an incontrovertible truth is heard. One heard it long ago about Auschwitz and Hiroshima, and more recently in other improbable stories about CIA assassins, germ warfare, a criminal President. But mine is a poor, one-sided intuition; alas, I have never learned to recognize the corresponding *ping* when I am being lied to. Right now I believe that probably none of the lawyers is telling the full truth, and yet every witness is telling his own truth. As for Patty, I am convinced to a moral certainty and beyond reasonable doubt that she, like my own fourteen-year-old daughter, Kathy, is one of those rare people who never, ever lies. All her life, Patty, again like Kathy, and not at all like me, has been a literal-minded girl, and bravely, even brazenly outspoken. At the age of twelve, after all, Patty was thrown out of a convent school for telling a nun to go to hell.

The trouble is that though I know Patty never lies, I am not so sure about Tania or Pearl or Pat—and one does not really know who is sitting up there in the witness box. The sense that every player in this courtroom masque is to some degree lying or, to put the matter another way, that everybody is to some degree telling the truth keeps one alert for cues to the reality behind the mask. One such cue is contained in Patty's answer to Browning's next question: Do you know whether there was a lock on the closet door? Yes. How do you know? "Because I tried to turn the doorknob once."

Once! The tiny word conveys, in a way that reams of lurid testimony never can, the paralyzing dread and hopelessness this girl must have felt during the month she spent sitting blindfolded, in darkness, on the closet floor while on the other side of the door the revolutionaries clicked and fired unloaded weapons, rehearsing war.

Patty looks now like an Edwardian chromo of an injured maiden arising from the veneered slab of the witness box. The prosecutor is reading the Hallinans' bail affidavit aloud, pausing every couple of sentences to inquire whether the statements are, in fact, correct. I can vividly recall my own hoots of disbelief when I first read the lurid tale, which concludes, "Finally, under the pressure of these threats, deprivation of liberty, isolation, and terror, she felt her mind clouding. . . . And everything appeared so distorted and terrible that she believed and feared that she was losing her sanity, and unless soon freed would become insane."

Browning asks, "Is that a true statement, Miss Hearst?"

"No."

Yet one now knows that the affidavit, despite its Day-Glo prose style, was *in substance* correct. So in retrospect one knows that one had heard the *ping* and, not for the first time, simply had declined to believe it.

" 'Meanwhile, after each meal,' " Browning reads, " 'she felt an aggravation of this condition, and all sorts of fantastic shapes and images kept coming and going before her eyes, so that the faces of the kidnappers and jailers appeared to her as weird and horrible masks; that she was able to properly comprehend only the reiterated statement, 'We are going to kill you.' Finally, under these pressures, her mind became more confused and distorted. Further weird concepts and images appeared before her, and she was unable to distinguish between what was real and what was imaginary.' " Now, is that a true statement? No. In fact, you were able to make the distinction, were you not? I think so, yes.

And this muddled answer, from this witness, is as clear a one as we shall ever get. When she describes guns, architecture, schoolwork—concrete facts of any kind—Patty speaks with meticulous accuracy and in explicit detail. She is ambiguous only when describing abstractions or dealing with emotional truths.

Many things in the affidavit admittedly are untrue: that her mind clouded, that she could comprehend only that "we will kill you," that her recollection of the time between the holdup and her arrest, seventeen months later, is "as though in a fog," that she lived in perpetual terror and could not distinguish fantasy from reality, that it was her own decision to return to San Francisco. Nonetheless, she signed the affidavit despite the penalty of perjury, is that correct? Yes.

(217)

ANYONE'S DAUGHTER

Browning moves toward deeper waters: Cinque's sexual torments and the brainwashing itself. But first, one question about another bodily function. Would it be fair to say that the kidnapping was a terrifying experience? Yes. Yet being kidnapped did not cause Patty to wet her pants, did it? No.

What does he mean? I would interpret the fact that she wet her pants when she was captured but not when she was kidnapped as evidence of emotional deterioration. But Browning has put the question so clumsily it is not clear what his point is. Possibly the prosecutor is trying to suggest that Patty was "in on" her kidnapping without actually saying it, since he has not a shred of evidence that such was the case.

Did Cinque pinch one or both of Patty's breasts? She really doesn't remember. A slightly different tone of voice here reflects either scorn or embarrassment, one is not sure. But if Patty herself cannot remember, how could Johnson have whispered that "he picked her up off the floor by her nipples"? Zombo, one fears, has been embellishing again.

Browning could be much tougher with Patty, pressing for more details or pointing out that Patty was not naked under her bathrobe, as Bailey had implied, but was dressed in the shirt and pants given her by the SLA. But the prosecutor is evidently as eager as Patty to get this part of his cross-examination behind him, for he sails into his next question with a Freudian slip that is almost a skid. "Now, at the time you made the first tape, Miss Harris," he begins, falters, starts again, and finally brings out that when the FBI issued a warrant for Patty as a material witness, she was not sure what the FBI might do to her, but she was *certain* the SLA would kill her. Under direct examination, the importance of these two threats had become reversed; Bailey had made it appear that the FBI was Patty's chief fear.

Browning is proceeding through his cross-examination like a novice downhill racer, ankles wobbling, poles twisting, skis crisscrossing, yet somehow staying on his feet and hitting all the important markers before coming to rest. He hits a crucial marker now—namely, the sixth tape, in which Patty confesses to the robbery and says, "As for being brainwashed, the idea is ridiculous to the point of being beyond belief." These were Angela Atwood's words, right? Yes. At no time did you believe you had been brainwashed? No.

"Do you now feel that you had, in fact, been brainwashed at any time, Miss Hearst?"

"I'm not sure what happened to me."

Truer words have not been spoken in this courtroom.

(218)

Browning suggests that what the defense calls "brainwashing" was, in fact, "an attitudinal change" and that Patty had described the process accurately in the "Tania Interview":

> I feel that the term "brainwashing" has meaning only when one is referring to the process which begins in the school system, and is continued via the controlled media, the process whereby the people are conditioned to passively take their place in society as slaves of the ruling class. Like someone said in a letter to the *Berkeley Barb,* I've been brainwashed for twenty years, but it only took the SLA six weeks to straighten me out. I'm not sure how many people actually believed the "brainwash-duress" theory that Randy and Catherine cling to—William Saxbe certainly didn't. However, a lot of people who didn't think that I was brainwashed decided that there must have been some other equally horrifying reason for my refusing to return to my family. Some thought there must be all kinds of bizarre sexual activities going down in the cell, and that I must have freaked out as a result of being gang-banged. Other sick-ass racists were hoping that I had fallen in love with Cin after getting a "little taste." The idea that I had been kidnapped by black men really played into a lot of people's fantasies, and many people immediately assumed that I had been raped.

Curiously, the first person who mentioned brainwashing to me was James Browning himself, back in May 1974. Once Patty was positively identified as having been in the bank, he had said then, "brainwashing becomes the only viable nonculpable defense."

A long table in the back of the Rathskeller, across the street from the Federal Building, is daily reserved for the defense team. Here the lawyers, who have been tied up in court, can confer over lunch with their investigators, who have been working on the outside, frequently sent dashing off to phones, jails, or other rendezvous, their food half eaten. Bailey usually knocks back a couple of Bloody Marys over lunch; Johnson stares glumly into his diet-plate special. The defense psychiatrists have now joined the defense lawyers at the long table and are eager to plan strategy, but Bailey doesn't seem much interested. He is by preference a hip-shooter. Let the shrinks do their job, and he'll do his. Today Dr. Lifton is worried; he thinks it would be unwise for the psychiatrists to comment individually to the press, especially before they have testified; he urges a united front. Bailey is noncommittal. He seems irritated when his experts try to play lawyer. At the other end of this long table the Hearst family sit alone, as they do every day, tightly bunched together, sixty-year-old Randy, surrounded by his wife and daughters, an abbot huddled with his nuns awaiting the barbarian invaders.

Outside, after lunch, blinking in the strong sun, I see the new *San Francisco Examiner* headline: PATTY TELLS OF SLA RAPES. Once more Bailey has scored in his "other trial": He has got the word "rape" into the headlines, and into the barroom and bus-stop debates about the case, without ever once using it in court.

The girl is going to need all the help she can get. This afternoon the moment everybody has been dreading will arrive: cross-examination on her activities during the Missing Year. First, a few preliminary questions. Browning establishes that the Hallinans got the information in the bail affidavit primarily from Wendy, but Wendy got it from the Harrises, Patty says, not from her.

Browning bears down harder. Patty has testified that when she was released from the closet, DeFreeze gave her a choice: stay and fight with the SLA, or be killed. But was it not, in fact, a choice to stay and fight with the SLA *or go home?*

"I said that's what he told me. But that was no *choice.*" Patty in her frail way has acquired some of Bailey's own arrogance. "I wasn't given any *choice.* I mean, that wasn't a *choice!*"

"Why not?"

Tears again. She crumples. "Because they wouldn't have let me go."

"How do you know?"

With great bitterness: "Well, I mean, maybe I should have taken a chance." Her lawyer grins wickedly at his client's put-down of the prosecutor.

Patty's characteristic answer is monosyllabic. She almost never explains, justifies, amplifies, so when Browning asks if she contacted her parents during the Missing Year, her response is unexpected. "No. Because . . . because I felt if my parents—" Tears come stronger.

"Pardon me?"

"I felt that my parents wouldn't want to see me again." This is said with tremendous pain.

"You felt your parents would not want to see you again. Well, did you ever think to try and write them a letter and explain what had happened to you?"

More sniffles. "I just didn't think they would want to hear it."

Browning is cross-examining the witness like an angry parent trying to deal with a naughty child who refuses to admit wrongdoing. I think of my daughter, who has never once written me a letter unless forced to. Not even a postcard. Nor would she write to her father when she was with me. Bribes and threats were to no avail. I don't know why. Maybe she could not bear to contemplate the gap between her two parents, two homes. Browning now sounds like me hectoring Kathy. Finally, he forces out the truth. Patty feared that if she wrote to her parents, they would have notified the FBI, and if the Harrises in turn had found this out, they would have killed her. Now Catherine Hearst begins to cry—moved by compassion or remorse, one is not sure. The fact is, Catherine *did* notify the FBI at every turn. She did not even hesitate to call them when she learned her daughter might have been involved in a homicide.

Yes, Patty and Wendy had had a falling out with the Harrises and, no, Patty did not fear Wendy. Or Steve Soliah, with whom she was living at 625 Morse Street when she was arrested. Where had she been previously residing?

"Object!" Bailey is on his feet. Judge Carter invites the jury to leave.

Bailey says he has advised Patty not to discuss the events of the Missing Year because they might be used to incriminate her in another proceeding. Once again, the lawyers are back on this critical point. "She has a right to refuse to answer to avoid incriminating herself . . . and I have asked for an order that the prosecutor not knowingly provoke the Fifth Amendment claim in the presence of the jury."

A claim of Fifth Amendment privilege has got to relate to some crime, Browning retorts, and so far as he knows, just being in Sacramento is not a crime.

Carter twinkles. "Having been in Sacramento myself many times, I do not take it to be criminal." The mirth of the bench makes me uncomfortable; it is the grinning of skulls. Carter offers the U.S. attorney an opportunity to interrogate the witness now, out of the presence of the jury, and the offer is quickly accepted.

Browning asks Patty where she went after Las Vegas. Bailey advises her not to answer.

CARTER: On what grounds, Miss Hearst?

"On the grounds that it may incriminate me."

So there it is. The fatal words are out. Browning asks the court to order the witness to answer.

(221)

"Well, I will not order her to answer something that will tend to incriminate her."

Browning attempts to frame his question in different ways, to no avail. Each time, she replies, "I refuse to answer on grounds I may incriminate myself." Her repeated refusals are an eerie replay of those of the four black witnesses, who had offered the same boiler-plate answer for the same reason. She does indeed sound like a Manchurian Candidate now. "Refuse to answer. Refuse to answer." Yet, as the litany goes on, I reflect on what a relief it must be to a beleaguered witness *not* to have to think. Oh, the *security* of being a Manchurian Candidate!

Browning continues to act bewildered by the defendant's unwillingness to discuss so neutral and merry a subject as Sacramento. Bailey says the prosecutor knows perfectly well what the grounds for refusal are. "We have had a three-way conversation about them with the United States attorney in Sacramento. So this claim that he is puzzled is nonsense." Bailey is very forceful, strong, and impressive here. "I am satisfied, as a reasonably experienced criminal lawyer, that her answer to any questions as to her whereabouts between Las Vegas and 625 Morse Street could and would be used by the United States government, and other governments, to institute a criminal prosecution." *What* other governments is not explained. Does he mean California?

Browning has one other question: Was there ever a time Patty was away from the Harrises during this period? When she again refuses to answer, Browning looks pained. Surely *that* does not call for an answer that could incriminate her!

"It calls for a very blatant answer!" Bailey snaps. "Suppose, Mr. Browning, that the Harrises were in a bank and she was not?"

While the jury is out Browning would like to discuss other evidence the defense objects to. He mentions "Bakery" again, "a document, with her fingerprints on it, that tells how to rob a bank!" The legal wrangle continues. Bailey, Johnson, and Patty, lined up in a row in front of the empty jury box, cast sidelong, wary glances at the bench. A ruling to admit "Bakery" would be a serious blow.

The prosecution cites *Brown* v. *U.S.,* a case from Carter's own Ninth Circuit, which held that when a defendant *voluntarily* puts in issue a particular matter—in Patty's case, that none of her conduct in the bank or her activities subsequent to the bank robbery were undertaken at her own instigation—he cannot then invoke the Fifth Amendment to avoid testifying about it. The judge agrees to rule.

Browning has a huge mass of documents taken from the two apartments that he wishes to have marked for identification and put into evidence, pending Carter's ruling. He holds up a green notebook, "containing handwriting and a list of answering and mailing services." Does Patty recognize it?

"I refuse to answer on the grounds that I may incriminate myself."

With Bailey at her side to coach her, she says the same words eighteen more times as other notebooks, several money orders, hand-drawn maps, book lists, and so on are presented for her identification. Bailey plays honky-tonk piano on the witness stand, drumming his fingers as they go over the exhibits. "Refuse to answer . . . Refuse to answer." As the Fifth Amendment litany drones on, Patty begins to giggle. Finally, she is giving rote answers without even bothering to look at the government's captured documents.

The judge calls for a recess. Outside, Dr. Singer notes that it is *her* science of linguistic analysis that is logical and the Lewis Carroll mode of courtroom logic that is absurd. Jolly West agrees, adding that yesterday, when Browning once, by mistake, called the defendant "Miss Harris" instead of "Miss Hearst," what had, in fact, occurred was a "psychological mistrial." He also puts reporters on notice that although tomorrow is Patty's twenty-second birthday, there will be no cake at the jail and no celebration; food gifts are not permitted, and Friday is not a visiting day. Does this bid for sympathy mean that now even the defense psychiatrist is trying his case in the press?

Many more documents are offered by the government, and Patty takes the Fifth on all but one—the cassette of her jail conversation with Trish Tobin, taped two days after her capture. Bailey says that "we did not raise the issue of voluntariness as to anything but the Hibernia Bank, and we were forced to do that by your ruling."

The judge doesn't believe he can examine all the evidence and rule on it before Monday. "You just threw a big package at me."

"The FBI threw a big package at *me!*" says Browning.

This irritates Carter, who sees it as a ploy to try to question Patty on the evidence before he has had time to examine and rule on it. "Stop playing ring-around-the-rosy! The buck stops here!" he barks, pounding his bench like his long-ago mentor, Harry Truman, the man who appointed him to it. Still spluttering, Carter orders the jury brought back.

Browning now retraces Patty's movements that summer between the two farm hideouts, in Pennsylvania and upstate New York, and then the ride back cross-country to Las Vegas, emphasizing her many opportunities to call for help. But when the prosecutor asks where in Las Vegas Scott dropped her off, Bailey lunges at the bench like a guard dog. Browning withdraws his question and moves to the matter of the final tape. " 'Cujo was the gentlest, most beautiful man I have ever known,' " he reads again. " 'Neither Cujo nor I had ever loved an individual the way we loved each other.' " Now, in fact, did you have a strong feeling for Cujo? In a way, yes. Did you love him? No. I believe that you testified that he raped you. That's right. When was that, Miss Hearst? While I was in the closet at the Daly City house, after I'd been there about a month. Was anybody else around aware of what was going on? In a flat voice: "As far as I knew, everybody was aware of it."

Was it a forcible rape? He gets no answer and repeats, "Was it a forcible rape? Did you struggle? Or did you submit because of fear?"

"I didn't resist. No."

"And why didn't you? . . . Was it because you were afraid?"

Bailey pounds his fist on the table. He finds this question outrageous. Browning says he merely wanted to get her fear on the record before inquiring whether she *later* developed a strong affinity for Wolfe. "You answered my earlier question, Miss Hearst, that it's sort of correct that you thought highly of him. Can you enlarge?"

"She didn't say that!" Bailey shouts, and simultaneously Patty says, "I didn't say that at all!"

"Well, what did you say?"

"I said I had a strong feeling for him."

"Well, what was that feeling?"

Browning has walked right into it. *"I couldn't stand him!"* Spectators gasp at Patty's audacity, her ferocity, and Browning's bum luck. Spasms of glee shake the defense table. Only in retrospect does it occur to me that Patty's outburst may have been a cheap Bailey plant, though I'm not sure how he could have set it up. One hears the *ping* of truth the next day when the mother of Willie Wolfe tells reporters, "My son was a revolutionary, but he was no rapist."

Browning asks when the rape by DeFreeze occurred. About a week later. "And then he gave you a ring, which you wore?" Yes.

Browning pauses a long time before putting his next question. "Where did *that* rape occur, Miss Hearst?" In the same closet.

The SLA members stood guard duty in shifts, throughout the night, at the windows at each end of the apartment. Patty stood guard, too, even before the bank robbery, but she was not armed. Where were the weapons kept? "Everybody slept with one or two," and the others were in an unlocked closet.

"So you could have gone and got one?"

"And done what with it?" she asks derisively.

"Well, you *could* have gone and got one. While the others were asleep. Weren't the weapons kept loaded at all times?"

"Yes."

It has been a rough day for Jim Browning. He really earns his $36,000 government salary. Every Perry Mason fan knows that a lawyer never asks a witness a question to which he does not already know the answer. Browning has violated this rule with such abandon that he has frightened the defense. "He must have a couple of bombs we don't know about," mutters a young defense investigator as we adjourn.

I say Judge Carter looked very tired today. "Yesterday he was fucking asleep!" Bailey grumbles. In the crowded lobby a reporter nudges the Hearsts' new bodyguard and says, "Packing heat, huh?" A sad-eyed woman holds up a homemade cake decorated with red candy hearts that spell out "Happy Birthday, Patty." "We'll see she gets it," says Al Johnson, tucking the cake box under his arm as if it were a football.

Friday, February 20

When Patricia Hearst was kidnapped, she was nineteen years old. She spent her twentieth birthday bound and blindfolded in a closet. We don't know about the twenty-first birthday; that one occurred during the Missing Year. But this morning, when she awoke on the lower iron bunk of a bare cell in the San Mateo County Jail, it was her third birthday as a captive. At daybreak a bomb threat was phoned to the jail, so the jailers varied the routine and drove Patty to the courthouse an hour early. But at ten o'clock sharp the questioning gets under way as usual. Browning is still hammering at her many chances to escape or call for help. She cannot recall the names of towns or motels, whether Scott bought gas with cash or credit cards. She wasn't allowed to visit rest rooms. Yes, she was alone in the motel rooms while Scott shaved and showered. What places did they stop at on the return trip? "One was . . . I think . . . Cheyenne, Wyoming?" The voice is dreamy, tentative. We seem to be watching a girl awakening from a trance in some remote, unspecified sanitarium in an Ingmar Bergman film, a girl unsure whether Cheyenne and South Bend are in the Midwest or Afghanistan. Patty's dress—a deep white cowl neckline—and her soft vagueness accentuate the nursing-home atmosphere. Browning will have to bear down harder.

"Now, Miss Hearst, I believe today is your birthday, is it not?" he asks, winding up to hand her a very cruel present. You are aware of the date of your mother's birthday, I assume? Your father's? Your sisters' birthdays? Yes. Did any one of these dates fall between April 1, 1974, and September 18, 1975? Yes. Did you ever send a birthday card to any one of those people? No. It is trial-by-Hallmark, and Patty stands convicted.

Yes, Wendy had advised Patty to get in touch with her parents and had even offered help. But "if I had done anything like that, and [the Harrises] knew about it, they would have killed both of us." This sounds a bit lame, and Patty's position doesn't improve when the prosecutor asks, "Prior to your kidnapping, did you consider yourself a submissive person?" Not really. You stood up for what you believed in, didn't you? And said what you thought? Sure, you did. And you occasionally had arguments with your parents, didn't you? "We had discussions, not arguments." Sweet reason prevails. Time to get tough again.

You went after Steve Weed when you were a high-school student and he was a teacher? "I don't understand your question," says Patty, but we all understand quite well. It has been widely published that when sixteen-year-old Patty saw the dashing new mathematics instructor at Crystal Springs, she announced to all the ninety-eight other girls, "I'm going to get him for myself." Patty was privileged and spoiled in the innocent, high-spirited manner of a slightly bruised Nancy Drew heroine. On her seventeenth birthday her adoring father gave her a sports car, a blue MG, and special permission for her to drive on campus was arranged. Patty did not disdain *all* the privileges of being a Hearst.

She acknowledges a few run-ins with teachers at her school. She admits she favored a union at Capwell's, the Oakland department store where she worked briefly before college. You were very vocal about that? No, I wasn't. But Browning has captured SLA manuscripts that indicate that she had supported the employees' demands for a union. So now it is trial by AFL-CIO. Furthermore, Patty did guard duty at

Golden Gate, just like the other SLA members, "so to a large degree, you *were* active. You *convinced* them you were a part of the SLA. . . . Are you a good actress, would you say?"

Bailey objects to the question, but is overruled.

"Are you good at acting, Miss Hearst?"

"Not particularly."

"Are you acting now?"

"*I object to that!*" Bailey yells. His sudden ferocity frightens me and scares hell out of his client, but the judge merely says mildly, "I'll sustain that objection. A little less heat and a little more light, Mr. Bailey. Proceed, Mr. Browning."

Where did you sleep at Golden Gate? In sleeping bags on the floor, Patty replies, starting to weep, her fragile composure destroyed by the outburst. There was also a Murphy bed, wasn't there, which was kept folded up in a very large closet during the daytime? Yes. "Are you sure that was not the closet *you* were kept in?"

"I am absolutely positive," says Patty, crying harder.

Comes now a discussion of the words scrawled on a wall at Golden Gate: PATRIA O MUERTE, VENCEREMOS. TANIA—"My country or death. We shall overcome." Yes, she wrote this, but only because she had been told to. That was the way the real Tania, the mistress of Che Guevara and a left-wing heroine, signed her letters.

Photographs of the graffito and of the Murphy bed are put in evidence. Now the weapons. How was Patty able to distinguish her gun from the others? It had a flat bolt, whereas the other carbines "had an M-2 bolt, which is round." When she entered the bank, she carried no spare ammunition, only the straight clip in her gun. Again one is astonished by the girl's easy familiarity with ordnance. The ugly weapon Browning is now waving around the courtroom does not make her uncomfortable; she answers his questions readily. "Well, I know now there is a clip release button. . . . I know quite a lot about that particular gun right now." But at the time of the robbery she had never fired it, nor did she remove the clip during or after the robbery.

You were acting the part of a bank robber, were you not? I did exactly what I had to do, sure. And you wanted to convince them, did you not, that you were one of them? I guess so, yes. Didn't they give you any extra ammunition? Well, I knew there was more ammo in the car outside. When you looked down at your weapon in the bank, you saw the bolt was open and turned, so that the gun wouldn't fire, didn't you? But you also knew, didn't you, that "in order to correct that condition, one would simply pull back the bolt and let it go forward"? Loud, metallic snap from exhibit 19.

Patty does not react to the sound, saying only, "I just wanted to get out of that bank." But *why* didn't she correct the half-open, inoperative position of the bolt? Wasn't she afraid of being punished if her weapon was in an inoperative state? "Because it didn't make any difference. I was in there just to get my picture taken. . . ." And if it had been necessary for you to fire some shots, too, as you did down in Mel's Sporting Goods in Los Angeles a month later, you would have had to do that, wouldn't you? No. No? Well, what was the difference?

Well, if anything had happened at that bank or any other time . . . Patty stops for breath, then bursts out, "I was always their ticket to get out of anything!" Tears come in freshets. "I . . . was . . . a *hostage.*"

Browning moves on to the mysterious subject of the wigs. If Patty was in the bank primarily to be recognized and have her picture taken, why did they first cut off her hair and then outfit her in a wig a different color from her own hair? Dully, she says she doesn't know.

Back to the captured documents, including one explaining why two bank customers were shot. "Because of our inexperience, we had some pretty rigid ideas about . . . the amount of force that would be necessary to control twenty or more persons inside a bank. Inflexibility is one of the hazards of inexperience. . . ." The last sentence is in Patty's handwriting.

Yes, Patty wrote it, but Emily dictated it. Why would she bother to dictate? . . . You wrote this on your own volition, now, didn't you?

"No. They asked me, strongly urged me, to write it."

"But they didn't dictate this word for word, did they?"

She is crying again. "Yes, they did. The handwriting part."

Browning is dogged; he almost has the rabbit in his teeth. The captured document says the SLA had expected more trouble from the bank's employees than from its customers. "That part is true, isn't it? That was discussed ahead of time?" Yes. And when the document moves into Q.-and-A. form and asks, "Why did you decide to rob a bank?" there is an interlineated answer, in Patty's handwriting, which Browning asks her to read.

"You want me to *read* it?" She is crying heavily now. Yes. " 'There were two reasons. We needed the money, and we wanted to illustrate that Tania was alive, and her decision wasn't a bunch of bullshit.' "

"Now, these words were written by you . . . and they are factual, are they not?"

"No, they're not."

Not factual! In what way are they not factual? The prosecutor is most puzzled. Amid floods of tears, Patty says, yes, it's her handwriting and, yes, the SLA needed money, but "talking about the fact that I'd made a decision to join the SLA" is not factual.

Who held open the bank door? Camilla Hall. Does Patty remember a woman in a nurse's uniform standing at the teller's counter? No. Does she recall telling one customer to lie on the floor? Pointing a gun at another? She has seen these events in the film, but they don't gibe with her recollections. Mercifully, Judge Carter now says it's time for recess.

It has been a rough morning. Questioned about her cross-country meanderings with the Scotts, the defendant has had to say "I don't recall" a dozen times. One wonders why Browning didn't pursue the "actress" theme. When we return, we learn some interesting underground survival techniques: purse snatchers and pickpockets frequently toss stolen wallets and purses into mailboxes, after removing the money, and these items wind up in a special bin at the post office. William Harris, a onetime postal employee, dipped into the bin whenever he needed new identification or credit cards, "and he had a big stack about this high." Jack Scott was "some kind of rip-off artist with credit cards" and also had ways of getting furniture on time and selling it. And he had something called Institute for Sport and Society, for which he received contributions.

The fugitives spent two months at an abandoned creamery in Jeffersonville, making tapes for Scott's book. But after the tapes were made and transcribed, the tapes were burned because the Harrises decided they didn't like them, and the back sides of the original transcriptions were used as scratch paper. Presumably, these are the pages that contain evidence that Patty was the most militant of the three SLA survivors and of the new recruits they attracted—the group Bailey calls the Second Gang. If this is so, it is not difficult for me to imagine the dynamics of her conversion, or seeming conversion. New converts, to anything, are always the most passionate. Consider the joy, the pure evangelical high, that converting Patricia Hearst, of all people, must have given to the others. How pleased her new "sisters" must have been, not to mention DeFreeze. If a poor ex-convict could convert a media princess, there was no limit to his power. He had real *mana.* And Tania, seeing the joy and importance she could confer on these people, whom she had so powerful a need to impress, would wish to give them more and more, would she not? So that the joy and the passion would reverberate between captors and captive, moving her always further and further left, into greater violence and terror, not so much to confirm their mad vision of political and social reality as to affirm their great triumph in converting *her*. This must have been the way it worked. The SLA never dreamed Patty would join up. The notion must have knocked them out! And their delight must have inspired her to try to please them still more, to become the baddest of them all.

"Did you first meet Wendy Yoshimura in the Scotts' apartment in New York City?" "Yosh-you-*muir*-ah" is the way Browning pronounces it, transforming the delicate cadences into a kind of fraternity yell. You were told she was a fugitive? Yes. Scott had once driven Wendy cross-country, posing as her husband. Did Patty know what Wendy had been arrested for? "She hadn't been arrested," says Patty, but is vague about the charges. She thinks it was "bombings and weapons." This is one of the few occasions when Bailey takes notes, awkward, crablike scratchings made with his left hand. The lawyer is self-conscious about his handwriting and rarely writes, but this testimony is evidently very important, though whether to protect Patty's friend or to use against her one does not know.

It is nearly noon, and Browning is asking for an early recess. The morning has passed with surprising swiftness. In the corridor Randy looks weary and defeated, but Catherine seems eager to talk, and buttonholes me. "My daughter is incredibly strong," she says. "If she weren't telling the truth, she couldn't be so strong. She's willing to testify against *all* those people! Why don't they indict the Harrises for kidnapping my daughter? She's *willing* to testify! Because it's all political, that's why!" The corners of her small, perfect mouth turn down bitterly.

"Things have to be in sequence," I say. "A has to go before B."

"Yes . . . but there's something that goes before A!"

I am still pondering these words and marveling at Catherine's flawless, tanned skin, the perfect pink lipstick, and sprayed coiffure as the elevator doors slide closed. A special kind of perfection also marks this woman's mind. It is not a perfection of stupidity, though her single-mindedness can make her appear that way, but a stunning one-track persistence. This evening, on television, Catherine says she hopes that at least she and Patty can spend Patty's next birthday together and points out that her daughter has now spent ten percent of her life in custody.

The next big problem for the defense is the Trish Tobin tape, the one made while the two girls were smiling at each other through bulletproof glass. The buggers were within their rights; only attorney-client jailhouse conversations are privileged, and all jails are bugged. Probably all criminal courthouses are, too, and it is routine for attorneys to warn clients never to say anything anyplace that they don't wish overheard. Whether the Hallinans failed to warn Patty or whether she was so glad to see Trish she didn't care what she said; whether she was foolish, or was a defiant and committed revolutionary, or was so "brainwashed," so self-destructive, or so traumatized by what had befallen her since her kidnapping, nineteen months earlier, that she was unaware of what she was saying—one doesn't know. But Patty said a great number of things to her friend that would be very damaging for this jury to hear, and her lawyers intend to try like hell to keep the Trish Tobin tape out of court.

First the jury is sent out, and then Al Johnson interrogates the sheriff in charge of the jail. It is a relief to hear a plain nuts-and-bolts lawyer, neither bumbler nor prima donna, leading a witness through the familiar locutions. We learn that the jail is on the fourth floor of the San Mateo hall of justice, five cells aligned in a corridor, with Patty's at the far end. She is housed in maximum security, both for her own safety and for jail security, though she is actually confined to her cell only for sleeping. The visiting room has "a bulletproof glass bulkhead containing phone contacts equipped with electronic monitoring devices." When a phone is picked up either by an inmate or a visitor, a light flashes in a control room, and a deputy patches in a recording device. Patty may occasionally have switched phones, and the deputy may not have noticed and failed to switch plugs, so that he was in fact recording a dead line. But other than these kinds of lapses—which did occur— all her conversations were taped. Eavesdropping is routine. The bugs are useful for discovering escape plans, anticipated crimes, and other threats to the public. As a matter of fact, the "attorneys' monitoring room" is the only place in the entire jail that is not bugged. On the sheriff's orders, an hour-by-hour log was also kept of all Miss Hearst's activities, movements, and visitors. Such logs are routine when dealing with celebrated cases or multiple crimes. "And it was certainly not your purpose, was it, Sheriff, to gain information on possible past offenses as regards Miss Hearst?" No, just to keep records.

Now, regarding the Trish Tobin conversation, is the sheriff aware of certain FBI tests later made on the equipment that detected "interruptions in the signal"? No, and he wasn't aware, either, that the log on

Miss Hearst was passed along to the FBI on a daily basis. This was done by his deputies without the sheriff's knowledge. But it is his practice to listen to each day's accumulation of Patty tapes before forwarding them to the U.S. attorney's office and the FBI. No, the sheriff doesn't recall whether he ever called the tapes to the attention of Patty's attorneys.

Johnson now moves to exclude the Trish Tobin tape from evidence on two grounds: It is an unlawful invasion of his client's privacy, and an FBI report just filed with the court implies that the tape may have been tampered with. The prosecution has a counterproposal: Until the judge rules, Browning would just like to ask Patty *about* her conversation with Trish; he will make no reference in front of the jury to the existence of an actual tape. But Carter isn't buying. "Human memory is a frail thing . . . this is why we say the written document speaks for itself." He will rule Monday and meanwhile will brook no more argument from the government. "To use a term of the streets, Mr. Browning, no matter how thin you slice it, it's still baloney."

The jury is brought back, and Miss Hearst resumes the stand. After the fire the three SLA survivors stayed two nights in a hotel in the middle of San Francisco, then went to Oakland, and finally moved to an empty Berkeley flat. Jim Kilgore and Kathy Soliah had the key "because they were supposed to feed the turtles." The notion of armed terrorists feeding pet turtles startles me, but it's all part of the game for Patty's lawyers, who look complacent and by now somewhat porcine. They have been eating well in their Hearst-paid suites but wear their new flesh differently. Johnson is as pink and plump as one of Disney's three little pigs; Bailey looks more like a wild boar, and equally dangerous. Browning, still bean-pole thin, has a large, round, forward-bent, bespectacled head and in silhouette looks very like a dental mirror. He is asking tedious questions about the gear found at 625 Morse Street. Cameras, loaded pistols, tennis rackets, and carbines—more startling juxtapositions.

Patty describes a life of perpetual terror, lived among people who were always armed, dangerous, and on the run. She dared not make even an anonymous phone call. If she were rescued from the Harrises, unknown SLA sympathizers could have killed her. The Harrises "weren't the only people running around who are like that. There were many others who could have picked up where they left off, and if they'd wanted me dead, all they had to do was say so."

What led you to believe the Harrises had this great power over your life? What caused you to believe that if they were safe in police custody

—if you'd turned them in—they could simply, by the snap of their fingers, turn around and have you killed?

"It's happening like that now on the streets."

"What do you mean, Miss Hearst?"

Suddenly Browning sees the trap ahead and attempts to withdraw his question. Bailey is on his feet, shouting, "He's asked the question! Let's have an answer! *A question is pending!*"

Smiling thinly, the judge agrees.

BROWNING: I'll withdraw the question, Miss Hearst.

BAILEY: *May* she answer?

CARTER: Well, I'll let her answer.

BROWNING: I beg your pardon?

CARTER: I'll let her answer.

BROWNING: I may not withdraw the question?

PATTY *(exultant):* San Simeon was bombed! My life was threatened if I took the witness stand! My parents received a letter! *Their* lives were threatened if I took the stand! And they demanded a quarter of a million dollars for the Harrises' defense fund!

The courtroom is in an uproar. Our heroine has come through and done it all by herself. She has given the tightly sequestered jury just the news they need; she has told them what Bailey wants them to hear more than anything else in the world—that terrorists are still around, to this day, *still* bombing, blackmailing, destroying property, extorting money, threatening death, and striking fear into the hearts of decent citizens. Patty has just given herself her own best possible birthday present.

Browning moves on to the moment when Patty was being booked. "Were you joking when you said 'urban guerrilla'?"

"It was the only thing I could think of."

"No objection!" Bailey interrupts again, hoping the jury will infer Patty's confused mental state at the time of her arrest.

Browning offers in evidence photographs of Patty giving the raised-fist salute. One became a *Newsweek* cover, as Bailey is quick to point out. Why did she make this defiant gesture? "I was doing what I was supposed to do," says Patty, looking totally zombielike once more.

The questions shift to Mel's. When Patty fired the M-1, dropped it, picked it up again, fired off the rest of the clip, then picked up another gun and continued firing, "It was like a reflex action. It all happened in a matter of seconds."

The second gun was a reflex, too? Yes, part of the same response. You knew people were on the street and in the store? Yes. You aimed at the top of the building? Yes. Did you tell Tom Matthews you were joyous at being able to free your comrades? Maybe she did, but it wasn't true. In fact, were they not your comrades?

"They were not," says Patty, her clipped and dry tone an uncanny parody of Johnson's, and with that dull, flat echo of Al's cop voice, the long cross-examination comes to an end.

The corridor buzz-talk is jubilant. Jim Kilgore, whom Patty named as the man who filled her apartment with New World Liberation Front leaflets, has definitely been identified as being one of the San Simeon bombers. Patty has held up strongly. The defense mood is very different from that of last Friday. Was it only a week ago that the trembling, blue-lipped victim described how Cinque had pinched her in the closet?

Bailey has a surprise witness on hand to open his redirect examination. Ulysses Hall is not like anyone we have seen before. He is hard-muscled, tense as a steel spring, very black-skinned, and sharply dressed in crisp new denims and shiny white cowboy boots. This one-time cellmate of Donald DeFreeze is a most unlikely White Knight to come to Patricia Hearst's defense and, since the cheery landlady, Mrs. Reagan, the *only* one. Though his posture is that of an athlete at rest, Hall is not relaxed; his body is almost quivering. Mr. Hall's present address is the San Joaquin County Jail. Only his nervous swiveling in his chair recalls the peculiar body tenseness of other convicts I have watched in courtrooms. Perhaps this constant, nervous movement is characteristic of any well-muscled creature that lives in a small cage. Hall stares intently at the jurors, determined, if he can, to achieve eye contact with each one.

In 1970 the witness was serving time at Vacaville and there he met Donald DeFreeze, whom the prisoners even then called Cinque. Both men were active in the Black Cultural Association, Hall as chairman of its entertainment committee and as a tutor in black studies. Bailey shows the jury a large, formal group photograph—the leaders of the Vacaville BCA formally posed alongside the city councilmen of Stockton, California, Hall's hometown. In any Mr. America contest, the cons would beat the councilmen hands down.

When Hall was paroled in 1973, he returned to his job in Stockton and became active in church work. Early in 1974 he received a telephone call from a person he recognized as Cinque, who told him he, too, was out of prison and "intended to get involved in a group." He invited his old BCA buddy to join him, but Hall declined, saying he was already active in prisoner rehabilitation in Stockton.

Hall speaks slowly, in measured cadence, pursing his lips and gracefully moving his hands to underscore points, his eyes sweeping the courtroom like an experienced lecturer's. "I asked where he was staying at, and he said he had no steady address at that time. So you will understand where I'm coming from, see, he made it plain, without saying it, that he didn't want me to know his whereabouts." But if Hall wanted to get in touch with DeFreeze, he should write a letter and head it "Letter to the People" and sign it with his Swahili name, Ngue, and place it on the bulletin board of Operation Reach in Oakland. The date on the letter would in reality be the date on which a second letter would be posted, containing a message or giving Cinque further details on how to get in touch with Ngue. An elaborate communications system, but not perhaps for ex-cons; it adds plausibility to what the witness says next.

When Ulysses Hall heard on television about the Hibernia Bank robbery, he recognized the names of Cinque and Willie Wolfe, whom he also knew from the BCA meetings, and hurried to Oakland to post a letter on the bulletin board. "My purpose was to find out why Cinque would use Patty Hearst, a person worth millions of dollars, and—like from what I read, she was a part of them, she was on their side—why take a person like that and use her in a ten-thousand-dollar robbery?" Four or five or ten days later, Cinque telephoned. "I asked him, 'What's happening, man? Why take a person supposed to be a comrade and front her off' when he could of sent her back home?"

Excuse me. You just used a word that I would like you to explain to the jury. What does "front her off" mean?

"Put her in a position where something bad could happen, she could get killed or arrested. . . . Why use her in a funky ten-thousand-dollar robbery? 'Funky' means something low and no good, you know. He could have sent her home and had a main line to—well, I couldn't even *estimate* the amount of money! He told me he had three alternatives. One was kill her. But I'd been knowing him a long time, and he really wasn't a killer, you know. The other was to send her home—but to cut her loose would just front off the SLA, because she knew who they were! They might get busted. Three would be to put her in a position where she became part of the group. Or should I say, front her off again? Put her in a position where the FBI, the CIA, whatever, would be looking for *her*, as well as *them*."

You mean, make her a fugitive? "Yes. Right. So the only people she could look for help to would *be* them. And I say the trick did work—because she's here today on trial."

At last! Amid all the phantasmagoria surrounding this case, we have encountered a realist, not surprisingly, a convict. Cinque confided to Ulysses that he didn't trust Patty, "so he told her that at the robbery she would have a gun pointed at her head, and if she did anything funny, she'd be the first to be shot."

When Patty was arrested, Hall attempted to get hold of her father and reached a Hearst factotum who journeyed to Stockton and interviewed Ulysses at the home of his brother, Waymond Hall, who is a member of the grand jury in San Joaquin County. Bailey puts a transcription of this interview into evidence.

"Is there any doubt in your mind, Mr. Hall, that the person you were talking to a week or so after the bank robbery was Donald 'Cinque' DeFreeze?"

"I'm sure."

"All right. Thank you."

James Browning uncoils himself to cross-examine. Gently, not alarming the witness, not in the least overbearing, he straightens out a certain sequence of events in Mr. Hall's memory: First he heard Cinque was involved in the robbery; it was only later that the name of Willie Wolfe and the other SLA members became public. Right, says Hall. Did Cinque tell Hall whether he had actually given Patty a choice of staying with the SLA or going home? No, he just listed it as one of his alternatives. Did Cinque ever mention that Patty was a prisoner of war? No. What is Operation Reach? A street drug program in Oakland.

Why was Mr. Hall so eager to reach DeFreeze? Because he was appalled at his buddy's political bad judgment. "I felt what he was doing was counterrevolutionary, against the interests of the people." We have just heard the first genuinely political statement—in a trial that deals with crimes allegedly committed for political motives. The Black Cultural Association did a good job of making its members politically aware. Hall stares hard at the jury for a long time; he wants to be sure they take his meaning. "The main reason the SLA was so hot, I figured, was because of Patricia Hearst's kidnap. If she was on their side, why not send her home? She still would have had access to the money." But Hall's purpose in contacting DeFreeze was not merely to offer a political critique. "You see, like when we all left the institution, we were all supposed to have did something to *help* the black community. And I felt that the thing *he* was doing—he didn't have the support of the black community. . . . I didn't want to *tell* him anything; I wanted him to explain to me *why* he was doing what he was doing." Ulysses Hall, I thought, was making more political and tactical sense than had any previous witness.

Has Mr. Hall ever been in Seattle, Browning inquires. Yes, but he was back in Stockton by the time the telephone call came through from DeFreeze. Will Hall please repeat the substance of that call? "I told you: that he had three alternatives. One was to kill her. The other one was to cut her loose. The other was to put her in a position where she would feel that the only support she had would be *them.*" And did he tell you he was going to choose the third alternative? "He had already chosen it." Did he tell you *why* he was not sure of her?

Hall is becoming exasperated with the prosecutor's seeming obtuseness. "Because the *position* that she was in! She was in the po-sition of being kidnapped with guns by force—what would *you* say under those conditions?"

The convict's logic is so unassailable that the audience bursts into appreciative laughter. Carter stiffens. "Just a minute, ladies and gentlemen. This is not a show. Give attention to this case, not to laughing."

But in the next instant the joke is extinguished as the first crack appears in the glossy façade of the remarkable Ulysses Hall. "Have you on occasion used narcotics, Mr. Hall?" Yes. But he was not using them when he got the call from DeFreeze.

"But you *have* been convicted of one or more felonies, is that correct?" Yes.

"I have no further questions," says the prosecutor, but today, as the fifth week of trial comes to an end, the jurors must have plenty.

Leaving court, a jubilant Catherine Hearst throws her arms around Bailey, and at his press conference the reporters exclaim at Patty's adroitness in notifying the jury about the bombing of San Simeon and the new threats. Bailey merely smiles. "I could spot it coming six questions in advance."

Saturday, February 21

I have been invited to give a talk at Pomona College, in Claremont, this weekend, about my life as a working woman. Certainly it has been a long one—my first job, on a newspaper, began the summer I was seventeen—and work has continued uninterrupted thereafter, despite the demands of education, travel, marriages and divorces and other vicissitudes. Now, in the dawn of the new feminist era, I am considered something of a "role model": Young women in college today like to hear about my life, in part, at least, because they see it as a "success." I see it as the reverse, not quite a disaster, perhaps, but very far from the happy picture of home, hearth, husband, and the vigorous troupe of sons and daughters I had imagined for myself when I was Patty's age. At that age, I was much more like Patty than I understood when I first began writing about her. More and more lately, I have found myself half-consciously matching, comparing, and judging all mothers and all daughters, trying on her life, as it were, and pinning up its seams against my own.

After the speech I will drive down to Los Angeles, where my parents live now, and bring my mother back up to San Francisco for a brief vacation. My mother knows San Francisco better than I do. She entered the University of California, Berkeley, when she was fifteen years old, a funny little kid, five feet two, eyes of blue, with long, blond Alice in Wonderland hair and some weird kind of Edwardian bobby socks, to judge by a torn old sepia photograph I once discovered in the top of a closet. The picture is a rarity. My mother does not keep things. She is not a sentimental woman. She never speaks of her own childhood except to praise her own mother, Fanny, who she says was a saint.

Fanny was a mail-order bride and my grandfather's cousin. He was the storekeeper in the mining town, and when he prospered there, he sent back to New York City for a wife. When Fanny arrived—"about sixteen," my mother said, with black hair and violet eyes—she didn't much like her cousin, who was a dour man, not handsome, and some years older than she. But when she wrote back to her father in New

York and said she wanted to come home, he replied that whereas it would be all right with him, the neighbors would think the cousin had rejected *her*, rather than the other way around—the neighbors being the other immigrant residents of teeming Hester Street, where this pauper–patriarch–wise man lived with his wife and six children, three of them daughters urgently needing to be married off. So Fanny married her cousin, and their first child, my mother, Cecelia, was born while Fanny was, I think, still a teenager. Cecelia probably felt more like Fanny's kid sister than her daughter. Two sons were born some years later; one was killed in a car accident while he was a Stanford student; the other became a doctor.

My father, who was born in Chicago in 1893, is an overflowing, endless fountain of stories, gags, and reminiscences of his boyhood, his eight sisters and brothers, their parents and neighbors, and he remembers new stories even today, but that's about all of my mother's story I know. I long ago gave up the quest for more details because every time I used to ask, my mother replied that the reason I didn't know was that I never asked, often adding that I never asked because I never cared. So I quit asking.

I used to ask a lot as a child because I didn't look at all like either of my parents or my sister. They told me I resembled the dead uncle, the Stanford student, but I suspected a hospital mix-up—or worse. By "worse" I really meant "better," or at least more mysterious, more melodramatic, more *fraught*. Secretly, I suspected that these strange people, so unlike all the other mothers and fathers I knew—fathers who *worked*, who were doctors or lawyers or businessmen; mothers who stayed home, planned menus, shopped—were not my real parents. My own daughter, who is adopted, came along rather unexpectedly, when she was six weeks old, after ten years of marriage and many miscarriages and other traumas. Does she long for her mother to be "real," I often wonder, just as I once yearned for mine not to be? Probably. I don't know. It is hard for her to talk about, especially to me. Now I look a lot like both of my parents, and strangers are always telling me that Kathy, my beautiful, myopic, blue-eyed daughter, looks exactly like me. Kathy and Cecelia have become good friends.

When Cecelia was graduated from Berkeley, she headed straight for New York City and the Columbia School of Journalism, not so much from an abiding interest in journalism—although, much later, when I was about seven, she got a job as a columnist on *Variety* and swiftly became the foremost movie critic of her day—as to escape from her strict Hollywood parents. (My grandfather by now had a prosperous clothing business, and Fanny owned and managed a small apartment house on Sunset Boulevard.)

While my mother attended Columbia she lived in Greenwich Village with Fanny's melodramatic, red-haired, green-eyed sister Anzia. Anzia's name had been Hattie Mayer, but when she decided to break away from the tyrannical, rabbinical patriarch of this impoverished clan and be a writer—an unthinkable notion then for a girl of her class —she changed her name back to its Polish-Russian original and became Anzia Yezierska. Anzia's books, with titles such as *Bread Givers, The Fat of the Land, Hungry Hearts, Children of Loneliness,* chronicle the struggles of poor Jewish immigrants from Eastern Europe, and they sold well and were much honored in the 1920s. But by the 1930s my great-aunt Anzia was in the WPA Writers' Project and lived in one meager Greenwich Village room, where she dressed—unfashionably then—in denim and sandals, and continued to scrawl her now-unfashionable stories in pencil on huge piles of yellow legal pads. Until she came to this country, when she was ten years old, Anzia spoke Russian and Yiddish. From the time I was about ten, she used alternately to demand and to beg that I visit and help her with her English. Anzia was nearly ninety when she died, and she kept writing in a larger and larger scrawl until her very last years. Today Anzia's short stories are in many anthologies of American writing, and graduate students at Berkeley do PhD theses on her work. She was a genuine American primitive, a distraught Jewish Grandma Moses of letters, and though as a child I was ashamed of my great-aunt's thick sandals, her foreign accent, her aggressive poverty, and, most of all, of her fierce passions on any subject, today I sometimes think Anzia is the ancestor I resemble most. Anzia, too, had a daughter whom she did not raise, come to think of it. (When she was grown, the daughter came back to honor and later to care for her mother, and Anzia became the daughter.) But none of this is the reason for the kinship I now feel. The connection is the lifetime struggle with the words on the yellow pads.

One day, while my mother was going to journalism school, living with Anzia, and trying on the side to become an all-out flapper (a role for which, I believe now, she had the zest but lacked the requisite silliness), she went on a picnic and met a talented and successful composer named Milton Ager, and pretty soon she married him, the service being performed in New York's City Hall by yet another songwriter, James J. Walker, who also happened to be mayor. Fanny came east for the wedding, and Milton adored her from the first moment they met, as everyone always did, including me.

I was born in Manhattan the same year my father wrote "Ain't She Sweet." Three years after that, somewhere after "Hard-Hearted Hannah" and before "Happy Days Are Here Again," came my sister, Laurel. Though we grew up in New York City, we made frequent summer trips to California to visit our grandparents, and in the late 1930s we lived for several years in Beverly Hills while our parents had movie-writing jobs. When *Life* magazine decided to transfer me from the New York headquarters to its Hollywood bureau in 1954, my entire family was ready to troop back west again. My parents and sister and her husband and daughter, Soft-Hearted Hannah, have lived in California ever since.

All this is by way of saying that my mother knows her way around, including around San Francisco, and that she is a woman to be reckoned with.

Although I had no idea how I could possibly smuggle her into Patty's trial, I knew she would never forgive me if I failed to do so. She has never forgiven me for any failure, ever. For a long time I thought it meant she didn't love me, and though I know better now, it still bothers me, especially when I'm feeling weak and worn out, which is a lot of the time. She feels the same way, and has been going around gasping for energy, complaining about insomnia, and saying she hasn't the strength to take another step for as far back as I can remember. I do much the same, but we both keep going, weak if not strong, so I guess it's just heredity.

Knowing Cecelia's inclination to be where the action is, I install her in the Stanford Court, and after a rollicking Sunday-night dinner with friends we go back to Cecelia's hotel for a nightcap. (We've always called her Cecelia. Our parents greatly respected language, and they didn't believe in baby talk, nor in any other special indulgence for children. Being forced to say "urinate" instead of "wee-wee" and "bowel movement" instead of "number two," as everybody else did, was bad enough. But when my sister and I realized we weren't allowed to say "Mommy" and "Daddy," either, we retaliated by refusing to call this pair of tyrants "Mother" and "Father.")

In the hotel bar Cecelia and I encounter a pale but game Al Johnson, and his company is so agreeable that it is after midnight before I get back to my small apartment, two blocks away. Al has said he will see to it that Cecelia is admitted to the trial, and I anticipate a blissful night's sleep. But as I open my door the telephone is ringing. Concord Academy is calling. They have been trying to reach me for more than six hours. Kathy has disappeared. About ten o'clock that evening, local time, somebody noticed she was not in the dormitory. Then they found the note on her pillow: "I've run away, I guess." The voice on the phone says not to worry that the temperature in Concord is only ten degrees above zero. Every state trooper and highway patrolman in Massachusetts is out looking for Kathy. As soon as they have any word at all, they will call.

Week Five

February 23–29

Monday, February 23

It is one o'clock in the morning. I feel stunned. I have no idea why Kathy has run away. There is no one to call: I've just put my mother to bed, it would be pointless to awaken my father or sister in Los Angeles, and my ex-husband, who is also there, would be sure to say it is my fault. In New York, where friends are, it is four A.M. So I stay up all night worrying and watching television and wishing I still smoked, and finally, at seven o'clock, just as the *Today* show is coming on, the phone rings. A voice says they've found her, in a Howard Johnson's, eating pancakes. She had taken her sleeping bag along when she left, and has spent the night in a field behind the school. She told the troopers who found her that she had about thirty dollars with her, and she was on her way to Los Angeles to visit her father and step-mother.

Next they put Kathy on the phone. She sounds a little scared but otherwise okay; rather pleased with herself, in fact. In a funny way, I am pleased, too; I admire her gumption, and say so. But when I ask if she thinks she can possibly finish out the year at Concord, she says no, she hates the place. So I say I'll call her dad, see what can be worked out. A boarding school is not a jail and couldn't and shouldn't try to keep a student who is determined to leave.

I hang up, cry like hell for about twenty minutes, then wake up Kathy's father in Los Angeles and tell him what has happened. Then I cry some more, take a long shower, and when I emerge, the *Today* show is just presenting an interview with Bill and Emily Harris, filmed at the Los Angeles County Jail.

For five weeks we have listened to Patty talk about these two people, and I have been stalking them, with no success, for two years. Now at last I can judge them for myself. William Harris looks slightly crazy, like the mad scientist in a horror movie, and Emily is sandy-colored and slim, with large, hypnotic eyes and a tight-set mouth. Frankly, the Harrises' version of HERNAP sounds every bit as plausible as the one we have been hearing from the witness stand. They say Patty was kidnapped by force and against her will but was never threatened with death at any time. The person who carried Patty to the car had a weapon slung over his shoulder, and the butt may accidentally have hit her cheek, but certainly she was never struck. The brutality, the threats and the sexual abuse are all fabrications. The prisoner was blindfolded, as much for her own protection as for the SLA's. They intended to release Patty when the Hearsts met their ransom demands, and it was best she not be able to identify her captors. The blindfold was dispensed with only after Patty made her surprise decision to remain with the group.

Sexual activity within the SLA was a matter of individual preference, and certainly there was no compulsion, the Harrises say. "I'll say for myself," Emily volunteers, "that I don't feel that one person, one man, can meet all my personal needs and that Bill and I have gotten a lot closer since we've allowed ourselves to get close to other people." Patty could not possibly have fooled the Harrises into thinking she was a revolutionary, they say, unless she really was. The number of times she could have escaped, had she wished to, is "mind-boggling." They didn't even know where Patty was living at the time she was arrested. Seven hours passed between the arrest and the moment Patty gave her occupation as "urban guerrilla," ample opportunity to request protection from the "killer" Harrises. But even then she never did. Asked if they would do it again, Emily replies, "We think that the Patricia Hearst kidnapping was a great success—as far as it went." I'll say!

For Patty's sake, I am glad she will be judged by people who have not been permitted to watch the *Today* show. It is nine o'clock now, time to get down to the courthouse. Cecelia plans to rest this morning, and perhaps will meet me for lunch. Time enough to tell her about Kathy then. I gather pad and pencils, cough drops and opera glasses, and ring for the elevator.

This is a critical day. The judge has promised to rule on the Missing Year and the Trish Tobin tape. On the big days people tend to dress up, as one would for a hanging, and today both Johnson and Patty wear new shirts, Catherine wears a sporty plaid instead of her usual black; even Jim Browning has a new suit. I am out in the corridor at a wall phone trying to settle matters about Kathy when a herd of reporters thunders toward the phones. Carter has ruled that the government may question Patty about the entire period between her kidnapping and her arrest because Patty herself opened it up when she voluntarily took the stand and gave testimony about the events at both ends of that period. He has also ruled to admit the Trish Tobin tape. The law is clear, he says, that a person in jail has no right of privacy, and the tape itself bears evidence that Patty knew her conversation was being monitored. The effect of the double ruling on the defense is incalculable but vast —a terrible blow.

I yield my phone to a reporter on deadline and rush back to my assigned seat. The Hearsts look utterly impassive in their pew, and F. Lee Bailey's face is redwood. He is arguing that Patty took the stand only because Carter forced her to. "In our early conferences with this court, I said we would like to try the Hibernia Bank case, and Mr. Browning would like to bring in everything under the sun. Now this defendant has taken the stand to explain that she did not voluntarily rob the Hibernia Bank. She objected vigorously to evidence of her conduct after the Hibernia Bank, and you insisted on permitting the jury to hear it. She was then required to explain that conduct. Mr. Browning brought in evidence of activity in Pennsylvania, through the 'Tania Interview,' and announced his intent to admit it against the defendant in rebuttal. [So] she had to respond to that. She did not wish to, but had to. . . ."

CARTER: Mr. Bailey, nobody made her take the witness stand.

BAILEY: If you are creating the rule that everybody who chooses to defend himself the only way he can in a charge must therefore incriminate himself *ad infinitum,* that is simply something we have to discover at a higher level. I am simply trying to say to Your Honor that you are wrong when you say that *she* invited these lines of inquiry. She had to explain the circumstances of her arrest when Mr. Browning put them in evidence, and you let them in evidence.

CARTER *(mild, bored, pleased):* Mr. Bailey, don't argue about it. I have ruled.

Bailey drops back to his second line of defense: the physical jeopardy

(247)

of Patty and her family, proved by fresh threats and extortion attempts within the past seventy-two hours. "We ask that she not testify for the very specific reason that in so doing she would name people, still on the street, capable of homicide, who would retaliate against her. Her family is fully exposed, without any protection whatsoever from the United States government."

Carter is losing patience. "Mr. Bailey, I will deny your motion. You can go to the Ninth Circuit, if you desire. Have at it!"

At 10:55 A.M. the jury is marched in, totally unaware that a big scene is about to begin. Carter overrules one last frantic objection by Bailey and directs Patty back into the witness box. Bailey is right beside her, feet wide apart, one arm stiffly braced against the witness box. His stance suggests a pool player lining up a tough shot. Browning's questions begin. Where in Las Vegas did Jack Scott drop her off?

"I refuse to answer on the grounds that it may tend to incriminate me and cause extreme danger to myself and my family."

Physical danger is not a legal basis for refusing to answer, Browning says. Judge Carter warns that if Patty persists in her refusal, he will have to cite her for contempt of court. "You should answer," he says.

Where did Scott drop her off? I refuse to answer. Who met you there? I refuse to answer. How long were you in Las Vegas? I refuse to answer. She refuses to answer questions about what happened or where she lived after Las Vegas, who was with her, what her relationship was with James Kilgore, Steven Soliah, or Kathy Soliah. Were any of these people members of the New World Liberation Front? "I don't know." She is coached in all her answers by Bailey, at her side. Questions about a hospital visit for treatment of poison oak during the Missing Year. Refuse to answer. About various retrieved documents—phony identification cards, notebooks, manuscripts, money orders. Refuse to answer. Refuse to answer. Bailey and Johnson are both beside Patty now, three heads together; the three-horseplayer lineup again, but now the handicapping system isn't working. The jury for the first time is not afraid to look directly at the press, not afraid to smile. One fears that what animates them is the sniff scent of guilt in the chamber. Several typewritten documents contain handwritten interlineations, Patty's in blue ink, William Harris' in red. The prosecutor places another of his plastic-sheathed exhibits on the witness stand. Do you see that statement in that document? Refuse to answer. You refuse to answer as to whether you see that statement on this piece of paper! Yes.

Very well, Browning is willing to climb down into the muck if he has to. This page of manuscript refers to Gelina's asking Patty whether she "was sexually attracted" to anyone in the cell. Patty has crossed out "sexually attracted" and written in "wanted to fuck." Isn't that true? That's not exactly how it happened. Well, tell us how it happened. It was part of a fight. "William Harris was writing this thing in a book about my having to have sex with William Wolfe, and I had a fight with him about it. And what I wrote in there was like the end of the fight because I didn't—I didn't feel like I ever wánted to talk about any of that again. And he gave me a black eye, and that was the way it was left."

But you also wrote in the document, "She said that she would like to sleep with Cujo." Isn't that true? Yes.

Is Patty on trial for fucking, or book writing, or bank robbing? The questions—and refusals—go on and on. Document 118? Refuse to answer. Document 120? Refuse to answer. Is this your handwriting? No. Is that your handwriting? Refuse to answer. Her appearance has changed. She's pale now and looks more furtive than nervous. I show you 135 for identification and ask you to examine the manila envelope and its contents as to whether you can identify any of *those* documents for us. I have examined them, and I refuse to answer. In all, Browning asks more than sixty questions and gets forty-two refusals, although he has not asked one question that touches even indirectly on the Sacramento bank robbery.

This part of the ordeal is at an end, but there is still the matter of Patty's conversation with Trish Tobin. Was anyone else in the visiting room at the time? Emily Harris. "But she was not a party to the conversation between you and Trish Tobin? It was not a three-way conversation, is that correct?"

"Not by any intention of ours, no," Patty spits back.

Browning reads from the transcript of this tape, in which Patty tells her friend she will make no statements until she can get out on bail. But the tape itself is a statement and, for one in her circumstances, a colossal indiscretion. Upon her release, she will speak in "a revolutionary feminist perspective totally. . . . I guess I will just tell you my politics are real different from way back when. Obviously. [Laughter.] Right. And so this creates all kinds of problems for me in terms of a defense."

And is it not correct that Patty's intended statement was to be "in terms of armed struggle"?

Patty says that was Emily's idea, and because Emily was in the room and could overhear her, "I felt that's what I should be saying."

In the course of their conversation, did Trish say, "My mom and dad said to send you their best. [Laughter.] My mom was so happy when you were found, I thought she was going to die"? And did Patty answer, "I was so pissed off, goddammit"?

"Was that your reply to Miss Tobin's remark?"

"Yes."

"I have no further questions."

It is the jury who looks pissed off, goddammit, as Bailey begins the redirect examination, in which he will attempt to demolish Mr. Browning's just-built palace of perfect guilt. Had Emily indicated to Patty what "posture" the group would take during their trial? Yes, lots of "jumping up, clench-fisting all over the place, shouting and defiance . . ." In other words, they would be revolutionaries to the end, right? And that's what Patty meant when she told Trish she was having difficulties with her defense? Yes. Furthermore, the transcript of the Trish Tobin tape is incomplete—"totally a partial transcript," Patty calls it—and Bailey manages to raise reasonable doubt, at least in my mind, about the integrity of the tape: It *may* have been doctored. Last Friday, Patty testified she was still in fear of the Harrises and others. "Do you know if the other people you fear are incarcerated?"

"No, they're not."

Bailey reminds the jury of the threats to the Hearsts and the bombing of San Simeon, and asks if there have been other bombings since. Browning demands the jury be sent out before Bailey makes his offer of proof. Then we learn of another explosion. Last night the New York City offices of the Hearst magazines were bombed. The jury is brought back and informed of the latest bombing. Patty herself learned of it last night in jail on the ten-o'clock radio news.

Browning asks for a brief re-cross-examination. When Patty was talking to Trish, Emily may have been present, but she was talking with someone else, was she not, at the other end of the visitors' room? Yes, "but I could have heard her if I had stopped and listened to her."

About the bombing last night, do you have any idea who did it? "I wish I did," says Patty gravely. (Later the New York City police report that the "explosion" was a firecracker, set off inside a can; no one was injured.)

"Who are these people who are not in custody?"

"James Kilgore, Kathy Soliah, Josephine Soliah, another woman, Bonnie somebody."

Bonnie Jean Wilder? Yes. Didn't you testify just the other day that you were not in fear of Kathy?

"I have reason to believe now that I should be very much in fear of her." Kathy's name has since been linked to the San Simeon bombing. But Patty still refuses to answer any questions about these people that would involve events of the Missing Year.

Browning and Bailey have another whispered bench conference with the judge. It is extraordinary how much of the script for this drama we are watching is known to the principals only—to Patty, the lawyers, and the judge. If I am as bewildered as I am, the jury must be utterly baffled.

No one can judge at this point how damaging Patty's Fifth Amendment pleadings have been or how much credibility Bailey will be able to recover when his battery of psychiatric big guns finally opens up.

At lunchtime a new diversion appears in the crowded lobby—a sandwich board with the guerrilla poster of Tania on one side and, on the other, Patty in her bridesmaid's gown. You can stick your head through a hole and have your picture taken from either side. A college girl has devised and constructed this potential gold mine and lugged the thing up here in the back of her Volkswagen. But she has had a change of heart, she tells me. "There's so much show business here already, I decided not to charge for the photos. I'm just giving them away." Good girl. But I doubt she'll get far in the media business.

After lunch, Ulysses Hall is back. Although Bailey objects that Hall's Seattle criminal record was known to the government and that it is improper to grant an opportunity to re-cross-examine Hall now, Bailey is overruled, and a very different-looking Mr. Hall takes the stand, glowering, frowning, avoiding eye contact with anyone, especially with Jim Browning. After reviewing Hall's testimony, Browning brings up the matter of Hall's police record in Seattle. He inquires about traffic tickets, false names, drunk arrests, parole violations, and several narcotics charges. The effect is to transform the formerly rather noble Ulysses Hall into the appearance of a squirming perjurer and multiconvicted felon. His credibility is beyond recovery, and the last image we retain is of his spotless white patent-leather cowboy boots clumping out the rear door, behind the jury box.

One phase of this trial is at an end. The jury has heard most of the facts—what did, or did not, happen to Patty/Tania/Pearl/Pat—few of which are in dispute. Now we are to hear the important part, at least according to the defense: not the *whats* but the *whys*. It is time for Commodore Bailey to go into action with his big guns. The first of these is Louis Jolyon West, MD, the bulky, genial, fair-haired, fatherly-looking man who now rises, buttons his jacket, picks up his briefcase, and crosses gravely to the witness stand. His professional credentials fill ten pages in the monumental West/Singer report. Today he lists only the high spots, which is like listing the high spots of the Himalayas. Dr. West is professor of psychiatry at the University of California at Los Angeles, chairman of his department and psychiatrist-in-chief of UCLA Hospitals.

His military service includes four years as an enlisted man and eight years as a regular Air Force medical officer. He left the service as a major in 1956. He is board-certified in psychiatry, and has taught at Cornell, Stanford, and at the University of Oklahoma, where he remained for fifteen years and became chairman of the Psychiatry Department. In 1969 he ascended from there to the sun-splashed academic pinnacle he now occupies. In addition, he has held numerous Class A hospital appointments around the country, and serves on the editorial boards of half a dozen professional journals. He belongs presently to twenty-three distinguished national and international professional societies. In 1958 he wrote a book, *Prisoners of War*, and he has contributed to more than a hundred other books and monographs on the subject. The overwhelming credentials are offered matter-of-factly but at enormous length, as if the lawyer is more impressed by them than the doctor is.

Bailey's questions begin on a historical note. During the Korean War, he reminds us, a number of the American pilots shot down over North Korea broadcast on Chinese radio that they had been engaging in germ warfare. This was untrue, and as an Air Force medical officer Dr. West's assignment had been to learn how the Chinese had produced these results in the captured pilots and to figure out what could be done to help future airmen resist these techniques. Systematic torture, hypnosis, and drugs—the traditional means of persuading a captive to change his mind or his testimony—had not been used. Yet of fifty-nine pilots who got the full Chinese treatment—whatever it was—thirty-six broke down completely. Dr. West and his colleagues identified a new triple-threat technique, which they labeled DDD—debility, dependency, and dread. "Debility" meant that the subject was allowed to become physically weak and run down but not dangerously ill. His "dependency" was enforced by making him turn to his captors for every comfort, for food, for his toilet needs. His "dread" was compounded of his fear of torture and death, and fear of reprisals to his family. To get the DDD process off to a quick start, the Chinese used "forceful interrogation"—rapid-fire endless questions to which the interrogator already seemed to know the answers. Isolation was also a factor in this initial phase, intensified by darkness.

BAILEY: Doctor, have you ever heard the term "brainwashing"?

WEST: Yes, I have.

CARTER *(waking up):* What was the term?

BAILEY: Brainwashing.

Ah, yes. The judge nods and closes his eyes again.

"Is that a term of any medical significance?" No. The literal meaning of brainwashing is "cleaning of the mind." Another common term is "thought reform," meaning political indoctrination accomplished without physical coercion. But the best term for forceful interrogation designed to produce compliant behavior is "coercive persuasion."

There follows a lengthy discussion differentiating "coercive persuasion" from confession; an analysis of the different ways Air Force pilots reacted emotionally to having confessed falsely to germ warfare; a long exegesis on the confession of Jozsef Cardinal Mindszenty, the Hungarian prelate arrested by the Communists in 1948 and who, five weeks later, confessed to being a criminal and an American spy. Dr. West terms Mindszenty's description of what happened to him in those five weeks "the classic passage in the literature of coercive persuasion."*

The signs that one has been subjected to coercive persuasion are "a marked degree of anxiety and pressure and an inability to deal with

---

*"My physical strength perceptibly declined. I began worrying about my health and my life. . . . My heart flagged; a sense of being utterly abandoned and defenseless weighed upon me.

"My powers of resistance gradually faded. Apathy and indifference grew. More and more the boundaries between true and false, reality and unreality, seemed blurred. . . . I became insecure in my judgment. Day and night my alleged 'sins' had been hammered into me, and now I myself began to think that somehow I might very well be guilty. Again and again the same theme was repeated in innumerable variations. . . . I was left with only one certainty, that there was no longer any way out. . . . My shaken nervous system weakened the resistance of my mind, clouded my memory, undermined my self-confidence, unhinged my will—in short undid all the capacities that are most human in man. . . .

"After the second week of detention . . . I could feel my resistance ebbing. I was no longer able to argue cogently; I no longer rejected coarse lies and distortions. Now and then I resignedly said things like, 'There's no need to say anything more about it; maybe it happened the way others maintain.' . . . Without knowing what had happened to me, I had become a different person." (Jozsef Mindszenty, *Memoirs* [New York: Macmillan, 1974], pp. 110–14.)

reality." Some repatriated American pilots wept uncontrollably and were unable for weeks afterward to give a coherent account of what had happened to them. Dr. West describes the famous Zimbardo experiment at Stanford University in the early 1970s. Even I knew about that one. A prisoner/captor game, using paid student volunteers, was set up by the Psychology Department. Although the experiment was designed to last two weeks, it had to be called off after six days because half the students pretending to be prisoners broke down completely under the stress, even though everybody knew the whole thing was just a game.

The foregoing testimony has become numbing in its boredom when, finally, Bailey says, "Dr. West, do you know the defendant, Patricia Hearst?"

Asking permission to refer to his notes, the psychiatrist says he first met Miss Hearst on September 30, 1975, and examined her thereafter for a total of twenty-three hours. His associate, Dr. Margaret Singer, whose experience also includes many Army studies on prisoners of war, spent seventeen hours with Patty. What were West's clinical observations of the defendant when they first met?

She was pale, very thin, with a strained facial expression, frightened and obviously on her guard. She had no complaints, however, and rather cheerfully showed the doctor her tiny cell. "But as soon as I asked her for any information about her previous nineteen-month experience it became extremely difficult. She would begin to cry, her eyes were downcast, her voice became almost inaudible, her pulse went up to a hundred and forty, she broke out into a clammy sweat, and she became pale around her nose and mouth." The psychiatrist believed he was watching "a person reexperiencing a profound fear." She could not remember things clearly. She had patchy amnesia." A neurologist who examined her independently found similar memory disturbance. She was hyperconcerned about her health and her bodily functions, and was unable to concentrate. An excessive concern with bodily functions is typical of prison-camp survivors and sometimes persists for years.

Can Dr. West tell from a person's answers to a battery of standard psychological tests whether that person is trying to feign mental illness? Yes, he can, and Patty exhibited no such signs whatever. On that note we recess for the day.

Tuesday, February 24

Prior to her kidnapping, Patty Hearst had no history whatever of mental illness. West tells the jury that her general mental state was not unlike that of other youngsters of her age and background,* but her unusual degree of freedom previous to her kidnap made her more vulnerable to her subsequent confinement.

Patty's transition to her life with her kidnappers was "about as violent a transition as I can imagine, or have ever seen, more violent than any military captive." Soldiers who become POWs have already been hardened by their military training. Patricia Hearst suffered an abrupt and brutal "plunge into another world," which in its acute phase —between the kidnapping and the bank robbery—lasted about seventy days.

When Doctors West and Singer interviewed the defendant last September and October, they concluded that she was suffering from "a psychiatric illness which was misunderstood both by the patient and by those around her." Now Dr. West wishes to read some passages from the clinical diagnosis he filed with the court at that time. A hush falls over the room. The defendant, supporting her chin on her hand, seems thoughtful and serene. As Dr. West drones on, Judge Carter goes to sleep.

The doctor's best estimate of the amount of time Patty spent in the closet is fifty-seven days. He cannot evaluate the effects of so prolonged a period of blindness. There are no data. Even people who go down in caves do not suffer such severe blindness for so long a time. After the second week Patty's time distortions and confusions became severe. But

*The youth scene, the New Left, the flower children, and rebellious youth in general are subjects in which Dr. West has special expertise. After some fieldwork in the Haight-Ashbury district, he published a paper with James R. Allen, MD, titled "Three Rebellions: Red, Black & Green." In it he writes, "The Red Rebellion is political, theoretical, intellectual, and radical. The Black Rebellion is economic, social, racial, and activist. The Green Rebellion is cultural, religious, mystical, and passively pharmacological." (Center for Advanced Study in the Behavioral Sciences, Stanford University, 1968.)

by putting together her own recollections with the recovered documents provided by the government, Dr. West figures that five weeks had gone by when Cinque decided that the best way the SLA could use Patty might be to force her to join their group. Little by little, she was given to understand that joining up would mean she would get out of the closet, need no longer wear the blindfold, and no longer fear death, at least from them. It was a classic example of coercive persuasion. Once she was persuaded to take on a certain role, she complied with everything they told her to do. "If they wanted her to clean a shotgun, she cleaned a shotgun. She tried to blend in. For her it was: Be accepted, or be killed."

The SLA had a little ceremony when the captive was taken out of the closet. She was allowed to eat with the others, and Cinque gave her her revolutionary name, Tania, in posthumous salute to an East German woman and a heroine of the radical Left who had once been Che Guevara's mistress. Patty had never heard of Tania before this.* Everybody in the SLA had a number; Cinque was No. 1, Patricia Hearst became No. 9. As plans for the robbery developed she became more and more numb. She was told that her part in it had a double purpose: to show the world that she had joined the SLA and to prove her own reliability. Cinque had told her that she was also free to leave. But for her the decision was not to stay or to leave. It was to live or to die. The bank robbery sealed her fate because it made her a common criminal. The Attorney General himself had said so. From now on it would be open season on Patty Hearst.

At the defense table, Tom May allows himself a half smile. He is pleased with the way things are going. But now Bancroft is on his feet, objecting that Dr. West is not just giving his psychiatric evaluation but, in effect, arguing the case. The judge reminds Bailey to "develop your thesis through question and answer," not narrative.

*The "real" Tania turns out to have been largely a CIA invention. On December 25, 1977, the New York Times reported: "One of the more intriguing CIA disinformation campaigns of recent years was its attempt to discredit the Cuban revolutionary movement in the eyes of other Latin American nations by planting the suggestion that it was controlled to some extent from Moscow. [The strategy] was to take an East German woman named Tamara "Tania" Bunke, who had joined Che Guevara's guerrilla band in Bolivia, and make her out to be the biggest, smartest Communist there ever was"—an East German secret agent and a KGB agent as well. Though Ms. Bunke is scarcely mentioned in Che's Bolivian diaries, the CIA arranged to "beef up" her part in the English translation of the diaries by feeding CIA-fabricated "material and background" on Tamara to Che's translator, Daniel James, an American author and former managing editor of The New Leader living in Mexico.

"When did her feelings of dissociation begin?" Bailey asks.

"Some began in the closet, where she had feelings that all this was happening to someone else." Assuming the role of Tania, writing "Venceremos" on the wall, taking part in the daily military drills, and so on, gave her a chance to dissociate more, to put the old Patricia Hearst out of her mind. It was like putting on psychological armor and learning to live moment by moment. Among prisoners of war, such dissociative behavior is common.

BAILEY: Doctor, how important is the human impulse to survive and not to die?

WEST: It's fundamental.

I'll say! Surely the impulse to survive is operating in this courtroom right now. If I were the prosecutor, I would ask Dr. West whether Patty's present confinement in jail, coming at this point in her misadventure—after the kidnapping, the closet, the bank, the fire, the Missing Year, and then her recapture by the FBI—is not even more anxiety-provoking than the closet ever was. Isn't her present confinement in the jail even more likely to make her willing to lie to the jury, betray her comrades, sell out, do anything to avoid *further* confinement?

What happens to the dissociated personality, Doctor, when the stress is removed? What is the healing process? That depends on how intense the confinement was, how long it lasted, how old the person was, and what his predispositions were. Our estimate in Ms. Hearst's case was that within three or four months, with good treatment, she would approach normal levels.

Did she also tell you about the incident at Mel's Sporting Goods? Yes. She kept saying, "I can't believe I did that. I cannot understand why I did it." We believe she acted as she had been trained to do by the Harrises without even stopping to think. This interpretation is supported by Patty's childlike question to the Harrises afterward—"Did I do it right?"—as if this were an army in which they were generals and she was just a private.

"Doctor, what is the purpose of drilling in military situations?"

"To diminish the amount of thought prior to action." At Mel's, Patty did what she had been trained to do. She grabbed the heaviest weapon first, squeezed the trigger, and bullets flew out. When she dropped it, she grabbed it again, and more bullets flew. Then she grabbed a second weapon and began firing. "We figure the total time elapsed was about three seconds."

What was the defendant's first reaction when the doctors asked her about the Hibernia Bank robbery? "After the usual tears and choking, her first words were 'It was like a dream.' " She remembered the sound of shots but thought people had been shooting at *her,* and she did not recall seeing the bodies of the two wounded men at all, even though she had to pass by them to get out of the bank. This sort of memory lapse is characteristic of the dissociated state brought on by extreme terror and stress. There are famous examples of concentration-camp inmates stepping over corpses and being unable to recall having seen them.

In making a medical diagnosis, the doctors took into account not only Patty's and Tania's history up to Mel's but "two more and longer phases" of her mutating personality: Pearl and Pat. Tania was her media name, but after the fire the Harrises and the others called her Pearl. She clung to the identity of Pearl even after she was arrested, as long as Emily Harris was around. Pearl grinned; Pearl clenched her fist; Pearl was the urban guerrilla. These acts were characteristic of a person with weak identity hanging on to her most recent personality until she was sure she was no longer in enemy hands. By the time Singer and then West met the defendant, a few days later, she had been separated from Emily, and now was Pat, "a person sort of without any identity."

What can the doctor say about involuntary urination "from a medical point of view"? Loss of bladder or bowel control under the first barrage in combat is well known among men. Less is known about female reactions, but they could be expected to be similar.

"And so, Doctor, what was your diagnosis?"

Oh, no, not again! The government objects as much as I do, but Carter says go ahead, so West plunges back into his notes. "Diagnosis: traumatic neurosis, acute and chronic, with dissociative features . . ."

As Dr. West plods on, describing a person who can't remember things, can't anticipate the future, and who has a profound uncertainty about her present identity and an unusual degree of stubbornness, it occurs to me that he could just as well be describing my own daughter or, for that matter, myself at fourteen. Mercifully, it is time for mid-morning recess.

On the phone I learn that the school will pack Kathy up and fly her to Los Angeles, where her father will meet the plane. Her father. Why did I stay married to him for fourteen years? To stay married, I think. Certainly he was not a charming man, not excessively brilliant, witty, kind, or rich. What great hold did he have over me? I still don't know. But, my God, he was domineering, and, my God, he could make me feel guilty, and he still can, and does, especially over the child, and *that* —I think—must always have been at the bottom of it. In him I had found not my adored father but a personality queerly akin to my domineering, seemingly unloving, constantly guilt-evoking mother, inside a male body. Maybe that is why I could never remain pregnant by him; if I had, it would have been a kind of psychological double incest —and transsexual to boot!

Similar psychological mechanisms must be a part of many women. Perhaps the lovers we choose are more like Daddy, but the husbands are more like Mommy. This is a dark side to woman's nature that nobody knows enough about. That need to be dominated, the feeling of female incompleteness, is very deep, worldwide, I think, among women. Women need men; women without men invariably are sad. In every tribe and race, women-with-women tell stories of sorrow, death, loss, babies dying, children gone, husbands run off or dead in battle. Women-with-women sing only the blues. Men sing the blues, too, but they sing about women or Mom or my buddy; they don't sing for the lost children. Men-with-men are happy all over the world; they go on hunting parties, war parties, they play war games and golf, they tell dirty jokes, they play cards, they get drunk. Men-with-men can relax. They are relieved of the tension imposed by the company of women. Men may need women, but not the way women need men. Freud was wrong. It has nothing to do with penis envy. Women need men because without men they cannot have children, and women who do not have children do not fulfill the biological imperative.

Some men learn to exploit the deep dependence of women on men with enormous skill and tenacity. Among other things, this sense of weakness is the basis of pimp psychology. How does a man get a girl to hustle for him on the streets of New York City and mail her earnings to him in Dallas? I don't know, but I know a prostitute who happily does that. Charles Manson and Cinque were each natural-born pimps; they understood that if you can get a girl to hustle for you, you can get her to do anything. Manson and Cinque were alike in many ways: talented pimps, gun freaks, jailhouse habitués, great fantasts and fancymongers, intrigued by hypnosis and other experiments in domination. Both were men from the bottom levels of society, obsessed with revolution; both were brilliant psychopaths. A psychopath is incapable of feeling guilt. Or love. He is deficient in anxiety. In Alan Harrington's book on psychopaths, which Doctors West and Singer will later urge me to read as a basic text for understanding the dynamics of this trial, one reads that in our age of anxiety, the psychopath is "the failed saint."

On the stand, Dr. West is clarifying his diagnosis: Patty's condition is not like the classic dissociations—dual personality, fugue states, or sleepwalking—but a *traumatic neurosis* (the trauma being the kidnapping) *with some dissociative features.* In repeat IQ tests administered just nine days ago, Patty's performance is up twenty-six points, from 112 to 138, "far beyond what chance could have produced." He attributes these improvements to San Mateo's "very humane jail" and to the Hearsts' and Bailey's and particularly Al Johnson's active, daily involvement with the patient. "Mr. Johnson, I think, was functioning as a psychiatric technician." As a result, Patty's mood has become more open, though she is still apprehensive and emotionally distressed. Her intellectual and verbal skills approach normal levels. She understands things better, and her memory is now near normal. There are still times of patchy amnesia, when she will say things like "If he says so, I'm sure it's true" or "I guess I must have done that"—characteristic devices to bridge the troublesome gaps in her memory. Now "the patient's fears are accompanied by some healthy anger. Nevertheless, Ms. Hearst still has not completely recovered from the symptoms of the *traumatic neurosis* itself. . . ." Dr. West ascribes this to "being kidnapped 4 February, 1974, battered, isolated, blindfolded, and confined to the small closet continuously for approximately fifty-seven days, tormented, reduced to a helpless and physically weakened state, threatened repeatedly with death, sexually molested and raped—"

BANCROFT: I object, Your Honor, on the same basis I did before. The doctor is lecturing and reading from his reports. I haven't heard a question from Mr. Bailey in about seven minutes.

CARTER: I'll overrule the objection.

BAILEY: Proceed, Doctor, proceed.

WEST: . . . repeatedly threatened with death, sexually molested and raped, humiliated in various ways, for example, literally shorn of her hair and so forth, rendered submissive and highly susceptible by the debility and dependency and dread, and finally left without hope of survival unless she gave the appearance of joining the group.

Despite the torrents of professional jargon, Dr. West seems to me a near-perfect witness; clear, modest, forthright; more like an ex-football coach (which he used to be) than a heavyweight psychiatrist. When he solemnly reports that despite her newfound anger, Patty still trembles whenever one mentions the SLA or Cinque or the Harrises; that when one mentions the closet, she turns pale, starts to sweat, and her pulse rate goes up by fifty percent; that she is still preoccupied with the danger of violent attack, you take the expert at his word. He is not the sort of man to indulge in hyperbole.

West would like to play a tape of one of his early jail interviews, to give the jury an idea of what poor shape Patty was in when he first met her. Bancroft objects that this would be "cumulative, unnecessary, and unprecedented." Carter sustains the objection, adding that both counsel are being especially argumentative today.

"I am not aware of that, Your Honor," says Bailey.

"Well, I am. And that's what counts!"

David Bancroft opens his cross-examination of this first expert witness with a solid punch. "Dr. West, do you recall who it was who said that 'perhaps the most insidious domestic threat posed by "brainwashing" is the tendency of Americans to believe in its power'?" Dr. West smiles and rolls away from the punch like a sportive porpoise. "It sounds like something I might have said myself."

Another punch. "Doctor, do you know of any case where by thought reform or coercive persuasion someone was indoctrinated so as to commit violent acts against their own kind?"

Another porpoise arabesque. "Oh, yes, Mr. Bancroft, many, many examples. Except that it didn't require what I would call brainwashing or coercive persuasion."

"No. That's why I asked it that way."

"There were literally tens of thousands of Chinese who had been in the Nationalist forces and, after a relatively short period of thought reform, joined the army of Mao Tse-tung and went back and were killing people in their own villages, even members of their own families."

"Has that been scientifically attributed to thought reform, Doctor?"

"That, in fact, is what it was attributed to."

"Where is the literature on that subject, Doctor?"

"Well, you have Dr. Lifton here. Perhaps when he comes to testify, you could ask him."

"No, I mean from you, Doctor."

"I think you will find it in the history books, Mr. Bancroft. And in Mao Tse-tung's own account of the revolution."

"Well, that's *his* account; that's Mao Tse-tung's account."

(261)

WEST *(very mild):* He was there.

Bancroft versus West will be a nice contrast of styles. The lawyer is about ten years younger than the doctor, dark and thin. There is something serpentlike in Bancroft's manner. The high forehead, horn-rimmed spectacles, and cool intelligence recall John Dean. The lawyer who will handle all psychiatric testimony for the government was born in Connecticut, attended Swarthmore College, was graduated from the University of Chicago Law School, and joined the Justice Department in 1963. Bancroft wanted to be a career prosecutor because "I was enamored of Bobby Kennedy and his organized-crime drive." He worked three years in Washington in the organized-crime section and then asked to be transferred to the San Francisco office so that he could stay in one place and "keep my family life from falling apart." In 1969 he took a year's leave of absence to become associate director of the National Commission on Reform of the Federal Criminal Laws; its report was originally made to President Nixon, and then became swollen and distorted into the infamous bill known as S-I. The commission's intent was to modernize the federal criminal law and remove many of its loopholes. Had Nixon survived in office, and the proposed reforms been put into effect, the course of the Patty Hearst case would almost certainly have been different. The new formulation of the duress defense "fairly explicitly recognizes a brainwashing defense, although only in misdemeanor cases," Bancroft told me after the trial.

When he was assigned to handle the psychiatric side of the Hearst case, Bancroft suffered reading through every word ever written by Doctors West and Orne and Lifton, including perhaps two thousand pages from West alone. "At forty pages an hour, maybe thirty—some of that stuff is pretty dense—I'd say it came to roughly a month of solid reading," he told me. But the month paid off. Bancroft is superbly prepared and near-sizzling with prosecutorial zeal.

Doctor, brainwashing actually forms a small part of your research, correct? Yes. You are also an expert on drugs, hypnosis, hippies, racial violence, alcoholism, civil defense, homosexuality, elephants, and scuba diving? Yes. You hold seven hospital appointments, belong to about forty-five societies, and serve on nineteen committees, councils, and boards? Yes. These activities require a lot of travel, I understand? More than I like. You also have administrative duties in connection with your university appointment? Right. That university, incidentally, is run by the California board of regents? It is. That hasn't left you much time to devote to the examination of criminal defendants, has it?

Dr. West has been involved in only three criminal cases. In the Jack Ruby case he was asked to examine Ruby after trial, and found him insane. He also found an Air Force child murderer insane, and there was an Oklahoma murder in which he again testified for the defense.

Doctor, is psychiatry an exact science? No, it is the practice of medicine. Is it as exact as engineering? Engineering isn't a science; it's a practice. Are some psychiatrists better than others? I'm sure that's true.

Bancroft inquires about a letter Dr. West sent to the Hearst family shortly after the fire expressing sympathy and urging them not to despair. If their daughter were returned to them alive, he wrote, she could be helped and possibly defended. Dr. West denies any ulterior motive. "It was a letter from one parent to another. I expected no reply, and I got none." Dr. West had told the court about his letter last fall, and also about a recent *Time* magazine interview in which he stated that Patty could still make a "healthy adjustment" to normal life if she were "carefully handled." Did he mean to suggest that merely being in jail is *unhealthy?* Hissing slightly, pushing his glasses up on his forehead, Dave Bancroft is turning into a most satisfying villain.

"I think being in jail is unhealthy for any young person," West says firmly.

On October 6, Dr. West, along with the other doctors who examined Patty, officially told the court that she was legally sane and competent to stand trial. But curiously, on October 24, West filed another report "of some length" and reversed his preliminary views.

"No, sir. I did not. I said I'd leave the question of *legal* competence to stand trial up to the court, but that medically and psychiatrically, I thought she was far from competent." It is a critical distinction that the doctor will make many times.

"Do you recall a conversation with me in Jim Browning's office, Dr. West, in which you stated there was *no way* you would appear in the mental-responsibility phase of this trial?"

Yes, Dr. West had thought he would be prohibited by law from appearing at the trial because he had served on the advisory panel.

Mr. Bancroft has a flat, deadly voice, as if a copperhead could speak, and mordant humor. Last fall, when I had asked the prosecutor his interpretation of the West/Singer report, he replied, "I think the doctor is planning to write a book. In fact, I think he has written one."

Dr. West acknowledges that he and Dr. Singer once went to the Hearsts' apartment for dinner. His purpose was to interview the parents of the person they were examining. "Did you feel that having dinner was a necessary part of that interview?"

"Not a necessary part, but I thought it might help."

Bancroft gathers that the doctor has gone to some lengths to get rid of the notion in the public mind that brainwashing is "some kind of unique thing, something like the Manchurian Candidate, requiring secret Kickapoo juice and the double whammy?" No, says Dr. West mildly, he hasn't tried to do that.

Bancroft's technique is to festoon the courtroom with long strands of quotations from the doctor's writings and then attempt to strangle the witness with his own words. You have written, have you not, about "the absence of any ideological converts . . . in the POW camps . . ."? Yes. But you didn't include any such observations in your big, fat report on Miss Hearst, did you? No, because I didn't find that Miss Hearst had been ideologically converted. Would you say that again, Doctor?

"I did not find Miss Hearst had been ideologically converted."

Judge Carter is out cold.

While in the Air Force Dr. West helped devise a scale of compliance to measure the degree of cooperation with the enemy. But among the pilots, unlike Patty, "behavior at the extreme end of compliance did not occur, did it, Doctor?" Well, none of them actually joined the Chinese Air Force.

How about sleep deprivation? Though Patty had no way of knowing day from night, Dr. West guesses that she—like the pilots—was probably getting less sleep than she realized. But she didn't complain, did she? "She complained of practically nothing, Mr. Bancroft. I had to pry it out of her, all of it." That Patty still does not complain, even two years later, is a major indication of how sick she was.

Are there other possibilities than the so-called survivor syndrome that could account for Patty's symptoms? Yes, many. How about the anxiety produced by a situation in which a young woman from a prominent family who had previously scorned her parents, now facing multiple felony charges, after one of the most intensive manhunts in a decade, is sitting in jail with loyalties torn between previous comrades and the help necessary to get her out of a heck of a fix? Could that not account for someone feeling sorrowful and regretful, for the racing pulse and clammy hands, and for not having the best of memories?

Jolly West's blue eyes are very steady, and he includes the jury as well as Bancroft in his slow, sweeping gaze. "I approached this examination in as objective a fashion as I could. If I had found her to be, let us say, trapped between the expectations of her family and the expectations of her comrades, that is what I would have reported."

Yes, Dr. West has heard the tapes on which Patty spoke scornfully of her parents, but he didn't put much credibility in them. "I have heard too many taped confessions, Mr. Bancroft." At this, Patty turns and gives her mother a quick, full smile.

Why should Patty first identify herself as an "urban guerrilla," then change her story? Was it not just a matter of trying to get out on bail? "I don't think she had any idea of getting out on bail. I quickly discovered she had great fear of being released—even to go to a hospital for a medical examination. She only felt safe in jail."

Midafternoon recess. We straggle out reluctantly. The contest is a good one. From a spectator's viewpoint, West versus Bancroft is a far more interesting tennis match than Bailey versus Browning.

Cross-examination resumes with a long wrangle about whether Patty's hands were tied in front or in back, and how much pain she endured. The doctor notes that Patty said it didn't matter much which way they tied her hands, though "it was better when they did it around the front." How on earth could he find *that* a "very significant" remark? Because nobody can lie in a closet for forty-eight hours with her arms tied behind her back and *not* experience great pain. POWs had told him the pain was "excruciating" after only a few hours. Even after allowing for differences in male and female anatomy, West was forced to conclude Patty was blocking out the pain she had felt. If she had been lying rather than blocking, she would have exaggerated the pain, not minimized it.

Weren't you interpreting what she said, Doctor? "You bet! All the time." Which way, Doctor? Whichever way I thought would lead me to the truth.

It is characteristic of survivor syndrome that whereas real complaints are minimized, minor physical problems become grossly exaggerated. In Patty's case, a small variation in the jail's morning urinalysis report was elaborated by nightfall into "a fear that she might need a kidney transplant."

"When she doesn't complain, you find that significant. When she does complain, you find *that* significant."

"If it's significant, that's how I find it. A normal person would have expressed some anger, some indignation, some recollection of pain and discomfort. Instead, here was this individual in a flat, bland way describing a long period with the hands bound behind the back, and in a vague way saying, Well, it felt better when they put it around the front. *Now, that's not normal!*"

Patty has changed her nail polish to bright red, and under the table her hands are twitching in her lap.

Dr. West admits Patty did not say much about the Missing Year. Well, then, since she was not forthcoming with you in the psychiatric interviews, and certainly was not forthcoming here on the witness stand, where she invoked the Fifth Amendment forty-two times rather than answer questions about that period, how could West say survivor syndrome still existed at the time of her arrest? Because West has now spent forty hours examining her and another hundred hours thinking about the case, reviewing materials, consulting with friends and colleagues. Yes, but what information did you have about that year? Did she describe to you going to Las Vegas?

Patty begins coughing softly, and sips of water from her Styrofoam cup don't help. The soft cough continues throughout the next sequence of questions: What was she doing, where was she living, whom was she with during the Missing Year? West says he is a psychiatrist, not a detective. He was more interested in her state of mind. As to her whereabouts, he relied on information supplied him by the government.

"Pray tell, Doctor. What information did the government give you on that score?" Heaps of recovered documents, journals, manuscripts, FBI interviews, and so on. "During the period after Los Angeles, Doctor?" Oh, no, not after Los Angeles.

"Oh, no," Bancroft mimics. "I want to be very specific. I'm talking about the period from Los Angeles to her capture . . . that's from May 17, 1974, to September 17, 1975." With thumb upraised like a dagger, he slices a slow, invisible arc of air to indicate the prolonged passage of time.

The doctor admits his information on "the whole Pearl period" is pretty sketchy, and he got most of it from *Rolling Stone,* not the government. Then "how could you testify that when she was found she was suffering from survivor syndrome, without knowing exactly what happened to her in the previous year and a half?"

Excellent point, Holmes, I note on my yellow pad; the witness is unable to tell us what his survivor has survived. Dr. West invokes his doctrine of "reasonable medical certainty." But Al Johnson is wearing a very odd, scrunched-up expression, and Patricia looks furtive and weary.

During a technical passage I notice the sixteen feet of the attorneys under their two tables. Bancroft is the only lawyer in this courtroom not wearing new shoes. For some reason I find this ominous. Also ominous is Judge Carter's new alertness on the bench. Bancroft bristles like a bloodhound catching the scent, and several times the judge must caution him against becoming argumentative. But the warnings are offered with barely suppressed glee; Carter enjoys a good fight.

Bancroft mentions the sentence-completion test in which Patty's answers included IF I *"was out of here, I'd like it."* MY GREATEST TROUBLE *"is the present and the past."* I ENVY PEOPLE *"who are free."* Dr. Singer characterized these responses as "unusual," showing how narrowly Patty's attention was focused on her immediate environment, but Bancroft finds nothing unusual in the replies, considering that the respondent is taking the test in jail. Dr. Singer also wrote that Patty's manner was "that of a young schoolgirl, trying to do what an older person requested . . . not flip, evasive, or putting me on." Bancroft reads two more test answers. MY IMAGINATION *"it runs wild."* MOST MEN *"are assholes."*

"Not trying to be a little flip, eh, Doctor?"

Far from it. That's the answer of a person who had "previously thought most men were pretty good and then had been brutally mistreated by some men."

How about her remark to Trish Tobin that if she issued a statement, "it would be from a revolutionary feminist perspective"? To Dr. West this signifies that Patty's attitude had changed from a rather conventional middle-class perspective "to a fierce concern with the extent to which women could be brutalized by men. . . ." Now West makes a fatal mistake; he gives more of an answer than is required. "I also knew that Emily Harris was sitting about eight feet away when she said that."

"How do you know that? How do you know that?" Bancroft is barking like a terrier.

"Same way *you* know it. From the patient, Miss Hearst."

"Would your opinion be any different, Doctor, if the jail records show that Emily Harris wasn't in that room at all!"

Smoothly smiling, Jolly West replies, "I'd find that fascinating . . . and quite understandable, from a psychological point of view." It would suggest that to Patty, Emily Harris was "a constant presence," whether she was really there or not.

Another sentence completion: I AM *"very strong."* Didn't you say, Doctor, that she was lacking in self-esteem? Yes. That's why the response is so interesting. "Here she is weighing at that time about

ninety-five pounds and looking like a good wind would blow her away"
and she writes, *"very strong."*

Perhaps she was talking about her mental conviction, not physical
strength? "As a matter of fact, her physical condition was surprisingly
good. She'd been running four miles a day and had excellent muscle
tone. Most of her debility was mental, not physical."

Dr. West had said that Patty's first scores on the lengthy Minnesota
Multiphasic Inventory test, which she was asked to take on her own
time and score herself, were so idiosyncratic that the doctors had to run
the tests over again. Bancroft suggests that perhaps the retests were
necessary because Johnson tried to coach Patty the first time. Dr. West
admits he "had to chase Mr. Johnson out of there," but there's no way
someone can be coached on that test. The doctors finally figured out
the reason for Patty's unusually high score on the F scale (F for "feeb,"
feebleminded, in psychologists' jargon). One section of the test contains
statements to be marked true or false, such as *I have had strange and
unusual experiences* and *People have been trying to harm me,* and "in
this woman's experience, those things were true!" Patty's curious situation, I realized with a start, was a novelty not only in the annals of crime
but in the annals of psychological testing as well.

Tonight I have a drink with Tom May, the Jesuit-educated former
Marine, former prosecutor, and nemesis of Boston hippies. An icy
warmth, or warm-blooded chill, radiates from his Torquemada-hand-
some eyes. I ask about the lie-detector tests, which Bailey said were
favorable to Patty. May doesn't like the polygraph. He prefers to go by
his own instincts, and he's worried. They're all worried. Bailey has
everybody watching that jury, especially the psychiatrists. But none of
them can tell much from the jurors' faces, not even Margaret Singer,
though she "is a witch, and should be prevented from testifying on
supernatural grounds." May worries that the jury will come to a "bad
man" conclusion: not that Patty did it, but that she is so bad she might
as well have done it. The client will be hanged for a sheep, he fears. It
should be a simple bank-robbery case, requiring no more than seven
days to try. "But this case is all full of shit that doesn't belong in it.
It's in her hat and over her ears." Mel's should not be in, and the
Missing Year certainly should not be in, because it always comes back
to *but for:* But for the fact that she was kidnapped, none of the later
things would have happened.

As an experienced prosecutor himself, May finds Browning "totally inept" and Bancroft "stupid. When you go in for fifteen rounds with Cassius Clay [to a man like May, the fighter will never be "Ali"], you play very, very conservative. You keep your guard up and try not to get hit. You certainly don't dance around! You ask very few questions; you don't open things up the way Bancroft's doing. When you ask a witness like West, 'Could there be another explanation, Doctor, for such-and-such behavior?' and he says, 'Yes,' you *never* say then, 'What could it be?' You wait until summation. Then you remind the jury that the witness said there could be another explanation and *you* suggest what that might be."

Patty's situation is profoundly upsetting to May because it represents the annihilation of free will. She is the Orwellian forecast come true in the present. To him, Patty deprived of her free will is more disadvantaged than the ghetto black kid, who has "at least a ten- to fifteen-percent chance of exercising his will. Patty had none." May's understanding of what happened to Patty psychologically is that "she exploded inside. The devastation is total." Every day he watches her narrowly across the defense table. "That poor kid," he says. "If she were my daughter, undergoing these indignities, submitting to this grilling on the personal details of life, with the results of her psychological tests put on naked display, I would get up and kill somebody."

The frustration of these defense lawyers is almost beyond telling. They are twelfth-century Knights Templars, a holy brotherhood dedicated to escort an innocent, endangered maiden through dangerous wildernesses. They would do the impossible: restore not only her freedom but her good name, rescue her reputation from the American middle class, who see her as Miss Rich Bitch. These lawyers *know* she is not. They *know* she has been most brutally, vilely abused. But they cannot get anybody to accept their interpretation. Men who pass their professional lives in courtrooms have lied and dissembled and gulled and bluffed and hoodwinked and humbugged so many times that now, when they have a genuine innocent maiden in their charge, people are disinclined to believe them. Oh, the frustration, the irony, of their predicament! All that latent rectitude crucified on the cross of cynicism, the pervasive cynicism that has soaked into middle-class, post-Vietnam, post-Watergate America. Their quest is hopeless *because of* the very same cynical climate they did so much to create.

One evening I chatted with a young foot soldier in the brotherhood, a novice, a penitent, a squire. Jim Neal is one of several free-lance lawyer-investigators who have worked on the Patty Hearst case. A few years back, when he was only a year out of law school and uncertain how to handle the case of a woman who had hacked her husband to bits, Neal had impulsively telephoned F. Lee Bailey. The star lawyer immediately flew out to Indiana, looked at the clippings and documents spread out on the bed in the young man's motel room, told him, "Okay, kid, you're handling it about right," and flew home. Neal has burned with loyalty to Bailey ever since, despite the psychological pressures of serving in his command. "Lee never *tells* you what he wants. You are just expected to divine it, do it, provide it." I understand. That is exactly how my mother ruled me. "Lee's second-greatest skill is lawyering," Neal says, meaning that his first is getting people to do what he wants, to follow him down any sacred way or garden path or across any bloody no-man's-land. When General Field Marshal Bailey gives a command, *you move.*

When Neal had arrived in San Francisco last fall, "the Hearsts were incredibly nice to me." They saw him sometimes discouraged in his labors—he had to replow ground already worn to dust by press, FBI, and other snoopers—and often invited him over for drinks and dinner. He felt almost like the son they never had. One evening, as he rang the doorbell, he heard Catherine playing the piano, and he begged her to continue. "If you play, I'll sing," he proposed, and the minister's son and the tycoon's wife spent two happy hours singing hymns together at the top of their lungs. On another occasion, Randy invited the young man to go duck hunting. He would have loved it, "but Lee would have been furious if he'd found out, and I wouldn't have dared *not* tell him."

The sin, one presumes, would have been fraternizing with the gentry. Once again, it comes down to barnyard pecking-order, the male brotherhood, the bond that transcends families, wives, loves, children. All the men of the brotherhood worship Bailey, and all at times feel underappreciated, used, abused by their leader. All have an absurd ideal of the Kiwi Fruit's power; their image of Linda seems to me preposterous—they perceive her as the Usurper, interposing her power between General Field Marshal Bailey and his loyal Friendly Sons of St. Patrick troops. The brothers are forever saying, "Lee would do *anything* for you." Unspoken in this is the quid pro quo: You are expected to do not less than anything for him. That aspect of the bond moves it out of the saintly class and over to the military model. The arrangement lacks generosity or charity, as I understand the terms. In its paramilitary structure, its demands of unquestioning loyalty and service to the organization, its emphasis on discipline, military preparedness, and other macho, rooster values, the Bailey brotherhood is a fun-house mirror reflection of the SLA. Possibly Patty, with her truly incredible luck— luck so fantastic it occurs only in Dickens' novels and boys' adventure books—had wound up with the most perfect man alive to defend her. It strains credulity to think that the poor Hearsts could have known they were hiring a paradigm of the SLA when they engaged Bailey and his men. But Patty is now captive to this Knights Templars–cum–U.S. Marines band, to be rescued against impossible odds, led across vast legal mine fields at the wanton expense of blood and nerve and daring and guts. If it is true that Patty has the lawyer she deserves, Bailey may also have the perfect client for his particular skills and psychological attitudes. One of the many psychiatrists who examined her in jail had asked Patty what her ambition was. To live at San Simeon, she replied. The rescued maiden would climb back into her castle, it appears, hoist the drawbridge, and all would be as before.

Wednesday, February 25

Dr. West, were you aware when you took this case that Mrs. Hearst sits on the board of regents of the University of California and also hands out money for research projects? Bancroft asks the next morning. Calmly the witness says he was not aware, but it wouldn't have made any difference. When West came to UCLA he had $1 million available for research. Now he has $12 million, all from federal funds, not a penny from the state of California. Furthermore, "I'm one of those persons known as a 'tenured professor,' so even if someone on the board of regents hated me, he couldn't fire me."

"But they could . . . up your salary?" Bancroft murmurs.

No, they couldn't do that, either, because it's already at the top level. Judge Carter laughs gleefully to see Bancroft riding into this trap.

But now, suddenly, the prosecutor has changed horses. Do you remember Steven Weed's telling you that the defendant's capacity for sarcasm is unparalleled? "I sat and listened to Mr. Weed for three and a half hours, during which I think he spoke constantly. He must have used a hundred to a hundred and fifty adjectives, which isn't bad for a Princeton man, and 'sarcastic' may have been one of them."

But Dr. West's own tincture of sarcasm is insufficient to grease his way through this slippery passage. Bancroft reads aloud some of the psychiatrist's own interview notes in which Weed is describing his former fiancée: "In many ways she was very immature. . . . She has a tendency to overstate things. . . . Her capacity to be sarcastic is unparalleled. . . ." Small wonder Bailey and Johnson were determined to keep this witness off the stand! In the moments that follow, Patty regards her parents and sisters with a sustained, smoldering, bitter stare.

Now, Doctor, your report states that this defendant attended some six schools in the past five years. You call these "self-instigated" transfers. Are you not aware of certain disciplinary problems? Forty demerits at Sacred Heart, to name but one example? "In fact you had information, did you not, that she almost got kicked out of Sacred Heart for telling a nun to go to hell?"

"Yes, I did have that."

A quiet, sad-eyed sixtyish little couple sit across the aisle from me. We have been exchanging smiles, and at recess we begin to chat. "Kids today," says the husband ruefully, shaking his head. "Especially rich kids! They don't know what to do with themselves."

"My kid just ran away from school," I blurt out.

"Join the club," says the man. *"Our* kid ran away from Oxford. And he was a Rhodes scholar!"

We introduce ourselves. Somehow I had not recognized them. They are Dr. and Mrs. Harry Kozol, the prosecution psychiatrist and his wife, and the son they speak of is the author Jonathan Kozol. We blink dazedly at one another like strollers who have collided in a fog and are suddenly intimates. He promises me a copy of his own fifty-page report on Patty, as well as a copy of Jonathan's new book, *The Night Is Dark, and I Am Far from Home*—an appropriate title for us all. Except for government and court officials, we are all fellow castaways here. The doctor is worried about his patients back in Boston. I remember Johnson yesterday making fun of Kozol, showing a group of reporters how the nervous psychiatrist relieves his own anxiety: by putting a forefinger on the crown of his head and dervishing like a *dreidl*, a Jewish top. We had giggled then at Al's imitation of the spinning shrink, but in the flesh he seems sad, his own *dreidl*, spinning and waiting in the wings.

Bancroft is ready to sum up. "Is it your view, Doctor, that a person who was politically embarrassed by their family situation, oriented toward the surface aspect of things, whose characteristic mode of expression is deep sarcasm, and if that person—prior to their acquaintance with political matters—in addition felt depressed or trapped—could that person not come to a sudden political expression of their own hostilities?" Damn good question.

West says the prosecutor has raised five points, and he wishes to answer them one by one. "By the way"—soft smile—"I assume we're talking about Patricia Hearst?"

A Halloween grin illumines Bancroft's face. "I certainly hope so."

West's reply to the extended question is an extended no, an archipelago of denial. She was not "depressed and trapped." She may have had personal, private reservations about marrying Weed, but "even her sisters didn't know about them."

My mind trails off. Private reservations, personal reasons. Politicians have flung themselves into presidential campaigns, emperors have flung their countries into war and destruction for personal reasons. How unusual would it be for a young girl having rather commonplace second thoughts about her impending marriage to fling herself into terrorist political activities for private reasons? This is the question a psychiatrist *should* be answering. . . .

Doctor, you have examined the SLA tapes and the "Tania Interview." Don't you find expression in both places of Patty's desire to be considered as an individual and her resentment for not having been so considered previously?

I find nothing of the sort. I consider them unmitigated propaganda comparable to the statements made by American prisoners of war. Some of the phrases sound as if they were copied out of the same book. . . . The SLA materials express the crassest perversion of the idea of individuality. When a small group of people goes around and kills other people to achieve their political goals, that's not individualism—that's terrorism! And there is nothing in her background to prepare her for that.

That's just it, Dr. West, I would like to jump up and yell. There is nothing in *any* of the SLA backgrounds, except maybe Cinque's, to prepare them for that.

Bancroft dangles before the prolific psychiatrist still another noose of his own making. Doctor, do you know who wrote the following passage? "Why does the new generation always seem to be corrupt to the old? Perhaps we repress the memory of our own youthful revolutionary impulses."

Wearily, West defends himself. Yes, it's out of context again, but it's from one of his own articles, "Psychiatry, Brainwashing and the American Character."

Suddenly a full-blown legal wrangle is going on; all the lawyers are on their feet and shouting about a footnote in Dr. West's report. The doctor, skilled by now in defending himself against being quoted out of context, says, "The sentence to which the footnote is attached is as follows," and again begins to read aloud:

"A traumatic neurosis was beginning to take shape." *Footnote:* "Neither Patricia herself nor her SLA captors were likely to have had any real understanding of this unconscious process. Cinque was looking for a successful political conversion in the well-known revolutionary tradition (Maoist) of thought-reform. His experience in prison had taught him also that following a period of isolation, solitary confinement or 'black hole,' where people are kept in darkness, an inmate would be unusually susceptible to political indoctrination. The others, as usual, followed his lead. Patricia subsequently heard this discussed."

"That's the context! Now, what was the question about it?"

The question was, did Cinque have any specific knowledge or experience with Maoist thought reform? Dr. West says he concluded that Cinque had picked up his Maoism from the others. "He was obviously a very bright man but not a great reader."

I lunch with Dr. West and his devoted assistant, Marcia Addis, who reports that the hotel switchboard is swamped with callers who want to tell Dr. West they are being brainwashed. Jolly smiles. "During *The Exorcist* we were deluged with people who'd been possessed."

West and I discover a mutual passion for elephants. I am literary midwife to and biographer of the first elephant ever born in the United States, a 225-pound blessed event I had described in *Life* magazine. It happened when Kathy was less than a year old, a time when my own interest in motherhood was at a personal and professional peak. At the same time that I was so fascinated by maternity, West was fascinated by LSD and its chemical similarity, if any, to the sex hormones of male elephants. To further his studies, West had obtained a large bull elephant from the same Seattle wild-animal importer who had provided the zoo with the parents of my infant elephant, and when his beast arrived in Oklahoma, West and his team injected it with LSD.

"What happened?"

"We must have miscalculated the dose." The elephant OD'd and died within the hour.

"Very interesting paper," says Marcia brightly, fishing up a reprint from her bulging briefcase.

At the far end of our lunch table the Hearst family are smiling and appear relaxed. West's genial mastery on the witness stand, his ability to resist the prosecutor while disarming and instructing the jury, has lifted their spirits as well as my own. In a rear private area of the Rathskeller, the jurors are having their own lunch. Faintly, over the clatter of the dishes, we can hear them singing "Happy Birthday."

On the front page of today's *Chronicle* is an artist's drawing of Dr. West in the witness box. The headline says, INSIDE PATTY'S HEAD, and Carolyn Anspacher reports that West sees Patty as "a person with a profound uncertainty about her present identity; one in which alternative personalities—the revolutionary Tania and then the fugitive woman called 'Pearl'—danced as if executing a fugue."

"What the hell is that supposed to mean?" asks a jealous reporter as we're waiting in the metal-detector queue.

"Fugue is when you've really checked out your baggage," Tom May replies. We are all shrinks here.

After lunch Bancroft asks Dr. West about Patty's statement that before she was kidnapped, she was "real depressed" and "couldn't do anything without thinking how I could kill myself while I was doing it." To the psychiatrist, Patty's statement is a rather commonplace form of emotional "rear projection," in which a person's current emotional state colors his recollection of the past.

Bancroft is undeterred. How about the statement in West's report that, to Patty, the robbery seemed "like a dream"? Does the film look to him as if she found the experience dreamlike? You can't tell anything from "Keystone Kop–quality movies," the witness replies.

Bancroft dangles his last noose. Did not West once write, in an essay on the problems of evaluating verbal reports of emotions, "To the psychoanalytically-oriented investigator, verbalizations are particularly unreliable indicators of subjective states, because such states are partially unconscious"? Yes, this was part of a long, technical article.

All right. With respect to the shooting at Mel's, did not Patty verbalize to Dr. West, "I can't believe I did it"? Yes, and she also asked, "Why didn't I just let them get captured?" But her query was retroactive; she had asked herself no such questions at the time.

Bancroft asks West to read aloud a transcription of his notes of an October 5 interview with the defendant. It is a good example of the doctor's extremely thorough style, complete with copious stage directions.

WEST: It's strange that you have trouble remembering that episode [*referring to the details at Mel's*] because I should think it would have been a very exciting one.

HEARST *(heavy breathing)*: It's like . . . oh . . . I don't know . . . just freak out or something. [*Sigh.*] You know, all of a sudden, something happens real fast. . . .

WEST: What happened so fast?

HEARST: _____. [*Cannot make out the words but think it was* shooting up *the sporting-goods store.*] Oh, yes. It's like I can't believe I did that. I can't believe I could just ——— [*and I think there is a word left out*] let them get caught and didn't turn myself in.

WEST: You were doing what you had been trained to do?

HEARST: [*Sigh.*]

WEST: And after which you wanted their approval, the Harrises, that you had done the right thing? [*I got that from somewhere . . . in fact, I had gotten it from Dr. Singer's previous interview. Hearst not saying yes. That was the reason. She just doesn't answer.*]

HEARST: [*Heavy sighs.*]

WEST: [*And I said:*] See what?

HEARST: Seems to switch around and backwards.

WEST: How so?

HEARST *(Sighs. Voice breaking.)*: I just keep thinking about this stuff and [*long pause; heavy breathing*] I mean, if . . . [*sigh*] we could have done that easy enough, I couldn't do it at all and [*sigh*] . . .

WEST: You mean, let them get caught, and yourself too? You could easily have done that—and yet you couldn't? Is that what you are saying?

HEARST: I mean, yes . . . Yes. [*Sighs. Long pause.*]

Does Dr. West recall a conversation with Patty at the beginning of this particular interview regarding legal defense strategy? Yes. Does he recall telling her, shortly after Mr. Johnson left the room, that "he explained to me something about the strategy they planned for the defense in this case"? And she inquired, "Which is?" And he then responded,

> Which is to emphasize the involuntary and violent way in which you were dragged out of a relatively normal life . . . the forcible and terrifying sort of indoctrination you got . . . the tremendous pressure of threats in the beginning to make you subservient and compliant with the leadership of this group so that they would be able to keep control of you. I think myself that's the best explanation for what happened. I haven't heard anything to make me think otherwise. Doesn't that sound logical to you?

"Do you remember telling the defendant in that conversation words to that effect?"

Mr. Bancroft, there wasn't a thing I said in that sentence that hadn't come from what the patient had already told all the doctors. . . . I was trying to ascertain her ability to stand trial . . . in order to do my job for the court. I wasn't *telling* her what had happened; I was *asking* her.

Did the doctor think it appropriate to tell the defendant that he was in agreement with the defense that was planned?

"I held it to be of no moment."

Does the doctor recall on October 11 giving Patty something called the postural-sway test and telling her, "You're relatively suggestible . . . easily deceived, I would say, especially if dependent on someone. You were so successfully coerced"? Yes. Do you think that might have affected her behavior in any subsequent psychiatric examination of her? No, I've never found it does any harm to tell a patient the truth.

What about the amnesia? It was patchy, extending from even before the kidnapping right up until the present time. In the period October 1974–January 1975, can you tell us where she was? Whom she was with? What they were doing? No, West didn't ask her those kinds of questions. Why not? Because I am not a detective. I am a psychiatrist.

During these questions Patty's eyes are downcast; she appears depressed and somewhat angry.

"Yes, Doctor, but what I am getting at is: How could you adduce a survivor's syndrome if you didn't know where she was during that period?" One of the distinguishing things about the survivor syndrome is that it persists, sometimes for years. I had the patient before me; I had the records, the history of capture and stress. So I knew that either she had been cured and then made sick again or else what I was seeing was a continuing medical illness.

(277)

Excuse me, Doctor, but you said she was suffering from a traumatic neurosis with dissociative features. But by the time we get to Mel's, you say she had developed some kind of multiple personality that she did not have at the time of the bank robbery.

No, Mr. Bancroft, that is not correct. She assumed the Tania role just before her release from the closet. She continued to play this role through the holocaust. "Pearl" was the chronic phase. I never said she had a multiple personality. I said she had assumed the role, for survival purposes, and used dissociative mechanisms, similar to those used by people who do have dual personalities, to keep herself from thinking about the past or the future.

The next item on Bancroft's agenda of innuendo will be more difficult for the psychiatrist to handle. West must now explain the circumstances of his letter to the Hearsts. Shortly after the fire, "when those of us who lived in Los Angeles thought Patricia Hearst was dead," and were being told by the press that the Hearsts were conducting an all-night vigil, "watching on television to find out if their daughter was dead or alive—that touched me." And so he wrote to her father.

Dear Mr. Hearst,

This letter is to express sympathy—sympathy for you and your family, concern for your daughter, Patricia, and the hope that her future may not be so blighted as recent events would seem to threaten.

Enclosed are a couple of reprints on the subject of so-called "brainwashing." From them you can see that considerable work from a medical and psychiatric viewpoint has been reported concerning the extent to which singleminded captors can profoundly influence individuals who come under their control. There's much that could be elaborated on the subject; but at this time, I would make the following points: One, there is a high degree of likelihood that a person whose behavior has been grossly distorted under conditions of captivity, or in the highly charged emotional climate of a cohesive small group setting, may return to a relatively normal state of mind and behavior. This can occur in a short period of time if appropriate rehabilitation procedures are carried out.

Two: there are historical precedents for special legal consideration of such a victim. Perhaps the most dramatic was provided by the United States Air Force in its rehabilitative rather than punitive treatment of fliers who gave false confessions of germ warfare while in communist captivity during the Korean War. . . . more than half of the Air Force officers who were subjected to the "full treatment" by their communist captors gave false confessions of germ warfare. Furthermore, this behavior was not induced by physical torture, hypnotism, stupefying drugs or conditioning techniques. Instead, socialization and group pressure together with subtler forms of debilitation such as sleep loss sufficed. Technically, the behavior of these men could have been classified as treason. However, they were not held culpable and in fact were not even tried by courts martial for such an offense, primarily because of the circumstances and conditions under which their behavior had been influenced.

If Patricia can be protected from physical harm and returned to her family, she stands a good chance of being restored to a mentally healthy and socially responsible state. Furthermore, in spite of the charges that have been filed against her, I believe powerful medical and legal arguments can be mobilized for her defense.

With every good wish. Sincerely Yours.

At this point, it seems a sentimental, self-serving, and almost ambulance-chasing letter. But it could have sounded quite different at the time. In any event, the Hearsts now say that in the floods of mail, they never received it. (Privately I wonder if the FBI was intercepting the Hearsts' mail. If the government had picked up the letter, that could account for Jim Browning's hitherto-inexplicable statement to me, only a few days after the holocaust, that "brainwashing is now Patty's only nonculpable viable defense.") One can be fairly sure that Jolly West now wishes he'd never written to the Hearsts. Nonetheless, he defends himself well. Because of the letter, he approached "the examination of this patient not only with my usual objectivity" but with excessive care, he did not want to let himself be biased and discover just the things he was looking for. As a further guarantee of objectivity, he insisted on having Dr. Singer with him every step of the way. "I feel that this case study of this patient is as honorable and unbiased and scientific as any psychiatric case study that's ever been done."

With that ringing statement, the cross-examination is finally ended. During the brief recess that follows, reporters learn that Al Johnson has been seeing about Patty's bail in Los Angeles, where she has been coindicted with the Harrises on gun and kidnapping charges. By this time it is hard to remember that all she is charged with in San Francisco is bank robbery.

Bailey's redirect examination of Dr. West deals first with the letter to Patty's parents. Are you in the habit of writing unsolicited letters to people like the Hearsts? No. But I have two daughters, one about Patty's age, and I thought, Suppose that was me watching the fire on TV and wondering if my daughter was dead or alive? My heart went out to them. I just thought that a little hope for these terrified people was something I might provide, so I sent it off and forgot about it.

"By the way, what was written at the top of the letter?" *Personal and confidential.*

Why did your report analyze Patty in so much detail? Bailey asks. It was part of what I feel is the changing challenge to psychiatry of what we *should* provide the courts. "In my report I cite the article by Judge David Bazelon [chief judge of the U.S. Circuit Court of Appeals in Washington] which says to us in psychiatry: Don't come into the court and play lawyer. Come and . . . give us psychiatric information and we'll take care of the legal judgments." Once Judge Carter ruled that Patty should be brought to trial, Dr. West was told to say nothing about his pretrial work to anyone. His report and all the notes as well would be under court seal until after the trial was over. "That's what I was told."

Lastly, Bailey must deal with the fact, brought out in Bancroft's cross-examination, that despite all Patty's suggestions to the contrary, Emily Harris was indeed not present while Patty talked to Trish. So the last thing the jury hears from Dr. West is his opinion that for Patty, Emily Harris was "a presence" whether she was in the room or not.

"Thank you, Dr. West." Leaving behind him the spectral presence of Emily Harris hanging in the courtroom air, the first and biggest of Bailey's three big guns steps down from the stand at last. One could have wished for a stronger finale to Dr. West's interminable testimony, but at 3:25 P.M. it is over at last.

"Dr. Orne, please." A rumpled, spectacled, mustached, well-fed son of Old Vienna waddles slowly toward the witness stand. An equally round and rumpled Mme. Orne leans forward in her pew, rapt respect smoothing her large, nice face.

Throughout her husband's testimony, Mme. Orne smiles seraphically and writes down his every word on a big yellow pad.

Martin Theodore Orne, MD, is a research psychiatrist at the University of Pennsylvania, a graduate of Harvard and Zurich universities and of Tufts Medical School. He is both a psychiatrist and a psychologist, and a lecturer in hypnosis as well. He has served on the faculties of many great medical institutions, has been a consultant to the Institute for Defens- Analyses, and has done a great deal of work for the Veterans Administration and much research for the Air Force in the field of "resistance training"—teaching men to withstand interrogation. He has also served for many years as a consultant to the League of Families of the POWs and MIAs. One can see the jurors react with approval to this obviously kindly man who has attempted at length, and on his own time, to help these bereaved families.

Doctors Orne, West, and Singer have met before. The trio first worked together at Stead Air Force Base in 1966, when the Air Force, troubled by the number of officers who were having mental breakdowns while still in training, was seeking ways to anticipate stress. It was especially important that newly captured officers not break down, or at least not too fast. No POW could be expected to hold out long, but if the men could be taught to resist for only two or three days after being captured, this would be sufficient to protect any tactical information they might have. Tactical information has a short life. Forty-eight–hour protection is enough, Orne says, sounding like a deodorant commercial. Accordingly, Orne and West helped devise a program of "survival training." They deposited a group of airmen in the desert, where they were forced to scrounge and "eat lizards" to stay alive. The next day they were "captured" by a "pseudoenemy"—other servicemen, dressed in strange uniforms and speaking a fake foreign language. The captives were kept overnight in "isolation boxes" similar to ones used in North Vietnam and were interrogated the next morning. The results of this experiment were shocking: Twenty-five percent of senior Air Force officers gave away not only the phony secrets of the survival-training exercise but real secrets as well! The training wasn't working at all. In fact, it made men weaker, not stronger. If a war game could have this effect on experienced military personnel, what would unexpected capture, confinement, and interrogation do to a nineteen-year-old girl?

Dr. Orne was shown the findings of all the other doctors, and only then did he examine Miss Hearst personally and alone, in December. He was surprised to find that the by now famous "patchy amnesia" extended backward in time into the period before the kidnapping. This "didn t make any sense" in terms of the patches' being self-serving. "I found, much to my surprise, that this girl was very troubled and would be *trying* to relate the events that had transpired . . . but it was just impossible for her to talk about the closet." The doctor provided all sorts of booby traps, but "she just didn't pick up on cues. It was really quite remarkable. Miss Hearst simply *did not lie.*"

Bancroft leaps to his feet, objecting, and Carter issues a solemn instruction to the jury: This witness has naively overstepped his province. He has stated that the defendant tells only the truth, but "that is *your* judgment. You and you alone have to make this ultimate decision, and no judge, and no psychiatrist, no lawyer, can do this for you."

Bailey thanks the court for making this critical distinction, and now he questions the flustered Dr. Orne more carefully, artfully shaping his questions to keep the bubbly Viennese, who has discovered this fountain of truth in a cell at the San Mateo County Jail, from pissing the case away. Once he has got his man quieted down, Bailey extracts the information that what Dr. Orne meant when he said Patty didn't lie was that "I couldn't sway her to tell me something by the way I asked the question."

"You invited her to adopt helpful suggestions you were making to her about her defense?"

"Yes, sir, that's what I—"

"And what did she do when you invited her to do that?"

"She didn't."

Dr. Orne is now safely back under the control of the architect of this defense, F. Lee Bailey, and it is a good time to recess for the day. The law is concerned exclusively with facts; psychiatrists deal in "subjective truth." In Dr. Orne's testimony and the government's objection to it, we have witnessed exactly the head-on collision between psychiatry and the law that has been inevitable ever since this trial got under way.

Thursday, February 26

Dr. Orne's examination of the defendant lasted an hour and a half, he tells us, and he threw her his entire range of curveball questions. When Patty told him about being in the bank under Cinque's gun, he observed, "You must have been very scared"; to which she replied, "I don't know what I felt. It was like a dream." This is an inappropriate response from someone who is "simulating," the doctor says. What a downy word—"simulating"! A neutral psych-lab term, lacking any moral knobs or prickles, so different from "lying." Patty "didn't protect herself psychologically" or try to defend herself from the pain of his questions. "If I'd ask about the closet, she would immediately begin to cry. This was a terribly difficult thing to talk about. But she would answer anything I asked her, though clearly in anguish. This is unusual. Many times a psychiatric examination is not a pleasant experience because one must ask about very private things which the patient doesn't want to discuss. But despite the hurt, she showed no evidence of trying to push me away. She appeared to be in intense pain but continued to cooperate."

What sort of personality does Patty appear to have had prior to her kidnapping? The gentle Viennese explains that some people are guided primarily by abstract notions of justice, whereas others respond more to people. "I found it striking that Miss Hearst had so little tendency to respond to abstract principles." When she expressed outrage to Dr. Orne about two department-store clerks who had been fired, what upset her was not the principle of the thing but the personal injustice to persons she knew. Had Dr. Orne thought about Patty's heritage— rather than just his own laboratory abstractions—perhaps he would have been less surprised.

What is the meaning of "dissociation"? It means ceasing to be "yourself," and varies in degree from the common kind of dissociation we all experience at a cocktail party when we simultaneously talk to someone and think about something else to its most extreme form, "fugue," in which amnesia wipes out the original personality and a second personality becomes the "real" one. In working with returnees from Vietnam, Dr. Orne has become familiar with dissociative mechanisms. . . .

His testimony, like Dr. West's, is becoming so boring that I, myself, begin to dissociate, reliving the glee of last night's women-only dinner party at the Yugoslav restaurant. This rousing, wine-drenched, high-spirited bash for female reporters seemed to disprove lesson one from my old mentor, Margaret Mead, on the difference between men and women. A few years earlier, when I was in considerable confusion and despair as the newly appointed editor of *McCall's,* I called on Dr. Mead and asked her to tell me what the differences were between men and women, besides what one could observe in the mirror while getting dressed. It was she who told me then that the one and only consistent and universal difference is that men in groups are happy, whereas women in groups are sad. I had clung to this stout plank of anthropological dogma ever since, like a castaway riding serenely on the rising tidal wave of unisex, until last night's all-girl good time. Some of us were over seventy and some barely twenty; all the usual opportunities for professional jealousy were present: high bitchery, low jabs, lots of wine; I even had my mother in tow. But it had been a superb party, more fun *without men* for us all. Patty and our common feelings about her—by now unabashedly maternal—had seemingly been able to dissolve inbred hostilities among women that anthropolgists still cannot fathom.

. . . And how does Dr. Orne account for the fact that Patty told him about having sexual relations in the closet with Cinque and Willie Wolfe but told Dr. West only about getting pinched? It means that she was improving. A ten-week interval separated the two psychiatrists' visits, and by the time Dr. Orne saw her, on December 15, "she was able to remember and think and talk about it, albeit with a lot of pain, tears streaming down, real suffering."

Patty is motionless, her long Egyptian eyes downcast and unblinking. Where is her mind? Is she dissociating now? There is never a smile, no facial response, no animation whatever. Bailey is ready to nail down his examination of Dr. Orne with a couple of solid final points. When did the dissociation begin? It began when Tania began. If she had been recaptured right after the robbery, there would have been no question about her behavior in the bank, and no trial. But the robbery made Patty an outlaw not only in the eyes of the law but in her own eyes. She knew it was a criminal act, and she knew there was no way back, so she was stuck with the role. As time passed, the role became more and more real. There was nobody around to whom she could say, I am only *playing* this game. In the Chinese prison camps, coercive persuasion didn't work well when the prisoners were housed two to a cell because, between interrogations, each man could talk to the other and revalidate his own identity. In Patty's case even a single other person could have made a difference.

This is the most coherent explanation we have heard of the persistence of Tania, or, rather, of Pearl, and although Bailey fails to mention it, this formulation also shows the crucial importance of Wendy, that first "other person." Attorney General Saxbe's characterization of Patty as a "common criminal" did not sentence her to life as an outlaw; the bank robbery had done that already. It merely put a period to that sentence.

Was the SLA organized in a paramilitary fashion, with ranks, responsibilities, numbers? Yes. Of the nine people involved in the army, what number did Miss Hearst have? No. 9. "She was the only private in an army of generals." The jury smiles, grateful amid the fog of

psychiatric jargon to encounter a simple image they can readily understand. But it is a line that will haunt the defense throughout the remainder of the trial, and will eventually be twisted back into a noose around
Patty's neck.

During Dr. Orne's testimony a growing awareness of the CIA has
crept up on me like an eclipse of the sun, unnoticed until quite suddenly
one notices it is dark outside—Koestler's darkness at noon. Martin
Orne must inevitably have worked for the CIA or some other branch
of military intelligence; West and Singer, too.* It is an uncomfortable
thought, especially when one recalls that Colston Westbrook, the Black
Cultural Association organizer, seemingly had CIA connections in the
Far East before coming home and organizing his BCA in the California
prisons. It reinforces the speculation that he was Cinque's "American
operator" and that as the war in Vietnam wound down, the CIA began
to redirect its elaborate intelligence capabilities toward what the "intelligence community," just like Manson and the SLA itself, perceived
would be the next war—black revolution in the urban ghettos—and
assigned its people to infiltrate the newly perceived "enemy forces."†

Bailey cannot let go of the absurd image of Patty as a private in an
army of generals. If Patty had really joined the SLA, would she have
remained a private? No, she would have demanded a promotion, says
Dr. Orne, with the logic of a captain of Hussars, and the SLA would
have given her one. But the SLA was no imperial army, merely a tiny,
terrorist rat pack, and before recruits No. 10 and No. 11 could join their
"army," everybody else in it burned up.

During recess the reporters marvel at Bailey's skill. "In ten years of
covering trials, that was the best direct examination I've ever seen,"
says Theo Wilson, one pro appreciating another.

Bancroft's counterattack is unexpected. How is it that Dr. Orne did
not attempt to inform himself of the additional background information
on Miss Hearst that was developed by the United States in the course
of preparation for trial? Had not Dr. Joel Fort, an independent psychiatrist consulting with the government, suggested that Dr. Orne examine
the government materials and also look into the legal definition of
"coercion"? Yes, but their conversation seemed to Orne somewhat

---

*Dr. West's ties were confirmed in a *New York Times* story of August 2, 1977, on the CIA's
long-term program and study of behavior control.
†Another conspiracy theory to which right-wing analysts incline is that in the beginning Cinque
was being run by "outside radical strategists"—Cubans or Chinese or South American Maoists.

improper. Bancroft pushes for a better answer. Finally Dr. Orne says, "I was quite outraged by what had happened with the examination of Miss Hearst, and I did not feel I wanted to contact the government." Precisely what outraged him is not made clear, but Bancroft has successfully raised the question of whether Orne's Old World sense of punctilio might not have overwhelmed his scientific objectivity.

For the past eleven days Dr. Orne has been present in this courtroom, together with Doctors West and Singer and, lately, Dr. Lifton, is that not correct? Yes. And do the doctors and their wives sit in the same row? Yes. Stay in the same hotel? Yes. Eat together? Sometimes. (One gets a renewed sense of what this defense must be costing Randolph Hearst.) Is Dr. Orne also being paid? For my time, yes. Is he, then, collecting a double salary? No, he is on vacation from his university.

Does he recall his testimony in a Los Angeles murder case three years ago: "Psychiatrists are not very good at recognizing the truth"? Yes. He was talking about "specific lies and specific truth. . . . This is not what a psychiatrist is trained to examine." Once more one hears the raw, scraping sound of psychiatry grating against law.

BANCROFT *(sharply):* In other words, if it were shown to you that Willie Wolfe never did sexually impose himself with this defendant, would it interest you?

An audible gasp of outrage from Patty. She and Bailey whisper to each other, arms entwined, as if arm wrestling.

You testified yesterday, Doctor, that the defendant told you the bank robbery "was like a dream." Now, if the defendant had already told Dr. West, "I was in a dreamlike state . . ."

"I didn't say that!" Patty whispers to Bailey.

". . . might it not be self-serving to say it again, in the sense that it would fit in with what she'd told the previous psychiatrist?"

The problem with all psychiatric testimony is that you can always take a single instance and make it seem ridiculous to the layman. But it is not the single instance that is the basis for Orne's opinion. It is the pattern of statements. The striking thing about Miss Hearst is her unwillingness to say things or even go along with things that are not completely what she believes.

Bancroft presses on. Aren't there several reasons why people minimize what has happened to them? Yes. That's why Orne was so careful. First he questioned the psychological tests. He checked to find out whether "Miss Hearst had taken any courses in psychology. She had not. In fact, she showed a remarkable lack of interest in psychology, for a young person."

It's perfectly possible, is it not, Doctor, for a person to give honest responses to a Rorschach test and still tell a phony story? Of course. Throughout his cross-examination of the defense's expert witnesses, Dave Bancroft has been formulating the same question in different ways: Is there not a second, equally plausible commonsense explanation of the defendant's curious behavior? Why is it necessary to see her as a victim of something so fancy as "coercive persuasion"? Why can't the symptoms she has exhibited since her capture be seen simply as the normal reaction of a scared kid who knows she's done something wrong and is now in one hell of a jam? It scarcely takes a psychiatrist, he repeatedly implies, to see that this is the truth of the situation.

Now the prosecutor is ready to ask his big question again. "Doctor, in determining the reason for the low marks [in the first IQ tests], did you consider, as a possible simpler reason than posttraumatic neurosis, that this was an examination given to a young woman from a prominent family who had publicly scorned her parents, who was deeply involved in a notorious terrorist group, no matter how, who had been the subject of one of the most intensive womanhunts in recent history, and was in jail facing multiple felony charges, and who was called upon to defend herself by possibly testifying against former associates, and having to face up to her family, and perhaps be humiliated by relying on them to *again* get her out of some trouble—wouldn't that have created a pretty stressful and rather depressed situation and feelings of hopelessness and destruction?"

But a psychiatrist is a psychiatrist is a psychiatrist; Bailey's three big guns are great experts in their fields, and they have come here, at great expense to the defense and at considerable inconvenience to themselves, to give these jurors the benefit of their combined expertise. No, says Dr. Orne, all that would not account for the decreased IQ. The tests did not show the pattern of a depressed person but of a troubled person. Patty shows greater anxiety in the retests than in the originals, an indication that the numbness of the repatriate was beginning to wear off. The doctor interprets this as a sign of recovery.

Suddenly it's lunchtime. It has been a particularly good show this morning. Bailey/Orne and Bancroft/Orne were both *mano a manos* worth watching, and everybody—with the possible exception of the defendant—appears to leave the courtroom in high spirits. The jurors

(287)

in particular seem to have been hypnotized by the palaver, and for the first time, they look reluctant rather than grateful to escape for lunch.

I have lunch with my mother and one of the television sketch artists, Rosalie Ritz, a political activist and an old hand at covering California criminal trials. To her, Doctors West and Orne are different from all the other expert witnesses she has seen. Most psychiatrists are very cautious, she says; they are fearful of saying anything that might encourage the death penalty, or result in punishment of any kind. "But these two are not like the others; they're not basically listeners, they're talkers."

Why were the SLA tapes introduced by the defense rather than by the prosecution? Rosalie thinks she smells a rat, and, exhilarated by a glass of wine and the scent of conspiracy, we climb up the Rathskeller stairs into the late-February sunshine. Rosalie spots a familiar figure up ahead. "Wanna see Rosalie Ritz embrace the FBI?" she shouts, and sprints down the block. "Hey, Perrone! You following me again?" She throws her arms around a stocky, middle-aged man in a gray suit and fedora.

The FBI man takes the toothpick out of his mouth. "Hi ya, Rosalie. D'ja get molested yet? Finally?"

After lunch Dr. Orne is at pains to explain his thought processes. "I asked myself, Why would somebody rob a bank? There were only three reasons. One, she really needed the money, which I excluded in this instance." So either she was converted or coerced. In trying to make up his mind, the doctor had to add up many scraps of evidence rather than base his conclusion on any one thing.

Yes, says the prosecutor, but how could Patty's failure to resist the sexual advances of Willie Wolfe, for example, provide a basis for judging her truthfulness? Could not the fact that Patty described herself as "helpless" during her encounter with Wolfe equally be interpreted as self-serving? It could. But "usually when you have a girl who describes a rape she describes *some* resistance. At least she says, I *tried* to push him away."

I don't know what happened to Patty, but once, long ago, I was raped myself, and there *was* a certain ambiguity to the experience. I knew the man and did not at first fear him, did not resist very much until things somehow got out of control, and by then I couldn't get away. I have since learned that my experience is quite commonplace. In any event, if some shrink had asked me about it afterward—indeed, come to think of it, when one did—I replied exactly in the manner Orne is now describing as usual: I responded with the most vituperative kind of false accusations: "He hit me! He forced me!" And so on. In contrast, Patty displayed a "strange flatness" when Orne asked her reaction to the attack. This was odd because it was an inappropriate response to forced intercourse with a man she didn't choose, didn't want, who "was filthy." . . . I wonder how this interpretation is coming through to the women on the jury, but there is no way to know.

When he asked specifically whether Wolfe had threatened to kill her, Orne couldn't even get an answer. "Her failure to make it a good story is what I found so impressive. She had a remarkable resistance to embroidering." Couldn't it be, Doctor, that she already had such a good story going? Isn't there a common TV commercial "I can't believe I ate the whole thing"?

What did Patty tell Orne she was doing during the Missing Year? One hears the unmistakable *ping* of truth in his reply: Orne says his concern was only with the bank robbery, not with Mel's nor with what happened after Mel's, because the motivation of man moves forward in time, not backward. The robbery would explain Mel's; Mel's wouldn't explain the bank robbery, and the Missing Year couldn't explain it, either.

But without inquiring of her about the Missing Year, isn't there some question about whether or not Patty really was a captive during that time? *Did* you ask questions about that? What investigation did you do into the backgrounds of the young female members of the SLA? Did you review the documents seized in the house in Concord or do any interviewing of the families and friends of other SLA members? Who told you that she was a private in an army of generals?

Here Dr. Orne has an interesting reply. *She* told him, and she also told him that at no time was she ever given any real responsibility. This was another indication of her true psychological state. If this person "got religion," as you call it, Mr. Bancroft, after being kidnapped, then she should have become a leader in the SLA.

Really? How is that?

Because she was a leader in her family, the daughter considered most responsible. If Patty had really been converted, then after the group was decimated by the fire and down to one general, one aide, and one private, Patty—as a natural-born leader—would have led the recruitment drive.

"Uh-huh," says Bancroft. For him, this testimony is almost too good to be true; Dr. Orne is making Bailey and Johnson's carefully tailored silk purse back into a sow's ear. He lets Dr. Orne go on.

People who get committed to political systems talk in abstract terms about justice, right, and truth because their conviction is conceived as an abstract idea. "A terrorist is someone who kills people to save them. I mean, that's the definition of a terrorist." This is, of course, only the gentle Martin Orne's definition of a terrorist, and his political notions are now perceptibly wacko. He was interested in Patty's declaration that she intended to issue a statement from "a revolutionary feminist perspective," for example, because "I was intrigued that her mother was a feminist."

This really *is* too good to be true. "Where did you get that?" Bancroft inquires. From the newspapers, says Orne, blinking his puffy eyes into the gale of laughter that sweeps the courtroom.

How about the statement in the "Tania Interview" that Patty's decision to become a guerrilla fighter was not a sudden conversion but a gradual development, similar to the emergence of a photograph in the darkroom? "Ah, but that's exactly my point!" Orne beams. "That kind of simile is not Miss Hearst. It's abstract, it's beautiful, but it is not the way she talks." Score one for the doctor.

Don't people who are closely associated over a long period of time tend to start talking like one another? Score one for the prosecutor.

It is Dr. Orne's view, in sum, that Patty was coerced at the time of the bank robbery, and thereafter a dissociation began that continued for a year and a half. The weight of the data is to him unequivocal. Is it not even *possible* that the facts could be interpreted in exactly the opposite manner? "Possible? Of course it's possible. I'm certain if it were not possible, we wouldn't be here, and I would never have been asked to see the defendant."

"Thank you, Your Honor," says Bancroft, deadpan.

In the corridor, Bailey is restless, rocking on the balls of his feet, jabbing with his cigarette, eager to get into action, sardonic about new death threats against him and the Hearsts. "We're gonna get the judge to issue an order holding them in contempt if they kill us."

When redirect examination begins, we learn the source of Mr. Bailey's high spirits. In the Los Angeles murder case Bancroft asked about, Dr. Orne testified as an authority on the polygraph. Though polygraph findings are considered inadmissible by most courts, by bringing up this particular case the government has opened up the polygraph question.

Despite strenuous objections from the prosecutors, Bailey can now try to shove his polygraph findings on Patty into evidence through the back door. To do so would extend this trial by at least two weeks, the United States says, but Carter rules that during cross-examination the fatal door has indeed been opened, and Bailey has the legal equivalent of a free throw.

BAILEY: For testing the truthfulness of an isolated statement, what is the most effective means?

ORNE: The appropriate administration of a polygraph test by a competent examiner under circumstances designed to maximize the accuracy of the test.

Thank you, Doctor. Call Dr. Robert Jay Lifton to the stand.

Lifton is tall, dark, and intelligent-looking. On a scale of Jewish intellectual good looks from one to ten, say from Woody Allen to Arthur Miller, I might give Lifton an eight. He has at least as many and as impeccable credentials as his two predecessors: Yale, Harvard, Ford Foundation grant for East Asian studies; Air Force psychiatrist at Walter Reed; author of twelve books on psychiatric subjects. During the repatriation of the Korean POWs, Dr. Lifton accompanied a boatload of them back to the United States and conducted ninety individual shipboard psychiatric examinations. He became so interested in what had happened to these men that he moved to Hong Kong and undertook a nineteen-month intensive study of Chinese Communist thought reform. Lifton's book is regarded by many as the definitive work. His POW researches led him in turn to study some extremist American religious groups, such as the Children of God and the Unification Church. Many troubled kids and parents come to Lifton for his counsel. In 1955 Dr. Lifton met Dr. Singer at Walter Reed. He knows Dr. West as well, and they all know the absent Dr. Edgar Schein, *the* authority, and in 1961 the principal author of the seminal book *Coercive Persuasion*.

Dr. Lifton had read about the Patty Hearst case in the newspapers, but his first direct contact with it was in early June 1974, when Steven Weed visited him at his vacation house on Cape Cod. "He came to me as a very confused young man. He couldn't understand what was happening." At this, Patricia Hearst looks interested in the testimony for the first time.

Weed had read Lifton's book and wondered whether some of the things that occurred in the Chinese prisons might also have happened to his fiancée. Lifton told the troubled young man that in a life-or-death situation, any behavior is possible.

(291)

After Patty was arrested, Lifton got many calls from newsmen. "Of course, I would tell them I could not make any specific comments on the case itself," says the witness, beginning to seem somewhat pompous, "but they would say, *Could* it be some kind of brainwashing or thought reform?" and Lifton would reply with a guarded "yes."

There had also been a call from the government, asking if Dr. Lifton might be interested in consulting with the prosecution on the case—if there *was* a prosecution. But it was just a preliminary inquiry, and nothing came of it. Then, in December, Lifton got a call from Al Johnson, asking if he was willing to be a consultant for the defense. With the mutual reservation that nothing would be decided until Dr. Lifton had had an opportunity to examine Miss Hearst, the psychiatrist flew to San Francisco. He saw Patty in January for a total of fifteen hours and saw her again just last Saturday for two more hours.

This appears to be a convenient place to break for the day. Outside the courtroom, we learn that various news organizations today received death threats against five people connected with this trial: Judge Carter, F. Lee Bailey, Jim Browning, and the witnesses Tom Matthews and Anthony Shepard. The sender(s?) remain unidentified.

Friday, February 27

Before the jury comes in, Bailey withdraws his motion to show them the results of the polygraph tests. The defense has decided, "as a legal matter," that the presentation of this evidence could be construed as a waiver of the defendant's right to appeal Carter's Fifth Amendment ruling.*

*Sometime later, Nat Laurendi, a New York City detective and lie-detector expert, who was to have served as a rebuttal prosecution witness, charged there were "indications" of deception on the test results. Bailey then said that the original tests had been "exploratory," and Johnson added that "the question of voluntariness was a test question. It was determined after asking it that she could not be tested on state of mind. As to whether or not there were threats made by Cinque, she answered yes and passed with flying colors."

Nearly a year later, Dr. David Raskin, the defense polygraph expert who administered the tests, said he believed Patty when she told him, on the third day of the testing, that the SLA had

When Bailey asks Dr. Lifton to list the steps in the process of coercive persuasion, I see Dr. Kozol reach for his notebook. The first requirement, Dr. Lifton tells us, is total control of all communication between the captive and the outside world. This makes the captors omniscient, so much so that even after their control ceases, the captive "still feels their presence inside." Thus the process begins with a terrific assault on the prisoner's sense of self.

The second element is the manipulation of guilt and blame so that the victim is held entirely responsible for his predicament. Everybody on earth has a psychological predisposition to feel guilty; it is part of the residue of one's very early life, part of one's sense of wrongdoing and the expectation of punishment. Police in every country make use of this built-in human guilt factor. (So do lawyers, I remind myself. And nobody makes use of it more skillfully or insistently than F. Lee Bailey. Cross-examining a witness or talking to a headwaiter, Bailey plays on the person's guilt with the assurance of a blind accordionist.)

On the heels of guilt comes confession. The victim, feeling deeply threatened, "begins to look for ways to satisfy his captors." He invents guilt in order to make his confession sound more "real." Mandatory self-betrayal is critical to the coercive process because it cuts the victim off from his old roots and loyalties. (Question: Is this not just what Bailey and West forced Patty, or Tania, to do to her SLA roots when they undertook to defend her?)

A feeling follows that one has reached the breaking point. This is a period of extreme anxiety about death, and in a sense, a kind of slow death has already overtaken these isolated, fearful, guilt-ridden people. Now comes a burst of leniency by the captors—the removal of the handcuffs or chains or the gift of a cellmate to relieve one's isolation. Though the reward is small, the prisoner feels tremendous relief and a renewed eagerness to live. He begins to search for a sure path to survival. Then the clincher: group and peer pressure applied by fellow prisoners. To prove to his peers that he has reformed, the prisoner

---

threatened to kill her and had told her to announce her name during the robbery. Bailey's failure to put Raskin on the witness stand may have cost Patty an acquittal, he charged. But Patty's answers to the first two days of questions were ambiguous and could have been difficult to interpret for the jury. Raskin blamed Johnson for insisting that ambiguous "state-of-mind" questions be asked at all—questions such as "Did you *willingly* go along with the SLA after they threatened to kill you?"—in order to bolster the defense claim that Patty had been "brainwashed."

When the polygraph proved unable to handle psychological ambiguity any better than the forensic process itself, the tests were scrapped, he told *People* magazine in December 1977.

struggles the harder to effect that reform. Behind this is what Dr. Lifton terms "a very simple but rather terrorizing principle: that the ones conducting the reform sessions take over the right to decide who lives and who dies."

What Dr. Lifton has been describing, he says, is a combination of traumatic neurosis and survivor's syndrome. The same patterns appeared among the survivors of West Virginia's recent Buffalo Creek disaster, in which a slag-heap dam collapsed and in ten minutes 125 miners and their families were flushed away. Lifton had helped to arrange psychotherapy for the survivors and he also helped to prepare the lawsuit against the mining company, which subsequently paid damages of $13 million. The significant part of that case was the establishment of a legal precedent of psychic damage, "built largely around my work."

When Dr. Lifton studied the survivors of Hiroshima, he was astounded to find people still exhibiting symptoms of survivor's syndrome seventeen years after the atom bomb. His book about it, *Death in Life*, developed the basic concept of survivor's syndrome, and is frequently quoted in the psychiatric literature. The study of "massive trauma," in which the experiences of survivors are directly related to traumatic neurosis, is a new and growing area of psychiatric inquiry. Reviewing the Hearst case in the light of his massive knowledge in this field (and from Lifton's demeanor, it is clear he agrees that his knowledge *is* massive), the doctor found that, one way or another, Patricia had had each of the eight experiences he has enumerated.

Could you document that, Doctor?

Lifton, the expert's expert, the Harvard man, clears his throat. One, she was thrust into the totally controlled environment—the closet. Two, the SLA gave her the sense they were omniscient. Leaning forward, inclining his large, well-modeled head toward the jury, wrinkling his lofty, intellectual brow, fixing them with his fine, bespectacled eyes, gesturing with large, shapely hands, the witness proceeds. "She said to me"—he leans still farther forward—"she told me, 'I confessed to anything. Because they seemed to know everything about me anyhow.' She also—"

There is a loud thud. "Just a moment, Doctor!" Judge Carter says. ". . . a brief recess, please . . ."

The woman juror closest to Lifton has pitched forward and passed out cold at his feet. A bailiff helps her up, and the rest of the jury straggle out behind her, clucking sympathetically. Lifton appears confused.

In the corridor, Tom Padden is muttering, "Ask that guy a question, you get four paragraphs."

When court reconvenes, an alternate has taken the place of the stricken juror—victim of a sudden intestinal attack—and the professor resumes his lecture. The defendant's sense of being totally controlled was present from the instant of her capture. "I felt like a 'thing' in the closet," she told Lifton. Patty's sense of guilt was very strong. She already felt guilty for being a Hearst and—Lifton turns directly to the jury—in addition, she felt the same guilt you or I would feel if we were put in a closet and accused. "Because all of us have a store of guilt. Not legal or moral guilt but psychological guilt," the mental capacity to experience oneself as bad or wrong. The jurors now pay close attention as if they at last have a glimmer of what all these psychiatrists have been talking about.

Overwhelmed by primal guilt and a desire to appease her captors, Patty began telling the SLA all sorts of things that weren't true. This was the self-betrayal, the enforced burning of all the victim's bridges. In Patty's case it took the form of making propaganda tapes and denouncing her family, although "the ultimate act of self-betrayal" was the coerced bank robbery, which was then further reinforced by the Attorney General's remark.

During her first two months of captivity Patty was threatened with death many times. Her very real fear was enhanced by the SLA's boasting about Foster's murder, the cyanide bullets, the omnipresent guns, and her confinement in the closets, especially the tiny second closet, in which she feels "already dead." Cinque visits her here and says, "Fight or die." Thus, he gives her the early signal, sometime in mid-March—the date is uncertain—of what her life will *have to become* if she is to survive. Later, when he gives her an "ostensible choice," she already has accepted the prior signal: Unless she stays, she will be killed. Her struggle from then on is to convince them that she really wants to stay.

Now the moment of slight leniency, the opportunity to adapt to one's captors. One is shown a path. Patty is reborn as Tania, comes out of the closet, and her hair is shorn. After the robbery she actually feels her ties to her past have been destroyed.

The doctor now wishes to differentiate between compliance and ideological or political conversion. The distinction interests him greatly, and he has questioned Patty closely. In his judgment, Patty was in a psychological state of "absolute compliance, but with virtually no ideological conversion." Lifton recognizes the clenched-fist salute after her capture as the "last act of compliance" he has so often observed in others. To Lifton, the parallels between Patty's case and that of the Chinese prisoners are so striking that he almost seems to see Patricia marching across the bridge into Hong Kong.

The witness was impressed by the speed with which the coerced ideology fell by the wayside as soon as Patty was arrested. By the time he met her, in early January, her only ideological set was "what I would call a mild-to-moderate feminism"—he speaks of this as if it were a fever or rash—"principally associated with Wendy Yoshimura."

Dave Bancroft objects that Lifton's testimony is "not responsive to questions." And, indeed, for some time there have been none.

"You want a question?" With burning contempt, Bailey inquires, "Doctor, would you have *liked* to see her when she was first arrested?"

Bailey's personality is so aggressive I think he could brainwash me in half an hour. Come to think of it, possibly he has. I consider the eight steps to perdition in this context. It started with our first meeting in Massachusetts, when I felt almost totally in his power. I attributed my feeling of helplessness to my ignorance of the law and insensibility to all strategies of defense. Whether in chess, criminal matters, love, or war, I have never learned to see the punch coming. My imagination has just never worked that way. By now, life has so often socked me with a Rube Goldberg boxing glove that I am used to it. But Bailey made me feel stupid. I was never entirely sure what he was talking about but didn't want to ask. I felt it was my fault and then experienced guilt or blame. To cover my ignorance, I would nod wisely and cast sincere, comprehending glances; this was my self-betrayal. Now the bridges were burned. Point five, the anxiety about death, did not occur with Bailey, but I certainly experienced an anxiety that my deception would be found out. Certainly my ties to my past have been cut. I have quit *Newsweek,* renounced all weekly-deadline journalism after a quarter-century. Many colleagues are skeptical of my current project—though none more so than I. Well, to hell with it. If Bailey has tried to brainwash me, I have survived it, just as I will prevail over the grinning imp of no-confidence who sits on my shoulder as I write. I shall observe this case from now on with a cooler eye.

Lifton wishes he had seen Patty earlier but even when he was brought into the case, in mid-January, "she still had a classical picture of post-survival syndrome."

Look! My homemade transcript already reflects my new, cooler attitude. "Bullshit," it says right here in blue notebook number four, bottom of page 169. NOTEBOOK: *Bullshit! Guys who want to see "classical" pictures always do. The landscape arranges itself in Ionian modes; Vivaldi plays as background music. Robert J. Lifton is so eager to believe, he is self-brainwashed.* F. Lee Bailey, with his understanding of another man's vanity, must have been reasonably confident this would happen to Lifton—and if it didn't, he could always dump him.

I find Lifton's extrapolation from his Hong Kong priests and doctors to Patty Hearst farfetched. To some degree, we all see what we want to see. Just now, for example, a physician has been describing some rather subtle observations he has made on a subject glimpsed only through a glass darkly, and long after the fact. Yet we have just watched the same man be utterly oblivious of the suddenly and obviously ill woman in the jury box, right under his nose.

It is coming close to noon. Catherine Hearst has slipped a compact out of her purse, and during the wrap-up expert-witness question we have learned to expect, she checks her flawless makeup. Do you have an opinion, Doctor, from all you have observed? Yes, this is a traumatic neurosis—no doubt in Lifton's mind. By virtue of both her tender years, the importance of which cannot be overestimated, and the sheltered life she had led, Patricia Hearst was less well equipped to withstand what happened to her than any other person Lifton has ever interviewed. "She was overwhelmingly more vulnerable. She had no extensive education, career, knowledge, or set of adult loyalties of any developed kind."

"Do you know any way, Doctor, of defending oneself against such onslaughts?"

"There is none. They can break down anyone. The result is compliant behavior and traumatic neurosis."

"Thank you, Doctor. Your witness."

Although the judge calls recess promptly at noon, one juror who hasn't bothered to wait is already fast asleep. It is feeding time now for the reporters, and the members of Patty's defense team enjoy slipping tidbits to favorites. Gonzales, the appeals expert, points out that the sleeper has made it an "illegal" eleven-man jury. McNally confides that the bank film has come back from Itek Labs and shows clearly that Patty was under Cinque's gun. Then how come the FBI claimed otherwise? "They lied." Behind a pillar, Jolly West coaches Bob Lifton in jury technique. "Speak slowly, and be very kind. Treat them like a group of slightly retarded children."

"Where's Al?" someone shouts.

Bailey crinkles his eyes. "He has been assigned to the brothels of Las Vegas to see what he can come up with."

Lifton may expect a rough cross-examination from Bancroft, but it begins, after lunch, quietly enough. Did Dr. West recommend Lifton for the defense team? Quite a number of people recommended me, of whom he was one. When the doctor and his wife arrived in San Francisco, they had dinner with Al Johnson, "but we did not discuss the case." I think, What an unusual evening that must have been! I have never spent five minutes with Johnson, Bailey, Lifton, Bancroft, or anyone else in San Francisco in which some aspect of this case was not discussed. That the government knows about the dinner reminds one how closely the FBI is watching everybody, including Bailey's trio of imported, expensive, pedigreed dogs—his expert witnesses.

Did Lifton seek out other evidence or view the bank film or read the "Tania Interview" before forming his opinion? No, though he read it afterward with great interest. It is a classic document of its kind. He has seen many like it, built around a kernel of truth but mainly intended to *hide* the coercion. The subject must appear to have come upon the new truth in a natural way, through a reinterpretation of the old data rather than through coercion. This manuscript is the result.

Did Lifton feel confident making a medical judgment on the basis *only* of his own interviews and the West/Singer report, without the "Tania Interview"? "I have to have it in front of me if you are going to ask me questions about it. Incidentally, I think there is one thing I should also add before you go off into this document. I conducted these fifteen hours of interviews, and I also then—when those interviews were more than half finished—carefully read the West/Singer report, including the psychological tests, in which, as I said before, I found confirmation both of my clinical findings and information in great detail about many of the documents which seemed completely consistent with the clinical findings that I had."

The doctor does himself no good with these windy answers. All the time he is rattling on, Bancroft is coiling himself to strike. "Doctor, where do you find any reference to the 'Tania Interview' in Dr. West's report?" Bancroft is wound so tightly that he asks questions twice over; it is like a nervous tic. "Where did you find any reference to this document in his report?"

The witness cannot answer. An embarrassing moment, and Bancroft makes it last as long as possible before passing on to his next question.

Since Lifton is aware that before he got to Patty she had spent approximately forty hours with Dr. West and fifteen hours with Dr. Orne, and that she was receiving regular visits from her own psychiatrist, Dr. Richards, will he admit that all these many hours spent with lawyers and doctors might have caused a slight shift in her attitudes since her arrest? No, I will not. Doctor, how many kidnapping victims have you known? None. How many persons you have examined in jail have been fugitives on felony charges for at least two years? None. How many young women have you interviewed in jails who came from prominent families and got involved in terrorist groups? None.

How many forensic situations have you been in? I haven't worked in any cases in which criminal responsibility was involved, but I have been very interested over the years in redefining the role of the psychiatrist in court proceedings, so that he functions less as a semilawyer and more as an expert in his own field of psychiatry. The leading judicial theorist in this regard happens to be Judge David Bazelon, with whom Lifton has held numerous discussions.

That may be so, but Dr. Lifton is allowing himself to become contentious, which earns a sneering rebuke from the prosecutor. "Anything else you want to tell us in answer to that question?"

I notice in one of your books that you interviewed twenty-five Westerners who had been imprisoned in China. Did you interview all twenty-five right after their release? If you'd read my book a little more carefully, Mr. Bancroft, you'd have seen that I interviewed one man three years later, in Germany.

"I wasn't sure the jury had read it, Doctor." Of the twenty-five, only one was female, I believe?

"Maybe I should have my book." Lifton reaches out a hand.

Another sneer: "I thought you had read it."

Another riposte: "I think I might understand it a little better than you do."

We have here a testy, prickly witness who resembles the dormitory bright boy, contentious by nature, smarter than the others, and bristling to take on all comers. But coercive persuasion of the examiner by the witness is a courtroom technique that can never work. Far better to be no more forthcoming than necessary. Cooperate, understate, and do not, for God's sake, elaborate. Once more, Bancroft is gathered to strike. Now, Doctor, do you know of anybody who went through the prisoner-of-war process who ever committed an overt act of violence against their own kind? An American pilot flying in formation with the

Red Chinese or North Korean air force? A good question; it grabs the jurors' attention.

"My sense of what the Chinese were after was false confessions of germ warfare for propaganda purposes. And they got them." A straight answer, as good as the question, though not perhaps so effective with the jury.

Bancroft reads a passage from the "Tania Interview": " 'The first time I took the blindfold off to take a bath, I couldn't focus very well. Everything was out of proportion. My eyes hurt. I couldn't open them for a couple of minutes, because they hurt so bad.' " Now, Doctor, is there any "canned" or "loaded language" here?

No, this is an example of how the victim is trained to reinterpret his experience. The paragraph "domesticates" a violent experience. A further example occurs on the next page. . . .

NOTEBOOK: *Lifton seems to be saying, Because she underwent violent assault and kidnapping, ergo she cannot have been genuinely converted. But why cannot both be true?* One difference between psychology and the law is that in the mind two things can be equally true, and sometimes three or four. The mind is oceanic; the law is snug harbor. For the past week Bailey's three big guns have kept up their continuous offshore barrage. But until the smoke clears, there is no way to know how much damage they have done.

Saturday, February 28

Over the weekend, Bailey expands his trial-by-media and takes his case to Stanford Law School. "If Patty had really become a flaming revolutionary," he tells four hundred students there, "she would be doing just what Emily Harris told her—jumping up and down and calling the judge a pig." As for Bailey, he would have turned down the case. During the question period he is asked why the SLA women —known to be feminists—would permit two of their male soldiers to rape a sister in a closet? His answer frightens me for Patty. "The SLA women were not real feminists. They just kind of slopped around. The rapists knew that physical resistance from Patty was out of the question, so they just walked in and serviced themselves."

Bailey has deeply misperceived the SLA. He fails to understand that Cinque was a black idol, the symbol of American racism—to the SLA men as much as to the women. Cinque was the necessary tent pole without which the entire SLA circus would collapse. His holiness and mystery were not only in his negritude but in his class, his ghetto background, his prisoner's stripes. Cinque was that stock American hero the sacred outlaw, dyed black according to the fashion of the times.

My third meeting with Wendy Yoshimura's defense committee takes place on Saturday afternoon, this time in the small, bright offices of her Oakland attorneys, and it is the worst yet. I still am not permitted to see Wendy alone; they still don't trust me or my motives, and it is apparent by now they never will. Despite Wendy's open face and open manner, she must be afraid of me, and now her well-meaning advisers, today a Japanese-American attorney and a Chinese-American radio reporter, are making a common mistake: They hope to control the story they want told. Anyone with a story to tell is foolish to believe he can in any way "control" its presentation by the media. Even such a master as F. Lee Bailey can't do it for long. Ultimately one will lose control; it is the nature of the media miasma that this be so. The big swamp is pocked with warning signs: PROCEED AT YOUR OWN RISK. One's public image can be controlled only by shunning all contact with mass communications. Climb up Simeon Stylites' pillar, haul up your basket and stay there. In theory, one can still pull a Salinger and hide in a house in the woods. But even this may earn for you, as it did for J. D. Salinger, a cover story in *Time* magazine.

The defense committee's paranoia is contagious; I catch it, and when the radio reporter sets up his tape recorder right beside my own (to check my veracity? to steal my interview?), I take offense, unplug my own recorder, and perform a brief, formal interview charade that I figure may be less discourteous than my getting up and walking out. Inscrutabilities and cross-purposes compound themselves.

Manzanar is "really nowhere land," says Wendy. "It's a place where you can't stay clean. When you eat sandwiches there, it's really a sandwich." She smiles at the weary old joke. In Japan, Wendy's earliest memories are of someone chopping wood, little people, a boat. "It was an island, but it wasn't like Tahiti." Yes, her parents still speak Japanese at home.

I use the word *nisei* and the attorney interrupts to instruct me gently in the correct use of these terms: *nisei* is a second-generation Japanese. *Sansei* is third-generation. These are simply the Japanese words for "two" and "three." Wendy's father is a *kibee-nisei,* meaning a person who was born in the United States but who went back to Japan to be educated. There are also *kibee-sansei,* "which is considered not so good." By then assimilation is expected to have taken a firmer hold.

My questions about Wendy's legal prospects are interrupted again when I use the word "Oriental." This time the radio reporter explains that he and Wendy prefer to be referred to as Asian-Americans. "Oriental" has an undesirable "exotic" connotation; the distinction is akin to that between "Negro" and "black."

Wendy's first line of defense in her coming trial on weapons-possession charges will be to challenge the fairness of the jury. The Asian-American racial level in jury selection has yet to be tested in court. It will be necessary to get hold of the proposed jury list, telephone each person, and ask about his or her attitudes toward the law and toward racial matters. The questioning will attempt to identify the percentage of persons who thought Wendy guilty when she became a fugitive; who identify her with Patty Hearst; who identify her with the SLA; who identify her with heinous crimes or with radical revolutionary activists, and therefore would tend to prejudge her. Talking to these people gives one a glimpse of the elaborate pretrial preparations that must take place before the curtain ever goes up on any courtroom drama. (Despite all the precautions, Wendy was convicted on January 20, 1977, of illegal weapons-possession, although the jurors deadlocked on the more serious charge of possession of an explosive with an intent to injure people or destroy property. Her conviction carries a penalty of up to fifteen years in prison, and the case is now being appealed.)

Wendy's cultural displacement, and her compound fracture of identity—racial, sexual, national, and even generational—is total. She is neither Japanese nor Japanese-American, not *nisei* or *sansei* or *kibee-sansei;* neither white nor Third World; she seems neither feminine nor masculine, and not lesbian, either; she belongs to no country, no nationality, no generation. Yet she is vivid, alive, *affirmed.* At her trial her lawyer will say that although people of Wendy's generation believe in speaking out against social injustice—unlike her tradition-minded parents, who believe that suffering in silence is a virtue—*sansei* also have "a strong tradition against stool pigeons." His client will refuse to give the names of anyone who helped her or who is not connected with the charges in her trial. "It would be morally indefensible and physically dangerous if she should be sent to prison." When the Harrises asked Wendy to help them find refuge, he will say, "she reluctantly agreed because she had been helped in the same situation." Rightly or wrongly, justifiably or unjustifiably, she acted out of "human concern."

Wendy herself will speak of the Japanese ideal of *on giri,* a concept that obliges one never to betray another who has helped him. Wendy's respect for and acceptance of *on giri* will earn her five citations for contempt of court.

Sunday, February 29

The morning paper reports that the FBI has raided "a terrorist bomb factory" and taken prisoner six members of the Emiliano Zapata Unit of the New World Liberation Front, which has been bombing the Bank of America, Safeway Stores, and other targets. The makeup of the unit is remarkably like that of the SLA: several recent dropouts from the straight life—the son of an Alcatraz prison guard who holds a college degree in criminology; a Sarah Lawrence girl working in San Francisco as a film editor; a trusted security guard from American Patrol Services. There is also one Third World ex-convict, with a record of heavy drug use, who got into left-wing groups inside prison, became romantically and politically involved with upper-class radical women after his release, and is now prepared to testify for the government against the others at the trial.

The story amounts to a case study in how the FBI infiltrates and suborns the underground Left. All you need to put the process in motion is one minority-group ex-con with some charisma, preferably hooked on drugs, and willing to do anything in return for freedom or reduced charges. The *Examiner*'s story is a reminder of why Patty is so dangerous just now. She is a ticking bomb, a grenade with the pin half pulled. Patty has *been there.* She's lived underground for over a year. It is increasingly apparent that during the Missing Year she had knowledge of, and may even have participated in, criminal acts. She met other fugitives. The *Chicago Tribune* reports that she met Kathy

Boudin. I have little doubt she also met Bernardine Dohrn, Cathy Wilkerson, Susan Saxe, Mark Rudd, and the rest. They would have been curious about her and would have relaxed their natural caution in order to see her, touch her, test for themselves the authenticity of her conversion, share the common pride in what the SLA had accomplished.

What must they feel now, these Boudins and Dohrns and all the anonymous others who helped, lionized, drove cars, rented safehouses, gaped at, or otherwise dropped their revolutionary guard because Tania was among them? Now Tania, but no longer Tania, has been on the stand, singing, and the whole damned Left is in mortal danger. No telling what she may do, given her flippy mental state, her evil parents' reassertion of control, the legal machinations of her lawyers, her lack of genuine political roots, and the dread conspiracy of cops and clunky FBI men who control fascist "Amerikkkaa." To the extreme Left, the fascist insect is the Old Man's granddaughter, the girl who has been sitting in the witness box in Judge Carter's courtroom, buzzing, buzzing, and spinning webs.

The Hearst family is a uniquely American dynasty. Its franchise is rooted squarely in the First Amendment. Its wealth derives directly from the public's appetite for news and gossip of a sensational, violent, mysterious, criminal, sexy, or expensive nature—and from the founding father's unparalleled ability to dish it up.*In the ongoing struggle between the press and the public, the people fight for privacy and the press fights for access. Or so it used to be. Now things work the other way around. Politicians, media freaks, and assassins fight to get on the front page, and editors fight to keep them from taking over. (At the Hearst-versus-HERNAP level, the media war is a lot more complex, partly because the protagonists are Hearsts.) Originally the constitutional guarantee of free speech meant freedom to speak out against tyranny, to denounce the king. Too often, of late, it has become the freedom to be prurient, to poke the lens under the dying man's blanket,

---

*The family attitude toward the family product was summed up in William Randolph Hearst's famous rebuke to his man in Havana, just before the outbreak of the Spanish-American War. Hearst had sent the artist Frederic Remington to Cuba to cover the early fighting, and in due course the boss received a telegram: EVERYTHING IS QUIET. THERE IS NO TROUBLE HERE. THERE WILL BE NO WAR. I WISH TO RETURN. REMINGTON. Hearst cabled back: YOU FURNISH THE PICTURES AND I'LL FURNISH THE WAR. Seventy-five years later, his granddaughter was furnishing both.

into the grieving widow's eye, under the politician's bed. Yet the country had been traumatized, no one knew how deeply, by Vietnam and Watergate, and if any group had pulled us through, it seemed to be the press. The latest American folk hero was turning out to be our old 1930s friend the crusading reporter: Superman *was* Clark Kent.

Today journalism is the most popular major on the American campus, and J-school enrollments have tripled in ten years. Enough college students are now studying the subject—which most working journalists believe cannot be taught in colleges—to replace every working reporter in the land. By the time Patricia Hearst was kidnapped America had become the most media-saturated civilization the world had ever known. The country was entirely wired up. Ninety-seven out of one hundred households had at least one television set, which burned an average of six hours and forty-nine minutes a day. In the course of a week television reached everybody in the country over the age of seventeen. Voyeurism had come into its Golden Age. To be a journalist in the 1970s was a way to get into politics without having to work for a candidate, a way to get into a profession without having to tell lies, a way to go to war without having to buy a ticket, a way to play games without having to get off the couch, a way to deliver opinions without having to think, a way to see the world without having to get out of bed, a means of leading a selective, chosen life. If the particular events of that life were chosen by somebody else, even by *circumstance,* what matter? Belonging to the press is a way to ride the highs and pass over the valleys of existence, to skim the cream of life and drink it through a silver straw.

I think it no accident that so many of today's successful journalists were orphans, outcasts, lonely kids, people born in trunks, reared in hotels, rootless children of divorced or loveless homes who escaped the chrysalis of childhood isolation to become vicarious butterflies in life's garden. Journalism is an endless sequence of highs—the borrowed highs of other people's lives. It offers the maximum of vicarious living with a minimum of emotional involvement. As an organism the reporter is more like a cabbage than a turnip: all top and very little root. Since this same rootless effulgence of surface, the same fear of involvement or connection, the same lack of sustained conviction, are characteristic of many nonmedia Americans, it is scarcely surprising that the fashionably named "investigative reporter" (what other kind *is* there?) has become everyone's favorite good guy.

A few years ago the historian Daniel Boorstin identified a modern news phenomenon he called the pseudoevent, the event that exists solely *in order to be covered.* President Kennedy's triumphal arrival in Berlin to make his "Ich bin ein Berliner" speech was Boorstin's supreme example. HERNAP evolved into an even more gigantic pseudoevent. It was created by a few Berkeley dropouts, and it didn't cost a dime, yet it became a multimedia extravaganza that had the propaganda power of a pseudoevent, but also had an act of terrifying aggressive reality at its core and strong roots in our unconscious collective fantasy. The story came along at a time when the news media's capacities to communicate, or overcommunicate, were larger than ever, and the volume of available news—*juicy* news, especially—was diminishing. The previous decade had been unusually violent, turmoiled by just the kind of action news that tabloids and television cover best: Assassinations, urban riots, antiwar demonstrations, the war itself, space probes, and moon shots. The media, especially the new form of television, had rapidly expanded to keep pace. Then, quite suddenly, nothing much was going on; it was as if a sort of "black hole" had occurred in the media miasma. After the hard chase of Watergate, the fox had (almost) been run to ground, and if the Vietnam War was not yet quite over, it was equally true that the American public was sick of looking at it. Enter, as if on cue, one missing heiress abducted by a bunch of commie-pinko-prevert-nigger-lovers, just in time to fill the big hole in the front page, the dread dead spot on the nightly news. The story seemed heaven-sent; a grandfather's gift from beyond the grave offered by the inventor of yellow journalism himself.

Not only was the press in a period of investigative ennui; another, more subtle shift was going on. As the war wound down, there had been such a severe falling off in serious news coverage and network commitment to investigative reporting that Columbia University, with Du Pont money, launched a two-year study of the "news slump." A major cause of the slump turned out to be increasing network reliance on outside news consultants and market researchers, people who tended to recommend attention-getting devices and tabloid-news techniques over responsible news judgments.

The trend had begun several years before, when the format of local television shows began to be revamped so as to emphasize chitchat, trivia, "warmth" and "personalities," plus consumer information, sports and weather, gourmet tips, fashion shows, gags, ad-libs, and other ways to enliven "dead air"—all at the expense of "hard news." Ratings rose. The formula, which originated at ABC-TV in New York and was widely imitated, came to be called happy-talk news. Paddy Chayefsky saw the trend and made a wickedly brilliant movie about it called *Network*. He even used an SLA type of guerrilla band in his subplot.

In *The Newscasters* Ron Powers contends that as happy-talk news became the norm the real news was drowned in freshets of trivia, and the news business partook of "the meretricious values of show business." The meretricious values of ladies' magazines, I would add, but I suppose it all depends on where you cut your wisdom teeth, and I have no wish to quibble with an ally. Powers believes that stations have a moral duty and a legal responsibility under the Federal Communications Act to inform their viewers and that happy-talk news evades this responsibility. He's right, and newsmen know it, so when HERNAP came along, hard news undeniably but hard news that *sounded like* soap opera, all the stops were pulled out.

As an added attraction, the central character of this melodrama was female. After ten years of war, the country was sick of looking at mostly men. There was still good old Jackie O, of course, but her image had become somewhat ambiguous: She was seen now as a dark queen, a vivacious widow who loved much but loved money most. On the home front, another revolution had occurred: The so-called Women's Movement was in full tide, and the charged-up air crackled with feminine emotions newly released. Female fury misplaced could be truly terrifying. After the Manson murders, in 1969, Weather Underground leader Bernardine Dohrn took to greeting her comrades with a signal of three fingers upraised. It was a gesture of approval for the kitchen fork left stuck in one of the female victims. (Interestingly, the Weatherwomen, in their frenzy of hate, had displaced the fork from the abdomen of Mrs. Nino La Bianca to the pregnant belly of the beautiful Sharon Tate.)

It was a time when millions of newly liberated women were so heroine-hungry that, as with sailors on shore leave, almost any woman would do. Patty became a candle on which to fix their bright gaze—whether of admiration, scorn, or compassion scarcely mattered.

When I returned to San Francisco, after Patty's recapture, and bought the family newspaper, it was like old times. Anyone who feared that the traditional Hearst Day-Glo style of journalism might be fading had only to look at the makeup of the front page. The biggest story was SLA'S PLOT TO INFILTRATE FIRMS. "SLA sympathizers" had applied for jobs at the Pacific Gas and Electric Company, it said, and had also prepared job résumés for the Oakland Police Department—which is some reach just to keep "SLA" in your largest type. Across the bottom of the page, THE ULTIMATE LOW IN PORNOGRAPHIC MOVIES, by-lined "Examiner News Service," described eight snuff films, showing actual on-screen murder and dismemberment of actresses after they had previously engaged in a variety of on-screen sexual activities. The third-biggest story detailed the voluntary death of a father of four, a kidney patient who chose to "put my life in the hands of Jesus" rather than endure the unbearable agony of further medical treatment. HOW KOOKY ARE WE? asked a banner across the top of the page, announcing a new series on violence. "Is the Bay Area really the Kook capital of the nation? Is there something about Northern California that brings out the demons among us?" The news that Patty Hearst had been indicted in Los Angeles was also on the front page, in a small box, but the story was carried inside. Terrorists infiltrating industry and the police; real murder committed for porno thrills; a small-scale family tragedy of suffering, death, and Jesus redemptive—all this in addition to the indictment of a fugitive heiress on eleven counts of kidnapping, robbery, and assault with a deadly weapon. Old Man Hearst in his wildest dreams could scarcely have imagined a better-balanced front page. At the *San Francisco Examiner,* it seemed safe to say, circulation might be dying, but tradition lives.

Several other truths about the press coverage of Patty's story also were now manifest, elements obscured until then by the emotionality on all sides. HERNAP was always more than a major media event; it was also a stunning media coup d'état. The SLA not only had staged America's first political kidnapping but had used Patty to score a propaganda triumph. The SLA didn't put Patty in the papers as much as it used Patty to put itself in the papers. Brilliantly. Every mad SLA demand had been slavishly met. Every word of its tapes and communiqués had been printed in full. Even the President of the United States had been unable to cut himself so fine a deal as did this phantom cobra band. Richard Nixon was subject at least to the "instant analysis" of Dan Rather.

HERNAP generated so little investigative reporting, it almost seemed as if no reporter wanted to spoil a good story by finding out what really happened. But that was not the case. San Francisco has always been a great newspapering town, spawning ground of Ambrose Bierce, Lincoln Steffens, and Jack London, not to mention the Hearsts, and in spite of the laughable/lamentable condition of its two daily newspapers, both of which regularly make the ten-worst-papers lists, the city still supports a collection of topflight reporters, columnists, essayists.*

What held good reporters back on HERNAP was not incompetence but humanity. They had been keenly aware of their obligation to weigh the public's right to know against Patty's right to live, especially in the early hours after her disappearance. When Patty's father at first requested an embargo on *any* coverage of the kidnapping, the entire press was willing to oblige. Only when the *Oakland Tribune* broke ranks twelve hours later was the scramble on.

At first the *Examiner* was extremely protective of the boss's daughter. The story about Patty's kidnapping was on the front page, but it omitted mention of the fact that Patty had been living with Steven Weed. When the SLA communiqués began arriving, the *Examiner* printed every word, as the terrorists demanded, and it was hard to see how the paper could do otherwise; it was not only the battered flagship of the Hearst newspaper chain but also the official mouthpiece of the victim's parents. Later, when vandalism and violence erupted in the PIN free-food giveaway, Hearst, fearing for his daughter's life, had asked his reporters to minimize the carnage.

When the SLA stuck up the bank, the *Examiner* was slower than the *Chronicle* to acknowledge that Patricia may have been "a willing participant," and it headlined its front-page story GUNS POINT AT TANIA IN BANK. But what was a father to do? In general, Randolph Hearst remained remarkably accessible to the press and courageously outspoken, even though he usually avoided holding press conferences until his own paper had been locked up.

The *Chronicle* was somewhat less guarded in its coverage, but still cautious enough so that after a few weeks its chief HERNAP reporter, Tim Findley, quit his job because he believed his work on the story was being compromised. According to John Bryan, editor of the *San Francisco Phoenix,* it was months before any major SLA story appeared in either San Francisco daily or went out over AP or UPI wires without first being cleared by Randolph Hearst.*

---

*The two San Francisco dailies have a somewhat symbiotic relationship. Although the *Chronicle* and the *Examiner* are independently owned (the *Chronicle* by the family of Trish Tobin) and consider themselves competitive, they share printing presses and advertising and business operations through a third company they jointly own, and they publish a combined Sunday paper. In September, the month Patty was captured, the *Chronicle* was selling 430,000 copies daily and the *Examiner* 158,000.

*John Bryan, *This Soldier Still at War* (New York: Harcourt Brace Jovanovich, 1975), p. 269.

The San Francisco press was well aware that it was being sucked in, co-opted, made to roll over and do tricks on the Hearsts' Oriental rug, then stand up on its hind legs and beg in front of the SLA fireplace. But reporters felt sorry for the kid and sorry for the parents.

The SLA had shown how easy it is today to stage a media coup d'état. All you need is a single dramatic situation, preferably in an enclosed space—a lone hijacker, even a streaker—or something more elaborate, such as Wounded Knee or "Son of Sam" 's letter to Jimmy Breslin. Once you stage your dramatic event and get it into print and on television one time, the media take over and do your job for you. They perpetuate the story and build it ever bigger, to feed their own insatiable appetite not only for product but for continuity and, if possible, for crescendo. Perhaps it would be more accurate to say, now that television's trick of instant replay is obliterating everybody's sense of history —while at the same time making us long for history the more, starving us for nostalgia—that the press has been not so much co-opted as become an integral part of the stories it covers. Very soon you wind up asking yourself, Who is really prisoner of whom? Is Patty prisoner of the SLA, or is the press prisoner of the SLA? Is the SLA the prisoner of the press, or are the Hearsts the prisoners of the press? The answer is four times yes.

FBI Director Clarence Kelley used to complain that he was "sick and tired of having people ask me at all my public appearances, 'Why can't you catch Patty Hearst?' " But once she was caught—or "rescued," to use her mother's preferred word—it was clear that the reporters had not just been covering the story but had been characters in it from the start. The first person publicly to identify the kidnappers had been Marilyn Baker, on KQED-TV. Later she gathered important evidence that had been overlooked by the cops in the SLA's abandoned Concord safehouse, and she somehow managed to obtain a copy of the bank's own film of the robbery and then have it shown on educational television. Within weeks of Patty's apprehension, *Rolling Stone* was telling the world all about where she had been and what she had been doing during the Missing Year.

This kind of wall-to-wall coverage provoked the lawyers on both sides into floods of self-justifying and self-promoting news leaks. Long before Patty came to trial, Browning was trying the prosecution case in the media at least as much as F. Lee Bailey was arguing the defense. The government's purpose was to put on a show trial and prove that the rule of law applies to rich and poor alike. Bailey's purpose was to prove the opposite. In their democratic zeal to treat the captured revolutionary like an "ordinary person," bench and bar now seemed to be trying, in Orwell's phrase, to make her "more equal than others"—which is to say, less.

Recently some industrial chemists left a mess of starch and fiber on their workbench overnight and in the morning discovered they had created a new compound with a seemingly unlimited ability to sponge up water. A chunk the size of a lemon could swiftly absorb sixteen gallons and swell up to look like a badly melted snowman. The chemists named their invention Super Slurp and predicted untold uses, including a revolution in the diaper industry. HERNAP was the Super Slurp of news stories, and the end, one feared, was not yet in sight.

One aspect of HERNAP as a media superevent was the mushroom growth of Patty Industries: books, novels, songs, and movies—porno and otherwise—as well as buttons, posters, T-shirts, bumper stickers, and more-or-less spontaneous happenings such as the 1975 Miss Universe Contest, held in a San Salvador hotel, at which Miss USA enlivened the opening-night festivities by dressing up in combat fatigues and pretending to stick up the joint. The automatic carbine she carried was real, and so were her support troops—government soldiers assigned to guard the hotel from possible attack by real urban guerrillas.

When she disappeared, Patricia Hearst slid as sleekly into world pop culture as a seal into a pool, and there were many other such "happenings."* But the major product of Patty Industries was always more media—film or printed matter—which could be divided into two categories: Pattypoop and Pattyporn. The first authoritative tally of Pattypoop-in-progress was published on June 24, 1974, on the front page of the *San Francisco Chronicle*. This story—in itself a way of prolonging HERNAP coverage despite the fact that all of the central characters had by then either been burned up or had vanished—reported at least eighteen writers sweating it out in San Francisco and environs on an imaginative assortment of literary pattycakes. One book-in-embryo was a memoir of Mizmoon, *In Search of a Sister,* by Patricia Soltysik's older brother, Fred. Another was *Cinque the Slave,* a nearly complete account of Donald DeFreeze's longtime career as a professional paid

*When COYOTE, the San Francisco–based prostitutes' self-help organization, staged its first hookers' convention at Glide Memorial Church, Patty Hearst was honored with a special award for "improving women's image in the media." COYOTE, understandably, instinctively appreciates Boorstin's law.

police informant and double agent. Its authors were Lake Hedley and Donald Freed, an ex-cop who was himself making something of a career of exposing police double agents.

Three more team-written books were being rollered through their authors' twin typewriters. Marilyn Baker was describing her adventures as a supersleuth with the help of a publisher-supplied ghost. Paul Avery, the *Chronicle*'s own man on the case, was doing a paperback for Dell with the help of Vin McLellan. And Tim Findley, who had been the *Chron*'s Woodward to Avery's Bernstein before he quit, had now gone over to *Rolling Stone* and, with the help of two young *Newsday* stringers, Carolyn Craven and Les Payne, was writing the straight Pattypoop for *Rolling Stone*'s book-publishing subsidiary, Straight Arrow Press.

The SLA can be thought of as a major and indeed seminal piece of media art, and, as such, an inquiry into its provenance was in order. One man well qualified to handle that was John Bryan, an experienced and innovative newsman. Bryan's book, therefore, would explore the origins of the SLA.

When everybody's central character turned up alive, if not well, in a house in the Mission District, the media were electrified into new spasms of overactivity, and on September 24 the *New York Post,* searching for new ways to keep the media ball rolling, issued a Pattypoop update and recount. Certain predictable media shifts had occurred. Curt Gentry had forsaken Patty for Charles Manson and written *Helter-Skelter,* the best-seller on the Manson murders, with Vincent Bugliosi, the Manson prosecutor. Bugliosi was now a candidate for attorney general of California, a campaign for which *Helter-Skelter* served as effectively ghoulish campaign literature. The first book out about Patty had been Marilyn Baker's *Exclusive!* It was written in three weeks and was almost exclusively about Ms. Baker, depicting the author as a female Dick Tracy, two leaps ahead of the cops. This was not exaggeration. Ms. Baker is fearless, angry, tireless, and tough. Because she particularly admired Patty's mother, who she felt had showed heroic strength of character, she was crushed when the Hearsts were critical of her efforts.

John Bryan's book was *This Soldier Still at War: The Story of the Vietnam Veteran Who Declared War Against His Own Country and Then Trained the SLA,* and it does a fine, fast job of reconstructing the motivation and genesis of the terrroist group, and of conveying the funky, paranoid flavor of once-gentle Joe Remiro and his deadly pals.

Then, two-thirds of the way through Bryan's story, half of Patty's California driver's license, a bunch of American Beauty roses, and a birthday card suddenly turn up on the author's own doorstep, along with a tape promising that Patty will be released within seventy-two hours. The reporter's conversion is faster than Tania's. Before Bryan can get his roses into water or the documents into a safe to secure them from the cops, he has become an actor in the drama, no longer an observer-interpreter. Now he sees his erstwhile brethren as "medialice" and Ms. Baker as "an aging peroxide blonde" throwing "her plastic-gutted weight around." Bryan's sudden strike against his colleagues makes him sound like a hissing cobra himself, but his temper tantrum does not occur until he has told most of his story, and told it very well. As Bryan describes him, Remiro is a more interesting, more tragic figure than Patty. It was this soldier's nightmare recollections of his participation in the massacre of Vietnamese peasants that turned Remiro into a killer-pacifist.

Steven Weed was within four pages of the end of his account of the affair when the damned girl turned up. Frankly, he wished it could have happened another three months later. Weed had been destroyed by HERNAP as much as anybody else had. Trying to make light of his loss, he joked that he had at least earned himself a place in the *Guinness Book of World Records* as the first man ever cuckolded on national television. By the time Patty reappeared Weed found himself, in his own word, "destitute," $45,000 in debt, and with a book manuscript on his hands that nobody much seemed to want. Weed had begun to write the book as a diary for his fiancée, so she would know what things had been like from his side of the looking glass. He needed to keep himself from going mad. "It's hard now to reconstruct the anguish I felt then," he had told me early in 1975. "I told myself, 'It's not gonna help to get sick.' But I found I couldn't function. I turned to writing because it was therapeutic. It was so difficult to grasp what was happening! My mind was going in circles, and I couldn't stop it except by writing."

At first Weed tried to do his book in tandem with his coauthor, Roger Rappaport, but the two men fell out over who was to control the content, and how much detail to include on Weed and Patty's sex and drug experiences, as well as how open Weed should be in his assessment of the Hearsts. Rappaport naturally wanted to throw it all in. Weed had personal concerns of taste and decency; like an amateur stripper, he was unwilling to take it *all* off. Weed wound up suing Rappaport, and though he did recover the rights to his own story, the cost was dear: "Between the kidnapping, the book, the lawsuit, and preparing for the trial, my identity has been soaked up," Weed had told me when Patty was still missing. "The first four or five months I felt *irreparably* damaged. It seemed like I was going to break. It couldn't be happening— being given your walking papers over CBS. It's kind of comical when you think about it. I'm still terribly dislocated, I don't have any schedule at all. I've been to about one movie in the past year, and I don't have any kind of sexual awakening that I've been able to ascertain, which has been a very curious thing for me. In nearly two years now I've been much more fidelitous, if that's a word, than I ever have been to anything in my life. Not because I think I owe it to Patty in any way. Just that I haven't been psychologically in any kind of shape . . . Up to the shoot-out, I was really impaired, much more so than it seemed on TV. In those days we were like the passive gang, whereas Patty and the SLA were the active gang. They were the ones that were motivated and in control."

I had felt sorry for Weed and had seen him several times during the Missing Year because he seemed nearly as damaged as Patty by their experience. He grew ever thinner and vaguer. I thought he was continuing to write his book not only to make money but because he badly needed to sustain, and if possible to extend into the future, his slender thread of identity: that he had once been the betrothed of Patty Hearst.

After Patty was found, I went to see Weed again. "Are you still having problems?" I asked.

"I'm down to anxiety, nightmares, phobias, and total impotence," he replied. After the falling out with Rappaport, Weed had started his book over again, working now with Scott and Mimi Swanton, his closest and almost his only friends. Swanton, an unpublished novelist, had been a fellow teacher with Weed at Crystal Springs. The trio of old friends tried to fashion a book that did not speculate excessively and that concentrated on Weed's own perceptions and experiences after the kidnapping. "But we found to our chagrin that the bottom had fallen out of the market. To state it more frighteningly, we found that most of our book had leaked out one way or another." Rappaport had published an article on Steve and Patty, including details of their sex and drug experiments, in *New Times* the previous March. "What was left we had to guard with our lives," Weed said.

But scarcely anything *was* left. One cannot make a semitough, nonbinding, informal pact with the devil. To enter the confessional lists of modern book publishing is a pledge to take it all off. If indecent exposure were a literary crime as well as a night-court offense, half the bookstores in the country would have to close down.

Although the Swantons had visited Patty, Weed was reluctant to call at the jail. Although he didn't wish to upset her unduly, he feared he might not upset her at all. The amount of rejection one man can take is unknown, but after talking to Weed, one suspects the capacity is bottomless. Weed was conflicted, too, about publishing his book, quite aware that he would lay himself open to charges of exploiting his romance for profit.

Sixteen months after the verdict against Patty Hearst came in, Ms. Janey Jimenez, the federal deputy marshal assigned to Patty throughout her trial, who wept so copiously when the verdict was announced that it was said she was Patty's only real friend, announced she was quitting the force. Janey, twenty-three, had a million-dollar book advance she said, and "they even offered to pay for my further education. I hope to get my master's degree and maybe go on to law school."

A book manuscript was a pivotal element in the case itself. The ashes of the holocaust in Los Angeles were not yet cold when Jack Scott, the self-styled "sports activist," went searching for Patty and the Harrises. Within days, it turned out, he had poked down into the underground with his own special dowsing rod and made contact with the three fugitives, who were then holed up in a fleabag in Oakland and desperate. Why did Scott arrange and pay for their rescue and himself drive the nation's number-one fugitive cross-country, with, for cover, his own mother and father in the car? Scott, too, wanted to write a book, and before he went to the Bay Area to find the beneficiaries of his "activism," he had gone to New York to seek a quarter-million-dollar publisher's advance.

When Patty and Wendy were arrested, a half-written letter from Wendy to her ex-lover, William Brandt, now in prison, was found lying on their kitchen table: "I hope you'll have a chance to meet P.H. She's incredible! I swear only the toughest could have come out of it as she did. What an ordeal she went through! I can write a book about it."

All the while the book boys were flailing away at their Remingtons, the movie people were keeping an eye on the box office. Otto Preminger was first to weigh in, with something called *Rosebud,* about a yacht full of rich American girls kidnapped by terrorists for political ransom. *Bud* was a dud, a knockoff of reality that never flowered, and will be remembered, if at all, only as the vehicle for the acting debut of John Lindsay.

By the time the real Patty turned up three Pattyporn movies were ready for release. *Patty* graphically detailed the heroine being drugged, tortured, raped, and at one point sexually assaulted by three snakes, this last being the pornographer's interpretation of an SLA initiation ceremony. Another movie was called *Snatched,* but despite his socko title, *Variety* said the distributor was worried that Pattyporns could become a glut on the market, so he called a press conference. "We're not really selling Patty Hearst. We're really dealing with contemporary drama," this pornographer said.

The most ambitious film, a $300,000 R-rated epic titled *Abduction,* was based on a pre-HERNAP porno novel called *Black Abductors.* This describes the kidnapping and sexual humiliation of a white heiress, followed in due and near-instantaneous course by her joyous sexual liberation by a troop of supremely potent and plenipotent black politicosexual adventurers. Shortly after Patty disappeared, certain journalistic adventurers and long-shotters employed by the *New York Post* had suggested that her abduction had been inspired by this very book, which unaccountably turned up in a *Post* editor's bottom drawer. In turn, Grove Press had tracked down the original San Diego publishers of *Black Abductors,* bought the book, and were preparing to reissue it, accompanied by appropriate movie stills, now that the time was ripe.

My mother having been a professional movie critic, one way or another I've sat through a lot of movies, but *Abduction* is the dreariest exploito-porn I've ever seen, wormy right down to its soft core. The film is unique on several counts. For one thing, it is the first time in the annals of cinema that the conventional disclaimer serves as a laugh line. "Any similarity of the characters in this film to real people living or dead is entirely coincidental," one reads on the screen, and gales of glee sweep the theater. Then the picture begins. A young girl walks into her boyfriend's apartment. They nuzzle on the couch. Humdrum acting, terrible dialogue, sleazy set, dismal tempo. No matter, we are riveted. He touches her breast. She slips off her blue jeans. *Splat!* A black gun is beside her cheek. Grab her, tie her, blindfold, gag. Knock him out. Wrap her in a blanket, drag her, kicking and struggling, past horrified bystanders into a waiting car that roars off. My heart has begun to pound. It pounds through every obligatory rape scene: White rapist can't get it up . . . get the black man . . . now the lesbian rape. But it wasn't the sex that upset me, and "upset" was not really the word. I was *terrified. Abduction* shook me up as no movie has since *Dracula,* seen when I was eleven. It was like taking speed. I thought my heart would break my ribs. At first I figured it was only me, that I had come to identify with Patty much more than I'd known. Then I calmed down enough to notice that the entire theater had fallen dead silent. I think the movie audience was gripped for the same reason the world audience was gripped by the real case. The emotions it touches, the fears aroused, are primal; the situation rakes over our most basic terrors, not only as children but also as parents.

"We could be anyone's daughter, son, wife, husband, lover, neighbor, friend," the "Tania Interview" said. Whoever had composed these lines —and the matter of their authorship would continue to be a major issue in Patty's trial—there was a far wider truth to them than straight America cared to admit.

Week Six

March 1–7

Monday, March 1

Today begins a grueling week for Bailey on two fronts. Expecting the Hearst trial to have been over by now, he had scheduled a week of paid lectures to trial lawyers in Las Vegas, a seminar he is unable or unwilling to cancel. So every afternoon this week, the moment the gavel comes down, he and Linda must leap into the big Cadillac, a present from Randolph Hearst, and make the mad dash down the freeway to the airport, where Bailey's $750,000 Rockwell Turbo-Commander is ready for takeoff on the thousand-mile round trip. Though his pilot comes along, Bailey often takes over the controls himself; he says flying relaxes him. At Las Vegas he strolls into his lecture, drink in hand, and speaks extemporaneously, and brilliantly, usually drawing a standing ovation. He gets home well after midnight. The physical strain of these trips, after a day in court, must be punishing, but Bailey claims to enjoy his iron-man act. "It's fun to be a superman," he tells reporters. Then he adds with typical cocky candor, "But that's a fraud. I attribute my appearance here to a very good physician who knew exactly what chemicals to prescribe."

In court, one alternate juror is down with the flu, and the jury is out again so that Bailey can argue the admissibility of Margaret Singer's testimony. The tall Mary Poppins figure settles herself once more in the witness box. She has gone over the SLA tapes and Patty's other postkidnapping literary productions, and compared them with Patty's earlier writings. This morning she filed a report that corroborates Patty's own testimony that although she spoke the words, she did not write them. She was not the *author*.

Dr. Singer has received several international awards for her work in language patterns, and Browning agrees that she qualifies as an expert. But he questions whether her field of study is "scientific enough" to put before the jury.

Dr. Singer became aware of the stylistic variations in Patty's language as soon as she heard the SLA tapes played on the radio, in 1974. Now that she has analyzed them, she knows that Patty made twenty-five separate speeches on seven tapes, of which five are spontaneous speech and twenty are readings from prepared scripts. After years of studying speech patterns, the witness can say this with scientific certitude and can identify the writer of each speech. When Browning looks dubious, Bailey leaps to his feet and growls, "Let the record show the United States attorney turned his back on the witness!"

Now everybody looks flustered except the witness, who says smoothly, "I have followed families for fifteen or twenty years, Mr. Browning, and after the age of seventeen, people's language styles do not change. You and Mr. Bancroft, for example, have quite different styles. I could analyze this trial transcript and detect which questions were asked by which man." She smiles. "That's what I won my two prizes on."

When students come to Berkeley from Iowa, Doctor, and become radicalized, doesn't their language change? No. They learn to say "Off the pigs!" and such, but these phrases get inserted into their own identifiable style of language usage.

Dr. Singer's method is simplicity itself: She counts up how many of a person's sentences start simply, with a noun or pronoun plus verb, and how many begin with a prepositional phrase or modifying clause before getting to the noun-verb action. She studies the qualities of phrasing. She watches for sentence starters, sentence length and variety, parallel constructions, and other covert patterns. Does the person write in a rhythmic, metered way, as Angela Atwood characteristically did? Cinque's first speech, on tape no. 1, and the one he reads on tape no. 3, for example, are in Angela Atwood's style; somebody else wrote Cinque's other speeches.

Patty tends to talk in the present tense. When she says, "I have been given the name Tania," that is Angela Atwood's style. Patty would have said, "I am called Tania," or, "They call me Tania."

Browning reads aloud a paragraph from the "Tania Interview." Dr.

Singer says its simple-start sentences—"About five days later . . . ," "I got real pissed off . . . ," and so on—indicate that Patty wrote this paragraph herself. She can identify which subsequent paragraphs were written by Patty, by Emily Harris, or by Bill. On page 19 she has found a single, strange paragraph beginning, "The world is in a constant state of change. Nothing is static or immutable . . . ," which is clearly in a fourth language style, perhaps a bit of interpolated revolutionary plagiarism. A thorough woman, Dr. Singer.

Most of the first fifteen pages of the "Tania Interview" are written in Patty's own simple style, worked over, edited, and fixed up later. This section is largely autobiographical and repeats what Patty herself told the doctor in jail: that she cannot clearly recall her early childhood, especially the first nine years. As for the seven SLA tapes, Patty's words on nos. 1 and 2, and the date verifier on tape no. 3 ("This morning the shah of Iran had two people executed at dawn"), are in her own style. Her words on tapes 4, 5, and 6 are in Angela Atwood's style, and Patty's portion of no. 7 is in the style of Emily Harris.

To determine this, wouldn't one have to study and analyze every single sentence? Yes. That's what I did. Browning tries another tack. Don't schoolchildren speak one way and write another? Yes, and this is also true of most professional writers. An interesting exception was Robert Kennedy, who spoke just the way he wrote. Is the converse also true? Have you read any books by Truman Capote, for example? Oh, yes, he's suitable for light reading when I am tired at night.

Margaret Singer is a deadpan genius. Last year, just for the hell of it, she and another professor made up several authentic-sounding kinky sex quizzes and sold them to *Playboy*. As a young girl in Colorado, her secret ambition had been to become a comedy writer for Jack Benny. But I discover all this only later. She does not allow herself to fraternize with the press while the trial is on. Bailey can hang out with reporters, but his crew of expert witnesses all take their roles in this drama too seriously for that. They are nearly as circumspect as the jurors.

Browning inquires about Patty's style on the Trish Tobin jail tape. He shouldn't have asked, because the question gives Dr. Singer a chance to say that the tape has been doctored, and she knows where the gaps are.

What is your opinion, Doctor, of tape no. 7?

A torrent of raw linguistic research floods the courtroom. "Okay. I laid out a count of complex versus simple sentence beginnings. And as you'll see, thirty-six percent, forty-six percent, and forty-five percent of the sentences Miss Hearst reads on tapes four, five, and six have complex starters. When Atwood reads her own speech or where she says, 'I am Gelina,' the speech has forty-two percent. See, that's the same general range of complex markers. And when Cinque reads his speech, which has *many* markers of Atwood's style, he has sixty-one percent complex sentence starters. . . .

"Now, when you get to tape seven, you have the two Harrises and Miss Hearst. With William Harris, we've got three speeches in which he says, 'I'm General Teko,' and on tape five, only twenty-eight percent of his initial sentences are complex. . . ."

It's too late to wish he hadn't asked, so Browning gets into the act and himself reads aloud Singer's "crudity count" from Patty's portion of tape no. 7. "Crudities: 'pig' twenty-two times, 'fascist pig' once, 'ass' four, 'fucked up' seventeen times, 'fucked over' once, 'horseshit' once." As Browning reads this, Patty wears a lovely smile. "What is the particular significance of this?" the prosecutor inquires.

The professor is ready. "Okay. In Angela Atwood's speech . . . her covert themes are *corporate, corporate state, corporate empire,* and so on. She uses the word 'corporate' twelve times and the word 'empire' seventeen. She doesn't use the word 'pig' once, and no crudities. So that 'pig's and crudities were not part of Angela Atwood's own speech style. But when you come to William Harris, on tape seven, you get lots of 'pig's—thirty-five 'pig's—six 'fascist's, and six crudities." Harris also uses the word "jammed" on this tape. In the Tania manuscript, page 9, Patty also "writes" that when she got out of the closet, "they jammed me around." But "jam" or "jammed" is a Harris word; nobody else in the SLA ever uses it. Emily Harris uses "love" repeatedly, more than any other writer, counterbalancing "love" with revolutionary themes. Now, on tape 7 Patty has twenty-two "pig"s, seven crudities, and seventeen "love"s. "Pig," "love," and crudities are all Harris words. Back on tapes 4, 5, and 6, written by Angela, they simply do not appear.

Has Dr. Singer applied the same analytic techniques to the Trish Tobin tape? No, there wasn't time. But she'd be glad to do so now if the government wishes. Browning recoils in horror.

Tom Padden is by now fully asleep, and I am fully awake, fascinated by Dr. Singer's science.* She handles words and percentages like a Persian carpet-weaver. Although Patricia Hearst has never looked so

---

*Other experts in linguistics, while maintaining that the field is indeed "scientific," have since disagreed with Singer's interpretation of the Hearst data.

content and pleased in court, Carter is not. "Mr. Browning, I would hope to conclude this."

"A very few more questions, Your Honor." Has Dr. Singer ever before been a witness in a court of law? No, but courts have sent writings to her for analysis, and she knows plenty of people in classified agencies of the government who do this kind of work all the time. "And they consult with me all the time."

Bailey mouths a silent "Hurrah." Patty laughs aloud. Browning doesn't seem to know what to do with this witness; he is a bird caught in a snare. Afterward the corridor is abuzz. Dr. Kozol says, "I loved that testimony." So had I. "If you think that was something, wait till next week!" Johnson pledges. Only Theo Wilson keeps her cool. "How can you say that 'This morning the shah of Iran executed two men at dawn' is in Patty Hearst's style?" Dropped into the heady excitement of this morning's wordplay, it is a good question.

A protracted wrangle between counsel ensues over the admissibility of Dr. Singer's testimony. It is one of the most difficult rulings Carter must make. On balance, he decides that her testimony would "add many hours without adding sufficient productive evidentiary value to make it worthwhile." Bang of gavel. Motion denied.

In that case, Bailey wishes to make an offer of proof and to put Dr. Singer's formal findings into the record, in view of a possible appeal. He would also like the right to cross-examine the government's witnesses as to *their* linguistic expertise when the time comes. Carter will do better than that. If the government's experts take the position that Miss Hearst not only spoke but authored all this material, the judge will not foreclose the possibility of bringing Dr. Singer back at that time.

The ruling against Dr. Singer is a serious blow, but Bailey at his prelunch press conference is feisty and unflappable.

"How do you think your case is going, Lee?"

"I think it would take a very harsh jury to say, 'We're going to hold her responsible,' at this point."

"How does Patty think it's going?"

"Her attitude curiously parallels mine. If the judge makes a ruling I don't like, she doesn't like it, either."

Back after lunch is Vernon Kipping, the photography expert. The FBI man's pale face and gray hair swim back up to the surface of memory. He is himself a drab photo in grainy black-and-white. Was it five weeks or five months ago that we heard him lecturing the jury on the resemblance between a movie camera and a sewing machine?

This time, Johnson will examine. "Now, Mr. Kipping, in conjunction with your duties, and in conformity with your orders from the United States attorney, did you have occasion to examine certain photographs made from the surveillance-camera photographs—or the surveillance-camera *negatives,* if you will?" Finally a lawyer who talks like one! What Johnson wants to know is whether the figure of Camilla Hall is not *substantially* different in the two versions of the photograph even though both sets of prints are made from the same negatives. In the five-by-seven prints Camilla Hall has been cropped out! And when she does appear, in the eight-by-tens, the muzzle of her weapon is pointed at Patty, is it not? Well, Kipping would prefer to say it is pointed in the general direction of the counter. In any case, the mistake was inadvertent. The automatic printer in the FBI's Washington laboratory masked the edges of the negative.

Did the movie as shown in this courtroom depict Camilla Hall or not? The witness is uncertain, so we must view the film yet again. Johnson offers Kipping the pointer—the better, presumably, to shaft himself.

During the film Johnson points out more than once that we cannot see Camilla Hall's face. The movie was made from the cropped photographs. Did the witness happen to see the film on television shortly after the robbery, and has he any idea how newswoman Marilyn Baker got possession of a film supposedly in FBI custody? Sheepishly, Kipping acknowledges that somebody at the lab must have pirated a print.

Johnson has saved his most damning point for last. He now draws from Kipping the admission that when the larger, eight-by-ten individual prints were trimmed, to remove the sprocket holes, Camilla Hall vanished from these pictures as well.

The debate over the photographs seems interminable. Browning cross-examines Mr. Kipping, then the same grainy ground is replowed a third time by Johnson on redirect and by Browning on re-cross-examination. I am half asleep when Bailey abruptly says, "If it please the court, that rests the case for the defense."

We have listened to twelve defense witnesses, including Patty, in eleven days. The purpose of the long wrangle over the film becomes clear when Carter asks the jury again to leave so that Mr. Johnson may make a motion out of their presence. The lawyer moves to dismiss all charges against Patty, on grounds that the government has withheld exculpatory evidence—namely, the seventy-three frames of bank film that fail to show Camilla Hall at the opposite end of the teller's counter from Donald DeFreeze. The newly discovered evidence, as the defense reads it, shows that Patty was in a two-gun sandwich between DeFreeze and Hall throughout the course of the robbery. "The government knew or should have known that exculpatory evidence was available. This has left the defense in the peculiar position of not being able to examine witnesses on what we now consider to be so vital." Even if the failure was inadvertent, its effect has been overwhelmingly prejudicial.

But it has all been a long run for a short slide. Browning says categorically that the pictures are not exculpatory. Whether Patty was under anybody's gun at the bank—Cinque's or Camilla Hall's—is clearly a matter of subjective interpretation.

In a last desperate move Johnson points out that the defense has complained continually of the difficulty in obtaining evidence from the government, owing to negligence or otherwise. That is almost an understatement, Judge Carter remarks—but he denies the motion to dismiss.

The jurors return with a note to the judge. They find it difficult to examine photographs and listen to testimony at the same time. Then we shall have no more testimony today, Carter says, and the jurors may use the final fifteen minutes to study in silence the enigmatic stacks of pictures and ponder what they may or may not mean.

Outside, we learn of a stunning development. In Los Angeles a judge has ruled that the FBI lacked a proper search warrant when it broke into the Harrises' apartment. The warrant has been challenged by a young, unpaid law-student volunteer on the Harris defense team, and the happy result is that not one speck of the voluminous evidence seized at 288 Precita Avenue can be used against the Harrises at their trial. What does this mean for Patty? Her trial is into its sixth week, and that same evidence, including the incredibly damaging "Tania Interview," has been used against her since day one. Even before. Not only had I read the "Tania Interview" the weekend before trial, but the government had leaked it to the *Chicago Tribune,* the *New York Times,* and elsewhere five months before that. Although the document was so damaging that the newspapers had refrained from publishing a word until after the jury had been sequestered, the effect of the still-secret manuscript on the minds of the *editors* of these large opinion-making organizations is incalculable and not inconsequential.

Before the trial a big unanswered question was *When did Tania die?* Was it during the Missing Year, or did the defense lawyers have slowly to strangle the life out of her during those grim four and a half months in the "iron telephone booth"? The task was made immeasurably more difficult because before she died, Tania had written a detailed autobiography. Without the "Tania Interview," it would have been far less imperative to explain Tania; the psychiatrists might even have stayed home. The jury could have seen and judged a straight bank-robbery trial, rather than the psychiatric and at times psychedelic carnival now irrevocably under way. Alone, Tania's SLA tapes might have been dismissed as the coerced ravings of a kidnapping victim temporarily crazed by fear or under the gun of her fiendish captors. Bolstered by the "Tania Interview," the tapes have a written concordance; the manuscript means that Tania exists or, at least, that she once did. But Tania without her manuscript is like Marx without *Das Kapital,* Luther without his letter, Jefferson without his Declaration; she is a revolutionary without a text. And now it appears that the fatal text was seized by the government illegally. It is as if, all along, the defense has been fighting a huge figment, an evil genie that could have been kept forever stoppered if only somebody had bothered to look at the bottle.

Tuesday, March 2

At six-thirty in the morning the phone rings. Kathy's father. "Kathy may be sicker than we thought. We don't quite know how to handle her. We think it might be good if you came down here to see her. We'll get a hotel room if you like. But it might be better if you stayed overnight with us. So you could be close to Kathy."

"Of course. Could I speak to her?" But she is asleep. I agree to fly to Los Angeles this afternoon and hang up, puzzled and frightened.

The government's rebuttal case begins this morning. The first witness is a self-employed electronics technician. Zigurd Berzins wears a corduroy coat, and looks—oh, impossibility!—like a dissolute Charles Percy. On the morning of April 15, Berzins was hurrying to the bank to make a deposit before going out on a service call. He vaguely noticed a car pull into a bus stop in front of the bank and saw some people get out. As Berzins pushed open the bank door he heard a metallic noise behind him and thought he had let the door hit someone. Turning, he saw a person down on one knee, just outside the half-open door, about eight or ten feet away from where he stood. A carbine lay across the figure's right knee. The weapon appeared in good condition; the wood was very shiny. Two ammunition clips lay on the sidewalk. They were straight, not curved. He saw a pair of hands trying to retrieve the dropped clips and noticed that one or two rounds of ammunition had also fallen. The kneeling figure wore a long, dark coat "draped to the ground," and he saw no face, only the hairline and the top of the head. Frankly, he was concentrating on the weapon. Unlike exhibit 19, which Browning shows him now, it had a straight clip, not a banana clip, and no holes in the stock; he is firm about that. The figure was female, with long, wavy auburn hair. Browning hands Berzins a carbine and asks him to demonstrate how the figure was holding the gun. It is apparent the witness knows weapons. We learn he is a three-year Vietnam combat vet. The government would like to show him a film and ask if he can identify the person he saw. "Aren't we showing it almost *ad nauseam?*" Carter says.

Very well. The government will rely for now on the still photos. What happened next, Mr. Berzins? Another person came flying into the bank, screaming, "SLA! SLA! This is a robbery! Everybody down on the floor!" She was only two feet away from Berzins, eyeball to eyeball, and had a gun with a banana clip. "I got down on the floor fast. I knew who this was, and I was very frightened. I thought there would definitely be some gunfire." He was inching toward what he hoped was a protected spot under a desk when someone grabbed him by the shoulder and walked him over to the check desk. Later, when he saw the movie of the holdup, he was able to identify this person as Patricia Soltysik by her knit cap. He saw himself, too, in the movie. Soltysik might also have told him, "Get down on the floor." He is not sure. The first person who shouted, "SLA! Down on the floor!" was Nancy Ling Perry. He does not recollect her using any profanity.

Was Nancy Ling Perry the person you saw kneeling in the doorway? No, sir. All right. Now, Your Honor, I *would* like to run that movie. Berzins steps down from the box, the room is darkened, the film begins to click through the projector, and when Patty, or rather Tania, skitters back into view, bouncing on the balls of her feet, a flat voice says, "This is the person I saw."

A few hours after the robbery, the FBI showed Berzins mug shots of three women, and he thought he could identify Soltysik and Nancy

Ling Perry but not the "person down on one knee." That person had better get down on both knees, and soon, because Berzins now says that the next day, when the bank surveillance-camera pictures were published in the newspapers, the identities of the three bank women became clear to him. By looking at the faces and comparing the type of weapon each woman held, he was able to sort them out. The person who grabbed his shoulder was Soltysik, the eyeball-to-eyeball person was Nancy Ling Perry, and "the person down on one knee" was Patricia Hearst.

Browning puts the newspaper photographs into evidence. When Bailey shouts, "No objection!" we begin to sniff the blood that is to come.

The week after the bank robbery, I had published a piece about HERNAP in *Newsweek*. Its final paragraphs read:

> Perhaps one can say only that while the story lives, Patty and the SLA live. When it ends, and no matter which way it ends, the illusion will die, too, and some small parts of ourselves as well.
>
> After that—I am sure—historians, novelists, playwrights and other amateur archaeologists like myself will sift the ashes of the event, and the dry, shuffling sounds of old newspapers and scratchy replayings of the tapes will testify to our efforts to understand the languages of our times.

Only two years later, I am seeing my prophecy come true. Berzins has brought his old newspapers into court, and they lie before him on the stand, already yellowed and beginning to crumble. When Berzins talked to the FBI the second time, he realized that the person on one knee outside the bank and the person who shouted, "SLA! SLA!" were two different individuals. Events happened so rapidly that at first he "had thought they were one and the same."

It is time to cross-examine. Bailey begins casually. "Mr. Berzins, I believe you described a degree of terror when you first noticed the person with the weapon, which increased when the impact of the meaning of the SLA flooded in on you. Was that your testimony, sir?"

"I was definitely scared for my life," says Berzins, sounding a little scared right now.

"Well, you knew they were cold-blooded killers, didn't you?"

"I had no impression. . . ."

"You had no impression?" Bailey's eyes are as reproachful as a bloodhound's. Then, hard: *"Were you in fear of your life?"*

"Yes, sir. Somebody points a gun at you, I think you would be in fear of your life, too."

"You bet!"

One way Berzins knew this was no "ordinary-type bank robbery" was that the gang entered "in a revolutionary fashion." He also had the impression they "wore commando-type makeup."

Mr. Berzins, precisely what did you do in the military? Commissioned officer, artillery branch, Fourth Division. Did you train people yourself? Yes. The soldier's concern must be to kill the enemy, right? Yet survival is well known in the military to be a continuing irresistible impulse, correct? Many people get frightened and try to stay alive, right?

Not to argue with you, Mr. Bailey, but we are not taught to fight a psychological war. We train an individual to be familiar with his weapon and with his duty as a soldier.

Do you recall, when you were lying on that bank floor, quite uncertain of your fate, saying a soft good-bye to every member of your family, just in case you never saw them again? I guess that thought went through my mind. How old are you, sir? Thirty-two. How many times have you thought you were going to die, sir? That's probably the only time.

I assume the morning began about like any other? You had no suspicion anything unusual was afoot? "No. It was a beautiful day. After Easter. It was income-tax day, but otherwise, no problems. It was a great day." How clearly Ziggy Berzins recollects this last shining moment before his involvement with the ambiguities of the law began!

Bailey's voice becomes gentle. I would like you now to forget all your conversations with the government and take yourself back to that April morning. Remember exactly what you did and did not see when you looked back through that door. Will you do that?

"Okay. I'll state it again ... I saw the weapon across her right knee—"

"Do you realize that, on direct examination, you said *'his knees'*?"

"I'm a little nervous up here. ..."

"Does nervousness change the sexes?"

Browning interrupts: For the record, his witness used the word "person," as well as "his."

Bailey's voice has a sudden tungsten edge. "As a witness-person, sir, will you tell me how you tell a man from a woman, from eight or ten feet away, looking through a door, without a physical examination?"

"The same way we all do. I'm not a genealogist."

"Gynecologist? . . . Nor, I gather, did you give an examination of that character."

"I did not. . . . But the hands I saw were not a man's hands."

"You can tell by the *hands!*"

Bailey has the witness somewhat flummoxed. "I'm telling you what I saw on that morning. What I saw on that morning was a woman, and it was female. The hands were female, the hair was female . . . if that person had a crew cut, I would probably have stated it was a man."

"Okay, then, the long hair is the clue?"

"It is one of the clues, yes, sir."

"Mr. Berzins, how long have you been in San Francisco?" Laughter from the audience and shouts of "Right on!"

"Do you know this gentleman seated at the end of the table—Mr. McNally?" Yes. "Didn't you tell him that you *never saw the face* of the person who bent over to pick up the clip?"

"I saw the top of her head."

"Can you identify a human being by looking at the top of his or her head?" Bailey's hand is on his hip, eyes narrow, chin thrust forward. Having demolished the facial testimony, he moves on methodically to the figure's coat-shrouded torso. "What do you use in looking at bodies to tell men from women?"

"I look at the face and perhaps the build."

"Forget the face, since you never saw it! Tell me about the body that you saw. Did it have the fulsome proportions of a voluptuous young lady? If you remember."

"Depends on what you call voluptuous."

"That's a correct response," says the somnolent judge. "What is voluptuous is argumentative. So . . . just stop using those argumentative words."

"I'm sorry, Your Honor. I thought they were descriptive." The apology is as sardonic as its provocation. Bailey's colleagues puff like little human steam engines running on swallowed laughter. Berzins looks miserable. "What is the difference between a man and a woman with respect to the shape of the chest that may provide you with a clue as to sex?"

"Well, a woman does have breasts."

"Fine. Did you notice any breasts?"

"I wasn't looking at her breasts."

"Now, as to a clothed human being whose face is not visible, is there any way to determine the sex?"

"If the individual undresses, I guess it can be determined."

"No, sir. I said *clothed.* You do know the difference between clothed and unclothed?"

The point of this cross-examination is to make the unfortunate Berzins seem ridiculous and thus to neutralize his extremely damaging testimony. Berzins is the first witness directly to challenge Patty's story that she was in the bank only as a docile captive. His assertion that she dropped her spare ammunition and stopped to pick it up suggests she was not under coercion. Worse, it flatly contradicts Patty's testimony that she had no spare ammunition, just the one straight clip in her gun.

"Absent the face, and absent the view of the pectoral area, is there any way, to your knowledge, to differentiate a man from a woman with clothing on?" No.

So Berzins' judgment was based on a look at the top of the head, part of the forehead, and the hands?

"Yes, plus that her general appearance was that of a female."

"I take it, sir, you have not spent much time down on Polk Street."

"I don't think you do, either."

"Right on!" the voice from the rear bench shouts again, and laughter rocks the courtroom. Polk Street is a homosexual promenade. Smiles in the jury box. The tension is broken. Later someone tells me the shouter was another neutralizer, a Bailey plant.

Berzins told the FBI that during the robbery he had heard a female voice say, "This is Tania Hearst." Yes, and that is exactly what she said. Sound equipment is Berzins' trade. Indeed, when he was later asked to come to FBI headquarters to listen to some SLA tapes and see if he could identify Patty's voice, he was amazed. He had expected an elaborate sound room, fancy equipment. But they had only a Sony tape recorder, "some type of Mickey Mouse amplifier," and an old car speaker.

"Kind of a sloppy setup?" Bailey grins.

Next comes a fast, brilliant passage of cross-examination flamenco, impossible to reproduce, in which the attorney stomps his heels, swivels his hips, beats a tattoo, and razzle-dazzles the witness until he scarcely knows what he is saying in the blur of noise and feet and dusty petticoats. Berzins by now has been interrogated by the FBI half a dozen times; his identifications varied somewhat; sometimes he made mistakes; sometimes the agents misquoted him; some but not all of the misquotations were later corrected and initialed in the FBI transcripts. At first Berzins appears to have thought that the kneeling figure in the doorway and the robber who shouted, "SLA! Get on the floor!" and the person who said, "This is Tania Hearst," were all the same woman. Later, slowly, he sorted out his impressions. Bailey's rapid-fire questions are intended to flummox us all, and to a remarkable degree he succeeds.

Struggling to climb out of the muck of words, the witness says, "The robbery, as far as I'm concerned, had three events: One, when I saw the person in the doorway. Two, when I was eyeball to eyeball. Three, when I was moved." He had been so frightened he didn't even recall the third episode until he saw himself, in the movie, being moved by the shoulder.

Describe the color of the hair of the person you said dropped the clips. Reddish brown. How long? Hanging on the shoulders. Did you describe the person in the doorway as a white female, early twenties, slightly built, with fine, medium-brown hair carefully arranged, probably tied back in a bun or pulled back from her face? *Did* you give this description? Yes, sir. *Was* the hair carefully tied back in a bun? No, I could only say it was very tight to her head . . . close to her face. You did not tell the agents the hair was carefully arranged and pulled back? It was carefully arranged, right. Use whatever words you want. I want to know what *your* words to the agent were. Did you tell him it was pulled back tightly into a bun? "I don't care if there was a flag tied to it! It was close to the ears, and that's what I saw!" Berzins' nasal, Sony-like voice is going too fast, high-pitched with anxiety. "You're trying to twist what I'm saying. . . . The person I'm describing is Nancy Ling Perry. It's Nancy Ling Perry."

The witness says this over and over. But *we all* know it isn't, having all seen the film *ad nauseam,* just as the judge has said. The jury looks blank, poleaxed. They, too, have been successfully confused by Bailey's staccato cross-examination. But of one fact Ziggy Berzins is steadily, unshakably sure. The stock of the weapon on the knee of the figure who dropped the clips had no holes in it. On this point we break for lunch.

The defense lawyers are feeling glum. Despite Bailey's battering, Ziggy Berzins is holding up. Bailey shakes his head in disgust; he is convinced Berzins is a perjurer. "I had him under subpoena, and I let him go."

I lunch alone in the building's cafeteria, worrying about Kathy. When I run into Al Johnson and tell him how frightened I am, he stares at me with astonished brown eyes. "Don't you get it?" he says. "The kid runs away from boarding school. Big deal. But now the excitement's over, and now she's stuck in public school. She's home with her dad, of course, but it isn't all that great. So she's reconsidering her decision. She is wondering if maybe she shouldn't have done it." He sounds so obviously right that I bawl with relief. Johnson knows human nature as well as anybody I've met.

Upstairs, the interrogation resumes. Bailey invites Berzins to step down out of the pulpitlike witness box and point out his and the robbers' various positions on the bank-floor plan, which still rests on its easel. Surprisingly, Berzins is no taller than Bailey. In the high, pulpitlike witness box the younger man had more authority. Standing next to Bailey at the easel, he has lost stature but gained humanity. Confusions about possibly mistaken identifications matter less. He is mortal, and he *was* scared in the bank; but he is dogged.

Was Berzins aware, at the time he was on the floor, eyeball to eyeball with Perry, that Patty was already in the bank, behind him? "That's impossible!" Berzins blurts, unless . . . He begins to think, to relabel the figures in his mind's eye another way, in order to accommodate Bailey's question, which he's not sure he correctly understands. But of one thing he is certain. "She said, 'This is Tania Hearst.' That's what she said." Berzins is a radioman by trade. His shop is called Tweeters 'N Woofers. His visual identifications may be a little off, but his ear is never wrong. He is certain of what he heard.

"And you think that was Miss Hearst's voice?"

It came from her position at the center of the bank, and it was similar to Miss Hearst's voice. Not just the position but the inflection . . .

"Tell me about the inflection."

Browning is on his feet and demanding a bench conference out of the jury's hearing. The government didn't bring up the matter of inflection on direct examination, and he suspects Bailey may be asking about it now as a means of sneaking in Dr. Singer's testimony. Carter overrules the objection.

The inflection is hard to describe, says Berzins, but very like Mrs. Hearst's inflection, which he has often heard on television. Really? Catherine Hearst! "Did you know, Mr. Berzins, that Mrs. Hearst is from Atlanta?"

By the way, did Berzins see the bank film on TV? "I think we've got a super-duper blond reporter here in San Francisco who showed it." Berzins grins. Bailey pounces. So he lied when he told the jury he first saw the film in January! No. A film is a film, whether it's still or moving; I saw it first in stills, in the newspapers, the day after the robbery. Where did you spend lunch, by the way? Upstairs, in the U.S. attorney's office. Did you discuss your testimony during lunch? No. I'll tell you what I talked about if you're interested.

Bailey cuts him off. "Mr. Berzins, have you the ability to recognize another person whose face you have never seen?"

"No, but—"

"That's all, thank you."

Let him finish his answer, please, Browning says. Berzins tries now to clinch it. He never said the girl in the doorway was Patricia Hearst. He is saying that the figure he saw in the doorway is the same person as the figure at the center of the bank in the film. "Whether she's Patricia Hearst or not is none of my affair. I know whom I saw in the bank as Nancy Ling Perry. . . . I know that wasn't Patricia. And Miss Soltysik—I know that wasn't her because I saw her later on in the film. So the only thing I'm trying to say is that the figure in the doorway was the figure in the middle of the bank, based on weaponry and the general appearance of the person."

"You mean you're identifying a clip and not a face." Bailey's voice is low and menacing. I am by now convinced he is dealing with a perjurer.

But Berzins is dogged. "*And* describing an individual. I'm not just talking about the clip."

"Even though you don't know it's the same face, is that correct?"

"I know the other faces in the bank. It wasn't Cinque. It wasn't Nancy Ling Perry. It wasn't Soltysik. And it wasn't Camilla Hall."

Bailey holds up two banana clips, back to back, as if they were taped together. This gets the desired rise out of Berzins. "No way, Mr. Bailey! No way you can fit 'em into the gun, taped like that!"

"Is that right?" Bailey is purring like Morris the TV cat. Sure enough, Berzins forgets witness rule no. 1: Never elaborate. Of course he never fired a carbine of exactly this model, but—

"That's all!" Bailey snaps.

Now the defense plays its last card: Bailey reads aloud the entire report of Berzins' first FBI interview, made on the afternoon of the robbery, using his rich voice to underscore Berzins' many errors: The robbery lasted seven minutes . . . the dropped shells he saw on the sidewalk were .45 caliber . . . the person in the doorway was Patricia Soltysik. But Browning, too, has a hole card: *He* reads aloud the entire report of Berzins' second FBI interview, in which the witness revises his statement after having studied the newspaper photographs: The kneeling figure looked most like the picture of the hatless Patricia

Hearst. It was not crop-haired Nancy Ling Perry whom he saw eyeball to eyeball. It could not have been Patricia Soltysik. She was wearing a knit cap. As Browning reads, Berzins is redeemed—once more a truthful man. Al Johnson squirts Binaca, which he does frequently when enraged, as if his anger had an evil smell.

I had visualized a jail matron as a Bella Abzug figure wearing a belt of keys, but the next witness is a leggy blonde in a purple miniskirt. When Deputy Sheriff Stephanie Marsh first asked the new prisoner her occupation, she got no response. When she repeated her question, asking if she were a student or had ever had a job, the prisoner replied, "Urban guerrilla." What was the expression on her face? No real expression at all. What name did she give you? Patricia Campbell Hearst. When I asked her if she went by any other name, she said, "Tania," and spelled it for me.

"Did you ask if she went by any *other* name?"

"Yes, I did."

"And what did she tell you?"

"She said, 'None that I would tell *you!*' "

I glance at the clock on the wall: 2:15 P.M. For some reason this moment feels like the exact fulcrum of the trial, a psychological balance point, which I note in my home-baked transcript. Up to now, I would have said the defense was clearly ahead. Up to now, not only has Bailey been outperforming Browning on the legal trampoline; the press and spectators have tended to believe Patty more than they do the government. Now, one senses, the balance may be starting to tip.

Al Johnson rises to cross-examine. (So *that* accounts for the Binaca!) Deputy Marsh met Patty first in the garage area of the jail about seven-thirty P.M., is that correct? Who else rode up in the elevator with them? Emily Harris. You had forgotten that? Yes, sir, I had. While Patty's property was being inventoried and she was being searched and booked, where was Emily? Six or seven feet away, being fingerprinted. Johnson leads Deputy Marsh back over her testimony. Her eyes and mouth harden; Johnson's do the same. Isn't this the way it went, Mrs. Marsh? That you asked her occupation, and she said, "Student," and you said, "You're not a student. What is your occupation?" And she said, "At home, I guess." And you asked a third time, "What is your occupation?" and she said to you, in the following fashion, "Urban guerrilla"?

"No, sir. That is not the way she said it."

This is the first head-on confrontation of the trial. No previous witness has been directly accused of lying. As the jail matron testifies Patty's eyes never move from her face.

The next deputy sheriff is a smashing creature in a red suit with gold buttons. Sherri Wood, who looks like a stewardess for a very jazzy airline, was on duty at the jail when the "great potassium scare" occurred. After a routine blood sample had been sent out for analysis, the lab called to report a lethal amount of potassium in Patty's blood. The jail doctor wanted to draw another sample, but the prisoner laughed and refused. In cross-examination, Johnson brings out that the jail medical staff is forbidden access to Patty; no needles can be used on her without the express permission of her own doctors or attorneys. The purpose is to protect her life.

The day's last rebuttal witness is a Stockton narcotics cop. In January of this year Ulysses Hall was again arrested, and fresh needle tracks were found on his arms.

"No questions," says Bailey. Ulysses Hall is best forgotten fast.

The jury is sent out so that the defense may now make a heroic attempt to piggyback on the good fortune and/or thorough legal work of the Harris lawyers in challenging the FBI search of the Harrises' apartment. If Carter agrees with the Los Angeles judge that the FBI broke into the apartment without a valid warrant, he will have to instruct the jury to disregard so much of what they have heard that there may be grounds for a mistrial. You can't unring a bell, you can't get a skunk out of a courtroom, and you can't count on anything in a criminal trial. But first, the lawyers must examine a transcript of the proceedings in Los Angeles, and as I leave the courtroom early, to catch my plane, this is being arranged.

Despite Al's reassurance about Kathy, the old, unnameable dread begins in the taxi to the airport, the worry whether I have ever had the capacity to raise my mysterious daughter; the shaky resolve not to interfere too much with the oak inside her acorn, nor to let its mistletoe strangle me. The plane lands in pouring rain. The cabdriver cannot find the house and drops me off at a neighborhood drugstore, where I telephone and, while waiting to be picked up, buy violets for the house.

A torn screen door, a neat house, a rambunctious puppy, a subdued girl, a tense dinner. Besides the child, there are four of us—the mother, the father, the stepmother, and a houseguest. While the adults make small talk the corner of my eye and the turnings of my ear are alert for any odd signs. Nothing out of the ordinary occurs until, over dessert, someone mentions the new public school, and somebody else leapfrogs onto the first question (I cannot remember if either question was mine) and some switch is thrown. Kathy screams one single, sustained, high-pitched note. I turn and see her open mouth. Silently the three other adults leave the table, and we are alone. The scream ends, leaving a vacuum of silence. I reach out. "Don't touch me, Mother," she says.

I don't move, but we sit together, saying nothing, for a very long time, perhaps fifteen minutes, before the stepmother comes and gently leads her away to the bathroom, where she takes a long shower and emerges with the fever gone. I believe, I hope, that what she was saying at the table but could not say was: Don't touch me, I feel too fragile, I might break . . . but stay beside me, Mother, please. At any rate, I've done that. Now I swallow a sleeping pill and accept a big drink and go to bed when she does, still not talking much, and we lie side by side in the beds where normally her father and stepmother sleep. As soon as I hear her breathing deeply I sleep, too, and do not remember my dreams.

Wednesday, March 3

The morning is a blur, a rush to school for Kathy, a silent run to the airport for me.

Back in San Francisco, Charlie Garry is outraged at the sloppiness of Patty's defense, in contrast to the diligence on the part of the Harrises' lawyers. "It's *elementary* to attack on search warrants!" he announces to me at lunch. "It's almost malpractice *not* to do so. I've won cases where it was all I had."* Looking rather fine in maroon jacket

*Three weeks later, in Oakland, a Superior Court judge ruled that the 1972 police search of Wendy Yoshimura's apartment was illegal because the Berkeley cops did not have a proper warrant. Four months after that, in Bailey and Johnson's hometown, a Boston judge ruled that guns and ammunition found in Susan Saxe's Back Bay apartment could not be used against her for the same reason: The police had no legitimate justification for being on the premises. Saxe, a former Brandeis University honor student and five-year underground fugitive, had been charged with armed robbery and first-degree murder in connection with a 1970 Boston bank robbery in which a patrolman was killed. At her trial the government presented twenty-four witnesses. The defense attorney abruptly rested, without putting the defendant on the stand. The jury deadlocked, and a mistrial was declared.

and navy polo shirt and gray-white hair, Charlie begins to steam in the gloom of the Polynesian restaurant. "The lack of warrants has already done so much damage in the minds of the jury that the only possible decision would be to declare a mistrial."

Garry is puzzled that Judge Carter did not admit Dr. Singer's linguistic testimony. The government's objections that such testimony would be cumulative, without precedent, and would unduly prolong trial are "all bullshit." Charlie can think of *two* precedents from his own casebook. In the late 1940s, at the New York trial of the Communist Party chief Eugene Dennis, Louis Budenz testified that Communists habitually used "Aesopian language," in which a phrase actually means something very different from what it appears to mean. And in *People* v. *Huey Newton,* Charlie produced an authority on ghetto speech to testify that Huey spoke in the Aesopian language of revolutionary black rhetoric; "Off the pigs" was just fanciful talk.

"Who do you think insisted on this particular defense, Charlie?" I ask.

The lawyer gives me one of his jury-withering looks. "The family." His words sound like dialogue from *The Godfather.*

"For its good name, you mean?"

"*What* good name? She was giving the family credibility!"

As for the Missing Year, Charlie assures me, "Patty's in it *up to here.*" As I gather up my things to rush back to court he utters a final pronouncement: "But anybody willing to undergo this defense gets an automatic acquittal. The trial is just a charade because the jury can't find intent."

Back at the courthouse, I run into a young television reporter who has been out all morning casing Sacred Heart, the school where Patty once told a nun to go to hell. She tells me that the convent cells there are far meaner quarters than the closets provided by the SLA. The two teams of lawyers have spent the morning and much of the previous night together, studying the Los Angeles transcript. Bailey winks at me. Patty wears her half smile. Her parents and sisters look cheerful. The presence in this courtroom for the first time of FBI special agent in charge Charles Bates indicates the importance of any challenge to the FBI's search-and-seizure procedures. A charge of false arrest at this point would be disastrous to the FBI's already tarnished image.

I had first met Charlie Bates in his office; he was sitting underneath a floodlit, flag-draped, life-size photograph of a Dick Tracyish man in horn-rimmed glasses whose breast-pocket handkerchief bristled in bayonet points—FBI Director Clarence Kelley. The portrait threatened to crash down onto Bates' head from the sheer gravity of the chief's expression. Bates is sallow, lean, and ugly but nice-looking; Bogart-ugly. A career FBI man who has worked in twelve cities in thirty-four years with the Bureau, he has been through a lot and looks it. He was J. Edgar Hoover's London liaison to Scotland Yard, then special agent in charge of the Chicago office at the time of the Panther raid in which Fred Hampton was killed, and after that a top man in the Washington headquarters. He wants very much to be liked; indeed, being liked is actually part of his job. Bates is an important front man for the Bureau, an exemplar of the FBI image, the image Hoover had left in pretty bad shape and L. Patrick Gray III had not improved when he admitted under oath to having destroyed Watergate evidence. Bates had the rotten bad luck then to be in Washington, as assistant director of the General Investigation Division, and it became his responsibility to supervise the investigation of the Watergate break-in. What happened next so sickened him that he requested a transfer, which is how he wound up in San Francisco in time to have the biggest, most frustrating kidnapping case in Bureau history explode right in his place of sanctuary.*

When I'd first met this man, in July 1974, he wore a look of costive anguish. By then his men had interviewed perhaps five thousand persons in the Bay Area alone, without finding a single clue to the whereabouts of the country's most wanted fugitive. "One thing bothers me terribly," Bates had said. "In the sixteen–to–twenty-five age group, *everybody's* anti–law enforcement. Nobody will even speak to you! I dunno why . . . the reasons are more complicated than the problem. You knock and say, 'FBI. Can I talk to you, please?' and they shout, 'Bug off!' and slam the door."

"Does this happen just with Patty?"

"No, we run into it on all kinds of cases. There's massive mistrust out there."

"*Everybody* mistrusts you?"

"The great silent majority still trusts us, I think."

---

*In February 1977, when he was fifty-seven, Bates suffered a heart attack. A few months later, FBI regulations forced him to retire, and he became an executive of Burns International Security Services.

Two elements are necessary to obtain a proper search warrant: positive identification and probable cause to believe that the evidence is there. The government claims it lacked both in San Francisco until the actual moment of arrest. At that time Patty's lover was Steven Soliah, a house painter, who was later tried for and acquitted of having taken part in the Carmichael bank robbery in which Mrs. Opsahl was killed. FBI agents testify that they got on to the Harrises because they were keeping a very close watch on Steven Soliah and his sisters, Kathy and Josephine. Their interest in the Soliahs is not explained now. Only later do we learn the full chain of events that finally led the FBI to Patty Hearst: After Walter Scott put them on to his brother, Jack, the trail led to a Pennsylvania farmhouse, where a fingerprint found on a newspaper stuffed into a hole in a mattress matched the prints of the three-year fugitive Wendy Yoshimura. This, in turn, led the FBI to check back on Wendy's boyfriend, William Brandt, who was still doing time. Brandt's prison visitors included not only the Scotts but the two Soliah sisters. (Soliah's full-time house-painting partner, Jim Kilgore, had been one of the three men arrested in 1972 along with Brandt for the Oakland bomb plot. Kilgore later became Wendy's lover. Steven Soliah became Emily's. For a while Emily Harris and Kathy Soliah were lovers—a complicated and sad daisy chain.) The FBI agents went to Palmdale, a small desert town northeast of Los Angeles, and called on Martin Soliah, a high-school English teacher and track coach, ex–fighter pilot, Nixon supporter, and devoted father of five, and asked his help in tracking down the three of his children who were living in San Francisco.

The entrapment of the patriotic Martin Soliah into helping the FBI snare his own children is one of HERNAP's uglier bits of minor narrative. Soliah was told that the FBI wanted only to talk to his kids and was assured that the inquiry had nothing to do with the Hearst case. He was persuaded to come to San Francisco at FBI expense and, as Soliah put it later, become their "Judas goat." After he made contact with his children through a mail drop, he took the kids out to a five-hour family dinner, during which he told them the FBI had been around asking questions. His son and daughters assured him they had no connection with any radical activities. "That's what I told them!" said the father, much relieved, and went on back to his hotel. The FBI paid Martin Soliah's hotel bill and reimbursed him with thirty pieces of silver to pay for the supper. They kept a tail on his three kids.

Two and a half weeks later, on the evening of September 17, the agents watching the Soliah sisters saw two people who they thought might be the Harrises walk into a Laundromat. One agent got within eighteen inches of the heavily bearded man and smiled at him, hoping the suspect would smile back and so reveal a peculiarity in his teeth that would enable the FBI to make a positive identification. The man did not smile, but he was dressed in shorts, and the agent observed a surgical scar on his right knee. Back at the Bureau, he found that while William Harris was in the Marine Corps he had a knee operation; this made the identification more positive but still not 100 percent. Emily Harris could be seen up close for only about two seconds, in a grocery store, and the agent remembers his comment to his partner because it has so often been quoted back to him: "I don't know who that young lady is, but I'll guarantee you it's not Emily Harris."

The FBI photographed the suspicious pair, and now the five-by-seven prints become an object of some legalistic merriment. "Does the defense wish eight-by-tens?" the prosecutor needles, and Bailey replies, "Let the record show the prosecutor is pulling my leg," to which Judge Carter adds, "It's not going to make you any taller, Mr. Bailey."

The day after the Laundromat encounter, while the Harrises were out jogging, FBI agents broke into their apartment through a window. Finding a locked closet, they broke into that, too, and saw guns, bomb parts, ammunition, and other contraband. They photographed the stuff without touching it, the agents testify, and only then went off to get a warrant. By then the Harrises had been under surveillance some thirty hours, plenty of time to get a proper warrant before breaking the window—or so it had seemed to the judge in Los Angeles.

Patty is looking faintly pink-cheeked today, as if for the first time she might have some blood inside her, as she giggles with McNally about the doltishness of the two FBI witnesses, who are indeed men under pressure. Bailey is smiling, too. The two agents seem wary, dour, and sullen. They have probably been up all night, and this may be what a man looks like who is watching his career slide down the drain. Bailey says these particular agents certainly had enough experience to judge whether probable cause existed or not. If they had probable cause, then they also had time to obtain a warrant.

Bailey is posing the "almost undecidable question I hear all the time," Judge Carter says, the critical matter of the sufficiency of the warrant. "From the government's point of view, you're damned if you do, and you're damned if you don't." If the warrant is insufficient, then the search is illegal, and the evidence seized will be thrown out of court.

If you wait too long, the precious evidence may be destroyed. "I would say the answer is: Be sure—then get your warrant."

Even if breaking the window was legitimate, the padlock on the closet should have sent the FBI to court for a warrant, Bailey argues. A closet padlocked from the outside is "a situation in which a fugitive is not likely to be found." Further, the warrant was "bootstrapped"—based on the evidence they broke into the closet to get. The day ends not with a bang but a whimper, a final bleat from Bailey that when a "bilateral mistake" is made in good faith by both sides—by which he means that both the prosecution and the defense in Patty's trial thought the warrant was legal—neither side should be penalized.

It is four o'clock. Carter smiles. "I think I will be able to decide this first thing in the morning. And when I say 'I think,' I am rather positive of it."

Mindful of Garry's questions, I buttonhole Bailey and Johnson in the corridor and suggest they look up the Budenz and Huey Newton cases. I ask to see their memorandum of law on linguistic expert testimony. They didn't file one. I ask why they never attacked the search warrant. Bailey has drifted away, but Johnson looks me in the eye and says sternly, "We do not go on fishing expeditions. No good lawyer does." Poor Al. He has to handle all the tough ones.

Charlie Garry calls me at home that night and explodes. "A lawyer's pretrial responsibility in this type of case is to attack the prosecution every inch of the way. I lecture all over the country on exactly this. That's chickenshit law work. Disgraceful! It's the lazy man's way. A lawyer who does that is not protecting the record and not protecting his client!"

I am puzzled by his vehemence. Just before this trial got under way, Professor Alan Dershowitz had been widely quoted as having said, "Bailey is virtually the only criminal lawyer I've met who has mastered the art of pretrial investigation."* Garry and Dershowitz cannot both be right. Is it possible that even the noted Harvard Law scholar is part of the defense pretrial hype?†

I tell Charlie there is no written memorandum of law, either, and he

---

*Time, February 16, 1976, p. 47.

†He later turns up as a member of the posttrial posse. After a federal appeals court upheld Patty's conviction, Newsweek, on December 19, 1977, reported that Randolph Hearst had hired Dershowitz to help prepare the ongoing appeals, the chief grounds for appeal being that the Trish Tobin tape was improperly admitted into evidence and that Patricia Hearst was forced to answer questions that were improperly raised.

explodes again. "That's horrible! It's elementary to do that! I couldn't believe what you told me at lunch. I don't like sloppy workmanship. ... How did the family look in court? Did Randy look happy?"

Yes, I report, adding that the defense lawyers and Patty all were smiling. "That's because they're waltzing together," Charlie says.

The next caller is Kathy's stepmother. Kathy seems much better, she says, and when I talk to my daughter briefly, indeed she sounds her old self again—whatever that may be. Perhaps it had been just an obligatory fourteen-year-old scene, something she thought she had to put on to justify having run away, maybe something inspired by *The Exorcist.* I don't know.

Thursday, March 4

Before court opens, Judge Carter has filed his singularly evenhanded ruling: The government may show the jury *some* of the evidence found in the Harrises' apartment, including the "Tania Interview," but not the Bank of America floor plan, which is partly in Patty's handwriting and bears her fingerprints. During *voir dire*, several jurors had indicated an awareness that the defendant was under investigation for a bank robbery in the Sacramento area in which a woman was killed. "If you are talking about Sacramento banks, you are raising the flag of homicide," Carter says. "When you start talking about banks, you start ringing bells." Bells or skunks, the pity is that, though the defense may not be able to undo them now, it might have kept them out to begin with.* Bailey's tone of voice is much muted this morning, and Mom is back in her funereal black dress, its white collar turning her costume into a curious parody of the judge's robes. Only Carter is feeling chipper.

Bailey would have asked for a change of venue, he protests, "but it

---

*In his ruling, Carter did not comment on the legality of the FBI search but held that the search "violated none of the personal constitutional rights of the defendant . . . since she is without standing to suppress the evidence obtained thereby." Patty had forfeited her "proprietary" interest in items found at the Harrises' when she testified earlier that she could not recall ever having been in the apartment, except perhaps once, for a brief moment.

was beyond my wildest dreams that you would admit *any* Sacramento evidence!" Then you admitted Mel's, on grounds that that wouldn't prejudice the jury because nobody got hurt in the store. "But there is a homicide in Carmichael. Some of the jurors know that. There is no way to wipe that from their minds. This is an invitation for them to speculate without guidelines." In his opinion, Carter's rulings up to now have so favored the government that Bailey has had, in effect, to try the Los Angeles case here. Even though he knows Carter will instruct the jury to disregard Patty's guilt or innocence on that charge, "I urge you not to let this case get dirtied up by this kind of evidence!"

Browning sputters, Bailey rails, Carter fusses but remains firm. He will admit the document labeled "Bakery," which Browning has described as a "laundry list," in Patty's handwriting, of instructions on how to rob a bank, but not the annotated floor plan of a specific bank. The press rushes out the front doors of the courtroom to phone in this important ruling just as the jury is marching back in through the rear doors—flow and counterflow continue its circular pattern. Important trial news flashes around the world from the bank of eight coin telephones outside the courtroom at the very moment that the jurors reenter our carefully padded cell—padded to protect the defendant from injuring herself unnecessarily.

Dr. Rod W. Perry, the next witness, was the intern on duty at San Francisco General Hospital on August 12, 1975, when a young woman suffering from poison oak came in. Her face was very swollen, one eye almost shut. Was this young woman pale? No. Did she seem to have low affect? No. Did she appear to be well oriented, rational, aware? Yes. The young doctor names the medications he prescribed, and the prosecutor puts into evidence three medicine bottles, each with Dr. Perry's name on it, recovered from Patty's apartment.

After the morning recess we are not called back into court. Patty is not feeling well. We are adjourned until two-fifteen P.M., and an impromptu bull session ensues among the press on Bailey's nightly flights to Las Vegas and his obvious fatigue. The reporters are astounded by his failure to challenge the Los Angeles search warrant.

We are waiting for the bailiff to call us to order after lunch when a wave of laughter ripples through the press section of the courtroom and a large sheet of paper passes from hand to hand. It is a cartoon drawn by one of the sketch artists. The next witness is to be Dr. Joel Fort, a psychiatrist who will testify for the government in its rebuttal of the defense. Dr. Fort is evidently a somewhat unusual character, well known to California newsmen, who frequently appears as an expert witness in sensational trials. About a week ago Dr. Fort had sent a long letter to the court, with copies to every news organization in town, setting forth his view of the proper role of the expert witness in criminal proceedings. The letter said he sought no personal publicity and would prefer, if possible, that his name not even be mentioned in press accounts of the Hearst trial. The notion of somebody connected with this case *not* wanting publicity strikes the reporters as preposterous, and they see the Fort letter as a ploy to gain publicity by feigning disinterest. The cartoonist has sketched Dr. Fort sitting on the witness stand wearing a big Safeway paper bag over his head. Dr. West chuckles hardest. "First laugh I've had in three weeks," he gasps.

Carter now orders the government to place in evidence various items taken from the Harrises' apartment: a green spiral notebook, money orders, old bills, shopping lists, maps, scraps of manuscript, a bankbook, a diagram of a restaurant, a document in Patty's hand headed "Consul General Of," another headed "American Revolution," and an envelope on which she has scribbled, "cat food, beef bouillon cubes, wine, hammer, screwdriver, stopper for tub." Johnson and Browning are quibbling over whether one side of a piece of paper may be put in evidence but not the other when suddenly Bailey is bent over me, whispering, "Have you got your copy of Fort's press release?" Being an out-of-towner, I never received one, nor even heard of Dr. Fort until today. But it is odd that Bailey lacks a copy. Again I am surprised by the seat-of-the-pants conduct of this defense.

Fort's lawyer arrives to plead his client's case for anonymity. Joel Fort, MD, who enters now through a side door, is shaven-skulled and wears a bold red-and-white-striped shirt, a mustache, and heavy glasses. He is grave and somewhat nutty-looking. Remembering the paper bag, I, too, am overcome with an urge to giggle. Carter wants Dr. Fort to understand that this trial is governed by the Sixth Amendment guarantee of a speedy and public trial by jury. The doctor's curious request suggests he may think he has some right to privacy. He does not. He doesn't have to testify if he doesn't want to, but whatever he says on the witness stand is open to public scrutiny.

All that Fort is really after is protection from exploitation by the news media, his lawyer says. But there is one other matter, a document that has been subpoenaed, a manuscript—

"A book. It says '*book*,'" Bailey interrupts.

All right, a book. But there *is* no book, only an outline and some lecture tapes. Several publishers have been approached: One has some of the tapes; another has an outline for a book, "Expert Witness," prepared from Fort's past lectures and research, and submitted before Fort was called into this case. He does not want to expose it to the public now in its present form. He feels he has some right of privacy on this, perhaps a First Amendment right, perhaps a Fifth Amendment right—

Carter's high forehead pleats up like an accordion. "You mean he has a First Amendment right to something he hasn't written yet!" Even Catherine gives a whoop of laughter. Dr. Fort glowers silently. "My business is creative thinking, Judge," his lawyer says.

Until now we haven't had any real heavies in this case, only real victims. After the fire in Los Angeles, the original villains all became martyrs and ascended to radicals' heaven. But over in a shadowed corner of the courtroom, slumped in a big leather chair, Joel Fort looks marvelously malevolent.

Invited to take the stand, Fort describes himself as a specialist in social and health problems, criminology, violence, youth behavior, and drug abuse. Has not Dr. Fort been asked by the defense to produce a copy of the press release he distributed to the news media? "I would call it an antipress release," says the unsmiling doctor. It came about when a *Newsweek* reporter asked for his opinion on how expert-witness testimony should be evaluated. The antipress release is read into the record. After stating that he has many years' experience with criminals and has served as an expert witness in twenty-two states, the writer wishes to

formally request that my name or photo not be used, now or if I testify. ... Over the years I have become convinced that crime and violence are so exploited and sensationalized by the media that it is destructive to society, victims, dependents, and their families.

I urge you individually and collectively to stop more than minimal coverage of this case, and instead devote your time and energy to exposure of incompetence and corruption in city, state and federal government; serious social and health problems which are growing worse; or other criminal trials involving ordinary people, and often more serious charges. ... I urge that the names of individual doctors, lawyers or family members of the defendant not be used, so as to decrease the symbiotic exploitation of crime. For myself, I request anonymity because of my right of privacy, my desire to avoid exploitation of crime, and my wish to avoid the personal danger which is engendered by media coverage. Also, I do not find it an honor to join politicians, actors, public relations creations, ads, and assassins as "celebrities."

Fort's memorandum goes on to define the role of the expert in criminal cases as "someone with specialized knowledge," perhaps a journalist, social worker, or ex-criminal, and not necessarily a psychiatrist, although "by default and by professional aggrandizement, psychiatry dominates. . . .*

"In general, expert testimony on criminal responsibility only occurs when a defense of insanity (or, in California courts, diminished capacity) is raised. . . . In the Hearst case, the judge has not yet ruled on whether he will allow expert testimony."

Regarding experts, Dr. Fort continues, the main questions one should ask are

1. Are they psychiatrists whose main experience is in the private office practice of psychoanalysis, or in academic teaching work, or in something else?
2. How relevant is their background to questions of criminal responsibility?
3. Have they over the years made themselves available to both sides, defense and prosecution? Do they search for truth or victory?
4. Does the expert regard a defendant primarily as his "patient" and uncritically accept everything told him by the defendant and lawyer as true?
5. What impact does the questioning of lawyers and doctors prior to a trial, especially when this amounts to hundreds of hours, have on a defendant's version of what happened?
6. How does the expert balance objective data (investigative reports, confessions, tapes, et cetera) against what the defendant tells him?
7. Has there been any collusion and/or peer pressure among the doctors brought into the case on either side?
8. With a special defense, such as—to make one up—"mind dirtying" —does it exist because it has been repeated time after time by a writer, lawyer or a doctor? . . . If it is a concept based on, say,

---

*The dispute over the proper use of psychiatric expert witnesses goes back at least as far as the Leopold and Loeb trial in 1924. The difficulty has always been the tendency of the expert— whether a psychiatrist or an auto mechanic—to function as advocate as well as detached witness.

Canadian sailors in Japan thirty years ago, how does it apply to American youth influencing other youth in the 1970s? And finally, how many things can dirty the mind, how long do they last, and how can a dirtied mind be washed?

Beneath this, in parentheses, the antipress release says, "These comments are summarized and excerpted from my book 'Expert Witness,' to be published by Norton, and held up by me so as not to conflict with any pending trials; and from the course material for 'Minds on Trial,' which I have given for the University of California."

This does indeed sound like a lightly veiled plug for the doctor's forthcoming book, a point that Bailey is by now fairly straining at the leash to make. My eye strays to Patty, and again I am struck by her mermaid aspect. Only the upper part of her body is ever visible. The rest is invariably hidden either by the defense table or the witness box. She rarely moves; sometimes she half smiles. There is something eerie about her. Perhaps she is a Lorelei, luring sailors to their doom. She may be doing that to Bailey and his crew even now.

Bailey goes down Fort's eight-point list, point by point, mocking it, daring him *not* to relate it to the Hearst case.

Fort's lawyer objects to "Mr. Bailey's nonverbal efforts to communicate with sneers, wiggling his eyebrows, looking at his watch, curling his nose, and other things."

"Oh, come on, George!" snorts Bailey.

"Overruled," says the judge.

"That's okay. I have no objection," says the spooky Dr. Fort.

Bailey continues to snap away at Fort's lawyer until Carter, anxious to hurry this case along, intervenes. "Gentlemen, I am calling a halt to all these procedural delays! I am advising you, Mr. Browning, and you, Mr. Bailey, that tomorrow morning at ten o'clock in front of the jury we are going to start taking evidence!"

Friday, March 5

It is a brilliant morning and I walk all the way to court, down the zigzag of sparkling white hills, humming summer hiking songs. After three or four years of grueling work, my friend Gail Sheehy has finally finished writing her book *Passages* and is in town to celebrate; last night we had a long, late dinner. Gail lives across the road from me in summer, and we have spent a lot of time barefoot in each other's kitchen, gossiping and cooking things. Gail's daughter, Moira, two or three years younger than Kathy, is a grave and levelheaded child with the balance of a Wallenda. We scarcely see each other in winter, but in the short, feverish burst of summer we are two single writers raising daughters, and our friendship pops into sudden, vigorous life like the radishes and zinnias we tend.

Last night I had found myself telling Gail all about Kathy, about her running away, about my visit to Los Angeles and my fears for my daughter. I confessed my fear of my own mother and the self-horror I had felt for years at being a childless woman; the joy and astonishment of Kathy's arrival long after we had given up hope; the collapse of the empty marriage; the particular guilts of that divorce; how Kathy grew up, lived with me, grew unhappy, moved away . . . I told Gail all of it, the whole thing. I had never put the entire story together before, not even in my own mind at midnight, but I had inhabited it, and it me, for decades. When I finished talking and leaned back it was past one o'clock, and I felt somewhat light-headed, exhilarated, in fact, because I understood then that at last I was over it. I could tell it and even experience it without having to bleed. The old wound had healed, and it would not hurt in the old way again. No wonder this morning I skip down hills and sing childhood songs.

In court a pompous FBI man named Ferguson describes some cards with matching codes that were discovered in the wallets of Patty, Wendy, and William Harris. The code was "a monoalphanumeric representation" of certain pay telephone numbers in the Bay Area. The key word was "Paintbrush," and the letters P-A-I-N-T-B-R-U-S-H stood for the numerals 1-2-3-4-5-6-7-8-9-0. One remembers the amorous house painters Soliah and Kilgore and their assistants, Kathy and Josephine. When it is Johnson's turn to cross-examine, he says, "It was a very simple code, Mr. Witness, was it not?" Yes, it had certain childlike qualities. A glint comes into The Great Zombo's eye. "Like the Captain Midnight code?"

"Not *that* simple."

"And how long did it take you to break this code, Mr. Witness?"

"About two weeks."

Johnson grins. "Thank you. That's all." Leaping to their feet in these small legal scrimmages like Tweedledum and Tweedledee, Bailey and Johnson have the odd ability to convey two opposed moods at once: fury barely held in check and the glee of roughneck kids in a snowball fight.

The government's next witness is an FBI handwriting expert. Patty's schoolgirlish script is copybook plain, as controlled and uninflected as her voice. The exemplars I have seen could have been produced by a handwriting automaton, which perhaps by now she is. Over a running series of objections from Johnson, who is striving to keep the contents of the documents from the jury, we get some tantalizing glimpses into SLA life. In court only the first lines are read aloud. "Toaster wire ... 10 sec." A grocery list commences with the words "cat food." Other documents begin, "The struggle against sexism in the SLA . . ." and "Contradictions of being urban guerrillas . . ." Out of court the government distributes the full texts to reporters. Most are from Patty's apartment, and all are in her hand. The cat-food list goes on to mention explosives. "Toaster wire" is on a list of parts needed to make a time-bomb trigger. That page ends, ". . . meet to talk about shooting—9:00."

Judge Carter is chipper, blue eyes twinkling above his bright blue shirt and tie, happy to see all this stuff logged into the record, to be *getting on* with it at last. Browning tries again to have the Trish Tobin tape admitted, but is overruled once more, and then it is time for the plaintiff's first expert witness to take the stand.

Joel Fort's testimony is prefaced by the usual catechism of credentials: medical degree from Ohio State University Medical School in 1954; PhD in clinical psychiatry; several years in the U.S. Public Health Service, and so on.

The doctor is resplendently attired in a gray suit, fancy gray striped shirt, and his Expert Witness tie—heavy maroon silk with a gleaming gold caduceus rampant on a field of uppers and downers. An expert

Expert Witness, Fort speaks directly to the jury, his back half turned toward the bench and counsel tables, and the jurors pay him very close attention. Dr. Fort has been an expert psychiatric witness in twenty-two states and in six federal-court districts, he says, and has consulted and testified in more than two hundred criminal cases, about 60 percent of the time for the defense. In cases with multiple defendants, he has testified for both sides in the same trial. Fort was an expert witness in the Charles Manson trial and in the subsequent trial of Tex Watson; the Kemper and Mullin mass-murder trials in Santa Cruz; the California sniper cases of Hicks and Sander; the trial of the two homosexual Houston murderers, Henley and Brooks, who tortured and killed twenty-seven young boys; the Timothy Leary drug trial; the 1969 *Presidio* mutiny; and the Lenny Bruce case. What a grotesque company in which to find the daughter of mild and humdrum Catherine and Randolph Hearst!

More credentials: Dr. Fort has taught courses at various branches of the University of California in sex and crime, drugs and crime, and rehabilitation of criminal offenders. He has made a number of educational films and tapes, and has written books and contributed articles to numerous legal and medical journals—though not nearly so many nor so prestigious as the outpouring by his three Ivy League predecessors, the defense experts. But Dr. Fort is often asked to testify at congressional hearings, and he has been a consultant to the World Health Organization, the United Nations, the Peace Corps, the Anti-Poverty Program, Vacaville Medical Facility, the Menninger Foundation, and the National Student Association, and to the governments of Canada, Thailand, and Australia. Though he once spent about 25 percent of his time in private practice, he has not done so for many years. In 1965 he founded Forthelp, a private, nonprofit center that helps young men and women with problems related to crime and violence, sex, drugs, and suicide. The place has no administrative offices, titles, or secretaries. It attempts to treat people as living-room guests seeking help, rather than as "sick people."

Now, Dr. Fort, Browning begins, what varieties of radicals have you dealt with? He has had extensive contacts with "the so-called hippie population" and with student radicals. In preparation for this trial he has done a special study of thirty-five kidnap victims, and, of course, he is familiar with the literature of urban guerrilla movements in other countries. He has consulted with CIA and Defense Department terrorism experts and has conducted perhaps fifty in-depth interviews with concentration-camp survivors. He has also known many victims of rape, mugging, assault, and attempted murder. In 1963 he had some experience with Chinese thought reform while interviewing Chinese refugees on a trip to Hong Kong. In sum, although Joel Fort's qualifications are somewhat different from the psychiatric credentials offered by the defense—more broad-based and less glossy—they are more than sufficient. The contrast between the two camps recalls the old academic distinction between town and gown, and the jury may well incline to the townies.

Lunch is over, and in a few moments Mr. F. Lee Bailey, a townie at heart, will get his long-awaited opportunity to cross-examine this man. Defense expectations and spirits are high. In the ladies' room, beforehand, Dr. Singer tells Catherine that for the hell of it she analyzed the Trish Tobin tape and discovered that whereas Trish used fourteen crudities, Patty used only ten. Offered lightheartedly, the information seems to require a joking response. Catherine Hearst crinkles her Chinese eyes. "Ah was never in the Hibernia Bank, and Ah can prove it. Ah was in Mexico. Ah have an *alibi!*" Nobody laughs.

We are all standing patiently in our queue at the metal detector when a long, hoarse, terrible scream slices down the marble corridor like a glass knife. Down at the end of the line some would-be spectator has flipped out. Marshals drag a screaming figure past us in a red blur, so fast one cannot tell if it is man or woman. The incident is never explained, but the sound was the sound of raw madness, the kind of thing one encounters in the locked back ward of a mental hospital, not in our neat and tidy world, not any more than one might expect to see a corpse rotting on a San Francisco street. The sound is a kind of overture to the last and most critical phase of this trial, Bailey's ongoing cross-examination of Dr. Joel Fort.

Before Fort can begin his expert testimony, the defense challenges his qualification as an expert. In a very mild voice at first, Bailey says, Dr. Fort, you've indicated a rather large range of interests. Can you tell me in what capacity you were retained by the prosecution? General consultant. Are you an expert in psychiatry? Board-certified, for example? No. "Was it any part of your assignment from the prosecution, or your responsibilities as you understood them, *to give legal advice as to this case?*" A sudden, very ugly edge has come into Bailey's voice.

"It was not part of my assignment, and I did not specifically see myself as giving legal advice."

"Do you know Mr. and Mrs. Hearst, sitting here in the front row?"

Certainly. "Have you met and talked with them?" I certainly have.

"Did you go to them, Dr. Fort, and try to fix this case behind my back?" Suddenly Bailey is bellowing like a bull. "Did you go to Mr. and Mrs. Hearst and try to arrange a meeting with Jim Browning without my knowledge and without my presence to try to dispose of this case? Did you advise Mr. Hearst how to go about avoiding a public trial?"

I raised one or two possibilities. I wouldn't call it making recommendations.

"Did you advise him to call a lawyer not retained by the defense?" It was an attorney already retained by them—William Coblentz.

"Did you advise them to do that without telling me?" Bailey's voice shakes with fury.

"I *had* told you, Mr. Bailey, *and* Mr. Johnson *and* Mr. Browning *and* Mr. Bancroft. It was done with the full knowledge of all four of you, and as a matter of fact, you praised me and my motives for doing so." Fort's voice is as cool and flat as a sheet of glass.

"Did you say, 'The problem with this case is that Bailey likes to try cases and Browning wants to be a federal judge'?"

"I never said that. I'll tell you what I did say that you have considerably distorted."

"Oh! Tell me." Bailey burns with such scorn one can feel its heat.

"I said that often the needs of the defendant in any criminal case . . . get lost in terms of other motives that are sometimes a part of the background of attorneys on both sides."

"Did you encourage Mrs. Hearst to meet with Mr. Browning directly?"

"No, I encouraged her to call Mr. Coblentz and ask if he thought such a course would be helpful."

"Without the defendant's counsel's knowledge!"

"That is absolutely untrue. I talked to both Mr. Johnson and you, as I did to Mr. Browning and Mr. Bancroft."

"That's absolutely false, Dr. Fort."

"No. You're lying about it, Mr. Bailey."

So there we have it, head to head: psychiatrist and lawyer each trying to sink his teeth into the other's neck.

Dr. Fort, did you tell Mrs. Hearst that this case should be disposed of because a trial would be agony for her daughter, and if she pleaded guilty the worst sentence she could get as a kidnapping victim would be six months' probation?

"Mr. Bailey, for the third time, I told Mrs. Hearst and Mr. Hearst, and I told you and Mr. Johnson, and I told Mr. Browning and Mr. Bancroft that if there was any way possible, I thought it would be desirable to avoid a public trial. A public trial, I felt, would be destructive to the defendant, to her family, and to society. I said no more, and no less, than that." The fat is in the fire, the gauntlet thrown.

Mr. Bailey would now like to discuss brainwashing. Sorry, but Dr. Fort doesn't like that term. Is "coercive persuasion" more acceptable? More acceptable, yes, but still somewhat vague; Dr. Fort prefers what he calls "attitude change." Here we go again; it seems unbelievable. Patty looks near tears.

Does Dr. Fort have experience with people who have been subject to the will of their captors? Extensive. What besides the Manson case? His special study of kidnapping victims, interviews with fifty survivors of concentration camps, twenty-five to fifty rape victims . . .

Excuse me. Which concentration camps? Which survivors? Did he write reports of these interviews? "No, Mr. Bailey. I don't write a book or make a movie out of every life experience I have." Another withering blast of scorn. This is like watching a duel between two comic-strip spacemen armed with death rays.

I see. Have you ever written *anything* on brainwashing, coercive persuasion, or attitude change? Or on kidnapping, for that matter? No, but Fort has made two films touching on these subjects, and a film often takes more work than a book. In his five-month study of kidnapping victims, his raw material came from the FBI, the official agency in charge of kidnapping in this country. After reading case studies on thirty-five victims of similar background, age, and social class to Patty's, he then did in-depth interviews with seven subjects and the father of one. Five were females aged fourteen to twenty-two.

For the time being, Bailey will not further oppose Dr. Fort's claim to be qualified as an expert. But before we can move forward, Browning has an urgent personal problem to clear up. "Dr. Fort, what does the word 'fix' mean to you?"

"It has a dirty connotation . . . bribing someone."

The prosecutor is at pains to bring out that he never urged Fort to say anything to the Hearsts, that he and Fort never discussed Browning's career aspirations and had never even met before this case. Dr. Fort suggested nothing in the least "under the table," no "fix," nothing beyond the proposition that a public trial might not be the best disposition of the case. Indeed, Dr. Fort felt that "Mr. and Mrs. Hearst would resent any kind of improper suggestion. They both seem to me to be very sincere and very concerned people."

How important is it, Doctor, that the expert have some familiarity with criminal behavior? Very important. The expert should know people who have committed crimes but have not been caught; know others who have been arrested, others who have not been arrested, others who have been convicted and put on probation or parole, and others doing time. In that way, one gets a sense of the continuum of human behavior and of what people are likely to say and do under varying conditions of danger and fear, stress and guilt. One should also attempt to visualize the person in a noncriminal or precriminal situation. Alas, most expert witnesses in criminal cases are psychiatrists with a background in office practice, where one sees mostly middle- and upper-class people suffering from neuroses; in academic research and teaching; and in hospital administrative work. The most common error made by this kind of expert witness is to accept uncritically and naively anything a criminal defendant says. One must also watch out for predisposing biases. For example, Dr. Fort was recently involved in a case in which the explanation for the defendant's criminal behavior was possession by the devil. In his opinion, training in Freudian psychoanalysis presents similar difficulties.

Can an expert be fooled, Dr. Fort? Certainly. What is mental illness? Swiftly, Judge Carter points out that the appropriate question to ask is what the term that has been used here—"traumatic neurosis with dissociative features"—means in relationship to the term "mental illness." "Now get to that, and we'll get someplace!"

Okay. Dr. Fort, would a diagnosis of traumatic neurosis with dissociative features at the time the defendant was captured be retroactive? Would it indicate whether or not she'd had it fifteen months before? Absolutely not. If the person were seen in jail, what is called mental illness could in part or in whole be caused by the jail experience. You would also need to consider whether the illness was of the same intensity or severity now as then. Mental illness can be mild, moderate, or severe; sometimes it is continuous, sometimes brief and abrupt. Sometimes it is incapacitating; more often, it is not.

Dr. Fort, can psychological testing determine a person's past mental state? Absolutely not, nor is there any relationship between such tests and criminal responsibility.

Bailey says these questions are irrelevant; there is no plea of insanity in this case. Judge Carter cautions the prosecutor against going into the question of mental illness; it is a dangerous door to open. But Browning plows stubbornly ahead. Doctor, how do you go about determining mental illness?

What Dr. Fort's five-minute answer boils down to is that you make a complete analysis of the patient's history, put it together with the present symptoms, look for internal inconsistencies, and try to rule out alternative possible diagnoses. This last is important because studies have shown as much as 60 percent disagreement between two psychiatrists on any given diagnosis. When a third psychiatrist is brought in, the differential may fall to 45 percent.

The first person to get in touch with Dr. Fort about Patty Hearst was Vincent Hallinan. Shortly after her arrest, he asked if Fort would consult on the matter of her mental competency. A day or two later, a call came from Bancroft. It was not the first time Fort has been invited by both sides to consult in the same case; indeed, he prefers to speak to both sides before agreeing to testify for either. Eventually he decided to testify for the government because the law says that the findings of the government's expert are available to the defense should the government decide not to use them, whereas the reverse does not obtain. Another factor in his decision was that there appeared to be a lot of behind-the-scenes shuffling of attorneys, if he might use that term, and Mr. Hallinan's involvement in the case seemed far from certain.

Finally, on about February 13, when the trial was already under way, he wrote a report based on his interviews with the defendant and on an exhaustive examination of data. . . . Fort plows through, listing his prodigious homework.

"Mmmmmm, when you come to a convenient place, Mr. Browning," says Carter.

"Suits me fine now."

"All right. We will take the afternoon recess." Bang of gavel. We all rise and, OD'd on facts, stagger into the corridor for a smoke. "Did you smell the brimstone!" says Tom May.

But on the matter of Joel Fort's research, folks, you ain't heard nothin' yet. We learn after the recess that the doctor has gone over every word of the jail tapes made by Doctors West and Singer, in transcript form when possible. He has read transcripts of FBI interviews with Christine Johnson, the black woman who was the last person to leave the SLA's Los Angeles house alive. He read interviews with Patty's sisters, her cousin Willie, and Steve Weed's collaborator, Mimi Swanton. He spent several hours at the house in Daly City, including one hour alone inside the closet, turning a radio on and off and trying to determine how much sound could be heard under various conditions. He drove to the apartments where Patty and the Harrises were captured, in order to ascertain the distance between them. He visited the kidnapping site in Berkeley and the apartment on Golden Gate. He made four visits to the San Mateo County Jail. He examined the sheriff's logs and spent an hour or so interviewing Al Johnson. During his interviews with Patty, incidentally, Johnson was always nearby.

Then there was his background reading. Dr. Fort has boned up on attitude change, radicalism, feminism, guerrillaism, the youth culture, criminology, religious conversions, the Moonies, Jesus freaks, Zen Buddhists, and similar groups, concentration camps, Maoist thought reform, suggestibility, sensory deprivation, hypnosis, and other altered states of consciousness. He looked at more than 200 books and 125 articles, and put in a total of 300 hours' consultation over five months before finally writing his report.

Now Browning is ready to put the specific question. "Did the defendant at the time of the bank robbery charged have any mental disease or defect—traumatic neurosis with dissociative features or anything else—which substantially affected her capacity to conform her conduct to the law, or to appreciate the moral wrongfulness of participating in that bank robbery?"

Bailey objects. This is not an insanity defense!

But yes, indeed, in Dr. Fort's opinion Patty "had no mental disease or defect at that time that would in any way affect her functioning."

Did she lack the mental capacity or awareness to know what she was doing? Again Bailey objects that this is not an insanity defense, and Carter sustains the objection.

Browning's third question: In Dr. Fort's opinion, at the time the bank robbery was in progress was Patty under any threat of grave bodily injury or death? Bailey objects even more violently. "If that doesn't go to the merits of the case, I never heard anything that did! Your Honor, that's a jury question!"

"Mr. Bailey, calm down. . . . Ladies and gentlemen, your function is to determine intent. This witness may give his opinion, but you are not bound by it."

Bailey has still another objection: Dr. Fort has no expertise on whether or not Patty was under the gun in the bank.

BROWNING: Do we understand three defense psychiatrists can get up on the stand and give their opinions, but the government can't give one?

Bailey says his witnesses made those statements as history, not as opinion.

If Bailey thinks Dr. Fort's testimony is improper, says the prosecutor silkily, perhaps he would join Mr. Browning in a motion that *all* psychiatric testimony be stricken?

"Be serious, Mr. Browning!"

"I am perfectly serious, Mr. Bailey."

Carter is woolly-minded as to when and how certain testimony occurred, but Bailey's recollection is meticulous. He will fight, at any cost, to prevent Joel Fort from expressing an opinion on whether Patty was in fear during the robbery because his case rests on the degree of her fear. If the jury finds the defendant in fear of death or great bodily injury, they cannot find her guilty.

The judge finally asks the government to defer its question; he will rule later. "Proceed, Mr. Browning."

In forming his opinion, did Dr. Fort use a single frame of reference, such as the POW experience, or more than one frame of reference? Multiple frames, of course. The doctor's level, bee-buzzing voice starts in again. One frame was all the elements that contribute to attitude-change—family life, education, the mass media, advertising and propaganda, peer-group relationships, business and organization relationships, religious experiences, psychotherapy experiences, and legal and criminal and police relationships. Another frame was the defendant's prekidnapping attitudes, since "the most important ingredient in any kind of alteration of behavior is what you already are.

"The third thing I thought was extremely important was the total context of the SLA. Who were the eight other members? . . . We need to explain how these people became SLA members if we are to understand what happened to the defendant. Seven out of eight came out of white, middle-class, affluent, educated backgrounds, and five were women."

The fourth frame of reference was the physical environment in which change occurred. What was the closet like, the radio noise, the food and drink, the toilet privileges? Next frame: the experience of other kidnapping victims of similar backgrounds. Sixth frame: concentration-camp survivors and POWs, rape victims, and veterans of Chinese thought reform. Of particular interest among many such people in the last category Dr. Fort studied was Jane Darrow,* the only woman among

*The pseudonym used by Lifton.

Dr. Lifton's eleven subjects. In January Dr. Fort telephoned her at the University of Michigan, where she is now a political scientist, and asked about the years she had spent in a Chinese prison.

Hearsay! Bailey objects. I cannot cross-examine a phone conversation not made under oath.

"Overruled," says Carter. "Proceed."

"What did Jane Darrow tell you with respect to her experiences, Doctor?"

"She said, first of all, that there's no such thing as brainwashing; it's a meaningless concept." Such a concept would mean a complete transformation of values, and she did not experience that. She went into the prison at the age of twenty, having lived in China most of her life and having been aware of its many social inequities. She came to admire many of the new Chinese social programs. She came to feel that the Western powers had not dealt well with China.

For myself, I find this information fascinating. Why is Patty paying so little attention?

In no way did Jane Darrow's ideology or values convert to Chinese values, she told Dr. Fort. She also told him that when she had agreed to be interviewed by Dr. Lifton, "it was with the understanding that it would never be written or repeated."

A great flurry from the defense. Dr. Lifton was never asked about this matter. If the government had this information, how come—

Fort interrupts. The government didn't have this information. Only he had it. Bailey doesn't believe him, but again the judge overrules and says to get on with it.

Is Dr. Fort familiar with various psychological experiments on attitude change, such as Milgrim's work at Yale? Like Zimbardo's work, Professor Milgrim's study is a classic. He measured conformity and obedience by seeing how far graduate students were willing to go to cause pain in order to follow the orders of an authority figure. To find out, electrodes were attached to a "victim"'s arm, and each time he gave a "wrong" answer, the test subject was instructed to turn up the electric current. The disturbing result of the study was that one can make an instant torturer out of at least two-thirds of our upper-middle-class population, at least at Yale. Was there any indication of mental disease or defect in any of these test subjects, Doctor? No, they were all perfectly normal Americans.

Saturday, March 6

This weekend my journalistic chickens come home to roost. *Newsday* has asked for a wrap-up piece, to be published after the verdict. It will need not only a reasonably fresh angle—no more difficult, at this point, than finding a fresh angle on Christmas—but a healthy shelf life. We settle on Bailey's often-quoted remark that a criminal trial is like a play. I have made a Sunday appointment to do the interview, and warm up beforehand by making a few yellow-pad notes on where I think the trial stands now:

The defendant is a Madonna dolorosa, a classic image of female suffering. She sits motionlessly, and tears fall from her eyes as in a Sicilian religious painting. Fine-featured, smooth-skinned, narrow, and pale, she is almost as white as the "Pietà" of Michelangelo. The corpse across her knees is the dead Tania, vibrant, defiant guerrilla girl. She has sat thus for six weeks, silently weeping, an Italianate image of agony. Strange! Despite its purity and classical lineaments, that agony has gone entirely unmentioned in this courtroom until the advent, some six weeks into the trial, of Dr. Joel Fort, a man whom the defense counsel sees as scoundrel-in-chief and devil incarnate, as the miscreant who went to the parents of the beleaguered madonna and tried simultaneously to "fix" the case, smear her counsel, and intrude himself ass-backward into Patty's limelight. Shaven-headed, swarthy, lithe, intense, with piercing eyes behind silvery glasses, Dr. Fort sometimes looks the part he plays in Bailey's mind. Others see the doctor as a psychological pragmatist, concerned to deal bluntly with the case at hand, and to hell with the lace-handkerchief formalities of academic disciplines and the overripened niceties of the law. But to me, Dr. Fort is beginning to look like the little boy in Andersen's fairy tale, the one who pointed to the royal procession and said, "The emperor has nothing on!"

In his first day on the stand, he has given voice to three ideas that have been buzzing around in my mind for six weeks now, and presumably therefore in the minds of jurors as well, without having once been articulated in open court. The failure of either side to mention them is astounding, as they are so manifestly *there,* hanging like a scrim of reality between the audience of jury and press and the lawyers' and doctors' kabuki show taking place onstage. What are these heretofore-unuttered statements of the obvious? First, the defendant is in manifest agony, which it would have been desirable to avoid if possible. Why the needless public spectacle? Why the sensational trial, the ordeal-by-media? Why hold this form of twentieth-century exorcism if a way around it could have been found?

Second, the opinion of the defense psychiatrists may indeed, and understandably, have been somewhat skewed, not only by their professional interests (people normally tend to find what they're looking for —brainwashing experts would tend to find brainwashing, not brain lesions) but also by their unique relationship to the defendant. Office doctors and academics *would* be likely to see Patty not as a neutral subject to evaluate but as a patient, someone who evokes their natural wish to effect a "cure," a wish not diminished by the fact that they are at least temporarily in the service of the patient's powerful, and powerfully suffering, father.*

Third is the striking but unremarked-on similarity between the defendant and the SLA women who captured and seemingly converted her. "Could this happen to *my* daughter?" America had asked itself for two years. It is the one question Bailey says he wants the jurors to ask themselves now. Fair enough. But, save for the kidnapping that preceded it, exactly this *did* happen to the daughters of a Goleta pharmacist, a Santa Rosa furniture dealer, a Midwestern minister, a New Jersey Teamster official, and a Chicago insurance man.

That these three vital matters have not been raised until Dr. Fort raised them may account for the charge of negative electricity sparking between Bailey and Fort now. I see three possible motivations for Bailey: He is trying to find a way to denounce the doctor *a priori* as a liar and fraud, in order to deflect the jury's attention from the damage

*After the trial Bailey told a reporter certain other dimensions of that suffering: Explaining some of the economics of the defense to the writer Peter Manso, who was preparing an article for *Boston* magazine, Bailey said, "I don't think her parents brainwashed her at all. . . . I don't rely on my own judgment, though. I rely on three people who are known as experts, and their opinions were not bought: West got nothing, Singer got nothing. Lifton and Orne charged pretty good, but both of them imposed conditions before they would take the case—namely, that her claims prove legitimate. I think the combination [fee] of the two was between $20,000 and $30,000, with Lifton getting most of it. We negotiated them down. Orne was easy to deal with. Lifton was not."

Fort is about to do his client; or he wants certain things said in the course of this trial about Patty's ordeal, and the best way to do that is to put the words in Fort's angry, scornful, believable mouth; or Bailey's ego is indeed as festering and rufous as it seems. Most likely, once again, all three explanations are true.

"Why is a trial like a play?" I ask Bailey the next day.

"Because it's a show for an audience—two audiences. One is twelve people. The other is the public, which unfortunately must view it through the eyes of an interpretive press."

"The reporters have been a most imperfect filter. We're *for* Patty, by and large, but you certainly wouldn't know it from reading the papers. What's the trouble?"

"Only the lawyers know what's really going on, and they bring a kind of selective truth to bear. However, the governing thing is not *Is it truthful?* but *Is it helpful?*"

"Does that account for your cross-examination of Joel Fort?"

"That may be legal overkill. I have this terrible feeling we're beating a dead horse. The so-called experienced press have been telephoning Al all weekend. 'Enough already!' they say. 'Fort's no threat. Wrap it up!' But a lawyer has to figure, Sure the press feels this; they *know* Joel Fort. So they think I shouldn't deck around with him anymore. But I can't take that chance. The *jury* doesn't know him. So I've got to sit down and wipe on him a while longer. The lawyer is not only the playwright but the director. He puts on the show, orchestrates it, and he is also to some degree the protagonist for his side. He decides on the order of evidence, how to treat witnesses, whether to examine them and, if so, how, according to the *effect* that he wants to leave with the jury. It's more like directing a play than a film or a television show because there are no retakes."

"As the playwright you are stuck with a certain set of facts."

"Sure, but so was Shakespeare. You've simply got to create your scenario around what you're stuck with. Plays are always written with something to bring down the curtain, so the audience can think about it during intermission. To accomplish that in a courtroom takes careful planning and some luck. But there is a fair opportunity to position your heavy points at certain times. Friday afternoon is always a good one. The turning points are the surprises."

"Have you had many?"

"The only surprise in this trial was Carter's ruling that she be required to take the Fifth in front of the jury, which I thought very harsh and legally incorrect. The basis on which he claimed she'd waived her rights is, I think, erroneous, and he's offering me no remedy. I said, 'Stop and let me go to the Ninth Circuit. You're about to wreck the whole trial.' He reacted like most judges. He said, 'If you want to appeal me, go ahead. But I won't stop the trial.' But if you don't stop the trial, there's nothing to appeal. The damage is done."

"If you'd been clairvoyant and known he was going to do this, would you have put Patty on the stand anyway?"

"I had no choice. She's the only access we have to her state of mind while she was in the bank. She's the only evidence we have of what happened after the kidnapping. *There are no witnesses.* . . . Letting all those documents in is very unhelpful. They're really trying her for everything *but* the Hibernia Bank. The bank case itself is terribly weak, but by getting in all this other stuff they're saying, 'Boy! What a bad girl she turned out to be! For that reason alone you ought to put her away.' What this play is really about is the punishment of Patty Hearst for ostensibly rejecting her parents, for her twenty months of absence, for being an ingrate, and for being rich."

Week Seven

March 8–14

Monday, March 8

Today Judge Carter is ready to rule on whether to admit Joel Fort's expert opinion. "While the ultimate issue here is the defendant's intent at the time of the offense, the initial situation—the defendant's status as a kidnap victim and whether this would deprive her of the requisite intent—is very unusual and beyond the common experience of jurors," he begins. Diminished capacity may or may not be part of the defense —Carter does not intend to "get into labels"—but if you look at the testimony of the three defense psychiatrists, "you must conclude they were talking about coercion."

I had been getting pretty confused by now by all these legal terms, so over the weekend I had looked up the law. What did each one mean? *Compulsion*, as defined in *Black's Law Dictionary*, is "constraint; objective necessity; duress. Forcible inducement to the commission of an act." *Duress*, according to the same source, "consists in any illegal imprisonment used for an illegal purpose, amounting to or tending to coerce the will of another, and actually inducing him to do an act contrary to his free will."

Another guideline, I learned, came from Devitt and Blackmar's *Federal Jury Practice and Instruction:* "In order . . . to provide a legal excuse for any criminal conduct the compulsion must be present and immediate, and of such a nature as to induce a well-founded fear of impending death or serious bodily injury; and there must be no reasonable opportunity to escape the compulsion without committing the crime or participating in the commission of the crime."

Diminished capacity is a native-born California product. The concept was developed by Charles Garry and is now accepted in other states as well. It says that though a person may be legally sane under the old M'Naghten Rule, that he may know the difference between right and wrong, for medical reasons he may have a diminished capacity to control his own behavior. As Garry has written, "The mental condition of the accused must now be considered as part of the defense; if a judge does not allow such evidence to be presented and does not instruct the jury that it must consider it, an appeal is almost certain to gain a reversal. The application of the concept of diminished responsibility has greatly increased the use of psychiatric testimony and has dramatically reduced the number of death sentences."*

The Hallinans had intended to mount a diminished-capacity defense. When Bailey took over, he chose instead to defend Patty on grounds of compulsion and duress.

Now Judge Carter is saying that Dr. Lifton's testimony for the defense was loaded with suggestions, discussions, and flat-out assertions of coercion. Therefore Dr. Fort's opinions may also be heard. Bang of gavel, and Bailey suffers another nail.

Before bringing Fort back in, Bancroft complains that the defense now has four separate subpoenas out to Dr. Fort and his publishers, trying to get their hands on his notes, journals, and time sheets. The government would like to quash these on the grounds that they are harassing, burdensome, and improper. Otherwise, he threatens to sub-poena all the defense doctors to return to San Francisco with records of *their* life's work.

"Mr. Bancroft, you are making me tremble with fear," says Carter. He will hear Fort's testimony first, then rule. "Bring the jury in." The jurors are followed by the mysterious Dr. Fort, outfitted today in a green suit and green shirt that make him somewhat more sinister-looking than usual.

Browning pops the big question. No, Fort thinks Patty "did not perform the bank robbery because she was in fear of her life. She did it as a voluntary member of the SLA." The jury has heard the dread words. Before the prosecutor can go on, the judge interrupts. "Ladies and gentlemen, let me repeat an instruction I have given you before. Only *you* can determine guilt or innocence. One of the issues in determining that is whether or not she was coerced and to what extent. The purpose of the psychiatrists' testimony is to advise

*Charles Garry, *Street-Fighter in the Courtroom* (New York: F. P. Dutton, 1977), p. 48.

(370)

you of their opinion. You will decide whether and how much of it to believe."

On Friday Dr. Fort was asked about various studies on human conformity. Fort again summarizes the history of such studies all the way back to 1935 and adds an important one he forgot to mention. *On Becoming a World-Saver,* by Laughlin and Stark, attempts to analyze how evangelical conversions come about and what makes people become Moonies, Hare Krishnas, Jesus freaks, or Children of God, as hundreds of thousands of Middle America's sons and daughters have done in the past decade. Fort outlines the world-saver study with great clarity and detail, speaking directly to the jurors. The evangelical process has a number of elements. The subject must have a dissatisfaction with his own life, an inner vacuum. Next comes a chance encounter with the evangelist or a group of disciples. The third and fourth variables are the degree of interaction, which will depend on how much affection the subject feels for the new group, compared to his or her emotional ties to others in society and family. Once the conversion occurs, the fifth variable is the amount of ongoing group interaction. The more of that you have, the stronger the new bonds become.

Fort is an excellent, practiced lecturer who uses no notes but never loses the thread. His testimony is like a copy of *Psychology Today* made into a talking book for the blind. "Now, in answer to your question, Mr. Browning, how these things apply to the defendant and what happened to her"—a question that must have been asked him at least twelve minutes ago—the witness finds it helpful to divide his answer into three time frames: first, prekidnapping, then the period between the kidnapping and the bank robbery, and, finally, the period from Mel's until the arrest.

Randy Hearst removes his glasses. Without them he looks naked and dejected. Patricia Hearst has gone gray-faced again.

Dr. Fort has carefully researched and reconstructed the defendant's prekidnapping personality, and "My findings were that she was extremely independent, strong-willed, rebellious, intelligent, and well educated, but not especially intellectually inclined." He cites Patty's numerous fights with nuns at school, the fact that she has been sexually active since age fifteen, and was notably independent about rules in general. He mentions Mimi Swanton's comment to Dr. Singer that Patty was "an amoral person who thought that laws she didn't approve of should be violated," adding that Singer, the master psychologist, found Mimi a "highly reliable" judge of character.

"This is thirdhand hearsay!" Bailey objects. Fort replies that his information comes from transcripts of Dr. Singer's interview with Mimi, material available by law to all parties but "which for some reason were not included in Dr. West's report." Mimi also told Singer, for example, that once, at the Santa Catalina School, Patty wanted to get out of taking an examination, and so she told the teacher her mother had cancer, knowing it was not the sort of alibi the nun would attempt to check. The defendant, in short, is not only a liar but a calculating one.

Patty's jaw drops, and she turns toward her sister Vicki in open-mouthed disbelief. Her claim that she was coerced by the SLA makes Patty's veracity the key issue in this trial. But Fort does not see the dumb show. He is faced squarely to the jury, telling them how Patty's parents and sisters and Steven Weed felt about her. All of them described her as independent, assertive, and self-assured. Though she expressed ambivalent feelings about her parents to Dr. Fort and obviously had poor communication with them, other materials support the belief that she disliked or hated them flat out and felt only a desire to get away from the Hearst name and role. Her race and class attitudes also were ambivalent; she described some very positive feelings about having taught in a black nursery school. She had refused to make her debut in society, and did not identify with the Hillsborough set. In short, she enjoyed her class privileges yet was uncomfortable about her social position.

Steven Weed, "her most important prekidnap relationship," had become a source of growing dissatisfaction. Her fiancé was becoming too interested in antiques and possessions, the legacy of San Simeon and Wyntoon in particular. Also, she considered him a sexual pig who thought she should be available when he wanted her but who did not respond to sexual initiatives from her. She resented having to do the cooking. She found her lover somewhat boring at times. She had idle thoughts of suicide. She felt committed to the marriage yet fearful of going ahead.

Patty's drug experiences are comparable to those of other young people, Fort says, though she began experimenting with pot and alcohol somewhat earlier than most. On LSD she always had "good trips," a further indication of strong ego and an intact personality. In sum, Dr. Fort would describe the prekidnapping Patty as "a true-believer type," very opinionated, sure of her attitudes, dogmatic, and authoritarian.

Is it your purpose to paint her as a bad person, Doctor? Absolutely not. One of the torments for me throughout this case has been my sympathy for her both as a kidnapping victim and as someone having to undergo a process like this trial.

Dr. Fort was particularly interested in the backgrounds of the other SLA members. Cinque aside, the seven others were people of similar background, education, class attitude, age, even religion. Seven times he asked himself the cliché question of the decade: How did a nice all-American girl or boy like this join a group like that? He found that each one of them had gone through a similar evolution—none was *born* a terrorist—and that all had done it in very recent years. They were ordinary, active, popular young people—at least from superficial analysis. Most had been high-school leaders. One must, of course, remember that family-communication problems run very deep in our society, so despite the fact that they went on to college and became cheerleaders, social activists, political workers—for Eugene McCarthy in one case and for Barry Goldwater in another—they all were probably somewhat ambivalent about the directions their lives were taking. Nor can random factors be overlooked. Chance is very important.

Were you able to develop any opinion, Doctor, about how these people viewed themselves? Yes, and that was where it all came together. All eight SLA members had some degree of self-hatred, some lack of self-esteem. All were troubled by feelings of alienation and a sense of being left out. All were dissatisfied with their accomplishments or appearance or family life. Many had experienced great frustrations in their recent emotional relationships. The whites all shared "an element of strong reverse racism." Instead of responding to blacks or to prisoners as people, and applying the same standards as they would to themselves, they tended to bend over backward to exalt or glorify such persons—in this instance, DeFreeze—because of their racial and criminal and ghetto background. In short, the SLA members suffered from a fatal combination of high racial guilt and low self-esteem. Fort's description recalls the dimly remembered concept of "critical mass" in the triggering of an atomic bomb. Two elements, and enough of both, are necessary to produce the desired explosion.

Many radical white women are especially susceptible to prison-reform ideas and hypersensitive to underdogs, Charlie Garry often said. "Movement women are idealists, genuinely militant, extremely sincere, and people who suffer from great guilt, especially as regards black persons." In the course of his years representing the Communist Party,

(373)

Garry had known many such women. "Blacks take advantage of them." One prison Pascal "fucked over one of his white lawyers so badly she still hasn't recovered." These SLA girls were not Marxists, but they *were* passionate. Patty would never have joined them, Charlie thought, unless she had been preconditioned by her own guilt feelings and was in "a condition of diminished responsibility—so that when the intruders broke into her apartment and put on the pressure to do or die —when they said, in a sense, 'We're not gonna fuck with you anymore, this is the zero hour, do you believe what you've been saying or not?' —she would have joined them. When these very idealistic girls get hit with these questions, they can't say no, because to say no would be to say no to themselves."

In a conversation after the trial Dr. Margaret Singer told me something similar. In her practice as a clinical psychologist she meets many young women who "simply feel that they're not worthy creatures." Instead of dating ordinary men of their own ilk, they become involved with Hell's Angels, convicts, brutal men. "They take up with sociopaths not really to help the damaged person but because of a kind of inner self-hatred. It amounts to thinking that, since they're women, they're not quite all right. And it's so *hidden,* this terrible feeling."

"They get it from mothers who feel *they're* not quite all right," I said.

"And then they take up with men who are *obviously* not quite all right. If you regard being a woman as okay, you find an okay man, and there's no acting out of that funny trip. But those SLA women had done the self-hatred, self-humilation, taking-up-with-the-bad-guy trip to a pathological degree."

Dr. Singer described another contemporary societal illness, which she calls "bad parenting," which, to a degree, afflicts not just Patty but all daughters, at least in white middle-class and upper-class families. Old-fashioned parents are criticized today for having been dogmatic and autocratic, but at least their children knew what they were up against and could react. Modern kids rarely see a parent take a hard, if unreasonable, stand. Because of "a misextension of egalitarian thinking," today's daughters, and sons, grow to adulthood entirely among "reasonable" beings. Consequently, most of them have never learned *how* to take a position, defend it, change the position in light of new knowledge—they don't even know how to feel free to *have* a position.

"There is a very complicated procedure that parents have to provide to show their position to their children and say, 'Okay, I have values, I have beliefs, and I want to hear what yours are, so we can talk about them,' " Dr. Singer said. " 'The more that yours are pink, and mine are green polka dot, the more *vividly* we hold them, the more you can learn why yours are good or bad, and the more I can learn why mine are good or bad, and together we'll learn that the other thing—a third possibility —is probably what's real.' "

Sheer dogmatism is no good. One must convey to the kids that they must provide an equal mirror image, "that they have to be similar to you, and reasonable, rather than a complement to you. Good parenting requires understanding this difference between complementarity and similarity. And if you expect your kid to be similar, you've got to let him give you a lot of flak." You have to show him how to be a person with strong values and opinions but also how to grant that same right and privilege to other people. It's hard. To kids like Patty, revolutionaries and others who take firm, dogmatic positions look like saviors. That accounts for the success of the Moonies. "At some point the kindliest thing to say to someone is 'No. I disagree.' "

Joel Fort is instructing the jurors on the meaning of the SLA Codes of War—a "basic document, their Geneva Convention," he terms them. The codes, which the world heard of for the first time in the April Fool communiqué, were read to Patty on her first day in the closet and were also discussed in the "Tania Interview" and on several of the tapes. These codes specifically forbade the killing of a comrade and made it clear such killing was punishable. They specifically forbade surrender to the enemy (significant in terms of what later happened in Los Angeles—both at Mel's and during the police attack on the burning house) and physical or sexual assault on any comrade, on the enemy, or on the people. Most importantly, they provided that if any members of the SLA should lose faith, "they may leave the SLA simply by announcing to the Field Marshal that they wish to do so, and they will be released in a safe area."

What do the Codes of War have to say about POWs, Doctor? Browning asks. They specify humane treatment, no violence, no sexual assaults, "even no cursing." In view of all the "crudities" we have just heard, this last statement is so patently foolish it weakens the impact of Dr. Fort's testimony—an unexpected bit of good luck for Bailey. At this point he can use it.

Can you tell us what is important about the second time frame, Doctor? Fort subdivided this period into the early time of extreme fear and terror, in the car trunk and in the closet, and the later period. Judge

Carter is asleep again. All psychiatrists bore him equally. He is inter-ested in the law and in the adversary contest, not in this interminable, vague "science" that can explain things into the ground.

Dr. Fort determined that the first closet was big enough for the prisoner to stand up, sit down, lie down, or roll around in, and was equipped with a two-inch foam-rubber mattress, a blanket and pillow, "and sometimes a reading light." It is true that in the beginning Patty's only human contact was Cinque, who threatened to kill her if she tried to escape. However, Fort believes that the gag probably came off the first day in the closet and that within the first week they had stopped tying her hands.

Judge Carter is still snoozing, and I begin to envy him as Fort delineates how Patty's "group interaction seemed to progressively in-crease" and "friendly contacts and mutual liking developed," especially with Atwood, Wolfe, and Perry. Who told you that, Doctor? Miss Hearst did, and it also comes across in some of the other accounts. The jurors look perplexed. Do they doubt what Patty told the doctor or what the doctor is telling them?

Can Dr. Fort contrast the closet with other POW settings he has visited? At Auschwitz, captives suffered fifty-mile forced marches, dys-entery, starvation, and freezing, filthy, cramped quarters. Prisoners were transported in cattle cars, herded with whips and dogs, forced to strip naked and to smell burning flesh. In Patty's case there was no evidence of sleep deprivation, no starvation. . . . Fort's testimony is becoming progressively less effective. His farfetched comparisons viti-ate the government case.

Browning moves on to time-frame two, part two—the period on Golden Gate Avenue. When did the conversion begin, Doctor? It is difficult to pinpoint because all prisoners have a blurred time sense, but in the "Tania Interview," Patty writes that she felt an attraction to the SLA purposes within two weeks of her capture. Nothing magical or brutal was done to convert her. The change came about through admi-ration for her new comrades, their sense of commitment, their enthusi-asm and motivation.

Oliver J. Carter is *still* asleep, but I am awake because I think Fort has just said it. The core of it, the Big Persuader for Patty, must have been the unusual commitment and belief she found in these young women and men in all other respects so like herself. On Golden Gate, Patty began to get out of the closet more, to take part in gun drills and political indoctrination, and to experience still more "group interaction." By about March 1, Fort believes, the defendant had voluntarily joined the SLA.

Doctor, did she mention anything to you about a "tiny closet" at Golden Gate? No. Did she discuss any sexual relations? She said she was asked whether or not she would like to have intercourse with Willie Wolfe, and she consented because, among other reasons, "I thought it would help save my life." She later had sexual relations with Cinque "without affection," but "she did not directly or indirectly suggest rape." (But surely a new-fledged feminist would consider enforced sex without affection *to be* rape, and I would agree.) She did not say where the encounter with Wolfe took place, "but it was clear to me it was not inside the closet . . . just somewhere in the room." Patty told Fort she had no sexual relations with any of the females in the SLA.

At lunch both Dr. West and Dr. Singer are extremely disturbed by the morning's testimony. "They should call that place of his Fort Sanctimony," Dr. Singer sniffs. West compares Fort to Senator Joseph McCarthy. The defense experts consider the government's man a "classic psychopath." They huddle together over a large book, *Psychopaths,* by Alan Harrington, underlining it for Bailey's benefit.

"He's not even a zealot, he's a pseudozealot!" Dr. Singer snorts. "And he says he has no prejudice against Patty as a female. Hah! If I were a science-fiction writer, I'd make him my main character."

Carter has ordered Browning to "speed it up," and in the ensuing *rataplan* of question-and-answer, two of Fort's replies stand out: When Patty said of her SLA comrades, "I can't believe I liked them!" this indicated she once *had* liked them; and although she refused even to utter the names of the Harrises, referring to them, when necessary, as A and B, at times she has said that Atwood, Wolfe, and Perry "were nice."

Doctor, were the other SLA members experienced enough to conduct some sort of mind conversion with respect to the defendant? No. Their radical philosophy, "which I would summarize as a superficial blending of Marxism, Maoism, and terrorism," was still in its early stages. They were committed to violent social change as a general principle but lacked experience in converting others. However, in DeFreeze's file, Fort found a prison book list that discloses the sources of some of DeFreeze's ideas: Janov's *Primal Therapy, Psycho-cybernetics* by Maxwell Maltz, and a pop-psychology book by the Overstreets on how to overcome fear. None has any relevance to radicalism or to the process of attitude change.

How, then, would Fort explain Patty's apparent conversion? Could it be due to thought reform, coercive persuasion, or anything similar to what happened to our POWs in Korea or persons in Chinese prison camps? Not at all. Fort sees the SLA as part of a broad social movement in the United States in the 1960s and 1970s, particularly among youth, involving the switching of attitudes and the changing of behavior of hundreds of thousands, perhaps millions of people—all the people who have been attracted to the hippie life-style or to exotic religious philosophies, to social activism and nonviolent social change. Very, very few were drawn to more violent activism. Such broad and deep movements spring from widespread social discontent and changing values, and are impossible to measure or count. Attitude change comes from the accidental interaction during a time of tension and low self-esteem between a searching person and some new chance force. The collision itself is what produces conversion—not drugs, not hypnosis, not something magical, not some new wave of political force.

Joel Fort's world view seems to posit a kind of ethical Velcro. Floating somewhere in moral space are millions of lost souls, hungry young people "searching for something meaningful in life." Random ideologies also float about—hippiedom, radicalism, food fads, exotic religions. At any chance collision between a searching person and a passing, free-floating ideology, tiny, invisible hooks interlock. With proper group support and postcollision reinforcement, personal glue is extruded and the bond becomes stronger. This process is what Joel Fort means when he talks about attitude change. As he sees it, Patty was just such a lost soul, searching for meaning without even fully realizing it, when she collided—rather more violently than most—with the highly energized, passionate, guilt-laden, and moralistic ideologues of the SLA, young people, otherwise so similar to herself, who had found a belief system they were willing to die for. The hooks caught and held.

Doctor, would you comment, please, on the effect of the defendant's prekidnapping personality on the attitude change that occurred after her kidnapping? Yes. She had been a strong, willful, independent, bored, and dissatisfied person, in poor contact with her family, disliking them to some extent, dissatisfied with Weed after their three years together, missing a sense of purpose in life. . . .

In short, she sounded to me a lot like any kid her age, but Catherine Hearst smiles scornfully, for Joel Fort has just spelled out precisely the version of reality that she and her husband and the defense attorneys have steadfastly refused to accept.

Browning moves on to the date of the bank robbery. Did Dr. Fort find any evidence of mental illness or defect at *that* time—any traumatic neurosis, for example? No. To elude the bank's burglar alarms, the whole thing had to be pulled off in ninety seconds, and somebody debilitated by severe depression or anxiety probably couldn't even carry out the actions shown in the film.

Incidentally, Doctor, is an act of violence itself a sign of mental disease or defect? Not at all. Not many first-time muggers, rapists, and murderers have a specific mental disease.

Is there any evidence of mental disease or defect in Patty's behavior *after* the robbery—say, at the time of Mel's? Quite the opposite. Fort gets a picture of the defendant sitting alone in a van, reading a newspaper, "and upon finding that the Harrises are being arrested, putting down the newspaper, picking up a gun and shooting in order to rescue them, and then driving away with them after they joined her in the car." To carry out so complex a series of acts so successfully would indicate the absence of mental illness or stress.

"Doctor, what can you tell us, from a psychiatric standpoint, with respect to the claim that she fired the gun at Mel's almost involuntarily or instantaneously?"

"I find it unbelievable."

"Oh, now, wait just a minute!" Bailey roars. "I object and move for a mistrial! Is this man going to tell the jury what to believe?"

Browning starts to sputter, but Judge Carter firmly interrupts and advises the jury, "In this respect, what Dr. Fort has said is no different than what Dr. Orne said." It is merely an opinion.

Browning moves along. Doctor, I'd like to ask you a few questions about the defendant's mental state at the time she was in the bank. Can you comment on her claim that she was there under fear of death? "I came to feel that was incorrect for a number of reasons." Not only had the SLA Codes of War given Patty the freedom to leave at any time, not only did she say on the tapes that she was remaining by choice, but Fort has interviewed at least ten bank robbers over the years, and it is his impression that they never take the slightest chance of something going wrong that might jeopardize their own survival. The other SLA members would not have taken a chance on someone less than fully committed.

"Doctor, in your opinion, was the defendant a private in an army of generals?"

"No, I think she was a queen in their army. She brought them international recognition. It was an exciting thing for her, and for the rest of them, that the media responded to the group the way it did." On this point, at least, I was in complete agreement.

What is the significance of the essay on radical feminism found at Patty's apartment? Fort doesn't recall any essay, but there was a book, *The Dialectic of Sex,* a call for an end of oppression and exploitation of women by men.

I recalled the book myself. The author, Shulamith Firestone, attempts to do for the war between men and women what Marx did for the class struggle. I had found her work the most impenetrable piece of feminist literature I had ever come upon. Nothing served better to remind me of the broad gulf between Patty and Wendy's brand of feminism and my own.

Did you see any signs of disease or mental defect at the time the defendant was in the San Mateo County Jail? She was certainly having what traditional psychiatry calls a depressive reaction, which is a long-winded way of saying she was kind of upset and discouraged and blue. But that's characteristic of anyone's first jail experience. What is the significance of the clenched fist, the guerrilla salute? I would interpret it as a reassertion of her SLA identity. It was very different from the way POWs behave. Released concentration-camp victims do not say *"Heil Hitler!"*

Browning asks Fort to contrast Patty with the thirty-five kidnapping victims he studied. All of them were frightened, and all tried to go along with their captors, but none changed his or her ideology to do so. They had confidence in law enforcement, and several tried to escape, including a fourteen-year-old girl. All were extremely glad to get back to their families—indeed, it was a renewal experience that brought the families closer than ever before. Patty, on the other hand, did not try to escape, despite what appeared to be multiple opportunities. The usual reaching out to the family, the enthusiasm at being home, seemed absent. Fort was impressed by the health and strength of the thirty-five people after their terrible ordeal. None required *any* psychiatric care, and some were back at their normal activities within hours. Often in the medical profession, and especially in psychiatry, we tend to emphasize the weakness and dependency of survivors. We should also emphasize the valor, strength, and resiliency of human beings—their survival strength.

Was there a difference in the level of brutality between this kidnap case and the others Fort studied? Well, one young woman was threatened with being buried alive, spread-eagled, repeatedly raped, and burned with cigarettes. Another young woman was put in a box and tortured with electrodes. Another was forced to undergo a whole range of oral sexual relationships with her captors, so—yes—a variety of extreme coercive measures was employed in these other cases, beyond the use of guns or other weapons.

During midafternoon recess the press is in high spirits. Joel Fort's delineation of the case has given a fresh twist to an old rag, and the headline he supplied is so catchy—QUEEN OF THE ARMY!—they'd forgive him anything. Journalistic juices rise in anticipation of the pleasure of writing today's file. Reporters clown around the corridors like kids at school recess, making up gag headlines: FORT CALLS HEARST CLOSET QUEEN! BAILEY HOLDS THE FORT! PATTY FRIGID AFTER DEFREEZE! By now our days in court are a lot like being in school. The group of reporters, court personnel, and lawyers spend the major part of each day together, enclosed in a building, cut off from home and family, in a studying or learning situation. We share lunch and bathroom breaks. Dave Bancroft is the smart kid in our class who won't let you copy his homework. Bailey and Johnson are schoolyard Robin Hoods, the boys who elect to beat up the smart kid and take his homework away. Browning is a boring teacher. Carter is the principal. Jolly West is the school nurse. Joel Fort is a sinister science professor. Margaret Singer is the music teacher, the one all the boys are secretly in love with, and the school cook is Martin Orne, a specialist in just desserts.

Recess over, the prosecutor is ready to wrap it up and tie the bow. "All right, Doctor, based upon all of your research and inquiries, is it still your opinion and conclusion, sir, that the defendant, Patricia Campbell Hearst, on April 15, 1974, was in the Hibernia Bank without immediate fear for her life or great bodily injury?"

"That is my opinion."

Bailey's re-cross-examination begins with another jab at Fort's credentials. The doctor readily admits that he took no master's degree at the University of Chicago, but he studied psychology for two postgraduate years. "I felt learning and knowledge were more important than a specific degree." He admits he no longer belongs to any professional organizations. Most memberships he let lapse, but he resigned formally f õm both the American Medical Association and the American Psychiatric Association in order to proclaim his opposition to many of their policies. "But I am still often invited to speak at their meetings."

He admits that as a part-time faculty member at the University of California, he is not a professor of criminology, only a lecturer at the professorial level. He admits that the articles he has contributed to scientific journals are now somewhat out-of-date. Bailey is dubious about Fort's claim that in three months he did a study for the World Health Organization of jails and prisons in sixteen nations. *Sixteen,* Doctor? Yes, I worked eighteen hours a day, seven days a week.

If Bailey cannot make Fort look like a sluggard, he will suggest he is a profiteer or a publicity hound. But neither tack proves promising. At Forthelp his time is donated, and he takes no expenses. The man's personal modesty and his contempt for the media and the uses of publicity seem sincere. He did not choose the name Forthelp: That was invented by a hippie volunteer telephone operator who liked to joke that he worked at the only nonmilitary fort in the nation.

Bailey carefully picks over Fort's other credentials. He has not been on any hospital staff in two years. "Most people cannot afford hospitalization, so I try to work outside the hospital system." How does the doctor earn a living? "I have no regular income. My income is intermittent, and is based on a combination of lecturing, writing, consulting, and teaching—all of them part-time activities."

"Would you describe that as a fairly modest income?"

"I'm sure it doesn't approach yours. But it's adequate . . . between fifteen thousand and twenty thousand dollars a year."

Doctor, you said that one reason you decided to go to work for the prosecution is that you were aware of changes in the defense. Yes, Joe Otieri, a Boston lawyer and mutual friend, told Dr. Fort he had recommended him to Mr. Bailey as a possible expert witness, but the call from Bailey never came.

Yes, but by the time Dr. Fort interviewed the defendant for the government, in January, he knew that the three defense psychiatrists had already been chosen, so if Fort was to get on the stand at all, it would *have to be* for the prosecution, right? On the contrary, Mr. Bailey. It was my hope that there would *be* no expert testimony in this case. I think a jury can make up its own mind. I would have preferred not to testify. The statement on how to evaluate expert-witness testimony was not a "press release"; it was a memo prepared at *Newsweek*'s request and then distributed to other news organizations. It was intended as "a guideline and a moral expression of concern. I had no expectations that it would be published." *Newsweek* agreed in advance to use neither Fort's name nor any direct quotes. "Unlike yourself, I have not chosen to have personal interviews with the media. I think it inappropriate while an important public trial is going on."

After the jurors are excused, the legal wrangling resumes. Bancroft would now like to find out how much time and money the defense has spent on *its* psychiatrists.

CARTER *(bristling):* You had the right to cross-examine when the doctors were here, and you didn't do it. Now, I'm not going to now hoist them and foist them back here by some sort of transmutation. The answer is no!

Although William and Emily Harris have refused to cooperate with the government in prosecuting Patty, they have mounted their own counterattack in the press. Today Part One of a long interview with the Harrises is published in *New Times* magazine. Reading it is like watching HERNAP all over again from the other side of the looking glass. First the Harrises discuss the SLA political objectives. They wanted to see if a Hearst could be used to bargain for the freedom of Remiro and Little, if the mass media could be forced to print revolutionary communiqués in full, and if masses of people could become involved in a guerrilla action through a free-food program. Put this way, it all sounds quite logical. A Hearst daughter was kidnapped, rather than her parents, to leave Randolph and Catherine free to work to comply with the kidnappers' demands. If Patty's cheekbone was injured during her abduction, it was not intentional, the Harrises claim. She was not struck; she was captured and held as a POW, like Remiro and Little. Her injury or death certainly would not have been in the SLA's interest. Her testimony about her treatment at their hands has been a pack of lies. In truth, the closet door was usually left open so the prisoner would not feel isolated, and her hands were untied. An SLA member did stand guard at the closet at all times, whether or not the door was open, and the blindfold was left on, but that was to protect Patty as much as the SLA. When the door was shut, a light was provided for reading or writing. She could go to the toilet whenever she wished, got a bath every other day, and was encouraged to exercise, although "it was like pulling teeth to get her to do it." Though she ate very little, Patty took her meals with everybody else, and was included in the general conversation.

Having Patricia Hearst on the premises seems to have been like keeping a dangerous but valuable pet in the closet, a boa constrictor or a leopard cub. Good care was paramount because, upon Patty's release, that in itself would "prove the humanity of the SLA." Come to think of it, this, too, makes perfectly good sense.

Angela Atwood, the first to "get close to" Patty, was astonished to find that the rich bitch whom she had expected to hate was in fact a likable girl, alienated from her family. Everybody in the SLA had assumed Patty was in love with Weed. "But she told Angela once that the emptiness of her life had driven her to the point where she was thinking of killing herself." If she felt that way then, it is hard for me to imagine what she must feel now, reading this article. The Harrises say that Angela wàs hesitant about asking Patty whether she wanted to sleep with anybody because it could be misinterpreted after her release. "Everyone kind of laughed about it at first, like high school kids." But when Angela did ask, Patty said yes—Cujo. "Once Willie gave her a stone relic in the shape of a monkey-face that he had bought when he was in Mexico—he called it an Olmec, or something." Wolfe fashioned a macrame chain out of some waxed brown string, and Patty wore his gift around her neck until he died. After that she carried it in her purse. The "wedding ring" in the group photograph with Tania had been made by Willie from the same string.

No one had been more astonished by the media portrayal of the Hearsts than Patty herself, according to the Harrises:

> There was a big propaganda campaign on to portray the Hearsts as the ideal American family. . . . The *Ladies' Home Journal* told how her mother did her own grocery shopping. . . . Patty just laughed. She said her mother has never done that in her life, never cooked, never did anything. . . . To hear Patty tell it, her father was a boozer, her mother a pill freak . . . I mean, her mother was the family buffoon. I think she even embarrassed Randolph half the time.
>
> The Hearsts weren't really socialites. They didn't go to all that many parties. They travelled a lot, but basically they wanted to be low-key, and Patty was brought up to think that she was not much different than anyone else . . . so she didn't understand the power part of it. She knew nothing of the history of her own family. She really wanted to get rid of the Hearst name. She said once that she had hoped her life with Weed would be the quiet existence of a professor's wife. . . .

The detailed news coverage of the hunt for the kidnappers filled Patty with terror for her own safety. A surprise armed raid on an Oakland house in which police thought Patty and the SLA might be hiding graphically demonstrated to the prisoner that she was endangered as much by her would-be rescuers as by her present captors.

She could not understand why her parents were taking so long to buy her back. "It was clear her father had the resources to meet the $6 million ransom demands. . . . She was amazed that he would risk her safety just so he could keep the American people in the dark about the extent of the wealth at his fingertips," the Harrises say. From listening to the defendant's testimony and watching her demeanor these past few weeks, I, myself, have a sense of the degree of her original confusion and fear. Reading the Harrises' version of HERNAP suggests how simple the "brainwashing" or "attitude change" or whatever it was must have been to accomplish. The *New Times* article makes the advent of Tania seem almost inevitable.

When Patty began to think about actually joining the SLA, the Harrises write, everyone laughed but Cinque:

> Cin was serious. Those of us in the SLA that were from more middle-class backgrounds were a lot less impressed . . . but for Cin, it was a heavy thing. . . . Cin felt that her renunciation of her family and her candid awareness of their role were really monumental changes. . . . It would represent the potential in everyone to change. . . . But the SLA made an error in accepting her decision to stay. . . . Everyone got too caught up in sentimentality.

The bank robbery had had a twofold purpose: to get money and "to verify that Tania had stayed of her own free will." As soon as the cameras started rolling she was supposed to fire a round into the ceiling and say, "This is Tania!" But her gun jammed.

The Harrises repeat what the "Tania Interview" already has told us: that Tania's anger and disgust with the Hearsts grew so great that her remarks on the tapes had to be censored. "The profanities, particularly in regard to her mother," were unrepeatable. "One thing she insisted on was that line about Hallinan, her father's lawyer, being 'a senile old fuck.' "

> We weren't surprised that they mobilized an army of 500 to kill six people [in Los Angeles], without even giving them a chance to surrender. . . . That was a search-and-destroy operation—any Vietnam vet who saw it knows that . . . and the folks in that house knew it too. That fire wasn't a fluke. It's standard practice—the scorched earth policy brought home.

Afterward, sure, we had problems. There were some hard feelings. But we were close. Just two or three months before we were busted, she told us that she loved us very much, that she felt more secure with us than with anyone else.

Emily Harris and Patty were together in jail for five days. "It was clear from the first minute that she thought she could cut some kind of deal for herself, that she believed she would get out on bail." She promised the Harrises and Wendy she would visit them when she got out. "She knew the power of the Hearst empire better than anyone. What she didn't realize was that part of the Hearst family strategy was *not* to bail her out—they wanted her in isolation to keep her from getting other legal advice, or support from movement people."

Although Patty now says Emily forced her to write "urban guerrilla," what actually happened is that Patty was booked first. Emily was in another area of the jail.

And she came over to me, kind of laughing, and said, "They asked me what my occupation was, and guess what I told them? *Urban guerrilla!*" . . . It was almost like, "I can say anything I want—my daddy's rich." . . .

Now she's getting on the stand and lying under oath to save her own ass. . . . Patty's more than a snitch. . . . What she's doing is fabricating things about other people—incriminating them with lies. . . . Even on the details—she now says that there was only a flashlight for reading in the closet, but she knows there was a hanging lamp nailed to the wall. Bailey is dragging the jury around to look at two closets that Patricia is saying she was confined in, when really she only spent time in the one in Daly City. By the time she moved into the Golden Gate apartment, she had already made her decision to stay with the SLA. . . . She was never hit by anyone. . . . She was never sexually molested by Cinque. . . . That garbage can was used to move bulky weapons because it could be carried into a house without looking suspicious—*she* was never in it. . . .

She'll get off, but where will she go? . . . What does she have left? She's basically compromised everything.

Every time the SLA moved to a new hideout they left a spoor of abandoned disguises behind. Shelves overflowing with makeup, eyeglasses, Afro wigs and red, gray, blond, and black ones, too; mustaches, hair dye, putty noses, shoe blacking, false beards and eyebrows, and even a "pregnant stomach" were found in Golden Gate, Daly City, and the Precita Avenue and Morse Street apartments. These people could not only change appearance at will; they could change identity. Membership in the cobra band conferred an instant and new *persona* on each recruit. It allowed people who in various ways had felt themselves to be "nothing" suddenly to be military commanders, "urban guerrillas," ghetto blacks, or heroines of the revolution, and attached to each new identity was the appropriate new viewpoint, like the celluloid nose attached to the phony eyeglasses. This extreme slipperiness of identity had always made it very difficult to hold on to my own identity while writing about these people. Even reading about them was perilous, and while I was reading it, at least, the Harrises' version of HERNAP seemed almost as compelling as the one I had been listening to in court.

Tuesday, March 9

Bailey arrives today with a fat sheaf of documents in hand, and, looking over the top, he inquires, "Dr. Fort, how many big trials have you been in?" Since the glowering Dr. Fort first darkened the scene, Bailey has attempted to portray him as a weirder-than-weirdo who tries to gain publicity by pretending to eschew it—in contrast to the honorable defense counsel, who go out to bark honestly for it, like trick dogs.

Fort names his three big ones and adds, "But I have never had a press conference, never sought attention, never hung around after my testimony, and was in and out as quickly as I could." Last June, Fort visited the Old Bailey to study the English approach to criminal justice, and that experience prompted his letters to Carter in an attempt to desensationalize coverage of the present trial.

When he sent his letter to the court requesting anonymity, with copies to a dozen major news organizations, was Dr. Fort unaware that most Bay Area publications had stories and even pictures of him in their files? Had he not, in fact, just seen his picture again in last Sunday's paper, in an article entitled "Bald Is Beautiful"? Smiles, titters, shy glances at the doctor's gleaming pate. But beneath the merriment, a rumbling tone of menace has crept into this examination on both sides. Just why did Dr. Fort send out this release if he was so eager for anonymity?

Frankly, I felt myself in a bind: I didn't want publicity, yet I wanted to provide an alternative to the kind of trial-by-press conducted by you, Mr. Bailey.

How about the unusual number of hours the witness has put into this case? Fort felt that because issues raised were so complex and there were no precedents, an unusual amount of study was required. Bailey would imagine Dr. Fort spends a fair part of his life being an expert witness? No, only a small part. He studies documents in advance and often gives telephone advice. His court experience began in Alameda County, about 1959, when, as a state examiner, he was called upon for his opinion on whether certain individuals were capable of taking responsibility for their own actions or should be committed to state hospitals. Responsibility for one's own actions is the cornerstone of Fort's moral philosophy; he returns to it at any opportunity.

It appears to me, watching the duel, that Lee Bailey is repeatedly hurling himself against this dark cloud, and losing, because he isn't dealing with Fort's positions, of which responsibility for one's own acts is key. It is a poor strategy to try to show up as a *poseur* a man who is obviously sincere. Bailey comes on like an angry, punishing parent trying to entrap, setting out fishhooks of guilt and snares of blame. But Joel Fort is purged of guilt. Singer and West would say it's because he's a psychopath. Fort would say he knows he's working for the good; he oozes righteousness. Bailey continues to threaten, bluster, and loom, but each time Bailey puffs with rage Fort grows quieter and more badgerlike.

Bailey holds up two documents, one of them the "Expert Witness" outline, the other a copy of Fort's bill to the government. The intent is to show up Fort as a plagiarist, mendacious gouger, and vendor of psychiatric and legal snake oil. But this gambit doesn't work, either. Fort readily admits the book outline contains inaccuracies and perhaps even exaggerations, but the hyperbole is the work of a too-eager ghostwriter. Fort should have blue-penciled it out; he did not, and he takes responsibility.

Fort's bill speaks of the "planning of strategy." "Do you consider that participation in the planning of strategy is an independent and unbiased function, or is it partisan, Doctor?"

"Well, Mr. Bailey, obviously the way in which you phrase questions is in keeping with your own lectures about what a defense attorney should do to destroy a witness." A gust of laughter sweeps the courtroom. Objecting that the answer was argumentative and should be stricken, Bailey whirls away from the witness box, turning his windburned face into the laughing courtroom in time to hear Carter say that, yes, the answer was argumentative, but so was the question. The smell of brimstone is stronger than it was yesterday. Bailey, facing into the laughter, looks like a man who probably realizes by now that he is losing but is too committed to draw back. He is playing the old-fashioned, thundering, flamboyant criminal lawyer, whereas Fort is the quintessence of the cool, open, California style: Yes, I made a mistake. I frequently do. Yes, I could have been wrong. No, I can't remember; it was some time ago. Several jurors, especially the rough-and-ready fellows—the mechanic, the postman, and the machinist—appear to react to the duel with gusto, as if the case excites them for the first time. Psychiatrists they don't understand; cockfights they do.

Patty looks smaller this morning, as if she's had such a bad night the steam has gone out of her. She may be having second thoughts about her defense, similar to the kind of retrospective doubts Al suggested were bothering my Kathy after she ran away from school: *Did I do the right thing?* All the practiced courtroom tricks of which F. Lee Bailey is an advertised master will not work against this kind of totally guilt-proof witness. If Bailey wants to shake Joel Fort, he should ask, How could a compassionate man such as you testify against an obviously wronged and unfortunate girl? *Are* you being helpful to society with this kind of destructive behavior? But Bailey appears blind to this strategy. Although San Francisco is overrun with mavericks, professional outsiders and againsters, renegades and fugitives from Eastern orthodoxy, liberated free spirits gamboling on San Francisco and Oakland and Marin hillsides, splashing and frolicking in the bay, the feisty, cocky, socially square, and politically conservative Boston lawyer seems never to have met a man like Fort before. West and Singer are absent for the first time. Perhaps Bailey has counseled them to stay out of the jurors' sight this morning lest they be spattered by the tar brush with which the lawyer is attempting to blacken the opposition.

Does Fort's book outline say that an expert witness on the prosecution side has a better time of it because one has better access to files and is even met at the airport by a chauffeured car? No, Mr. Bailey, the ghost-writer got that one turned around. It is the defense expert who gets met by the chauffeured car. This provokes another gust of laughter.

Bailey's tone of voice is always accusatory: Did you, or did you not, put your hand in that cookie jar? With Fort it doesn't work. He just smiles and licks his fingers.

At recess the reporters are not pleased. "Let's get rid of this guy!" "He didn't give us a lead!" "Patty wasn't even mentioned!" "Fort's just a mouth! He talks and talks. He used to work as a sex therapist on a housewife's call-in show, *California Girl.*" "I covered a trial where a guy cut up seven people with an ax and kept his mother's head on the mantel in a bottle, and Fort said he wasn't crazy!" "The surprising thing is that Bailey doesn't have more to hit him with. Joel's been around this town for years. Doesn't Bailey *know* about *California Girl?*" "San Francisco juries are used to oddballs."

Al Johnson circles the clucking reporters, dropping crumbs like a poultry feeder. "Patty's down to ninety-two pounds," he says. Beyond Al, a more porcine, more ominous presence looms: Larry Schiller—photographer-exploiter of the lurid and doomed. Later Schiller will become famous as the business partner of the convicted murderer Gary Gilmore and the Sol Hurok of Gilmore's execution by a Utah firing squad. But the press has known Larry for years. He was the jailhouse companion of Jack Ruby, the Manson girls, Lenny Bruce. Schiller is a special species of media hound. Whoever is in the headlines and in trouble, preferably of a lurid and terminal variety, can expect to find Larry Schiller turn up like the angel of death, camera in one hand, management contract in the other. Sign with me, and at least we can make your family some money out of your terrible tragedy. People in trouble always need money; the gambit always seems to work. Schiller's arrival on a story is a threat to press standards. William Randolph Hearst would have loved the guy. His presence here today becomes more ominous when we learn that he is "merely" here to visit his fiancée, the British bird who by coincidence happens to be a friend and the constant companion of Linda Bailey.

"Lee's working on this thing too hard, night and day," Schiller says, shaking his fat cheeks. "I don't know how he can last a year."

Not to worry, says another reporter. He has stunning news from back East that passes through our gaggle of writers like an electric current and may, in fact, account for Schiller's sudden advent: Bailey's book deal has firmed up; Putnam's will pay an advance, they say, of a quarter of a million dollars, win or lose. (The contract contains a clause promising that no other writer than Bailey will have access to his client for a period of eighteen months. She is his exclusive literary as well as legal property. This contract will become part of the basis for the August 2, 1978, appeal by Patty's new lawyer, George C. Martinez, to set aside her conviction on the grounds that Bailey gave her an inadequate, incompetent defense. The motion reveals for the first time that two days after her conviction Patty signed a covenant with Bailey "not to compete with the intended book of trial counsel. . . .") At such prices and terms, Bailey can afford to set a low fee for his legal services and anticipate substantial ancillary revenues from book and perhaps movie sales. I can anticipate that the noncooperation of the Hearst family in my own enterprise will now be total. Fine. The news at this point is a boon and a blessing. It will oblige me to continue working the way *New Yorker* "Profile" writers used to, in the special style devised by Harold Ross, the *New Yorker*'s founder-editor, when he invented the "Profile" form back in the 1920s. Ross wanted the writer to talk to as many friends and enemies of his subject as possible, to view him from all sides like a pigeon walking around a statue, never alighting, never speaking to the central figure directly, but finally processing all the other people's points of view through the writer's mind and typewriter. Hence the term "Profile."

After the recess Fort returns to the witness box. Dr. Fort, were you a friend of the now-deceased comedian Lenny Bruce? I was an acquaintance. You never prescribed for him? No, but in 1963 Fort had testified in Los Angeles that in his opinion Bruce was not a drug addict. And the outcome of that case, Dr. Fort, was that the judge sent Bruce away for ten years? No, Mr. Bailey, you appear to have two cases confused. I testified for Mr. Bruce in a civil commitment proceeding.

One is again surprised by the flimsiness of Bailey's preparation. Too often his big guns fire blanks.

A few years earlier, Fort had testified in a Massachusetts case designed to test the constitutionality of that state's marijuana laws. The prosecutor was James St. Clair, recently more celebrated as counsel to Richard Nixon.

BAILEY: Did you describe that experience in this fashion? "Aided by a vast state-funded staff, St. Clair had researched and catalogued every article and speech of the author's, and everything written about him. His cross-examination was detailed, lengthy and aggressive. At the end of the day, both were perspiring freely. The author had been 'taken to the edge,' but had not yielded, and St. Clair was to comment that he had brass balls."

No. This was the doctor's ghost-writer overselling again. The truth is that Fort did not bother to rewrite the outline, because he felt hopeless by then about ever actually getting his book published. By the way, he adds, he never contemplated using any material from the Hearst case in that book or any other. Fort would be very pleased to renew that commitment and "suggest that you agree to do the same, Mr. Bailey."

"May the doctor's recommendation be stricken as nonresponsive?" asks the lawyer. The judge agrees.

What so infuriates Bailey may be that Fort, like himself, makes books, or proposes to make a book, out of his courtroom adventures. That "Expert Witness" is, in fact, only a rejected book outline, written by an overeager ghost, does not diminish Bailey's fury. It seems to exacerbate it. Way back at the beginning, when I had first seen the HERNAP aquarium, I had wondered what would cause Bailey, the shovel-nosed shark, to turn upside down and attack. One could not then have guessed that the stimulus would be an unwritten book, but a work nonetheless aimed squarely at the contents and assumptions of all Bailey's own work both as lawyer and as author. What's upsetting Bailey now has little to do with his client; it is, in fact, dangerously distracting the jury's attention from Patricia Hearst. What's upsetting Bailey is the damage this expert witness can do to Bailey himself, to both the fabled criminal lawyer and the inner man, the tender writer. For the ghostly "Expert Witness" is an all-out, Valhalla-style attack on the adversary system by which Bailey operates. Unwittingly and tragically for many people besides Patricia Hearst—tragic for the distinguished trio of psychiatrists who, wisely or not, have hooked their own bright stars to Bailey's comet; tragic, too, for the future of forensic psychiatry, and of courtroom reform in criminal trials, and of reform of the rules by which the media govern themselves in covering sensational, violent, or terrorist events—Dr. Joel Fort has found F. Lee Bailey's exposed jugular and is now needling away at it. Yet all this is largely accidental. Joel Fort has no built-in psychic sonar to direct him to the man's most vulnerable area. Only Bailey knows where his secret weak spot is, but in the necessity to defend and protect it, Bailey has begun to piss his case away. Not just any case, but the Big One, the one that would permit him to pay back his debts, recover and enhance his glory, and then, in the fiscal splendor to which he aspires, retire awhile from the gladiatorial lists and compose the courtroom classic he has dreamed of writing for twenty years.

The jury is again asked to leave, so that the defense may make a motion out of their presence. Bailey claims to have uncovered evidence that Herrick Hospital found Joel Fort unqualified to administer psychotherapy. Fort's lawyer says the records state the exact opposite. A third attorney, representing the hospital, reminds Carter of a recent law that says such records are privileged and may not be read in open court. The judge will consider the matter over lunch.

A curious shift in emphasis is going on. The defense seems to be chasing not only a red herring but a deadly one. The last thing the jury heard before leaving was Bailey reading the summary of the final chapter of Fort's book outline, "Towards Better Expert Witnessing":

> . . . this chapter will make specific recommendations for improving both expert testimony and the "justice industry" as a whole. . . . Among its proposals would be an end to the adversary system; more universal jury service, with decision by two-thirds vote; an end to plea bargaining in first-degree murder cases; stringent control of handguns and daggers; and restrictions and reduction of the power of psychiatrists and the "mental health industry" in dealing with prisoners, suspects, and human life.

A pity Joel Fort is sitting here. He should be home writing that book.

It is one-thirty P.M. The jury is still not present. Carter says the hospital records include a report signed by seven doctors saying that Fort was not competent to handle psychotherapy, that he couldn't understand his patients, manipulated people, and aroused hostility in others. But there are also a great many complimentary letters in the file, and by going into the pros and cons of Dr. Fort's hospital record, Carter says, "you are losing sight of the Hearst trial." Besides, this case has nothing to do with events at Herrick Hospital nearly twenty years ago. It seems to the judge that the lawyers are "having some sort of contest to see which side stinks the most," and he does not intend to referee a stinking match.

But Bailey has to destroy the doctor's credibility because the jury must disbelieve Fort in order to believe Patty. "Your Honor, I think I'm entitled to challenge his diagnosis. Dr. Fort wouldn't know a traumatic neurosis if he fell over one." He begins to read aloud:

"Fort . . . arouses hostility in others and is frequently unaware of his own hostility. . . . On occasions, to gain his own ends, he manipulates others in an irresponsible manner. . . . He lacks empathy and only *appears* to learn. . . . He arouses anger . . . is insensitive to the needs of people . . . has a rather rigid approach . . . fails to see the forest for the trees . . . pays lip service to concepts . . . and has a tendency to become dogmatic, negativistic, and sulky."

The description could equally well apply to the man who is reading it, and is a reminder of how evenly matched the two contestants are.

Carter refuses to admit the records, and the jury is brought back. Bailey reviews Fort's oft-repeated criticisms of our criminal-justice system: that only about one percent of the crime committed in this country is actually punished, that rehabilitation is a myth, that the psychiatric profession considers nearly everybody abnormal, and that the most widespread example of psychopathy in American life is the American politician.

Did you also say, Doctor, "The law is an ass"? No, Charles Dickens said that. Did you say, "I think the problem lies with the philosophy of the lawyer in an amoral, adversarial, expediency-oriented system: that is, that you win at any cost. The object is either to get the defendant convicted, or get him off. Acting, in the courtroom, is an acceptable part of that role. . . . Totally ignoring whether or not the person is guilty is acceptable. . . . The legal canons of the American Bar Association make that something to be rewarded rather than something to be condemned"? Yes, and Fort has also said in his lectures that juries are highly unrepresentative, as well as unfair.

Bailey's attempt to trip up the witness with a transcript of a year-old extemporaneous lecture doesn't work, because whereas Bailey quibbles over exactly what Fort said exactly when, the witness is responding with expressions of general, long-held beliefs. The defendant and her doctors and lawyers remind me of people huddled in a lifeboat. Just now the lifeboat is shipping a lot of water, but all these people have delivered themselves into Captain Bailey's hands, and it is too late to change. Did you say, "I think we need better judges, and judges should work longer hours"? Yes. "Did you say in conclusion that if there is one word that summarizes American society, it is 'hypocrisy'?" "Yes, I did."

"Doctor, is it fair to say in summary that there is very little about the system of justice that you are able to admire in a fifty-six-minute speech?" No, he doesn't think that is fair. "What things do you recall complimenting, if any?"

Browning objects that the questioning is becoming irrelevant. Bailey asks that Fort first be allowed to reply. Browning, suddenly firm, says, "Well, no! I would like to ask the court for a ruling on my objection before he answers the question, Counsel. As I understand it, *that's* how our system works." The courtroom bursts into applause.

When at last we debouch into the corridor, those same "halls of the Hall of Justice" where Fort has said that much of the courts' work actually gets done, the reporters agree that the doctor is holding up remarkably. He reminds me of Vladimir Sokoloff in *For Whom the Bell Tolls.* No matter how the melodrama twists and turns, the old peasant sits impassively in his corner, puffing his pipe and repeating in his curious Russian accent (curious, at least, in a cave of Spanish partisans), "I don't pro-woke." Fort don't pro-woke, either, no matter how Bailey jabs, and the result is a standoff.

Fort is an accomplished counterpuncher, as is Bailey. But whereas Fort has one enemy—orthodoxy—which assumes multiple forms, Bailey has many. Bailey is against ambiguity, change, newness, stupidity, losing, boredom, inactivity, and anonymity. But the greatest of these is losing.

Bailey ridicules the book list Fort submitted to the prosecution. Among 267 titles on psychiatry, sociology, the press, and the law, many of which Fort admits he has read before, are *Alice in Wonderland, Through the Looking Glass,* and Kafka's *The Trial.* Fort denies trying to use Lifton to get in touch with the pseudonymous "Jane Darrow." Nor did he trace her through the FBI. Dave Bancroft found her through a mutual friend. Although Fort talked to her on the phone for an hour and a half, he still does not know her true name. "But I certainly wouldn't think a person interviewed by a doctor or lawyer becomes the exclusive property of that doctor or lawyer," he adds, unaware that just such an exclusive-property arrangement exists right now between this particular client and her lawyer and the lawyer's publisher.

Doctor, when did you talk to Mr. Randolph Hearst? Mid-January. I remember a more specific conversation with Mrs. Hearst, but I advised Mr. Hearst that it would be a good idea to seek an independent opinion and that it would be desirable, if at all possible, to avoid a public trial. I suggested he discuss the matter with William Coblentz, his attorney. Did you have the permission of Mr. Browning to do this? No.

I informed the government, as I did you, Mr. Bailey, that it was my own professional and moral opinion that this attempt should be made; there was no discussion. Did you tell the Hearsts, "Browning says it's okay to talk so long as you understand that it's one hundred percent my idea"? Yes. Did you tell Mrs. Hearst this trial was being held principally because Bailey was out for publicity and Browning wanted to be a federal judge? No, Mr. Bailey, that's what Mrs. Hearst told me. Catherine's head is shaking slightly, and her mouth is open. One cannot be certain whether she is laughing or crying.

To "speed things up," Bailey requests yes or no answers. Was Patty crying through the first fifteen minutes or so of their interview? Yes. Did she say she liked horses? Yes. That she was transported in a plastic garbage can? Yes. In your judgment, was she already a member of the SLA when she was put into the garbage can? I don't know whether she *was* in the garbage can.

It is a few minutes before four o'clock. Bailey asks to adjourn early; it appears he wishes to stall. Carter grants his request, after drawing from Bailey his assurance that tomorrow morning this cross-examination will finally end.

Nobody in the real world looks exactly like Catherine Hearst. She is the Platonic ideal of Lana Turner made flesh, and even in fury the flawless façade does not crack. Reflected now in the ladies'-room mirror, Catherine is raging at Fort, vowing, "I'll shove those words right back down his throat!"

The all-day duel has been dramatic, sharp, weird. Dr. Fort versus Dr. West—how do they stack up to me? At home I jot a few impressions on the yellow pad: "The chief defense psychiatrist has a frame like a fullback's and a name like one of the Seven Dwarfs, personality to match. I distrust a psychiatrist named 'Jolly' for the same illogical reason I am wary of a writer who doesn't drink. He doesn't do that, either. Or smoke. (Neither does Fort, I later learn.) I distrust West's creepy incandescence. Next to 'Jolly,' Joel Fort is a narrow-minded, hermetic monk. I distrust my distrust."

Wednesday, March 10

High hilarity shakes our press queue. Last night, in the subterranean garage, Joel Fort caught Larry Schiller trying to take his picture and swung at him, Schiller claims. Possibly Fort just tried to grab the camera—one cannot be sure from the big, blurry prints of the enraged doctor, still wet from the developing bath, which Schiller is gleefully handing out. Last night I had telephoned Forthelp, eager to meet this increasingly interesting character. A young lady with a wispy, drifty voice said that might be difficult but she would give the doctor my message.

This morning another juror is excused, owing to a death in the family. Now only two alternates stand between us and a mistrial. Bailey asks Fort whether he has read the chapter on brainwashing in a standard textbook of psychiatry. "Will you look at it, please?"

"Will you let go of it for a minute?" So much for the flavor of the morning's dialogue.

Bailey produces Fort's November–December bill to the government: $2,450 for forty-nine hours' work. Then he dumps an enormous stack of file folders on the witness stand and begins to question Fort in detail about his study of thirty-five kidnapping cases. Bailey, Fort, Browning, and Carter all seem to have swallowed irritability pills. Browning demands to know when this interminable cross-examination will end. It's already been four days! Five, says the witness. If only Fort wouldn't give such long answers, Bailey complains, pantomiming migraine. Fort says his answers have been considerably shorter than those of the other experts; the tricky way Bailey phrases questions requires long answers. Carter nods. "Mr. Bailey, Dr. Fort is not the only one giving long answers."

"I heard his statement, Judge." The knife of contempt in Bailey's voice would cut silk. "Dr. Fort, do you know of any cases you studied where the victim of the kidnapping was prosecuted?"

"No." It is the shortest answer to the best question of the week.

Experienced trial hands are dismayed by the direction this trial has recently taken. "It's a textbook example of how not to cross-examine a witness," F. Steele Langford, the clam from Washington who is keeping a special Justice Department eye on this case, remarks during recess to our veteran expert, Carolyn Anspacher. She agrees. "He's digging a hole for himself, but nobody in there is strong enough to stop him, and he can't stop himself."

The end, however, is near. Bailey mentions Tania and asks, "What is the significance to you, Doctor, when somebody changes his name?" It commonly signifies a dissatisfaction with the previous name. It can also indicate an allegiance to a new group, as when Black Muslims take the name "X." Mmmm-hmm. And you were born in Steubenville, Ohio, on September 30, 1929? Yes. And what was your name then? My family name was Friedman. And you changed it to Fort? No, my father did. Actually it was changed twice. My father was a Russian immigrant, a freed serf, and when he arrived, he had an unpronounceable name, which an immigration inspector changed to "freed man," or Friedman. The family later changed it to Fort. "What is the significance of that question, Mr. Bailey?"

"I'll ask the questions, Dr. Fort."

In January, had Fort found occasion to tell Al Johnson that if his report were favorable to Patty, he would certainly send over a copy, even though by law he was required to do this anyhow? Yes, and as a matter of fact, "I was then biased toward the defendant and toward you, Mr. Bailey. I found you to be very persuasive."

But only after this trial was under way had Fort finally concluded that the defense was not credible. The reason, Bailey again insinuates, is that by then Fort knew that unless he testified for the government, he would not be able to get on the stand at all. Fort denies this. "I see. And so, as an unbiased party, who might well wind up with an opinion favorable to the defendant, you were paid in November and December for advice to the government on planning and strategy, is that right, Doctor?"

"No. That's your fifth misstatement on that, if I recall."

Well, you typed up the bill, Doctor, and it includes the words "planning and strategy." *"Was that an honest presentation?"*

"You don't have to holler, Mr. Bailey. I can hear you." It was honest, but despite his 300-odd hours' work—and here it is Fort who for the fifth time reviews the range and variety of his study—he did not think it was essential. "I feel this jury was entirely capable of deciding the case on its own."

"Was the bill paid?"

I beg your pardon?

"Was it paid?"

One feels as if Mr. Bailey for five days has been constructing some vast and elaborate trap for this witness that somehow has never sprung. "Does that conclude your cross-examination, Mr. Bailey?" Carter asks in dubious tones.

Yes, says Bailey, already at the defense table, his face brick-red. One had not even noticed him sit down.

Any redirect examination, Mr. Browning? Yes, Your Honor. I shall try to be brief.

Browning sets about rehabilitating the educational background and professional qualifications of his witness after the mauling at Bailey's hands. He also carefully brings out that the government imposed no conditions on Dr. Fort of any kind. Whereas Fort read the opposition experts' psychiatric reports, he did not read Kozol's reports. Nor does he sit in court with him, socialize with him, stay in the same hotel with him, or even eat with him.

What is the standard government fee for psychiatric consultants? Fifty dollars an hour. But Fort would have been willing to take $35, as "it has been my practice throughout the years not to make my main decisions on the basis of monetary values but in terms of social conditions." We are back to the kind of sanctimonious moralizing that drives some cynics, including Bailey and me, up the wall. What is the usual hourly fee in *private* practice? Between $65 and $125 for a fifty-minute hour. (This seems high to me, but when I check later with Dr. West, he confirms it as the going rate in once-and-future America.)

When was the first time it was called to your attention that there was something improper about your meetings with the Hearsts?

"When he [Bailey] made a violent attack on me in this courtroom."

Even after Bailey and Browning have run out of questions, Browning is still searching for "relevant" documents. But Carter has finally had enough. "No more material will be admitted! Dr. Fort, you're excused!" The witness exits silently, swiftly, through a side door, a Kafka survivor of an inexplicable ordeal.

At two-fifty P.M. Dr. Harry Kozol is called to the stand. Gripping his briefcase, the funny little man walks stiffly, like someone who has been sitting down for three months, which he has. Patty's face is the dead-white color of a fish's belly. In a high voice and with a slight lisp, Dr. Kozol recites his credentials: education in Boston public schools and a 1927 degree, *magna cum laude,* from Harvard. Speaking extremely slowly, he describes his studies in law, criminology, abnormal behavior, and physiology. "Physiology . . . is . . . the . . . science . . . of how . . . things . . . function." The absurd high voice, the lisp, and the lugubrious tempo are comic relief after the tensions of the past week, and an irresistible urge to giggle sweeps the courtroom. Soon Carter, Catherine, and even Janey Jimenez, the marshal, are laughing openly. Kozol drones through further credentials: Rockefeller fellow, University of Rome, University of Mexico, Johns Hopkins, Royal College of Psychiatry, Boston Society of Neurology and Psychiatry, American Board of Psychiatry and Neurology, American Psychiatric Association, and so on. Kozol's fiftieth Harvard class reunion will be coming up soon if he—or any of us—lives that long. He terms himself "a physician at heart, not a specialist, just a general practitioner in psychiatry." Most of his work over the last twenty years has involved young people, and his primary interest is in violence. Why are kids marching in the streets, blowing up college labs, wrecking computers? He is not condemning these young people so much as he is concerned about his own children and grandchildren.

Dr. Kozol expresses his concerns in a curious way, it seems to me. For the past sixteen years he has been director of the Bridgewater, Massachusetts, Center for Criminally Dangerous Sex Offenders. Its thousand or so inmates are rapists and killers, not mere exhibitionists and Peeping Toms, and Kozol's mission is to learn to identify the kind of person who really enjoys killing and maiming. He searches for "the man who rapes and stabs a twelve-year-old boy, spends ten years in prison, gets out, and repeats the crime within six months, killing and burning the next victim's two little brothers as well." Bridgewater's inmates are treated for life, if necessary, rather than released back into the population. Kozol has appeared as an expert witness twenty to thirty times in thirty to forty years and has often served as a court-appointed psychiatrist. His personal familiarity with prisoners of war goes way back to Spain in the 1930s, though he claims no special expertise. He has also dealt professionally with Russian, German, Italian, Canadian, and Japanese war prisoners.

Dr. Kozol spends half his time at Bridgewater and half in private practice, and works seven days a week. Many of the sex criminals under his care have kidnapped women, children, and even old ladies for purposes of rape, so Kozol and his wife have known many female kidnapping victims. Ruth Kozol, chief psychiatric social worker at her husband's institution, has interviewed 350 such women in order to get a victim's-eye view of the aggressor in action. Kozol interviewed thirty-five of the women, himself, while acting as his wife's chauffeur. This fuddy-duddy, benign couple look like cookie figures in a Hänsel and Gretel forest, not people who spend their professional lives running a cageful of dangerous, crazy sex criminals. The courtroom's other old man, Judge Oliver Carter, nods benignly. Unlike Fort and Bailey, neither of these gentle, elderly men appears to be *of* the violent world in which each wields so much power.

When Dr. Kozol was first asked by the government to consult on the Hearst case, he replied with the standard letter "that they had no assurance, and I made no commitment," as to his findings. What materials did you study, Doctor? Kozol's voice winds down to a truly excruciating slowness. Yes . . . he . . . also . . . has heard . . . all the psychiatric . . . testimony . . . in this courtroom and has filed his own sixty-three-page report. His first impression of Miss Hearst was that she was not feeling well, though she tried very hard to do her best. "I started out with questions about her interest in being a veterinarian— I'd got that from Weed. Miss Hearst seemed a little startled." She told me about her mother's helping her clean up the dog mess before her father came home and began to shout that if children wanted pets, they should learn to take care of them. I got an insight from that into a very motherly, warm, normal type of home. Kozol goes over the familiar ground.

At recess we stroll out. Encased in her matching navy-blue dress, stockings, and tiny pumps, Catherine Campbell Hearst is plump-to-bursting with good health and inner glow, whereas her frail, fading daughter looks drained of blood. The afternoon paper says that today Steven Soliah went on trial in Sacramento for the $15,000 bank robbery in which Myrna Opsahl was killed. If convicted, he faces a life sentence. Although the authorities have publicly attributed the crime to the SLA, and four armed bandits were seen in the bank, Patty's former lover is the only person charged.

Tonight five of us women reporters do a round-table discussion of the trial on a local television station, after which we go off for another hearty, all-female dinner. There is no question among us, either publicly on television or privately over wine, that despite this last difficult week of testimony, all five of us remain staunchly on Patty's side.

Thursday, March 11

Patty is sick. "A severe malaise," fever, swollen glands, Jolly confides at the metal detector. Judge Carter announces that he will recess the trial until Monday and use the intervening time to handle matters that do not require the presence of the defendant. First, Dr. Singer will take the stand in order to complete the offer of proof on her expertise, now that she has obtained additional documentation of Patty's style—term papers, interviews, and five postcards to Weed.*

These turn out to have "only three percent complex beginnings," whereas in the October interviews with West, only five percent of Patty's sentences have complex beginnings. Dr. Singer, herself, has already told the court that Patty in this period was a low-IQ, low-affect zombie. Her testimony is a fine example of what the psychiatrist Dr. Thomas Szasz calls the "prostitution of the expert in the toils of the law," even if it is the unwitting prostitution of a noble-browed semidivinity like Margaret Singer. Skilled advocates unfurl possibilities before the expert: Display your arcane knowledge before the world, validate the work of a lifetime, escape the cart-horse routine of academic life, be "in on" the story of the decade, help save an innocent girl. It is all too much to resist. What's a professor to do? The silk is too pretty; the expert winds up in the witness box. This morning offers a fine lesson in democracy and the value of the ordinary juror in a criminal trial. The juror knows something that Margaret Singer does not: Any analysis based on 3 percent of sentence beginnings on five postcards is absurd.

*Patty's absence this morning has gouged a corresponding blank in my memory. I cannot remember what happened. My home-baked trial transcript is no help. Without the crutch of memory, the blue notebooks, too, are inadequate. When I consult the official trial transcript, over a year later, to find out what happened this particular morning, I find a curious notation at the top of the page: "Thursday, March 11, 1976: (Pages 3746 through 3754 of the original transcript transcribed and sealed, to be held by the Court and not made a part of the public record.)"

The defense press conference today is an extended medical bulletin in near-presidential detail. Al Johnson received the news that his client was ill at eight A.M. She was taken directly to a hospital, but "I am not at liberty to disclose the name, for security reasons. I *can* tell you she looked very pale, with chills and shakes, and red eyes. Her illness is not psychosomatic. We considered having Patty sit at the defense table wearing a surgical mask, but that might be inappropriate during a bank-robbery trial." The reporters chuckle, but the fact is that she did wear just such a mask earlier this morning for the benefit of news photographers, managing to convey the impression of—at least—bubonic plague.

Friday, March 12

With Patty still ill this morning, the lawyers meet informally with the judge to settle on his instructions to the jury. A skeleton crew of reporters is on hand, which means that Bailey can still get his message out to the public—which includes possible future judges, jurors, and litigants in future Hearst trials—and, perhaps most important, to the members of the board of the Hearst Corporation. It appears more and more likely that these faceless people are chiefly responsible for dictating strategy and paying Patty's legal fees. Today's message is a broad hint that the client, if acquitted, will turn state's evidence against the Harrises and others.

Browning is worried because "I don't know how many people have come up to me on the street and asked, 'Why don't you put the Harrises and the Scotts on the stand?' " and the jury may be wondering the same thing.

"They also want to know why you haven't indicted them," Bailey shoots back.

"All in good time. As soon as we have a witness who will testify before the grand jury."

"She's sick right now!" Bailey snaps. Another part of his message is that had the trial been limited to events in the Hibernia Bank, he would have relied strictly on the bank film and not even put his client on the stand, let alone his battery of psychiatrists. His defense would have been that Patricia was a kidnapping victim and, if not literally under the gun in the bank, at least under imminent threat of death if she had failed to cooperate. But once the machine-gunning at Mel's and her confession to young Matthews were admitted, it took psychiatrists to explain them. Then came the "Tania Interview" and other documents, including descriptions of banks and notes on homemade explosives in Patty's handwriting. These materials strongly suggested that Patty was now in the business of robbing banks, and psychiatrists were required to explain that Ms. Hearst was kept in a *continuing* state of terror and fear for her life until the moment of her arrest, and that her irrational-seeming fear of the Harrises, the police, the FBI, and her parents was, in fact, a quite normal response to her abnormal situation.

Back at my apartment, with the afternoon off, I begin to organize accumulated newspapers and to check my stacks of clippings against my blue notebooks for the first time. The late-winter mist rises and obscures the iron-red bridge in my narrow, slice-of-San-Francisco view. Ten days from now, on a plane back to New York, I will realize that this was the day I began to feel like a person again, something more than the piece of media, the human tape recorder, the HERNAP junkie I had by now become. Today I no longer feel helpless, mired in legal thickets, confused, suspicious, exhausted from trying to figure out who is lying how much about what. This is the day I begin to see they all were lying, and I have been lying, too, or at least perceiving it all through a highly personal eye. This is the day when I begin again to become myself.

The sky turns violet behind the Roman-red bridge, white above the thick sea fog. A rustle at my door—the evening paper. BOMB AT HEARST ESTATE! The terrorists have struck Wyntoon, the rustic Bavarian *folie à grandeur* that was Patty's own favorite family hideaway. Her grandfather had loved the place, too, and so had Marion Davies, Hearst's "great and good friend" for the last half of his life. *Time* magazine had coined this euphemism to describe their remarkable thirty-two-year relationship. My own favorite description of it is by Orson Welles, who wrote in his foreword to *The Times We Had,* Miss Davies' bubble-headed memoirs, that the delectable comedienne for whom Hearst built both San Simeon and Wyntoon "was never one of Hearst's possessions; he was always her suitor, and she was the precious treasure of his heart for more than 30 years."

In her book Miss Davies describes it all in dippy, delicious prose. I am particularly fond of the section about WR and Marion's World War II evacuation of San Simeon. From the air the place "looked like a birthday cake," she says, and might seem to the Imperial Japanese Air Force an irresistible target. But Hearst does not want to leave; he favors hiding underground in the palatial cellars. Marion argues, "I don't want to be blown up just for a castle."

"Well, I'm not evading the war!" the patriot replies.

"I don't want to be shot for no reason," she says, explaining to her readers that "it would have been perfectly okay if I'd had a gun and could fight somebody—which I couldn't, because I'd wiggle. But I didn't see why we should stay right in the line of fire. They could see us from miles away, and WR had been the one who first started to write about the yellow peril."

So the entire baronial establishment decides to remove to Wyntoon, Hearst's vast enclave of chalets—an entire rustic village, in fact—tucked into the densely wooded mountains of northern California.

Miss Davies' account of wartime austerity at Wyntoon relates that

WR ran the papers from there with a wireless and the ticker. We knew when the Japanese got loose one night. They had an internment camp about 30 miles away. One was electrocuted in the electric wire. The rest were headed our way. We had extra guards out; the Japanese hated WR at that time. They couldn't have gotten in, but if they had, you know what would have happened to us.

I didn't know what they were complaining about, because they had lovely menus in their camps; I had a copy of the menu. They had the most wonderful breakfasts, and chicken for luncheon, and anything they wanted at night. But still they were dissatisfied. They created a furor all the time, and it was a constant strain all during the war.

In another of these California internment camps, Wendy Yoshimura had been born, and now, more than thirty years later, Wyntoon has been bombed by SLA sympathizers—surely the only instance, at least in recent political history, of terrorist attack by canoe. This evening, on his own front page, Randolph Hearst is quoted as saying that the terrorists are trying to frighten his daughter into silence. But, as so often happens in this remarkable story, when the screws are tightest the better remark is Catherine's: "The FBI plays checkers while the terrorists play chess."

(405)

At the start of the trial, when Judge Carter threw out the press during *voir dire,* I spent a day at the San Quentin Six trial because as a novice court reporter I needed to warm up. An hour's drive north over the Golden Gate Bridge, the state of California was prosecuting the six men accused of murder and assault in connection with the prison uprising in which George Jackson and five others died. Nobody said much about Jackson anymore. It had all been so long ago, and the only people who seemed to remember had been the SLA, and they all died in a fire that seems very long ago now, too. But if there had been no George Jackson and others to dramatize so vividly the hellholes of our prisons, there would never have been an SLA, and Marcus Foster would be administering the schools of Oakland, and Mrs. Steven Weed would be a California housewife. Like a reverse telescope, the San Quentin Six case was a lens through which HERNAP could be viewed. Now I got out my Marin County Courthouse notes and compared the two trials.

Although the San Quentin Six trial already was the longest and costliest in California history, it received no attention from the media whatever. It all took place behind a $40,000 Plexiglas shield inside a fortified, bulletproofed courtroom watched over by armed guards. Five of the six defendants wore chains around their waists and ankles at all times, and were shackled to specially built chairs.* Convict witnesses were chained to the witness box. The security on the other side of the Plexiglas was almost as extraordinary. Visitors had to register with sheriffs' deputies, have daily mug shots taken, pass through two separate metal detectors, have all possessions inspected, and submit to a body search. Women visitors got their bras and crotches patted by a lady cop.

The unlikely setting for all this was the spectacular courthouse designed by Frank Lloyd Wright in a repeated circular motif—circular walls, circular courtrooms, circular judge's chambers, circular drinking fountains and toilets, circular stairs, circular everything. From the freeway the building always reminded me of a giant octopus, its round pink suckers clamped tight to the hillside. Marin is one of the five richest counties in the United States, and San Quentin, an old and evil maximum-security prison, is located at its remote outer edge. Functionally, the new courthouse has been converted into an extension of the old prison, a total-security pseudopod sticking out from the invisible

*The sixth defendant, Willie Tate, had been paroled, so chains were not required.

San Quentin, twenty miles away, into the green and pleasant hills of Marin.

Charlie Garry, who drove me to Marin, had been commuting to this legal madhouse four days a week for eleven months, and that morning he had been good and mad. It was really too much, the last straw. When the Supreme Court had ruled, some months before, that a criminal defendant has the right to choose his own lawyer, one of the San Quentin Six defendants had fired his attorney and elected to represent himself. Prison makes every man somewhat crazy, but Hugo "Yogi" Pinell has been diagnosed by prison psychiatrists as a dangerous paranoid schizophrenic, Garry told me. "The *judge* loves having Yogi in there because he fucks up the case for the rest of us." That extended the trial three or four months right there. So far the trial had cost $2 million. If the judge were to accommodate any of the motions to sever Pinell's case from the others, he would have to declare a mistrial, and the entire $2 million would be down the drain.

Garry represents Johnnie Spain, another of the convicts. The actual indictment reads: *People of the State of California* v. *Stephen Bingham et al.* But only "et al."—the convicts—were in court. Bingham, the last visitor to see Jackson the day he died, had been a fugitive ever since. Garry drove in silence for a while, then burst out, "The system created Yogi Pinell. The system deserves him. *But I don't deserve him.* And my client doesn't deserve him!"

Like Patty's, this, too, was a "show trial," the intent being to show the prisoners—and the public—that they can't get away with it; that "et al." are crooks, criminals, and bad guys, not revolutionaries, urban guerrillas, and freedom fighters. The government must show this if government and law and order are to continue to exist. In show trials there is frequently a glass box. In the Eichmann trial the defendant was put in a glass box. In the Nuremberg trials a group of defendants—a government—was put in a glass box. In this trial, as in Patty's, "the system" was in the glass box. What was really on trial in both courtrooms was America—the Pie itself. The preceding decade had raised fundamental questions: Does government under law prevail? Are politicians honest? Is the judiciary corrupt? Do the media now run the show? Will the truth always out? Most important perhaps in the world's greatest and oldest democracy, can a poor man get a fair trial? To prove it we were trying a rich girl in California with the entire world looking on. No one was watching this other California trial. The day of my visit, fewer than two rows of seats were occupied, and only one other reporter was present besides myself.

Nothing prepared the visitor for the creepy atmosphere here. After the metal detectors, the search, the Polaroid, and the fingered bra in the sunlit corridor, one entered a darkened door into a circular courtroom, two-thirds of it walled off behind ceiling-high double thicknesses of bulletproof plastic held in place by stout six-inch oaken beams. On closer inspection, the beams were not oak but steel pasted over with Con-Tact paper to look like wood: a strange nicety.

Just inside the smeary "glass," with their backs to it, sat six large, muscular black men, average age thirty, in bright electric-blue swivel chairs bolted to the floor. Each man was tethered to his chair like an organ grinder's monkey, his handcuffs attached to a waist chain that dangled to the iron stanchion beneath his chair and was secured to his ankle chains by its own padlock. Because all that chain made it difficult to swivel the chair, each man had a pocket mirror, to communicate over his shoulders with spectators. Farther into the murky depths of the bulletproof chamber sat the lawyers. Along the left side, disappearing into the gloom, were the double row of jurors and, behind them, most indistinct of all, the judge, his clerks, and the witness box. The distortions caused by the milky plastic made the cheeks and jowls of the judge and the witnesses puff and waver in the distance as if they were underwater. Patty's trial reminded me of watching an aquarium. This one was taking place in a real tank. When I saw them, the six defendants seemed in high spirits, flirting and preening with their mirrors, but I was told that on some days they were grim, depressed to the edge of tears.

All the prisoners were taking notes, the judge and jury were taking notes, and the lawyers were taking notes, yet nothing was really happening. Adding to the visual distortion, it was very difficult for spectators outside the glass to hear. Everyone inside had a microphone, but the mikes were not turned up very loud, so members of the audience frequently waved their hands at the judge to indicate they couldn't hear, and then the volume would be raised slightly. It must have been a strange sight to Judge Henry Broderick, this frieze of waving black and white hands against the far wall. To the people inside the plastic shield we spectators were perfectly clear, but from our side of the plastic everyone seemed distorted—not only underwater but frozen in ice.

Defendant Dave Johnson, called "Jap" because of his squinty eyes, had slung one shackled foot up over the arm of his chair and was ostentatiously reading a newspaper. Willie Tate, smaller and wiry, wore a loud yellow shirt; he was the one out on parole. The others wore rough prison denims. Luis Talamantez flirted with a blond girl seated just behind him, one of the groupies in daily attendance. The pair held love notes close to the glass. Luis's notes were attached with bright green chewing gum. Number four was Fleeta Drumgo, one of the three original Soledad Brothers. Seeing him, I remembered attending a hearing in 1974 at which a prison doctor testified about a visit to San Quentin to treat Fleeta for diabetes. The convict had burst into tears; it was the first time in six years that he had been allowed to be alone in a room with another human being without having to wear the chains. When I saw him now, Fleeta was grinning and smiling even more than the other five. Whenever the door opened behind us and a new cop or spectator came in, Fleeta would twist clumsily around to look. Johnnie Spain wore a blue artist's smock over his denims, and two daisies were stuck in a buttonhole. At the far end was Hugo "Yogi" Pinell. Like three of the others, he wore thick-lensed, wire-framed, Ben Franklin–style glasses. Vision deteriorates, along with bodies and brains, after long years in a dark cell.

The witness on the stand was James "Doc" Holiday, another chained and shackled convict. Every time a prisoner had to be moved, whether from the witness chair or the prisoner's dock, the judge ordered the jury out, so they wouldn't witness the chaining and unchaining, and this meant that everybody in the spectator section also had to file outside, taking all his belongings with him.

In the front row of spectators were eight white women and one white man. In the second row were four more white women, two white hippie chicks, and one black man. There was no one else except for the sheriff's deputies, all white. Inside the glass sat two or three burly guards from the California Department of Corrections, usually black, but as shifts changed, an occasional Oriental, brown, or white guard appeared.

On the morning I was there, not one of the questions that Yogi Pinell was asking his witness was admissible. Judge Broderick said repeatedly, "Mr. Pinell, put a proper question to this witness, or I shall conclude your examination."

Trying to get certain information into the record, the convict lawyer tried another tack. "Do you know the meaning of 'militant'?" he asked. The judge said again, "That's irrelevant." Pinell said, "Many political people have been killed for their beliefs," and this was why he wished to get the word "militant" into the record. The judge said, "Mr. Pinell, I will caution you one more time against speaking out," but it was no use, and finally Broderick declared a recess.

On the round bench in the corridor I met the other journalist there, Mark Shwartz, of Pacific News Service. He had covered the case since its inception, and was eager to give me his version of the political intrigue behind it, beginning with Jonathan Jackson's seemingly suicidal rescue operation. The original plan had called for Huey Newton's Black Panthers to lend support to the desperado mission, but at the last moment Newton withdrew the Panther support, and Jackson was doomed. In reprisal, George Jackson, from Soledad, put out a contract to murder Newton. This made it necessary for Newton to eliminate Jackson. Shwartz believed it was Newton who persuaded Stephen Bingham to cooperate, at least to the degree of smuggling the gun to Jackson to set him up for the escape attempt in which he was killed.

Garry's overall defense plan, however, was to show that Stephen Bingham had *not* brought in the gun. The only other possibility then would be that a guard had brought it in, in order to set Jackson up. This is a relatively simple defense. The guards brought in knives; they brought every other kind of contraband into the Adjustment Center; why shouldn't one of them have brought in a gun? It was this carefully prepared defense that Pinell was now trying to knock down. Pinell, a member of the Black Guerrilla Family, a more militant prison group than the Panthers, believed that the Panthers and Bingham were responsible for George Jackson's death, and in trying to present his own defense, Pinell was destroying the defenses of the other five.

After recess Judge Broderick said, "Mr. Pinell, you've got to be aware that at some point in time your defense must end. Now, you've mentioned six more witnesses that you intend to call, plus your mother. You've got to give us some idea when that will be." The other defendants had become restless. When they moved, their chains rattled against the stanchions and sounded like the cable cars that go up and down the San Francisco hills.

It was hard to realize that preparations for all this had taken four and a half years. It looked more like a human zoo than a fair trial. Under such circumstances, what happened to a defendant's presumption of innocence? The presumption of the chains was that without them the defendants might do injury to the court or jury. But that unspoken suggestion made the entire trial a mockery. Because the spectators were safely outside of the bulletproof glass, the chains implied that the judge and jury, the lawyers, clerks, and marshals—that is to say, the court and the law and justice itself—were the potential targets of the chained-up men.

The present situation added up to injustice in 3-D. Had the case not been reinstated by a higher court, three of these men would have been paroled by now. Then there was the injustice to his codefendants of the intransigence of Pinell. Everybody agreed that Yogi was crazy, too dangerous to appear in court without chains. By refusing to sever his case from the other five, the judge and prison authorities were in effect using the presence of Pinell to keep his codefendants also in chains.

At lunch with the defense in the courthouse cafeteria—a half-dozen lawyers to one journalist—I was pelted with information. Since 1850 there have been more than four hundred revolts in U.S. prisons, but the San Quentin Six trial was historically important because it dealt with the first of the big prison blowups of the 1960s and '70s, Attica being the second. Bracketing the country geographically as they do, Attica and San Quentin raised to nationwide public consciousness the appalling conditions in all prisons. This case was also important because it involved the death of George Jackson. It was also associated in the public mind with assassination, and might even involve a Watergate type of conspiracy against the Left on the part of prison authorities. So that although what was happening here appeared to be all in the past, it was very significant in the long run. If another miscarriage of justice were to occur here, the authorities might be unable to handle the result. If the men were acquitted, it could signal a new era in the prisons.

This trial, like Patty's, showed how easy it has become today to politicize people from the very top and very bottom levels of society. The reason is that the system stinks and everybody knows it, but few people do anything about it. The majority are like Moonies, passive followers of the system. The trial reminded me of childhood visits to the Museum of Natural History in New York to see a vast diorama behind glass of creatures from the ice ages or before. Maybe we were looking at dinosaurs now. Certainly very little that was happening behind the glass in Marin County was relevant to what was happening in the outside world.

Although Yogi Pinell had been diagnosed as a paranoid schizophrenic, he could be the only sane one in the chamber of dinosaurs we were looking at. He believed that there was a conspiracy, a real conspiracy against his person, by the California Department of Corrections; he believed that he was their own Private Yossarian, and maybe he was. Now that prison had helped drive Pinell mad, he was being punished for being mad.

As for Judge Broderick's role in the insanity, the lunchroom lawyers called him a "volunteer fool at a two-million-dollar error." Recent California trials had cost the taxpayers $750,000 to prosecute Charles Manson, $750,000 for Angela Davis, $800,000 for Sirhan Sirhan, and $1 million for the second Ruchell Magee trial because of the extra security involved. "And in each case, except for Angela and the Magee trial, you had a judge who was not up to the legal demands of the case," the lunchroom lawyers said. Why not use the taxpayers' dollars for top prosecutors and judges? Broderick was inexperienced in the criminal field. He had been an ardent campaigner for Ronald Reagan and had a Reagan attitude toward criminal justice and the prison system. He was handling this case in a Ronald Reagan way, a Department of Corrections way. Furthermore, he knew that if he stayed with Reagan, and if Reagan prevailed on the national scene, perhaps got to be President, he, Judge Broderick, would rise up the ladder to the California Supreme Court or to the Ninth U.S. Circuit Court of Appeals, where he longed to be. It was in the service of these ambitions, the lawyers think, that Broderick had volunteered for this case and was now over-managing it. As he said over and over, "We're not going to try the death of George Jackson in this court. We're not going to try prison conditions in this case. The five other deaths—three white guards and the two trustees—those are the only deaths that are going to be tried in this case."

Back down in the round lobby, my young friend Shwartz was waiting. He had no use for lawyers of any stripe, particularly radical ones, and he pointed out that Garry was being paid forty dollars a day by the Bingham family to come to this trial and defend Johnnie Spain. Shwartz especially does not like forty-dollars-a-day lawyers. He had covered the Angela Davis trial and other prison trials, and time and again, he told me, he had seen these "intellectual lawyers" gang up against men like Ruchell Magee and Yogi Pinell just because they were not lawyers. The real lawyers didn't like the amateurs; the professionals didn't like the primitives. The whole San Quentin Six trial "is all a lawyers' game." To Shwartz, the whole country is a lawyers' game. Watergate was a lawyers' game. "Lawyers are not interested in truth, they are interested in acquittal. Criminal lawyers like Lee Bailey are interested in money and reputation. Prisoners like Pinell or Magee may be crazy, but they are interested in truth."

"Truth is not the point of any trial," I had said, quoting some half-remembered civics book. "Justice is not the point. Acquittal is the only point." That had been back on Monday, February 2. How sure of myself I had sounded! Now, six weeks later, an old trial hand, I was sure of hardly anything.

Week Eight

March 15–21

Monday, March 15

After four days' recess, Dr. Kozol scampers into the witness box. Everybody else seems somewhat subdued. Patty looks terrible, paler than she has since the trial began.

Kozol now tells Browning that he had asked Patty about Willie Wolfe. "I told her that on the June seventh tape she had provided a eulogy in which she spoke of Cujo so lovingly, so tenderly, so movingly that she made it come alive.

"She seemed to get upset and said, 'I don't know how I feel about him!' deeply moved, as if sobbing inside. 'I don't know why I got into this goddamn thing! Shit!' Then she ran out of the room." She came back with Mr. Johnson, and there was no more interviewing that day.

In the next interview, Kozol invited Miss Hearst's own psychiatrist, Dr. Richards, to sit in. Miss Hearst described her abduction rather curtly. When Kozol asked for more details, she began to seem so upset and uncomfortable that he said, "Never mind." She said, "I don't *want* to tell you this part but I'm *going* to tell you." And then she told him that while sitting in class, four days before she was kidnapped, she was overwhelmed by a premonition she would be kidnapped. It stayed with her for four days, and she couldn't shake it. She thought, in her terror, of running home to her parents, where she would be safe—and then the very thing she'd dreaded occurred.

Patty told Kozol she had been assaulted twice. Catherine Hearst's eyes are again downcast as the fifth psychiatrist relates how Cinque pinched her daughter. Did you specifically ask her, Doctor, if he ever sexually assaulted her again? No, but my feeling was that this had not been a sexual assault but rather an angry assault that had a sexual connotation. (In Kozol's line of work, one figures his opinion carries special weight.) Because the West/Singer report seemed ambiguous, Kozol had specifically asked Patty whether DeFreeze had ever threatened to rape her. Definitely not, she had replied.

When Dr. Kozol asked Patty to draw a floor plan of the Golden Gate apartment, she drew a circle to represent the bedroom–living room, with lines indicating the location of the Murphy-bed closet, where the arms were stored, and another, overlapping circle to represent the kitchen area. She marked the locations of all the windows and the bathroom, and Kozol finds it significant that she failed to indicate or even mention a second closet. She described the daily SLA regimen: up at eight, exercises, chores. No time for fun and games, only Spartan living. The standard fare was dried foods and beans. "No candy, and no ice cream, either," the witness says sorrowfully. "Mr. Cinque felt that treats would soften their life-style."

Today Kozol has abandoned his notes, making him a far more effective witness, but now Patty is scribbling furiously on a yellow pad.

What did she say about the Missing Year? Just that she was in Sacramento until two months before her arrest. Did you also discuss the Trish Tobin tape? Yes, I asked her if Miss Tobin knew Emily Harris personally, because she spoke of her as "Emily." "I'm not going to say *anything* about the Harrises," Patty replied. When Kozol asked the reason for her interest in revolutionary feminism, she said, "Because I am a woman." In relation to the person we have been watching for seven weeks, this answer is burlesque Garbo, not to be taken seriously. Patricia Hearst does not seem like a woman but like a wound that will not heal.

When Kozol asked if she didn't find other things important—poverty, unemployment, racism, for example—she replied, "None more important than the liberation of women." Here I agreed with her. "The liberation of women" is also a far more radical idea, and more dangerous to the established order—established since the days of Abraham, Isaac, and Joseph—than any idea Marx or Lenin or the SLA ever thought of. It is the most radical idea to come along since Jesus suggested we love one another and turn the other cheek, and probably just as antithetical to the archaic biological imperatives we still carry around in our little stacks of X and Y chromosomes.

I have been puzzling for a long time over the significance, if any, of the SLA's female leadership. How would a terrorist band run by women differ from a traditional outlaw group? How might a political ideology conceived and constructed by women differ from previous radical political constructs? It had always seemed to me no accident that "symbiosis" was this group's core word and organizing principle. "Symbiosis" is more than "synthesis": It is a biological term, meaning a state of mutual interdependence, and it refers to organisms that cannot exist except in that state.

"Liberation," as the SLA appeared to employ the term, meant the liberation of everybody who is not now free: the poor, the blacks, the workers, the young, the convicts, women, military conscripts, victims of corporate capitalism—literally *everybody*. And "Army" meant that the only way to achieve this liberation is to fight for it. But I had not been able to go beyond this point until, quite by accident, I picked up a frayed paperback and read, ". . . in the beginning of human history sexual relations were promiscuous, therefore only the mother's parenthood was unquestionable. . . . She was the authority and law-giver— the ruler both in the family and in society." With that, I heard a *p-i-n-g*. The book was *The Forgotten Language: An Introduction to the Understanding of Dreams, Fairy Tales and Myths,* by Erich Fromm.* I turned another page. "[The] religion of the Olympian gods was preceded by a religion in which goddessses, motherlike figures, were the supreme deities. . . ."

The notion of an archaic reign of mother-goddesses, I knew, was scarcely limited to ancient Greece. Anthropologists describe similar, dimly recalled matriarchal eras at the dawn of history among the peoples of every continent. Under the now universal patriarchal system, to summarize Fromm's long and tortuous exegesis, the people worship gods, and the social order is hierarchical. The father heads the family, and a king or president or prime minister heads the state. Marriage is sacred and monogamous. The family is a closed unit; love is restricted to family members. The paramount duty within the family is filial respect and love. The paramount crime is patricide. What matters most in the larger society is man-made law, obedience to authority, rational thought, and man's effort to change natural phenomena, that is, science and "progress."

In a matriarchal system, goddesses are worshiped, not gods. Open sex rather than monogamy is the norm. The most sacred tie is not the

*New York: Grove Press, 1956.

one between man and woman but between mother and child. Matricide is the major crime. The most important values are ties of blood and ties to the soil. A "primitive" harmony with the natural world replaces "civilization" as the primary value. Instead of a hierarchical social order with its premium on obedience to authority—be it god, state, or king—one finds in matriarchy a value system in which all people are equally important, as all are equally the children of mothers as well as sons and daughters of Mother Earth. Because mother love is based on parenthood only, on the the fact that the children *are* her children, without regard to merit or achievement, all children are loved alike.

Relating all this to ancient Greece, Fromm tells us that its archaic, matriarchal world was defeated by the patriarchal order, as represented by the gods on Mount Olympus, under the leadership of Zeus. Implicit is the belief that if ever the mother-goddesses do reassert their dominion, human society will exist on a higher, more moral plane than is now the case.

Comes now a discussion by Fromm of the Oedipus complex: the unconscious wish of every male child to kill his father and marry his mother, a desire that Freud believed to be "the kernel of all neurosis." Fromm interprets the entire story of Oedipus as a counterattack by the defeated mother-goddesses on the reigning patriarchal hierarchy, using Oedipus as their agent. Reading that, I am really hooked.

When at about age ten I had first come across the writings of Sigmund Freud in the Modern Library edition, I recall leafing through the pages looking for the dirty parts, and my gleeful discovery of "penis-envy"; and then I remember a growing sense of dismay. According to the master, all girls had penis-envy, and my trouble was that I didn't. Try as I might, I simply could not summon up a trace of what Freud assured me was a universal female feeling. All that Freud gave me was penis-envy envy, which is a pretty rotten feeling for a ten-year-old girl. Reading next about the Oedipus complex and its companion, the Electra complex, did nothing to restore my self-esteem. The Electra complex—the daughter's unconscious wish to kill Mommy and marry Daddy—seemed to me vague and unformed, a Freudian afterthought, and downright tacky when compared to the savage brilliance of his original (male) insight.

Having concluded at a very early age that in my search for self-knowledge I could not count on much help from Sigmund Freud, I commenced to look elsewhere—a lifelong habit. But the old hurt must still have rankled because now, when kindly Dr. Fromm seemed to be offering me a second chance to stroll through the maze of myth and see it all again from another, non-Freudian perspective, I eagerly seized his outstretched hand.

It turned out to be quite an expedition. Fromm himself has a guide and companion, a nineteenth-century German authority on myth, J. J. Bachofen, whom Fromm regards as coequal to Freud: "With an unsurpassed penetration and brilliance [Bachofen] grasped the myth in its religious and psychological as well as its historical meaning." Bachofen was the first to say that the earliest human civilization must have been organized along matriarchal lines and that humankind had goddesses long before it had gods. Because early man and woman were sexually promiscuous, he reasoned, the mother's identity was always sure, the father's never. Hence the only certain consanguinity and continuity were through the maternal line. This made the mother rather than the father the supreme authority and law-giver, not only within the family but in the larger society as well. But at some point in the long, dim ages of prehistory, the stronger males asserted themselves, subdued and eventually defeated the ruling mothers, and themselves assumed the leadership. In order to preserve male domination in all spheres, it became essential to outlaw open sex and to impose strict monogamy, at least for most women. (So long as most females remained monogamous, promiscuous behavior by men could not upset the new social order. And so far as I have been able to observe, it still does not.) Religion followed reality, and, the earth-mother–goddesses having been dethroned, "man" now worshiped "god."

Following Bachofen, Fromm sees not only Oedipus but all the other father-murderers of Greek mythology as agents of the older, suppressed female supremacy. They act as killers of the fathers and destroyers of male authority in an attempt to reassert and reestablish the matriarchal social order. There are many renderings and variations of the basic myth, but Fromm, like Freud, goes by Sophocles' version. An oracle prophesies that the king of Thebes will be killed by his own son, who will then take his mother to bed. To prevent the murder of her husband, Jocasta, the queen, gives her infant son, Oedipus, to a shepherd with instructions that the boy be left in the woods with his feet bound, so that his death is certain. But the shepherd disobeys, and Oedipus grows up unaware of the prophecy. He kills the old man, solves the riddle of the Sphinx, and saves the city of Thebes. The grateful citizens invite their savior to marry their widowed queen. Thus does Oedipus come to fulfill the terrible prophecy and plow the field where he was sown. Forced to see truth, he tears out his own eyes, and Jocasta kills herself.

Fromm looks at the story not as a symbol of primal sexual desires but rather as another of the "fundamental aspects of interpersonal relationships, the attitude toward authority." Fromm's analysis illuminated for me many of the hitherto incomprehensible SLA attitudes toward authority. The original mystery in the SLA story was the choice of Marcus Foster (King Mark the First, First Mark) as the SLA's first-strike target. Looked at logically, it had never made any sense. Foster was no one's enemy. He was a civil servant, an outstanding man performing a near-impossible task—the pacification, degangsterizing, and orderly administration of the Oakland public schools. Trying to look at his murder symbolically had got me a little further, but not much: Possibly Foster's plan to post police on the school grounds and require students to wear photo-identification badges gave particular offense to the convict mind, a mind of one warped by years of being locked in cages, locked under police guard, forced to wear a numbered badge, to dress in numbered clothing, to perform a numbered task, to answer a numbered roll call; the mind of one whose rank is zero, whose name means nothing, who has *only* a serial number. Combat grunts in Vietnam, men like Joe Remiro, also lived only by serial number.

But that explanation, too, seemed farfetched. Now Fromm and Bachofen were suggesting another symbolic interpretation: Perhaps the bizarre choice of Foster was the women's doing, the work of new-fledged women terrorists who were making an extreme, all-out effort to be like and *think like* men. But women are not men; we have different values, and among women the primary bond is not between man and woman but between mother and child, and for one to kill the other is the primary crime—the mirror of matricide being infanticide or less drastically, child abandonment.

Thinking about the Greek myth in relation to the woman-driven SLA, I found it useful to look at the old story from Jocasta's point of view. Like every other tragic figure, the mother of Oedipus attempts to challenge fate. But her loyalty at the moment of crisis is patriarchal—to authority, to her husband, the king. To save his life, Jocasta gives away her child. Worse, she orders that he be abandoned, so he will surely die.

To the male, then and now, child abandonment is not a special crime. Husbands often disappear; fathers literally abandon tens of thousands of children every year. On a symbolic level, abandonment occurs each time man withdraws from woman and arises from the bed. "The night my father got me, his mind was not on me. He did not once consider the thing you see," as Housman expressed it.

The advent of so-called women's liberation has done nothing to change these old, sex-determined attitudes toward abandonment. In fact, women's lib has exacerbated the problem. The same easygoing series of casual sexual encounters that young men perceive as "sexual liberation" is experienced by many of today's young women not as serial monogamy but as serial abandonment.

To the SLA women, *and to Patty,* Catherine Hearst must have seemed a Jocasta-figure, willing to sacrifice her child to maintain authority and the moral order. Indeed, Catherine saw herself the same way. She literally became a regent, or, more accurately, was reborn as a regent for another sixteen-year term, at just the crucial moment in Patty's ordeal. With that, she appeared to have abandoned her daughter to what seemed certain death. She might as well have left her on a hillside with her feet bound. The SLA's special fury against the mother in black now made a kind of symbolic sense.

If the old myth had spawned the Oedipus complex and the Electra complex, why not a Jocasta complex? To interpret the SLA, Patty's role in it and all of HERNAP from the point of view of the Jocasta complex supplied mythic logic and consistency to a hitherto baffling sequence of events. In *Oedipus Rex,* the first play of Sophocles' trilogy, Jocasta at first seems a contradiction and a denial. If Jocasta symbolizes the motherly principle, why is she destroyed? Fromm answers, "Jocasta's crime is that of not having fulfilled her duty as a mother; she had wanted to kill her child in order to save her husband. This, from the standpoint of patriarchal society, is a legitimate decision, but from the standpoint of matriarchal society and matriarchal ethics it is the unforgivable crime."

Seen from this point of view, the myth's whole tragic chain of events becomes Jocasta's fault. By committing the unforgivable crime, she sets in motion the chain of events that eventually destroys her child, her husband, and herself. In the second and third plays, *Oedipus at Colonus* and *Antigone,* one finds numerous references to the "Queens of dread aspect." Who are these "Awful Goddesses" who rule the sacred grove, and why is it here that Oedipus dies, in peace at last? Fromm says that "Oedipus, although himself a man, belongs to the world of these matriarchal goddesses, and his strength lies in his connection with them."

Here I found a startling parallel to the role of Cinque in the SLA. Later, when Oedipus speaks of his beloved daughters, Antigone and Ismene, and compares them to his hated and disowned sons, I felt I was meeting the archaic, mythic ancestors of Fahizah and Mizmoon.

> Now, these girls preserve me, these my nurses, *these who are men not women,* in true service: but ye are aliens, and no sons of mine.

King Oedipus also compares his daughters to the Egyptian matriarchy.

> O true image of the ways of Egypt that they show in their spirit and their life! For there the men sit weaving in the house, but the wives go forth to win the daily bread. And in your case, my daughters, those to whom these toils belonged keep the house at home like girls, while ye, in their stead, bear your hapless father's burden.

Again the SLA parallel is striking: When Donald DeFreeze escaped from prison, it was Patricia Soltysik who first took him in, hid him, became his savior and bedmate. And then, that summer, while Mizmoon and Zoya and Gabi and Fahizah went about the SLA's daily business—practicing their marksmanship at the rifle range, drilling in the hills, visiting prisons, and recruiting new members to the secret cobra society—DeFreeze stayed at home in the tiny cottage cooking up black-eyed peas, chitlins, and corn bread for everybody's evening meal.

Fromm next takes up the matter of the mysterious and terrifying death of the blind Oedipus in the grove to which he had been guided by Theseus:

> . . . holding his hand before his face to screen his eyes, as if some dread sight had been seen, and such as none might endure to behold.

Once Fromm showed me that the foregoing was a veiled reference to the fact that in death Oedipus was not drawn up to the heavens with the gods but back down to his true home, the netherworld realm of the mother-goddesses, I saw more: This passage is a paradigm of the death of Cinque and his followers in the burning house.

The theme of conflict between the matriarchal and patriarchal principles is expressed most fully in *Antigone,* in which Creon emerges as the tyrant of Thebes and the prime embodiment of the supremacy of the law of the state, "of obedience to authority over allegiance to the natural law of humanity. Antigone refuses to violate the laws of blood and of the solidarity of all human beings for the sake of an authoritarian, hierarchical principle."

In his clearest formulation of the difference between the two realms, Fromm says, "The matriarchal principle is that of blood relationship as the fundamental and indestructible tie, of the equality of all men, of the respect for human life and of love. The patriarchal principle is that the ties between man and wife, between ruler and ruled, take precedence over ties of blood. It is the principle of order and authority, of obedience and hierarchy." Another *p-i-n-g!* In the foregoing I heard a direct expression of the ideas of the SLA, of Camilla Hall and Emily Harris' overweening respect for human life and love; I saw the blood relationship symbolically achieved by the SLA decree of open, shared sex; I recognized an echo of Nancy Ling Perry's passionate belief in the equality of all men. In the reference to the ties between man and wife, I found expression not only of the much-advertised bond between the Hearsts but of the sacred ties between all the parents of SLA members, ties from which these young people had turned away in search of some "finer," more "open" relationship. (It had always been of great interest to me that although the SLA members had certainly rejected their parents' values and way of living, only Patty rebelled against her parents; none of the others had called them "pigs." Rather, in the letters they wrote home before dropping from sight, the children begged the parents to try to understand what they felt compelled to do. Moreover, these parents did try to understand; their deep concern is evident in all their statements to the press, both before and after the Los Angeles holocaust. To me, this fundamental difference between Tania's state of mind and that of the other SLA members was more convincing proof than any of the psychiatric testimony that something was awry within that mind. I could not understand why it was never brought out in court.)

When Creon says he would kill his daughter rather than "nurture mine own kindred in naughtiness," he seems to be speaking for the Hearsts, or at least for the defense counsel retained by them. And his words prefigured exactly the words of another authority figure, a bank president who was my dinner partner one summer night twenty-five hundred years later, just after the SLA died in flames. This man's only daughter was a student at Harvard Law School, and after the vodka and over the gaspacho, he addressed the table thus: "You know what I'd do, don't you, if *my* daughter held up a bank? I'd kill her." The other guests on the moonlit terrace nodded assent, a modern Greek chorus exactly echoing the cadences of Creon long ago:

> ... I will slay her. .... Let her appeal as she will to the majesty of kindred blood. .... He who does his duty in his own household will be found righteous in the State also. But if anyone transgresses and does violence to the laws, or thinks to dictate to his rulers, such a one can win no praise from me.

> ... disobedience is the worst of evils. This it is that ruins cities; this makes homes desolate; by this, the ranks of allies are broken into headlong rout. ... Therefore, we must support the cause of order, and in no wise suffer a woman to worst us. Better to fall from power, if we must, by a man's hand, than we should be called weaker than a woman.

It was in just this state of mind, it seemed to me, that the Los Angeles authorities, defenders of law and order, had given orders to open fire on the house.

In modern translation, Sophocles' "ruler and ruled" become the whites and blacks, the jailers and convicts, the rich and the poor. And the "principles of order and authority, of obedience and hierarchy" today are embodied in the FBI, the Los Angeles Police Department, the California Department of Corrections, the university's pedagogical hierarchy, the corporate state, the multinational corporations, and every other institution on which the SLA members had declared war.

The reason men like Randolph Hearst, William Saxbe, Raymond Procunier, and Mayor Bradley—the men of the police and prisons and industry and order—*must* oppose the SLA is that otherwise, as Creon explicitly says, if Antigone is *not* defeated, "Now verily I am no man, she is the man, if this victory shall rest with her and bring no penalty." To prevent this loss of his manhood, Creon is willing to see Antigone buried alive in a cave; to have her literally as well as symbolically returned to mother earth. Symbolically, the SLA girls were buried alive in a cave and returned to mother earth when they died in the burning house, and by 1978 Patricia Hearst and Emily Harris had been buried alive in prison's metal cave for more than three years.

Since the very start of Patty's trial I have been fascinated by what the court stenographers do, and when I have had occasion to check their official transcript, in order to fill in a gap in my own unofficial one,

I have been struck repeatedly by the many tiny but sometimes dangerous errors in their work. During the next recess I buttonhole a court
reporter and ask him, Why not install permanent tape recorders in the
courtroom, just as permanent bugs are installed in the courthouse
walls? Ah, there is a *union* of court stenographers. I see. Additionally,
the stenotypists have the right to sell copies of the public record to
anyone at a rate of a dollar a page. This is one reason why criminal
defendants have difficulty filing appeals; a simple trial transcript is apt
to run four or five thousand pages. The system appears to be a guarantee
of unequal justice. Why not change it? Not only is the present transcription system rife with opportunities for error that we would not have
permitted back when I was a fact checker for *Life* magazine. In today's
Xerox and computer era, every citizen surrenders part of his precious
personal privacy forever. In return for feeding himself into government
computers, he gets his Social Security card, driver's license, and other
necessities. Surely he also has a right to a free Xerox transcript of
whatever criminal prosecution the government may bring against him.

Just before the bailiff raps and the judge returns, I feel a light tap on
my shoulder. One of the young reporters on the *Los Angeles Herald-
Examiner* is my cousin, a fact both of us are attempting to stay cool
about. During recess my cousin has managed to copy Patty's notes off
the yellow pad, but since he is a Hearst man they are of no use to him,
and he hates to see good reporting go to waste. "Dr. Kozol kept trying
to equate the women's movement with violence," one note says. "I
repeatedly told him: (1) Violence has no place in the women's movement. (2) I didn't feel it was possible to make lasting social changes in
our society unless the issue of women's rights was resolved." The other
note says, "I paid the rent, bought the furniture, bought the groceries,
cooked all the meals (even while working eight hours a day, and carrying a full course load). If I wasn't there to cook, Steve didn't eat."

Browning, the woodpecker of prosecutors, continues tapping away
at his witness.

Summing it all up, does the doctor have an opinion with respect to
the defendant's mental state when she walked into the bank? Did she
walk in voluntarily?

"Objection! Witness is not an expert on voluntariness."

"Overruled . . . with the same instruction to the jury. You have to
determine intent in your own minds."

"I think she entered the bank voluntarily in order to participate in
the robbing of the bank. This was an act of her own free will."

"Did you also form an opinion with respect to whether she joined her captors voluntarily?"

"Same objection!"

"Overruled."

"I have an opinion. I think she joined the people who had captured her some weeks before."

Doctor, you said earlier that you considered the period just before her abduction significant in reaching your opinion. Would you comment on that? Well, she entered into this relationship with Weed with the most conventional aims. She wanted to marry, she wanted a ring. But Patricia also had private reservations. This very proud, dignified girl felt disappointed and frustrated. She was cooking for his friends, who were not her friends. Then she'd do the pots and pans. He did very little; when she wasn't there, he lived on toast. These things, together with some subtle hostility she had developed toward her parents—well, the girl who got kidnapped was a bitter, confused person, angry at authority, angry at power, angry at hypocrisy, angry at Steven Weed. . . . She really was revolted by this man's sense of values. So this is the girl who was picked up. . . . She had gotten into a state where she was ripe for the plucking. I don't think she was in a *clear* frame of mind, but she was in a receptive frame of mind. She was ready for something. She was a rebel in search of a cause. And the cause found *her.* In a sense, she was kidnapped by the cause. A terrible, terrible, terrible misfortune that of all the movements she might have got involved with —revolutionary feminism, for example, which she came to a year and a half too late—she had to be captured and therefore exposed to the violence and hatred of *this* group, which in a sense echoed how she herself felt. She turned her back on her parents, her sisters, and everyone else who loved her, and their values. Why? Why did she stay with the Harrises? Why did she drive east with the Scotts? Was she handcuffed? Put in the trunk? No.

During this testimony Al Johnson and Lee Bailey look more glum than I have ever seen them. They stare at each other, slowly shaking their heads, and the color of their gaze is a dark, gun-metal gray. Dr. Harry Kozol may have seemed a fuddy-duddy Kewpie doll once, but he is very believable right now.

Patty was an ordinary girl, he goes on. Her parents were trying to provide a good home, a very normal home, but, "well, who knows what terrible things develop in the heart of a child?" A voice echoes back from long ago, from my own childhood. "Who knows what evil lurks in the hearts of men?" our favorite radio program used to ask. "The Shadow knows." Now we are the adults, and we wonder what terrible things may have developed in Patty's heart or Kathy's heart and in the heart of the Kozols' child.

How do the tapes bear on the doctor's conclusions? They map the change in her. Dr. Kozol consults his own report. On the first tape, for example, she mentions the IRA. Obviously the kidnappers were dictating what to say. Why in the world would a terrified girl sitting in a closet in Daly City be worrying about the Irish Republican Army?

On the second tape she sounds a little stronger. Some of this tape may be hers, but she would never pick on her mother for not allowing Eldridge Cleaver and Angela Davis to speak at the University of California. "That wasn't spontaneous on the young lady's part. . . ." The third tape contains only a few words by Patty, to prove she's alive, but there seems to be a general escalation of hatred by the others. The fourth tape is one of terrible fury, great anger at her parents, and it contains expressions foreign to the old Patty. She is speaking the new rhetoric of her new world. This is the strongest language of all, in some ways more dreadful even than tape no. 7. It's almost as if she were saying she has given up and telling her parents, You have failed to get me out—so the hell with you! It seems to Kozol that her basic turning point was somewhere in this period. (Al Johnson is taking notes of this testimony at top speed.) Then, on April 3, Cinque tells Miss Hearst she is free to go, but Patty says, I have chosen to stay and fight. "So I see an incredibly rapid development of events." She was kidnapped on February 4. By March 9 she is very angry. By April 3, she has joined them!

Harry Kozol is winding down like an old gramophone, undercutting the impressive aspects of his previous testimony as he dwells on the abusive statements Patty made about her parents on the final tape. "And that was the last word these parents heard from their daughter. Until they came to visit her in jail the night she was arrested . . . they didn't know if she was alive or dead. . . ." Kozol's voice trails off; is he again talking about his son?

"I think this was all *in* her. In a sense, she was a member of the SLA in spirit, without knowing it, for a long, long time." Rebels grow and develop; it doesn't happen overnight. Patty had been rebellious since birth. For the first nine years of her life she was taken care of by a very harsh and arbitrary governess who beat her with a hairbrush. The early appeals by the child to her parents about the nanny apparently fell on deaf ears. Now, I don't say this *is* what happened; I wasn't there. I say this was *her* image of her early life: an abandoned child, abandoned by her parents to the caprices of a cruel and arbitary governess. (But this was once my image of *my* early life! Abandoned to a cruel German governess, Miss Bodda, who made us count out ten grains of sugar on the morning Wheatina, and never allowed us to play with other children in Central Park for fear of "catching germs," and forced us to walk home down Seventh Avenue backward "so the wind won't blow in your mouths." And Kathy! Kathy's favorite book when she was seven and eight was called *The Abandoned.* She wore out three copies.)

But there is another side to the picture, the doctor is saying. She did have a great deal of indulgence; she did have pets. . . . (*I had no pets!* Cats and dogs weren't suited to a New York City apartment. I can feel the old rage and longing. Finally, I got a chameleon my father bought at the circus, where the little lizards were sold as souvenirs. But it wouldn't eat. In a couple of weeks it had shriveled to an apple-green skeleton, and on a Saturday morning we took it to Central Park and set it free. So it could find food it liked, we said, but I knew it was going to die. I can feel the desperate certainty even now. When I was eleven and we moved to California, somebody at last gave us a puppy. In less than a week it was at the vet's, where it died of distemper. I can still hear my father shouting about the thirty-six-dollar bill. Much later, many unborn children of mine died mysteriously in miscarriages or bizarre gynecological mishaps. After Kathy came, was adopted, our marriage died, and when we were divorcing, I bought my daughter a pair of Christmas kittens, and three or four cats after that, and one after another, they all died. All this flushes back in a retch and vomit of a seven-year-old's memory.)

Kozol is saying that as a teenager Patty became awfully upset about her elder sister, Catherine; she thought her parents were ashamed of Catherine because she was so little. (*My God, I had a sickly "sister,"* too—*Little Shana!* A distant orphan cousin, whom my grandmother had adopted. When my grandmother died, Little Shana came to live with us. I was a teenager then, and I wept every night for the child. She was fat and ugly and sad, and had to live in the maid's room. I thought my parents were unbelievably cruel to her. I fancied myself as her "good" mother and tried to comfort her; I took her on the endless doctor visits for mysterious allergies and ailments. But as soon as she could, as soon as she grew up, she moved away, and none of us ever heard from her again. A few years ago, I ran into another remote cousin, who told me Little Shana had been dead for a long time.)

Patty didn't think of her sister Catherine as a curiosity or a midget, Kozol is saying, and she took Catherine's side against her parents. Also, "she was so upset by the fights between her parents she asked to go back to boarding school." (My own feelings had been identical. I thought the fights meant they hated each other. Now my parents are old. I hear exactly the same quarrels going on today and now find their burden of deep devotion almost unbearably moving. My father and mother have been married for fifty-six years. Tough, vibrant, enduring marriages like theirs are all but gone now, gone forever. My adored parents are like a pair of beautiful snow leopards, exotic, tufted white, rare, almost extinct. . . .)

On the other hand, says Dr. Kozol, the Hearsts were a family that traveled together, enjoyed holidays together . . . it is a mixed picture. . . . But there was enough turbulence in Patty so that she had developed a sort of separation in herself, an alienation, though he would like to avoid the imputation that all this is due to her parents. "Parents ought to have something said for them, too."

"Thank you, Doctor. No further questions. You may cross-examine."

Bailey rises. "Doctor, I notice that since you have come back after lunch, your speech has been accelerated rather markedly. Is there some reason for that?"

"It must be the coffee, Mr. Bailey. It must be the coffee, Mr. Bailey."

"What's that? I didn't hear your answer."

"He said it must be the coffee, Mr. Bailey," Judge Carter says. We are in for a rough afternoon.

Doctor, have you worked with any prisoners of war? Not formally, but I have read a good deal about it by my colleague and old friend Dr. West and the distinguished Dr. Lifton.

Are they recognized authorities on POWs? West, yes; Lifton, no. His people were not POWs; they were people living in China. Some had been in China more than forty years. Are you saying you're discounting all his testimony under oath—of Dr. Lifton? Certainly not! I don't disagree with all he said. But I disagree with much of what he said as it applied to Miss Hearst.

Bailey shows the witness the bibliography on coercive persuasion in the *American Handbook of Psychiatry*. It contains seventy-eight titles, and he asks Kozol if he is familiar with each one. The tactic seems ridiculous. As Bailey drones along I recognize about a third of the writers myself. What does that prove? "Biderman? . . . Farber? . . . Harlow? . . . West? . . . Freud? Grinker? Spiegel? . . ." There is a sudden crash in the jury box as juror no. 7, the aircraft maintenance worker, nodding off asleep, falls out of his chair.

Note the small, Greek arrogance of Lee Bailey's posture, bent right arm braced against the witness box, one foot up on its ledge, heavy-chested, narrow-hipped, fancily suited, probing for guilt like a man with a mine detector. Since Dr. Kozol has no experience with POWs, did he consult with any doctors who *are* familiar with survivor syndrome? No, but my problem was to evaluate a young American civilian convicted of a crime. I am familiar with many children of well-to-do families who got into trouble with the law.

"How many were kidnap victims?"

"Not one."

Kozol says that, like the previous expert witnesses, he would not agree to consult on the case until he himself had examined the defendant.

An honest expert can never go into a case without swearing that, can he, Doctor? I didn't know that. . . . I have no idea what goes on between you and the people whom you hire.

Comes a sudden snarl. "Doctor, do you know a man named Nicholas Groth?"

Calmly: "Yes. This is a man I fired. A clinical psychologist . . . for misbehavior with a patient . . . It was a terrible thing to have to do . . . he sort of looked on me as a father. But like so many fathers, I had a great deal of disappointment with this man. . . ."

You say you fired him. You do not mention the fact that you were overruled for extending your authority and that the firing was revoked.

I was not aware of that until this day. But I told him to resign. I have not discussed his offense, and I hope I don't have to.

I told him I wanted his resignation, or I would have to suspend and discharge him. He refused, so the next morning, I wrote a letter notifying him he was suspended and barred.

Bailey develops and builds the story of Dr. Kozol and his underling Groth for another five minutes, perhaps ten, leading the increasingly agitated witness through interminable false starts and half sentences. Was Dr. Groth working at your facility the day Patricia Hearst was arrested? Yes. I fired him eight days later. Following the arrest, and while the publicity was front-page, did you say to Dr. Groth, "The Hearsts are disgusting and venal. Mrs. Hearst is a whore"?

Never! Please let me complete my answer. I have never met a Hearst, and—

"Did you say to Dr. Groth, 'Mrs. Hearst is a whore'?"

"Ne-e-e-v-er! That is not my language! That is inconceivable and incredible! A misstatement and a lie, in exact keeping with some of the reasons why I had to fire this man."

"Did you say, 'What is she trying to do? Look like Zsa Zsa Gabor? At least Zsa Zsa Gabor makes no pretense—she *admits* she's interested in money!'?"

"No, I didn't. This is too disgusting to discuss."

"Did you say, 'I understand Patty referred to her father as a pig. Well, they *are* pigs!'?"

"No, I didn't . . . oh, dear . . . I don't think I even knew what the word 'pig' meant until I got here. . . .'"

At this moment Harry Kozol reminds one very much of the White Rabbit. Quite possibly he did say this. But so what? Bailey says a recess would be convenient at this time. In the corridor, just outside the door, Al Johnson is waiting. "We have Groth's letter of dismissal," he tells reporters. "Groth went to New York with a couple of inmates to raise money for a film on the horrors of Kozol's institution. Kozol accused him of going for immoral purposes."

The recess ended, Bailey digs in again. How is it that you called her "little girl" in your examination and referred to "Mister Cinque" in your testimony? The White Rabbit twitches his nose, dumbfounded, and his interrogator snaps, "Did you suggest to her she got herself kidnapped?"

"Not in a million years!"

Bailey cross-examines like a Chinese Ping-Pong player, every question delivered with a spin, an edge, a twist, a curve.

From your broad view of the case, Doctor, tell us when you feel that her fear of the SLA and Cinque was dissipated. I think it dissipated gradually. She writes in the "Tania Interview" that they started leaving the closet door open after the first two weeks. I don't have a specific date. Fear doesn't drop off like a mantle. Nonetheless, by the time Patty made the April 3 tape she was "not a prisoner" and was "free to go."

Hearing Dr. Kozol say these words, I realize that this is what I, too, have now come to believe—not from any single bit of testimony but from the drop-by-drop accumulation of the weight of the evidence, even though, bone-weary by now in our eighth week, and coming down with the flu, which last week San Francisco doctors said was epidemic in the city, I cannot clearly remember the train of evidence that brought me to this conclusion.

Under the circumstances, Doctor, "when she knew the voices of these people and had other information about the place of her detainment and where they had picked her up without masks on, do you think it perhaps a reasonable judgment that she would not believe that she could simply walk home so she could get them arrested?"

"That is a little complicated sentence for me to remember."

"If it's too complicated for you, Doctor, I will revise the sentence." One, do you think she was aware that they knew she had seen them? Two, do you think she was aware that they knew she might be able to lead the authorities to their hideout? Three, do you think she was aware they knew she might recognize their voices?

Dr. Kozol believes Patty *was* free to go, just as Cinque said. "I would take the word of that dead black man."

"Despite the fact that he had served time for armed robbery, illegal possession of firearms, participated in the execution of Marcus Foster, kidnapped Patricia Hearst and publicly threatened her execution, and extorted one point eight million dollars out of her family and demanded four million more, and demanded the release of four killers—you would take that black man's word! Is *that* your testimony, Doctor?"

"I would, in respect to the promise that no harm would come to her. Because harm did not come to her. They didn't kill her."

"Is that the proof—that they did not kill her?"

"Well—did they?"

"Doctor, she is sitting in this courtroom today exactly as they planned! You know that, don't you?"

"Exactly as she chose, Mr. Bailey."

"And you say it's just a stroke of coincidence they happened to arrest a victim who was primed and ready for the kind of life they offered? Is that your expert opinion, Dr. Kozol?"

"No. It's stronger than that. It's a tragic misfortune for her that this coincidence took place—"

Now, Doctor, you have described her as a rebellious, bitter girl, ready for action. In other words, she was a bad seed growing. Is that about the size of it, Doctor? I don't use the term "bad" in that sense. Why, I thought you said she was rebellious at the moment of birth! Wasn't that your medical opinion?

Judge Carter warns Bailey against badgering the witness (an offense in law seemingly similar to the combined football violations of being offside and of unnecessary roughness) and reminds him that it's now 4:03 P.M.

Bailey must batter away as long as possible at Dr. Kozol's catchy phrase "rebel without a cause." Doctor, kindly look at these reports and tell me where you find her "rebellious." Was her employment record at Capwell's department store an indication of rebelliousness? No, that was commendable, to be a champion of poor people. You mentioned tape six, her "confession" to the robbery. Have you considered that it was the actions of the U.S. attorney that might have produced that tape? That the day after the robbery, Mr. Browning said perhaps she was a victim, but the next day, when his boss, Mr. Saxbe, said she was a common criminal, "the SLA could help itself by publishing her confession? Did that thought run through your mind, Doctor?"

"No, it didn't, and it still doesn't."

"Does the phrase 'Once freed . . .' in a confession of a supposedly free person have any importance to you, Doctor?"

"Not necessarily," Kozol replies. And he is right. This is the answer I have wanted to hear ever since Bailey first raised the obscure point.

In an abrupt switch worthy of one of his own lectures on cross-examination techniques, Bailey asks the witness if he recalls walking through the metal detector out in the corridor this morning. Yes. Did you recognize the gentleman who was right behind you? No. Do you recall a photographer who took your picture recently for a national magazine? No.

"Stand up, please, Mr. Schiller." The dark, eggplant-shaped man in the audience rises, poker-faced.

"Larry!" Dr. Kozol beams. "Sure, I recognize Larry."

"Did you have a short conversation with him? Did you ask him where his lady friend was this morning? Did he tell you she'd gone to the bank? Did you say to him, 'Too bad she's going to miss my performance'?" Dr. Kozol looks bewildered.

"Thank you, Doctor, that's all."

With this cheap shot, the cross-examination of Harry Kozol is at an end. It is late, already four-nineteen P.M. But more sleazy stuff is to come.

The prosecutor begs for just twenty minutes more, in which to present three brief witnesses. First, Tom Padden returns to confirm that he was the arresting officer and to identify plaintiff's exhibits 176 and 177—the one an object, the other a photograph.

Bailey interrupts. "To save time we will stipulate that the stone object around her neck in the photograph once belonged to Willie Wolfe, now deceased." But the items are produced, and Browning plods ahead. The photograph is a blowup of the SLA group picture recovered from the ashes in Los Angeles. Browning asks Padden where he found no. 176, the stone object? "I got it out of the purse of Patricia Hearst."

"So stipulated," Bailey barks.

The second brief witness is the Los Angeles police sergeant who examined the dead bodies in the ruins of the fire. Browning hands a small object to the police sergeant and asks him to identify it. This was found under the body of Willie Wolfe when the corpse was turned over. At the defense table, Patricia Hearst appears troubled.

"What is it?" Judge Carter asks, peering down.

"I'm sorry, Your Honor. A small figurine." Patricia Hearst takes a deep breath and assumes a queer half smile.

Browning's third brief witness is Clement Meighan, a UCLA professor of anthropology and archaeology, whose work deals with "prehistoric human remains in the New World."

"So stipulated!" Bailey shouts, and then adds, as Browning begins, wormlike, to burrow into the professor's academic qualifications, "We'll waive any foundation."

The professor is frequently called upon to identify a certain category of ancient Mexican artifacts that are plentiful, easy to find, and generally called *monos,* which in English means "monkeys." Exhibits 176 and 178 are *monos.* Now Browning wishes to replay a bit of the SLA's final tape. "One day," Patty's voice says again, "Cujo and I were talking about the way my parents were fucking me over. He said that his parents were still his parents because they had never betrayed him, but my parents were really Malcolm X and Assata Shakur. I'll never betray my parents. The pigs probably have the little old mack [phonetic]* monkey that Cujo wore around his neck. He gave me the little stone face one night. . . ."

BROWNING: Professor, did you hear the voice on that tape saying, "The pigs probably have the little Olmec monkey that Cujo used to wear around his neck"?

MEIGHAN: Olmec is a style named for very early culture in Mexico for a particular class of archaeological artifacts.

CARTER: O-l-m-e-c?

MEIGHAN: Yes, O-l-m-e-c.

*This spelling is from the official FBI transcript of the tape.

These figurines are commonly sold in Mexico as authentic Olmec monkeys, but the professor thinks these two *monos* are both fakes. Poor Patty. Once more, it would seem, somebody has given a Hearst a piece of second-rate, phony old art.

Bailey's cross-examination is a model of brevity. You are from UCLA, Doctor? Yes. You came up here from Los Angeles? Yes. Thank you. No further questions.

Does that conclude the government's case? Yes, the government rests, Your Honor. Then Mr. Bailey may begin his surrebuttal tomorrow morning. Fine. If Your Honor has no objection, may we begin at nine-thirty to *ensure* getting this case over? Yes, if there's no objection by the jurors? A quick, birdlike glance over at the jury box, where the men and women, fourteen see-no-evil Olmec monkeys, now slowly shake their heads.

The corridor buzz-buzz is louder than usual around the U.S. attorney, who is looking slightly pleased with himself. "You know, we didn't get onto that monkey thing until just this very morning," Browning says. But he did, and so the trial of Patricia Hearst has wound up with a Perry Mason flourish, after all.

Tuesday, March 16

This morning my worst fears are confirmed. I awaken with fever, earache, headache, eye ache, total flu. I telephone the only doctor I can think of, and Jolly says not to worry about finding a druggist, he'll bring me some stuff himself, and he is waiting, paper sack in hand, when I step out of the courthouse elevator. He has three different things to swallow, each at a different interval, and precise, typewritten instructions are attached to each. I get them all down just as the bailiff bangs his gavel.

The jury is not present. Bailey is still trying to shoehorn Margaret Singer into this trial. This morning he has filed a brief citing as a precedent some twenty-year-old law-review articles on psycholinguistics, and an expert from the University of Michigan is now en route to San Francisco to testify. "I am sorry the brief could not be here sooner, but we have had perhaps the three brightest students at Stanford Law School working on it all weekend." Why they were not working on it three months ago is not asked. Bailey has also subpoenaed the records of the American Psychiatric Association, in an attempt to prove that Dr. Fort did not resign over policy but was kicked out for nonpayment of dues.

"Excuse me, Judge, but Mr. Bailey is trying to make up for a deficiency in his cross-examination."

"Mr. Bancroft, will you look at what the record says!" Bailey snaps.

"Would *you* address your questions to the court!" Bancroft snarls. Seasoned reporters are offended by the unseemly wrangling. "You are listening to the government of the United States unravel here," one says. "These guys are going at each other like hired guns. Compared to this, Leonard Boudin in the Ellsberg case sounded like Adlai Stevenson!"

Bailey's next couple of witnesses, a private detective and a lawyer employed thirteen years ago by the late Lenny Bruce, do nothing to elevate the tone of things. Bruce was attempting to overturn a Los Angeles conviction for narcotics possession, and he became frightened that these two men might quit the case when they saw so much drug paraphernalia at Bruce's home, even though the medication—Methedrine—was entirely legal. To prove the drugs were legit, Bruce put the private eye on the telephone with the doctor who had signed one of the prescriptions, a certain Joel Fort. "This guy's a real ball-buster," Bruce had told the detective. "He really knows how to fuck up psychiatrists in court." Cross-examining, Browning swiftly brings out that Bruce's conviction *was* reversed on appeal, thanks in large part to the helpful testimony of Dr. Fort.

As for the legal eagle, now a prospering Miami real-estate lawyer, he was a bright kid just out of law school thirteen years ago and a whiz at constitutional law. Seeking advice on the constitutional implications of his conviction, Bruce flew him to Los Angeles for two weeks of day-and-night consultations, during which time Bruce lived in a variety of motels, apartments, crash pads. Browning objects that Mr. Bruce is dead. What is the relevance of where he lived? Browning is right; the defense has taken on a necrotic stink.

"The prescriptions in his home [were] signed by Joel Fort," says the obsessed Bailey, and the objection is overruled. Bailey is smiling, red-faced, charging ahead, the $10,000-bill suit once more earning its fee. One morning the witness went to Bruce's motel and found his room a shambles—bloodstains on the walls and mirrors, drugs in the wastebasket, a woman in the bed. Bruce got out of the bed and stood naked with a bottle of drugs in one hand and three or four prescriptions in the other. As long as he was able to get drugs and prescriptions from Dr. Fort, he said, he could keep going and have a great time.

At this testimony, I feel my own heart lift. Surely now Patty will go free. Even though I think Fort and Kozol's interpretation of what happened was probably largely correct, I do not want Patty convicted, and the image linking Dr. Fort to Bruce's motel room must be very damaging in the jurors' minds.

"What was that drug in the vial, if you know, sir, on which you saw Dr. Fort's name?" Browning asks.

I never saw the name. He told me it was Dilaudid, and he said Dr. Fort had given it to him.

In other words, you cannot establish that Lenny Bruce was not just using Dr. Fort's name, as an excuse, to legitimatize the presence and possession of drugs? No. Now, through your law-school training, are you familiar with something called the attorney-client privilege? Yes, and even though Mr. Bruce is dead, I consider it an ongoing privilege.

"Sir, was possession of Dilaudid a crime in California when you saw Dilaudid in Mr. Bruce's house?"

"He didn't testify to that," Bailey says. He said only that he saw prescriptions. . . .

It is recess before I recognize that West's three prescriptions have worked on me with magical effect. I feel incomparably better. Jolly smiles tenderly.

Fifteen years ago, in the San Francisco Public Health Service, the next witness, James Stubblebine, MD, was Joel Fort's boss. He testifies that Fort, contrary to his own claim, did not start the Center for Special Problems, later known as Forthelp. He adds that Fort was fired from his public-health job and produces the "termination letter" signed by his own superior. This contest, one feels, is sinking lower and lower.

Browning accuses the defense of "the worst case of bootstrapping I have ever seen. . . . This trial is moving into a barrage of collateral matters; I don't know where they're going to end." But Carter allows Stubblebine to continue. Then I notice the tall girl standing at the back of the courtroom. She is large, healthy, blond, and tan, a perfect specimen of the genus *California Girl.* She and Patty smile radiantly at each other across a distance of fifty feet.

"Dr. Stubblebine, are you familiar with Joel Fort's reputation for truth and veracity in the medical community?"

"Yes. He is untrustworthy and not to be believed."

Browning has no questions, and the witness is excused. Before calling his next witness, Bailey prepares to read the "termination letter" aloud. Browning objects to the "publication" of this evidence before the jury, since he has not been permitted similarly to "publish" the Trish Tobin jail tape.

"She's the next witness, so you'll get your chance."

"Great!" Browning exclaims, and now the California Girl in rose-tinted glasses and flower-sprigged frock ascends the witness stand and settles herself with a shake of her shiny yellow hair. A spritz of Binaca, and Al Johnson is at her side. Miss Tobin lives at home, does she not? Yes, with her parents, Michael Henry DeYoung Tobin and Sarah Fay Tobin. To a San Franciscan, these are Founding Father names, Bay Area equivalents to Washington, Jefferson, Adams. Trish Tobin represents the fifth generation of an already prosperous Irish family who arrived in San Francisco via Chile in the nineteenth century, founded the Hibernia Bank, and ever since have been diligently stockpiling wealth and piety while simultaneously trying to prove themselves "nice people" and "not rich." I recall being at lunch with Trish's parents on the Sunday morning that Mrs. Martin Luther King, Sr., was shot in church. At the news, Trish's father looked up from his corn on the cob and remarked, with the sort of wit that daily sets ice cubes atinkle at the Burlingame Country Club, "Some places in this country, it isn't even safe to go to church anymore."

Patricia Cooper Tobin and Patricia Campbell Hearst met at the Burlingame Country Club "in the summer after fourth grade." Would you describe yourself as being her best friend? "Yes, I would," says Trish, with a melting smile. What was her relationship to other members of her family? She had a very warm relationship with them. What were the defendant's political views? We never discussed politics. What were her views on revolutionary matters? Feminist matters? Radical matters? We never discussed any of those things. Trish maintains that her best friend has *no* views, on anything, which *is* the authentic Hillsborough point of view.

What was her friend like on the day after her arrest, when they talked on the jailhouse phones? Patty had no animation or vitality; she just droned along and sighed a lot. She looked terrible and "seemed really dazed." At times she didn't seem to understand what I was saying, and I couldn't follow her. I had no idea we were being taped, but I said to the deputy as I was leaving, "I guess you taped us, huh?" He said, "No, the tape machine was broken." But later Dr. West had played the tape for her, and their conversation had been edited, of that she is certain. Trish felt Patty spoke in a very "canned" sort of way, "as if her mind wasn't in it." She never heard Patty say anything like the words "revolutionary feminist perspective." But she does recall Patty saying other things that are not on the tape, for example, a comment about the SLA that "these people are so *crazy* or *weird.* . . . "

Trish is trying too hard to help her friend; her testimony sounds overblown. One wonders who "prepared" Trish, and why the decision was made to put her on the stand. The bond between Trish and Patty is clearly one of utter loyalty, but it is girlish and mindless, the loyalty of midnight marshmallow roasts. I believe scarcely a word of her testimony, but I do respond to her sincerity. Trish believes she is acting according to a "higher" integrity than whatever forces may be at work here, and on that point I think she is probably right.

"Now, Miss Tobin, if I told you that yesterday Dr. Kozol indicated that, prior to her kidnapping, Miss Hearst was a rebel looking for a cause, how would you describe his comment?"

"As totally false."

"Thank you." With a nod to Browning: "You may cross-examine."

Why did Trish resist talking to the FBI soon after the bank robbery? I didn't feel I had any more to say to them. Trish is assured and aglow with the naive arrogance of her class. She is a lot like the circle-pinned, beaver-coated, long-legged girls who had terrified me so at Vassar back in the 1940s. (Later, when Mary McCarthy published *The Group,* I had met my classmates' older sisters.) Now here is one of their daughters on the witness stand. The witness wears the impenetrable and utterly controlled mask of Hillsborough. Here sits the girl Patricia Hearst would have been if the SLA hadn't kidnapped her. Looking at her, I prefer the injured Patty to this snippy, smart-ass girl. She has a ladylike invulnerability that makes me want to smack her in the perfect white teeth. Al Johnson smiles a tiny, wicked smile. She is just the sort of girl Al Johnson would think of as Real Class. I would dislike her more were it not for the twinkling good humor, barely suppressed even now. Trish would be a splendid companion in a practical joke; her high spirits are her best feature.

You told Patty Hearst you wished you were a lawyer so you could represent her, didn't you? Agreeing, the witness dissolves into attractive giggles, and the judge smiles. Trish had attended Patty's arraignment and bail hearing in disguise, under an assumed name. All during the Missing Year, she maintained a special post-office-box letter drop on the chance her best friend might want to reach her. Her testimony has overtones of girls' adventure books; Patty and Trish could be characters in a mystery.

We await the bailiff to announce the afternoon session. Over lunch, Theo Wilson and Linda Deutsch of the Associated Press toted up the list of people Patty will be accused of selling out so far in this trial—seventeen names. Schiller boasted of personally having dredged up the raw materials for the Lenny Bruce testimony. "I pulled it all out of my old files in Bekins Storage," he says, proud as Jack Horner. Bailey has vowed to discredit Joel Fort for all time, "so he can never appear in court again." He will continue to pour on the hostile witnesses until the judge cuts him off. Looking up at the big United States seal over Carter's head, the furious eagle of the Republic positioned like the sword of Damocles, I realize Schiller is right. Bailey is obsessed. He will hang in there and squeeze until the eagle screams and the seal barks. At the defense table, Patty is laughing, showing big dimples, and pouring water from a thermos jug as if it were Bacchic wine.

Then the jury returns, the joking stops, and Patty's best friend resumes the stand. The government is now ready to play the Trish Tobin tape for the jury. In that case, Johnson says again, he wants to play a tape of an early conversation between Patty and Dr. West, but Carter again defers that decision.

On the Tobin tape, Patty sounds drugged. The judge cannot understand her. The tape player is faulty again. Repair the machine, Carter orders, and meanwhile, work from the transcript. Browning reads it aloud. The dialogue sounds almost subliterate. "I'll tell you that, well, God, once I get out of here, I'll be able to tell you like all kinds of stories that you just wouldn't even believe, man. [Laughter.]" Had Patty ever refused on the tape to talk about Emily? No.

When Patty said, "I guess I'll just tell you like my politics are real different from, uh, way back when . . . so this creates all kinds of problems for me in terms of my defense . . ." Trish replied, "Right!" and later, "Yeah, it does. . . . That's the thing."

"What did you really mean by that?" Browning asks.

"It was just something to say."

On redirect, Johnson asks why Trish didn't go to the FBI when she became suspicious the jail tape had been doctored. She assumed they had doctored it.

The double doors behind us swing wide, and Bailey and Henry Gonzales stride purposefully down the aisle with their next witness, a tan, compact man in blue suit and gray sideburns who turns out to have been yet another attorney in the proceedings against Lenny Bruce. Joel Fort had also advised this lawyer on how to question psychiatrists, and he, too, had seen drugs at Bruce's homes in Los Angeles and Miami with prescription labels bearing Joel Fort's name.

What a cheesy processional this has all become! The next witness is the anguished-looking Dr. Groth, of whom we heard in the Kozol testimony; he is now chief psychologist, Department of Legal Medicine, State of Massachusetts. He has dark hair and a pale, angular face. The week before he was fired, Groth relates, he dropped in on Dr. Kozol and saw a newspaper with Patty's picture lying in his office. Kozol had said, "The Hearsts are venal and disgusting. Mrs. Hearst is a whore. At least Zsa Zsa admits what she is!" Kozol had recently watched Zsa Zsa on a TV talk show, and when a fellow guest admitted he was rich, Zsa Zsa said, "You should have told me before I married my current husband, dollink. I would have married you instead!" Kozol told Groth, "If you had grown up in a family like Patricia's, you would know what she is rebelling against. They are pigs."

The incident occurred before Groth knew he was to be dismissed. The provocation for that was a trip to New York City to appear on a television program about rape. At NBC's request, Groth brought a convicted rapist and his wife to the studio to talk about it. He returned to Massachusetts and Kozol fired him.

When Groth heard on his car radio that Patty Hearst had been brought to the edge of hysteria by a government psychiatrist—in fact, Harry Kozol—he presented himself at Bailey's Boston office. He is here now under subpoena, and has been in town for two weeks, a secret witness, waiting under wraps to destroy the government's expert.

But one does not feel the full story has come out yet. Groth describes his personal relationship with Kozol as one of mutual respect and love. "Professionally, we disagree." As to Kozol's professional manner, says Groth, the sad truth is that his behavior with patients was at times so accusatory and demeaning it amounted to harassment. The witness is receiving no fees for his testimony, although the defense is recompensing him for the salary he loses by being away from his post.

Browning's cross-examination is brisk. Is it fair to say you feel you were treated unfairly by Dr. Kozol? Yes. The witness seems tense, with a new tightness to his voice, and Kozol looks equally unhappy. Perhaps

(443)

the younger man was once a kind of son substitute for the rebellious Jonathan.

In any event, one is grateful when this sad, edgy confrontation ends, and surprised by Bailey's next change-up. "Call Mr. Hearst, please!"

What a relief, after all these little fish, to see Big Randy stand up and glide serenely over to the witness box. Patty's father has lost fifteen or twenty pounds during the trial. He is Ray Milland in horn-rims. Did you see much of your daughter before the kidnapping? "Oh, sure," he says, in his giggly, Ed Wynn voice. We often had lunch alone together. What kind of girl is she? "A very bright girl. Pretty. Strong-willed and fun to be with—*I* think."

A girl could not ask for a more devoted and sincere and adoring father. Randolph Hearst in the witness box appears relaxed, easygoing, *nice.* Yes, Joel Fort had come to the Hearsts' apartment to ask questions about their daughter, as had the other psychiatrists, and, yes, he said that a public trial would be very bad for Patty, that she was pretty run-down and depressed, and that the adversary system was bad. He suggested I inform myself about plea-bargaining, though I don't think he used that word.

In cross-examination, Browning asks, "Was it your impression, sir, that Dr. Fort was trying to fix the case?"

"I wouldn't say he was trying to fix it."

Bailey's next surprising witness is J. Albert Johnson himself. Blushing, Al climbs into the witness box and affirms that he has been here in San Francisco most of the time since Patty's arrest. The law partners maintain their dog-and-master good humor even on the witness stand. But *why* has Bailey put his partner on at all? To my surprise, he is still gnawing away at the Fort bone. The fat man explains that early on, Dr. Fort came around and told Bailey and Johnson he had grave doubts about whether he would testify for the government, in which case he would be available to them. The next thing Johnson knew, Fort had proposed to Catherine Hearst that she get Coblentz to try to stop the trial.

Perhaps *this* is the fulcrum of Bailey's fury. It had been inconceivable to Bailey, from the beginning, *not* to try this case, just as it had been inconceivable to the Hearsts not to seek vindication of their good name. If the Hearsts had not wanted a big public trial, would they have hired F. Lee Bailey? Perhaps they would. Nobody has ever accused a Hearst of foresight, probity, or a sense of the consequences of one's acts. In its striking lack of just these characteristics, the Hearst clan is peculiarly

American. Perhaps in the special moral numbness that is the family heritage, further cocooned by Hillsborough, nurturing their good name, lusting after good taste, and living quietly in the perpetual haze of country-club life, they could envisage nothing but a razzle-dazzle, Fourth of July, Bailey-style defense. Then along comes this oddball Joel Fort with a crazy plan to avoid the very trial the family, the Hearst Corporation, and the American public have been gearing up to for two whole years! Fort's off-the-wall proposal to avoid a trial, cop a plea, turn state's evidence, or plead guilty and throw herself on the mercy of the court would also have deprived a man widely regarded as America's greatest criminal lawyer of the capstone of his career. Bailey was at, or almost at, the pinnacle of success. He had achieved an eminence so high it would soon provide sufficient time and money and fame for the first time in his tumultuous, striving, world-beating life to relax, to reflect, and to write the Big Book, the courtroom novel about two titans of law locked in mortal courtroom combat. No wonder F. Lee Bailey hated Joel Fort. The wonder was how deep the hatred became.

Johnson says Harry Kozol visited Patricia Hearst three times, and each time, she ran from the room sobbing and trembling. On the third occasion she was in a state of near collapse. The night before, Dr. Fort had advised Johnson that in *his* medical opinion Patty's physical and mental condition was so poor she could not be examined the next morning by anybody. In view of all this, Johnson told Kozol that he found his persistence deplorable—more like an inquisitor than a psychiatrist. Kozol replied that he was the better judge of Patty's mental state, that he intended to continue with his examination and had a court order to do so.

Bailey may hate Fort, but he is still willing to use the medical opinion of his enemy if it will impugn the medical competence of Harry Kozol. All's fair in love and law.

Cross-examining, Browning asks what Dr. West's fee is. Nothing. Zero. Who is picking up the tab at the Stanford Court, Mr. Johnson? I don't think it's been paid yet, but *I* intend to pay it. From his seat, Bailey says, "All right, Mr. Browning, I will stipulate that *I* intend to pay it. . . ."

"And if Mr. Bailey doesn't pay, I will!" Johnson repeats.

The level of euphemism in all this is growing thicker than the Stanford Court's carpets, wider than its canopied double beds, higher than its prices—already the highest in San Francisco. A two-room suite at the Stanford Court, such as the Baileys, Johnson, and each of the psychiatrists occupies, costs over $150 a night. Lodging, food, and drink for the high-living defense entourage cost the Hearst Corporation well over $200,000 by the end of the trial.

On redirect, Bailey and Johnson plow the thrice-plowed ground once more. On the evening of January 6, when Fort told Johnson it was a shame Miss Hearst had to face trial, and wondered if there weren't some other way the matter could be resolved, what had Johnson replied? "That I had asked Mr. Browning a number of times to dismiss the indictment, as they knew she was absolutely innocent."

"What a bunch of self-serving claptrap!" Browning shouts.

Your Dr. Fort opened the door, Mr. Browning, Bailey says. When Carter finally restores legal order, Bailey asks meekly, "May Mr. Johnson be excused, Your Honor?" Blushing like the half choirboy, half con man that he is, Zombo steps gently off the stand.

Carter promises this case will be wrapped up tomorrow morning. After that, there will be no more witnesses. His assurance is welcome news. Bailey's attack on Joel Fort recalls the Los Angeles Police Department's response to the SLA—total, hysterical overkill. For more than a week the defense of Patricia Hearst has been diverted and subverted into an all-out personal assault, a legal firefight, a ruthless search-and-destroy mission into the background and character of one little man. And it isn't over yet.

Wednesday, March 17

Green suits, green shirts, green ties, even green baseball jackets—it is the densest array of green haberdashery I've seen anywhere, Third Avenue bars included. I didn't think I knew a man who owned a green suit, but a half dozen of them are visible in this courtroom this St. Patrick's Day morning. All eight federal marshals are clothed at least partly in green; Al Johnson wears total green—suit, shirt, and tie; so do Gene Driscoll, the court clerk, and Tom Padden. Bailey wears his $10,000-bill suit and a neon-green silk tie. Bailey's boys all sport the green silks, even Henry Gonzales, the Florida lawyer who looks like a Mexican heavy in a B Western. Browning wears a conservative green-plaid tie. The three black newsmen, the only sharp dressers in our generally frowsy press corps, wear funky green; a green-enamel shamrock floats on Catherine Hearst's full-sail bosom; and white-faced Patty sweeps in wearing a sea-green blouse. The gavel raps, we rise; Judge Carter has a green shirt and tie beneath his robes. Surely this green explosion is as much in celebration of the end of the grueling trial as it is of Ireland's saint.

The jury is brought in, and Bailey calls his last witness. Catherine Hearst, wearing a close-fitting pigeon-brown dress and pink scarf, walks very slowly to the witness box. What kind of girl was Patricia? Catherine flashes the Double-Mint smile. "A very warm and loving girl."

Was she sometimes strong-willed?

"She was. I wouldn't want anything I say make you think it is an easy job to raise five children, Mr. Bailey." Catherine says Dr. Fort told her that if Patty pleaded guilty, the worst sentence she could get as a kidnapping victim would be six months' probation. "The trouble is that Bailey likes to try cases," Fort had said, "and Browning wants to be a federal judge, and everybody has forgotten about Patty in the process." Fort told Mrs. Hearst the government would besmirch Patty's character and do everything it could to damage her reputation, including presenting evidence on sex and drugs. "They would say things that were very harmful to our family."

Our family. That is what it all seems to come down to in Catherine's mind. If our family must be protected at all costs, then Patty must shed her "bad girl" image; she must have been brainwashed if the honor of our family is to be preserved. But if our family must be protected, even at the cost of one's daughter, then Patty has lost, whatever the verdict.

Did Patty have a close relationship with her sister Catherine, despite what Dr. Kozol said here yesterday? Yes, very close. How were the family's relations with the FBI? In the beginning, special agent in charge Bates made daily visits. But the FBI never really told the Hearsts much. At one time, did they bring you a garment to be identified? Catherine's voice begins to shake. Yes, the blue bathrobe in which Patty was kidnapped. They found it in the Golden Gate apartment.

So the case is ending as the drama began, wrapped in folds of Madonna blue. I raise my borrowed opera glasses to check out Patty, and discover I am shaking, too. But I cannot see her at all. She is entirely hidden behind John McNally's massive bulk.

Cross-examination is brisk. Mrs. Hearst, did I ever tell you I wanted to be a federal judge? "Mr. Browning, I am an Establishment person. I think it's a very laudible ambition if you *do* want to be a federal judge." McNally tilts his chair backward, roaring with laughter, and Patty comes into view, smiling wanly.

Catherine testifies that William Coblentz advised her that trying to stop the trial would be a bad mistake. The U.S. attorney's office "would give it to the newspapers, and it would look as if we were trying to fix the case."

Does Mrs. Hearst interpret the word "fix" to mean that money changes hands? No, she thinks of it more as something like plea-bargaining.

"You equate plea-bargaining with the word 'fix'!" The U.S. attorney is understandably appalled. Plea-bargaining is a large part of what his office does.

"Well, I don't know exactly what you mean," says Catherine, backing off. But the jurors are not very attentive to her testimony anyhow; this is the *mother*, after all. Bailey's use of her at all seems bizarre. Is he trying to wind up his show with a mom-image front and center, or is Catherine there at her own request?

In a brief, savage redirect, Bailey asks, Mrs. Hearst, in January did you learn that all your conversations with your daughter over the past three or four months had been secretly recorded and delivered to the United States attorney? Yes. Thank you, no further questions.

It is time to play the Trish Tobin tape. Incredibly, the sound equipment is still faulty, and the first sentences are barely intelligible. But Patty's vagueness and confusion come through. Listening to the girlish voices, one feels disgust at the government snooping and dismay at the puerile level of the conversation. Their girl-talk is so minimally articulate, we might be listening to a conversation between a couple of what the psychiatrists have referred to as "feebs." But it's just authentic Hillsborough teenager lingo; one had forgotten how vapid it could sound.

The jurors have heard about this tape for days. Now they listen intently as the girlish voices fill the stone-quiet courtroom.

"How's Hallinan?" Trish asks.

"He's good. Like I really trust him politically, and personally, and he, like, I can tell him just about anything I want, and he's cool."

Patty does not sound afraid of Emily when she talks about her. When she mentions reading one of the Pattypoop books, she seems to be enjoying her own celebrity. The torrents of crudities are as shocking as anything we'd heard on the SLA tapes. Glen Robinson and Janey Jimenez, the two marshals who are Patty's special partisans, look grim. Trish assures Patty that her father, the bank president, will forgive the robbery: "Fuck the ten thousand dollars! We don't give a shit about the ten thousand dollars!" Patty's and Al Johnson's eyes are downcast. The longshoreman language is a severe blow to the classy image of the girls that the defense has tried to project.

One detects something else in this conversation, too. Patty appears to be waiting or looking for someone. Is it someone she loves or someone she fears? She asks Trish repeatedly who else is waiting to see her. Who else had been in court during her arraignment?

"Who else is out there? . . . No other visitors? How come?"

" 'Cause we were allowed, and your parents were gonna come, and they decided not to, and I tried to see you this morning, and they wouldn't let me."

"Right . . . So they turned away all the other visitors?"

"They've come and gone. It's past visiting hours."

"No, I mean to see me. Is there anybody else out there?"

"Well . . . well, they . . . see, if you call, they say that you have to be family, at the moment, except for during visiting hours, and—"

"This is visiting hours?"

"This is not visiting hours now. It's over."

"Oh. They don't let us [Patty and Emily] visit during visiting hours. Yeah, they keep us [garbled]. They're really doing a trip. I mean . . . they keep us isolated from everyone. They say that we're gonna get stabbed. [Giggles.] That's probably about the last thing . . . You should *say* that when you go out 'cause there's press out there, right? You should say that that's what they're doing, and that, you know, like, they keep us isolated from everyone and, like, they don't let anyone say anything to us, like . . ."

"Who's in here? Just you and Emily?"

"Yeah. Right. We're, uh, we're in isolation, and then everyone else is like in dorms, out back in the rear."

"Yeah. Yeah, 'cause like the way it is, if you're like in maximum . . . They say that everyone's visitors come, and then yours come. So if someone came here at eleven, uh, uh, they have to wait until the whole crowd cruises through, and then they come, so that's like it's three o'clock."

"Yeah. Umkay. Uh . . . also, could you, like, umm, did you notice anybody in court that you like knew, or had seen before, other than like Cecil Williams [*] . . . that kind of thing?"

It sounds to me as if, two days after her arrest, Patricia is still hoping for armed rescue, still hoping someone will storm the San Mateo County Jail, just as the SLA had planned and dreamed so long of storming San Quentin to rescue Remiro and Little; just as Jonathan Jackson had stormed the Marin County Courthouse to rescue his brother George. Poor, pitiful Patty. If this is so, it means she is still militant and also still crazy, still fearful, still entirely alone. No one will come, no one will ever come, no one but her mother bringing fresh flowers and clean underwear, and Al Johnson in his bus-driver suits, with his jokes and his baby talk and his other talk about how she's gonna have to dump it all out . . . dump it all out.

At twelve-twelve P.M. the tape ends. The evidence is now finally closed, Carter says, and we shall recess for the day. Final arguments are to begin the next morning, and the following morning, Friday, he will instruct the jury in the law. They will then retire, and their deliberations will take place in the judge's robing room, directly behind the Great Seal of the United States that hangs over his head. These last weeks, the giant disk has seemed to loom ever larger and lower while the courtroom itself has been growing smaller—Poe's nightmare image of pit and pendulum squeezing down inexorably upon us all.

Thursday, March 18

"A couple of cons got out of the bucket last night," Ted Kleines whispers as we take our seats. "Any *more* death threats, they'll have to lock up this whole place!"

Patty is back in the navy blue with a white bow at the throat. Her skin is bone-white; you can see the skull beneath. The jury files in. It is nine thirty-five A.M. when Judge Carter begins to speak. "All traffic

*The activist black pastor of the Glide Memorial Church, who was one of the people with close ties to the Left through whom Randolph Hearst had tried to make contact with the SLA.

in and out of the courtroom during the closing arguments will be stopped. . . . Anyone who desires to leave may leave at this time. If not, we are going to lock the doors and start."* Federal marshals with guns and keys at their belts turn the bolts, and the courtroom is "locked down," making us the judicial counterpart of San Quentin, across the Bay.

Browning's suit is wrinkled, his nose is red, he looks awful; the flu epidemic has hit him, too. Bailey, by contrast, is animated and well pressed in dignified dark blue. A new podium and microphone have been placed directly in front of and only a few feet from the jury box. Carter swivels to face it and speaks in his patient jury voice, as one would address a small child. Fourteen deadpan faces stare back, solemn as stone.

Ladies and gentlemen, arguments are a time-honored process, so you will understand—in the adversary system—the opposition views of the case. Out of that process usually develops truth. Counsel are skilled in this process, and you should give careful attention to their arguments.

Mr. Browning, on behalf of the United States, will make the opening argument. Mr. Bailey will make his one defense argument, and then there will be the closing argument of the United States by Mr. Browning, who knows that he must make a rebuttal argument only. I do not believe in the practice of laying back in closing arguments and sandbagging. Mr. Browning, you may proceed.

Sniffling slightly, the U.S. attorney steps up to the special podium. One does not expect much.

Judge Carter, counsel, ladies and gentlemen, I don't mean to insult your intelligence by reviewing things you already know, but I would be remiss in my duty if I did not mention that you can take any evidence into the jury room, and I urge you to do so.

Ladies and gentlemen, we expect that Judge Carter will instruct you as to the elements of the crime of bank robbery. Essentially, there are four: One, the United States must prove that somebody took some money from a bank. Two, this was accomplished by means of force, violence, or

---

*HERNAP makes minor legal history again! Judges sometimes lock the courtroom while charging the jury, but so far as anyone around San Francisco can recall, no judge ever before has forced press and public, as well as jurors, to listen to what opposing counsel have to say in summation.

intimidation. Three, it was accomplished by an assault or by the use of a dangerous weapon. Fourth, that the acts have been done willfully. There is no dispute in this case with respect to the first two elements.

As to the third element, there has been some question raised as to the operability of the defendant's weapon. We do not concede it was inoperable, but aiding and abetting others would be enough, under federal law. So the sole question it boils down to is whether the defendant was in that bank voluntarily and whether she acted willfully with criminal intent.

The burden is on the government to prove the case beyond a reasonable doubt. A reasonable doubt is a doubt based on reason. It is not a possible doubt.

Carter looks quiet, thoughtful, alert, and, yes, judicious.

In judging this case, consider the evidence: motion pictures made in the bank, documents in her own handwriting.

Browning's own hand is very nervous. He cannot find the proper documents. Neither can his FBI aide, Park Stearns. But, then, for nineteen and a half months they couldn't find Patty. Ah, here we are.

Exhibit 63/96, part of the "Tania Interview": "Why did you decide to rob a bank?" And in the defendant's own handwriting we have the words "There were two reasons. We needed the money, and we wanted to illustrate that TA [Tania] was alive, and her decision wasn't a bunch of bullshit." On the next page, the handwritten text of the defendant. "We didn't go into the bank with the intention of shooting someone. That would be crazy. But we also expected people to cooperate with us and not freak out."

So you have, in addition to the movies, the defendant's handwritten account. [And] you have her voice on tape stating that she and her comrades expropriated—I believe that was the word she used—over $10,000 from this bank and that the idea of her having been brainwashed is ridiculous.

Rarely has so much evidence of apparent intent been available to a jury. But in addition to the evidence of apparent voluntariness and intent, I want to talk about some of the testimony of the witnesses and some of the circumstantial evidence. . . .

Let me reconstruct what I believe happened. Mr. Norton went in that bank first. Berzins entered almost at the same time as the robbers. He lets this front door fly, the five bank robbers almost at his heels. The defendant collided with that front door and dropped some bullets and some clips. Nancy Ling Perry came around the defendant, who was down on one knee gathering up her clips and her bullets, and confronted Zigurd Berzins in the entryway, "eyeball to eyeball," right here, at point one. So whom did Mr. Norton at this time see in the area of the rapid deposit? It wasn't Cinque. Mr. Norton could have told a man from a woman, a male from a female voice. Soltysik did not have a carbine; she had a handgun. Camilla Hall had a shotgun. Nancy Ling Perry was the one confronting Mr. Berzins. Who does that leave, ladies and gentlemen? It leaves the defendant, Patricia Hearst.

Bailey and Johnson take no notes, but watch the jury intently.

Now, let me comment on the film itself. The more you see that film, the more things you see in that film. You will see the defendant appear to glance at her watch. She immediately swings her weapon. She does not look over to Mr. DeFreeze or Camilla Hall, to see whether she should swing it. You see her mouth open. She may have yelled an order to those customers—"Come in!" or "Get down!"—just before Nancy Ling Perry fired the shots. There is no evidence any of the other four were holding a weapon on Patricia Hearst. It is possible to make this interpretation, but only out of context. In context, it is impossible. If they had intended Camilla Hall to cover the defendant, with her shotgun, she might well have wounded DeFreeze or Perry, due to the spray effect of the shotgun pellets.

But the evidence, ladies and gentlemen, does not depend only upon the witnesses and upon the film to establish the defendant's intent. You must also consider three other broad categories . . . circumstantial evidence, psychiatric testimony, and the credibility of the defendant.

In dealing with intent, we can't unscrew the top of a person's head and look in. You cannot take the person's word. There is too great a motivation to lie, if it means being convicted of a criminal offense. So we have to look at extrinsic factors. There is just no direct evidence that proves intent because there is no way of fathoming or scrutinizing the operations of a human mind. But you may infer intent from surrounding circumstances. Incidentally, the law makes no distinction, despite what laymen think, between direct evidence and circumstantial evidence. It is what convinces you, ladies and gentlemen, whether circumstantial or direct, that is important.

(453)

The most crucial segment of circumstantial evidence is the events at Mel's Sporting Goods store and the following day and night. Why? Well, first of all, I suggest that it is reasonable to believe that a person who is in fear of being killed by her captors does not, when confronted with an opportunity to escape from the captors, fire weapons in the direction of other persons in order to free the captors and does not fail to try to escape, given an opportunity. If the defendant had been aiming at the top of the building, as she said, is it likely that the bullet holes would be in the divider? If a gun bucks at all, it bucks upward, not downward. I suggest the evidence shows that she aimed directly at Mr. Shepard and the others that she saw, and it's only by the grace of God that others were not killed. She attempts to explain this by telling us that it was a sort of reflex action. If that is true, ladies and gentlemen, there were three reflex actions. The first had to be when she picked up the gun, and then it fell out of her hand. So the second reflex action is when she picked it up and started firing again. The third reflex action is when she exhausted the bullets in that weapon, put that weapon down, picked up a second weapon, and fired several shots out of that. Can you, as reasonable people, accept the story that they forced her to rob that bank when, one month later, she is spraying this area with machine-gun fire in order to free the very people she claims forced her to rob the bank? Finally, don't forget that the defendant told Tom Matthews that very same afternoon that it gave her "a good feeling" to see her comrades come running across the street.

Other items of circumstantial evidence would include the words "Patria o Muerte," written on the wall of the Golden Gate apartment in the defendant's handwriting. As I understand her testimony, they did not make her write it on the wall. They also trusted her enough to stand guard duty with a loaded weapon. Is it reasonable that the captors would entrust their safety to their hostage?

You can say, I suppose, the defendant simply put on a good act. Where does a good act leave off and voluntary participation begin? Consider the fact that after the bank robbery they all counted the money. And they split it up nine ways. If you, as a reasonable person, heard that a person in a bank with a weapon had helped count the money and had received an equal cut thereof, would you conclude that it's reasonable to believe that that person participated willfully? I submit that you most certainly would. So there again is an item of circumstantial evidence for you to consider.

Fourthly, I want to mention to you the concept of flight. Flight is a very old concept in American jurisprudence and in English common law, almost as old as the law itself, and it holds simply that a guilty person usually flees. Flight tends to indicate a consciousness of guilt. So does concealment of a defendant after a crime that is a fact. Here we have a defendant who was missing for some seventeen months after the bank robbery. You might say she didn't call us; we called her. She didn't turn herself in. And you may consider that she had opportunities to escape or at least to get some word back to the authorities; she did not do it.

Browning reads a segment of Tom Matthews' testimony. Al Johnson's eyes never leave the jurors' faces.

Now, you may recall that Mr. Matthews also testified that he and the defendant were alone in that van for almost a minute without the Harrises, and yet the defendant not only didn't say, I want to get out of here, she didn't even say, Look, these things I have been telling you I have been forced to say. Get word to my parents, get word to the FBI, get word to somebody. Is it reasonable, ladies and gentlemen, to believe that a person must recite a confession of that type due to fear, and yet not say anything to contradict it when you're alone with another kidnap victim? The defendant tells us that she was in great fear of the FBI during this period of time, but she did not substantially acquire any fear of the FBI, even by her own account, until she saw the shoot-out and fire on television.

Then we have another matter I think you should consider, and that is the confrontation between Tony Shepard and the Harrises and, I submit, the defendant, on Glen Ellen Drive. Admittedly, Mr. Shepard's identification of that person was very poor. I think we have to bear in mind that he'd been wrestled with, shot at, been in a wild chase, and now he's being confronted with a person carrying an automatic weapon at port arms. It's not too surprising that he didn't get a very good look at this person because he wanted to get out of there as quickly as he could. But he does know that it was not William Harris, that it was not Emily Harris, and there wasn't anybody else present!

I suggested to you earlier that the operability of a weapon bears upon her intent. I want to come back to that.

Browning steps over to Gene Driscoll, who hands him the carbine with its flapping tag.

If the defendant was in the bank with an operable weapon, it is more likely that she was there with willful intent, and not, as Mr. Bailey

characterized it, as a "prize pig." In other words, if you're going to rob a bank and you're not sure about one person, you certainly don't give them an operable weapon with live bullets. You give them a simulated weapon that doesn't work. You recall she testified that she looked down and she saw that the bolt was turned. It's rather difficult to keep the bolt in that turned position, so that it is not all the way forward. You will recall when Mr. Sibert, the firearms expert, demonstrated, simply by tapping the gun against the corner of the table, that the bolt would slide forward all by itself.

Browning taps the gun once, twice. The bolt doesn't move. *Something* assuredly is the matter with this carbine. Hastily he changes the subject. It is already ten-forty. The time is going by very fast.

Ladies and gentlemen, let me say a few words about the psychiatric testimony. It is not alleged that she has a mental disease or defect that causes her to lack the mental capacity to commit a crime. It is not an insanity defense. Under the instructions that you will receive from the judge, you will hear that you are free to accept or reject the opinion of an expert witness, a psychiatrist. The psychiatrists weren't there at the bank robbery; they weren't there at Mel's; they don't have any ability to unscrew the top of a person's head and look in and take a picture of what the intent was any more than you or I do. They are trained, yes. But I hope you decide this case on the facts because that is, frankly, where it's at.

A duress defense is what is being proposed in this case—that somebody was threatening to kill her unless she robbed that bank and that she was in imminent fear of death or great bodily injury as a result of those threats. You don't need a psychiatrist to tell you whether that is true or not. You can decide that just as easily as anybody else can. . . .

All the talk about mind control, psychological coercion, et cetera, et cetera, apparently was injected in this case by the defense in the hope that if duress does not stick to the ceiling, maybe something else will. I urge you not to be misled by that, because brainwashing and coercion are totally inconsistent concepts. If a person is brainwashed, there is no necessity to coerce her physically. And the converse is equally true. Duress or coercion is a factual defense. It depends upon physical evidence that you yourselves can look at, that any individual who is familiar with human affairs is capable of evaluating. You don't need an expert.

I want to ask you to bear in mind that the doctors who were called by the defense in this case are basically not experienced in examining persons who are charged with criminal offenses, as were Doctors Fort and Kozol. Every one of them referred to the defendant as "a patient," not as a subject or a defendant but as "a patient." Most of these doctors are used to working with individuals who come to them for treatment. There is a great difference between that type of a relationship and one in which you are evaluating persons charged with criminal offenses. Such persons often lie in what they tell the doctor.

Secondly, the psychiatric experts called by the defense are academicians. They are not forensic psychiatrists. They are apt to find in any subject a varying degree of the particular malady they happen to specialize in. A specialist tends to find his own specialty.

Thirdly, all the doctors, that is, defense and prosecution, seem to agree that the other members of the SLA came from similar white upper-middle-class backgrounds, and they all found that significant. Apparently something changed those other white upper-middle-class females; something made them become urban guerrillas or revolutionaries. What was it? Was each and every one of them brainwashed? And, if not, is it all that surprising that Patricia Hearst could have made the same voluntary conversion, attitudinal change? I submit to you that it is not.

We take a short midmorning recess. The reporters are subdued and impressed. The prosecutor has revealed himself as a fine carpenter who has built a solid case, and he is now hitting each one of his points squarely on the head. He tells us he doesn't intend to talk much longer. It is 11:04 A.M. when the marshals relock the doors.

The easel and charts that have stood for eight weeks at the edge of the jury box have been removed, and we have an unimpeded look at the jurors for the first time: fourteen Olmec monkeys in profile. Reporters, jurors, and spectators sit in total, fishlike silence for three long minutes until Carter comes in, wearing his tiny smile, and the rumpled Browning rises to his feet, eager to go back to work.

Ladies and gentlemen, I know it's not easy to sit there and listen to a harangue for two hours, and I do thank you for your patience. You recall that Dr. West was the leadoff witness for the defense. But they all talked about brainwashing or thought reform, and they all took the SLA babble rather literally. They found, in effect, that they were an army, eight young middle-class people, college-educated, from professional backgrounds, filled with guilt, led by a black man but overwhelmingly female. This was the army. The SLA announced they were at war.

The SLA, in rather pompous rhetoric and to dazzle the media, called Patricia Hearst a POW. So the defense psychiatrists found that she was, in fact, a POW. And the conclusions followed not from an analysis, we submit, of hard evidence, but from a rather literary description of her. Once they find that Patricia Hearst was a POW, they conclude that everything she did was coerced—notwithstanding, ladies and gentlemen, that they are unable to cite to us a single instance of a POW ever committing an overtly violent act as a result of the mind control or brainwash. They conclude she couldn't escape during well over a year and a half, notwithstanding that she was not in a POW camp behind enemy lines and the fact that many of the POWs who were did undertake successfully to escape.

Incidentally, I throw this question out to you: Did the so-called SLA possess the expertise to brainwash anyone? Mr. Bailey said in his opening statement that he would show Mr. DeFreeze read books on brainwashing while he was in prison. But . . . there is absolutely no evidence in this case that Mr. DeFreeze had acquired any special expertise at all in the art of brainwashing.

And during the time Dr. West was on the stand we heard some rather remarkable testimony. We heard that Dr. West had written a letter to Mr. and Mrs. Hearst on June 3, 1974, before he ever saw Patricia Hearst. I would like to read you the last two paragraphs of that letter: "If Patricia can be protected from physical harm and returned to her family, she stands a good chance of being restored to a mentally healthy and socially responsible state. Furthermore, in spite of the charges that have been filed against her, I believe powerful medical and legal arguments can be mobilized for her defense."

Restored from what? He had already made his diagnosis, ladies and gentlemen, in June of 1974!

Right now the defendant's appearance gives testament and corporeal reality to the television term "whiter-than-white."

It seems to us that Dr. West went beyond the charter the court appointed him for. You should consider that in his October 4 interview with the defendant, he tells [her], "The strategy they plan for your defense is to emphasize the involuntary and violent way in which you were dragged out of a relatively normal life, with a forcible and terrifying sort of indoctrination that you got and the tremendous pressure of threats in the beginning to make you subservient and compliant. " And so Dr. West puts his own Good Housekeeping *Seal of Approval on this strategy. . . .*

Dr. West's interviews, however, did turn up some rather interesting things, such as her unparalleled capacity for sarcasm, her maladjusted relationship with her parents; that she was "independent and especially bold on matters that she knew little about, like politics"; that she was "self-motivated, " often became extremely involved in ideas or programs advanced by others, had felt trapped, had suicidal thoughts and had felt dead-ended before the kidnapping; and that the defendant had an all-or-nothing reaction to people. Do those things really sound very different from what Doctors Kozol and Fort found—that the defendant at the time of the kidnapping was a rebel in search of a cause? I submit they did not.

Turning to Dr. Lifton, again we have a professorial academician describing himself as a psychohistorian. Dr. Lifton read Dr. West's report and then formed a conclusion. That's what he testified to. He apparently did not listen to the SLA tapes, did not examine the bank-robbery exhibits or the documents seized on the occasion of the arrest, or listen to the Tobin tape or any other primary materials. Would you say as jurors that all you have to do in this case is to listen to the defendant's testimony and then you could make your minds up? That's just about what Dr. Lifton did.

Browning's presentation is so orderly, so measured, I find I can write down almost every word in longhand. But I also see that the jurors are taking no notes and, accordingly, I decide to slack off myself.

It is interesting to note that Dr. Lifton found one of the integral matters in psychological conditioning to be isolation from the outside world. But we know by the defendant's own words that she knew people on the outside were worried about her. I direct your attention to the first and second tapes. In the defendant's voice, we hear these words: "I mean I know it's hard, but I heard that Mom was really upset. . . . I hope that this puts you a little bit at rest and that you know that I really am all right." Second tape: "I know that a lot of people have written and are really concerned about me and my safety and about what you're going through. . . ."

Finally, notwithstanding Mr. Bailey's claims in his opening statement that the defendant was subjected to grueling interrogations, so far as we know in the record, ladies and gentlemen, the interrogations consisted of a few hours by Mr. DeFreeze.

What emerges from all of [this] ladies and gentlemen, is that psychia-trists and—just as Judge Carter said—lawyers as well have no corner on being able to tell when somebody is lying. The time-honored and tested commonsense way to look at these matters is for you to decide, based on the evidence, with your own collective intelligence and your own good sense.

Let me speak to a very, very important matter in this case, and that is the defendant's credibility as a witness. You may look to the substance of her testimony, that is, what *she says, as well as* how *she says it, in determining what credibility to ascribe to her testimony. When a defend-ant makes some statement tending to show innocence, and this explana-tion or statement is later shown to be false, you may consider that falsity as circumstantial evidence pointing to a consciousness of guilt. In this connection, I urge you to consider the affidavit that Miss Hearst signed with respect to bail. We find in the affidavit not one reference to a second closet. We find in the affidavit that she heard "constant threats against her life and saw her captors were armed with revolvers, shotguns, and other weapons." Later she admitted that was not a true statement be-cause she was blindfolded. She states in the affidavit, "Meanwhile, one of her captors, armed with a gun which was kept pointed at her, had told her in advance that if she did anything except announce her name, she would be killed immediately." But she testified she was supposed to make a speech in the bank. The affidavit was untrue again.*

Finally, the affidavit says, "Under the pressure of these threats ... she felt her mind clouding." As I recall her testimony, she said that was not true. . . .

Does it surprise you ladies and gentlemen at all that this affidavit was signed two days after the conversation you heard yesterday, wherein Miss Hearst says to Trish Tobin, "I can tell you things you wouldn't believe." I won't belabor you, ladies and gentlemen, but that affidavit was signed under penalty of perjury, just as the oath she took when she appeared as a witness in this case.

When the chips are down, Jim Browning knows exactly when to shut up, and he does so now. We hear not another word about the perjured affidavit.

There is another matter that you should consider in gauging Miss Hearst's credibility, and that is the matter of her refusing to answer questions. The law holds that when a witness refuses to answer a question after being instructed by the court to answer, that fact may be considered by you in determining the credibility of the witness and the weight her testimony deserves. The court also will instruct you that fear of death is no legal privilege to take the Fifth.

There are some other matters bearing on the credibility of the defendant. She said she gave the clenched-fist salute and talked the way she did on the Trish Tobin tape because she feared the presence of Emily Harris. And yet we know now, pursuant to stipulation after the facts were checked, that Emily Harris was not in that visitors' room at the time of that conversation.

I urge you to consider the Tobin conversation itself, in gauging her credibility. She told Trish Tobin she was "pissed off, goddammit," about being arrested. Those were her words. That is how she felt, and you have to consider that in evaluating what she told you from the witness stand.

One very, very, very important consideration in determining her credibility is the testimony of Mr. Zigurd Berzins. You will recall that the defendant testified that she did not know whether her gun was loaded. She testified she never had any bullets on her person when she walked into the bank, and she never examined the clip to see if it contained any live rounds. Zigurd Berzins testified that what he saw on that pavement were two straight clips. He never varied on that. He knows what he's talking about. And he knows the difference between a straight clip and a banana clip. He's had a great deal of experience in the military.

As Browning speaks he gestures with the straight clip itself. Black with a bright yellow label, it flickers in the air like a tropical bird.

Only Patricia Hearst had a straight clip in her weapon. You can tell from the bank-robbery photographs that Mr. DeFreeze had banana clips taped together, Camilla Hall had a shotgun, Nancy Ling Perry had a carbine with two banana clips taped together. The only straight clip in that bank was the one the defendant had.

Now, this claim about her fear of the Harrises. She was living at 625 Morse Street. She stated in her testimony that neither Harris—Emily nor William—had ever been to 625 Morse Street. And yet we are asked to believe that she had loaded weapons on those premises and a loaded pistol in her purse because she was afraid that William Harris might pop in sometime. Is that reasonable, ladies and gentlemen? I submit it is not.

And then we have the opportunities that the defendant had to escape, to make telephone calls, even to turn the Harrises in. Yet she didn't do it. She didn't even follow Wendy Yoshimura's suggestion that Wendy assist her in getting hold of her parents. . . .

Is this business of the haircutting reasonable? First to decide to put the defendant in the middle of a bank robbery as a "prize pig" to show her off, then to cut off nearly all of her hair, and then have to find her a wig so she would look like herself again? I suggest it's more reasonable to believe that she wanted a wig to disguise herself. Persons who rob banks do often disguise themselves to make apprehension and identification more difficult.

All this sounds so reasonable, as Jim Browning lays it out, that one wonders, marvels even, at the easy, friendly trust we have held this girl in, in this courtroom—not only in the early weeks of trial, when she looked so wan, but also in later weeks as she began to look merely pale and familiar. *Nothing* is appealing about the defendant right now except her plight, which is heartrending.

Finally, ladies and gentlemen, I want to talk just a bit about the alleged forced sexual intercourse or rape by Willie Wolfe. . . .

I glance over at the defense table and see three astonishing faces, the same two men and young woman who at the beginning of this trial looked like three lucky horseplayers handicapping the big race. How the weeks have changed them! It is a relief to look away.

You will remember that the "Tania Interview" talks about radical lesbian politics, women's closeness . . . sisterhood: "We, the women, struggled to build close personal relationships among ourselves. We wanted to be able to go to each other for love and support instead of feeling we had to go to 'our main man' for this. . . . Almost all our energy was put into developing military and survival skills. In this environment, the men were able to assert themselves in traditional roles as 'instructors' and 'leaders,' while the sisters struggled to become guerrilla soldiers. But without realizing it, our concept of a female guerrilla was male-defined! We were so helpless (so womanly) . . . we were willing to put every other liberation struggle ahead of our own!"

That's from exhibit 133, ladies and gentlemen, what I call the "Essay on Sexism." I think the men on the jury may wish to ask some of the women on the jury whether, in their view, someone strongly into radical lesbianism, or women's liberation, or radical feminism, would ever per-

mit herself to have been raped by one of the males in that group? Also consider Miss Hearst's testimony when I asked her what her strong feeling was about Willie Wolfe. Remember that? "I couldn't stand him," she said. "I couldn't stand him!" Of course, that was after she testified he raped her. Sure. And on the occasion of her arrest, a year and a half later, after he "raped her," she had this little stone face in her purse!

Browning turns out to be a surprisingly good mimic. He lifts his lanky arm and holds aloft the little monkey charm while rising slightly on his toes, like a matador, after the fancy capework, about to go in over the horns for the kill.

She "couldn't stand him." And yet there is this little stone face that can't say anything. But, I submit, it can tell us a lot.

I glance to my left, at the girl. Stone faces all around. The prosecutor has begun his wrap-up by reminding the jurors of two lines on the last tape: "The pigs probably have the little Olmec monkey that Cujo used to wear around his neck. He gave me the little stone face one night." He reminds them that the charm *was* indeed recovered, from Willie's body. He reminds them that in the same house where the corpses lay a charred photo was found that shows Tania wearing her matching Olmec monkey around her neck.

In short, ladies and gentlemen, we ask you to reject the defendant's entire testimony as not credible. She asks us to believe she didn't mean what she said on the tapes. She didn't mean what she wrote in the documents. She didn't mean it when she gave this power salute, this clenched-fist salute, after her arrest. That was out of fear of the Harrises, she tells us. She didn't mean it when she told the San Mateo County deputy sheriff that she was an urban guerrilla. She says the Tobin conversation wasn't the real Patricia Hearst. The Mel's shooting incident was simply a reflex, ladies and gentlemen; the untruths in the affidavits were simply some attorney's idea. She was in such fear she couldn't escape in nineteen months, while she was crisscrossing the country, or even get word to her parents or someone else. The confession to Matthews was recited out of fear. She couldn't stand Willie Wolfe, yet she carried that stone face with her until the day she was arrested!
It's too big a pill to swallow, ladies and gentlemen. It just does not

wash. I ask whether you would accept this incredible story from anyone but Patricia Hearst. And if you wouldn't—don't accept it from her, either.

It is 12:03 P.M. when the prosecutor sits down. He has talked for two hours and introduced 295 pieces of evidence in making his orderly, detailed, and factual argument.

Elevator doors, lobby doors, restaurant doors, courtroom doors—we are all actors in a Feydeau farce of doors. The jury is sitting in its box after lunch, the spectators waiting, when the courtroom's rear door opens and F. Lee Bailey hurries down the aisle, his hair rumpled, his face flushed, a thick sheaf of notes in his hand. Asking Judge Carter's permission to use a hand microphone—"I cannot quite stretch myself across this podium, Your Honor"—he rises on his toes and detaches the podium mike from its cradle. In so doing, he leaves all his notes behind him on the table. No matter. Speaking in a low but vibrant voice, looking directly at the jury, holding the mike in his hand, he bends his body across the awkward, chest-high podium as if it were a rack. The crowd is tense, ready for Joan Sutherland, Bobby Thomson, and Sam Liebowitz rolled into one.

Ladies and gentlemen, those of us who do this thing for a living have a lot of questions about what our function is when it comes to summing up. . . .
There are many concepts in the law. The SLA was so right about so many things that I, as a citizen, am a little bit ashamed that they could predict so well what we would do. But I think an overview of this case is more appropriate than talking just about bank robbery. This is not a case about a bank robbery. It is a case about dying or surviving. How far can you go to survive? People eat each other in the Andes to survive. The big question is—and we don't have it in this case, thank God—can you kill to survive? We do it in wartime, but that is a different set of rules. We allow ourselves all kinds of special privileges when we fight the enemy. G. Gordon Liddy would have been an international hero if it was only the Russians who caught him instead of the reporters, and ultimately the Department of Justice. A novelist once wrote a most disturbing book— you may have heard about it. It was a best-seller and a movie. A man who was condemned to hang for killing his wife killed his executioner

*to survive, and then it was determined that he had not killed his wife.
And a judge had to decide whether or not he could be tried for that second
killing. Does one have an obligation at some point to die? It was called*
A Covenant with Death, *and we all have a covenant with death. We're
all going to die, and we know it. And we're all going to postpone that date
as long as we can. And Patty Hearst did that, and that is why she is here
and you are here. And the manner in which she did it is the subject of
this trial.*

*There has been much contradictory evidence of peripheral matters. I
don't agree with Mr. Browning that we are in no better position to judge
the truth than you are. We are skilled at this sort of thing. There are
specialists in deception and simulation, and you were privileged to hear
from one of the very best alive today, whose opinion you may accept or
reject because, in the end, we come back to a nonperson.*

Is this reference to Fort? Orne? Patty? One is not sure. Bailey's train
of thought is erratic.

The reason we don't try these cases, ladies and gentlemen, before one
*of you is because we don't, and have not for hundreds of years, trusted
a single human being to be that kind of balance that can make this
awesome judgment. But we do trust the collective.*

*What happened in this case? We all know what happened and we
watched it happen. The news media kept us informed of every detail. The
interest of the news media in this case has been so intense that it was
necessary to protect you from it. A young girl who absolutely had no
political motivations or history of activity of any kind was rudely snatched
from her home and taken as a political prisoner. She did rob the bank.
The question you are here to answer is why. And would you have done
the same thing to survive? Or was it her duty to die, to avoid committing
a felony? That is all this case is about, and all the muddling and
stamping of exhibits and the little monkeys and everything else that has
been thrown into the morass don't answer that question.*

*The one thing we don't want and can't stand is a mistake by you that
lands on her. The government can well afford it. The government always
wins when justice is done. And it would be nice to say we impaneled you
to do justice, but please don't get those kinds of grandiose ideas. We know
that is normally beyond the capability of human function. We impaneled
you for a very different reason: Patty Hearst has a lot going against her.*

The escape that Mr. Browning and Dr. Kozol think she should have welcomed—she said, "I had nowhere to go"—has resulted in only a change of captors. But at least now, as long as society is her captor, she does not have to worry about being killed. Freedom may be a more awesome alternative—but you are not here to decide that.

The SLA predicted this trial. They also predicted your verdict and persuaded her that coming back would get her twenty-five years. If we can't break the chain in their predictions, there are going to be other Patricia Hearsts.

This is the first of several implied threats that Bailey will make to the jurors in the course of an increasingly rambling and emotional appeal: If you find Patty guilty, you will be serving the SLA. You will be responsible for future Patty Hearsts.

The SLA said, This is a political prisoner, paying for the crimes of her parents. I don't perceive they committed any crimes. An enemy of the country perceived that, a bunch of crazy psychopaths that Harry Kozol had the unmitigated gall to delineate similar to the defendant. In what possible way? They killed people because they liked to kill people. They wanted to insult the world in which we live. They perceived us as bad, and some of them died for that belief. I ask you to remember that were it not for Mel's Sporting Goods, Patricia Hearst would be dead, too, and you wouldn't even have a body to try.

This is the last bastion of our system of justice. The Attorney General of the United States couldn't resist temptation. He's been a hip-shooter for a long time. Everybody knows Bill Saxbe. He is the one who said President Nixon was like the piano player in the house of ill repute who didn't know what was going on. He is the one who walked into the Supreme Court of the United States to argue the case of Sam Sheppard and talked about Sacco and Vanzetti by mistake. He is the one who said she's a common criminal. To him, the presumption of innocence didn't count for much.

The prisoners made their confessions knowing—or hoping and believing—that back in the States, people would know they didn't mean those kinds of things. Patty probably hoped that, too.

Mr. Browning is, by the way, a decent man. Do not interpret anything that I say and argue in this case as a personal attack. There has been some convolution of his desires because of what Dr. Fort did.

Bailey gestures broadly with his left, upstage hand and a loud crash-and-tinkle ensues. We cannot see what has dropped, but a tiny smile winks across Judge Carter's face.

This case had to be tried. The public would not have stood still for its dismissal. It had to be tried. Joel Fort just tried to put together a deal so he could write another chapter in his book, the one to tell you how he saved Lenny Bruce.

By the time I got here that awful affidavit had been filed by my predecessor. The main thrust of it is true. Some of it is exaggerated by lawyers trying to do too much too fast. Doctors had been appointed. The judge had to decide the very difficult question as to what we are going to do with this girl.

Before this case, I never heard of Louis Jolyon West. But I am very glad that I met him. My delight is nothing compared with the good fortune of this defendant, and this jury, that that man, impartially selected by the court, knew the subject matter, was a man of great expertise and known integrity.

The beating of prisoners is no longer in fashion. The trick is to get them to confess, get them to embarrass the people that they came from—in this case, you and I, Randolph and Catherine Hearst—embarrass in every way they can, to break down the confidence of the structure that is that society, and mount the attack to make a new one. That is how this case began. . . .

Bailey drops his voice very low.

. . . You heard a little girl saying, "Please, please, do what they want! Don't come bombing in here like you did in Oakland. There will be gunfire, and I will be the first one to get it. Don't do that. Be nice to them. Do everything they want." And she might as well have said, As I have done. And she did, and she survived. In every kidnapping case there are only two kinds of victims: those that survive and those who don't. But, as Dr. Fort discovered, while the government paid him to try to become the expert he pretended to be, all of the ones who survived do exactly what they are told to do when they are told to do it.

Patty Hearst robbed a bank. The case boils down to the fine line between whether she wanted them to believe she was voluntary—or really wanted to be there. Dr. Orne said there were three possibilities. First, she needed the money. Second, she wanted to be there as a rebel. And third, she had no choice.

As the judge will instruct you, frankly the machinery of the law is a hedge against mistake. When we put somebody's liberty at stake, first we give her the presumption of innocence, and she is wearing that today, and will continue to wear it—unless you take it away from her.

Again one hears the undertone of threat in Bailey's words, hears it faintly, for he has long ago discarded even his hand mike and is speaking to the jurors directly, in a throaty whisper. He switches now from threats to a patriotic appeal.

With this case, in my view, we were into something American citizens had never seen before—because the military had long ago given up prosecuting these kinds of POW cases. But those of you who perhaps have not had much military service, not had to look at a weapon from both ends, not had to discover, quite contrary to what Mr. Browning thinks —and I perhaps could dramatize the point by pointing it at you, but I was taught not to do that a long time ago—when you're looking at the business end of anything that fires a bullet, your attention is on that business end with one hope in mind—that is that a bullet does not come out. You are scared to death. And it does not serve the United States government well, in my judgment—indeed, I think it offensive—when five witnesses in a row—Shea, Norton, Washington, Shepard, and Berzins—were able to find it in their hearts to change what they thought they saw from a story not helpful to the government, as they first gave it to the FBI, to a story that was helpful to the government.

Eden Shea was the deaf bank guard. Eddie Washington, a minor witness, had observed the bank robbers changing getaway cars on a nearby street. Bailey now has switched again, to a theme of personal honor.

I did not foist off on this jury box the likes of Joel Fort. Indeed, if there is anything left in this case that still shines, that still gives color and integrity to the judicial process, it consists of three eminent men who came here to teach. They came as doctors. She had been beaten to a pulp, and they know these cases. "We've seen them before, and we are specialists." Now, the government wanted to contradict these eminent men. All they could come up with is a couple of people whose only claim to fame is that they testify a lot. I plead guilty to bringing in academicians, each of whom is a full professor at eminent universities. I plead guilty to bringing you men who don't have much experience on the witness stand, and I tell you with sorrow that the lawyer's dilemma is, Shall I get a good doctor as a witness, or shall I get a doctor who is a good witness?

You may have been puzzled why I was standing here, hour after hour, letting Dr. Joel Fort shoot his mouth off. Well, I think you found out the answer Tuesday. If you think I was angry, I was. If a witness says something harmful to the case, the lawyer's obligation is to stop him from walking by knocking him down. I do not suggest that my friend Mr. Browning deliberately asked anyone to lie. I'm sure that he did not. I do not suggest that, until it was exposed in open court, he had any idea that he had called as an expert a psychopath and a habitual liar, purporting to know something about a subject he'd never studied and charging the government $12,500 to read 274 books, including Alice in Wonderland. *But, nonetheless, he called him. And as a service to human decency, I thought that my duty was to cut his legs off, so that he never disgraced an American courtroom again. . . .*

When I considered defending this case, I had a great concern. I do not tolerate people who think a United States courtroom is the place to put on a show—whether it's Squeaky Fromme or the Chicago Eight. Because when the court's orders are not obeyed, the system of which I am a part is failing. I said to myself, If I walk in and find this is a flaming revolutionary, who's going to insist on the right to jump up and protest and insult all and sundry from the witness box, I think I want no part of that—much as I grieve for the plight of Mr. and Mrs. Hearst.

The problem did not arise. You have the word of the court-appointed doctors as to what happened. When Tania's American operators were removed from the scene, the "urban guerrilla" died, gradually and slowly, and all that was left was fear—and hatred. A real fear, of undergoing this trial, and being told not to testify, by people who were now demanding $250,000 to save those who have destroyed your life, punctuated by a bomb that blows up a building with the name Hearst on it.

Bailey's voice drops so low now, he is all but inaudible in the spectator section of the courtroom. In effect, he sequesters himself with the jury and whispers directly, intimately, to them alone to conclude his argument.

Patricia Hearst was not a bad girl. She is not famous for anything she did before February 4. She's famous for what happened to her afterward. And what did happen is up to you to decide. If—and this is a pretty far-out theory—if she really liked these people who kept her in the closet, the closet, the closet, the closet—the one Dr. Fort thought was reasonably comfortable, I gather . . . If you can be duped into believing the preposterous notion that Dr. Kozol said he believed, that when Cinque said, "She is with us," she really was . . . "I believe that black man," were Kozol's words. . . . You consider whether you would stand up to that closet. Not your daughters or your sisters but you, yourself. You have heard some eminent men say no human being is equipped to do that. . . .

That bank was robbed for the same kind of simple coercion that would have caused each and every one of you, without any fifty-seven days anywhere, to do exactly what Cinque said.

Bailey steps out from behind his podium, walks right up to the jury box, grips the rail, and leans in, saying directly into the jurors' faces the words he pictures Cinque saying to Patty, "Either do what I say—or —I—will—blow—your—head—off." The moment is no less frightening for the words' being delivered in an almost inaudible whisper.

Once I have seated myself, my job is done, and I must be forever silent. Mr. Browning has the opportunity to answer any questions I may have raised, and you will get the court's instructions, and then you are on your own until you come back and give us a verdict. And that will either be the most horrible saying that Patricia Hearst has ever heard, in one word —or the symphony the SLA says we couldn't deliver, in two.

Bailey stops talking, but he doesn't move. Is this the end? Not quite.

This case is riddled with doubt. It always will be. Perry Mason brings perfect solutions to all cases. Real life doesn't work that way. No one is ever going to be sure. They will be talking about this case for longer than I think I am going to have to talk about it. But there is not anything close to proof beyond a reasonable doubt that Patty Hearst wanted to be a bank robber. What you know, and you know in your hearts to be true, is beyond dispute. There was talk about her dying, and she wanted to survive. Thank God, so far she has. Thank you very much.

Bailey turns away with tears in his eyes and straps his wristwatch back on. He has talked less than forty-five minutes. The court declares a short recess, and the lawyer trudges wearily out of the courtroom between the defendant's parents, one heavy arm thrown across the shoulders of each. From the rear, the sagging central figure supported by two stalwarts suggests certain Italian religious paintings. But when we return to our seats after recess, all the defense lawyers have re-grouped around their table, laughing, flushed, and gasping like knights after a hard-fought victory. Browning promises his closing argument will last no longer than half an hour. Thank heaven. I don't think any of us can take much more of this. We are OD'd on information and stuffed and trussed with legal theory.

I think it's important to consider what the defendant would be today if she hadn't been arrested. What would she be doing today? Whether she was reprogrammed or what, she is a different person today than she was on the day of the bank robbery. I submit to you, ladies and gentle-men, that the evidence you have heard, and some of it from the defense psychiatrists themselves, does not bear out the picture of Patricia Hearst that Mr. Bailey would have you believe.

Read the "Tania Interview." Look at the Tobin tape. Look at her bail affidavit. Look at her clenched-fist salute in this very courthouse. Can you really believe she did all of those things because of fear from the Harrises? Or was it because she was reprogrammed by the psychiatrists, by the defense attorneys, in order to explain all of the things that the defense knew would be brought before you? Some of them are very difficult to explain, and they know that. And so they say, time and time again, "They made me do it. It was the fear that made me do it."

I am sorry Patricia Hearst was kidnapped. I am sorry when anybody is kidnapped. I wouldn't want to be kidnapped. Neither would you. But to make the assumption that she remained a kidnap victim for the next nineteen months strains credulity.

Now, counsel mentioned in his opening argument and again in his closing argument the matter of a portion of the sixth SLA tape in which the defendant says, "As for my ex-fiancé, I'm amazed that he thinks that the first thing I would want to do, once freed, would be to rush and see him. The fact is, I don't care if I ever see him." Counsel seems to perceive that because the word "freed" was used, Angela Atwood, who is supposed to have written this portion of the script for this tape, slipped and catego-rized the defendant as a kidnap victim rather than as a comrade. I submit to you, the content of that sentence does not bear out that interpre-tation. Miss Hearst at this point is talking about what Mr. Weed thinks, not what Angela Atwood thinks.

Mr. Bailey spoke of the five witnesses who he claims changed their story somehow to accommodate the government. I'm not going to rehash their testimony at this time, ladies and gentlemen, but I leave you with this thought. People in a fast-moving panic situation are apt to make mis-takes.

Now, with respect to Dr. Fort. Counsel categorized him, I believe, as a psychopath and a habitual liar. That sounds like character assassina-tion to me of Dr. Fort. We would have preferred that Mr. Bailey closely question Dr. Fort with respect to the substance of his testimony. Instead, we are told about his dues in the American Psychiatric Association. We are told about Lenny Bruce. And then we heard from Mr. Bailey what perhaps was the most remarkable attack on any witness that I heard in this trial, and that was a question to Dr. Fort: "Dr. Fort, didn't you go to Catherine Hearst and try to fix this case behind my back?" What does that word "fix" mean? Does it mean money under the table? You bet it does! Where is the proof of that, ladies and gentlemen? Don't be misled by the smoke screen, ladies and gentlemen. Judge this case on its merits; judge this case on the relevant evidence, not on those collateral matters. There is absolutely no evidence that the SLA predicted this trial and the verdict and any twenty-five years.

BAILEY *(interrupting):* Your Honor, the defendant testified precisely to that, and I think it improper for Mr. Browning to assert otherwise.

CARTER: The defendant did testify, ladies and gentlemen. You are the jurors, you have heard the testimony, and it is your memory that counts, and you consider the testimony as you understand it, not as counsel are saying it.

If I am incorrect, I apologize. The bottom line here, ladies and gentle-men, is to use your good sense in arriving at a verdict in determining whether the person inside the Hibernia Bank on April 15, 1974, was a person who fired the guns down at Mel's in Los Angeles a month later. The person who gave the clenched-fist salute in this courthouse. The person who described herself as an urban guerrilla upon booking. The person who, time after time, failed to escape, to notify her parents. The person who spoke with Trish Tobin on the tape, said that she was pissed off about being arrested. The person who signed that affidavit. The person who said she had no bullets when she went into the bank. The person who, in short, the evidence shows had become a revolutionary and robbed the bank voluntarily.

We ask you to return a guilty verdict on both counts of the indictment.

It is three-thirty P.M. when we adjourn. I feel high on flu drugs, low in spirit, strung out emotionally, exhausted in body, and dreading the television spot I must tape that evening, my last from San Francisco. Yet when I return home from the studio at midnight, I find myself unaccountably wakeful and alert.

Child psychologists recently have identified a mysterious new category of people whom they call "invulnerable children." The mystery the doctors set out to answer is why some kids simply do not break down, despite the most stressful, deranged, impoverished, bereaved, punishing, and catastrophic of childhoods. "These splendid children," one doctor writes, "have this extraordinary equanimity." He illustrates his point by telling a story about three dolls, each one hit by a hammer. One doll is glass, one is plastic, and one is steel. The first shatters, the second is scarred, but the third gives off "a fine, metallic sound. It's that sound that we're all trying to investigate," the doctor says. Patricia Hearst, too, has been hit by a hammer. Yet with her, one still hears no sound at all.

Friday, March 19

Catherine Campbell Hearst comes down the aisle like a new-made widow, wearing on her crumpled face the Celtic certainty of disaster. She is leaning hard on Vicki's arm and weeping openly; even her chrysanthemum hairdo is wilted by grief. Judge Carter announces that the rules of reason have come down to us through the history of jurisprudence, and, he adds, smartly stacking a thick sheaf of papers on his desk top, the same principles will now be stated in varying ways.

Now that you've heard the evidence and the arguments of counsel, it becomes my duty to instruct you in the law. Justice through trial by jury must always depend on the willingness of each individual juror to try the issues. The law does not permit jurors to be guided by sympathy, prejudice, or public opinion. Do not assume I hold any opinion. You as jurors are at liberty to disregard any comment I have made. You should not show prejudice to an attorney or client because an attorney has made objections. To make objections is the attorney's duty.

The law assumes a defendant to be innocent of crime. The defendant thus begins the crime with a clean slate . . . so the presumption of innocence alone is sufficient to acquit a defendant. It is not required that the government prove guilt beyond all possible doubt. The test is reasonable doubt. A reasonable doubt is a doubt based on reason and common sense—the kind of doubt that would cause a reasonable person to doubt to act.

The burden of proof is always on the prosecution. It never shifts to the defendant. A reasonable doubt exists whenever, after careful and impartial consideration of the relevant evidence, the jurors do not feel convinced to a moral certainty that the defendant is guilty of the charge.

Carter defines the difference between direct evidence and circumstantial evidence, and says that the law makes no distinction. The presumption of innocence exists in this case until it is overcome by competent evidence, direct *or* circumstantial. "And that is the very purpose you are here for." Al Johnson is listening more intently to this charge than I have ever seen him listen before. Dr. West looks shorn. He has had a real haircut, as well as the symbolic one delivered that morning by Carolyn Anspacher, who has written in the *Chronicle* that in the Hearst case psychiatry has been put on trial and found guilty.

Bailey wears his ice-cream suit this final morning, and Patricia a black sweater. On this day it is she, not her mother, who is dressed in mourning, and her complexion has gone a powdery, dusty gray—as if she has already begun to molder inside her closet-cupboard.

The judge's instructions include a stipulation:

The Harrises, the Scotts, the Soliahs, Mr. Kilgore, and Ms. Yoshimura are unavailable to both parties as witnesses, and no inferences are to be drawn as to their absence.

The next matter is the credibility of witnesses.

Once more, you, as jurors, are the sole judge. Expert witnesses may testify only as to their opinions. They may also state their reasons for their opinions. You must give their testimony such weight as you think it deserves, or you may disregard it entirely.

What Carter is, in fact, doing is explaining the rules of the game retroactively, after the game has been played. He is making it possible for me to understand much more of what has been going on here these past two months. What a pity none of us, and none of the jurors, heard these rules at the beginning of the trial. That would have made it all so much clearer.

Evidence of flight or concealment is not in itself enough to establish guilt, but it may be considered in light of the other evidence. The fact that a witness refuses to answer questions may be considered by the jurors as evidence in determining credibility.

The sobbing Catherine Hearst of today suggests the distraught Patricia Hearst of eight weeks ago. The strength and vulnerability that are polarized in this mother and daughter have subtly changed places.

By ten A.M. Judge Carter is reading aloud the grand jury's indictment:

Count One. On or about April 15, 1974, in the City and County of San Francisco, State and Northern District of California, Patricia Campbell Hearst, defendant herein, and others not named in this indictment, did by force and violence . . .

It is six months to the day, less three and a half hours, from the moment Tom Padden crashed through the door of 625 Morse Street, shouting, "FBI! Freeze!" and causing one of the occupants to wet her pants. On the bench in front of me, the sketch artist Harry Aung has already completed his daily portrait for the New York *Daily News* and is at rest, arms folded. Carter, still reading, is down to Section 2113, Subdivision (d) of the United States Criminal Code, and the legal language has become so dense it makes the judge stumble badly, despite a lifetime of riding comfortably at anchor in vast seas of such verbiage. I sense trouble for Patty from juror number nine, a middle-aged woman wearing an odd smile. I check my jury fact sheet: Number nine is a hospital nurse, so this is the smile imprinted by tens of thousands of admonitions to "open wide" and "roll over"—a professional smile.

I begin to handicap some of the other jurors in my yellow pad. "Number twelve is a good guy . . . number four also . . . another one is an Archie Bunker. . . . Another is the one I can never see. He is out of my line of vision, an invisible man—or woman. Juror number five, the good-looking, part-Japanese United stewardess from Hawaii, is a mirror image of Patricia Hearst, across the courtroom. Number eight is a pragmatist, impatient of bullshit. . . . Number eleven is intelligent, I think. . . ."

Carter's voice drones on, laying down the boiler plate.

An act is willfully done if it is done voluntarily and intentionally. Motive and intent must never be confused. . . . A good motive alone is never a defense when the act committed is a crime. . . . Whether or not the evidence convinces you the defendant possessed an operable weapon at the time of the robbery, if the evidence convinces you that she acted willfully and knowingly in conjunction with others who did possess operable weapons, then you may attribute to her, as an aider and abettor, the use of a dangerous weapon.

Coercion or duress may provide a legal excuse for the crime charged in the indictment. However, the compulsion must be present and immediate and of such a nature as to induce a well-founded fear of impending death or serious bodily injury, and there must be no reasonable possibility to escape the compulsion without committing the crime. If the evidence in the case should leave you with a reasonable doubt whether, at the time and place of the alleged offense, the accused acted, or failed to act, willingly and voluntarily—that is to say, whether the accused was forced in effect to commit or aid in the commission of the crime charged in the indictment by coercion or duress, as just explained—you should acquit the accused.

I do not understand the second part of his charge, but the judge is already back on the subject of expert witnesses, and my pencil and mind are racing to keep up.

The purpose of expert psychiatric testimony offered in this case by the defense has been in an attempt to explain the effects kidnapping, incar-

ceration by the kidnappers, and alleged psychological and physical abuse at the hands of those—of these kidnappers—may have had upon the defendant's mental state is relevant to the asserted defense of coercion or duress, upon which you have already been instructed.

So it is clear, I will read it again. It says: The purpose of expert psychiatric testimony . . .

I cannot follow this! Judge Carter reads his instructions so badly he seems to throw the law at the jurors like rice upon honeymooners. But the effect of this confusion should operate in the defendant's favor because it strengthens the adjuration "When in doubt, vote innocent." What Carter's boiler plate seems to boil down to is: Use common sense.

Keep constantly in mind that it would be a violation of your sworn duty to base a verdict of guilty upon anything other than the evidence in the case. And remember as well that the law never imposes on a defendant in a criminal case the burden or duty of calling any witnesses or producing any evidence. Remember also that the question before you can never be: Will the government win or lose the case? The government always wins when justice is done—whether the verdict be guilty or not guilty.

It is ten-twenty-six A.M. Catherine Hearst's seat is empty. Other reporters tell me she left a few moments ago, sobbing heavily, leaning on a marshal's arm. "I guess I chickened out," she will say later.

Carter directs the twelve jurors to leave the room. The two alternates will be kept in separate sequestration, and may not deliberate. They have drawn the roughest duty of all. These two ultimate losers are returned to the Holiday Inn. Bailey is on his feet, demanding the text of Carter's instructions be sent into the jury room, obviously because the spoken instructions were read so haltingly. Browning prefers the jurors to "come out here and ask. That's the accepted manner." Carter unwittingly omitted reading certain instructions altogether, and Bailey has picked up one serious slip: Instead of saying the defendant "begins the trial with a clean slate," Carter said, "begins the crime." So the twelve jurors must be recalled; already they look different. Fourteen people look like fourteen people, but twelve people look like a *jury.* Carter reads them his additional instructions.

A lawyer's statements are not evidence. A witness has no legal privilege to refuse to answer questions put to her on the grounds of physical fear of harm either to herself or to her family.

Then he untwists his earlier remark:
The defendant does not begin the crime *with a clean slate; she begins the* trial.

It is appropriate in this screwy trial that the last words the jury hears is the fuddled judge correcting his own Freudian slip.

Saturday, March 20

This was to have been a weekend of entire, blissful escape. Nobody expects a verdict until at least the middle of next week. Late yesterday afternoon I drove an hour out of San Francisco to a glamorous, easeful ranch house in the wine country north of the city. The six or eight people I might like most to see in the whole world just now happen to be gathered here under one moss-grown, vine-heavy roof, the new, spring leaves just appearing like tiny green hands. It will be a weekend of excellent company, fine wine, superb food, linen sheets, long snoozes, breakfasts in bed, handsome men and women with good things to say about the world and one another, a time of rest and succor, generosity, intelligence, and trust. I could not find a more perfect hospice. Except that after one candlelit, perfect dinner, one fitful night in the linen sheets, I am jumpy as a water bug. When I try to work on my blue notebooks, the jumpiness gets worse, so this morning, even before lunch, I slam notebooks, suitcases, and myself back into my rented Hertz without quite knowing why, startling myself and insulting my host, and then I barrel top speed back toward the city, country music blasting from the car radio and me singing along at the top of my lungs. As I make the turn onto Van Ness the disc jockey interrupts to announce that the jury in the Hearst case has just sent a message to the judge. My foot mashes the accelerator, and in ten minutes I have thrown the car into an empty lot and am back up on the nineteenth floor, breathless. Marshals in sport shirts are hastily setting up their metal scanner, and all the rest of the cast, most, like me, dressed in sneakers and jeans, are hurriedly assembling for the last scene. Only the lawyers, who have been keeping round-the-clock vigil at the court-house, wear suits and ties. McNally is sweating lightly in his blue serge. Johnson looks gray, Bailey waxen-faced; Tom May looks like a bruise. Catherine's Chinese face is perfectly composed; Randy's is set like cement. The windows in the courtroom doors have been covered over, masked appropriately, with old newspapers neatly taped onto the glass. When it's time to lock us back in, we fit ourselves into our old seats as Puritans into stocks. But when we rise this time for Judge Carter's entrance, we all remain standing, as if awaiting the blessing in church. Patty stands up at her table, braced by her pink-enameled fingertips, mouth slightly open, cheeks hollow. The jury files in, staring straight ahead. Patty's mouth opens wider. My own heart batters my ribs with a force I would not have believed. Judge Carter bites a cuticle. The foreman hands a paper to the clerk. A split second before he reads it aloud, Patty sways toward Bailey and says one word in a low but clear voice: "Guilty."

"We, the jury, find the defendant guilty on the first count and guilty on the second count," the clerk reads. Then the jury is polled, and each person tonelessly repeats the word "guilty." But Patty said it first, and said it aloud, and right now that millisecond's lead in saying "Guilty" before everybody else says it, too, appears to be her only victory.

Carter sets a date to return for the sentencing and thanks the jurors for "a long, hard, difficult trial." Patty regards them with a rueful smile; Janey Jimenez is sobbing. "Don't try to second-guess yourselves later," Carter cautions. "Judgment day is always very difficult."

The government lawyers have closed faces; nothing to be read there. Carter thanks the press. "I know I chastised you for laughing. If I have offended any of you, I apologize." He praises the skills of the lawyers. "You gentlemen performed with honor and in accordance with the high calling which you have accepted as your station in life. Now, then, we will be at recess, and the defendant will be remanded."

Dazed, we straggle downstairs to the last television press conference from this special room. We feel as if we have all reached Mecca together at last, only to find the holy city inexplicably blasted to bits. The victors open the show. "The verdict bears out what most persons believe—that the criminal-justice system works pretty well," Browning says. He thinks it could have gone either way. "It was not a dead-bang case. If the jury had voted for acquittal, I was gonna tell you that she had to be tried because the grand jury indicted her. Though I think any bank robber is a danger to the community, I have nothing but sympathy for her family. I have children of my own. I believe the defendant robbed the bank because she got caught up in rhetoric and momentarily joined the SLA."

Out in the corridor shadows, Al Johnson leans against the wall, smoking. Bailey lurks nearby. Nobody looks at anyone else; the place feels like a locker room after the team has lost the Big Game. Squinting through tired tiger eyes, Bailey just says that Cinque's prophecy has come true.

Upstairs, the battered old pre-Patty press room is an equally dispir-ited place. Not only is the trial over, the high gone, the case lost, but somewhere the girl seems to have been sold down the river, and justice smeared; the marshals, jurors, parents, friends, lawyers, all are in de-spair. Not even the prosecutors seemed joyous. As for the members of the press, they are destroyed by this miracle of bad timing. No matter which way it went, no one had expected a verdict on Saturday after-noon, when there are no newspapers and no big television news shows, either. After all the buildup, the reporters cannot write the finale to the story of their lifetimes. The Sunday papers have already gone to press, and by Monday morning their wrap-up stories will be most suitable for wrapping fish. Once more the veteran print reporters will get scooped and the story picked dry by the flashy piranha boys and girls from television, and even for them there will be no regular news show until Monday night.

So on Saturday afternoon in this blowsy press room, after two years of HERNAP, we all wind up with nothing to write, nothing to say, nothing to drink, nothing even to feel. Act III seemingly has ended in a total, perfect, universal bummer. "*Somebody* must be happy about this," a voice says. "Just one person. Somewhere."

Dave Felton, the mordant man from *Rolling Stone*, fits another cigarette into his holder. "Yes. Somewhere a little sister of the Sacred Heart of Jesus sits in a rocking chair, not saying a word. She just laughing and rocking, rocking and laughing."

Closing
Reflections

It used to be that Merlin made the magic but the king made law. Today law *is* king, and Merlin has become a psychiatrist. At the trial of Patricia Hearst the two systems—external order as represented by the law, and internal order as represented by psychiatry—appeared to collide head-on. Many persons besides Patty were injured in the wreck: her lawyers Lee Bailey and Al Johnson, her previous lawyers the Hallinans, the Hearsts themselves, Doctors West and Fort, and Judge Carter —to name only the most obvious casualties. Nobody came out of the thing well; HERNAP seemed to bring out the worst in everyone. A trial staged at least in part to prove the System worked seemed to prove just the opposite.

By the time it ended I sensed, as we all did, that something had gone terribly wrong, and I spent the next months shuttling uneasily back and forth between kings and wizards, trying to disinter truth from the wreckage. Joel Fort had been right to bone up on the works of Lewis Carroll, but a single looking glass was inadequate to reflect these curious goings-on. To do that job properly would require a tailor's three-way mirror that could show what I saw, what the experts saw, and what the jury saw—three reflections; in effect, three different trials. The effort to sort them out made me queasy. It was like watching a screening of *Rashomon* at which the projectionist had got the reels mixed up.

I saw what had happened to Patty Hearst as a tragedy and her trial as a travesty. In the collision of necessities, the defendant's day in court had been turned into a psychiatric carnival, a media swamp, a legal circus, and a modern-day witch trial. Probably it would have been easier on everyone, Patty included, to have thrown her into San Francisco Bay and seen whether she floated.

Long before her trial, Judge Carter had injudiciously allowed that the trouble with Patty's story was that you didn't know whether to cry or throw up. During jury deliberations, I would shortly discover, they had done both. Perhaps, under law, they could have reached no other verdict than they did. But they reached it in tears and vomit, I thought, because they, too, have daughters, as we all have daughters, and when any one of us asks, Could this tragedy have happened to my daughter? the only answer is yes. Yes, it could.

The next time I saw her, after the trial, Patricia Hearst was reflected in the shiny roof of a police car, gazing down at her image as dreamily as Narcissus in his pool, hair curling softly around her sunken cheeks, beautiful, wistful, blank—an icon of herself but otherwise still a cipher. A photograph of this was made in May as she left a courthouse in Los Angeles, where she had been brought from prison to answer charges growing out of the events at Mel's Sporting Goods store. Patty and the Harrises had not seen one another since September, after their arrest. Now, during the nearly three-hour proceeding, she stared blankly ahead, never once looking at her codefendants. Nor did she speak or even enter a plea. Instead, Johnson cited the section of the state penal code that reads, "A person cannot be tried or adjudged to punishment while he is mentally incompetent," and his client stood mute. That is to say, the lawyer was telling the court that she was neither guilty nor not guilty. Patricia Hearst's relation to the law was accurately reflected at last.

As for the individual wizards and kings, they reminded me of the six blind men and the elephant. If Dr. West saw a dissociative reaction as a result of a traumatic neurosis, well, Robert Lifton saw a victim of survivor syndrome. Martin Orne saw a person who could not lie. Margaret Singer saw bad parenting and linguistic counterfeiting. Harry Kozol saw an ungrateful child. Judge Carter saw himself as the even-handed referee of a fair fight (an opinion upheld after his death by the Supreme Court).

Ask Joel Fort what had gone wrong, and he would say just about everything. He saw the wizards and kings making asses of themselves and of one another, and himself as David vanquishing Goliath. But his archenemy was the System itself. Though he operated within it, even

—as a semipro expert witness—by grace of it, he despised its every Laocoönian coil. Fort seemed to be of the small, fierce tribe of men who conceive of themselves, in James Cagney's term, as "professional again- sters," tirelessly dedicated to the exposure of every injustice, every absurdity, every hypocrisy devised by the minds of other men.

On the Friday the case went to the jury, Fort had finally arrived at my apartment for an interview. His conversational icebreakers were startling. "I can see you are the kind of person who likes children," he ventured. I said I had one child. He said he had two and wanted a third but since his wife did not, he had been "looking for a woman who wanted the experience of pregnancy but was not interested in keeping the child." "I should think most women would prefer the child to the experience," I said. "What were you planning to pay this brood sow?" "Gee, I hadn't thought of it that way," he replied.

By the end of the trial, I said, the Bailey-Fort duel had begun to seem like a grappling between an angel and Satan, though I wasn't yet certain which was which. The lawyer in his summation had called the doctor a pathological liar, adding that, in the interest of clean jurisprudence, he hoped to cut Fort's legs off. Outside the courtroom he amended "legs" to "balls."

Why had the demolition of Fort become even more important to Bailey than the vindication of his client? I invited the doctor to specu- late. Up close, Fort really does have a piercing eye, and when he looked at me, I felt stapled to my chair. We talked all afternoon and many other times until I had stored up enough impressions to formulate a cosmos, the world according to Fort. This is a prickly, ungenerous place, short on justice and truth, long on hustle and hype. Its inhabi- tants worship only the almighty dollar, and, not surprisingly, its rank- ing high priest, at least for the present season, was F. Lee Bailey, a figure whom Fort saw as Mr. Expediency, a combination of Uncle Sam as Eagle-Eye Fleagle and Vince Lombardi in striped pants. Fort saw the trial as a ladder of legal errors: Bailey's first major mistake was not o plea-bargain, his second was to permit his client to take the stand, is third was to bring in expert witnesses, and, finally, "The sim- pleminded notion that 'brainwashing' can account for complex behav- ior such as this defendant engaged in is no better an explanation than possession by the devil used to be. But I think Mr. Bailey not only saw brainwashing as a plausible and clever defense; I think he partially believed in it."

As for me, I saw Fort's own contribution to the trial as a triumphant rub-a-dub of plain speaking. The turning point for me had been the day I heard him make three simple statements of the obvious that, unaccountably, had not been mentioned by anyone else: One, this trial was a pity. The girl seemed to belong in some kind of rest home, not in the docket. Two, psychiatrists would quite naturally tend to regard her as a patient more than as a criminal defendant. The bias was natural; why deny it? Third and most important, five other young women and two young men from backgrounds not too dissimilar to her own had embraced the SLA's politics *without* having been kidnapped. The effect of the glaring triple omission was to make one wonder what else was not being said.

Fort agreed with what Bailey had told me himself back in December: Patty needed to be "reverse-brainwashed" before she could safely take the stand. This process, the tenderizing of the easy meat, was begun by the Hallinans, Fort believed, but the key figures in it were Dr. West, Dr. Singer, Johnson, and Bailey. To Joel Fort, Patty was a victim of the traditions of psychiatry and of the law, of the ambitions of individual psychiatrists and lawyers, and of society's institutionalized ageism and sexism as well. Before that she had been a victim of a temporarily frightening kidnapping, and before that "a victim of her family's lack of understanding, their lack of communication, and, most of all, a near-total lack of feeling, represented particularly by Mrs. Hearst." She was also a victim, he thought, of Steven Weed.

Fort's view of orthodox psychiatry is that it knows very little about natural, normal, healthy behavior and that its practitioners meet few criminals, radicals, or terrorists. Patty's experts not only were naive about criminal behavior and the law, they did not even know what it says. They did not know that "duress" in federal law "requires that you be under *immediate* fear of death, and that there be no opportunity to escape."

My own impression of Patricia of necessity was based on her courtroom persona, and here again, said Fort, the System intervened. A trial is inevitably a staged performance. The defendant is clothed and coiffed in a certain way; even the language is controlled. "Whether you're a Patricia Hearst or a Hell's Angel, you're a totally artificial person on that stage. This is a result of surrendering total autonomy to the lawyer. One of the most heretical things I did in the case was to suggest to Patricia Hearst that *she* run her lawyers, rather than her lawyers running her. I also suggested to her parents that they had the theoretical control of the lawyer, rather than the other way around. One of the most dangerous things in the legal system is that it invites human beings to give up their freedom to a totalitarian system in miniature, and to individuals such as Bailey and Johnson, who are basically authoritarian personalities."

Had the defendant been Fort's own daughter, he would have advised her to plea-bargain. As a twenty-year-old first offender, whether her name was Hearst or Fort, he saw a 99 percent chance that she would get probation. One reason the Hearsts did not attempt to plea-bargain, he thought, was that Bailey wouldn't allow it. Plea-bargaining would have yielded him only a few days of publicity; the trial promised many weeks. Besides, he expected to win. "No one believed his own publicity more than Bailey himself."

Fort had little better to say for the other participants. Carter was "probably the worst judge I've encountered in any courtroom. I found him confused, inarticulate, sometimes sleeping. I think he made a number of key mistakes, the most blatant of which was to think he had already ruled on the question of expert testimony and then to allow the expert testimony to proceed. Had there *not* been expert testimony, then *I* would not have been able to testify, and I would have been glad not to have had to do it."

Most judges are political appointees, Fort reminded me, and federal judges feel unduly secure. There is even less control over the federal judiciary than there is of state judges, who at least are watched over by a judicial council with disciplinary powers. A federal judge can be disciplined only by congressional impeachment, which is almost as difficult as impeaching a President. "They believe themselves to be godlike, and people react to them that way. This particular judge also showed incompetence and unheard-of bias in allowing the Hearsts to be present in the courtroom during jury selection. It's never been done before. I think all of his decisions favored the defense—except where the law was so clear that he had no choice, such as his ruling on the Fifth Amendment."

The Hallinans had been the first to try to project the image of a poor little sick girl, and Fort's scorn for them was fierce; since they were radical lawyers themselves, he found it doubly hypocritical when they depicted other radicals as "inherently sick." The fatal image of the rich little sick girl was reinforced by Carter's competency proceedings and emphasized again when a private psychiatrist was hired to treat Patty in jail.

(487)

There is no such defense as brainwashing in federal or state law, Fort reminded me, only in military courts, and there it has an opposite connotation: Soldiers claiming to have been brainwashed were tried for *having been brainwashed.* It wasn't used as an excuse for getting them off! Carter was wrong in accepting it and wrong in using that as a criterion for picking so-called experts like West. The final absurdity was that the law says a competency proceeding is only to find out whether the person knows the charges against him and is able to cooperate with his lawyer. "Instead of accepting that, West and Singer, very inappropriately and at great financial and time costs, went into her whole history. They did that, in my judgment, because it had already been decided that they, particularly West, would be the coarchitects along with the lawyer of a 'brainwashing' defense. Therefore they had to compile this report about how sick and weak and dependent and gullible and convertible she had been, so it could become the foundation for the later testimony. I like him personally, though."

Although Fort said he felt considerable affection for Patty, too, he is scarcely one to permit personal feelings to undermine his scientific objectivity. When I asked him for a word picture of the enigmatic young woman, he said in his classroom lecturer's measured voice, "If I went by her demeanor, I would have had to conclude that she was passive, immature, and seriously depressed." But when he put together their four interviews, his reading of the jail logs, and so on, "she came across as an independent, strong-willed person who was not acting. I can't read people's minds, and unlike another doctor who testified, I'm not able to tell whether somebody's lying to me just by talking to him." But if that great expert on fakery, Martin Orne, had fallen for a pair of phonies like Bailey and Johnson, why should he not also have been deceived by Patty Hearst?

Was it possible, I asked, that Patty was actually the most violence-prone member of the SLA, as the Harrises had recently charged? Possible? It's only natural, Fort said. "Any new convert tends to be overzealous. But as for the idea that Patricia Hearst had four distinct personalities, that, I think, is pure, unadulterated crap! Pearl was the name given to Patty by the Harrises for a very legitimate reason: As a fugitive, she needed an alias. To manufacture out of that a case of multiple personality was absurd."

Fort had no doubt that at one point Patricia was genuinely in love with Willie Wolfe, although her story on the stand differed markedly from what she had told him in prison—that she went along with the sexual proposals because she thought it would help save her life. "It also seemed plausible to me that she got horny frequently. She's been sexually active since the age of fifteen, which I consider very healthy. I think if you'd had a period of deprivation and isolation for a few days or a few weeks, you'd want to have sex all the more—for pleasure, for companionship, and so forth."

Fort saw two possible explanations for the "rape" testimony. One was that Bailey is an extremely racist person. "I base that on some of the things he said about me. Also, he's a very classist person, and Cinque was a ghetto figure. Equally plausible is the notion that it was just one more lie in a scenario designed to get her off at any cost."

When I invited Fort to speculate on the dynamics within Patty's family, he did not hesitate. Because Randolph has the name and the money and the power, he is the boss outside the home, Fort thought, but inside the family, it is Mrs. Hearst. "Her attitudes, her instability, her biases, other facets of her character, control the children and the husband. Through the years I think he's probably gone through hell. I think she's a constricted person emotionally, with little human warmth, very rejecting of the children, and extremely authoritarian." That was why she wanted the most conservative nuns to bring them up and why she employed a very strict and apparently punitive governess for a good many years.

"She tends to lash out at people and to be highly bigoted, and yet at the same time she is afraid of showing her own feelings about herself or toward her children. It's complicated, very hard to explain."

But he didn't have to explain. When I grow angry at my own daughter, I often feel exactly the same way.

The world according to Fort by now contained a falsified legal track record, an incompetent judge, a couple of sellout radicals, several bubble-headed psychiatrists and attendant stooges, some lazy, self-serving reporters, a variously victimized, tough-minded, or depressed defendant, and her superficial, bigoted parents. It was time for the entrance of the lying lawyers, and they appeared right on schedule. "One requirement of the 'good trial lawyer' is that he be able to lie with a straight face. Bailey and Johnson are professional liars. The assertion that she kept the Olmec monkey because she loved good art is absolutely absurd, but isn't it also absurd that so many reporters would disseminate this with a straight face? Her interest in art history never included *any* Mexican art. I talked with her in detail about what things she had read and what art she liked. I also saw all the art books she used at their apartment in Berkeley. There is absolutely nothing there involving Mexico—or Olmec, Mixtec, Aztec, Mayan, or anything else."

Fort knows a great deal about the appeals process, and even though the Hearst appeal had not yet been filed, Fort was reasonably certain of what its general tenor would be. "A 'good defense lawyer' always plays the sour-grapes game when he loses. Having earlier expressed respect for a jury, he now criticizes them, and he always appeals. He tells the appellate court, in effect, Although the jury was good, they were wrong. Or if not the jury, the judge was wrong. It's part of a process, beginning with the defendants themselves, of not accepting responsibility, again a process that's emblematic of what's going on in our whole society. People who are unwilling to accept responsibility for their own actions either deny to themselves that they've done it, or lie about it, or blame somebody else."

Patty's evolution away from the SLA had probably begun with the death of Willie Wolfe, Fort believed, and was strengthened by Wendy and the turn toward revolutionary feminism. But before Patty could renounce violence completely, she was captured again and jailed. "You have to understand what it means to be in jail. Your attorney absolutely controls and filters all input to you. You have no phone, no access to the outside world, no funds. She didn't know *what* was going on. That's part of the reprehensible manipulation of the accused by the system. Part of the maneuvering was that she was denied any contact with ordinary people, including her past friends and acquaintances and any new friends that she would have made. By January Bailey and Johnson had spent about two hundred and fifty hours with her, and the trial was another four hundred hours. I suspect maybe it wasn't so easy to get her to repudiate Willie Wolfe."

"Brainwashing" by her own attorneys and doctors produced her trial testimony, and not all of it was lying by any means, Fort assured me. "Many of the things she said she had actually come to believe, through this process of conversion combined with isolation from ordinary human contacts." The best thing for Patty would have been to let her out on bail, let her associate with Trish Tobin and others with whom she felt a sympathetic relationship. Let her readjust to her new environment and make some choices for herself. If that had been done, Fort doubted she would have given her lawyers and doctors so free a hand. "Strangely enough, although she probably hates me, I see myself more on Patty's side and supportive to her growth than her so-called defense

team was. If Cinque ever did make any prediction about her future—
and we don't know that he did—what actually happened to her was just
the reverse of his prophecy. It wasn't the government and her family
that did her in. It was a team of doctors and lawyers *hired by* her
family."

HERNAP had more than one urban guerrilla in its cast of characters. By the time the trial was over I was persuaded that the champion
urban guerrilla of them all had been F. Lee Bailey himself. I disagreed
with those critics who said that Bailey was a simple *poseur,* an incompetent, or a publicity freak. I thought he had won his impressive string
of victories by working up tremendous rage, rage at injustice, rage at
the system, rage on behalf of the little guy, and an extra measure of
pure, inchoate fury. He seemed to have the ability to mobilize all his
adrenaline, all the hormones, to collect a huge wad of aggression and
use it to fuel his extraordinary intelligence and alarming physical energy. The legend of his heroic pretrial homework might be a myth. But
the herculean throwing of himself at his task, his total commitment to
winning at any cost, is in Bailey's nature. He is a fighter pilot; he really
is Jonathan Livingston Bailey.

But this time there had been no need for rage; there was nobody to
be angry *at.* This case needed empathy, and Mr. Bailey doesn't have
much of that. If the SLA had survived the holocaust, they would have
got his bucket of rage full in the face. *They* would have been vilified as
the psychopaths, the anti-Americans, the evil, wild-eyed fanatics. But
they were dead, and the only available target for Bailey's fury was one
dead, no-account black man, one mild little revolutionary fanatic and
his wife, already in jail in LA, who for whatever reasons had helped his
client stay alive for nearly two years. And there was Joel Fort. Bailey's
rage is a very ugly thing, and frightening to almost everybody, especially other men. Ask the Bailey brotherhood, the Knights Templars.
Ask Steve Weed, who got only a flick of it and crept away. But the rage
didn't scare Fort. It turned him on.

Bailey was also a victim of his own class attitudes. He saw the trial
as the judgment of the rich by the proles and the middle class, and saw
himself as the defender and champion of the rich against the *lumpen*
proles—though perhaps only *lumpen* rich, like the Hearsts, would have
chosen a man like Bailey to represent their daughter.

Why did Randy hire him, I wondered, and why did he continue to
keep him? "I have to go with the man's track record," Hearst had told

me a few days after the verdict. But Bailey's track record—the visible part—is a series of ax murderers, wife poisoners, sex maniacs, and massacre agents. He defends the indefensible as much as the undefendable. His presence in a courtroom telegraphs to the jurors, and to the world, that his client has very likely done something wrong. Either her parents believed Patty was guilty as hell and needed an advocate of Bailey's stripe, I thought, or else the choice was political. Possibly the Hearsts or the Hearst Corporation, which would have to come up with the money to pay for it, always knew precisely the defense they wanted and had spent the Missing Year shopping for the man who could sell it. If the defense was to be that only brainwashing could account for a daughter of the Hearsts betraying her class to join the Left, then of necessity a trial would have to be held in order to lay out this script before the world and to show her contrition. In that sense, "political conspiracy" could be said to have existed between the Hearsts, their doctors and lawyers, the government and the court to keep Patty in jail and not grant her bail lest she return to the arms of the Left before the easy meat could be tenderized. If this was the real strategy, it *worked*—with one hitch: The jury failed to acquit. But such a political position would have to be maintained, and that perhaps was why Randy did not dump Bailey even after the verdict. A final factor was Randolph Hearst's own character: In a conversation with William Coblentz shortly after the trial, I had asked him if Hearst was a stubborn man. "I'll say he's stubborn! Stubborn beyond belief!" Coblentz at the time was begging Hearst to fire Bailey and Johnson, pay them off, and get competent counsel for all the legal white water still to come. But it took Coblentz more than two years to convince his client to take his lawyer's advice.*

Whichever combination of factors was responsible, it struck me that in the course of HERNAP, F. Lee Bailey had achieved his lifetime ambition despite all. He had composed his long-dreamed-of masterwork and played its starring role, or rather both of them. In Act III we had seen F. Lee Bailey go down in flames. We had watched a great criminal lawyer destroyed in a courtroom by a

---

*HERNAP continues to crackle with liaisons betrayed. On May 1, 1978, in San Francisco, two weeks before Patty was to return to jail after the Supreme Court refused her appeal, Johnson announced that Bailey had quit the case. Patty's new lawyer would be George C. Martinez, a local attorney who was also representing one of Patty's bodyguards in his divorce case. Although Johnson said he would still represent the Hearsts in certain peripheral legal matters, the bodyguard, Bernard Shaw, was also said to be Patty's new boyfriend.

great criminal lawyer. Bailey himself brought Bailey down, and that is the definition of tragedy.

Immediately after her sentencing on Monday, April 12, her lawyers had wound up the Patty doll and she had begun to sing to a select and private audience. She did not leave the Federal Building until late that night, and all day Tuesday her siren song continued. Her listeners included eleven assorted local, state, and federal prosecutors and a small posse of FBI men, all gathered around a huge square table in Browning's office. After cutting up the act, or rather booking it— deciding where their captive mermaid should sing first and how long a number she should do—the tableful of prosecutors appeared on television that very night. Patricia Hearst had switched allegiances, they told us, and was now helping authorities in the prosecution of SLA members and associates. She was trading her knowledge of activities by her former revolutionary comrades in return for a lenient sentence. By telling all, she hoped also to receive immunity in connection with the SLA robbery of the branch of the Crocker National Bank in Carmichael, a suburb of Sacramento, in which a woman was killed. She had apparently told the FBI she was stationed outside the bank at the time and reportedly identified seven other participants, including the triggerperson.

That same day, in Sacramento, at the trial of Steven Soliah for having taken part in the holdup, witnesses had identified him as having been inside the bank. It was not yet known whether Patty herself would testify against her former lover. Browning said he could not confirm or deny reports that Patty might do this without endangering her life. Well, *could* Patty escape prosecution *if* she decides to tell all, someone asked?

"It does sometimes happen," he said.

But it was all too much for our failing Ondine. The next morning, when Patty was due in Los Angeles to be arraigned with the Harrises, San Francisco woke up to learn that she was in Redwood City Hospital instead. The previous evening her right lung had collapsed. "Spontaneous tension pneumothorax," the hospital bulletin called it. But Doctors West, Orne, Lifton, Fort, and Kozol might have understood better what really happened. This young woman's body now was fighting itself on two fronts. For over a year her womb had been bleeding without surcease; now her breath had threatened to crush her heart. "Patricia

Hearst today is in considerable pain but in very good spirits," the next hospital bulletin said.

In April, the day before I left San Francisco for good, Al Johnson came to see me for the last time, bringing along his faithful secretary, Sue Maddox. Throughout the trial Sue had been to Al as Al was to Lee: loyalty incarnate, the defense team's Della Street. Now Al carefully placed his briefcase with its secret tape recorder alongside my rented blue couch and launched into three long and rambling stories, Zombo's last and most creative embellishments. I wasn't sure which one of them Sue was there to witness: the lung collapse, the firing of the Hallinans, or the legal hanky-panky preceding the Soliah trial, which was still in progress.

For openers, Al showed me a tiny, ten-ounce portable telephone also hidden in his briefcase. Like a kid with a new toy, he scampered with it into the bedroom, and sure enough, in a moment the ordinary phone at my elbow rang. "Hiya! Only FBI and CIA guys carry these gizmos," Al whispered. "They cost twenty-five hundred bucks!"

Al came back into the living room, replaced the briefcase against the couch, and said that on the evening of Patty's second day with the panoply of prosecutors, his secret phone had rung. "Al, something's really wrong now," Patty said. "The pain is terrible." The jail doctor got on the phone and said the prisoner's lung appeared to have collapsed, the Hearsts were away, and the sheriff could not be reached. So Al had baldly ordered Patty brought to the hospital emergency room in a police cruiser, and when Johnson arrived, he could see it himself on the X rays: Patty's right lung was almost totally flat, and the air pressure inside the chest was pushing the heart into the left lung. The doctor told Al he could wait no longer.

"We were standing on opposite sides of the table. He looks at me and picks up a scalpel. I nod, and he just sticks the thing right in her, no anesthetic, nothing. Patty looks up at me and says, 'Oh, Al, what else can happen to me?' He had made a one-and-a-half-inch incision in her rib cage, *then* he injected the novocaine. Shana, I almost shit. I'll remember it to my dying day." After the emergency surgery Al reached Patty's parents on his special telephone, he said, and after that he sat by her bedside holding her hand all night long.

It was a swell story, but it must have been an unusual emergency room. Spontaneous pneumothorax is a rather common occurrence among young adults and usually causes mild discomfort. If the X ray shows severe displacement, the standard procedure is first to inject an intramuscular anesthetic, then to make an incision just large enough to insert an air tube to restore the pressure. Later the incision is closed with a single stitch.

Zombo's next tale concerned his first visit to the jail. Before he had even met his client, he said, he ran into Dr. West, who reported that Patty was in a curious mental state. "She gets to certain parts of her story and just shuts off," the psychiatrist said. He recognized that some of the forgetfulness was due to a mental block, but other areas of her amnesia were feigned. "Things like the names of other people which she says she cannot remember—somebody is telling her to do this," West advised Johnson.

Lawyer and client met in the iron telephone booth for the first time. "She didn't know me from a hole in the ground," Al related, "but I told her, 'Patty, I don't know what your intentions are. But if you intend to conduct a political defense, if you intend to cover for other people, I'm going back to Boston with Mr. Bailey.' "

To me, this sounds like another threat; it sounds, in fact, like precisely the sort of intimidation Lifton, Orne, and West have described at such length. But Al appears unaware of the implied ultimatum: that unless Patty played the game his and Bailey's way, they would desert her just as everyone else has.

"Do you trust me?" Al asked her next, and Patty told him yes. When Al asked why, she said, "I don't know." When Al asked who had been telling her not to be fully forthcoming with Dr. West, Patty said it was her lawyer. "Terence Hallinan had advised her to deny recollection of anything that happened after the Hibernia Bank. No names, no dates, no places. Patty had no amnesia. She remembered it all. But Kayo had told her she would get killed if she betrayed her comrades.

"I was furious. I stormed out of there and drew up a letter and went over to that crummy office of theirs, taking Ted Kleines along as a witness. I gave Kayo the letter and said, 'The only way out for this kid is to tell the truth.'

"Kayo jumped up in the air and screamed, 'You've killed me, you've killed me! . . . You don't *know* these people.' He *threw* the letter back at me. Well, I popped my cork. I stood up to defend myself, but Kayo threw himself onto the floor instead and started beating a leather chair with his fists, still screaming, 'You don't know them!' "

The choirboy eyes narrowed. "Kayo, are you telling me you gave her this advice not to tell the truth *because you wanted to protect other clients of yours who are involved in radical movements?"* Zombo thundered. Then, to me, in a stage whisper, "Remember, I had Kleines there with me as a witness.

" 'Kayo,' I told that little punk, 'that was the most unethical thing you could do! I want your withdrawal from this case before the judge by nine o'clock tomorrow morning, or I will take drastic action.' I would have gone right to the judge and the California Bar Association and got both the Hallinans disbarred, and he knew it."

Zombo's second tale might better be termed a case of disembellishment. I had seen the younger Hallinan at Patty's bail hearing. This "little punk" is over six feet tall, and had been heavyweight boxing champion of the University of California.

Zombo's third and most elaborate tale dealt with the manner of his client's cooperation with various authorities in connection with the Carmichael bank holdup. Patty had been giving evidence against her former comrades for some time, it seems. She had spent the day of the lung collapse telling authorities that it was Wendy Yoshimura who drove the getaway car and that Emily had fired the shotgun that killed Mrs. Opsahl. She had identified the roles and positions of all eight bank robbers, herself included, and she had repeated something she had actually told Soliah's prosecutors many weeks before his trial began: Steve Soliah was part of the gang, but he was never inside the bank.

This information, Al tells me now, was first imparted to authorities secretly on March 10, the day before Patty seemingly was stricken with flu. The truth of the surgical mask so prominently displayed in the evening paper the next day (the same day, incidentally, that the trial transcript contained its hitherto-incomprehensible notation about pages 3746–54 being sealed, to be held by the court and not made a part of the public record) was that, behind the gauze, the girl had begun talking to U.S. Attorney Dwayne Keyes and his assistant. Johnson had smuggled the two prosecutors from Sacramento into the Federal Building with Judge Carter's approval, he told me, and they had met with Patty "so that substantial injustice would not be done." The meeting was so secret that "not even Jim Browning knew."

Patty's story connected her former lover to the crime, but it also saved him because it flatly contradicted two eyewitnesses who had told the grand jury they had seen Soliah in the bank. The government decided to put its "eyewitnesses" on the stand anyway and to disregard Patty's story, Al said. But the Sacramento judge had got onto the discrepancy between the "eyewitnesses'" version of what had happened and Patty's account, and so had Soliah's attorney, who had now subpoenaed the entire roomful of prosecutors. The attorney had also asked the judge to order Patty to tell the Soliah jury about those first, secret courthouse confabs back in March.

On April 20, the morning I left San Francisco, the newspapers carried Al's story, adding that Patty's latest illness, the lung collapse, now made it appear "highly unlikely that her delicate physical condition would permit her to take the witness stand." Poor Zombo. Evidently he intended to go down fighting, and I felt sorry for him. Seemingly his client's credibility had been damaged so severely by her own trial that the government feared future juries at future trials would never again believe anything she said. If such were the case, it would have serious consequences not only to her legal position but to her chances of remaining alive very long, in prison or out.

"She has knowledge of other crimes, and I'm terrified for her," Al had said. The refrain was familiar. In urging their client last September not to name names, not to talk to anybody—especially psychiatrists— and to sign the bail affidavit, the Hallinans had taken the identical position.

Dante reserved for lawyers the second-lowest level of hell, there to spend eternity slinging boiling pitch at one another, and Dante would have loved the San Francisco posttrial scene. All over town—all over the United States, I later discovered—lawyers were shouting *"Malpractice!"* and *"Malfeasance!"* Some, being lawyers, even shouted *"Misprison!"* According to the Monday-morning quarterbacks of the bar, a catalogue of defense legal errors, in no particular order of importance, would include the failure to check with the property clerk at the jail on the contents of Patty's purse, or the failure to read about the Olmec monkey in the *New Times* article, or the failure to make a connection between the two, as the government had. It would include various failures to check out witnesses and submit pretrial motions, including one on Margaret Singer's qualifications as an expert in linguistic analysis. On the matter of the treasure trove of evidence in the Harris and Hearst apartments, it would note that Patty had needlessly forfeited her proprietary interest in the Harris-apartment materials, including the lethal "Tania Interview," by her testimony that she had practically never been there. To say as much was to acknowledge she lacked standing to contest the warrant, and such testimony could have been avoided. But the most glaring error was the failure to file a routine challenge to the warrant.

Foremost among Dante's mudslingers were, of course, the Hallinans. As Vince told an audience of journalists and lawyers at the San Francisco Press Club less than a week after the verdict, dring the trial he had felt like Marcus Welby watching another doctor perform an operation. "And as he observes the manner in which his successor handles the scalpel and ties the ligatures, he thinks, 'My God, he's going to kill her!' And he did."

When Al Johnson rose wearily to defend himself, noting that he had been invited to the press club to "enjoy a meal," not "a boot in the tail," he pointed out that Hallinan had only one opportunity to speak to Miss Hearst, after which "he and his son declared to the court that she was incompetent. Notwithstanding, Hallinan and his son filed an affidavit which, in fact, was *the cause of* the psychiatric examinations, which affidavit in fact they knew was false at the time they asked her to sign it, and which affidavit later was used to impeach her credibility at trial. Is that the type of professional conduct which Mr. Hallinan would ask you to believe was *not* the type exercised by Mr. Bailey and myself?"

Then Terence Hallinan, speaking off the record, explained that he had stuck his neck out as much as he had with the affidavit because he felt the judge's order revoking bail prior to trial was probably illegal under the Federal Bail Reform Act and would be reversed on appeal. "The only things Patty Hearst was ever caught lying in were the things that came up after I withdrew from that case. . . ."

Dante would not have been surprised when, a few days later, Vince Hallinan mailed me a tape of his son's supposedly off-the-record remarks and invited me to drop by the next time I was in town. The Hallinan law offices are a triumph of restored Victorian finery—Turkey carpets, frosted glass, marble fireplaces, damask walls—and spang in the middle of all this sits another triumph, Vince himself. At seventy-nine, the old radical looked like an ancient but still alert Irish lizard, duded up in a sharp green suit and tie.

Vince got into the case, he told me, when a reporter telephoned him in Hawaii to say Patty had just been arrested in San Francisco. Vince told the reporter, "Get hold of Kayo and have him tell her to keep her mouth shut." Although Jim MacInnis, an old-time Hearst lawyer, asked the judge to have Patty transferred from jail to a psychiatric ward, Kayo advised his client to stay cool and talk to nobody, especially not to any psychiatrists, until he could arrange bail.

Then the Hallinans filed their affidavit, and things began to come apart. "So out comes Bailey, or Barnum and Bailey, as I call them, and sells himself to the Hearsts. Randy tells me, 'We've got to have Establishment people in this, Vince. You're too radical.'" But if Hearst thought that Hallinan and Bailey somehow could work in tandem, his fragile hope was shattered immediately when "Bailey panics Kayo by threatening to get him disbarred by telling the judge that Kayo advised his client to lie!" The old lawyer's voice shook with outrage.

Hallinan showed me Bailey and Johnson's two-page letter outlining the new defense strategy and stressing that it was essential that Patty cooperate fully with the court-appointed panel of psychiatrists. "As soon as this happened, the case was flushed down the sewer," he said, because although Carter promised to keep the psychiatrists' reports under seal and never let them be used against Patty, he may have lacked jurisdiction to make such a promise. Furthermore, "It would take a hell of a lot of brass on her part to tell one thing to the psychiatrists and another story to the jury." It would also take a very foolish person because she could never feel certain that the privileged information she had given to the doctors would remain under seal forever. "The position those clowns put that poor dame in is really tragic. They're con men, not lawyers. They're *bad birds.*"

"What do you think of the Harrises?" I asked.

"Bill Harris is a dangerous madman. So to put Patty in a position of *naming* people—why, I wouldn't give you fifty cents for her life after Bailey did that to her! If you let her out in public now, she wouldn't have a chance. They *couldn't* protect her! Ever hear of the Baader-Meinhof Gang? The whole world is infected with terrorists—twelve thousand in Japan alone. You can hire one and have him bump off anybody you want."

Bailey's letter specifically advised Patricia Hearst to avoid saying "I can't remember." But "it's a hell of a lot better to say 'I can't remember' than to take the Fifth Amendment forty-two times," Hallinan said. "If you're gonna give your client a defense, give her a believable one, for Christ's sake! A drug-induced psychosis can last a day, a week, a year, a lifetime. It can account for total amnesia and selective forgetfulness. We figured the jury would feel sympathetic to her, so all they would need was a legal excuse to acquit. Any lawyer could have won that case. It was a cinch! The LA situation was much more difficult. And Carmichael was a hell of a dangerous thing because somebody was killed. We wanted a formula that could cover all three. Drug-induced schizophrenia couldn't have missed. Brainwashing would have worked, but there is no such thing in law. Brainwashing is an excuse *not* to prosecute."

Terence had told Patty, "If you're gonna be a revolutionary, you gotta stay outta jail." The new advice, from Bailey and Johnson, had been exactly the reverse: Stay in jail, where it's safe. Why had Patty so readily accepted it? I wondered. Or had she? "We were representing *her.* Bailey was representing the Hearsts, and Patty was just a pawn in his game," Vince said. "We would have allowed her to keep her humanity. Now she looks like a liar and a squealer. The one thing the Hearsts and Bailey had from the beginning standing like the Colossus of Rhodes over the whole damn thing was that that girl had been kidnapped and kept in captivity and isolation. *And they threw it away!* Here's the way I feel: It was as if I had owned a beautiful horse, a thoroughbred, a magnificent animal, and I sold the horse. . . . A year later I came back and I saw my horse broken down and spavined and sick. Those two mountebanks took that beautiful horse and broke it down."

Charles Garry analyzed the debacle quite another way, but he had no quarrel with the Hallinans about the villain of the piece. "Lee Bailey fucked up the case. A simple defense was available which he didn't use. One week before the robbery, the SLA was offered four million dollars for Patty's return. *This information was never imparted to the jury!*" The failure to do so was professionally inexcusable because it would have shown that the SLA didn't need to rob a bank to get money; the robbery must have had another purpose. The $4 million was in trust. If Patty had been a free agent and if the SLA trusted her, she could have let herself be ransomed, let her new comrades collect the loot, and then rejoined them. After that, she could even have signed over her trust funds. "Instead she becomes a chickenshit bank robber. This makes sense only *if* they were fronting her off. After the bank robbery she became a free agent, but by then she was confused, branded as a criminal, uncertain whether people would believe her or not, and in a state of complete depression.

"At the trial she should have said, You can do with me what you wish, but I don't intend to become a stool pigeon just to salvage my life that I've already fucked up. I don't intend to destroy other people. If she'd done that, a lot of people would have come and testified for her. I'm sure the Scotts would have."

"Then why put on a brainwashing defense?"

"Because Mom wanted it. It was the only explanation she could accept. But no attorney with any self-respect has to take shit from the mother of his client!" The brainwashing concept destroyed the defense by opening up the possibility of admitting testimony on subsequent events in Los Angeles that could tend to show the defendant's state of mind at the time of the crime. The judge chose to admit it, as there was considerable precedent, Garry said.

"The sexual testimony was outrageous. The 'rape' by Cinque simply never happened. Bailey made it up. As for Willie Wolfe, Patty should have said, 'We were in love,' instead of 'I couldn't stand him!' That was the truth, and the jurors would have bought it because the facts of the case would have proved it—the elegy on the last tape and the Olmec monkey. But I don't think Mr. Bailey knows very much about the facts of this case."

"If what you say is correct, Charlie, then how did her lawyers get her to repudiate the dead lover?"

"Because she's a cold, calculating bitch. She got in with a gang of thieves and she became just like them. She was the kind of person who would participate in anything to protect her own skin. Maybe she wasn't a bad girl before she was kidnapped. She was barely formed. She had no principles. But when she was kidnapped, the jungle came out in her."

"Did Patty get a fair trial?"

"She got a trial of her own choosing. She got a very sympathetic judge. It was not the court's fault, nor the jury's fault, that the case was presented in such a way that it could not have been won. The jury wanted to acquit her and the truth would have. The defense Bailey chose presented the jury with an impossible problem: They *couldn't* acquit her!"

Garry would never have attacked Fort. He would have asked him, Do you agree she was kidnapped? If the answer was yes, he would have asked, Do you know how long she was kept under restraint and when she became a free agent? Did you know there was four million in escrow in cash, providing the defendant surfaced by a certain date? Then why did they risk a chickenshit ten-thousand-dollar bank robbery? We would all like to hear your explanation of that, Dr. Fort.

The fact that Patty is a stool pigeon now could also have been used to indicate that she never truly joined the SLA. If she had really been a member, she would not have betrayed them. "All you gotta give a jury is some basis of reasonable doubt," he went on. "You'd need very little psychiatric testimony, just a profile on Cinque. Did they play the tapes for the jury?"

"Yes, but Cinque sounded crazy on them."

"All the better! Why not ask, How was she gonna get out of there alive? She was told by her lover, Willie Wolfe, there was only one way: She had to pretend. She was told *how* by her lover. The jury would have bought that. It was opera, high drama, a beautiful case to try!"

Dave Bancroft surprised me because he was unwilling to be a Monday-morning quarterback. He didn't think his adversary had done a bad job at all. And he was not at all sure Bailey was the real villain in the case. When I asked him why he thought Bailey hadn't chosen one of the other defenses available—straight insanity, diminished capacity, or actual conversion—he replied, "I came to feel there were forces at work in this trial of which I never gained firsthand knowledge. One of the things I want to do, just to satisfy my own curiosity, is find out exactly how Dr. West came into this case." When the doctor first visited the U.S. attorney's office, he had brought a secretary, a big briefcase, and two or three tape recorders, and he did two things that stuck in Bancroft's mind. He said that under no circumstances would he testify, for the prosecution or for the defense. It struck Bancroft as an odd comment, and the lawyer told the doctor that if he examined Patty for the court, he could be subpoenaed by the defense. That's the law. "He expressed some surprise and then asked me for a formulation of mental responsibility—that is, sanity versus insanity. I said that was an odd request in light of the fact that he'd just told me he did not want to participate in the trial. He said nevertheless, for his own information, could he have it, so I Xeroxed it and gave it to him."

I told Bancroft I thought the person fundamentally responsible for bringing in West was Bill Coblentz, the family lawyer. The same day last fall that Bailey was flying out to San Francisco, Coblentz had told me about a doctor who would be flying up soon from Los Angeles. The fellow might really be able to understand Patty and help her, Coblentz hoped, because he had done a lot of work studying hippies and dropouts during the Haight-Ashbury heyday and really knew his stuff. Coblentz had got the man's first name wrong, but he had called him "Dr. West," and I had always assumed that he had also mentioned this well-qualified person to Ollie Carter, his friend the judge, who was looking for well-qualified persons just then.

As soon as Bancroft read the report West and Singer submitted to the court, he told me, it was clear to him that the authors intended to testify for the defense. "Most competency reports are one or two pages long. When you get a 136-page document that dwells in detail on what kind of childhood braces somebody had or whether Mr. Hearst is allergic to bee stings, but neglects to talk about a period of a whole year —well!"

Any lawyer knows that putting on a psychiatric defense is taking a calculated risk that the prosecution psychiatrists may prove more persuasive than his own. Why had Bailey done it? The longer Bancroft thought about this, the more certain he became that "client pressure" had to be the answer. But client pressure was only part of the new lawyers' problem. A "trial script" also was lacking. "What happens is, new lawyers come in and they see a hard cookie. They know it's gonna take three, four months to bring this person around. Al Johnson did a hell of a job with her, by the way. If she had been tried right off, she would have taken that stand and lifted her leg on the entire courtroom."

"Why not plea-bargain?"

"If you're going to cop a plea, it's always preferable you do it right away—the sooner, the better—and with this young lady that wasn't possible. So the defense should have said to us, We realize that technically she's guilty. If we can bring her back, we'll come in and plead her guilty. They should not have said to us, What she did was wrong, but she didn't mean it. They should have said, She meant it—with a small *m*—but she realizes now that she was on a fling, and it all happened in such unusual circumstances—with such devastating consequences to herself and her family—that she shouldn't be judged harshly."

But although Bancroft found Bailey "adept at having his cake and eating it," Bailey's legal strategy put his own experts in an impossible position. Using the word "brainwash" instead of "duress" had been just guerrilla theater on Bailey's part, he thought. "But it also meant Bailey could use his experts only at half-horsepower—to say she was duressed, but not say she was converted. She suffered the kind of brutal maximum exposure you get from a psychiatric defense. For half a gain, she suffered a full loss. The defense chosen for this client meant a great cost in exposure and humiliation."

I said that Patty appeared to perceive herself now as a kind of universal victim and that I was inclined to agree. Bancroft demurred. "Isn't part of the tragedy that we do tend to see her as a victim? Weren't these really her own choices, however foolhardy? She must have a hell of a lot of inner strength! I put myself in that position, down there in jail, all my supports kicked out from underneath me, all my friends in jail. I have to face the humiliation of being forced to come back to my parents on their terms, not mine, and be at the mercy of *their* attorneys. All those things that I did I not only have to betray, I have to deny they were even *me!* Some parts of this strike very deep. I happen to think that the affection for Willie Wolfe, the genuine affection that she had probably for Wendy Yoshimura and probably Steve Soliah, are things it's awfully hard to rob somebody of. There just aren't very many times in one's life when one can come to feel as close to something, or somebody, as she probably did at times. It was probably very vibrant, very real."

Bancroft's empathy with his victim astounded me. The prosecutor didn't really see Patty as a victim. He thought it likely that those who did were in reality somewhat jealous of "the pungent life-sense she had during her period of active participation in the SLA. She wasn't an infant who was snatched away by a pack of wolves, weaned at the tit of some wolf sow, who then comes back to her village as a wolf. At nineteen years old in this day and age, you know what most of it is about."

Bancroft thought what had really happened was pretty simple: At the time she was abducted, Patricia Hearst felt a lot of half-conscious hostility toward her parents. Like most kidnapping victims, she was thankful to her abductors for small favors.* Once her terror subsided,

---

*The process by which a political hostage comes to identify with and may even "fall in love" with his captors has been well described by Brian M. Jenkins, a senior staff member of the Rand Corporation, who specializes in the study of political violence.

Surprisingly, few hostages bear any grudge against their captors for turning them into human pawns. Indeed, they frequently develop positive relationships with them. They chat and share sandwiches inside embassies surrounded by soldiers and policemen. Upon release, hostages and captors often part company amiably. . . .

Sometimes the hostages go beyond compliance at gunpoint and actively collaborate. They may even try to protect their captors. Several years ago, when police stormed a bank vault in Stockholm, one hostage held by two bank robbers shouted to police, "I won't let you hurt him." [This incident was the genesis of the so-called Stockholm syndrome.] A stewardess, once held at pistol point by a highjacker, continued to bring him gifts in prison long after his arrest.

Political extremists may lecture hostages on their political goals, but seldom make any serious attempt to indoctrinate, convert or recruit them. More often, the hostages are informed that they are simply pawns, bargaining chips, against whom the captors bear no personal malice, but who, unfortunately, may have to be killed if the demands are not met.

These are hardly ideal conditions to forge even temporary friendships. How do we explain it? Some of the reasons are simple and obvious. Others reveal how the human mind deals with the maximum threat.

The hostage instantly tries to establish his own identity, some human bond with his captors. He knows he must move out of the category of human item to be bartered and become a human being whom, he hopes, it must be harder to kill.

The hostage also quickly recognizes that his interests and those of his captors coincide. Both would like to see the demands met. The hostage's life depends on it.

But these obvious reasons alone do not account for a change of heart. Another process is taking place. Its essential ingredient is the inescapable threat of death, with the outcome a mere matter of whim from the hostage's point of view. The captors may kill him whether their demands are

she even found the experience exciting. "If I had to put it in one word, I'd say she was buccaneering. The real rich have a layer of confidence about them. It's not just money, it's not just power, it's another dimension, a sense of *I can do it!* And *I'm gonna land on my feet!* It's a great thing to have, that kind of self-confidence. But then I think she slowly came to realize what a real twerp Bill Harris was and what a pain in the ass Emily was. By the time she was picked up she was sick of the Harrises and ready to bomb off somewhere else, with Wendy or Steve Soliah, and now feels regretful, in that she's having to pay her price."

"If she had been your daughter, how would you have defended her?"

If he had the Hearsts' money, Bancroft would have done exactly as they did, except that he would have defended her on a diminished-capacity argument. Or if she were willing he might have advised her to plead guilty. "No doubt about it." But on second thought he had doubts because a guilty plea would mean the defendant would have to end up testifying against other people, and Bancroft wasn't sure he'd want to put a daughter in that position. He was unable to separate his feelings about what he thought best for his daughter from what he views as a moral duty to put bad people in jail. Not surprisingly, the prosecutor's sense of moral duty was well nourished and exercised; it bulged out of his persona like a fierce, overdeveloped moral biceps. When I spoke of Wendy Yoshimura as the only person who had tried purely to help Patty, Bancroft expressed a fleeting warmth. "Why do we have to prosecute people like Wendy? It's weird. Yet she should be prosecuted. She's a very different person now from what she was in the internment camps. Sure, she suffered as a child. No question. So did I. My mother was put in an insane asylum when I was five years old. She stayed there fourteen years." The moral ice cap had closed over.

Bancroft expressed regret at Patty's present predicament—not her residence behind bars, which he viewed as just, but the fact that "she's

---

met or not. It is entirely up to the captor, omnipotent, a virtual god, before whom the hostage is helpless, humiliated, virtually an infant. Under these circumstances, the hostage unconsciously begins to assimilate—and even imitate—the attitudes of his captors. ["Do What They Ask. And Don't Worry. They May Kill Me But They Are Not Evil Men," *The New York Times,* October 3, 1975.] Surprisingly, these points were not well brought out in the trial by either side. There was plenty of talk about brainwashing, dissociative reactions, coercive persuasion, attitudinal change, and so on, but for some reason, the infantalization of the hostage—the utter helplessness that *drives him unconsciously to imitate his captors*—was scarcely mentioned.

going to have to live for the rest of her life in the fantasy world created by her defense. Al Johnson is one of the most persuasive persons I've ever met, and—"

"What fantasy world?" I interrupted.

"Why, she was robbed of the opportunity to feel blameworthy! She was entitled to her guilt. Even little children have that. But she's been *evaporated.* Accountability is the name of the game, and they took her accountability away."

Bancroft felt another twinge of moral outrage—it amounted to compassion, really—for a predicament he sensed his colleague, Mr. Bailey, might be in. "You have to realize one thing," he told me. "Bailey was in receipt of a report, from a doctor who was highly credentialed, saying in no uncertain terms that his client was not responsible for her conduct. Now, that puts a lawyer in a corner. I mean, if he is *then* going to go in and try to plead guilty, he'll have to do some pretty fancy footwork, or he can later be accused of malpractice. That's why I happen to think that Dr. West was the architect of the defense in ways that perhaps even F. Lee Bailey does not recognize."

By April 15, the second anniversary of the robbery at the Hibernia Bank, I had talked to all the kings and nearly all the wizards. Only Merlin himself remained, and the mystery of Dr. West seemed to be at the heart of the matter. The various interpretations of the trial all seemed to suggest that his intervention had been crucial and, to critics, devastatingly wrong.

Merlin's castle was no ivory tower. The vast UCLA campus was abloom with spring flowers and happy students when I arrived in the impressive suite of offices occupied by Professor Louis Jolyon West, MD, chairman of the Department of Psychiatry and director of the university's prestigious Neuro-Psychiatric Institute. In an outer room three smiling secretaries, pert as Mouseketeers, glowed with the pure joy of service one used to see on the faces of the actresses playing novices in movies in which Loretta Young played the nun. In a few moments the inner door opened and Jolly himself appeared.

In the ordinary academic, every stray notion, theme, or correspondence the front end encounters is instantaneously captured, processed, pollinated, and cross-fertilized to be issued out the other end in the form of an academic paper, report, speculation, reflection, or footnote. The alimentary model is not, however, appropriate at the rarefied level at which Dr. West functions. Nonetheless, reviews, critiques, papers, and monographs drop from him like hen's eggs. One Mouseketeer is always at his elbow, ready at an instant to catch, tape, and transcribe the least stray insight or sudden synthesis. No *Eureka!*—however faint—goes unrecorded. At the drop of an idea, L. J. West reaches for fountain pen and tape recorder like a sneezing man going for Kleenex.

Dr. Jolly brims with tender loving care. Hearsts, Mouseketeers, me, the world—all are potential patients. He feels with his patients, empathizes, bleeds. Or does he? That central mystery, still unsolved, was American Pie's invisible plum. Could Dr. Jolly be an utterly, absolutely cold fish, colder even than F. Lee Pickerel himself?

The doctor ushered me into his large, pleasant inner office lined with bookshelves and expensive cabinets packed with reprints of the occupant's prodigious academic output. The door to this *sanctum sanctorum* can be shut firmly for as long as the doctor wishes. A university car is ever at his disposal. The big teaching hospital is next door. I am in the domain of a psychiatric Big Chief, a man who presides over a 250-bed hospital and a staff of more than fifty psychiatrists. But this year the professor was on sabbatical leave. He had plenty of time to talk, and enormous inclination. The week had begun badly. On April 11, the day before Patty was to be sentenced, someone—West could not imagine who—had leaked the West/Singer report to the newspapers, leading the press to conclude that its authors were the ones chiefly to blame for the disastrous brainwashing defense.* "Immediately after Patricia Hearst was arrested last Sept. 18 on armed bank robbery charges, she was ready to negotiate for leniency in return for a guilty plea," the *New York Times* story began. "Instead, lawyers and psychiatrists began to talk with her. From those talks emerged a defense plan based on a story that pictured her as the brainwashed victim of a revolutionary conspiracy." The tone of the article was distinctly unfriendly. The effect was as if a large, wet, half-decomposed sea monster had been dredged up and deposited on the analytic couch.

Dave Bancroft had been right about something else, I learned: West

*Later, Bailey would say that in a conversation with Judge Carter on June 13, the day before he died, the judge verbally released the West/Singer Report from court seal, thereby enabling Bailey to quote from the report in a magazine article entitled, "Why Patty Hearst's Trial Was Unfair." Nor was this the last time Bailey would raise Carter from the dead. In May 1977, for example, in his oral argument for Patty's appeal, Bailey told a three-judge panel that he had made a pretrial deal with Judge Carter to keep all Los Angeles matters (Mel's and Matthews) out of the trial. In its written rebuttal, the government denied that this was so. Browning was present at every pretrial conference with Carter. If necessary, he told a colleague, he and both of Carter's clerks were willing to submit personal supporting affidavits that Bailey's oral claim was untrue.

and Singer *were* planning to write a book. "The heart of our study will be the report you read."* Its title, "A Different Person," was taken from Cardinal Mindszenty's memoirs: "Without knowing what had happened to me, I had become a different person." The book would attempt to present the case in "the Bazelonian way." The doctor and Judge Bazelon were old friends. They had often discussed the need for reforming the way in which psychiatric testimony is usually presented in criminal trials. Doctors should offer medical opinions only, they believed. A doctor on the witness stand should present the case to the jury the same way a hospital physician presents a case to a review committee of his fellow doctors. "But what Bazelon couldn't predict was: Once we did it, the court wouldn't want it."

It was midday on Thursday, April 15, when West and I sat down to talk, and he kept going almost nonstop for two days, right through Passover and Good Friday. Everything we said was taped, later to be transcribed by the Mouseketeers. When the transcript of our marathon conversation arrived in the mail sometime later, it made the West/ Singer report look like a slender pamphlet. Just reading through it all again was head-breaking. Really understanding what it contained and then cutting this hunk of paper up or down into an intelligible document were going to require an icebreaker, and not the conversational kind—the kind the Coast Guard has in Alaska.

In the course of my icebreaking chores over the next several months, I talked to a great number of psychiatrists on both coasts and collected some brutally frank assessments. One of Dr. West's most prestigious colleagues characterized him as "an opportunistic psychiatrist-executive who has never in his life made an original contribution to psychiatric thinking . . . a high-level hack." I suppose there is some truth to that. I also suppose that had Dante known any psychiatrists, he would have assigned to them a circle in hell several levels lower than the place he put the lawyers.

There was other bad news. Trade gossip had it that Dr. West's protracted involvement in the Hearst case had done him more harm than good, professionally speaking; it had, in fact, probably destroyed

*Dr. West eventually decided that the profits of the book, if any, would be given to charity; but the manuscript was never completed. Although both West and Singer worked for more than a year at fashioning alternating chapters, ultimately, like the author(s) of Joel Fort's "Expert Witness," these experts, too, lost heart.

his hitherto-excellent prospects for achieving the longed-for pinnacle of his career: the chairmanship of the American Psychiatric Association. So HERNAP had injured kindly Dr. Jolly more seriously than most.

All this being said, I was particularly sorry to learn from him that nobody in the Hearst family ever asked Dr. West for his professional opinion of their daughter. (West decided to offer it anyway. While the jury was still out he called on Patty's parents and told them that regardless of which way the verdict went, they should understand that their daughter was "a sick cookie" who was going to need a lot more care than she or they realized. She was incapable of planning for the future in any realistic way, he explained, particularly in her relationships with men, even though on the surface she appeared normal.) Each time I hacked into the mammoth transcript my sorrow deepened because, once one heard Dr. West's opinion in full, and understood it— which, in my case, required several readings—the weight and value of the thing was unmistakable. Inside this ice jam, this Antarctica of paper, was the most accurate reflection of what had really happened to Patricia Hearst that anybody was ever going to be able to get.

The elves, having got us settled and coffeed, with our Sonys all hooked up on that April morning, now respectfully closed the door. "Jolly," I said, "how did you get into all this?"

Carter called me the day the bail affidavit was filed. A lot of people don't want to get involved. I don't usually want to, either, and won't. I don't like the use of psychiatrists to oppose one another as expert witnesses. But Patty Hearst was a different matter. This was a court asking for help prior to a trial. I told the judge that I was not interested in serving as a witness, and he assured me that was not a part of this assignment. I told him that before he appointed me there were a couple of things he might want to consider. I had given an interview about brainwashing in which Patty Hearst's name had come up, and I had written a letter to the Hearst family. He said, I know the Hearst family, but that isn't going to prevent me from trying this case, and as long as you feel that you can be objective, that's good enough for me.

So I said, All right. Now I've got some conditions. I'm going to want to order a lot of studies. I want a complete medical/neurological workup. I would like to have you appoint a fourth person to the panel. I want a woman, and a psychologist. He pointed out that I could engage her, but I told him I felt she should be working for him, not me, as an equal panel

(509)

member, and that her findings should be available to the other doctors. He agreed again.

Well, that's how, with some trepidation, Margaret Singer and I got involved. I was willing to serve, and it fit in well with my sabbatical plans. Here was a victim of violence, and one of the big categories in the UCLA Violence Study Plan on which I had worked for some years had been victims and what happens to them. This seemed like a legitimate way to invest some time, and it was a hell of an interesting case. Besides, the lawyer had been claiming "brainwashing."

Before I ever saw Patricia Hearst, I jotted down a little list of alternative possibilities. (Dr. West went to his blackboard and chalked an outline.)

I. No Kidnap
II. Kidnap
    A. Psychiatric Disorder Preceding
        1. Psychopathic Personality
        2. Severe Passive-Dependent Personality
    B. Converted Politically
    C. Pseudoconversion (through coercive persuasion)
        1. Feigned
        2. Role Identification (doesn't sustain)
    D. Psychotic (no trial)

The first possibility was that she was a coconspirator and the kidnapping was a phony event. The second possibility was that she was a bona fide kidnapping victim but was also a mentally unstable person of some kind —either a psychopath who got turned on by excitement or a pathologically dependent, passive person who would respond to any suggestions made by anybody.

A third alternative was that she could have been a genuine political convert. A fourth was that she could have experienced a "pseudoconversion," either completely feigned, or a role identification that didn't maintain itself when circumstances changed. (An example of circumstances changing is the repatriation of a prisoner.)

Now, as a court-appointed person, the charge was to consider all the available information from all sources. I asked Browning point-blank: Was this a bona fide kidnapping or not? He said yes, it was. I said, Give me everything you've got about Patricia Hearst. He turned it over, and I set up headquarters in a motel near the jail and settled down to study

the material and the patient. Everything the government had was supposed to be handed over. But they had a bunch of stuff they didn't show
us, and then in court they asked us about it. I'm not sure how much of
the withholding was deliberate on their part and how much was just
confusion.

By the time I began to examine her Bailey had just been called in,
but the Hallinans were still involved. Margaret and I could both see
that whatever was wrong with Kayo, he was telling the truth: The essential basis for his oddball affidavit was that his client was unable
to give him a totally rational, inclusive, historical account of the bank
robbery or anything else. She still hadn't been able to tell anybody what
had really happened to her in that goddamn closet—which was part of
the reason we said she should have treatment before she had to prepare
a defense.

My notes, dictated after I saw her that very first time, describe how I
chased Hallinan and "a little fat fellow" out of the room. At the time,
I couldn't even remember who he was. I think now that Al Johnson
probably did more to bring her back than anybody else. What was taking
place in that jail in the months before the trial was this: Someone who
had been out of touch with reality to a considerable degree—not because
of insanity but because, in a sense, she had been living under a spell—
was bit by bit having a guy like Al Johnson dragging her or forcing her
to face the real world, real people, the real FBI. Not the ogres of her
fantasy but people like Tom Padden and Park Stearns, who were doing
their job and wouldn't hurt a fly. I don't call that reverse brainwashing.
That's what you do with a psychiatric patient, and the people who do it
are not the psychiatrist who sees you once a day or three times a week
but the psychiatric technician who's right there hour by hour, playing
cards, talking about what's happening in the newspapers, and what we
call, in technical jargon, reflecting reality back to a person who is not in
full touch with it.

After I met Patty the first time, I made it a point to talk to Bailey and
Johnson right away because up to then they didn't really have a picture
of what had happened to her. Also, I realized there were other trials
pending, and I knew that her lawyer, Hallinan, had advised her that
since all my notes were available to the prosecution, she shouldn't name
names to me. By not pushing her into a position where she had to say,
I don't want to talk about that, my lawyer tells me I shouldn't, I could
maintain the relationship in which I work the best, a doctor-patient
relationship, which I consider to be very legitimate, not a dirty word.

(511)

One of the documents I had was Hallinan's affidavit. Hallinan is no fool. When your patient—correction, when your client—can't tell you what happened, how in the hell are you gonna prepare a defense? He knew there was something wrong. He just didn't know what to call it. So he made this affidavit up in order to get her out on bail. But Mr. Kayo Hallinan is about as psychiatrically sophisticated as a chorus girl, so I just settled down to do what you always have to do, and that's to examine the patient yourself.

Margaret and I both had the distinct understanding from our conversations with the judge not only that our report was sealed but also that we were somehow immune from any further involvement. But after Lee and Al saw our report, Johnson asked me how I would feel about testifying for the defense. I said, "I understand I am not available for that under any conditions." He said, "That's not true. You could be a witness. There are ways." So I said, "You have my report. Just show it to the jury. If they want to know what happened to Patricia Hearst, here it is. If you need psychiatric witnesses, call up any of the people who really know their onions; they'll find the same things I've found." He asked me for names and I gave him several, the first two being Lifton and Orne.

Johnson called me next on New Year's Eve and said, "Doctor, we've got a problem with your report. We can't get it introduced unless you come and testify." I thought he was telling me that unless I appeared as a witness, the jury wouldn't get to read it. But I still didn't want to do it. If I appeared in the courtroom, called by only one side, then my report would lose its value as an objective document. So I declined again. He called back a week or ten days later, saying they just had to have me. I said, Well, I certainly don't want to hold back if it means that this information I went to such great pains to prepare would not come before the jury, so I would do it on the condition that Margaret would participate. I also told him he should understand that I was not doing it for a fee. I couldn't afford to pay travel and per diem costs, but I was not going to serve as a paid defense witness.

Then Lifton called and asked if he could come through LA on his way back to New York and just talk about the case. A Sunday it was, I remember, because I missed my tennis. Martin Orne telephoned Margaret. That was the extent of the contact between us before we actually appeared on the scene.

When I first saw Patty she seemed withdrawn and downcast, but I didn't take that at face value. I had read reports saying that she seemed pretty cheerful around the jail. I went and talked to some of those officers and they said, "When she's with her lawyers or you doctors she looks like that, but when she's with us she doesn't seem so depressed." It wasn't until the third session with Patricia that I realized what I had—a full-blown dissociative reaction.

At that point, as I understand it from Lee, he had not yet made his decision on what her defense would be. But after he read my report he decided to base his defense on it, and once he decided to accept my diagnosis, I don't know whether he had any options other than to go to trial.

Looking back, it seems to me a lot of things were unfair about the trial. Before it even started, Judge Carter had a report from four experts he, himself, had appointed, and every single one said that this person needs treatment before having to defend herself in a contest at law. Rejecting that was the first unfair thing. Two, the court decided to present to the jury all of the prejudicial material deriving from the period after the bank robbery until the time of her capture, and even after. I know this was supposed to provide retroactive information about her state of mind in the bank, but I think that is a spurious argument; even if she had become a convert later, she still might not have been one at the time she was in the bank. This ruling allowed a third unfairness: The government knew that things had happened during that year that she couldn't afford to testify about. So essentially they required her to either incriminate herself or take the Fifth Amendment. A fourth unfairness is that the jury was allowed to see all kinds of documents, some of which were in dispute as to authorship, but never got to see our report—which both sides knew was the only complete account. It was just ruled out. I swore to tell the whole truth, but the only way the jury was going to get the whole truth was to read it for themselves. There's no way that you can equate what a group of twelve people can grasp and retain of information gotten in question-and-answer form and what they could get by studying a carefully worded document.

I also felt it was very unfair to let the jury hear the Trish Tobin tape. It had been edited and two passages were removed. In one she describes her fear of the Harrises and says how bad they are; in the other she asks Trish to tell her parents not to believe the stuff she'd said on the tapes. The jury was allowed to hear the Tobin tape, and the SLA tapes, all of which were prejudicial to Patty, yet they weren't allowed to hear the jail tapes that I made, which showed her in a completely different light. The government feared that if the jury heard them, they might understand better what had really happened. They knew goddamned well she was innocent! Browning knew it just as well as I did. He was prosecuting the case because winning is the name of the game, and in order to win, you do whatever you think you can possibly get away with. On both sides. One of the main points of the adversary system is supposed to be that fair play will bring everything out. But one of the things that staggered me was how much of the energy and craftiness of the lawyers, again on both sides, was spent in keeping information away from the jury, with Margaret Singer as the most dramatic case in point. Also, the adversary system is based on the idea that the number-one value in our society is fair play. When you change the number-one value from fair play to winning, you go beyond duty, as I think Browning did.

Judge Carter's decisions appeared to me to be responsible for much of the trial's unfairness. Carter would make a decision that seemed to kind of equalize the two sides and then say to the lawyers, Now have at it. Have at it! Like a referee who wants to make sure that the guy that just got knocked down is allowed to stand up and clear his head, and have the rosin brushed off his gloves, and resume boxing once more on equal terms. But this wasn't a boxing match between Browning and Bailey. It was Patricia Hearst's life on the line.

Furthermore, the government has no appeal. If she were acquitted, that was it. So if he had been one-sided, his decisions were never going to be reviewed by a higher court. And the world, which was watching Carter's last case—the one that makes his name a household word—would say, Patricia Hearst was acquitted, but you have to admit the judge didn't give her a single break. He was very tough-minded.

The search for truth and the use of a systematic or scientific method —that's what the university life is all about. Maybe the courtroom isn't a very good place to express that. Before the trial I had faith in the fairness of our judicial system. I had a deep-seated belief that the truth will come out and that fair-minded people, if they're faced with the truth, will know it when they hear it. Now my faith is shaken badly. My whole life is tied up with the idea of being a good doctor, not with being a good witness in a trial. Part of that is being true to yourself. Compassion is one thing, but doctors don't make diagnoses out of compassion. If they do, they aren't very good doctors.

This trial was the most disillusioning thing that ever happened to me. I mean the behavior of the government. You must understand that I am a patriot. I enlisted at age eighteen. I spent twelve years in uniform. I

*put in twenty-odd years of active duty. I owe a tremendous amount to
my government. They paid for my education. Without the government,
I'd be just another lumberjack.*

We had been talking for more than four hours. It was time for me
to leave. "By the way, what *is* a dissociative reaction, actually?" I asked
as I was putting on my coat.

Jolly slid open a cabinet door. *"The* paper on dissociative reaction,
if I may say so." He smiled and pressed fifty-five more Xeroxed pages
into my hand. It was a reprint of an article by L. J. West, MD. Then,
helpful as any one of his Mouseketeers, he insisted on personally driving
me back to the hotel. En route, he could not stop talking. "The poor
child must feel like a character in a Kafka novel by now! Her kidnappers are on the *Today Show,* and she's sitting in jail, convicted of bank
robbery!"

"Jolly," I said the next morning when we were again seated, coffeed,
and hooked up to the tape recorders, "when did you realize the jury
wasn't buying it?"

In addition to Patricia Hearst herself, who was almost resigned to
being found guilty, Dr. West knew of two others who were very doubtful: Gonzales and himself. Back when the three defense psychiatrists
had completed their testimony, West felt confident the jury did grasp
that something bad had been done to the defendant; otherwise she
would not have been involved in a bank robbery. But as the weeks
passed—that testimony, and her own, fading into the background while
the government hammered away at other issues, which West could see
that the jury was listening to—he grew increasingly pessimistic. The
night before the summation, Bailey called the entire defense team together. In *his* opinion, he said, the most effective moment of their joint
labors had been when West told the jury that at the time Patricia Hearst
made up her mind to play the role of Tania, she believed her only
alternative was to die. He planned to base his summation on this.

At that point in the game, the distinguished doctor and the famous
lawyer were in a condition of considerable mutual awe, despite West's
unease about his own moments in the box. Throughout the trial Dr.
West, like the other defense experts, found it disconcerting to take the
stand without knowing what question Bailey might throw next. But
although they made repeated attempts to sit down at night with Bailey

and map the terrain of the next day's questioning, the lawyer was elusive. Not that he was unwilling to talk; he just wouldn't talk about trial strategy. Eventually the doctors decided that the lawyer's real message to them was: Look, I'm the legal expert around here, not you. Trust me to bring out what is in the best interests of our common goal, which is not to let you fellows show off how much you know about a very complex case. It is to acquit an innocent person. Having got the message, Bailey's expert witnesses, like his clients, put themselves completely in the lawyer's hands.

But despite his discomfort on the stand, West also considered F. Lee Bailey, then and now, the most naturally gifted lawyer he had ever seen. His aggressive instincts, his mind, his voice, his presence, his personal magnetism, his dramatic flair, his talents as a raconteur, his rapport with the media, and his extraordinary intellectual ability to organize complex information so that it becomes intelligible to jurors—all these traits combined to make the man ideally suited for trial work. What's more, he was aware of his own gifts, and knew how to exploit and vary them according to need. He could throw any pitch. He could use himself as an instrument, the way a great actor does or, for that matter, a great psychotherapist. Before meeting him, West expected the lawyer might be little more than a flamboyant, artful manipulator. But once they met he came to share the team's genuine awe for Bailey's ability.

When Bailey did finally call a first full-group defense-strategy session, during the evening of St. Patrick's Day, it was to discuss what everybody thought his summation should contain. Flattered by the news that Bailey considered one of his spontaneous remarks the linchpin of the entire case, Dr. West was emboldened to speak out forcefully on what *he* thought the proper summation should contain. He envisioned a three-part performance, with the first part very long and detailed. He sensed that the jury still wanted to hear a lot more from the great F. Lee Bailey himself. They had seen his razzle-dazzle skill at cross-examination, but they hadn't heard *from* him in the same sense they had heard from Browning and Bancroft. West recommended that Bailey take up each of the prosecutors' points one by one and show how invalid or irrelevant or dubious it was. Anyone could have carried and dropped the rectangular clips, for example, and either type of clip fits the guns. None of this had been brought out. West didn't know why. He was a psychiatrist, not a lawyer.

As a psychiatrist, he also thought the Olmec monkey business had to be explained to the jury with great care because the obvious conclusion was that Patty *had* kept it as a love token, then lied. West, the expert, recognized how much more complicated it really was: The Olmec monkey was the only talisman of a terrified girl who had been kidnapped half-naked, and thereafter literally had no way to clothe herself except with the gauze of her new Tania role and nothing to hang on to except the *mono.* The jurors also had to be made to understand the psychological nuances of her relationship to Willie Wolfe. They had to understand that when she blurted out, "I couldn't stand him!" it was the present Patty talking, the girl in the box, not the person who psychologically had costumed herself as Tania. Also, she was speaking specifically about sex. Sexually, Wolfe probably smelled bad. They made love without privacy. But at the same time, Patty was aware that their relationship was helping her remain alive.

Suddenly Wolfe and most of the others were dead and, magically, she was *still* alive. Perhaps somehow the monkey had protected her. West could not imagine Patty throwing away the little stone face after that, not even if she had hated Willie Wolfe's guts. Although West was not at all sure a jury was capable of grasping these kinds of subtle psychological nuances, nevertheless he felt they had to be carefully spelled out to the jurors in order to offer an alternative explanation of Patty's curious and damaging behavior. The objective of part one of the summation was slowly and painstakingly to bring the jury back to the reality of what they were being asked to decide about: a bank robbery, not all the bizarre, lengthy goings-on over Joel Fort.

Part two would be devoted to reminding the jurors of the person Patty was before the kidnapping and also to making them reexperience what happened to this nineteen-year-old girl whose door was suddenly broken in, her sanctuary invaded, her mate struck down and, she thought, killed. He wanted them then to reexperience the imprisonment in the closet and to relive with her the seventy days leading up to the bank robbery, so that they could understand, as he did, that there was not one shred of evidence that Patty, in this period, was "a rebel in search of a cause." He wanted the jurors reminded that if Patty had been captured directly after the robbery, no one would have perceived her as a real bank robber, despite the SLA tapes. Instead, the world would have seen a helpless captive of some very terrifying people.

Then, two-thirds of the way through his summary, West thought Bailey should stop and say, Ladies and gentlemen, this is where it all ends. Remember that. All she is on trial for here is the bank robbery. But remember, too, that life is a one-way street. After the robbery

Patty's bridges were burned. After the robbery she had no choice but to continue with the SLA.

The actual summation that Bailey delivered the next day left West stunned. The lawyer had been brief, slurred, rambling, at times almost incoherent. West tried to describe the pathology of the botched summation: Throughout the case Bailey had been an actor playing to two audiences, press and jury; and at the end he may have got the two mixed up. Furthermore, because of Bailey's many absences, much of the legal work had fallen to Al Johnson. But Johnson wasn't trying the case, Bailey was, and in a courtroom, as in an operating room, one cannot have two first surgeons. On top of that, West thought it likely that experienced trial reporters had come to San Francisco in a skeptical mood, expecting to hear a snow job from Bailey, and then had gradually come to understand that with respect to Patty's queer condition the lawyer knew what he was talking about. Unfortunately the press took pains to tell Bailey as much; worse still, he listened. The result of all this positive feedback from his buddies in the press box could have given Bailey the impression, by the time he was ready to sum up, that he had already won, and all that was necessary was to reiterate his central point: survival.

But the main trouble with Bailey, West thought, was a kind of creeping deterioration in the great man himself. For West, each of HERNAP's major characters had a literary analogue—Cinque was Emperor Jones, Patty was playing the lead in *Sanctuary*—and the crumbling of Bailey so reminded West of Jack London's novel *Burning Daylight* that after the trial he hunted up a first edition of the book and sent it to the lawyer as a kind of consolation prize.

Burning Daylight describes the downfall of the strongest, most gifted man in Alaska, a brute who can lift nine hundred pounds and wear out two Indians carrying the mail across the Arctic waste. His nickname is Burning Daylight because he's always the first one up in the morning, shouting at the others as soon as the sun comes up, "Get moving! You're burning daylight!" He makes his big gold strike; he challenges the outside money operators and wins again. In triumph, the gold-rush king comes to California and settles into what he calls "the game." But he fails to realize that it isn't *his game* anymore. Because his orientation always was that life is a gamble, he begins to gamble in too many ways. He spreads himself too thin. The transformation of gold miner into tycoon is accomplished at a great price. As the hero gets further and further away from nature, and the sources of his greatest strength, he becomes a heavy drinker and grows physically soft. To West, the story illustrates how "a great man with all that is manly lets himself slip, investing himself and his energies in things that are not really in harmony with the source of his own greatness; how he betrays himself."

After the trial West severed all his ties to HERNAP. Nonetheless he hoped that his farewell gift to his old comrade-in-arms might prompt Bailey to take himself in hand a bit, concentrate on the law more, and spend more time in exhaustive analysis of his current cases and in tough, lonely scholarship. In short, he hoped Bailey would become more like West. He hoped the lawyer would become more Spartan in his personal habits, go on the wagon, stop smoking so much, get some regular exercise, take things easier, find more time for solitude and for a little more family life; whatever would save him from a progressive dilution of his tremendous talents.

Bailey might be burning himself out, West feared. It was no accident that he had come to look so much older than his actual age—forty-two. Come to think of it, the lawyer had been repeating himself a lot lately, too. West thought there might be real damage there.

Certainly it would be understandable. The trial happened to take place at a time when Bailey was under greater strain than he himself realized. It came at the end of a long period of personal stress, during which his whole career was in jeopardy. The Glenn Turner fiasco had taken two years out of his life, just about broken him financially, and almost destroyed his law firm. During this period his main concern had been to try to hold all his enterprises together, including his helicopter business, which West believed was on the brink of disaster.

For whatever combinations of reasons, West could not be sure, but by the end of trial Bailey abandoned the thought-reform–traumatic-neurosis sequence that had been so painstakingly presented by his doctor witnesses and in his summation gave a simple coercion defense. Possibly Bailey had despaired of the jury's ability to grasp the complex psychiatric formulation and preferred to paint his final portrait in simple black and white. And the jury went for the black. On the other hand, Bailey may have been so exhausted that he just had to keep it simple—"because he didn't have the patience and will left to undertake the subtle and complex work to make the other thing come off. In a situation when he needed every bit of skill and strength he ever had, plus a lot of extra care and effort, time and chance caught him at that moment when he didn't have it to give. The will was not there. He was an exhausted man and didn't realize it." At bottom, Bailey's *machismo* may have been to blame. "He had pushed himself—his brain, his body, his reserves of strength and energy, his capacity to absorb alcohol—further than he realized, so that in the end he wasn't able to do what he had done so splendidly so many times before."

The truth was that the trial had been an enormous physical and emotional strain on West, too. In some ways the doctor's post-HER-NAP convalescence would take more time than Bailey's. The lawyer, after all, was accustomed to all-out courtroom free-for-alls; indeed, he relished them. But nothing in West's professional experience as a psychiatrist was in any way comparable to the self-imposed physical ordeal of flying an airplane back and forth every night to Las Vegas for a week, in the middle of a trial. The feat staggered West's imagination, and he knew what he was talking about: West had spent years as an Air Force flight surgeon.

No one, of course, had been under greater stress for a longer period than the defendant. After the closet only the dissociation of affect had made it possible for her to function, West believed. After the bank robbery the public came to feel that the one sure way Patricia Hearst could redeem herself to posterity was to die. After the verdict West worried that Patty herself might agree. Now everything had let her down: the government, the SLA, her parents, her lawyers, her closest friends (in the sense that the Trish Tobin tape was really what did her in), and, finally, even her own body. The spontaneous pneumothorax accident that placed the heart in territorial contest with the lungs had occurred just as Patty began her song to the prosecutorial posse. West felt very sympathetic to the war within, to "the body's fight for its own integrity," and he was more worried now than he had ever been. In the depths of depression a person plain despairs. But as the depression begins to lift he or she reaches a point where there is still enough despair left to make life seem hopeless, yet sufficient resolve so that one is at least able to do something about it. The risk of suicide therefore is greatest about halfway up the slope of recovery.

West had been unhappy when Patricia was put on the stand. He knew that her true psychological condition, after her capture or before, was not well understood by anybody. There were certain things she knew how to do: to smile, to tell about how she took part in the bank robbery. That was the beginning of it, that was the mold, and she kept on doing it thereafter. She said, "Right on!" She said, "Off the Pigs!" She raised her little fist and gave a big smile, which even she really didn't understand. He doubted that the Harrises understood, either. As to whether she enjoyed being "the queen of the SLA," the one objective observer whose account we have—Wendy Yoshimura—saw her as almost a zombie: depressed, withdrawn, subservient—and Wendy tried to help. She even tried to help Patty get back in touch with her parents, as Wendy herself had managed to do. Joel Fort called Patty "the queen of the underground" or "the queen of the SLA" to suggest that she relished her role. West didn't see any evidence for this or for Kozol's assertion that she was "a rebel in search of a cause." Wendy's description of how she and Patty broke with the Harrises didn't remind West of a proud and joyous queen enjoying her prestige and pizzazz underground. It sounded like the rescue operation of a pitiful child.

West was scornful of Joel Fort's assertion that Patty was eager for sex because she was a sexually active girl and had been so at an early age. A person who is terrorized and depressed isn't feeling sexy. All the data from prison camps suggest that sexual feelings are about the first thing to go. West saw Fort's testimony as that of a healthy, well-fed male having a neurotic fantasy about a woman in a closet.

A final reason Patty paired off with Willie Wolfe—though not brought out in the trial—was her dread of becoming common property. This would have included homosexual liaisons, a prospect of which Patty was terrified.

The main difficulty West saw in the testimony of both Dr. Fort and Dr. Kozol was that neither of them *examined* Patricia Hearst. They merely had conversations with her. They did not do a proper psychiatric work-up and interpretation of medical and psychological facts based upon observations, tests—the data that were available. In jail or out, a medical examination is a doctor looking at a patient, not a detective looking at a criminal.

When West first met Patricia, she was at a ragged edge. Gradually her emotional condition improved, up to a point early in the trial, he thought, maybe through the time of her own testimony. Deterioration began again with the cross-examination. One could see it taking a toll. She seemed to be getting smaller. She was starving again, partly because she couldn't eat, for emotional reasons. In Browning's cross-examination Patty was subjected to yet another interrogation on which her life was going to depend: "We are asking you questions to which we already know the answers, and the answers incriminate you." This had been Cinque's message to Patty, and it was almost verbatim Browning's message. West felt in advance that this was going to be traumatic. As a court-appointed psychiatrist, he had been extremely reluctant to see Patty subjected to cross-examination, and had said so in his report. But the decision whether to put her on the stand was up to the attorneys. Bailey had read the warning about cross-examination in West's report, but there were legal factors to be considered as well as psychiatric ones, and by the time West arrived in San Francisco Patty's testimony already had begun.

Any young person subjected to the stresses that Patricia Hearst was might have succumbed the same way she did, he was certain. Furthermore, if the same tragedy had befallen his own daughter, as a father West would have been very likely to follow Bailey's advice to the letter. If he had said the girl was innocent and therefore should not cop a plea, West would have gone along with that. If he had said, In order for us to win the case, we have to put her on the stand, West would have thought, God, can she stand that? But he would have gone along.

West had spent his previous sabbatical year studying young people in America during the mid-sixties, and he had identified and color-coded three distinct varieties of rebels: the blacks, the reds, and the greens—the last being the flower children and other superpeaceful counterculture types. Knowing Patty's tender nature as well as he did —her early ambition to be a veterinarian and care for sick animals, her later enjoyment of her job as a nursery-school teacher in a poor neighborhood—West was certain that when Patty's normal adolescent rebellious instincts surfaced, she would have "gone green." Like his own daughter, she would have felt drawn to a commune, not to the barricades.

But when one agrees to play a role, even voluntarily, the influence of the situation is enormous. Since that role was all Patty had, however, she made herself play it. Then, as soon as external circumstances changed significantly, she began to revert in the general direction of her previous identity; this further indicates that hers was not a conversion at all. Otherwise one would not know. But after only three or four days away from the direct influence of the Harrises, living in a neutral setting, seeing her parents, talking to her pal Trish, being in touch with the larger reality that her role had kept her from—the role dropped away. "And what was left was a goddamn blob." Patty was just beginning to grasp the meaning of some of the things she had said on the SLA tapes. "God, she didn't want to hear those tapes! And when you played them for her, she collapsed!" West felt like a brute forcing her to listen. It was not that she was unaware of what was on the tape; it was that she couldn't stand to hear it and didn't want to think about it. She sounded to West like a three-year-old being asked to stick her hand in the fire. "Do I have to?" she would ask him pitifully.

The difference between Patricia and the other SLA members was that only she had been forcefully dragged out of a normal life and thrust into this one. All other choices had been taken away from her. If through her identification with the SLA role, and as a person suffering from a traumatic neurosis, she was *unable* to see alternatives for herself, if she came to believe that her only hope was to stay with the group and be Tania, then she was bound to the SLA, not through her own choice but through a consequence of what they had done to her. It thus was clear to West where the responsibility lay: with the SLA, not with Patty. *Because she herself did not make the choice.* Any other train of logic leads to the same kind of garbage conclusion that holds the German Jews responsible for their own destruction because they did not put up more of a fight.

In saying Patty should have taken responsibility for her acts, one also says that the brutes who captured her were *not* responsible. Most people have no difficulty taking this point of view, because they don't like to think of *themselves* as being weak, helpless, and at the mercy of others, especially of dangerous people or persons whose values are inimical to their own. "Exactly the same thing could happen to me" is a very difficult thing to acknowledge. And because one doesn't want to believe it could happen to oneself, one refuses to believe it could happen to someone else. And so the tendency is to tell oneself that it really didn't happen to Patty—she's lying. It's a natural reaction. West understood why the jury and 80 percent of the public responded by saying, It wouldn't have happened to me. I would have found a way to escape. But how many Patty Hearsts had they ever examined? How many dissociative reactions had they had to treat? How many returned prisoners had they had to sit with and listen to as the men attempted to account to themselves for what they had done? West had seen many men who would rather be punished, be convicted of treason, even executed, than admit they had assumed a new identity in order to survive. In many ways it is even more frightening to lose one's identity than it is to die. At least when one is dying, one knows *who* is dying, but to lose one's identity is to face a kind of unknown that most people cannot grasp. Very comforting models exist of identity after death: heaven and hell and Nirvana. Every religion ever invented by mankind, from the pharoahs onward, even from the prehistoric times of the mother-goddesses, throng with them. But there are no models to help one imagine what it is like to not be oneself anymore.

The marathon interview with Jolly West left me dizzy but still on my feet and certain at last which *Rashomon* view was my own. Patty *had* been brainwashed. She had undergone a pseudoconversion, brought about through coercive persuasion, which resulted in role identification that after her capture she could not sustain. If Dr. West himself had been permitted to put the case to the jury, as he had to me, if the jurors had not had to hear him "in translation," so to speak, I was sure that they would have bought it.

Sure until I talked to the jurors, that is. Locked in sequestration, penned on the other side of the looking glass, the jurors had seen a third trial, different from what the press or the experts saw; they had been moved by different levers and fulcrums and emotional block and tackle. This, then, is the third reflection: what the jury saw.

By the time they retired the jurors had listened to 66 witnesses, and the defense had offered 512 exhibits, the prosecution 295. They looked at almost none of these objects and documents. They shut the door to the windowless, green-painted jury room that Friday morning and immediately elected the senior man in the group foreman. He was William Wright, a retired Air Force colonel. "Thank you for electing me," he said. "We have a job to do here."

They had been locked together and locked away from the world for nearly seven weeks, and at that point each of them felt he or she knew each of the others—fancies, foibles, weaknesses, strengths—better than any other living beings. The circumstances of their sequestration had added up to a marathon group-therapy session.

Besides the colonel there was a nurse, a retired housing inspector, an airplane mechanic, a letter carrier, a potter, a dental assistant, a receptionist, an airline stewardess, a commercial artist, a boat operator, and a housewife. Seven were women, five men. Ten were Caucasian, one was Japanese-American, and one was Mexican-American. Most appeared to be middle-income and middle-class. Eleven were married and eight had children, of whom four were close to Patty in age.

"I think we're all thinking the same thing," their foreman continued. "We might as well take a vote . . . unless somebody wants to examine some evidence first?" No one made a sound.

But Colonel Wright had guessed wrong. On the first ballot only nine persons voted to convict. Three held back. Later two of the three would explain that they were hoping someone would come up with a persuasive argument for acquittal; that is, they weren't *yet* ready to convict. But by the next ballot one gave in, and the vote stood ten to two. Their third ballot was eleven to one, but by then two jurors were in tears, and the group decided to adjourn. It was proving very difficult to ignore personal feelings, as Carter had demanded, and judge Patty only and strictly by the weight of the evidence.

"Legally it boils down to a question of whether you believe her—you don't know whether to cry or vomit," the judge had said. That night, in their rooms at the Holiday Inn, the jurors did both. Every juror later agreed that the decision to vote *guilty* was the most difficult one of his or her lifetime, more difficult, specifically, than the decision to get married, get divorced, have a child, or change jobs. But they felt they had no choice: By the time the trial ended the jurors found it impossible not to believe Patty was lying. Even so, their inner turmoil and guilt were excruciating. The vow not to discuss the case had meant they had been able to share everything except the main thing: the mounting anguish growing inside each one of them as they listened and watched the trial unfold. A measure of their aloneness is that each of the nine persons who felt compelled to vote *guilty* on the first ballot was positive he or she was the only person who had reached that unbearable but unavoidable conclusion.

The twelfth juror, the overnight holdout, had an odd personality quirk: He was the kind of impassioned defender of lost causes who is able swiftly to reduce any political or social gathering to a hopeless, joyless shambles. The others had seen Twelve use the trick to disrupt every lively argument they had got going during the long weeks of sequestration. When the third ballot was going around the table, the others watched Twelve do it again. He also intended to switch to *guilty* this time, they believed, but before it became his turn to vote, the one other pro-Patty juror also changed to *guilty.* This gave Twelve an irresistible opportunity to switch back temporarily to *not guilty,* and single-handedly hang up the verdict. The others did not press him. They were only too happy to go home, and they knew their man. Sure enough, on Saturday morning, after everybody had looked at two pieces of evidence, more or less for form's sake—the "Tania Interview" and the Trish Tobin tape—they voted again. This time it was unanimous. By the time the distraught group sent word to the judge several of the women and one of the men were weeping openly.

(525)

The very next day, one of the jurors sent word to me. After being locked up so long, he said on the phone, he found himself afflicted— as I was myself—by a kind of careening total recall, and his need to "dump it all out" was overwhelming. He would have liked to tell his wife, but she hadn't *been there.* The choice, as he saw it, was either to pay a psychiatrist to listen to his churning bellyful of emotions or, through me, to try to tell the world. The other jurors had similar feelings, and the following account more or less represents the feelings of all.

In a general way, all the jurors were aware of what had happened to Patty Hearst before she went on trial—the kidnapping, the robbery, the aftermath. But until they actually got into the courtroom and recognized the faces of some of the television reporters present, they didn't know they might be asked to judge her. When they understood, they began to worry about the length of time it would take. Four weeks or so seemed plausible; eight did not. Their $20-a-day wage could not possibly compensate them for two months away from their jobs and families. Although they had been told they would be "sequestered," they did not really know what the word meant.

The night before final selection, Carter had told all thirty-six remaining candidates to have someone drive them to court the next morning so they would not have to park a car, and to bring a suitcase. Only when the twelve jurors and four alternates left the courtroom and descended to the basement and were told to get aboard a dilapidated bus did they begin to get an inkling of what they were in for. The old gray '51 bus normally used to transport prisoners had seats for only twelve, although sixteen jurors, plus two or three marshals, always had to cram themselves inside. The wire-cage windows were pasted over with butcher's paper. It was frustrating never to see where one was going in this aged, airless vehicle stinking of gas fumes.

"They're the most pampered jury in history," Charles Burrows, a Justice Department expert on jury-handling assigned to this case by the United States Marshals service, told the *New York Times.* Needless to say, the jurors didn't read the story, and they certainly didn't feel pampered. They felt as if they were in reform school. Their domestic arrangements seemed harsh and arbitrary, applied at judicial whim. They lived for sixty-six days without radios, television, newspapers, or magazines in single rooms equipped with alarms that rang if the door was opened after ten o'clock at night. Until the knock came at six or six-thirty the next morning, each one was entirely alone.

The only opportunity for autonomy related to food: A juror could either eat alone in his room or go to a restaurant with the group. But since all sixteen had to eat together, it was difficult to avoid people one didn't like. The two drinks one was allowed before dinner were insufficient to relieve the tensions of the day. The boredom and inactivity were such that in seven weeks one juror gained twenty pounds.

I thought about my own emotions at the end of a day in court. When I got home after that kind of intense concentration, I was so tired I could scarcely review my notes. All I wanted to do was to relax, have a few stiff drinks, a visit with good friends, and a chance to talk over and sort out the impressions of the day—in Dr. West's jargon, to find someone to reflect reality with me. The jurors could have none of this, not even a nightcap before bed.

In court, concentration on the evidence and the testimony was exhausting, and still worse was the anxiety over not knowing what was coming next. Out of court, there was no way to break the tension. Golf, jogging, and most other customary recreations were impossible because each juror would have required his own marshal. The weekend diversions—a group walk on the beach or a movie—were chosen by democratic vote. But the choice of *which* movie was made by the marshals. When they saw *One Flew over the Cuckoo's Nest,* the jurors chuckled grimly: *Their own bus* was on the screen. "We were all *in* the movie. *We* were the loonies, the nuts."

On working days, general conversation and a long-running whist game were the sole diversions. Persons whose habitual relaxation was to open a beer and watch *Kojak* were simply out of luck. Even worse than life in the common room at the motel was sitting around in the backstage jury room in the Federal Building, a bleak, twelve- by eighteen-foot windowless chamber with a table and chairs down the middle and a bathroom at either end. Incarceration here could last for five minutes or two days; one never knew. The boredom was intolerable. A coffee urn was provided and sometimes, but not always, a few magazines. One woman hooked a rug. One man drew endless cartoons. Sometimes people simply lay down under the table and went to sleep. Ventilation was poor, and nonsmokers were very uncomfortable. The worst things were never knowing the rules, never being able to anticipate, and the constant sense of being "stepchildren."

"For the people who were going to have to make the decision, we were the last to know anything!" more than one juror said resentfully. They did not even know if they could or should take notes. When someone asked the marshals, the only answer was that some judges allow it, some don't. So no one did. In the absence of any information channel, instruction manual, or briefings of any kind, people comported themselves literally according to what they could remember from *Perry Mason*. They knew the judge was in charge and that they could send him requests for clarification via the marshals, but the system seemed too cumbersome. The jurors could not understand why, if they were here to make a difficult decision—a responsibility that they took with utmost seriousness—the conditions of their sequestration were such as to make decision-making extremely onerous.

The lack of any sexual outlet was a severe deprivation to some. Nor could one risk picking a fight. The waiting around was unbearable. Why, if breakfast was at eight, were they awakened at six? Why were they always the last to leave the courthouse at lunchtime and the first to return? It was worse than the army. Reporters awaiting the verdict had noted that the jurors had shown up early Saturday morning to resume their deliberations. It didn't seem odd to the jurors; they were *always* early, everyplace they went.

At times it seemed to them that everybody in a criminal case had rights to be protected *except* the jurors. "They're concerned with only one thing: guilty or not guilty. That's all they care about."

After a while, it grew awkward even to see one's family, and Sunday became the hardest day. At least during the week one had a job to do. Lonesome as they were, jurors began almost to dread the family visits. "Living in two different worlds" was too difficult.

Despite all, or perhaps because of all, the jurors became very close. "Almost like a family" was a phrase used by many. But when it came time to make the most difficult decision of their lifetime, each one had to do it entirely alone, without the normal support from spouse, friends, clergyman, psychiatrist, lawyer, accountant, or any of the other figures on whom one relies to help make a difficult judgment about a fellow human being.

Ignorance of the law led the jurors into many erroneous assumptions while the trial was in progress. Often they thought the opposing attorneys were attempting to hoodwink or razzle-dazzle them when, in fact, only sheer coincidence was at work. For example, when the jurors were shown the group SLA picture, no one noticed the object hanging on a macrame string around Tania's neck. Later, when a blowup of that portion of the photograph was shown to them, several jurors thought, How clever of Browning to have planted the earlier picture! But there had been no such intent in the prosecutor's mind. The jurors were very conscious of variations in the defendant's tone of voice. Usually she was vague, but whenever the questions switched to rifles and shotguns, she became precise, and her replies were sharp and swift. But they interpreted this change as the result of some kind of multiple personality. Still believing her innocent at that point, they assumed that the vague talker was Patty; the precise one, Tania.

Surely the wackiest misperception had occurred during Bailey's summation when he gestured so broadly with his left, upstage hand that he spilled a pitcher of ice water down the front of his trousers. (*That* was the mysterious crash-and-tinkle we spectators had heard!) Bailey's failure to pause or to react to the accident in any way was interpreted by the jurors as evidence of the famous lawyer's steely self-control.

As far as their verdict went, the crucial week was that of March 1. It was only when Ziggy Berzins took the stand that they began seriously to doubt Patty Hearst's veracity. His simple, blunt way of reasoning to figure out who was who at the Hibernia Bank seemed similar to their own. But by Friday of that week, with Dr. Fort on the stand for his second day, the trial appeared to be veering off in some mysterious new direction. Sitting through four *more* weeks of baffling interrogation now seemed to be a real possibility. One juror wrote the judge a note that Friday saying she couldn't stand it any longer; she wanted to be excused. But on Saturday morning, when she saw Carter in chambers for the first time, she changed her mind. Here was a mortal, reasonable human being, not a robed abstraction. "I didn't really expect him to let me out at that point, and he said he wouldn't. But he promised the trial would be over in about a week, and it was! When I said we didn't know what the hell was going on and had no idea even what sequence of events to expect, he told me, and I was very relieved. By the end I was awfully pleased with the judge. Seeing him in chambers had a whole new effect on me. He was just in a sport jacket, and he seemed so alert, so responsive; he appeared to have a handle on things. Before that, it looked like the attorneys were determining things between themselves. I've read since the trial that there was a lot of contesting as to what was admitted and what wasn't, and apparently he *was* in much more control than it seemed to us at the time."

Fort's testimony was unsettling to the entire jury and emotionally draining. Because they were unaware of Bailey's savage personal attacks while they were out of the room, the dogged recalcitrance of the government's expert didn't make sense. Nor could they understand why the lawyer never cross-examined the doctor on the substance of his testimony; it failed to occur to them that he didn't dare.

Al Johnson appeared to the jurors to be the more capable and forceful of the defense counsel. Most of them surmised that Johnson was the true architect of the defense, relying on Bailey as the "orator" and "front man."

The most upsetting evidence had been the SLA tapes. Several jurors thought that playing them was a deliberate defense attempt to frighten them—and it worked. "We all got very upset and uptight." The visit to inspect the two actual SLA hideouts, coming, as it did, midway in the sequence of seven tapes, was especially scary. When the jurors climbed out of their blinkered bus and saw the huge crowds in the streets, they grew panicky. Then they were shown the closets, but no one bothered to tell them which apartment was which. They never understood that they had visited the SLA's second hideout first.

The moment of pronouncing sentence "was very heavy," one juror told me. "At that point we had a very strong bond. All during the trial, when you can't discuss the case, the bond is forming. At that particular moment everybody was going through the exact same feelings that I had, the pounding of the heart. We were so glad to get out of that courtroom! Back at the hotel there was an obvious feeling of warmth and affection and respect and trust for people who two months ago were total strangers and whom you never would have met under any other conditions.

"Then, all of a sudden, you're taken out of *that* environment and put back into your home environment, where the people cannot relate to what you've just been through. They've seen the newspapers and television but they didn't go through it, and it's very difficult to relate to *them*. That shock was even greater than the shock of being sequestered. During the trial I had been desperate to go home, but now I didn't really want to, and even when I was home, for the first two or three days my body was there, but I was still with those other people at the Holiday Inn."

The most striking aspect of my talks with the jurors was to hear the testimony from their point of view. While Patty was on the stand they believed her. Before the experts began to speak, there was no question in any juror's mind but that Patty was innocent or at least that there were reasonable grounds to doubt her guilt. But the total effect of the expert testimony, the defense doctors' as well as the government's, had been to erase that possibility of doubt.

Dr. West looked to the jurors like "Mr. Right." He had the right credentials, the right background, the right appearance. They did not understand why they were not permitted to read his report. But the appearance and demeanor of Dr. Orne—rumpled, overweight, balding, and speaking with a Viennese accent—impressed them even more than Dr. West. He was not only believable; he was lovable. "When he got up and said that she was absolutely not simulating, he was the strongest defense witness," one juror said. Dr. Lifton seemed weakest "because he got personally involved. I got the feeling that he didn't want to be there, that his was almost a textbook study of the case, compared to the personal concern that West and Orne had."

But in hindsight, after they decided Patty was lying, the jurors came to view the defense doctors' testimony quite differently. "Reasonable doubt" had existed in all the jurors' minds long before they were assigned to the case. At the trial Browning's task was to erase that doubt, and he would have been unable to do so without the "help" of the defense psychiatrists. The cumulative effect of their testimony and the defendant's own had been to overstate the case, in effect to write Patty a "blank check" that covered two years' time. It was too much. Ultimately, none of the jurors could buy it.

The other factor that weighed heavily against Patty was her appearance. At first they had not even recognized her. The tiny, dowdy, downcast creature at the defense table bore no resemblance to any of the famous newspaper photographs—neither the smiling debutante, the gun-toting Tania, nor the defiant urban guerrilla. "I thought she'd be pretty, but she was just unattractive, not pleasant-looking at all," said one male juror. "I started to take it apart: Why do I get this feeling from her? Her hair looked terrible. You'd look at her mother, with every hair in place, and *her* hair looked like it had been cut by somebody shearing sheep. There was no coloring at all in the face, and very hollow, depressed eyes." Because he still believed her truthful, he couldn't figure out *why* she looked so bad, and he ascribed it to the rigors of her captivity. "But for some reason I just couldn't relate to that person sitting in the courtroom." Then Bailey had introduced the *Newsweek* cover, the "urban guerrilla" photograph, "and all of a sudden this picture comes around of a vibrant young woman who's *alive,* feeling, showing her emotions, attractive, lipstick on, a big smile." They seemed to be two entirely different people, one of them animated, one a zombie. "At the time I couldn't figure out what the hell was going on. But I realize now that that's when my real serious doubts set in."

When the jurors still believed Patty innocent, all of her explanations, including her behavior at Mel's, seemed plausible. When they began to doubt her, nothing seemed plausible. Finally, the judge's instructions made a *guilty* vote seem mandatory.

After it was all over, the troubled jurors felt that since the law had forced them to make such an uncomfortable and difficult decision, the law should also give them a voice in determining the degree of the sentence, which they deemed far too harsh. The jurors were ignorant of the fact that the term of sentence was not entirely up to the judge but was itself delimited by law.

In retrospect, the jurors wondered, as I did, whether the severe sequestration served the course of justice or interfered with it. "During the cross-examination of Dr. West and Dr. Orne, a great deal of time was spent questioning them as to where they were staying, who was buying their meals and putting them up. But they never looked at who was putting *us* up, who were *our* custodians, who became *our* authority figures, who shaped *our* environment."

As one of the marshals said later, "The trouble with sequestration is that the cure is worse than the disease."

When sequestration began, many jurors still did not understand the term, even though Carter had just explained it. But the fact is that on the second anniversary of the world's most celebrated kidnapping, the twelve people whom society was asking to judge this kidnap victim's subsequent behavior were themselves, in effect, kidnapped. Treated more like prisoners of the Republic than honored citizens, they were asked to become modern vestal virgins, sacred keepers of the flame of justice.

The sequence was all wrong: First they watched the game; then, after it was all over, they were told the rules. Then, after that, they were asked to decide who won. In hindsight it appeared to me that the uncertainty, isolation, discomfort, and inhumanity of the jury's sequestered existence, combined with their ignorance of the law, are what did Patty Hearst in. This pattern may have worked in simpler days, when Anglo-Saxon justice was just getting organized, when a jury of the defendant's peers was insurance that a simple citizen not be dealt with arbitrarily or unfairly by the nobles or the king. But I wonder if it makes sense to try to preserve these arrangements any longer, now that all of us—jurors, lawyers, defendants, officials, witnesses, and reporters—inhabit a pervasive, media-drenched miasma in which the boundaries of time and space themselves have been obliterated; when every place is Here, and the time is always Now.

The defendant in CR. 74-364-JC would not have received a more "fair trial," but surely she would have received a more *human* judgment from her peers had they been permitted to see and hear all that we saw and heard. If those jurors had known what the people who watched the entire trial knew, Patricia Hearst would not have been convicted and would not be in prison today. But as Patty said after the verdict, "I don't blame them. Unless they had been *there,* there was no way they could understand."

Later a juror told me, "At some point everybody has to face up to the fact that the media are essential and central to our lives, and life can't be given out in spoonfuls. In a trial of this nature, where people all over the world wanted to know what was going on, and you had reporters there from all over the world, why not let the people decide? Why not televise the whole thing, if that's what people want, just as they do congressional hearings? If something's that important to society that *that many* people have to cover it—then instead of some judge saying, 'Well, you can't cover this part, or you can only have drawings, not photographs'; instead of using the imperfect filter of the media people who are there—why not put the whole thing on the tube?"

Why not, indeed?

The last time I saw her was on December 16, 1976, about a month after the new judge, William Orrick, released Patricia Hearst on $1.5-million bail in the custody of her parents. She had then been in prison for fourteen months, and if all appeals failed, she would have a minimum of fourteen more months to serve. To mark Eurydice's return, Bailey had arranged a final *CBS Special Report,* this one hosted by old Uncle Credibility himself. Walter Cronkite explained the ground rules: no questions on Mel's, on the Harrises, on the Hibernia Bank. Which is to say, it would not be an interview at all—with the possible exception of Carmichael, these were the *only* three questions of substance—but a final mazurka in the carefully orchestrated presentation of the newspaper heiress in the news media.

An opening shot showed three strolling people outlined against blue sky. Pan down to San Simeon's gaudy gardens, huge clumps of blue agapanthus and spiky orange bird of paradise. The stagy "uplift" setting recalled *The Sound of Music,* but what we got was the sound of self-justification juiced up with garish flora. *CBS Special Report*s are sold to sponsors, and appropriately enough, Patty's swan song was brought to

(533)

us courtesy of the itch, burp, and headache healers of at-home America. As for the players, Patty, in bright red pants, was flanked on the one side by Bailey, sleek and cheetah-eyed, and on the other by the CBS reporter who had covered the case, Harold Dow. They looked like a commercial for themselves: In lawyers, buy the best; to play the hotshot newsman, hire a handsome young black; for a criminal defendant, get a long-haired and smiling girl. The background shifted to a fancy interior: a flaming, Vatican-size silver candelabrum illuminated an immense flower painting and a delicate settee. On it, perched beside Dow, Patty now wore a glowing gown of Madonna blue, and diamond ear-drops. The classy setup would have made a swell opening for an X-rated movie; it was just right for this "interview." First, Dow guided his leading lady through an instant replay of the trial, almost as ritualized by now as the stations of the cross. Yet, after all these months, her answers still were marked by hesitations and long pauses.*

"The SLA knew all about me and all about the Hearst Corporation." Did they ever really intend to release her? DeFreeze told her the choice was to stay with him or get killed.

COMMERCIAL: Emeraude, a "mysterious" perfume, by Coty. Sears appliances.

Patty readily told Dow—despite the previously agreed-upon "restrictions"—that during the holdup her gun was not operable. "I looked down. The bolt was wide open." After the two bank customers were shot, Patty had no memory of leaving the scene or of riding in the getaway car. Yes, "they *would* have killed me if I hadn't done it right."

"How about the communiqué you sent after the robbery?"

Long sigh. She has told this so often, she knows better than anyone how unbelievable it sounds. "A script was written up . . . and I read it. . . . If they hadn't *believed* it, I wouldn't be sitting here now."

"What were your thoughts during the shoot-out in Los Angeles?"

"You see it on TV, and you think, *They* think I'm in there! I believed that if I tried to get away, the same thing would happen to me. . . . And

---

*Later Dave Browning, of CBS-TV, who produced the show, told me that right behind his cameras in the small, cramped room—actually a guest house four or five miles from the San Simeon castle—were Bailey and Mr. and Mrs. Hearst: Willy-nilly, Patty was playing to that three-person live audience. Browning would have preferred them out of the room but could not think of a polite way to ask the Hearsts to leave. The fact was, Browning was uneasy about producing this particular show at all. But Bailey had insisted on it. Dave Browning is the brother of James Browning, the prosecutor, "which made this assignment a little ticklish for the Browning family. I kept thinking, Why would Lee Bailey be giving an interview to the brother of the guy who put her in the slammer? It was pretty screwy all the way round."

then, on June 7, I ended up eulogizing those people . . . who . . . after what they did to me . . ." Deep breath, then: "I feel they got exactly what they deserved. *Exactly* what they asked for. I don't feel sorry for them at all!"

Patty looked straight at the camera. One could see her eyes at last. They are large and beautiful, with well-defined lids, but there was nothing in them, nothing to see there after all.

"Were the SLA successful in making you feel your family didn't love you anymore?"

"Yes."

COMMERCIAL: Vicks.

"Patty, the jurors were bothered most by two things: that you never tried to escape or call home, and the other thing was the Olmec monkey."

"Well, I know it's hard to understand. Because it's hard for me now to understand how I really could have thought that way. It's crazy!" So much for not calling home or escaping. As for the monkey amulet, "All the SLA knew I had it. One reason why I wouldn't throw it away is that all my life I have been surrounded by art."

Are they kidding? "Vissi d'arte"! Puccini wrote it better.

Dow asked about future plans, and she said she'd like to work and travel. But when he mentioned getting married, she broke into strange peals of laughter.

Another camera angle. Now Bailey spoke. "During the trial, evidence was introduced that Patty was a 'bad girl.' " They said she hated her school. But everybody hated that school, "and if getting demerits in high school means you're out looking for terrorists, well . . ." The cheetah-eyes narrowed; the sideburns quivered with disdain. "How do you feel about your family now?"

"Oh, I love them!" This is accompanied by a silvery tinkle of delight. "Tomorrow we're getting our Christmas tree!"

It had been a long time coming, but Patty's statement that the SLA members who were burned up in Los Angeles "got exactly what they deserved" released me from this girl at last. A person in her position has scant business making moral judgments. Patty sounded like Charlie McCarthy sitting on Bailey's lap or Fay Wray clutched in King Kong's hairy paw. Only persons who see things in King Kong moral terms would have permitted this view of the family castle and its sparkly princess in blue. Out of the courtroom setting I found it offensive to hear Patty say that she believed the SLA when they told her her parents had abandoned her, that the FBI was out to kill her, that the police didn't care about her, that she had nowhere to go, that the sight of the televised incineration of her quondam friends made her think that "if I tried to get away, the same thing would happen to me." It was unpleasant in particular when she showed no awareness that had she not opted to join the SLA, had she not decided to play "girl guerrilla," the TV barbecue would never have happened. Six people were burned alive *because* Patty had joined them, or because some cops believed Patty had joined them. If she had gone home after the April Fools' tape instead of announcing, "I have chosen to stay and fight," there might have been no firefight. If the cops had not thought Patty was in the house, there might have been no firefight. If Patty had not opened fire at Mel's, the day before, drawing attention to herself and the Harrises, it would not have been necessary to flee and commandeer another van, leaving behind in the old van the parking ticket that led the police to the location of the SLA hideout. Had Patty not chosen to stay and fight, two young men who possibly had nothing to do with the assassination of Marcus Foster might not now be serving life terms in prison. The Hearst/Bailey insensitivity to these matters was shocking.

Most offensive of all was the pap about the Olmec monkey. "I was told it was two thousand years old. I would never throw something away that was that old. All my life I've been surrounded by art." Did they really expect people to believe this, either that the monkey *was* two thousand years old or that Patty thought so? True, all her life she had been surrounded by art, much of it very bad or fake, but none more fake than the artifice of this cynical "interview," especially its fulsome words of praise for her family. "Oh, I love them. They've been so fantastic!"

Was this, then, to be the true ending—the princess back in her tower, safe and sound, loving Mommy and Daddy, and insisting all those wicked people "deserved exactly what they got"? Bad girl! Nanny spank! Had the girl reverted to type? Was she as mean-spirited, grandiose, opportunistic, vain, and contemptuous of the public as this "interview" made her seem? Was she a throwback to her grandfather after all, even unto the arrogance about "art"? Maybe the kidnapping and subsequent experiences had forced her to become a Hearst, after all. Or maybe she *was* just Charlie McCarthy, sitting on her lawyer's knee. Perhaps it would have been more accurate all along to describe Patty not as a POW but as an MIA. Somewhere in Act II, during the long pretrial preparation by attorneys and psychiatrists, the newly recaptured Patty had disappeared. The kidnapped girl had come in from the cold and vanished. And *now?* Was she a battlefield casualty? A POW of her doctors and defenders? Was she still missing in action? Despite her trial and the *Rashomon* that followed, one still could not be sure.

Was Patty tried for what she *did* or for who she was and what she *became*—perhaps, at least partially, as a *reaction* to what she did? The jury judged her for what she did; they concluded she had willingly participated in robbing a bank and in the unlawful use of firearms. As the judge read them the law it is hard to see how they could have come up with any other verdict.

However, there is a difference between what she was *tried for* and what she was *judged guilty of*. She was tried in the press for what she became—a revolutionary. She was *put on trial* by the government, *and she was permitted to go on trial by her family* (because, at least subliminally, her parents acknowledged that their daughter bore a guilt that needed to be expunged), and she attracted the attention of some fancy psychiatrists because of what *they thought* she became.

In a way, HERNAP could be seen as the victims' revenge. Everybody in the SLA was a victim or perceived himself as a victim—of class, race, or sex. They were an intricate tangle of victims, all of them violently lashing out, which is what made them such a poisonous nest of vipers.

Very few people, professionals included, had been able to look at HERNAP and disentangle the interaction between the child-cum-revolutionary—who is out to accomplish the private rebellious activity of establishing his individual identity apart from that of the parent—and the political rhetoric. If Bailey's defense had prevailed, then all political dissidents could be declared mentally incompetent!

A lawyer often defends a person he knows to be guilty. Under our adversary system, he will try to raise reasonable doubts in jurors' minds, which is all he is required to do. He will also defend persons he knows to be guilty because, on balance, misconduct on the part of the government is so much greater a threat to society than the misconduct of a single criminal citizen. He will not, however, if he is ethical and prudent, present evidence he knows to be false. But to him, "psychological evidence" is different. His sense of legal ethics does not inhibit his urge to play amateur shrink. On the contrary, it encourages him to dope out a defense he thinks will "work" and then to hire the experts to back him up. Bailey did it. Hallinan did it. Garry did it. They all do it.

Perhaps the assignment of responsibility for human conduct is too important to be left to professionals—whether of the bar, psychiatry, law enforcement, or the press. HERNAP's professionals were as deeply steeped in self-serving, self-perpetuating concepts as bureaucrats. But sensational and invasive as the media had been, the members of the press clearly had comported themselves better than the other pros.

I now believe that in the United States, as in England, pretrial publicity, by either side and by doctors and attorneys, should be barred. How would it interfere with the Bill of Rights if the courts were to gag the lawyers rather than the press? Fort is right: A symbiotic relationship does exist between publicity-seeking lawyers, a celebrity defendant, and a sensation-seeking press. A defense attorney should not be allowed to smuggle information, and attitudes, into the minds of jurors by broadcasting these attitudes to the community before the jury is selected.

It must happen more than rarely that certain cases come to trial over the better judgment of some of the parties involved, whether those parties be prosecutors, plaintiffs, defense attorneys, other government officials, psychiatrists or other doctors. But no matter who asks the question—Why did this case have to come to trial at all?—the answer is always the same: The public demanded it. The excuse that "the public demands it" was used forty years before HERNAP in the prosecution of Bruno Richard Hauptmann in the Lindbergh case.

Who makes this determination that "the American public demands vengeance"? And *what* public? In each instance, that of Hauptmann and that of Hearst, the determination that "the American public demands vengeance" was made by prosecutors who wanted to prosecute, in cooperation and collusion with politicians with axes to grind, puppeteers with strings to pull, and defense lawyers who like to try big cases. In each instance a family wanted its family honor restored or upheld and was at the same time immeasurably anguished, and perhaps impaired in its common sense and ability to make good judgments, by a massive press assault on family privacy in a time of private crisis. In retrospect it seems clear that the early press stories, unmuzzled, might have brought Patty home in three or four months, rather than thirty-four months, and with far less physical and mental damage to herself. Indeed, more open coverage could well have prevented the televised barbecuing of her six mad, suicidal comrades. But in retrospect, *everything* seems clear. Retrospect is the spyglass of all retired admirals.

True, too, that many members of the bar thought that the Bailey-Johnson legal work had been execrable; true, many psychiatrists were shouting that other psychiatrists didn't belong in courtrooms at all;

true, there were shouts in the streets; and in the press, moralists of every stripe scrutinized with narrowed eyes every wriggle and blunder of the suffering Hearsts, who were pinned like butterflies on a public bulletin board. But there was no public *qua* public shouting for vengeance.

At bottom there *is no* American public. There are only persons and pressure groups and professional interests that—for reasons of self-interest—presume to speak in the public's name. These people can be lawyers, politicians, psychiatrists, family members, or press. In the Hearst case they all spoke. Each invented a hypothetical "American public" to suit his own purposes. The situation is not unlike the philosopher's example of the tree that falls in the forest: If no one is there to hear the crash, does it make any sound? Until the big case actually comes to trial, who clamors for vengeance? An "American public" demanding vengeance or, indeed, demanding anything else simply does not exist. There are only the hypothetical public(s) of the various opposed forces in the case, each group waiting—unknowingly—to be mobilized into reality and given voice.

As for myself, it no longer mattered whether Patty was a POW or an MIA. For me the curettage was complete, over. The television interview served to cut her out of my heart and my concern. If she were a zombie, I could not help her. If *she* were the adventuress, not I, so be it.

Not that HERNAP was over. It would go on, I knew, and on. From here on out, we were in for Jabberwocky time in Dixie. Bailey would continue to try his case in the media. One could have guessed that as the public slowly recognized what had in fact happened to Patty, public opinion would swing back in her favor. But the precise expression of those feelings was delicious: Imagine a Free Patty Hearst Committee led by California's newest citrus in national politics, Senator S. I. Hayakawa, hand in hand with that staunch avatar of the freedom fighter William F. Buckley, the saintlike Cesar Chavez, and John Wayne and the four of them marching down the yellow brick-road trailing a phalanx of forty-eight U.S. senators and congressmen, *and* the editorial writers of the *New York Times*, all demanding of the White House that it grant a presidential pardon to Patty Hearst!

The Committee for the Release of Patty Hearst would learn to use the media with the same skill the SLA once employed. The "Free Patty" campaign, led by a young Episcopal priest, Ted Dumke of San Jose, would now churn out FREE PATTY buttons, bumper stickers, and

T-shirts, and Patty herself would take to wearing one around the jail. In jig time, tens of thousands of anonymous persons would write to President Carter demanding a presidential pardon for the Prisoner of Pleasanton.

On September 5, 1978, at the suggestion of the late Democratic congressman Leo Ryan, who represented the Hearsts' Hillsborough district, Charles W. Bates would write a letter to Attorney General Griffin B. Bell asking him to recommend to President Carter that he grant clemency to Patricia Hearst. In order for Bell to proceed, Patty had first to file a petition with the President. The Hearsts had been reluctant to do this, but Ryan finally convinced them. When, on the day the Harrises pleaded guilty to having kidnapped Patty, someone put a dead and rotting rat on Patty's jail bunk, "she found that to be very upsetting," Ryan said then, adding that he feared for Patty's life. "She is a constant and inviting target to others." A scant two months later Ryan himself was dead, shot along with three newsmen and a young woman in Guyana by members of a sect of religious refugees from San Francisco. Then most of the nine hundred members of the sect either committed mass suicide or were murdered by poison—cyanide again— to prove their loyalty to the People's Temple. Two weeks after that, George Moscone, the mayor of San Francisco, was shot dead in his office by a disgruntled former city official who also murdered another city supervisor and gay-rights leader, Harvey Milk. At that point, one could only pray for them and remember Lenin's words: "The difference between revolutionary violence and counterrevolutionary violence is the difference between cat shit and dog shit."

Bates' letter to President Carter meant that a retired senior FBI official now was urging his old bosses to grant clemency to a red bank robber! Jabberwocky time. Bates' letter made it clear he was not joining Dumke's grass-roots "Free Patty" campaign but was basing his plea on a lifetime's professional experience in law enforcement, as well as his intimate familiarity with the details of this particular case.

Bates wrote that experience in hundreds of bank-robbery cases led him to conclude that "Miss Hearst has served sufficient time," and he listed three reasons why: Unlike Miss Hearst, most convicted bank robbers have a record of prior felony convictions. Second, Miss Hearst was never involved in any criminal activity prior to her association with the SLA. Finally, rehabilitation was not an issue in this case, as had been stated by the sentencing judge. *O tempora! O mores!* By these same criteria, the U.S. government also did not give a fair shake to William and Emily Harris, either. Jabberwocky time.

Since HERNAP's very beginning, linguists coast to coast had been a-gurgle over the various Patty texts and tapes. Now, amid the latter-day flood of high academic Pattypoop, much of it from doubting colleagues of Margaret Singer, came a glittering paper entitled "Authorship Attribution in a Forensic Setting," presented in Birmingham, England, with the help of the American Council of Learned Societies. The author was Richard W. Bailey, a professor of English at the University of Michigan and an expert on authorship. During the trial this Bailey had been a consultant to the prosecution. Later he would observe that it was scarcely surprising that statistically differing results could be obtained from various comparisons of linguistic traits. "Unfortunately," he continued, "there is little reason to assign such differences to authorship. . . . In fact, a *failure* to find differences between writing and speech may itself be a cause for doubting common authorship. Unskilled authors have great difficulty in writing a plausible imitation of speech. . . ." Although Professor Bailey, an extremely impressive author himself, was unable to reach any firm conclusions in regard to the defense claims that Patty was not the true author of the first six SLA tapes, he was inclined to think that Emily Harris, not Patricia Hearst, had written both the eulogistic seventh tape and the "Tania Interview." But Professor Bailey also took pains to point out that he, like Judge Carter, felt that what was important about the tapes was not *authorship* but *sincerity*. As Judge Carter had put it in his ruling not to admit expert testimony by Dr. Singer, the question was "whether she [Patty] meant what she said."* Jabberwocky time.

Although I knew Jabberwocky time would go on and on, I didn't know in what directions. Who could have foretold that the proprietor of Mel's Sporting Goods would file a million-dollar damage suit against Randolph Hearst, claiming that when the publisher's daughter shot up his sidewalk, the premier gun merchant of Inglewood, California, was thereby rendered impotent? Who could have foretold that Tom Matthews would have filed another suit, claiming that on the day he was kidnapped, he was to have been scouted by the American League and that Tania therefore had destroyed Matthews' big-league baseball career. Dozens of civil suits were filed against the Hearsts. The PIN

---

*After the trial, said Professor Bailey, Carter privately admitted doubting the merits of his own decision.

program had been set up so hastily that no proper insurance had been taken out, and now platoons of injured parties said they had been run over by forklifts, or suffered similar disasters.

Who could have foretold that Charlie Bates would write a book, or at least an unpublished manuscript, entitled "Get Patty Hearst!" and that it would become the basis of an ABC television movie about the FBI search? This film, produced by David Frost—*that could* have been foretold—was timed to be televised on February 4, 1979, the fifth anniversary of the kidnapping. Considering the prodigious FBI time and effort consumed before the ultimate kitchen confrontation between fearless Tom Padden and the FBI's target, the girl in the wet underpants, "Not Get Patty Hearst" might have been a more accurate title. Jabberwocky time.

That Patricia Hearst would have fallen in love again was predictable, even inevitable, given her years and romantic nature. But with one of her own bodyguards? With a policeman! Yes, even that was predictable, given what one knew now about the Stockholm syndrome. Still, Patty's newest fiancé, Bernard Shaw, seemed a lot like Cinque in whiteface. The couple had met on November 20, 1976, Patty's second night out on bail, when she and Johnson and her special U.S. marshal, Janey Jimenez, had gone to the Top of the Mark to celebrate her release. Shaw—one of a squad of fifteen to twenty bodyguards hired by Al Johnson at Randolph Hearst's request—was standing, or rather sitting guard, at the next table. A bomb threat to the hotel ended the impromptu cocktail party, and the next day the citizenry of San Francisco was outraged that on Patricia Hearst's first night out in public she was endangering the tourist industry of the entire city.

As for the romance, it took some time before love's own Velcro caught, and held. Patty had dates with other men, under Bernie's guard, but she was having a hard time getting along with them, just as Dr. West had predicted she would. "They didn't understand what had happened. Bernie did. So did the other policemen on duty. A real camaraderie developed with the guards," Patty later told a reporter in a jail interview.

People magazine, on November 6, 1978, published a cover story on Patty and Bernie, announcing the couple's intention to wed on Valentine's Day the following year, in jail or out. "It seems like it just happened in a pretty natural way. I remember Bernie liked my dog a lot," Patty said of their romance. Arrow is the trained German shepherd guard dog given to Patty the day she got out on bail. "If anyone didn't love my dog, I would know he didn't love me."

For his part, the thirty-three-year-old Shaw, a fireman's son who decided to go into police work after thieves shot and killed his younger brother, said, "I think I liked the way Patty was so giving of herself to people. She always went out of the way to remember and celebrate birthdays and anniversaries." Finally, it seemed, inmate #0077-181 at the Federal Correctional Institution in Pleasanton was taking Dr. Kozol's advice and sending birthday cards. Jabberwocky time.

After the jury had found Patty Hearst guilty, Bailey had set to work simultaneously writing her appeal and writing his book. In October 1976 Johnson had telephoned me to inquire how my book was going, and to report that Putnam's had decided not to publish Bailey's book after all. In August 1978 Bailey told me he had written another book, this one a novel. By then Patty's latest attorney, George Martinez, had asked that Patty's conviction be set aside and that she be released from prison because Bailey's defense had been inadequate, incompetent, venal, and in violation of her constitutional rights. The Hearsts had fired Bailey some months before; or more accurately, they had permitted Al Johnson, who was still hanging on by his gritted teeth, to announce through same that Mr. Bailey had withdrawn from the case.

That the Hearsts and Bailey-and-Johnson would fall out was probably inevitable. Nor did the Bailey-Johnson bust-up and the resultant squabble over fees much surprise anyone. That it was Al Johnson who had recommended George Martinez to Patty and boyfriend Shaw as the man to handle Shaw's divorce, and that Martinez then ganged up with Patty and Shaw to bounce Zombo added a picaresque touch. So did the fact that Harold Dow of CBS-TV now was meeting with George Martinez about setting up further televised jail interviews. Meanwhile, Ronald Reagan had taken to rumbling, in public: "Is Patty Hearst in jail *because* her family has money?"

That nobody got a dime out of it—your standard *The Treasure of the Sierra Madre* finish—could have been expected, too. The defense fees turned out to have been relatively modest. Bailey revealed that his initial retainer was $125,000, which he and Johnson split one-third, two-thirds. Later they billed the Hearsts for another $50,000 for the appeals work, reversing the split.

That Bailey expected to clean up on his own Patty book was known, too; he always did that. That nobody would publish the book after he lost the case was a great loss to the ever-expanding literature of Pattypoop. But consolation could be found in comments Bailey made on the fallout to Peter Manso, a free-lance journalist.

On the matter of his own Patty book, Bailey told Manso that Patty's latest charges of conflict of interest between Bailey as advocate and as *auteur* were an "absolute lie. . . . If I wanted an exclusive on her story, why the Christ would I put her up in a public courtroom and give every other writer a crack at it?" The agreed-on publisher's advance, negotiated while the trial was in progress, had been $210,000, Bailey said, adding that to eliminate literary competition, Patty had been happy to sign a posttrial agreement with him, three days after the guilty verdict, "that she herself didn't intend to have a book out until ten months after publication of my own."

Perhaps my favorite slice of Bailey Jabberwocky was that "the government made a terrible judgment, essentially a political judgment, that if they didn't prosecute Patty with tremendous vigor, it might have hurt the Republican Party nationally." I was also partial to his comparison of the two bank robberies: "Initially, we were defending a girl for a bank robbery involving ten thousand bucks. Nobody got killed. Sacramento, on the other hand, is a ninety-nine on a scale of one hundred. Hibernia was maybe a forty." I also enjoyed Bailey's revelation that in the course of interviewing many other potential jurors around the country for subsequent cases, these persons dismissed Patty and Martinez's charges against her former counsel as an obvious "loser taking her last shot."

Other criminal lawyers leaped gleefully into the newest Bailey-Johnson-Martinez-Hallinan fray, nearly all of them defending their beleaguered colleague(s). Bailey, in order to serve his true client, the senior Hearsts, had *had to* pander to their fear of other dangerous radicals still on the loose who might do harm to their daughter. "Bailey's just the kind of lawyer the government loves to have around," lamented one radical lawyer. "He attempted to try the case from a right-wing point of view; he tried to *become* political." But he couldn't. Not that he didn't have the smarts; his own political conditioning, or lack of same, made him unable to deal with the concepts. Bailey himself never really understood the difference between brainwashing and coercive persuasion. "What Lee Bailey couldn't deal with was that she *was* brainwashed. The jurors caught it, though. Because they can smell fear." By the time Bailey finished defending himself against Patty and Martinez's newest list of charges against the competence of the Bailey-Johnson defense it sounded as if the person most in need of the protection of the attorney-client privilege was not Patricia Hearst but F. Lee Bailey. Jabberwocky time.

The lawyers proclaimed Patty's claims of immunity against further prosecution if she were to testify against Bailey simply preposterous. The Justice Department cannot even grant immunity; only judges can do that. Patty Hearst by that point had no immunities left of any kind to anything. She had "taken it *all* off" long ago. It did seem a pity to learn that only now could Patty pay her own legal counsel. At the time of her arrest she had had no access to her own money. During the Missing Year her trust funds had been cut off or tied up to prevent Tania from giving family money to the SLA. Jabberwocky time.

Still, there was not the least doubt now that, as always, Randolph Hearst at all times had had his daughter, not his money, as his uppermost or *only* concern. Patty could have requested any lawyer on earth and her father would have gladly paid that person's fees *if* he had confidence in the man's or woman's ability.

Poor Jimmy Carter. Challenged to come up with an example of political prisoners in the United States, Carter's human-rights and United Nations man, Andrew Young, Jr., had named Patty Hearst. Then, in a nationwide editorial written by clan chieftain William Randolph Hearst, Jr., the entire Hearst press came out in support of Young's position. This assertion provoked former prosecutor David Bancroft (he, like Browning, is now in private practice) to write in a letter to Patty's dad's newspaper that "to call Patricia Hearst, as you do, a political prisoner is most inappropriate. If she is, then so is Haldeman, James Earl Ray, Charles Manson, and anyone else whose crime or trial might be 'socially metaphored.' A decent respect for the common meanings of words in the English language does not permit such a characterization. Even if Miss Hearst is someday deserving of a pardon, she surely does not deserve a 'political' one."

On November 7, 1978, the Jabberwocky shut off—at least temporarily—when Judge Orrick denied all of Patty and Martinez's petitions to set aside or reduce her sentence. He was a tough judge, and the Prisoner of Pleasanton was just going to have to be tough, too, and do her time like everyone else. If the campaign for a presidential pardon failed, Patty's earliest possibility of parole would be July 1979. She then would have served thirty months of her seven-year sentence.

By the time Orrick ruled, F. Lee Bailey's legal and helicopter businesses were both thriving again, and he had just published a novel, entitled *Secrets,* about a case involving not two great lawyers but *three,* the third being a famous English barrister. In fact, things were going so well for Bailey that he had all his airplanes back and seemed to be ascending, phoenixlike, in his own aircraft. At that point the feisty lawyer met Giovanni Agnelli, the billionaire industrialist, for the first time. After this encounter Agnelli said he did not know or much care how good a lawyer Bailey was: The man was heads and away the finest salesman of helicopters that the Fiat king had ever met in his life.

That year, for the first time, lawyers permitted themselves ethically to advertise for new business, and, not surprisingly, the first classified legal ad to appear in tiny letters on the bottom of Page One of the *New York Times* was placed there by F. Lee Bailey, who described himself as a lawyer "practicing in the representation of wrongful death and injury cases arising out of aircraft disasters."

By the end of the year, the long-whispered rumors of trouble in the Hearst family became public knowledge when Randolph and Catherine announced a formal legal separation after forty years of marriage. The following day, President Carter hinted that the destroyed family might expect a happier New Year: Patty's release seemed to be in the works. On February 1, 1979, it came through, and early that morning, under heavy police helicopter cover, Patty walked through the prison gates, jubilantly waving her commutation papers high above her head.

Assuredly Jabberwocky time would go on. And on. But the point for me was that *I* was off it, out of it, over it—rid of my obsession and free now to tie up the bundles of chapters and move on. After the CBS-TV show in December 1976, I never saw Patricia Hearst in the same way again. I almost quit watching her, in fact, and at my typewriter one fine morning the following spring, pink-gray sunrise over fields of soft green rye and steaming, plowed brown, I remember looking out the window and quietly saying good-bye to her.

Good-bye, Patty, and God bless.

Index

(549)